D0274820

CATHERINE COOKSON

CATHERINE COOKSON

Hamilton

Goodbye Hamilton

Harold

PEERAGE BOOKS

Hamilton first published in Great Britain
in 1983 by William Heinemann Ltd

Goodbye Hamilton first published in Great Britain
in 1984 by William Heinemann Ltd

Harold first published in Great Britain
in 1985 by William Heinemann Ltd

This edition first published in Great Britain in 1991 by
Peerage Books an imprint of
Reed International Books Ltd
Michelin House
81 Fulham Road
London SW3 6RB

ISBN 1 85052 218 9

Printed in the United Kingdom by
Collins & Sons Ltd

Acknowledgments
The extract from the words by Harold Harford of the song
'I Hear You Calling Me' (Music by Charles Marshall) is printed by
permission of the Copyright Owners Boosey & Hawkes
Music Publishers Ltd

'One Day When We Were Young' Author Oscar Hammerstein II
© Leo Feist Inc., 1938, Chappell Music Limited London.
Reproduced by permission.

Contents

HAMILTON

Part One
THE CHRYSALIS

Chapter 1

I've done it! I have really done it. After thirteen years I've done it. How long have I wanted to do it? Oh, for the whole of the thirteen years. Yes, all of that time. Now I don't care what happens to me. I don't. I don't.

I'm sitting here in this dreadful place wondering why it should have happened at all, and to me. I'm what you call inoffensive. Well, that's how most people see me. Some even think I'm odd; and, of course, that's without them knowing anything about Hamilton.

When did I first meet up with Hamilton? Oh, it must have been when I started talking to myself when I was seven years old. I didn't call him that then, though.

I remember very little before I was seven. Some people can go back to when they were two or three and recall instances as plainly as if they had happened yesterday. But there are only two I can recall before that time. One was my first day at school when the children stood me against the wall and measured my arms, making me hold them out straight in front of me when they would try to pull my left hand to meet my right, and when they couldn't, Katie Moore, who lived three doors down, explained to them that God had made my arms like that to get even with my mother who thought herself better than anybody in the terrace and she had no right after what had happened.

Long after I was seven I tried to get Katie to tell me what had happened to make my mother like she was, but she didn't seem to know.

The other event I can recall before that early age is of my mother knocking a book out of my hand, then sitting staring at me, and me sitting staring at her too frightened to speak, until she yelled, *"Why? Why?"* at the same time swiping with her hand a cup and saucer and jug off the kitchen table. And then she cried.

But from when I was seven I could give you almost a day to day report of things that happened. My first vivid memory is of George. Oh, I liked George. Oh, I did, because George was common. Funny, how soon I discovered that all the nice things were common, such as eating ice cream out in the street; or, when it was raining, running along a gutter and kicking the water up in sprays; or jumping in the garden and screaming as you jumped because of a wonderful feeling inside you which regrettably lasted only a second; or wiping your bacon dip up with your bread. But the most common thing was to say what you were thinking, especially if they were funny things. This wasn't only common, it was low; and George was both common and low in this respect, and his mother was even worse, and nicer.

Why did my mother marry George who was four years younger than her? I've never been able to fathom that one out. I understood that my own father popped off when I was two. I didn't know then whether it was popped off dead, or just popped off, because the only time I mentioned him I got my ears boxed.

Thinking he might have popped off dead I started to pray for him. That was when I became a sort of Catholic. You see George was a Catholic, a wooden one as he said. I couldn't understand that at first. But it wasn't the reason he couldn't marry my mother in the Catholic church but had to go to the Town Hall to have it done. He took me to church one Sunday. It was the very first time I had been in a church and my mother let me go for they had only been married a fortnight and she was still in a good temper. In spite of not understanding a word that was said, I liked that church very much. What with all the bobbing up and down, it was as good as the pictures.

George didn't go to church every Sunday, just now and again. Some Sundays he took me to see his mother, and she said to call her gran. But the first time I referred to her as gran at home my mother took me into the bedroom and, grabbing me by the shoulders, shook me as she said, "You're not to call that woman gran. She's an awful woman, common."

One thing I learned early, my mother was everything but common: she didn't talk common, she didn't act common, she didn't look common. She was about five foot four in height and had a lovely figure and was pretty. She had large grey eyes, dark hair with a deep wave in it, and a small mouth, and she always spoke nice, correctly. She was an only child and she had been born in this house, 7 Wellenmore Terrace,

Fellburn. Her father had been a draughtsman, drawing ships' insides, so I understood from the few times she spoke about him. Her mother had been a music teacher. She didn't talk very much about her either. They had both died before I was born.

So why, her not being common at all, had she to marry a man like George, because you couldn't get anybody more common than George: he smoked and he drank, and he used language; he laughed a lot and very loudly; and then he wasn't a nice eater, he guzzled.

But George was nice. He altered my life . . . for a time. I always used to associate him with colours. When he came into the house it turned bright yellow; when he left, it dropped back into its extremely clean and extremely tidy, extremely well-furnished grey.

George travelled, that was, when he did the job he liked best which was driving a lorry. But he often lost his job because he didn't get the lorry to where it was going. When he got drunk on the way he just slept in it, and on one occasion when he was making for a port with some big crates, it was twenty-four hours after the boat had sailed when they found the lorry in a lay-by. He was still asleep in it.

Sometimes he worked digging ditches; other times he'd help knock buildings down. He didn't seem to mind any job that he did except the one that took him down manholes, because then he smelt.

They began fighting towards the end of the first year because my mother knew by then she had let herself down in marrying George. But I was glad she had because I'd never had a companion like him. Whenever he met me outside he would always take hold of my short arm. And sometimes on a Sunday - this would be a Sunday when he hadn't a bad head first thing in the morning - he would take me to church with him and we would come home along a tree-lined path through the park which led to the field bordering our terrace. There he would say, "All right?" and I would look up at him and laugh and say, "Right ahead!" And then we would both hitch along, like Katie and I did. He was very big and bulky, and watching his feet leave the ground and flop down again seemed to me to be very funny, and always before the end of the path I would lean against him and laugh until my body shook. And then there was that memorable Sunday when he suddenly lifted me up until my face was level with his and he said, "Maisie Rochester, it's a bloody shame. All round, it's a bloody shame."

I couldn't make out why the laughter should suddenly cease and he was quiet on the way home. I only knew that in that moment I loved George Michael Carter and I loved his mother, and to me they were the most wonderful people in the world . . . my world.

I was thirteen years old when George left us, and there was no question about how he popped off because he came and told me that he was going. My mother had gone to a meeting of the Literary Circle. Apparently she had been a member for years before she married George, and then she stopped going, until six months ago when she started again.

It was on a Thursday night. We'd had our teas and I was washing up. I did most of the washing up and in spite of my short arm I rarely broke anything. There had been no conversation at the tea-table: Mother was talking less and less to George, and they weren't fighting openly any more like they had done when they were sleeping together in the big bedroom; for a long time now George had slept in the back room.

Our house was quite big. It had five bedrooms, the bathroom and a small storeroom, with a long attic above; and downstairs there was a big kitchen, a sitting-room, a dining-room and a smaller room that my mother always referred to as the study, because her father's books were arrayed on shelves all round the room.

When my mother came downstairs this night she looked very pretty. She was dressed in pale blue and her face was made up, and as I looked at her I wished I loved her like I did Gran Carter.

"I'll be back at half past nine," she said. "You be in bed by then." She rarely looked at me when she gave me orders. When I come to think of it she rarely looked at me at all if she could avoid it.

She did not speak to George, but as soon as the door had closed on her he looked towards it for a moment, then went upstairs.

I finished the dishes; then I, too, went upstairs and into my room, because I had to do my homework and I always did it in my bedroom. But on that night I stood looking out of the window because the sun was still shining brightly. It was early September and it had been quite hot all day. As far as I could see there were deckchairs in most of the back gardens. I could see as far as the Stickles' garden and the top of Mr Stickle's head that came well above the back of the deck-chair.

The Stickles had only lived in the terrace for about six months. They rented their house, which in a way made them different, for most in the terrace owned their property. But the Stickles weren't common. Mr Stickle lived with his sister, and was looked upon as a sort of gentleman. He was a little old, being twenty-three, and he dressed very smartly. Katie Moore's mother said he'd have to because that was his job, being assistant manager in a high-class gentleman's shop, which Katie's mother said wouldn't last very long because men weren't wearing suits now.

It's funny about that, I mean the things that people say: men weren't wearing suits now. When Katie told me that, my mind did a funny little skip and I saw men going about in their shirts and underpants. It made me giggle inside. I had the habit of doing this, but nobody knew about it. Oh yes, they did, George knew. I had told him once and he had laughed and laughed.

I couldn't get down to my homework this night and I sat scribbling in my spare book - it was an exercise book that I wrote things in such as names and things I wanted to remember, and also sayings that sounded funny to me - when George's voice came from outside the door, saying, "Maisie."

I ran and opened it, and he came in and sat on the edge of the bed. He had his best suit on and his hair was wet and well combed back. His big face was shiny and somehow as I looked at him I thought he did resemble Oswald. That's what I called the bear he had bought me when he first married my mother.

I sat on the bed beside him and, when he didn't speak, I said, "What's the matter, George?"

He still didn't speak for a time, but then he muttered a blasphemy: "Christ Almighty!" he said.

I didn't flinch as my mother might have done because Gran Carter often said things like that. Gran Carter was always calling on God. She could do it in so many ways too. And now George turned to me and caught hold of both my hands, and I looked down on them as they became lost inside his, and he looked down on them too as he said, "I'm going, Maisie."

"Going where?" I said stupidly, knowing that there was only one place he would be going to and that would be his mother's. And he said this: "To me ma's." Then he looked into my face and his eyes were sad as he went on, "I can't stand it any more, Maisie. You know what I mean. This isn't life, this isn't living, it's hell. I suppose I'm to blame for part of it but not the main part. She's hopeless . . . your mother. Well, you know that, I don't have to tell you, you've had her longer than me. And God help you from now on. You know something, Maisie?"

I gulped in my throat and told myself not to cry, but then I started to cry and he said, "Oh, pet, pet, come on. But look -" He brought my head towards his shoulder and as I sniffed I inhaled his particular smell of cigarette smoke, soap, and body sweat that was so comforting, and his voice came to me now, muffled as he said, "I might as well tell you, Maisie, I've stayed as long as I have just because of you. Me ma knows that an' all, 'cos as I said to her, that woman isn't human where you're concerned. I want to tell you something." He put his broad thumb under my chin and lifted my face up. "If she ever gets physically cruel, I mean with her hands, she's an expert with her tongue we know that, but if she should take up the other way, you come straight over to us. Now promise me?"

"Yes, George." My voice sounded like a squeak, and he smiled wryly now as he dried my eyes with his handkerchief, saying, "You've not only been unlucky with your mother, you've been unlucky with your fathers, although that poor bloke has my sympathy. Wherever he is, good luck to him, I say. He got away in time: he had only two years, I've had six of 'em."

"He got away? You mean he isn't dead?"

"No. Well, I don't know, lass; he wasn't dead when he left her. Went to Australia, I understand. Well, now she'll be divorced for the second time. Oh, Maisie." He now stroked my hair back from my face as he said, "I wish to God I could take you along of me. I do. I do. You mightn't have the bloody cold elegance you've got here, but you'd know love, and appreciation, aye." He smiled widely now as he tapped my forehead, saying, "People don't know what goes on in there, do they? I think I must be the only one that's discovered what you've got up top. Anyway, what you've got to do, Maisie, at least for the next three or four years. . . What are you now? Thirteen? Aye, well until you're sixteen and you leave school, what you've got to do is don't answer her back, let her get on with it. But then you don't answer her back, do you? Perhaps it would be better if you did. Oh God, I don't know. . . Anyway try to make the best of it, because you can't do anything now as she's legally got the right over you."

We sat staring at each other. Then of a sudden he sprang up from the bed and pulled me into his arms and kissed me before going quickly out; and I turned to the window, and the sun had gone in and the world had changed.

I sat down on the dressing-table stool and looked in the middle of the three mirrors. Because I was crying so much I could make out only the outline of my face But I knew what it looked like: two small round eyes, a nose that would have looked all right on anybody else's face but didn't seem to fit mine, and my mouth too, too big for the size of my face. My teeth weren't bucked, but still I had a job to keep my lips closed all the time. And my hair like tow, neither fair nor brown, mousy-coloured. Again it would have looked all right on somebody else's head because there was plenty of it, and it was thick and coarse, but there wasn't a kink in it. As for my figure, I was straight up and down. Gran Carter said it would be all right, I was a late developer and I'd have a bust like nobody's business in a couple of years' time. I wasn't troubled about having a bust, but my face troubled me even more than my arm, because I could keep my arm waist high and put my schoolbag on it and hardly anybody noticed it then. But you can't hide your face, and it was my face that my mother didn't like because no part of me resembled her. She was ashamed of me in so many ways. This thought was very clear in my mind as I blinked the tears away and dried my eyes. It was as if the six years that George had been in the house were as a tick of time, they had gone; and once again I was seeing my mother in a tantrum and hearing her voice saying, "God! To have to put up with you an' all and looking like you do. Why? Why?"

Chapter 2

I should really start from the time I was seventeen, and yet what happened between when I was thirteen and that time set the pattern for all the years following.

The effect on my mother of George leaving was varied. When she returned that night and read the note he had left, she laughed and laughed. I hadn't gone to bed as she had ordered, because I had felt in some strange way she would need comfort. But what she did was to throw herself on the couch in the sitting-room and laugh. In amazement I watched her lift her slim legs from the carpet until they were on a level with her hips, spread her arms wide, then throw her head back. Her small mouth was wide open and I could see her tongue wagging in the cavity. If she had cried and thrown things I'd have been less afraid. But this reaction of hers seemed to give me an insight into the complexity of her character.

Within days her reactions changed. Perhaps it was the neighbours that caused the different eruptions. Yet how could she know what they were thinking because she wouldn't let them into the house. I knew what they were thinking because of Katie. Katie said her mother said some folks thought it was the best thing that could have happened, because George was a big drunken slob. But others said that it was a wonder he had stuck to her so long, because they were oil and water.

I learned a lot from Katie on our journeys to and from school. I liked Katie. She was my best friend; in fact she was my only friend, and because of that I had to forgive her when she hurt me saying things about George and telling me what her mother said about me looking as I did. We quarrelled once and she said her mother said a pikestaff wasn't as plain as me.

It was on a Saturday about a week after George had left that my mother startled me by almost springing on me and taking me by the shoulders and shaking me with a strength that was out of all proportion to her size as she cried at me, "You go near his mother's and I'll murder you. Do you hear? And if you see him in the street and speak to him I'll thrash the skin off you." Her voice and everything about her had ceased to be refined; in this moment she sounded as common as the people she despised for being so. She was thirty-four years old at this time and had no lines on her face. Yet such was her expression that she appeared older than Gran Carter who was very old, almost sixty.

"Speak!"

I couldn't speak.

"Do you hear? Promise me you'll never go near that house or go near him."

I couldn't promise.

When one hand left my shoulder and came in contact with the side of my head, my vision blurred. I heard a noise in my ear like a train choo-chooing in a station and I fell to the side and grabbed the kitchen table; and I stayed like that for some minutes. And when I pulled myself straight and looked slowly around, there was no one there.

George had said if she started with anything physical I had to go to him. Well, if I had taken him at his word, I would have run to him at least once a week during the next six months.

It was on my fourteenth birthday when I received the card from George that she really did seem to go mad. It was a beautiful card, what I saw of it. It had a pretty girl on the front holding a bouquet of roses, and I had just opened it and read. "From George and Gran with love to Maisie", when it was snatched from my hand. As I watched her tear it into a dozen pieces and without uttering one word, it was then the voice became audible, but only to me.

Oh, you cruel thing. I hate you. Do you hear? I hate you. I'll go to Gran's, I'll go this very day. I will. I will.

I knew my mouth was opening and shutting as if I was saying the words, but, like her, I remained silent.

Gran Carter lived in the lower end of Fellburn, Bog's End where all the common people lived. She lived on a council estate. It was an old council estate. The houses looked like rows of rundown barracks, but inside Gran's house everything was bright, cheerful and cluttered. I knew the first time I saw the furniture that it was common; but it was comfortable, and she always had a fire on, a real fire not an electric one with artificial logs like we had. And she made toast at the fire and put dripping on it mixed with the sediment from the meat. I'd never tasted anything so wonderful as that first piece of toast and dripping. And on that Saturday morning I longed with a longing that was painful in its intensity to get into that house and to sit close to Gran Carter and perhaps see George. But my mother watched me like a hawk all day, silently, no word passing between us.

On Sunday morning when Katie called and asked if I could go for a walk with her, my mother said to her, "Where do you propose to go?" And Katie said, "Oh, as far as my cousin's at the bottom of Brampton Hill."

Brampton Hill was the real posh part of Fellburn. Most of the big houses had been turned into flats and Katie's cousin lived in one of them, but the name Brampton Hill was still a passport and so I was allowed to go. But no sooner were we outside the house than Katie said, "Will you do something for me?"

And I immediately said, "Yes," because I would do anything for Katie. "Well," said Katie, "I met a boy. He . . . he's nice. He goes to Paynton High School. But he's nearly seventeen and I daren't let Mam or Dad know 'cos he's so old, and he looks older. He's very tall." She smiled widely at me. "Anyway, I told him I'd try to meet him round by the lower park today. I told them I was going out with you. You won't give me away, will you?"

I looked at her sadly: how could she say such a thing? She said quickly, "I know you won't, but . . . but I want to be alone with him for a while."

The idea sprang like a ray of light into my mind and I gabbled at her, "How long d'you want to be alone?"

"Well, I must be back for dinner-time, that's at one, and it's now quarter past ten. Say an hour and a half. Would you mind, I mean, being on your own?"

"No. No, I wouldn't. Look, there's . . . there's some place I want to go an' all, so let's meet back at the market place at half past twelve, eh?"

"Good. Yes, good."

We held hands and ran now towards the market, and from there my feet might have had wings on them, they moved so quickly, and I was gasping when, ten minutes later, I knocked on Gran Carter's door, and when she opened it she took a step backwards as she cried, "Why, pet! Why, pet! Well, you're a sight for sore eyes. Come on. Come on in.

Georgie, look who's here!"

The front door led into a small hallway that gave off to a passage, and there at the far end, looking as if he had just got out of bed, was George, and he appeared beautiful to me.

"Why! Why, hello, lass!" He came slowly towards me, his hands outstretched. "You've flown the pigeon loft then?"

"Yes, George." I gazed up at him into his shaggy bear-like face, and he put his arm around my shoulder and led me into the sitting-room. It was rather untidy, but nice, and there was a smell of cooking and Gran Carter said, "Can you stay for a bite of dinner, hinny?"

"No, Gran. I'm very sorry. I'll have to get back."

"However did you manage to get out?" She bent over me as she spoke. She had a round face, not unlike George's, but her skin was softer. Her hair was a reddy brown; she had it touched up once a month; she was wearing a hair net. She flung out an arm now, saying, "You would catch us on the hop, wouldn't you? This is like Paddy's market. But it's Sunday an' we were both in late last night." She nodded towards George. "I was at the whist drive, an' I won again. I'm the luckiest so . . . body on this earth. They're tryin' to say I'm a card sharper." She put her head back and let out a laugh very like George's. "They're green. I won the lot last night, twelve pounds. What are you gona have, hinny? A cup of tea or cocoa? . . . Have we got any lemonade left?"

"We never have any lemonade left when there's beer in the house an' you want shandies, you know that." George plonked himself down on the sofa beside me and, pushing his mother with the flat of his hand, he said, "Go on, woman, this is a special occasion, give her coffee. You like coffee, don't you, Maisie?" And without waiting for an answer, he looked back at his mother and said, "She likes coffee. Of course" - he pulled a face at me now - "it isn't the real stuff, not like . . . well, in 7 Wellenmore."

His mother went into the kitchen laughing, and he turned towards me and, his face straight, he said, "How is she?"

I couldn't answer him.

"Like that, is it?" he said, and he jerked his chin. "Has she said anything about divorce?" He didn't wait for an answer but added, 'Well, if she has or she hasn't, it makes no difference: if I have to wait I'll wait and gladly, and put in some practice for the next time." Then he added quickly, "Well, what I mean is, I'll shop around and not make the same mistake twice. Well, you know what I mean."

I knew what he had meant in the first place and I knew that he thought I was too young to understand. And on the surface I was, but under it there was this other being that knew about some things without in a way having learned them.

"Did you get our card, pet?" Gran Carter's face came round the kitchen door and I looked towards her and opened my mouth twice but no sound came out. It was as if I was watching my mother tearing it into shreds again. And when I eventually did speak, I stammered, saying, "Ye . . . yes, thank you."

George must have noticed the effect the question had on me because he turned my face towards him and looked at me silently for a moment before he said softly, "You didn't get it, did you?" I nodded at him and muttered, "Yes. Ye . . . ye . . . yes I did."

"Well, she found out about it, eh? And what did she do, tear it up? Now, now, don't upset yourself." He was whispering now. "But say nothin' to her." He nodded towards the kitchen. "If she thought that had happened she would go round there and belt her face for her, she would that, 'cos she went into Smith's and took a long time to pick that card for you. I was with her." He smiled. "There was something in the little lass's face on the card that reminded me of you."

How kind, how kind George was. Suddenly I thought of the statues of the saints in his church. He was better than all the saints.

"Here you are, hinny. And have a chocolate biscuit."

As Gran Carter put the cup of coffee and a plate of biscuits to the side of me I knew for a certainty from where her son got his kindness. She now put her hand on my hair - I had taken off my school hat - and said, "You know, you could do something with that hair. You get that trimmed at the hairdresser's and it would look real bonny. It's strong hair. They always like strong hair. They have a devil of a job with mine." She now pulled the net upwards from her head. "Peggy Wicklow" - she nodded towards George now - "she says she can count me hairs on the top an' why did I pass on what hair I had to you. She said you should go to her and she'd trim you up."

"Aye, she'd do more than that, would Peggy Wicklow." They both laughed and he added, " See me goin' into a woman's hairdresser. I hate to go to the barber's; I'm gona be like the young chaps, let it grow down me back."

"You do if you dare! All them young bug . . . people look lousy."

George became so doubled up with laughter that he spluttered as he said, "Why didn't you say it, Ma, she won't drop down dead? She's heard it afore an' she's had her bellyful of politeness. Haven't you, pet?" He pulled me towards him, and the voice inside me said, "More than me bellyful, George. Oh yes, more than me bellyful." At this moment all I wanted was to be like them, and be common. Oh, I did want to be common.

After I'd drunk the coffee and eaten three chocolate biscuits I said I'd have to be going, because I was to meet Katie at the market. Why, asked George, had I to meet Katie at the market? But I paused before telling them why, because I thought I was giving Katie away. I knew though I could trust these two people with Katie's secret. But I couldn't see what was so funny about it when George put his arm around his mother's shoulders and she put her arm around his waist and they hung together like that half over me while they laughed, and George said, "Eeh! the things that go on." Then he ended, "But you thank Katie for us. Thank her 'specially, and tell her you'll stand in for her every Sunday."

"I'll tell her."

At the doorstep they both kissed me, but then walked down the short front garden to the gate, and when I reached the end of the row and turned, they were still there and they waved. But after turning the corner, all the joy left me and I was filled with such longing and a great urge to run back to them and be loved and be common.

That word common was coming into my mind more and more every day. And Katie was using it too. Such and such a girl was common. Such and such a thing was common. Such and such a place was common. But mostly she was saying nowadays that such and such a one talked common. How did one talk common? Perhaps she was meaning the people who talked in broad Geordie. But why were they common because they talked like that? This word common was in a way troubling me, because I knew that everything nice that had happened to me in my life had been common.

Katie was not at the market place. I waited until one o'clock and when the Town Hall clock struck, I turned in agitation and made for home, and as I neared the terrace and saw Mrs Moore leaving our door I knew what was in store for me.

I went in the back way and through the kitchen. She was standing in the middle of the hall, and what she said to me in a quiet voice was, "Where did you go when you left Katie to do her dirty work?" I didn't answer, but that voice inside me said, She's got a nasty mind; Katie wouldn't do anything bad.

"Where did you go? I'm asking you, girl."

The voice said, Speak. Say you went for a walk. Say something. If you don't, she'll hit you.

"You went along to them, didn't you?" She was standing close to me now. I hadn't seen her walk towards me; I think my fear had dimmed my vision.

When she did hit me it wasn't with the flat of her hand but with her fist. She had a small hand. It looked delicate but the bones seemed to go right through my skull. I was falling to one side when a blow came on the other side of my head. This time it was the flat of her hand. And now she was using both on me, flap-flap,flap-flap. I was crouched on the bottom stair, my face pressed tight now against the carpet on the third step and the fingers of one hand gripping the edge of the flat brass stair-rod.

I didn't hear her leave. The house was quiet, so quiet that I heard the sparrows chirping in the nest they had built above the cup of the drainpipe. I crawled up the rest of the stairs and then, bent double, made for my room. I knew I was crying a lot and yet I was making no sound, not outwardly at any rate, but inside the voice was yelling at me, Go to George's. Go to George's. He said you had to. I answered it, No, no; she'll get wrong; not only from him she'll get wrong, she'll get wrong from other people. . .

When I lay on top of the bed I shivered and for the first time I realized I hadn't my coat on. I remember my hat flying off my head but I couldn't remember her tearing my coat off me.

The next few hours became a blur. I must have fallen asleep, and I woke up with a dreadful dread on me because I felt I had gone blind. Something had happened to my face; it was stiff and I could scarcely open my eyes, but through their narrowed slits I saw her standing over me. The electric light was on so I knew it was night-time. As I shrank back into the bed her voice came to me soft and in a tone that she had never used to me before. "Sit up and drink this," she said.

It was a great effort to do as she told me, and she put her hand behind my back and it felt firm and gentle. And I found difficulty in sipping the tea because my lips were swollen.

When I couldn't manage any more she took the cup away, then stood looking down at me. Her hands were clasped tightly against the collar of her dress and her voice was a mutter now as she said, "You asked for it. You know you did, you asked for it. You shouldn't have done it. You asked for it." And as I peered at her I realized she was frightened, and the more this became clear in my mind the more my own fear of her ebbed away. . .

The following week is lost in mist because at times I knew I was in bed and yet at other times I felt I was some place else: sometimes at Gran Carter's; sometimes hitching along the park path with George; and more than once I seemed to be in a room that was lined with books and laughing at a man sitting across a desk. He was a nice man and I knew I liked him until he turned into a policeman, and he took my hand quite gently and led me into a cell-like room with bars on the door.

When everything else during that week turned into a misty blur, that last picture remained in my mind, foretelling the future.

My mother brought up meals and tried to make me eat, but my face was so stiff that I could only swallow liquids. She very rarely spoke to me and I never spoke to her at all, at least not during that first week. But sometimes during the second week, I said to her, "I . . . I must go to school. They'll be wondering." And she answered, "I've sent them a note and told them you've had a slight . . . a slight accident." She drooped her head now and turned to the side as she added, "You've got to say you toppled down the stairs. You understand?"

I understood, but I said nothing. "You brought it on yourself," she said again. And then she muttered, "I just couldn't bear it, the . . . the indignity, the . . . the. . ." When she turned away I knew she was almost crying and when she left the room I no longer hated her but felt sorry for her.

It was on the Monday of the second week that I saw my face for the first time. It was mottled blue and yellow. My eyes were black, my cheeks were swollen and my large mouth looked even larger. The voice said: No wonder she's frightened. She could have killed you.

Yet in some strange way I was glad it had happened because I had lost my fear of her and I knew also that she would never again raise her hand to me; she mightn't be able to stop her tongue, but the result of her rage had in a way entirely altered our relationship.

During the following days I sat by the back window, but not too close and my view only showed me the McVities' garden to the right of our house. The weather had turned colder so there was no one sitting outside. It was during these days that I first experienced aloneness. It wasn't exactly loneliness, it was if part of me was locked away and had no urge to get out. Yet this part of me seemed real, because nobody knew about it, not even George. I tried to put it into words in my exercise book but it didn't read right. Anyway, if I wanted to write in my book I had to keep alert in case my mother came in, for she would want to read what I had written. She had more than once torn out sheets from my book because she said she had never read anything so infantile in her life; a child of five could do better.

I always wanted to write down things that I thought when I was with Gran Carter, because everything she said sounded funny. Even when she was sad she sounded funny.

What I didn't write down was what had happened over the past few days, because that was beyond words; it was all feelings, feelings that couldn't be expressed.

Then on the Thursday night we had a visitor. When I heard his voice downstairs I clamped my hand over my mouth. The doorbell hadn't rung, so I knew he had come in the back way and he was yelling, "You try an' stop me."

When he burst into the room I was standing with my back to the window and he took only two steps before coming to a halt; then he shook his head as he whispered, "God Almighty!"

My mother was standing behind him and she was yelling at him, "She fell downstairs. She fell downstairs. I tell you, she fell downstairs."

I watched him turn slowly towards her and his voice now was low and his words slow as he said, "You're a bloody liar. Fell downstairs. Who do you think you're trying to hoodwink? It's me remember, George. I'll have you for this. By God, I'll have you for this. I warned you, I did. I warned you time an' time again when I saw what you meant to do. But you've done it. Well, it's the last time you'll lift your hand to her. By God, I'll see to that. Come on, hinny." He thrust out an arm towards me; but I didn't move from where I was standing, and he said again, "Come on, lass."

"I'm . . . I'm all right, George." I saw my mother's eyes on me, her lips were quivering, in fact her whole body was shaking, and then I was amazed to hear myself saying in a calm-like way, "I want to talk to George, Mother."

I saw her throat contract as she gulped, and I wasn't surprised when she turned about and left us alone.

George had hold of my hands, and as he stood looking down into my face his big head moved from side to side and when he muttered, "Poor bairn," I wanted to fall against him and cry. I wanted to feel his arms about me. I wanted to say, "I'll come with you now," but there was this other voice that seemed to belong to someone who had more knowledge and understanding than I had and it said to him, "I can't come, George. I can't leave her. She . . . she'll never do it again."

"By God! she won't. By God! she won't, lass."

"She's sorry. She's . . . well, she's frightened."

"An' well she should be. If this happened a week gone Sunday as I reckoned it did from what I've heard about you supposed to have fallen downstairs, she as near killed you as nothin'. Me ma only heard the day about your supposed fall. Some girl that goes to the same school told her mother, an' me ma soon put two and two together. I . . . I didn't even stop to wash. Look at me!" He held out his work-grimed hands; then dropping down on to his hunkers, he said, "If you came and she took the matter to court and they saw a picture of your face as it is now after all this time, she wouldn't stand an earthly of keepin' you."

"She's lonely, she hasn't got anybody."

"Oh, hinny, you don't know her. She'll get somebody; she'll have some other man in here afore you can say Jack Robinson. But he won't be like me." He smiled wryly now. "A different type altogether. She's got over my phase, digging in the dirt as she once termed it. The next one will be some white collar bloke with an interest in music and such. You know the kind."

I didn't know the kind, but I understood what he meant.

His hand came out and he gently touched my still swollen face and all the time he was muttering to himself; then he asked, "What did the doctor say?"

"I . . . I haven't seen him."

"You haven't?" He screwed up his eyes. "Well, it's about time you did then, isn't it? Has anybody been from the school?"

"I . . . I don't know."

"Somebody must have been around, you off school a fortnight. . . You're sure you won't come?"

"I . . . I want to come, George, you know that. I want to come more than anything, but . . . but somehow I can't. If . . . if I came I would be thinking about her all the time."

"You're daft, do you know that? She's put an old head on young shoulders an' she's not worth your little finger, and she won't thank you for stayin' mind, she won't. I know her."

He was right. I knew that she wouldn't thank me for staying, not in the way I wanted, not by loving me. She was only afraid of me going because of what the neighbours would say and the publicity that might follow if she then took the matter to court. But as for thanking me; no, I knew that she would never even like me. I was, in a way, something that had spoiled her life. I . . . I was a sort of cross.

George stood up now and as he did so a sprinkling of light-coloured dust fell from his clothes: he was working on the buildings, knocking them down again. He now said, "I'm gona tell her that if you don't appear at our house within the next fortnight, when your face goes down that is, I'll be back again. And she won't like that because the neighbours' tongues will be waggin'. I passed two of them on the street as I came in. One was old Mrs Pratt and her lower jaw dropped so far her teeth nearly fell out."

I wanted to laugh but couldn't, and when he bent and put his cheek against mine the smell of lime and brick dust and sweat and cigarette smoke was like perfume to me.

At the door he turned and said, "You'll see a doctor an' all, yes you will." He nodded twice, and then he went out.

I sat down with my back to the window, my joined hands tight between my knees and my head on my chest, and my mind was crying: Oh, George, George, George. . .

My mother acted as if he had never been; but the following

afternoon the doctor called. His name was Doctor Kane.

Over the years there were periods when my mother visited the doctor regularly, and at these times she took a lot of pills. I hadn't seen Doctor Kane for years and had only a faint memory of a man with a hairy face. I had never been really ill except with whooping cough and measles. The faint memory of him went back to a time when I fell on the elbow of my short arm and it swelled up and he stuck needles in it. After a time the swelling subsided but it continued to pain. And now here he was looking at me.

He looked at me for a long time before he said, "Well, well, so you tumbled downstairs. When did this happen?"

"A . . . a few days. . ." His head seemed to snap round on his shoulders and he looked at my mother and said, "She's got a tongue, hasn't she? She can speak for herself. . . Now, when did this happen?"

"Over a week ago," I said.

"Precisely how long over a week ago?"

I daren't look at my mother. "A week gone Sunday," I said.

"A week gone Sunday. Well, well. And so I'm called in to see you now. . . Why?" He was looking at my mother again and her voice trembled as she answered, "She . . . she didn't seem to be recovering as she should."

"From the aftermath on her face I should say she's recovered remarkably well. She must have looked a pretty mess when she reached -" his eyebrows seemed to go up and his beard drooped down as he finished, "the bottom of the stairs."

There was a silence before my mother said, "She . . . she didn't look all that bad at first."

"You surprise me. But still, I'm used to surprises. Well, miss, how do you feel?"

How could I tell him how I felt. Could I say I feel lonely, unloved? But that would be a lie, because George loved me, and Gran Carter loved me. Could I say I feel lost and part of me feels I'm not grown up enough to know anything, and the other part of me feels I don't need to grow up to know? I know it all now, which, when I thought about it even then, was ridiculous.

"Come on, you must know how you feel."

"Not very good."

"Not very good," he repeated; then said, "Now we are getting somewhere. Where do you feel not very good?"

He was a difficult man to talk to and my other voice which I used only to myself now came out, saying tersely, "That's a difficult question to answer, because to tell the truth I don't know where to begin." His whiskered lips moved apart and he showed his teeth as he said, "Now we are really getting someplace, it's up to me to start eliminating, isn't it? By the way" - he turned and looked at my mother - "do you think there could be a cup of tea going?"

I saw her blink rapidly; then she looked at me. "Yes, yes; I'll make one," she said.

As soon as the door had closed on her he sat down on the edge of the bed and stared at me for a moment. "Well, now," he said, "let us use our horse sense, shall we? And I'm sure you've got quite a bit of it tucked away in that napper of yours."

I hadn't time to think that in a way he could be like a cross between George, Gran Carter, and a gentleman - for doctors were gentlemen - all mixed up, because the most strange thing happened at that precise moment, a weird surprising thing, for what did I see but a great horse which galloped right over him. I opened my eyes wider than I'd done since that particular Sunday morning when I'd come through the kitchen and saw my mother waiting for me. My mouth fell into a gape too, for although the creature was galloping, it had its head turned towards me; its eyes were full of knowledge and its lip was back as if it was laughing. It had a long white tail and two white front feet and a great flowing mane, a white spot on its nose, and its body was shining black and as sleekly as a seal's.

"I bet that's the first time you've tried to smile."

"What?"

"I said, miss, I bet that's the first time you've tried to smile. What were you thinking about? Do you find my face funny?"

"Yes, I do a little bit." The horse was galloping around him.

"Well, we are getting somewhere but not along the road I expected. Young ladies should learn to be tactful. You should have said, No, I think you're handsome."

That would have been stretching it. . . . Eeh! my goodness, I had nearly said that, and the horse was laughing.

Was I going a bit funny? When mother punched me like that, had it done something to me? No, no, I wasn't going funny, because I'd always talked to myself, only I hadn't seen a horse before, a dog when I was younger, and there had been a little girl whom I called Jennie. She had gone when my mother married George.

I blinked my eyes a number of times and the horse faded away.

"Does your face still pain?" His voice was quiet now, no humour in it, and I said, "No, it's only a bit stiff."

"How did you manage to fall downstairs?"

I looked to the side before saying, "I tripped."

"Yes, you must have. Oh, yes you must have." He was nodding at me. "Do you get on with your mother? I mean do you argue and fight?"

I was staring unblinking at him and he at me and neither of my voices would give him an answer. Now he leant towards me and said, "If you should fall downstairs again with a kind of dizzy spell, which I suppose that's what it was, wasn't it? You must come straight to the surgery. Do you understand me?"

I understood him all right. His attitude was the same as George's, only he was using different words to express it. "I must tell your mother to come to the surgery," he said, "and I'll give her a prescription for a tonic. She's not looking too well herself . . . You still haven't told me which part of you feels the worst."

"I . . . I just feel low and tired."

"Do you have any trouble with your arm these days?" He reached out and took my hand and waggled it up and down as if he were weighing it, and I said, "No, none at all."

He now put his head on one side and surveyed me for some seconds. "You've grown a lot since I last saw you," he said. "But I think you could do with a little fat on your bones. Do you eat well?"

"Sometimes."

He now let go of my hand and stood up and, taking his case from a side table, he mumbled something before saying, "I'll have that cup of tea downstairs with your mother and I'll send you a bottle along that'll make you jump about a bit. Good-bye."

"Good-bye, Doctor. . ."

I don't know what passed between her and the doctor that day but almost until the day she died she visited him regularly every week. And from when I was fifteen I saw him regularly too.

Chapter 3

My mother had nerves, and I got them. They became evident when my left eyelid started to flutter and the corner of my mouth to twitch.

I had imagined the business of seeing the horse galloping across the doctor to have occurred because I was a little light-headed at the time, but I was to see him again on my first visit to the doctor and it was he who once more brought him into being.

I was to discover that Doctor Kane often used the term "horse sense", and on this day that he saw me . . . and alone, for he told his nurse to tell my mother to stay in the waiting-room, he said to me, "Now, miss, what's all this about? You haven't tripped and fallen downstairs this time. What's troubling you? And don't say you don't know, use your horse sense and tell me." And there it was again, this beautiful horse, galloping right across him, its white tail flying, its two fore-legs in the air, its head turned towards me, its upper lip back showing its big teeth in a grin; and it said, Tell him. Tell him that she doesn't hit you any more, but she talks at you. Tell him you've heard her story from when she was a pampered little girl to what she is now, a nerve-ridden hag, a hundred times.

Eeh! don't talk like that about her.

"What's that you say?"

"I . . . I said, it's my mother's nerves. She keeps talking."

"Yes, she keeps talking. And yes, it's her nerves." He nodded at me. "And her talking is getting on your nerves, isn't it? In fact, it's got. Well now. . . By the way, how old are you?" He looked at the open folder on his desk.

"Fifteen gone."

"How are you doing at school?"

"Not bad."

"What's your best subject?"

"English."

"What do you intend to do with yourself when you leave school? Going to try for university?"

"Oh no." I shook my head. "I'm not clever like that."

"You should leave that to others to say. What makes you think you're not clever like that?"

"Well, I'm only good at English and drawing."

"Well, either of them should get you somewhere; and God knows, they want English, real English, because they've forgotten how to speak it in this country. If you want to hear English spoken correctly you've got to go abroad, because now and again out there you'll hear words pronounced as they should be. The English spoken today is like most doctors' writing, not understandable."

The whiskers on his face parted and I was looking at his lips: they seemed to be the only evident flesh on his face and I was surprised to see how many teeth he had and all large and white. He had always seemed to me to be pretty old. He was forty, but that, to me then, was as old as the Ancient Mariner. "Now" - he was leaning across the desk and wagging his finger almost in my face "what you've got to do, miss, is to get out and about. Do you dance?"

"No."

"Can you dance?"

"No."

"Well then, you'll have to learn. Take dancing lessons. Join a club."

"I . . . I couldn't."

"Why not?"

"I don't make friends easily. It's . . . it's my arm."

"*Nonsense.*" He pulled himself up straight and banged my case folder closed. "You've got two legs, haven't you? People don't dance with their arms. Come on, spit it out, get it off your chest. Tell me why you don't make friends; why you don't join clubs or go dancing."

Go on, tell him. The great black horse had stopped galloping and was looking at me. Its mouth was closed now, but its eyes were speaking. Go on, it said, tell him the truth. He's the only one you can talk to who will understand. You can't tell George because he would just bang about and tell you lies, because he doesn't want to hurt you. This man won't do that. Go on, right now, tell him. And tell him Katie hasn't spoken to you since the Sunday business because she blames you for splitting on her. And anyway, her mother has forbidden her to have anything more to do with you. Go on, tell him.

I didn't tell him that, what I said was, "It's my face."

"What!"

His eyebrows had moved upwards again; his eyes looked huge round brown balls.

"I'm . . . I'm plain . . . very . . . not nice looking."

He sat well back in his chair now and let out a long sigh, pulled his beard onto his chest and nodded at me as he said, "Yes, it's true, you're plain, but as regards not nice looking, there's a difference. It's no use telling you that the ugly ducklings turn into swans, because I've found out already that you've got quite an amount of horse sense in that head of yours."

There! he had said it again, and the horse was at his antics once more and laughing now.

"But the last term, not nice looking, that doesn't apply," the doctor said. "Plain things can be nice. You will find that in life very few handsome men marry beautiful women. Some of the cleverest and most prominent women in the world are ugly. Do you know that?"

"No."

He paused and stared at me, and my lip began to twitch.

"The big fellow didn't come back?"

"No."

"Well, one can't blame him. But your mother was a fool there, that's the type she needed, not that she would admit it. Well now -" he rose from the desk and came round towards me and, putting his hand on my shoulder, he said, "you come and see me next week. And I want to see you looking . . . nicely plain. Do you understand? Nicely plain." He sighed now as he added, "Send your mother in. . ."

He was to say those four words to me a number of times during the following year. There were times when I had no fluttering of the eyelid and no twitching of the lip, but there were other times, generally following her bad bouts, when it seemed that the corner of my mouth was trying to reach my eye. But during this time I had one consolation, I acquired a companion. My horse came to stay and I christened him. It was funny how the christening came about, because in a way it was connected with real horses. Up till that day he had just come and gone at odd times, mostly when I was talking to the doctor. But then he began to appear when my mother kept talking at me while we were sitting eating a meal, one each side of the table, in the kitchen; or when I was feeling very lonely. At these times he would always try to cheer me up. Then this day I was coming from school and while passing the Bentley Street traffic lights that had turned red, there stood a horse box and almost on eye level with me were the words in small print: B. Hamilton, and immediately I said to myself, Hamilton. That's a nice name, Hamilton. Then there he was almost skipping over the crossing in front of me, as if he was pleased with the name. And so from then on he became Hamilton. It was as simple as that.

It was on my sixteenth birthday when I received the birthday card and a little parcel from George and Gran Carter that my mother had the first seizure.

I hadn't seen much of George during the last year. He was working again on the long-distance lorries, and whenever I managed to visit Gran's, he had just come or gone. Twice, when I saw him, he had the woman with him. She was the hairdresser that Gran had referred to that Sunday, that memorable Sunday, and from the beginning I didn't like her. Not that I was jealous of her. Yet I suppose I was a bit. But at the same time I wanted George to be happy and I knew that he had to have a woman in order to be happy. Right from the start though I thought that George should have a better woman than Peggy Wicklow because she was common, really common.

It was on my first acquaintance with Peggy Wicklow that I realized all common things or all common people weren't nice. She was a different common from George and Gran, she was loudmouthed. Of course, Gran shouted when she talked, and so did George, but not in the same way as Peggy Wicklow.

Just as I didn't approve of her, so I knew she didn't approve of me. And I knew it was a mystery to her what George saw in me to make a fuss about, because at our first meeting he led me to her and said, "This is Maisie, Peggy, and she's my first girl." And at this Gran had cried, "There you are! After me bringin' him up he pushes me aside. I'm nothin' to him now."

It was all in fun but I wished they wouldn't do it because deep inside I knew they were putting a false value on me, a value that nobody else could see. I loved them for it, yet was sometimes irritated by it.

It was when I arrived home from school that I saw the parcel and the card. Neither had been opened, but she was there when I undid the sticky tape that was round the parcel. When I unwrapped the paper and revealed a little red box, I paused before lifting the lid and looked at her. She wasn't looking at me but at the box. I told myself not to open it, but my fingers wouldn't obey me and when I lifted the lid there was a gold watch lying on a bed of red satin. I lifted it out and held it between my finger and thumb. The wrist band was gold linked and when slowly I pulled it over my fingers I found that it stretched. It was an amazing feeling that these small solid links could stretch. It was as if I was witnessing magic.

"Take it off!"

"But . . . but. . ."

"Take it off! Do as I say, take it off."

It was while I hesitated that it happened. She opened her small mouth wide and gasped at the air as her hands clutched at her throat. When they moved down to her chest she toppled over and fell to the floor. I tore the watch from my wrist and flung it on to the hall table, and bending down to her, I cried, "What is it? What is it?"

She rolled on to her side now and began to groan. The colour had gone from her face, her eyes were tightly shut, her mouth was open and she was gasping at the air.

I must get the doctor. Mrs Atkins had a phone three doors down. I rushed to the front door and out on to the path, and there I saw Mr Stickle and I grabbed at him, "My . . . my mother's taken ill. I . . . I've got to get the doctor. Mrs . . . Mrs Atkins has a phone."

"What is wrong with her?" His voice was cool and polite.

"I . . . I don't know. She's in a kind of seizure."

"Is she in bed?"

"No, no, she's in the hall." I jerked my head backwards.

"Well" - his voice was still cool - "you go and phone from Mrs Atkins's and I'll see what I can do." He passed me and went up the path, and I dashed down to Mrs Atkins and rang the bell three times. When she opened the door she looked surprised to see me. Again I was gabbling. She got the gist of what I was saying and said, "All right. All right. I'll phone him for you. You get back."

I dashed back and into the hall to see Mr Stickle putting a cushion under my mother's head. She was still on the floor, and he glanced at me and said, "It looks like she's had a heart attack. She'd better not be moved." Then straightening himself, he stood looking around the hall, his eyes lingering longest on the open door that led into the sitting room. After a while he spoke to me again, saying. "Has she had bad news . . . a shock?"

I didn't answer. But yes, she'd had bad news, a shock. Nine days ago she'd had her thirty-seventh birthday and the only thing she had received was a card from me. I'd written formally on the bottom of it: Happy Birthday, from Maisie. I couldn't say anything else. She hadn't received a present of any kind. I never had any money now to buy anything. Since George left the only money I handled was my bus fares, and at times the precise amount if I was going to the pictures. The exception was when I went to see Gran Carter. She often gave me a shilling, and George always put a half-crown in my pocket when we met, and I bought chocolates on the side with the money.

My mother, I knew, was quite well off; her parents, although not wealthy, had been saving people. How much my mother had been left I didn't know, only that she drew just so much out of the bank every week for the housekeeping. But on her birthday she hadn't received a present from anyone, and yet here was I, her nondescript daughter, her thorn in the flesh, as she called me, the recipient of a beautiful gold wrist-watch. It must have been too much for her.

When I didn't answer Mr Stickle he moved towards the front door, saying, "Well, I must get back to business," and he pulled the lapels of his coat together as he spoke, then adjusted his neat tie. I stared at him, wanting to say, Don't leave me. Before this I'd only glimpsed him, but now I was looking him full in the face. Without his trilby hat he didn't look so old as I imagined. He was tall and his face was round. The shape didn't suit his length. His skin was pale as if it had never seen the sun; his eyes I noticed were blue and his lashes quite long for a man; his nose was thin towards the tip, and his mouth small, like my mother's I thought; he spoke precisely, his words clipped. He paused on the doorstep and stood as if thinking for a moment; then turning to me, he said, "I'll go and tell my sister. She'll stay with you until the doctor comes."

"Thank you." I felt deeply grateful to him for his kind thought. I went back to my mother and knelt down by her side. She was moaning gently as if in pain and I asked her if she was: "Are you in pain, Mother?" I said, but she didn't answer.

Some minutes later when I heard the footsteps on the pathway I rose and went to meet Miss Stickle. I had never looked at her fully before either: she was as tall as her brother but twice as thick; she looked hefty, strong and much older than him. She seemed to bounce into the room. Her voice was loud: "Well, well," she said; "she's collapsed, has she? Dear, dear." And she bent over my mother and asked her, "Are you in pain?"

When she got no reply she straightened up and, looking at me, she said, "Looks like a heart attack. One thing sure, she won't be able to get upstairs for a while. Have you got a couch, I mean in your sitting-room?"

"Yes." I pointed, and she marched forward, right to the middle of the room, and there she stopped and stood looking about her, her eyes seeming to rest on one piece of furniture after another. I stood in the doorway watching her. Presently, she patted the chesterfield couch, saying, "This should do in the meantime. When the doctor comes we'll get her in here." And she again looked round the room before turning to me and saying, "Nice, nice. It's bigger than most rooms in the terrace. How's that?"

"I . . . I think it was two rooms at one time."

"Oh, yes, yes" - she nodded - "I can see now." Then she pointed to the windows. "Good idea, plenty of light." She came back into the hall now and, looking down at my mother and her voice low, she muttered, "Hasn't been well for some time, has she? Nerves, suffers from nerves?" She glanced towards me, and I said, "Yes."

"All nonsense really; lack of will power."

I was amazed at her talking like this and felt upset when I thought that the whole neighbourhood must know my mother had nerves. I wished the doctor would come. . .

It was fifteen minutes later when, seemingly reluctantly, he came through the open doorway and, after glancing first at Miss Stickle, turned to me and said, "What's this? What's this?"

"She's had a turn."

He knelt down by my mother's side and, taking her hand from her chest, he felt her pulse. Then quietly he said to her, "Mrs Carter, its all right. It's all right," then rose and looked about him. Addressing me again, he said, "The couch in the sitting-room, we'll put her on there." And now turning abruptly to Miss Stickle, he went on, "You can give me a hand."

I was now surprised to hear Miss Stickle say, "She's had a heart attack; is it wise to move her?" especially after what she had previously said.

"What do you suggest, madam, leave her on the floor all night? Take hold of her legs and help me lift her."

Miss Stickle obeyed him, albeit somewhat slowly, and between them, with me hovering at the side, they managed to settle her on the couch in the sitting-room. And now he turned to me, saying, "Get some bedding and cover her up, then make a hot drink."

"Don't they usually send them to hospital in such cases?"

"What cases, madam?"

I stopped for a moment and looked at them. They were both bristling.

"I think she's had a heart attack."

"You're not paid to think about such matters, that's my job. Now, I'd be obliged if you would leave us."

As Miss Stickle marched from the room, I followed her, and in the hall I caught up with her and said, placatingly, "Thank you. Thank you, Miss Stickle, for your help." But all she said was, "That man! He's most unprofessional."

However on the doorstep, she turned and said quite kindly, "If you need me, you'll know where to find me."

"Thank you. Thank you, Miss Stickle." I sounded grateful, and indeed I was: neither Mrs Nelson nor Mrs McVitie would have come in and helped. I knew that.

Blankets. I dashed upstairs and brought some, and a top sheet, from the linen cupboard, and when I entered the sitting-room Doctor Kane was sitting by my mother's side talking to her. "Come on," he was saying. "Come on. There's nothing wrong, not what you think. The feeling will pass. I'm going to give you something to make you sleep, really sleep, then we'll have a talk. Now you are going to be all right."

Nothing wrong? Nothing wrong?

He turned to me and motioned me out of the room, and in the hall he said, "Don't look so worried, it's nothing."

"Nothing?"

"Hysteria."

"What?"

"Nervous hysteria." He nodded. "I'm not surprised; I've been expecting it."

"Hysteria?" I repeated.

"Yes, that's what I said, hysteria. Her nerves have got the better of her, causing her to show all the symptoms of a heart attack. It happens again and again: they think they're going to die, they don't. But one thing I do know." He wiped his fingers. "She should go away and have treatment. I've been telling her this for months past. What brought this on? Some climax, eh?"

"I . . . I got a present; it's my birthday. George had sent me a gold watch."

"Oh." His eyebrows made the usual effort to disappear into his thick brown wiry hair. "That would do it. Dear, dear. These women." He shook his head. "Ah well, I'll be passing this way in a short while and I'll drop you in some tablets. See that she takes one at night; it'll make her sleep. But don't encourage her to stay on her back during the day, she'll be much better going about. And tomorrow make her a tasty light meal; and get her to eat it."

At the front door he turned and, looking at me, he said kindly, "No use wishing you a happy birthday, is it?"

I didn't answer, for, holding the door half closed, I was thinking: A tasty light meal. I knew nothing about cooking: she had never let me try my hand at anything in the cooking line. Dust and polish, yes, and clean brasses, especially the stair rods. She would see that I took them from their sockets every week. In fact every piece of furniture in the house was moved every week, especially those pieces standing on carpets, so the moths wouldn't get a chance to breed.

The sun coming through a narrow window near the front door fell on to the wrist-watch on the side table, and the glinting light drew me to it. I picked it up. It was beautiful; and yet it had been the means of causing her to have hysteria. On thinking about the word and its implications, it didn't surprise me because, looking back, I could see that she had always been hysterical. Yet what did surprise me was that the effect could resemble a heart attack.

I went back into the room and drew a chair to her side. After a while I realized she was awake but she didn't open her eyes, and so I said softly, "You are going to be all right. The doctor says you are going to be all right. He's bringing some medicine."

Her only response was to turn on her side, her back to me, and as she did so it came to me that she was not only wide awake now but had been so all along.

Chapter 4

It was from my sixteenth birthday that May Stickle became a regular visitor to the house. Strangely, my mother took to her. And it seemed natural that her brother Howard should at times call in too.

His manner towards my mother was very sympathetic: he spoke to her as if she was an invalid, and she seemed to enjoy this. I knew she looked forward to his visits but, as I put it naively to myself, she couldn't fall for him because he was only twenty-six and she was thirty-seven. But then, George had been younger too. Anyway she was still married to George and divorces took a long time. So this situation didn't worry me; in fact, I was pleased when he came in because he was always very nice to me. I say very nice, he was quietly polite, asking me how I was; and how was I progressing with my secretarial course which I'd taken up since leaving school. Looking at him as I often did now, I realized he could have been very good looking if he'd had a body like George, but he was too thin, weedy . . . scraggy.

During this time, as Gran Carter put it, George was going strong with Peggy Wicklow; and Gran Carter wasn't altogether too happy about it. Flibbertigibbet, she called Peggy Wicklow. What George wanted, in Gran's opinion, was a steady lass who would give him bairns, because he loved bairns. That was why, she said, he was so fond of me. And he was fond of me; she emphasized that he thought the world of me.

During the months that followed, my life seemed to enter a quiet period. I spent a lot of time up in my room; and I talked a lot to Hamilton. I'd had to have an understanding with Hamilton. He had sat on the foot of the bed one night, and he looked no bigger than myself, and this was strange about him because most times when he appeared, he did so as a full-sized stallion, and generally on the move, either galloping in front of people, or pawing the ground, or flashing his white tail from side to side. Yet this night, there he sat, his fore-legs tucked under him, his back legs stretched out, his tail gently flicking the counterpane, and his face, his beautiful big strong face, looking fully at me. And when I said to him, "Now look here, Hamilton!" he said, Look where?

"Don't be silly," I replied.

Well if we can't be silly here, we can't be silly anywhere, can we?

That was right. I had to be on my guard when I was talking to people. If they were people I liked, then he rarely appeared, but if I didn't like them and I felt any animosity at all, he galloped like mad around them. Sometimes he kicked them in the bottom and let out a great neigh. And at these times I had to mumble and explain myself in some way or other. It was very disturbing. So I talked to him plain this night. "Look! it's all right for you," I said; "you haven't got to stand the racket."

You're talking like Gran Carter.

"All right. I could do worse," I answered.

True. True. He threw his head back and his mane bounced and a piece fell down between his eyes and covered the white spot on the top of his nose. I said now, "Promise me that you will keep your place when I meet strangers or someone I don't like."

Well now. Well now. He jerked his back legs out. That doesn't rest with me, it's up to you, isn't it?

He was right in a way. Yet I didn't seem to be able to do anything about it. Every time I thought contrary, there he was.

As I stared at him, I said, "I wonder if other people talk to horses . . . or . . . or things or . . . ?"

Yes; yes, if they're like you they will.

"I doubt if there are many people like me."

You'd be surprised. You can never judge anyone by their outside. Take your mother for instance. Everyone thinks she's such a refined creature, but you know she's not. Don't you?

"I don't want to talk about my mother."

Better if you did.

"Who would I talk to? There's only George and Gran and it's like giving her away to talk to them."

There's the doctor.

Yes, there was the doctor. I nodded my head, then added, "He knows all about her in any case."

But he doesn't know all about you, does he? Or about me.

I looked at him. His eyes were on me, great dark orbs, and after a moment he said, That would be something, wouldn't it, if you told him about me. What do you think would happen then?

"He'd think I was up the pole. He'd likely want me to see a psychiatrist."

There's no doubt about it. But don't worry; if he does I'll go with you.

"Oh, Hamilton." I threw my notebook towards the bottom of the bed and it went through him and hit the wooden foot and he was gone.

That night I wrote about Hamilton for the first time. I filled ten closely written pages telling how I'd first made his acquaintance, and after I had finished it I saw him for a moment. He was standing near the bedroom door, full-sized now, and he said solemnly, I would tear that lot up if I were you; it's dangerous to leave it about. She's only got to see that and . . . well. . .

I knew he was right. So the next day, which was Saturday, I waited until she had gone out, then went up into the attic. I had a job to pull the swing ladder down, it was a tricky apparatus. Only once before had I been up here, and that time George had carried me up.

I tore the ten pages out of my notebook and put them in a brown envelope, then looked for a loose board under which to place them. I hadn't far to look, there were numbers of them, mostly where the roof sloped down sharply towards the floor. I chose one, prised it up and there, underneath, were the rafters and, about nine inches below, a layer of plaster.

I laid the first pages of Hamilton gently down on the plaster, replaced the floor board, then hurried towards the trapdoor; but on nearing it my eye was attracted to a trunk stuck in the corner to the left of me. It was covered with foreign labels. I lifted the rounded lid and saw it held clothes. Putting my hand down by the side, I felt the layers and layers of them. The material felt like soft silk, but in the dimness of the room I couldn't distinguish exactly what they were. I pulled down the lid again, telling myself that someday I would come up here and go through it. It would be exciting. When I eventually did, it was, and saddening, so saddening, that I cried for the torment my mother had created in herself.

Chapter 5

My mother died a fortnight before my seventeenth birthday and four days before her own. She'd had two pseudo heart attacks during the past months, the second one occurring shortly after Miss Stickle told her that Howard had become engaged to be married. The third and final one occurred when there appeared on television one evening the smiling face of George being interviewed by a B.B.C. man and being praised for his bravery in rescuing a mother and two children from a burning building. He laughed about his hair being singed and his lack of eyebrows and made light of his bandaged hands. The interviewer had eulogized this man who had gone back into the blazing house again after bringing out the mother and one child. He had dropped the second child from an upper window into safe arms, then had, himself, been almost overcome by smoke and fumes but had somehow managed to get downstairs before collapsing. The woman he had saved had put her arms around him and kissed him and George had laughed his big hearty laugh.

I was sitting wide-eyed, my mouth agape and my heart beating rapidly with pleasure, and my mind was crying: Oh George, George. I knew you were a brave man, I always knew you were a brave man. Oh George, George.

The television screen went blank. My mother had turned it off, and she stood and stared at me before rushing from the room. I heard her run upstairs; then I heard her call. When I got into her bedroom she was writhing on the floor.

I didn't send for the doctor but helped her on to the bed, saying all the time, "It's all right. It's all right. It'll pass. You know it'll pass. Lie still now, lie still. I'll make you a cup of tea."

I wasn't long downstairs making the tea but when I brought it up she wasn't on the bed. The bathroom door was closed, so I put the tray down and waited. She was likely being sick. I waited for ten minutes before I knocked on the door, saying, "Are you all right, Mother?"

When I got no answer, I tried the door. It was locked.

For the first time in my life I experienced panic.

We had by now got the phone in and I rushed downstairs and phoned Doctor Kane. When the nurse said he was busy in the surgery with patients, I yelled at her, "It's important! I think my mother has done something silly."

At that she put me through to him, and after a moment he said, "Quiet. Quiet. Tell me what happened." And when I told him and finished, "She's been in there now over a quarter of an hour, more," he said, "I'll be round directly."

He was as good as his word. He, too, tried the door but couldn't get it open. He called, but there was no answer. He told me to stand back, and then took his big foot and rammed it against the keyhole. There was a crunching of wood but the door didn't open. The third time he kicked at it, it sprang back.

She was lying on the floor. There were two empty bottles near her and one on the basin top. He said quietly, "Go and call an ambulance."

I rushed to do as he bade me. The ambulance was there within five minutes; within another five minutes she was in hospital. I went with her, and I know they worked on her for hours, but she died at eleven o'clock that night.

George and Gran Carter were with me. I don't know how they got to know but they reached the hospital about half past nine. I slept at their house that night.

At the inquest the verdict was suicide while the balance of her mind was disturbed.

After the funeral George and Gran sat with me in the sitting-room.

"Well, lass" - George looked at me - "what you goin' to do? I know you're goin' to this typing school, but you can't live here on your own. My advice to you is to sell up and come and live with us. You were never one for fancy things. As you know, it's no palace, but you'll be happy."

I knew I would, but at the same time I also knew that somehow I didn't want to leave this house. Why? I couldn't explain. It wasn't only because I'd been born here; perhaps it was because I knew that this house was mine now, I actually had something of my own, I wasn't dependant on anyone. What money my mother had left would be mine too. I should know tomorrow when I went to the solicitor.

Gran Carter took my hand and said, "He's right, lass; you couldn't live here on your own."

I surprised them by saying, "Yes, I could, Gran. I . . . I could live here happily, comparatively happily anyway, now there's no one to . . . to. . ." I had almost said, torment me, but I replaced it with "look after"; then added, "In a few days time I'll be seventeen; and so I should be able to look after myself."

"You're still a bairn." George had his hand on my shoulder, rocking me gently.

"I don't feel a bairn, George. Well, I mean part of me doesn't. And yet another part feels so simple, I sometimes think I haven't been born yet." I smiled at him.

"It isn't good for you to live on your own," he said.

"Well, I won't be on my own really. I shall be at the school most of the day, and then I could pop in on my way back to see you, that is when you're not off gallivanting." I nodded towards him even jovially. And he, taking it up, said, "Aw! now, now, don't be like me ma; let me have me fling when I'm young, I'll never be eighteen again."

Oh, George was funny.

Gran Carter now said to me, "Does that Stickle woman come in often?"

"Yes; she's been very good, very kind."

"Some piece that." George grinned. "A pickle of Stickle to handle, that one. Once round her, twice round Penshaw Monument."

"It was nice of them to come to the funeral," I said, and looked from one to the other.

Now they both nodded, saying, "Aye, yes, it was."

Apparently the manner of one's dying still affected many people and some in the terrace must have stayed away from the funeral because my mother had killed herself.

Then Gran said, "Does he pop in often, young Stickle?"

"Sometimes he did, to see Mother; that was until he became engaged."

"Oh, he's engaged to be married? That's good. That's good." Gran nodded at me, and I said now, "And he's not young, Gran, he's nearly twenty-eight I should say."

"Oh is he? Well, that's a terrible age, isn't it?" Gran pulled a face at me. "It makes our Georgie here old enough to be his father."

"Oh, hold your hand a bit, Ma. Hold your hand a bit."

And so went the talk in the sitting-room. Only when I persuaded them that I was quite all right and that I would be happy on my own, did they leave me; but not without qualms, I knew.

The door had hardly closed on them when Miss Stickle came in the back way. She had the habit of tapping on the door and at the same time opening it.

"How are you now, dear?" she said.

"Oh, I'm all right, Miss Stickle."

"You must call me May, dear. Miss Stickle sounds so stiff, so formal, and I'm your friend."

I didn't think I could ever call her May. She didn't look like a May. May trees bloomed and smelled nice, they were the harbingers of summer. Miss Stickle conjured up a thistle in my mind, proggly, not to everybody's taste. Yet she had been very kind to me.

She now walked through the kitchen, then through the hall and into the sitting-room.

She seemed to like our sitting-room. When she sat down on the couch, she put her hand out and drew me down beside her. It struck me for a moment as if it was she who was at home and I the visitor.

"Well, what are you going to do, dear? What are your plans?"

I answered calmly, "I mean to stay on here, Miss Stickle."

"You are not going to sell the house then?"

"No."

"It'll be very lonely for you."

"Oh, I don't mind that. I'm used to being alone."

"But you'll miss your mother."

I paused, "Yes," I said, "perhaps. But I . . . I know what I'm going to do. I'm going to finish my course at the typing school."

"Yes. Well, that's wise." And her head on one side, she added slowly, "I suppose you would like to be a secretary?"

She said this as if she thought there was very little chance of my ever becoming one. It had surprised the teacher at the school that I had taken to the typing so well. When I had first applied for the course she seemed dubious that I would be able to type at all. But all I did was sit slightly sidewards, draw my right arm in and stretch my left one to its full extent. It had been natural for me to do so many things this way, and I didn't feel awkward. In fact, she asked me if I had been practising at home. One of the pupils had said spitefully when she thought I was out of earshot, "She'll pass in shorthand without taking exams."

That was one of the times Hamilton had appeared and galloped all over her.

I answered Miss Stickle now by saying, "No, I have no intention of putting in for such a post, but I would like to set up a small business at home here." I looked about the room now. "Do typing for other people, writers and such."

"Oh, that's a very good idea. But . . . but in the meantime will you have enough to live on?"

It was a question and I said, "Yes; yes, I suppose so. I won't get details until tomorrow when I see the solicitor."

"Oh well, I hope everything works out as you would wish. Anyway, you know we are always at hand. Howard is very concerned for you."

"He is?"

"Yes; yes, he is. He was just saying yesterday that you've had a very sad life; that you never seem to have much fun or pleasure. Not that he thinks young girls should gad about. Oh, no, he's got very strict ideas, but as he said, there are limits, one must have a little recreation. We used to play tennis a lot when Father was alive. We lived in Gosforth then and our circumstances were so different from what they are now. Oh yes, so different." She sighed, then went on, "Howard wasn't intended for the tailoring, you know. Oh, no; it was rather a come down. But there, that's all in the past. As he says, life must be faced squarely. But my dear, I'm not at all in favour of the partner he's chosen to spend his future life with."

"You're not?"

"No. No, I'm not. Between you and me she isn't of the same class. You understand?"

I remained silent.

"Common. Utterly, utterly. She's in the office of the establishment. Proximity, you know. This is what it's all about, proximity. Half the people wouldn't be married today if they weren't thrown together haphazardly by fortune. Proximity."

Proximity, proximity, proximity. Hamilton was galloping round the couch. I followed his progress and when he stopped at the end of it, his head over Miss Stickle's, I looked at him imploringly and when he bared his teeth and took a strand of the top coil of her hair, I closed my eyes for a second, and opened them quickly again as Miss Stickle's hand came on mine saying, "You're tired, my dear, and slightly overwrought. I can see that. I'll go and let you get to bed. You're sure you're not afraid to sleep alone?"

"No, no." I rose hastily from the couch, she more leisurely, but as she preceded me down the room there he was again right behind her, and he turned his back on her and kicked her, as George used to say, in the back of the front, because my mother had objected to his frequent use of the word backside. I saw her rise in the air and land in the middle of the hall.

In the hall she turned to me and said, "You're half asleep now, you're dropping on your feet; I'll say good-night, my dear. But don't forget, we are always near, we are always thinking of you. You need never be alone."

After bolting the door, I came back into the hall and I thought of Hamilton swivelling round on his forelegs and kicking our guest, and I started to laugh.

My mother had been buried that day and here I was laughing. Was there something wrong with me? Perhaps, because the fact that Hamilton didn't like Miss Stickle at all should have warned me. Yes, it should have warned me, but it didn't. I just thought it was that funny side of me that would emerge at the most odd moments. Some years were to pass before I realized there was more to my funny side than that, much more.

I look back on the months that followed as a happy time. And so many things happened. I passed my typing exam and got top marks; and as a result of this I put an advert in the paper:

Home typing done. First-class work.
(I thought I was qualified to say that.)
Grammatical corrections.
(That was a bit of a nerve; but still I'd been very good at English at school, especially essays, and seldom had red ticks against my punctuation or grammar.)
Paper provided. One and six per thousand words.

Gran Carter saw the advert and was highly delighted; especially, as she said, about the grammar bits. Professional like it sounded, she said. And I laughed at her and hugged her when she went on, "How about giving me a few lessons, 'cos eeh! I know I talk awful."

I knew she talked awful. Often when thinking about her, my thoughts would run as she was apt to talk: "What time it is!" she would say. I'd even said this out loud once or twice, only to hear my mother cry, "There you are! There you are! That's what comes of that association." And then there was her habit of interspersing the word "like" at the end of every sentence, or sticking it in the middle of one: "You know what I mean like. As I said like. Eeh! it was awful like. I nearly had a fit like."

I often wondered how this word came to be used as it was. However, my advert promised to do away with such deficiencies, at least in the writing of them. But when I saw the advert in print I went hot from head to toe. Who was I to say that I could correct people's writing when my own went rambling on, especially when I was writing about Hamilton. Sometimes I could do a full page on him without one dot or curl of punctuation.

During this time, too, my appearance changed a little but I don't think for the better. Gran had me go to Peggy Wicklow's to have my hair done. Peggy Wicklow had two assistants but she did me the honour of attending to me herself. The result was startling to say the least. She had cut my hair shoulder length, permed it and curled it, and the reflection from the mirror showed me a mass of frizz with a small face in the middle of it. And the face looked all eyes and mouth because they were both wide in astonishment.

"Now, how d'you like that?" she said.

What could I say? I said, "I look different."

"Yes, you do, you do, indeed. It's an improvement, I should say. What d'you think?"

"I . . . I'll have to get used to it." Once outside the shop I took my scarf from beneath my coat and put it over my head, pulling it tight in an effort to hide the corkscrews surrounding me.

When five minutes later I took off the scarf in Gran's kitchen, she looked at me without speaking for a moment, then said, "Aw, lass, I don't think that style suits you. She should have done something different."

"Can I wash it out, Gran?"

"You'll have a hard job, pet, it's a perm. Still if you get at it with one of those wiry brushes you might get it flattened a bit. Eeh! you know something?" She screwed up her face. "She's a bit of a bitch. And our Georgie is finding that out, for since he's got free, you know, since your mam died, she's been at him to get hooked . . . you know, married."

"Yes, I know. Doesn't he want to, I mean get married?"

"Not to her, lass, not to her. She was all right on the side. You know what I mean?"

Yes, I knew what she meant. I imagined I knew a lot of things by now. It was a pity that I had to learn later and painfully that I knew nothing about life or people; I was infantile, and an idiot as far as reading character was concerned.

"You know what?" Gran handed me a cup of tea now, then sat down on the black imitation leather couch fronting the fire. "He's for doin' a bunk."

"He . . . he hasn't done anything wrong? I mean. . ."

"No, no. That's me, not explainin' meself properly. Although mind, it wouldn't surprise me if afore long he hadn't to do a bunk . . . that kind of a bunk, because Peggy Wicklow's brother is on the fiddle in more ways than one - runs a bloody orchestra if you ask me - and they've pulled our Georgie in with them, things droppin' off lorries, you know."

It was I who now screwed up my face as I looked at her and repeated - I had a habit of repeating people's words; this is what I suppose caused many people to think I was dim - "You mean . . . dropping off lorries?"

"Aye, I mean just that, lass."

"Stolen goods?"

"Well, not exactly stolen. You know what I mean. Lightenin' the loads on lorries you know, a bit here an' there. Oh, the bosses can afford it. An' they're all at it, 'specially them drivin' stuff to the docks. Wicklow's brother is one. But he's got to have a lifter, somebody to pick up the stuff when it's dropped, if you get what I mean."

I got what she meant all right and I felt a bit sick. Fancy George doing that. But worse still, if he ever got caught and was sent to prison.

"Anyway, his heart's not in it. He's not that type, our Georgie: he'd give his boots off his feet then go an' buy a pair of laces an' find he had nothin' to put them in. That's how his mind works. He does things without thinkin' and then when he thinks after, he thinks what a bloody fool he's been and says it'll not happen again. It usually doesn't, not in the same way, but there are lots of other ways left. Still, that's our Georgie. Anyway, it wouldn't surprise me if he goes off down south and not afore long, and oh God! lass, I'll miss him. But I'd rather he go than get hooked up with Wicklow. And he'll be killin' two birds with one stone, getting out of her brother's clutches an' all. As I said to him, fancy goin' along the line for a box of safety razors. They thought they were gettin' small radios, you know the kind that the bairns carry round with them, but no, hundreds of little safety razors, when most men are using 'lectric ones! He brought a box here" - she thumbed towards the back kitchen - "and I said to him, 'You can get that lot out of here, an' quick. Anyway, what the hell did you bring them for? What can we do with safety razors?' An' he said, 'I thought you might want to shave your legs.'"

She pushed me and knocked me almost sideways on the couch and we both laughed as she cried, "Me, shave me legs! Look at me varicose veins." She twisted her leg towards me. "The knots are standing out like plonkers. Shave me legs, my God!"

Her legs were a dreadful sight. Yet here I was laughing at them, almost doubled up. Then I happened to turn my head towards the corner of the room where the sideboard was, and there was Hamilton. He was sitting on it, looking like an enormous dog. His head was back, his mouth was open, and his lips were not only revealing his teeth but his gums, and, like me, he was shaking with laughter.

"What is it?" Gran said, following my gaze; then she exclaimed loudly, "Oh, don't look over in that corner; I'll get down to the sideboard sometime. There's no place to put anything, so everything gets pushed on there. Paddy's market isn't in it."

"Oh, I wasn't looking at the sideboard, Gran. Well, I wasn't thinking about it, just about you and your legs." I laid a gentle finger on her knee.

"Oh, don't worry about them; they'll be here as long as me. You know, I remember reading a story somewhere when I was young and it had a rhyme in it and it went: It wasn't the cough that carried her off, it was the coffin they carried her off in. I can never remember where I read it, but I often think of it an' laugh."

"Where's George now?" I asked.

"Oh, somewhere across the channel, as far as I can gather; he's taken on the long journeys. He enjoys them. Hissy on parlour francis. That's what he said when he came in that door last week. Eeh by! I hissy on parlour francised him, 'cos he was tight."

Ici . . . on . . . parle français. Oh, her granny was a scream. Better than going to the pictures.

When I left her on that particular day her last words to me were,

"Does that woman still come in . . . big May?" And I said, "Yes; she often pops in."

"Does she ever try to borrow anything?"

"Oh no." I shook my head.

"Well, that's a good thing. I believe in the saying, never a lender or a borrower be." Then with a wicked grin on her face she leant towards me and whispered, "Have you got half a crown to spare until Monday, hinny?" before pushing me away. . .

Two things happened that week.

It was about nine o'clock on the Friday night and I was up in the attic hiding away some more bits I had done on Hamilton. I'd only asked myself once why I should hide scraps of writing, and the answer was that if I were to die through an accident or some such and anyone was to find them they would think I was nuts. Well, sometimes now I thought I must be nuts, because Hamilton was becoming more real to me than the people I met during the day; that was except Gran and George. May, although I saw more of her than of anyone else, was excluded for some reason or other; Hamilton didn't even take to her. Yet she continued to be so kind and thoughtful.

Anyway, I knew why I hid these bits of writing; I also knew why I didn't like going up into the attic at all now. I had been through the trunk that I'd looked into the night I had first hidden my writing on Hamilton and the condition of the contents told me more about my mother's life than a whole book could have done, for under the layers of silk underwear I found what remained of her wedding gown. I say what remained, the gown was all there. It was white satin and cream lace, but it was torn into shreds. There must have been at least a hundred pieces of it, but these had been meticulously laid out on tissue paper, one layer to form the skirt, another layer to form the bodice, and the third layer the long narrow sleeves.

Sitting on the floor with the evidence of despair around me, I cried and cried for her. Whether she had done it before my father left her or after I don't know. But she had done it, and systematically ripped the symbol of marriage into shreds.

Poor Mother. I had at one time hated her and felt I had reason to, for she had never given me any love, but now when she was no more I loved her with a deep compassionate love.

I had replaced everything in the trunk as I found it, but on my journeys up to the attic my eyes were always drawn to it and the sight made me sad, for in it lay a life of disillusionment that had led to despair.

But there I was, the floor board in my hand, stuffing some more Hamilton sheets down to join the others when I heard the doorbell. It was the front door bell, so I knew it wouldn't be May.

It rang four times before I reached the hall and opened the door, and there stood George.

"What's kept you so long?" he said, passing me. "I knew you were in; the light's on in the sitting-room. Where've you been?"

"Up in the attic."

"In the attic! What were you doing up there? . . . Can you pull the steps down?"

"Oh yes; I'm a big girl now." I grinned at him and he put out his hand and ruffled my hair, which still wasn't flat, and he remarked on it: "By, she made a mess of you, didn't she? Me ma was flaming mad. She didn't let you know that, but she was. She did it on purpose, I mean Peg. She's a bitch you know, a jealous bitch. Have you got the fire on? It's enough to freeze you out."

"Yes, the electric's on in the study. I'm using that as a kind of office now."

"Oh, aye. I hear you're in business. How's it goin'?"

"Up till now I've been swamped with silence."

"Aw, never you mind; it takes a time to get started."

When we were seated in the study, one each side of the electric fire, I looked at him and noticed he had on his best suit and overcoat. I said to him, "Aren't you going to take off your coat?" And he answered, "No, pet. I haven't much time. I'm meetin' a fellow round quarter past ten in the market."

"Oh, George." I lowered my head and he came at me now, saying, "What d'you mean, oh, George, like that?"

"Well, Gran told me. You'll get into trouble."

"Aw, lass." He reached out and took my hand. "He isn't that kind of fellow. He's just a man who's giving me a lift down south."

"You are going down south?"

"Yes. I'm popping off once again. People are always popping out of your life one way or another, aren't they, lass? And you know something, I hate to go for one thing, no two: I'm going to miss you and Ma. But I've got to get away. You see, it's Peg. She's aiming to get me up the aisle. Now things weren't too bad when your mother was alive, there was a time limit afore I could get a divorce, but these last few months since she's gone, oh, my, the pressure's got so bad. It's funny what pressure does, it sort of pushes your eyes open, makes you see things. If the hand is light on you, so to speak, you can carry on happily, never trouble to work things out, come day go day, God send Sunday, so to speak. You know what I mean. But once the pressure starts it gets your old napper workin'" - he tapped his forehead - "and you ask yourself how you would look at this kind of life if it was legal like. An' that's what I've done, and I know I'm not up to it."

He leant towards me now, patting my hand. "I'm a bad lad. I ran out on your mother, now I'm runnin' out on another. I don't seem to pick 'em right. Now if I'd met a lass like you when I was young . . . well now, things would have been different, wouldn't they?"

I made no reply, my throat was full. Of all the people in the world, I loved George. He was all the fathers I had dreamed of; he was a protector; he was a knight in shining armour; he was the bulwark against all foes; as long as George was at hand, nothing much could go wrong for me. If anyone really got at me I could go to George and he would . . . settle their hash. That's what he used to say during my schooldays: "You tell me if anybody gets at you in that school yard and I'll go and settle their hash for them."

"Ah, don't cry, pet; I'm not goin' to the ends of the earth. Look, I'll send you postcards, naughty ones with big fat women on." He pulled his chair closer to mine and put his arm around my shoulder, and I leant my head on his chest. He smelt nice tonight, soapy nice, But I noticed through my blinking tear-filled eyes that the bulge of his stomach was getting bigger. That was his beer drinking, added to which he was always eating chocolate. He said it helped to keep his strength up on the long runs. We sat quiet for a time; then he said, "You still all right for money?"

"Oh yes." I lifted my head and nodded at him. I was slightly puzzled. Then I said, "I still feel that you should have had it."

"Oh, no, no. She knew what she was doing all right." He pursed his lips. "And she was right, she put it in hard writing that you had to have everything."

"But you should have had something. You could have claimed."

"I could have claimed nowt, lass. Well, I would have had to get a solicitor and by the time the case had gone through, he would have had the bulk of it. Anyway, I didn't want a penny of hers; I didn't feel I was entitled to it; and it was a mistake from the beginnin'. You were the only good thing that came out of it."

"Oh George. Look, will . . . will you let me . . . ?"

"No, no, not a dime. No, thank you, lass. Anyway, with the money I've been makin' lately I'm in clover. And the old dragon's kept half of it for me." He patted his chest pocket. "Me wallet's bulgin' an' I'm gona take care of it till I get set on somewhere. Oh, I'm gona be a reformed man, you'll see."

I was still puzzled that he had asked me if I was all right for money. My mother had left four thousand, three hundred and fifty pounds, besides the house and the furniture. Part of the money came through an insurance. George knew how much I had and he would know too that it would be impossible for me the way I lived to spend that money in so short a time. Anyway, I expected it to last me for years, even if I didn't earn anything. And then he gave me the answer, "Don't mind me saying this, pet," he said, "but those two along the street, the Stickles, have they ever asked you for a loan or anything like that?"

"No, no, George. Gran asked me much the same question. What makes you think they would?"

"Oh, I don't know. To my mind they're a queer couple."

My voice was very low as I said, "They've been very kind to me, George. I know they are not like you and Gran. I don't get on with them like that, I . . . I feel awkward with them, but they've still been very kind, more so than anybody in the terrace. Do you know Katie Moore who I used to be so friendly with? She's married now, but she passed me in the street the other day as if she didn't know me; and her mother merely nods at me. Yet at one time I was always going in and out of their house. She . . . she was the only girl friend that I ever had. And those next door, the Nelsons and the McVities, they hardly speak."

"Oh, well, both of them are stiff-necks." He laughed now, saying, "Remember the time when McVitie's terrier jumped the wall and cocked his leg on Oswald, you remember that day?"

I did not smile or laugh for I did remember that day. My mother had picked Oswald up by the few hairs left on his cloth ear and, taking him into the kitchen, had lifted the boiler top and thrust him into the fire. George seemed to have forgotten the result of that incident. I had been almost dumb with sorrow for a week. And George had said, "Well, now, she couldn't have done anything else, not after the dog had widdled on it. Now could she?"

I remember my reply to this; "He could have been washed, and . . . and he looked like you," and the great roar he had let out. He had, I remember, bought me another bear, but it was never Oswald. I don't know what happened to it.

At the front door he stopped and kissed me, not on the cheek but on the mouth. It had the most strange effect upon me and I clung to him, crying, "George. George." He had to push me from him back into the hall; then he went out, pulling the door closed behind him. . .

The other thing that occurred that week was May almost bursting in the back door one evening when I was preparing my meal, and her first words were, "Sardines on toast again! You know this will never do; you must cook yourself a meal . . . or let me come and do it for you." This was the first time she had made such a suggestion, and she went on, "I'll give you lessons, for there's no doubt you need them." She laughed her exposed gum laugh. And then she told me the reason for her hurried visit. "Howard has broken off his engagement," she said. "You have no idea of my relief. She was so unsuitable; she was a person who would never have learned. As I told you, common wasn't the name for it. I was surprised he couldn't see it himself. But at last, fortunately, oh yes, fortunately, it has got through to him." And then she added, "Oh, you are pleased an' all. Howard's very fond of you, you know, very fond."

Was he? I hadn't noticed. He was polite to me. And was I looking pleased? I always used to think he was still serving customers after the shop had closed. Or perhaps it was just his height that made him bend slightly forward when he was talking to me. And sometimes he would raise his hands to his shoulders as if he was putting on an imaginary scarf. I was to learn he was adjusting his tape measure. . .

It was about a week later that I went to dinner at the Stickles'. Up till then I had never been further into their house than the hallway. But here I was, sitting in their dining-room and, to use May's own expression when speaking of most things and of people outside the house, the furniture looked common. It was what you would see in any of the shops on the main street that were always having sales. However, what the room lacked in refinement the meal made up for it.

I really did enjoy the meal. I couldn't say as much for the conversation that took place afterwards in the sitting-room, which by the way, like the dining-room, was very poorly furnished. Sitting there looking about me, I could understand why May considered our house . . . my house as I thought of it now, was so nice, because it was a palace compared with this.

The conversation ranged around Howard's hobby which was collecting bottles. May enthused wildly about it. Howard had little to say until May said, "Take her up and show her your collection, Howard." Then he looked at her and said, "Oh, she wouldn't be interested in bottles." Then he turned his head and looked at me and ended with, "Would you?"

"Oh, yes. Yes?' - I made my voice eager - "I would very much like to see them. I've heard about people collecting bottles."

For the first time I saw a look of bright animation in his face; my reply seemed to have changed him altogether, because, getting up quickly, he said, "Come along then. Come along." And I followed him up the stairs and into a room that was the same size as my bedroom. When he switched the light on there I saw the bottles for the first time. There were hundreds of them, arrayed on shelves all round the room, with more on a long narrow bench running under the window and even more on the floor.

I stood and gaped and said truthfully, "I've never seen so many different bottles in my life."

"They are lovely, aren't they?"

Like a man showing off some precious possession, he lifted a bottle from a shelf. It was square. It had a glass stopper and I watched his fingers stroking the glass as if it were the most delicate porcelain. "This is my favourite," he said. Then he pursed his small mouth and wagged his head and added, "But I really haven't got any favourites. She's lovely though, isn't she?" At this instant Hamilton peered over his shoulder and, his nose on the bottle, he turned his eyes towards me and there was a deep enquiry in them. He was asking the same question as I was: Are there male and female bottles?

"Oh." Howard had noticed my glance was directed upwards. "Oh, you've got your eye on Bluey, have you?" he said. And reaching up, he took down from a shelf a large blue bottle with a glass stopper; then holding it out towards me, he said, "He's an old chemist's receptacle. I have a few dozen of his cousins."

Hamilton's head was at the other side of him now peering down on the bottle, one eye seeming to look at the bottle, the other eye turned in my direction: So they are male and female, he said. Not only that, there's families. My, my! What have we here?

"This" - Howard lifted another bottle from the shelf - "saucy thing has the maker's name in the glass. Look." He held it out towards me, saying, "Middle of last century, and she was a sauce bottle. Indeed, indeed, yes."

One thing that was revealed to me before we finally left the bottle room was that Howard Stickle was a different man when he was with his bottles: the shopwalker had disappeared; the assistant manager of Hempies' the high class tailor was lost under myriad pieces of glass and stone. Oh yes, there were stone bottles too, all shapes and sizes. Those on the table were ready for classification he informed me. The ones under needed to be washed and dressed, his own words, before they found their everlasting home on one of the shelves. . .

"There! What do you think?" May greeted us in the sitting-room sometime later. And I said, "It's most interesting. Unbelievable how many bottles there are about; I'm really surprised." But if I'd been truthful, my surprise, I would have added, was not so much about the number of different bottles, but with the discovery that Howard Stickle was just an ordinary fellow, and not someone superior who had once played tennis in Gosforth. . .

That evening was the beginning of a number of meals in their house and of an equal number in my own. Prior to the latter, May would come and supposedly show me how to prepare the meal while doing it mostly herself. There was one thing about May, she knew how to cook.

So things went on smoothly, progressing, I should say, as May intended for some months.

During this time I received a number of cards and one letter from George and generally showing different postmarks. The letter said he was enjoying himself, meeting different kinds of people that he never knew existed, and that the south wasn't as black as it was painted. No, not by a long chalk: there were some decent fellows down there . . . and lasses an' all.

Gran missed her Georgie, mostly, she admitted, last thing at night before she went to bed because she had always waited up for him no matter how late he might come in, except, of course, when he was on the long lorry journeys. But she kept herself going all right during the day for she had a part-time job in a factory now, packing dresses.

I, too, managed to keep busy during the week but I hated Sundays. Sundays were interminable. I had discovered long ago that no matter what you did you couldn't change a Sunday. You could alter your pattern, go someplace, or stay at home, even be sick in bed, but you still knew it was Sunday. I always had the longing to talk to somebody on a Sunday: strangers in the park even; or to go and knock on May's door. And I might have done if it hadn't been for Hamilton; he was very attentive on Sundays. . .

The first invitation to go out with Howard came one evening in May. I had been to supper with them and he was walking me back to my door, and he looked out over the playing field towards the park and said, "It's a lovely evening. May is a lovely month, a quiet month, it has so much promise."

He sounded so poetic that I stood looking up at him, and as I did so, Mrs McVitie passed us and Howard raised his hat to her. He always wore a hat even on a short journey. "Good evening, Mrs McVitie," he said, and she mumbled something and went into her gate.

We then walked on and he said, "May, as you can imagine, was born in this month. It's her birthday next Wednesday. I really don't know what to get her. Perhaps you would come and help me choose something?"

I was staggered by the invitation, and I must have appeared so because he hesitated in his step and, looking down at me, said, "You will be too busy?"

"Oh, no, no." My voice was two tones higher than usual. "I would love . . . I mean I would like very much to come and help you choose a present. And I must get her something too."

He was standing at my door now as he said, "It would be nice to end her birthday at a play or something. They are putting on *H.M.S. Pinafore* in the Town Hall on that particular evening, it should so happen. Would . . . would you like to come too?"

"Yes; thank you very much. Yes, I would."

I'd never been to a place of entertainment with a man in my life before. I'd never even been to the pictures with George. I thought the suggestion wonderful.

"Well, that's settled then. Now I must away because tempus fugit." Oh! that saying. How I came to loathe it. Tempus fugit, time flies. When years later I told Gran about it, she said, "Oh, that's an old one: tempus fugit, said the man as he threw the clock at his wife."

Nevertheless I thoroughly enjoyed that evening out; it was my first taste of Gilbert and Sullivan. The following day as I dusted, I skipped from one room to the other singing snatches of the songs.

This night out began a pattern of evenings out. At first May accompanied us; then one night - we had made arrangements to go to the pictures - she had a severe cold and insisted that Howard and I went alone. I must admit that I felt rather proud of being escorted to the pictures by this tall presentable man.

It was on a night in late August that Howard proposed to me. We had again been to the pictures and for the first time as we sat in the dark he had taken hold of my hand, and there flowed out from me to him a great wave of gratitude. That this man could find it in his heart to make this gesture towards me was so overwhelming that the tears poured silently down my cheeks. It happened to be a very sentimental picture, and when it was finished he chided me playfully about my concern for the heroine.

Later at home, I had just made some coffee and we were in the sitting-room. The electric logs were glowing and the pink shade on the standard lamp was adding to the warm radiance when once again he took my hand and this time said, "Do I have to tell you, Maisie, that I've become very fond of you?"

I was about to say, thank you very much, Howard, but I remained quiet, staring at him.

"You know I had a broken love affair some time ago?"

"Yes, Howard. I was very sorry about it."

"You needn't be." He pressed my hand. "I've got over that, entirely over it, and I know now it was a great mistake in asking that certain person to be my wife. But I also know now" - I watched his Adam's apple flicking up and down, as I imagined, with emotion - "that I'm making no mistake in saying to you, Maisie: Would you consider being my wife?"

I stared up into his face. There were small beads of sweat on his brow. That I was amazed by this offer was putting it mildly; yet at the same time I asked myself why I should be, because hadn't he in a way been courting me? But how silly. Just because he had taken me to the pictures once or twice and we had been to see some amateur theatricals, sometimes accompanied by May, was that a sign of courtship? From my point of view, they had both been kind to the extent of taking pity on me. But here he was, this presentable man, asking me to be his wife. Never in my wildest dreams had I expected to be married. I had thought the only romance that would come my way would be through the written word: once I began a love story I couldn't put it down, eager to know the heroine's desires, the fulfilment of her longings, the overcoming of her frustrations. And if the writer should explain that the heroine was no beauty I would glow as she did when at last the proposal came.

And now here was the proposal and I wanted to glow. I should be glowing, but there he was, that Hamilton with forefoot raised ready to kick Howard in the back of the front. In order to do that he would have had to bring his hoof underneath the couch; but Hamilton could do that, Hamilton was capable of doing anything disturbing.

From the back door of my mind I yelled at him, "Go away! I shall never get this chance again. All right, if it is a mistake I've got to make it. Who else do you know will ask me to marry him? Look at me."

"What did you say, dear?"

He called me dear, and I said, "Look at me. Well I suppose you don't really need to, you've already done so, but have you taken into account my arm?" I lifted up my shorter arm and then went on, "And what is more, I'm a very plain person.
I . . . I mean my features, and they are not likely to improve."

"Oh, my dear, my dear" - he had a hold of both my hands now - "your humility does you credit."

Yes, he had a way of talking like that. I wasn't taken very much with it, but nevertheless at this moment I lapped it up.

"Plain women," he said, "are often the most interesting; and after all, beauty is only skin deep. There is a beautiful woman asleep in every plain one. And what's more, plain women are known to make lifelong companions, and that's what the partnership of marriage is all about to my way of thinking, companionship. What do you say, Maisie?"

It sounded too beautiful. In a daze I nodded: "Oh, yes I agree with you, companionship is important. Oh yes, yes," I said.

No word of love had been spoken, not even liking, but at the time it didn't strike me as odd. I had nothing to compare this proposal with except the romantic stories I had read; and these I knew at bottom were but fragments of the authors' imagination, nice figments, but nevertheless, figments. So when he said, "Well, my dear, what do you say?" I said politely, "Thank you, Howard. I would like to, I mean, become engaged. Yes, thank you very much."

At this he leant towards me and slowly put his lips on mine. I didn't see what his face looked like because I closed my eyes. But his lips were moist and soft and sent a shiver down my spine.

"That's settled then." He rose from the couch and buttoning his waistcoat - he was always buttoning his waistcoat; odd, but I never saw him unbutton it, yet he was always buttoning it - he said, "I must now go and tell the happy news to May. She'll be delighted. She's very fond of you is May."

I made no answer to this. Even if I wanted to I couldn't because there he was, that great black shining beast with the white tail, the two front hoofs and a spot of white between his eyes, galloping round the room like mad. He was kicking things right and left and as I walked towards the door with Howard he galloped between us and I stepped quickly to the side and Howard put his arm out, saying playfully, "Oh dear, you're tipsy. It's all the drink you haven't had."

I managed to laugh.

I opened the door and he stood on the step for a moment looking out into the night, saying nothing; then abruptly he patted my arm, said, "Good-night, Maisie," and was gone up the street.

When I turned into the hall, there was Hamilton sitting on his haunches, his front legs well apart, his head thrust forward, a wild angry expression on his face. As I passed him he said, Don't kid yourself he's in love with you or. . . And I snapped back, "I'm not kidding myself. As he said, it's for companionship. In a way he seems as lonely as I am."

Lonely, me foot. You know what he's after. George knew what they were both after. You must have been blind if you haven't seen May's envious eyes round the house. And they don't own their property either. And they know you've got a bit of money.

"Shut up!" I thrust open the study door, went to the desk and started to write.

I wrote to Hamilton rather than talked to him because I always seemed to come off second best when I talked to him, and at the moment I was upset. I was engaged to be married, I told him; I knew that no word of love or affection had been spoken, but that I didn't expect it, I was lucky to get a proposal. All right, all right, May might have encouraged her brother along the line he had taken with her eye on this house, but I wasn't marrying May, I was marrying Howard. May would have her house, Howard and I would live here. I would clear out the end room and he could bring his collection of bottles with him. He'd like that. And I must really learn to cook. I could never hope to serve him meals like May, but I would improve on what I was turning out now. So Hamilton, there it is, I wrote, it's as much as I can expect from life, more, because you know I never thought any man would ask me, or would want to live with me. I have no brilliant conversation, I've talked too long to you to be at ease with people, but he seems to understand me, and . . . and I shall try to make him happy. So there, this chapter is closed, Hamilton. Once I am married, I . . . I'm not likely to want you any more and you can go back to . . . well, wherever you came from in me. But I'll never forget you, never, because you have given me moments of glee that I would never have known otherwise.

I took the pages, went up into the attic, raised the floorboard and put them among their companions, thinking, That episode of my life is finished.

Some hope. The voice sounded like Gran Carter's, but as I turned round there he was, jumping out of the attic, down on to the landing. As I myself reached the landing I saw him galloping through the window in the end wall, then right across the playing fields, across the park, on, on, that beautiful, shining, magnificent friend that my mind had given me for comfort during all the lonely trying years.

Chapter 6

"Aw, lass. What have y'been and gone and done? Promised to marry that fellow!" The look on her face made me squirm and I turned my head away and walked to the fire and held out my hands towards it. And when she said, not intending to cause me any pain but nevertheless doing so, "Lass, if he's proposed to you he's after something, and it isn't far to look. It's your house and all the fine bits that's in it, and your nest-egg. I'm sorry to say this but he's the type, that man, and his sister an' all, who don't do things without a motive like. Aw, don't be upset, lass, I mean it kindly. I . . . I think too much of you. You're like me own and I don't want to see you makin' a mistake."

I turned to her, blinking the tears from my eyes as I said, "I won't get the chance to make many mistakes, Gran, not me. All right, it might be a mistake, but I've got to take it."

I watched her sit down on the couch with a plop, then bend forward and lift up the bottom of her skirt, turn the hem towards her and start picking at it as if she were pulling at the threads, and as she did so she muttered, "Eeh! I wish our Georgie was here. He'd know what to do."

"Gran" - I sat down beside her and took her hand - "I'm going to marry Howard. I know you won't be the only one who'll think he had ulterior motives in asking me, but over the past months I've got to know him and I think he'll make a good companion."

"Oh, to hell with that, lass!" She threw my hands off her. "Bugger companions! That's not what you want out of marriage at your time of life. That's all right for the old 'uns. Even me, you wouldn't get me at this stage taking anybody just for a companion. Don't you know what it's all about?"

"Yes," I said, "I know what it's all about."

"Well then, all I can say is if you do, you're a bloody fool to go on with it. Companionship!" she snorted, then rose from the couch and went into the kitchen.

I'd said I knew what it was all about. But what did I know all about? Quite candidly I knew nothing about marriage except what I'd read in the romantic books. There had been no whispered conversations in corners with other girls for me; there had been no innuendoes; no hints that I could pick up and dissect. Katie hadn't been like that. And she was married and she would know all about it now. But she must have been unhappy for she had left her husband. If we had still been friends, we might have talked. . . I hadn't understood Katie's changed attitude towards me, nor her mother's, not at that time anyway. It was her father who explained it to me. I met him in the street one day when he was very drunk. He had doted on Katie and so he was very bitter about this, and he said to me, "Life's funny, Maisie. Aye, it's funny. The wife was against you and my lass being pally because she thought it would spoil Katie's chances, you being as you were then. She thought Katie wouldn't be able to meet any suitable fellow if you were along, and who did she meet? That rotter. I never liked him, not from the word go. But here's you now, comfortably settled in your own house. And you've filled out a lot, you've changed. And what is our Katie's life? Two bairns, and separated from her husband. Life's a puzzle, Maisie, life's a puzzle."

I remember at that time I too thought it was a puzzle and how wrong he had been in thinking I was changed.

But here I was at Gran's, and she was dead set against my marrying Howard. Yet I knew firmly in my own mind that I would go through with it, Katie and her unsuccessful marriage were far removed from my mind.

Perhaps it was she who sent Father Mackin to the house, thinking that if I was set on going through with it then it should be done properly. Anyway, there he was one day when I answered the door bell, cheery and chatty, but both these facets of his character hiding a deep purpose. As he once said to me, there were different ways of driving a cuddy besides kicking it. And on that day and for weeks following he did his best to use these ways to drive this particular cuddy into the Catholic Church. And he might have succeeded if it hadn't been for Howard.

"Now this is a nice house," Father Mackin said. "Oh dear me, what a surprise." And he looked round the hall and through the open door into the kitchen. The ceiling had imitation rafters and the units were all scrubbed oak. My mother had had them specially fitted. Then laying his hat down on the hallstand and rubbing his hands together, he said,

"'Tis nippy outside. It is that, very nippy."

"Would you like a cup of tea, Father?"

"Now whoever said no to a question like that? Yes, I would indeed, I would love a cup of tea. What is your first name again?"

"Maisie."

"Oh . . . Maisie. It's a very friendly name that, Maisie. Yes, Maisie, I would love a cup of tea. May I go and sit down?" he said, already walking towards the sitting-room door. This was half open and I pushed it wide and he entered, exclaiming loudly, "Well, whoever did this had taste: grey walls and a blue carpet, and those dull pink curtains. Now who would ever think about those colours combining into such harmony. 'Tis a lovely house. Have you been here long?"

"I was born here, and my mother too. My grandparents came into it when it was first built, but since then there's been a lot of alteration done."

"Well now" - he sank on to the couch - "if I lived in a place like this the church would get the go-by, I'd promise you that."

I went out laughing and hurriedly made a tray of tea. And when I returned to the room he was examining some pieces of china in the cabinet that stood between the windows.

"You don't mind me being nosey, do you?"

"No, Father, not at all."

"These are nice pieces. I know something about porcelain and I can say these are nice pieces."

"I understand my grandfather brought them from abroad."

"Yes, he would do, he would do."

He sat down on the couch once more, and I poured out the tea and handed him a plate on which there were some scones, and after biting into one he exclaimed loudly on its merits. But I had to tell him that I hadn't baked them, that a friend of mine along the terrace was a very good cook, she had done them.

"Now then, if she can bake scones like this, I bet she's not single."

"There you're wrong, Father, she is. And she is soon to be my sister-in-law."

"Oh, yes. Yes - " he put his cup down on the side table, wiped his mouth with a coloured handkerchief then said, "I heard that you're to be married. And really, to tell the truth, because I must do that sometime, mustn't I?" - he grinned at me - "that's partly why I've come, to see what arrangements you are going to make for the wedding."

"Oh, Father." I made to rise from the couch but his hand stopped me, and he said, "Now it's all right. It's all right. Don't take off in a balloon, I know that you're not in the church yet, but I've got a strong feeling that you would like to be. I understand you used to come to mass with your stepfather at one time, so as I see it, just a little push and you'd be over the step."

"I'm sorry, Father, but my fiancé is not that way inclined at all."

"What do you mean? He's an atheist, he doesn't believe in either God or man?"

"No. Well, I think, if he's anything, he's Church of England."

"But at present he's nothing?"

"I'm not really sure. We haven't discussed it."

"Well then, if you haven't discussed it, perhaps he and I can get down to a little natter, eh?"

"No, Father, please. He has already suggested we get married in the registry office."

"Oh, now, now." The smile went from his face. "Registry office." For a moment I thought he was going to spit. Then someone did spit. Sitting behind him, just to the right, there was Hamilton. I gasped because I hadn't seen him for some long time now. His head was turned and he was looking towards the floor, and then he brought his big lips into a pout and he spat. And I heard myself say, "Oh dear me."

"Now, now, there's no need for you to get worried. But I maintain that a registry office marriage is no marriage, not in the eyes of the Headmaster."

"The Headmaster?"

Father Mackin now turned his eyes upward until little but the whites of them could be seen, and, his voice lowered, he added, "Aye, the Headmaster, the Headmaster of men."

He was referring to God as the Headmaster of men, and I heard myself saying almost skittishly now, "And what about women, Father?"

"Oh" - he put his head back and laughed - "that's good, that is, that's good. Well, it's a mixed school. A . . . ha!" He was leaning towards me now, his head bobbing, and he repeated, "A mixed school. And there's coloureds in it too, yes coloureds: blacks and browns and yellows and a few Red Indians if I'm not mistaken."

We were both laughing now and I wasn't looking at him, I was looking towards Hamilton, and he was mimicking me. His big mouth wide open, his lips baring his teeth, he was doing a horse ha! ha! ha! bit. I could see that he didn't dislike the priest but that at the same time he had taken his measure: the iron hand in the velvet glove so to speak with a dusting of laughing gas inside it.

I don't know what made me think of that bit except that up in the attic I had come across a glove tree. It was in its own box with a canister of dusting powder; it must have been used by my grandparents at some stage.

He had three cups of tea and four scones and when he took his leave he put his hand on my shoulder and, his face and voice devoid of all laughter now, he said, "Think seriously on this Maisie. It's a big step and it's for life. Never take marriage lightly. It's for life."

How often I was to think of those words in the years to come, it's for life.

Chapter 7

I was married on the second Saturday in February 1969, and before the day was out I was to experience humiliation as I had never really known it before, although I'd been acquainted with it; but terror, with which I had had no acquaintance, was almost to paralyse me.

It was ten days later when I ventured to Gran's. She was out, and the woman next door said she had gone along to the Community Hall. The Community Hall was only two streets away, and so I went to the door and asked the volunteer porter if he would ask Mrs Carter if I could see her a minute. "Why don't you come in, lass," he said, "an' see her yourself? They're having a sing-song."

"I'd rather not," I said.

"Is it important?" he said, and when I nodded he left me.

A minute later Gran was standing on the pavement looking at me, saying, "Aw, pet. Aw, pet."

"Can you come home, Gran?"

"Yes, like a shot, lass. What is it? Aw, don't tell me. Let's get inside first."

Inside the house, the first thing I did was to burst out crying and she held me in her arms, saying, "There now. There now. Oh, my God!

What's happened to you? Your face is like a sheet of lint. You never had much colour, but you never looked like this. Sit yourself down till I make a pot of tea, and keep talking. Aye, keep talking."

I sat on the couch, but I didn't start to talk, I didn't know how. It wasn't until I gulped at the hot tea that I looked at her and said bitterly, "Why didn't you tell me, Gran?"

"Tell you what, hinny?"

I turned my head away, only to have it pulled sharply round towards her again, and with her hand on my face she said, "I asked you, and you said you knew all about it. Is it that? That's upset you?"

"Oh, Gran." I bent my head deep on to my chest as I muttered, "I never dreamed. It . . . it was awful. It still is."

When she said no word I lifted my head and looked at her, and after a moment, her voice low, she murmured, "That's marriage, lass. That's marriage. Was he rough?"

I gulped in my throat and turned my whole body away from her. My head almost in my shoulder, I stared wide-eyed down the room. "Was he rough?" she had said. Was a hungry lion rough? Was an insane man rough? Because that's what he had been like. The only thing I was thankful for on my wedding night was that it took place in my own house and not in an hotel, for my screaming protests would surely have caused a disturbance. I wondered now if Mrs McVitie hadn't heard me, but then the bedroom was to the front of the house and both hers and Mrs Nelson's bedrooms faced the back. Anyway my screams had been smothered by his hand over my mouth and, his face contorted out of all recognition, he had hissed at me, "You are my wife."

The following morning was, in a way, as big an astonishment to me as the events of the night before, for his manner had reverted to the ordinary; it was as if nothing had happened between us, that dreadful struggle before the exhaustion overcame me had never been.

I dreaded the second night coming, and when it did he spoke quite calmly to me before he got into bed. Standing by the bedside he looked down on me and said again those words, "You are my wife. I am only taking what is my due." I remembered stupidly reminding him what he had said about companionship. And his lip had curled as he reacted, "Don't be so stupid, woman." It was the first time I had been called "woman". I was eighteen and hadn't felt up till then that I was a woman; however the previous night seemed to have made me into one. I begged him, "Please, please, don't." And again he said, "Don't be so stupid. You surely knew what to expect: being associated with a woman like George Carter's mother you couldn't have remained all that innocent."

Being acquainted with George Carter's mother, I *had* remained innocent, not only innocent, but ignorant, blind. Not only was I afraid of the savagery of the intimacy, but I knew now that I didn't even like the perpetrator. As for companionship, how could you make a companion of someone during the daytime who tore at your body like a savage repeatedly in the night?

"Was he rough?"

I didn't turn round as I muttered, "Terrible."

"I would have put you wise, lass, but you seemed to know. And you know, hinny. Look. Look at me." I looked at her. "It can become a sort of beautiful thing like. Yes, yes, it can."

I almost bounced up from the couch and began walking up and down the room, my hands gripping each other. Talking rapidly now, I said, "Gran, you don't know. He acted like a wild beast. No words, nothing. Just a sort of an attack."

"He didn't love you? I mean, fondle you like, lead up to it?"

"No, no, nothing like that."

"He's a swine then. Aw, pet." She too got up now and stopped my pacing, and holding me tight she said, "I knew from the beginnin' it was wrong. But you were for it. You thought nobody else would want you. You silly lass."

"Can I come and stay with you?"

"*No, lass, no!* You can't." Her tone was emphatic. "This is something you've got to work out; you can't run away from it. And anyway, what would happen if you left that house? He wouldn't leave it, nor his sister. They would be planted there for good. But that's what they were after from the start; it's the best house in the terrace. I've heard a lot about him since. He was engaged to a woman in the office of the shop and when he broke it off she left. Nobody seemed to know what had happened atween them. I understand from Florrie Ridley, whose lad's an apprentice there, that the lass's mother was for setting about him 'cos the lass got a lot of bits and pieces together. Now I ask you, why should he break that off and turn to you if he hadn't a deeper motive? To my mind that big lump of a sister of his arranged everything. So . . . well lass, as much as I'd like you to come here, an' I'd welcome you, but if you did, it would be just playing into their hands, and you'd have a job to get that property back, I'm tellin' you. And a house like that is worth thousands. You'd have to get a solicitor an' likely go to court, and that'd cost something, and in the end he'd get his share. Men are for men when it comes to the push and, if I'm not mistaken, there's some law about it. At one time the husband could claim the lot. I don't think it's the same now, but they've still got some rights along that way. I'll look into it. In the meantime, make a stand against him. If he starts any more hanky-panky, rough like, take a hatpin into bed with you. It's been done afore. Oh aye." She nodded at me, her face solemn now. "I'm not jokin'. . . What has big May to say about it?"

"Oh, I couldn't say anything to her."

"Do you see much of her?"

"Too much. She's always in and out. Yet at the same time I'm sometimes glad of her company, especially at night when he's in."

"Look, pet" - her brows knitted and her eyes narrowed - "are you really frightened of him?"

I hesitated before answering, and then it was only half an answer, "In a way I am," I said. "Yes, in a way I am."

"What do you mean by that?"

"Well, looking at him in the daytime he doesn't seem to be a frightening person. It's . . . it's just at night. He . . . he seems to change entirely once we're alone upstairs. It's strange, odd."

"Oh, hinny" - she turned away from me - "I wish I could do something for you, explain things to you. But I can't; you only come to this kind of knowledge through experience. Everybody's different. Every man's different. An' you never know how different until they get you in that bedroom. Yet I've had nothin' to grumble about. No, indeed, no. Georgie's father was what you call a gentle man." She turned to me again. "You know it's a pity you hadn't come across somebody like our Georgie. He doesn't know B from bull's foot education like, but about livin' and lovin', well, there isn't much he doesn't know. He's like his da. A man like that would have suited you down to the ground. If you only had waited. Aw!" She shook her head violently. "But what's the use? It's done. But you go back now an' brace yourself an' make a stand, because that's your home and I know you love the house. You were happy in it from your ma died, you could see it in your face, and you kept it nice, as nice as she did. And I know one thing for sure, pet, you couldn't put up with this kind of life for long," and with outspread arm and hand she indicated the room; "you cannot swing a cat here. And there's no privacy around these quarters. Why, you can hear when Mrs Pratt, two doors down, has been to the lav. No, lass, this kind of habitation isn't for you. So go on home and stand up to him. You've got a lot in your napper that hasn't come out, I know that. Our Georgie used to say that an' all about you."

I picked up my hat and coat and as I put them on I said, "Have you any idea when he's coming back?"

"No, lass. He seems to have settled in Falmouth these last few weeks. He's likely found a dame down there. One thing's certain, he won't show his face here till Wicklow gets hooked up with somebody. I don't go back to her for me hair. She came round here and raised the house on me after he went, as if it was my fault. You should have heard the names she called me. But she learned a few new ones afore she left, I can tell you that." She smiled her old smile; then putting her arms around me, she kissed me and said, "Look, I'm in most days atween one and half past two. If you need me slip round then. Or atween five and six round tea-time. But I suppose that's his time for coming in."

"No," I said, "he doesn't get in most nights until half past six." And as she led me to the door she said, "What does he do nights?"

"He mostly goes upstairs and arranges his bottles."

"Arranges his bottles! What bottles?"

"Oh" - I hesitated - "well, I didn't tell you but he collects bottles."

"Beer bottles?"

"No; all kinds of bottles."

"*Bottles?*" Her lips remained wide apart when she finished the word.

"Yes, sauce bottles, ginger beer bottles, vinegar bottles. Any kind of bottle that's ever had anything in it. He's got hundreds of them upstairs."

"Oh . . . my . . . God!" The words were spaced. "Have you married a nut?"

"I . . . I understand lots of people collect bottles."

"Well, that's the first I've heard of it, except beer bottles. But they don't collect them, they take the empties back, if there's anything on them. And he's got them all up in the bedroom?"

"No; I've given him a separate room. It takes a full room."

"Eeh!" - she looked upwards - "Gordon Highlanders! Go on, lass." She pushed me towards the door. "I'll be lookin' forward to seein' you the morrow. And do what I told you, mind, make a stand."

I went out down the street and walked across the town, then through the park, and for the first time since I'd been at school, I sat down on one of the seats opposite the pond and looked at the ducks. It was very cold. The world seemed empty. The future seemed empty. What was I going to do? Were all my days going to be like this? Gran had said, make a stand, but how could I do that? . . . Oh Hamilton what have I done?

I'd continued to keep Hamilton at a distance for some time now, but there he was standing at the end of the park seat. His coat didn't look so bright and shiny. He looked as if he had been galloping through bad weather; his mane looked wet, his tail drooped. His eyes were sad. I spoke to him, first apologizing, saying, "I wouldn't listen to you; you were right."

What's done's done, he said. The question is, how are you going to go on from now? Would you consider following Gran's hatpin suggestion? His upper lip moved slightly from his teeth, but I couldn't raise the slightest smile in return. "I could never do that kind of thing," I said. "You know I couldn't."

Then what do you propose to do?

"I don't know. Can't you tell me?"

Use your elbow, he said.

"My elbow?" I looked down at my arm, the foreshortened forearm resting as usual across my waist. This part of my arm had very little flesh on it compared to my right one. The doctor had referred to it as withered. The elbow was very bony. I had once playfully jabbed Katie with it and she had cried, and I was so contrite I swore I would never use it again in that fashion.

I looked at Hamilton. He was standing straighter now, and looking not so shaggy. I said to him, "But what am I going to do in all the days ahead?" And his answer was, Take one thing at a time. What you could do is take up your writing again, about me or anything.

"Oh, I don't know about that," I said. "I get all flustered when he's in the house, even when he's up among his bottles, and I haven't attempted to do any of my kind of writing in case I say something about him or May, for as sure as I did he would come and say, as he did the other evening, "What's that you are writing?" And when I said, "The grocery list," he retorted, "Do you never find anything better to do! May will see to that."

May was taking over. With a greasy smile on her face and a soft tone, her progress into the house was insidious. The little liking I'd had for May had evaporated.

When Hamilton came and stood by my side, his legs astride the park seat, I turned my head and looked at him as I said, "I feel trapped, Hamilton, and I . . . I feel I've been tricked."

You can say that again. Well - he brought his thick lips together and his head bobbed up and down - you've got to play them at their own game. He hasn't given you any money for housekeeping, has he?

"No."

And you paid the bills last week?

"Yes."

Well, stop paying them. He's got a decent wage; he's taken on the title of husband and head of the house, let him see to them.

"But he knows I've got money."

Well, use your napper, as Gran would say; think about it. If you hadn't any money what would he do then?

I turned my head and looked over the lake. The ducks were quacking loudly. One was skimming across the surface leaving a white arrow of froth behind it.

Go to a solicitor, put your money in Gran's care.

My head jerked round towards him again, "Could I do that?"

Go to a solicitor and find out. He seemed a nice enough man, the one who made the will out for your mother. You could pass the lot over to Gran with certain provisos, such as, she would hold the money in care for you, and that if you should die, it had to be split between her and George, or all of it go to the one who survived.

I smiled for the first time in days. "You think of the cleverest things, Hamilton. What would I do without you?"

I don't know, he said. I only know that life is very dull at the moment and it's a long time since we had a laugh together. I've never kicked anyone in the back of the front for some time now, although it isn't that I haven't wanted to. But you weren't about. Or you were but you had shut the door on me, and it's no good a horse acting the goat on its own; anybody who's capable of acting the goat needs an audience.

I rose from the bench feeling somewhat better. I would beat them at their own game as far as the money was concerned and I would see to that as soon as possible. And as for my weapon, well, I might even put that into use before tomorrow.

I did.

At half past six when Howard came in, May was there. She had brought a shepherd's pie down, saying, "I know you give him his dinner but he also likes a warm snack at night, and he needs to be fed. He was very delicate as a child," which made me almost snap back, "He has the strength of a bull now;" but that certainly would have led to questioning.

When he came in his face was bright as if with excitement. Even before he had taken his hat and coat off he called through the hall to May, "What do you think I've heard today?" And she, passing me, went to the kitchen door and said, "What, dear?"

"They're making tennis courts in Brampton Hill Park."

"No."

"Yes."

"How lovely!" May turned to me. "They're making tennis courts in Brampton Hill Park. Isn't that exciting?"

When he came into the kitchen he actually put his hand on my head in passing as one would on a dog's. Yet the gesture was so unexpected that it made me smarmy and I could have kicked myself for saying, "You'll enjoy that, being able to take it up again." He smiled at me as he said, "Oh, yes, yes indeed," and looking at May, added, "We were very good at it one time, weren't we, May?"

"First-rate." She jerked her chin upwards and repeated, "First-rate. We were always picked to represent the club. When will they be ready?"

"A couple of months' time, I think. And oh, by the way, I'll have to be off again in half an hour." And noticing that the table was set for the high tea, his eyes resting on the casserole dish, he said, "Shepherd's pie. Oh! May; I'm sorry I won't be able to do justice to it because -" He paused and his glance took me in now as he said, "I've been invited to supper at Mr Hempies'. What do you think about that?" His eyes did a flicking movement from one side to the other of us; then to me he said, "Put me a clean shirt out and my brown shoes. See they're polished, will you?"

I paused a long moment before leaving the room, and I was at the foot of the stairs when I wondered what brown shoes he wanted. He had four pairs. I returned towards the kitchen door again but stopped to hear him say, "He seems impressed at my being married. I think it's the house; and he seemed to know about her mother and that she was quite well off. It can't be anything else; eleven years I've been there and this is the first invitation."

"Didn't he ask to see her?" This came from May. And my breath stuck in my throat as I waited for his answer. "Yes, he did," he said, "but I made excuses, saying that she wasn't at all well. And that's how she's going to remain, if I've got anything to do with it."

I took three silent steps backwards before turning, and I slowly crossed the hall to the stairs, and there I stopped and looked upwards to see Hamilton. His head was lashing from one side to the other, his mane falling over his face. I went up and into the bedroom - he had preceded me - and I spoke aloud now, really aloud: "Tomorrow the solicitor." And he nodded his head twice, saying, Yes, tomorrow the solicitor. . .

Howard was late coming in. I had fallen asleep, and he woke me up to tell me all that had taken place at Mr Hempies'. "And you know something," he said; "his is a semi-detached in Durham but it isn't half as substantial as this. Nor is his furniture anything like ours."

Ours. My dulled mind repeated, ours.

I couldn't bear to watch him undress and I turned on my side and buried my face in the pillow but couldn't shut out his chatter. Then I stiffened as he said, "If you made yourself a bit more presentable we could have him here. That would show him. You want to go and have your hair properly done and get something done about your face. There's places. They can alter noses to any shape; and mouths an' all. And if you put make-up on. . ."

I swung round in the bed and glared at him now as I cried, "I am as you married me and like this I stay. I'm not changing for you or God Almighty."

That he was surprised by my retaliation was evident, but he was more surprised a few minutes later when, on my side once more, his arm came on me in a grabbing movement, for it was at this point I took my elbow, and *wham!* I stuck it into his ribs. The squeal that he let out was comparable with those he had wrenched from me on the night of our marriage. And now gasping and holding his side, he said, "What do you think you're up to? You . . . you could injure me. You have. You have."

He screwed round and sat on the edge of the bed. The bedside light was still on. That was another thing: he never put the lights out until he was about to sleep; he seemed to enjoy watching my torment. I watched him now pull his pyjama coat open and look at his ribs, and pathetically he repeated, "You could have injured me." And then his tone suddenly changed: he glared at me and growled, "Don't think you'll get the better of me by using that stump."

When I said, "Well, it's either that or a hatpin," his face seemed to stretch to twice its length.

"You're mad!"

"I shouldn't be a bit surprised; I must have been to fall into this trap."

"What do you mean?"

"You know what I mean. Would you like me to put it into words for you?"

He bent over me now, one hand still holding his side: "You've found your tongue all of a sudden, haven't you? May said you were out all afternoon. Where were you? Along at the old hag's again? Did she put you up to this?"

"My gran's not. . ."

"She's not your gran. She's your stepfather's mother, and she's an old hag, a common old cow."

Hamilton was rearing at the foot of the bed, standing right on his hind legs as I yelled, "Don't you dare put that name to Gran!"

"I'll put what name I like to ....*Gran!* She's an old ...." And he came out with a mouthful of short four-letter words that up till now I hadn't heard anyone voice - I'd seen them written on the walls of toilets and the subway that led to the station - and nothing he could have done could have affected me more, this tall, thin, well-dressed, gentlemanly looking individual who had the appearance at times of an ascetic monk as portrayed in the films, using the foulest of language.

I felt immediately it was a mistake to let him see how it affected me; but I couldn't have known then that I had given him a weapon which was to be his main line of attack down the years. If I had told anyone that Mr Howard Stickle was a foul-mouthed individual, not only would I not have been believed, but I would have surely been accused of slandering a gentleman; indeed one of nature's gentlemen. I'm sure that even May wasn't aware of this trait in him.

It was some long time before I went to sleep somewhere in the middle of the night. And when, across the breakfast table the next morning, he looked at me and said, "You look tired, you should get more sleep," and he laughed, I thought, I can't stand it. I won't be able to stand this. He can have the house and all that's in it.

Yet once he was gone and I was alone, I walked from room to room. Hamilton went with me, and as I stood in the sitting-room he said, Don't do it. Don't make it easy for them. Do as you said yesterday, go and see the solicitor.

"Oh," I said, "I've got to start that woman's story."

You can work late tonight. That'll keep you out of bed. Go on, go now, else you won't go at all.

They called the solicitor Mr Pearson. He was middle-aged and very nice. He said yes, such a thing as I proposed could be arranged but could I tell him why I was taking this step.

Could I tell him? Could I say that although I knew deep within me my husband had married me for my house and for what money I had, I wouldn't have minded except that he had turned out to be a horrible individual. How horrible was only known to myself. What I answered him was, "I have good reason for doing what I'm doing, Mr Pearson." He stared at me for some seconds before saying with a slight smile on his face, "I'm sure you have;" then adding, "I've always thought of you as a very sensible girl, not at all like your mother, if I may say so, who was more erratic in her dealings. What you must do in this case is to take your grandmother to see your bank manager." He stopped here and pulled a slight face as he said, "Aren't you afraid of her spending your money?"

"No, not at all. She wouldn't do that. But if she did it wouldn't matter; there's nobody I'd like to have it more than her or my stepfather."

"Well" - he stood up - "you seem to like your relations better than most and it's a very nice attitude to come across. Although at the same time" - his face now took on a solemn look - "I am sorry that you feel obliged to do this."

"I am too, Mr Pearson."

We parted with a handshake after I had asked him not to send the document concerning the matter to my home but to Gran's address.

"You must be up the pole, lass. God in heaven! you can't do a thing like that."

"I have done it, Gran."

"Look, lass, all that money. What did you say? Nearly three thousand pounds worth of bonds an' all that money in the bank an' building society. Eeh! lass." She backed from me and leant against the little kitchen table. Then rubbing her hands across her mouth, she said, "What if our Georgie gets his hands on it?"

"He would act the same as you do, Gran. Anyway, you are just sort of being guardian to it."

"But you say it's in my name an' I have to go and see the bank manager?"

"Yes. And if I want any money I've got to come and ask you."

"Eeh, bugger me eyes! I've heard everything now. But what's made you do this, lass?"

I could tell her what had made me do this, even about his vile language, and she surprised me by saying, "Oh, that's not uncommon that. I know that at first hand, 'cos you see I went into service when I was fourteen. It was over Morpeth way. Gentry they were; not the top drawer but the riding, shooting, fishing kind. They had six bairns and the master was a warden in the church, an' all the servants knew about his language. Butter wouldn't melt in his mouth during the day, but at night-time he went for the mistress as if he was talking to a whore from the streets. His drink was port and brandy mixed. Men are queer cattle, lass, but yours is a dirty-minded bugger to take that line with you. One thing you mustn't do, pet, is to let him see it upsets you. That would give him satisfaction. An' if he gets too bad you go and tell your doctor."

I couldn't see myself going to Doctor Kane and saying, "Will you speak to my husband, please, because he uses bad language?" I could hear him over the distance exclaiming, "Who doesn't, woman! Who doesn't!"

But there was a difference in bad language and swearing. Gran swore. George swore. All the people in this district seemed to swear - as I walked down the street you could hear them, and the children too - but in a way it was clean swearing compared to the words that Howard used, and it was not only the words but the way he had of saying them.

The fact that I was penniless was not brought to Howard's and May's notice until almost six weeks later, when a final demand was sent for the electricity bill. I had left the previous bill together with the coalman's bill, the butcher's bill and a bill for wood that Howard had ordered to make more shelves for his bottles, and when on this Friday night, as once again I had received no housekeeping money, I quietly placed the bills in front of his plate, he looked down on them, then at me, and said, "What's this?"

"What does it look like? They're bills."

He turned now and glanced at May who had given herself a permanent invitation to our evening meal, which I must admit she herself provided very often. And it was May who, smiling smarmily, said, "But you see to the bills, dear."

"No, I don't." I hadn't sat down at the table; I was standing to the side of it and I shook my head like a little girl might as I repeated, "No, I don't."

"What do you mean, no, you don't?" His voice had taken on the bedroom tone.

"Well" - I looked at him - "how do you expect me to pay bills when you never give me any housekeeping money, you give it to May."

I saw him grind his teeth; then with his hand he swept the bills towards me, saying, "Don't you take that tack, madam, with me! You pay those bills like you've always done."

"I can't. I haven't any money."

Now they both screwed up their faces at me before turning and looking at each other, then back to me again.

"You haven't any money?" His words were slow. "Yesterday you had more than three thousand pounds and today you haven't any money. Have you gone really mad?"

"That's what I used to have, but I haven't anything now." I watched him slowly rise up, and even from the other side of the table he towered above me, his thin length seeming to stretch with each second of the silence that followed, until I broke it, saying, "I gave it away . . . legally."

Again the brother and sister exchanged glances; and now May was on her feet. "*You what?*" They both spoke together, and I repeated, "I gave it away legally. It's all been signed and sealed by my solicitor."

Slowly he came round the table now until he was my short arm's length from me, and I saw his jaw working backwards and forwards. His pale skin had turned almost purple, and for a moment I thought he was going to choke before he brought out the words, "Who did you give it to?"

"Well, you would know who I would give it to, wouldn't you? There was nobody but Gran, and failing her it goes to George." He turned slowly from me, only I think to prevent himself from striking me to the floor, and then he took his hand and swept it across the table, and in its passage my plate of fish pie, my cup and saucer, the sugar basin and the milk jug, all went flying; and then he let me have it from his mouth. "You bastard! You deformed stinking little bastard." And there followed a spate of words that not only shocked May, but surprised her into protest, and she cried at the top of her voice, "Howard! Howard! Stop that! No! no! Stop that, please. Such language."

"Shut up!" He rounded on her now. "You got your way, didn't you? You . . . you got your way and this is the result. Tied to that!" He thrust out his arm and pointed to me as if I was some crawling creature; and he made me feel like that. Yet I felt not the slightest remorse at what I had done. I had paid him back. I had paid them both back in part, even though I knew that wouldn't be the end of it; he being who he was would make me pay.

And he did.

Part Two

THE EMERGING

Chapter 1

The years that followed I look upon as the doctor and dog period because Doctor Kane became my bulwark and I fell in love with dogs. Hamilton didn't seem to mind, for, as he said, dogs were much more trustworthy than people.

My real association with Doctor Kane began one Wednesday morning. I had felt sick in the morning for some time now and when I told Gran about this she said, "My God! lass, you're pregnant."

Pregnant? Yes, I should have realized that; I was stupid. So I was going to have a baby. How wonderful! How marvellous! Yet, no, because it would be a part of Howard, if not all of him. People turned out like that, all of one or all of the other. But then equally it might turn out to be like me. Oh, no, not physically anyway. Oh, please. I found I was praying, until Gran said, "Now don't get upset. It's just normal, I suppose, only I would have wished for a better father for it. Still, you'll be its mother and it can't go far wrong with that. You'd better go and see the doctor."

"Well, well; so you think you're pregnant. How far have you gone?"

"I don't know."

"You don't know? Well, you should; if you don't know, nobody else does. Get your clothes off." He pointed to the screen.

A few minutes later he said, "Put your clothes on again." And when I was once more sitting before him he looked at me in silence for a moment, his hands joined on the desk in front of him, and he asked quietly, "How do you feel?"

"About what?"

"Oh, my God!" He turned his head to the side; then looked back at me again, saying, "About everything: the fact that you're going to have a baby; how you are finding marriage; about life in general. How do you feel?"

I smiled weakly at him as I replied, "Taking it in a lump, awful, except I think I'm pleased about the baby."

"Taking it in a lump." The hairs on his face moved in different directions as he twisted his mouth from one side to the other. Then he asked abruptly, "Why did you have to do it, marry that man?"

I answered truthfully, "Because I thought it would be my only chance."

"And now you've found out your mistake?"

"Yes."

"I'm surprised at you, you know. Behind that quiet exterior, I always thought you had a lot of horse sense."

There, he had said it again, and as before Hamilton appeared, standing behind the doctor's chair, his forefeet on the back of it, nodding at me.

"Don't look over my head when I'm talking to you; I'm not wearing a halo, not yet anyway." The doctor grinned at me now and, leaning forward, he said quietly, "You want to get out of the habit, you know, when people are speaking to you. You're always either looking up or down or sideways but never to the front. It gives folks the wrong impression of you. As I said, I always give you credit for some horse sense at least, and you should have known a fellow like that who looks as if he'd been let out of a band-box wasn't marrying you for your looks. Oh, yes, yes, I know. I'm being blunt, but then you've faced up to it long before this. That's why I could never understand why you did it. Now if your mother had done it, and she might well have at that, I could have seen a reason for it, a good reason for it . . . Anyway, how do you find life with him?"

"Awful."

He sat back in the chair as he said, "Really?"

"Yes; yes, really. He's two different people."

"What do you mean by that?"

"Well, he appears to be a sort of gentleman to all outsiders but" - I now forced myself to look him straight in the face "savage would be the kinder word I'd use with regard to his attitude towards me, my . . . my person, I mean."

He said nothing, but continued to stare at me.

"And . . . and there is something else."

He waited, and now I did look to the side and above his head and down to the floor before I said, "He talks at me in vile language, every night, just sits up in bed and talks at me."

"What do you mean by vile language? He swears?"

"No, not just swearing. I don't mind swearing. It's vile, filthy."

He leant forward and started to scribble on the blotting-pad as if he was doodling and there was silence between us for a moment; then lifting his head abruptly he almost bawled, "You brought this on -" only to realize he might be heard in the waiting-room for he lowered his voice as he ended, "yourself, girl." Then his head to one side, he said, "Have you refused him? You know what I mean?"

I knew what he meant and I said, "Yes; at least, when I can. "

"Well, that's not going to help you. If you could try."

I moved in my chair as if my body was shrinking down into the seat as I repeated, "I can't. I can't. He's so cruel; no thought, nothing."

"What are you going to do about it?"

"I . . . I don't know. I thought about leaving the house but I think that's what they want, him and his sister. I know now that she pushed him into marrying me. She liked the house . . . and the fact that I had a bit of money. But" - I pulled a slight face - "I potched them there."

"Potched them? What did you do?"

I told him. And when I was finished he sat back in the chair gazing at me; then, his big hairy head flopping back on his shoulders, he let out a great laugh. I don't know what the people in the waiting-room thought because it went on for quite a while. And then he had to take his handkerchief out to wipe his eyes, and as he did so he said, "I was right. I was right about your horse sense. Well, if you had the courage to do that, girl, you will have the courage to work things out for yourself. Go on now. I'm not going to worry about you any more. Oh no." He got up. "Pop in again next week. Eat plenty, and take exercise. What do you do with your days?"

"Well, I'm running a little business, typing manuscripts and such."

"Oh, well now, you've got something there. That's good, good. But still, that's sitting; so get yourself out and march round the town at least once a day."

At this I saw Hamilton walking through the door into the waiting-room. His knees were almost coming up to his shoulders; his tail was flashing from side to side in rhythm as a soldier's arm does when marching. He stamped out into the street and I followed him, smiling to myself. I liked Doctor Kane, I did.

I didn't tell Howard my news; I told May. If it had been conveyed to her before they had known I was virtually penniless, she would have clasped her hands together at her breast and exclaimed, "Oh, how beautiful! How delightful! Howard will be pleased." What she said was, "I hope you make enough money at your typing to engage a nurse when the time comes;" then she added, "I don't think Howard will be overjoyed."

Howard wasn't overjoyed. He was now having his midday meal out and she must have either gone to the shop or waylaid him on his way home. He came in as usual, took off his hat and coat in the hall, hung them up in the cloakroom and washed his hands, then came into the kitchen. I was frying some fish that May had brought in earlier; she still did the housekeeping.

He paused in the doorway and looked at me. I turned my head from the stove and looked back at him. He didn't speak until he was seated at the table; nor did I make any remark but as I placed the meal before him he gripped my wrist and, looking at me, he said, "So we are going to have an addition to the family, are we?"

To this I replied, "As May says, we are going to have an addition."

"It would have been nice, don't you think, if there had been a little extra money to provide it with the essentials of life."

"Most husbands I know of provide for their children," I replied; at which, he threw my hand from him. It hit the side of the table, causing me pain, and he said, "Most husbands have women they can call wives."

"And most wives have husbands who don't act like savage illiterate brutes," I snapped back. I don't know why I put the illiterate in, and I think this upset him as much as the other adjective, for he sprang up, his arm raised, his fist doubled; but at the same time my right hand shot out and gripped the frying pan. It was still hot and had the fish fat in it, and, holding it in mid-air, I screamed at him, "Don't you start that! Just don't start that, because if you do, you'll get as much as you send. I cannot retaliate by uttering filth for filth, but I can physically, and every time you hit me you'll get double in return with anything I can lay my hands on. I promise you that. Now, let's come to an understanding: you leave me alone and we can live in this house together, but you attempt any physical force on me and, you know, this house will go where the money went. I promise you that." I now lifted up my short arm, and my forefinger wagged to the side of my face, emphasising what I'd said. And I repeated it: "I'll sell this house. You can't stop me, nobody can. I've gone into all that an' all. So you have your choice. Your main purpose was to live here. All right, you may, and if I have a child I would like it brought up here, but not at any price." When he jumped back from me, I realized that I was waving the frying pan and the hot fat was spilling on to the tiled floor. Slowly, I replaced the pan on the stove; then, skirting the table, I walked just as slowly out of the room, leaving him purple with rage. And I knew he was utterly dumbfounded.

I had won another battle. Even so, I felt that the war had just begun.

Looking back down the years, I wonder how I could have tolerated this state. Could the loss of the house and its possessions have been such a force as to tie me to that man? Yes, I suppose it could. Well, it did. But there were other factors. Where would I have gone had I left there? To Gran's? Gran was wise. She knew I couldn't have stood living in that house in that quarter, as much as I loved her. The surroundings would have stifled me. I myself would have become like a caged animal in that one room, and perhaps become tired of Gran's mode of expression. It was amusing, taken in small doses, but with no variation, would I not become tired of listening to it?

Yet, I ask myself, what variation had I in my own home? Only the sound of my own voice talking to Hamilton most of the day. But then, that was the point, in my own home I could talk to Hamilton, but in Gran's I would have been unable to do that, for there was no privacy from the neighbours and the whole council estate would have soon known of the daft lass in Gran Carter's who talked to herself. She should be put away, they would have said. And they were not the only ones who would have been of that opinion, had I tried to explain about Hamilton.

So I stayed on in my house, and six months of my pregnancy passed.

Towards the end of this period I had joined a writers' circle. Oh dear me! it was a surprise. I had expected to be enthralled listening to literary geniuses; I had expected to be overawed by the possessors of literary merit. What I met with was a conglomeration of people who really looked as dowdy as myself. They were mostly women, and half of them wrote about kittens, dear little kittens and dear little cats. They wrote short stories about them, and poems about them. There wasn't so much said about dogs; it was always kittens or cats.

Howard never gave me one penny, but I was making enough now from my typing to buy odds and ends I felt I would need when the baby came. Life in the daytime was tolerable. Life when I entered the bedroom until the lights went out was almost unbearable. The nights when I wasn't being obscenely talked at, he handled me, and my elbow wasn't always a deterrent.

I was just on six months gone when I said to him, "I'm going to sleep across the landing."

"Like hell you are!" he said.

"Like hell I am!" I repeated.

"I'll make it worse for you if you do," he said.

"I don't think it's in your power to make it any worse."

"You know nothing yet."

I looked him straight in the face, and I said quietly, "Howard, if you start any new tactics with me I shall go to Doctor Kane and tell him exactly what happens." This seemed to deter him; as also did my manner of speaking; yet he came back with, "And what can he do?"

"He will know that I have registered a complaint against you, and it will help me when I tell you to get out of this house or I decide to sell it. Now I'm going to sleep across the landing. It's up to you to decide what the future holds for you."

What he said to me now was, "You ugly, pig-eyed, little snipe, you! If you think you're going to get me out of this house, you're mistaken. And I'm going to tell you something else. I'm bringing May in here to live; I don't see the reason to pay rent when there's rooms going empty. And anyway, she looks after me now as she's always done, because you damn well don't."

"I won't have May here permanently."

"You'll have her whether you like it or not."

"I mean what I say, Howard. You force my hand, and I'll sell this house. As much as I love it, I'll sell it. I will not have May here permanently."

I could feel his hand coming up again and the effort it took him to refrain from hitting me. . . .

It was a Saturday night when I began to feel ill. It couldn't be the baby, I told myself; I had felt it kicking vigorously only a short while before. I couldn't quite put a name to my feeling of illness, but in the middle of the night, sleeping alone now in a single bed and the door locked, I became worried; more so when the feeling of illness was still with me on the Sunday morning.

How I struggled to Gran's on the Sunday afternoon, I don't know. As soon as she saw my face she said, "My God! lass, I think you're for it. How much are you gone?"

"Six and a half months," I managed to say before collapsing onto the couch.

I came to myself sometime later, with the bushy face of Doctor Kane hanging over me. "It's all right," he was saying gently. "It's all right. You're going to be all right. Now listen carefully, Maisie. You're going into hospital; your baby's on the way. It's a little early, but you're going to be all right. You're going to be all right." . . .

I lay in hospital a week, and they were so kind to me, but I seemed to know from the beginning that I was going to lose the baby. When they eventually took him away from me, he had been dead for some little time. . . .

After I returned home, Gran came every day to see to me. But she left the house before Howard came in. May hadn't visited me in the hospital, nor did she come and see me at the house. I understood she wasn't well. And this was true, she wasn't well; she was so unwell that Howard spent most of his evenings with her.

For weeks after returning home, I couldn't pull myself together; my body seemed depleted and my mind in a very low state. If I saw Hamilton at all he was bedraggled, his tail between his legs, his head drooping, no shine to his coat. He was no help to me. And what was worrying me now was that my lip was jerking like it used to.

It was some time later when I went to see Doctor Kane. He had come to see me on several occasions, but the last time he visited me he said, "A walk won't do you any harm. Pop in next week." Poor Doctor Kane, I was to pop in every week for months on end, until he was to become sick of the sight of me and, candidly, I of him. . ..

On this particular visit, he said to me, "Now what I've got to tell you is going to be disappointing: you're made in such a way that you can't carry babies."

"Why not?" I said. "My body seems all right to me."

"Oh, your body's all right. It isn't your body really, at least it's a part of it, it's your blood."

"What?"

"I said, it's your blood."

"What's wrong with my blood?"

"You're what is called Rhesus negative."

"What?"

He took a long breath and said, "I said you are what is called Rhesus negative."

"I know what you said, but what does it mean?"

"Well, it's to do with monkeys."

"*Wh . . . at?*" As if I were imitating the creature, I rose up from the chair as if about to climb the wall. My whole body was stretched with indignation, until he said, "Get off your high horse -" It was odd how he always connected me up with a horse. "It's an experiment they did during the war with monkeys."

"And I've got the same type of blood?"

"No. Most women have an antigen in their blood which is also in the blood of a Rhesus monkey. You haven't such an antigen. I don't know a lot about it, but it does happen in such cases as yours that the blood of the mother and that of the child are not compatible, and so she is unable to carry the baby. Some women have had six, seven, eight miscarriages, trying to carry through, and failed."

"Monkeys?"

"Don't take on like that, girl. It's just a name. I've explained to you

you've got no monkey blood in you. But still" - he gave a short laugh - "the fact of the presence of these antigens does open up a big question of evolution via the apes. Was there a Garden of Eden? Hell no; I plump for the monkey blood coming down through the ages."

"I . . . I won't be able to have children then?"

"As far as I can see now, my dear" - his voice was soft - "you would be able to conceive again, but it's the carrying of them.
But you have one consolation, you're just one of thousands who are in the same boat. Under other circumstances I would suggest adoption, but not in yours, not the way you're placed."

Oh no, he was right. Certainly, there wouldn't be any adoption the way I was placed.

"How are things, any improvement?"

"I have a room to myself. I don't know how long it will last."

"I could have a talk with him. I think I should. You're in a very poor state of health at present, very low. Tell him I want to see him."

"I don't know whether he would come."

"Well you can tell him and we'll see." . . .

I told him. Surprisingly, he made no comment, and he went to the surgery. But when he returned later that night he came into the study where I was typing. He stood just within the doorway and there was a sneer on his face as he said in that flat toneless way he had when spewing obscenities at me, "Monkeys. That explains it. My God, yes, that explains a lot. I always thought you should be in a zoo."

When he closed the door, not banging it, just drawing it slowly and softly into its place, I laid my head down in the crook of my arm on top of the machine, and the swelling in my chest burst up through my throat and the tears poured out of my eyes, nose and saliva out of my mouth, and from that great unfathomed depth of me there emerged a new pain that made me cry out to God and ask Him why He had put me into this world to make me the victim of such people as, first, my mother, and now this man. Wasn't it enough that He had made me plain to the point of ugliness, besides having deformed me. Why hadn't He gone the whole hog and made me mental, then I wouldn't have been aware of my state?

When I raised my head Hamilton was gazing at me. He didn't look like himself somehow: he was a horse and yet he wasn't; the white of his tail seemed to have spread all over him. He said quietly, You'll get your answer; just work at it.

I dried my eyes and, strangely, for the next few days I felt calm inside.

Then I met Bill.

I had been to a printer's on the outskirts of Bog's End. I found I could get a good quality typing paper cheaper there than I could from an ordinary stationer's. To get to the building I had to pass along the waterfront. I liked this walk. Before you got to the high dock wall you could glimpse the ships along the quayside, and, too, everything around this quarter seemed to be full of bustle.

I had bought three reams of paper and was making my way back along by the wall now when I heard the screeching of brakes and above that a pitiful cry of a wounded animal. I swung round and saw, some way behind me along the road, a small lorry had stopped. For a time, nobody got out of it. From where I stood I could see this dark bundle lying in the gutter writhing and whimpering. After I reached it, the man got down from his cab and, looking at me, he said, "The damn thing ran right under the wheel. It's a wonder it wasn't knocked flat." I had put my parcel down on the edge of the pavement and was now bending over the dog, yet afraid to touch it. I liked dogs, although I'd never had one of my own, and, remembering my mother's warning, never to stroke a stray dog, I stayed my hand. The animal tried to raise itself from the ground, then flopped back again, and from there turned its head and looked at me. It wasn't a nice looking dog; it had a sharp pointed face and a blunt head, and its dark coat had white patches on it.

Another voice now joined the driver's, saying, "Oh, it's that bloody animal, is it? He's been runnin' round here for the last three weeks. It's a wonder he hasn't caught it afore now. Somebody gettin' on one of the boats must have dumped it. A bull-terrier he is, isn't he?"

A bull-terrier. The name sounded ominous. Yet, as the animal continued to look at me I put my hand down and touched its head, and for a moment it stopped its whimpering.

"What are you going to do with it?" The voice was from above my head again, and another answered, "Knock it on the head. It would be a bloody kindness to knock it on the head, because nobody's been looking for a lost dog around here. And anyway, they don't go in for bull-terriers. Whippets more like."

"You can't do that." I turned to look up at the men. "It's only his foot. It could be attended to."

"Aye, but who's going to attend to it?"

I turned my head and saw that the animal was still looking at me. What would Howard say if I took a beast like this home? Anyway, I couldn't take it home; it would have to go to a vet first.

"Is there a vet near?"

The second man answered, "Yes, there's one in Roland Street."

I looked at the driver and asked him, "Will you take him there?"

"What! Me? Look, I've got a job to do."

"I'm only asking you to carry him for me, or let me ride in your lorry with you. I'll ... I'll have him on my knee."

The two men looked at each other; then the other man said, "Well, if you don't you'll have to report it, won't you? It doesn't matter when it's a cat, but when it's a dog I think you've got to report it. But if she wants to take over ... well, let her."

This seemed sense to the lorry driver and so without further words, he stooped down and quite gently lifted the animal from the ground. Then looking at me, he said, "I do run into them. By God! I do run into them."

I knew he wasn't meaning running into dogs, but running into misfortunes.

The other man gave me a hoist up on to the seat, and when the driver put the dog on my knee I was amazed at the weight of him. I also thought it very strange that although he was lying at an angle, he turned his head and kept looking at me. It was as if there and then he had decided that he wasn't going to let me go.

When we reached the vet's the lorry driver helped me down from the cab, placed the dog in my arms again, then drove off without a word.

When eventually we met the vet, his approach to the problem was that stray dogs were a nuisance; they should be sent to the pound. Did I realize what I was taking on?

"What exactly do you mean?" I asked, and the reply I got was, "This is a stray dog, you say. Are you intending to keep him? If you want his foot seen to, and this will need an operation because the bones are shattered and the ligaments torn and he will be in plaster for some weeks and then need further attention, it is going to cost you money."

"I'm aware of that," I said.

"That's all right then," he said.

"Well, that's all you can do for now. Just leave your name and address with Miss Fennell, and then come back tomorrow and take him home."

I looked at the animal lying on the table. He was quiet now. I said, "Is he an old dog?"

"No, no. He's little more than a pup, I should say. Not quite a year old."

"Really ... that's nice."

He looked at me narrowly, and I, embarrassed, now said, "Well, what I mean is, he's not going to die shortly after the operation then? I . .. thought he might have been thrown out because he was so old."

"No, he's not old; but he's the runt of the litter I should say." My eyes questioned him, and he went on, "Legs too short for a bull-terrier and the body much too heavy. There's been a slip up somewhere, I think. Anyway, there's one thing certain, miss, he'll never win any prizes for you."

"That won't matter to me. I've never won any prizes myself. Good-afternoon."

Why on earth had I said that?

As I gave his secretary my name and address, I saw him looking through the top half of the glass door at me. I was in two minds about him: I didn't know whether I liked him or not. But it didn't seem to matter. Yet at the same time it did: if he was a nice man, he'd be careful in his treatment of that poor animal; if he wasn't, and knowing the dog was a stray, he might hash the whole business. . ..

Mr Biggs turned out to be a nice man, a very nice man. We were to become well acquainted over the coming years.

It wasn't until I reached home that I discovered I had left the new packet of typing paper on the kerb.

I wasn't going to mention the dog to Howard. It was to be a *fait accompli:* I'd install him in the house and that would be that. . .. Or would it? But he happened to be at home when I arrived at four o'clock, which was most surprising. I didn't ask why he was there because, looking at my blood-stained light grey coat, he said, "And what's happened to you?" in a tone that indicated that he wasn't interested but would just like to know out of curiosity.

"A dog got run over. I took it to the vet's."

"Huh! If you concerned yourself with humans it would be more to the point. May's ill. But do you care? Oh, no. You go to the rescue of stray dogs. Or sit talking to that moron of a council house woman." Then, turning swiftly from me, he said, "I'm bringing May here," only to turn swiftly towards me again, and, his arm outstretched, his finger almost touching my face, say, "And don't you put any obstacle in the way. May's ill. She could die. She's coming here."

I hadn't seen May for a fortnight; the last occasion only for a few minutes. She had been very quiet, not her usual self. And so I said now, with some concern in my voice, "What is the matter with her?"

I saw him swallow deeply. It was also obvious that he was very worried, and it was a moment before he brought out, "Leukemia. She's got leukemia."

"Oh no."

I had a very guilty feeling as I hurried from the room. I hadn't realized she had been so ill. I had thought that since the business of the money, she had been putting it on as an excuse for not cooking the meals any more, sort of letting me get on with it, and making a hash of it, as Gran had once said. . ..

I was shocked at the sight of her when he brought her into the hall. I went up to her and said softly, "I . . . I have your room ready, May." And she said, "Thank you." Her voice was quiet; all her boisterousness seemed to have disappeared.

Up in the bedroom, when I went to help her undress, he pressed me aside, not roughly, but firmly, saying, "I'll see to her." I hesitated and he turned and looked at me and repeated slowly, "I'll see to her." And on this I walked out. I thought it was odd.

But during the next four weeks, which was all she had before she died, I learned that if he loved anybody, it was her. Not once during that time did he go near the bottle room. From he came in, he fetched and carried and saw to her till he went to bed. During the day my own hands were more than full, for I also had Bill to see to.

So changed did I find May that, the day after her arrival, I felt I could tell her about Bill, because that's what I had christened him in my mind, and I asked her if she would mind if I slipped out and brought him home. And she answered quietly, "No, of course not. I'm perfectly all right."

I was confronted by Bill standing on three legs and what looked like a thick white stick. The plaster cast, the vet said, would have to remain on for some time, but I had to bring him back next week.

Bill could walk in a dot-and-carry-three fashion. The funny part about it was, he kept stopping and looking back at his leg, then looking up at me, as much to say, what are you going to do about it?

When I got him home I made a bed in the clothes-basket for him, and gently pressed him into it and told him to stay. I had taken two steps away from it when he got up. The "stay" business went on for about five minutes before he got the message.

I then ran up to May to see how she was. She seemed to be sitting in bed exactly how I had left her, her hands on top of the cover, her head propped up against the pillow. She said, "Did you get him?" And I said, "Yes. But he won't cause any trouble."

Surprisingly, she now said, "I've always wanted a dog, but never got round to having one. Perhaps you'll bring him up sometime?"

"Oh yes." I smiled broadly at her and again said, "Oh, yes." That she should like Bill would surely give him an entry ticket to get past Howard.

That evening, Howard came in the back way hurriedly, then stopped dead on the sight of the anything but beautiful three-legged-and-one-white-stumped dog. I'd heard the back door open as I came downstairs, and I raced to the kitchen, there to see him and Bill surveying each other, mutual dislike evident in both their faces. And Bill was giving voice to his in a low growl. As I bent and patted him I looked up at Howard and said, "I had to bring him home."

"Well, he's not staying here, not that thing."

"He is."

"I said, no."

"You can say what you like, Howard, he's staying. And May wants to see him. She tells me she's always wanted a dog, and . . . and she wants to see him."

"May said she wanted to see him?"

"Yes. Ask her yourself."

For the evening meal I had cooked some lamb chops, potatoes, and vegetables, and I had May's tray ready to take up when Howard entered the kitchen. Looking down on it, he said, "Where's the gravy?" And I said, "Well, I didn't think you would need gravy with chops; I've . . . I've put some butter on the potatoes."

"Don't need gravy with chops! . . . Stupid!" He drew in a quick sharp breath, then grabbed the tray from me and went out.

And I stood and repeated, "Stupid!"

The following morning I took Bill up to see May. I had a job to get him up the stairs. It was evident he had never had to manipulate stairs before and we were only half-way up them when I sat down and laughed; and he licked my face and gave one whoof of a bark as if he was enjoying the joke. But I silenced him, saying, "Shh! Shh! No barking in the house."

When May saw him, she smiled and, looking at me, she said, "You do pick them, don't you, Maisie?"

"I couldn't do anything else," I said; "I was so sorry for him." And then I added, "It isn't so much me picking them, as they picking me." She stared at me for a long time, and then, her head drooping, she said, "Yes, you're right, they picking you. I've done a lot of thinking lately, Maisie. . . .. You know I'm dying?"

"Oh no! Oh no!"

"Don't be silly." Her voice sounded as of old; but she paused before saying, "I've faced up to a lot of things, and one of them is, I know I did wrong by you."

I stared at her silently. Then she went on, "I liked your house . . . this house. I never expected to die in it though. The main thing was, I wanted security for Howard; I felt he hadn't had his rightful chance in life. I was wrong. But there, the excuse I have is that so many mothers are wrong, and in a way I've always looked upon myself as Howard's mother, because I've mothered him from the day he was born. I think it's because I knew early on that he'd be the only man in my life. You see" - she moved her head slowly now - "I've . . . I've never been able to like men, except . . . except Howard. But I'm not blind to his faults. And Maisie -" She put her big bony hand out towards me, and I lifted mine from where it was resting on Bill's head and let her clasp it, and now, her words halting and her eyes cast down, she said, "I . . . I know you've had a hard time with Howard. I didn't imagine he would be like that. You are a girl who would have responded to kindness, been grateful for it. I recognize that, and I thought that, once you were married, he would see the other side of you, the kindness, and . . . and would therefore come to . . . well, care for you in a way. But from what I understand now, I fear that can never be. And . . . and I feel full of remorse for saddling you . . . for saddling you both with each other, when you are so unsuited."

I could not look at her. I turned my gaze down on Bill. His eyes were on me. And now she said, "We made a mistake about you. I . . . I imagined you were very amenable. We didn't realize that behind your sort of inoffensive manner there is a strong character."

I now raised my eyes to her, my mouth was slightly agape. I didn't know I had a strong character: I had looked upon myself as weak, easily led, rather inane. Her head drooped back on the pillows now as if she was tired, and I rose slowly from the bed and was about to release her hand when her grip tightened slightly and she turned and looked at me again as she said, "I shouldn't say this, but I must: stand up to Howard. He'll respect you more for it. If . . . if you let him get the better of you, he will treat you like . . . like . . ." She closed her eyes and swallowed deeply, and I heard myself murmur, "It's all right. It's all right, May. Don't worry. But . . . but thank you." She opened her eyes and looked at me, and I repeated, "Thank you, for talking to me as you have. And . . . and if I can help it, you'll not die; I'll look after you." I bent towards her, smiling slightly now as I ended, "I'll even cook you a tasty meal." She gave me an answering smile and said, "That'll be the day."

I laughed outright now. "Just you wait," I said. "Just you wait. I'll make a hash that I won't make a hash of."

I found I had to get out of the room quickly. There was no need to call Bill; he followed at my heels. And out on the landing, I stood with my hand pressed tightly against my cheek, the tears were blocking my throat, and I muttered aloud, "Please, God, don't let her die. We could be friends now. I could see that, we could be friends. She understands the situation. Please, please, don't let her die. . .."

During the following days that were left to her I learned to make junket, egg custard, and light pastry, and I served her these appetisingly. But as time went on she ate less and less.

The atmosphere of the house had changed completely. Different people from the terrace came in to see her. And Doctor Kane visited her every day. It was during the middle of the fourth week that, after coming downstairs, he put his hand on my elbow and led me into the sitting-room, and there he said, "I don't think it will be long now."

I couldn't speak for a moment; then I said, "Shouldn't she be in hospital getting special treatment? Couldn't they do something there?"

"No, they couldn't do anything for her now that isn't being done here. I would have had her in weeks ago, but she refused. There's only one good thing that has come out of this sad business; she speaks very well of you now. Strange that, isn't it?"

"Yes, yes, it is," I said.

"It was she who pushed you into this marriage. I know that and she knows it. But in her own way she's been trying to make amends, although if that'll have any effect on her dear brother, I don't know. We'll have to see what happens when she goes, won't we?"

I made no answer to this, just stood looking into his face. I seemed to know every hair on it. I had seen it every week for months now across his desk, mostly on a Monday morning. It was something I had come to look forward to. I knew all the regulars who visited the surgery. I had very little to say to them, but I listened a lot, and the snatches that came to me made me want to laugh, even when I didn't feel like it. There was one woman in particular who, when she sat beside me, would say, "You here again?" Hamilton laughed his head off about that. He would sit on his haunches in the middle of the round table where the out of date magazines were and rock with laughter. You here again? he would mimic. She would then give me a running commentary on her ailments: "'Tis the neck of me bladder. He says it wants seeing to. Me water's like nobody's business, 'cos I've had it all taken away, you know. Hysterectomy, you know; yours is only nerves. By! you're lucky. But you're always here. Men don't understand. He said to me, me husband, 'Well, what about it, are you or aren't you? Come on, make up your mind; it's either that or I go to the club.' So I said, 'All right,' and we got down to it and papered the front room. But I didn't feel like it."

On that occasion the women on the other side of her spluttered and choked. They had evidently placed the wrong construction on her words.

I don't think it had dawned upon the woman that she was as frequent a visitor as I was or else she wouldn't have known I had been there so often.

As I now stood looking at him, there came a scratching at the door, and when I went hurriedly and opened it and Bill marched in, the doctor turned his gaze down on him. "Who's he?" he said.

"Where did he spring from?"

"It's Bill," I said; "he's a bull-terrier. I've had him for some weeks. I keep him in the kitchen. He must have got out."

He stared down at Bill. Then looking at me, he said, "You could have picked a better looking one. Where did you find him?" When I told him, he smiled and said, "Maisie, you're a funny girl."

"Funny ha-ha, funny peculiar, or just funny?"

"A bit of all three, I should say."

Yes, he would.

At that moment Hamilton appeared. He was standing in the corner of the room, and I thought, Yes, if I were to tell him about you, it would be the middle one that would head my certificate. At times I longed to tell someone about Hamilton, just to see what effect it would have on them. Would they think I was barmy?

Definitely, they would. Well, I didn't feel barmy, and I wasn't barmy. Then why did I talk to Hamilton?

I didn't know, not really. But talk to him I did. I felt I always would. I saw him now walk slowly across the room and stand by my side, facing the doctor. I say, stand by my side, he seemed enormous, my head only came to his shoulder.

"What's the matter?"

I blinked at him, "Nothing."

"You worried about something besides . . . ?" He jerked his head backwards.

"Not really."

"Not really? What do you mean? Has he been at his games again?"

"Oh, no, no. He spends all his time, every evening, with May until very late. I . . . I think he cares deeply for her."

He turned now and walked up the sitting room towards the door, saying, "A man like that cares for just one person, Maisie, and the quicker you realize it the better. That person is number one. "

I wanted to say, you're wrong there, he cares for May, but I remained silent. At the door, he said, "If you see any definite change, give me a ring, straightaway."

"I will. Thank you."

*

I wasn't in the room with her when she died. It happened suddenly one evening. I went upstairs with a tray on which there was a glass of hot milk. I opened the door, and there I saw Howard sitting on a chair, his body bent forward, his face buried in the coverlet near her limp hand.

I didn't speak; there was nothing I could say. Her face looked white and thin; the flesh had dropped off her of late; her cheekbones stretched the skin. I went quietly out, taking the tray with me, and down in the kitchen I sat on the chair, my elbow on the table. I put my hand over my eyes, and found myself muttering, "Good-bye, May. Good-bye, May. I'm sorry we didn't get to know each other better earlier on. But you're all right now. You're safe now. Good-bye, May. Good-bye, May."

I had to make an effort to stop myself talking. It was as if she was in the room. As I made to get up I had to push Bill aside. His muzzle had been against my knee, and I looked down at him and said, "She liked you. Yes, she liked you. That was something, wasn't it?"

I went to the phone and told the doctor. He came almost directly, and when half an hour later he left, he stood on the doorstep and looked at me and said, "He's all yours now, Maisie. He's all yours now. It's up to you how you deal with him. The only thing is, don't let him trample on you, or you'll be finished for good."

I stood in the hall and looked up the stairs. May's presence seemed to have gone from the house. There was only his in it now, and in this moment I asked myself how I was going to prevent him trampling on me, because I didn't think that anything May might have said to him before she died would make any difference in our association.

Chapter 2

It seemed that I was wrong, because for the first few weeks after May's funeral he treated me almost like a human being. During this time I did my best to make the meals attractive. Usually before, whenever we had eaten together no word had passed between us; now, he began to talk, but it was all about May. I didn't mind that in the least, as long as he talked, and normally, without that dreadful sneer in his voice. May, he told me had been everything to him, mother, sister, friend. He didn't know what he was going to do without her. When I said, "You will have to go back to your collecting and take up tennis again," he nodded at me, saying, "Yes, yes, that's what I must do."

When this situation had gone on for about four weeks I began to think he was right, regarding companionship, as he had suggested before we were married. Perhaps, I thought, if he continued in this way I could forget what had happened and life would be tolerable, more than tolerable, perhaps enjoyable. He would have his pastimes and I would have mine.

I was trying to catch up on the orders for typing, and I was also beginning to write myself, not just scribbles, not just about Hamilton, but little pieces about different things that had happened to me. Like the day I took Bill to the vet's to get his plaster off.

Only one unusual thing happened on our way there: we passed some buskers, and Bill stopped and, putting his head back, howled to the accompaniment of a man playing a fiddle and another a mouth-organ. A third was going round with a cap. Try as I might, I couldn't get Bill away from them as long as they continued to play, and a lot of people stopped, and the man who was playing the mouth-organ shook with laughter and his mouth became so full of spittle he couldn't go on playing.

As soon as they stopped playing, Bill allowed me to lead him on. But the man who had played the mouth-organ called after me, "Will you loan him to us, miss?" which caused the crowd to laugh.

I was always addressed as Miss, no one ever took me for Missis.

As I led him along in his dot-and-carry-three step I thought, Oh, my goodness! If he starts that every time he hears music, we are in for something. Yet I'd had the radio on and there had been music and he hadn't reacted in this way. I was to learn that he was only affected by reed or wind music such as the flute, the mouth-organ, and yes, brass instruments; the piano and the violin didn't seem to take his fancy.

I was brought to another halt at a butcher's shop. Bill tried to tug me into the shop, and I kept saying, "No, no, Bill." The customers in the shop turned round and laughed, and the butcher, leaning over his block, shouted to me, "If you want him cut up, bring him in." And, of course, this caused more laughter.

When I eventually got him into the surgery after a slight contretemps in the waiting-room when Bill took a strong dislike to an Alsatian and then showed his preference for a cat whose head was poking out of a basket. The owner of the cat laughed when Bill wanted to lick her charge. She said she had never seen anything like it. Nor had the owner of the Alsatian. Her dog never fought, she said, he was as quiet as a lamb. I nearly asked her why he was baring his teeth at Bill. Of course. Bill wasn't only baring his teeth at the moment, every stiff hair on his body seemed erect. I was to learn that Bill loved people, but didn't like any of his own kind. And, too, being contrary, he tolerated cats. Once he brought a young kitten home in his mouth while the mother was trying to tear him to bits. I think Bill was a male who should never have been a male. There are a lot of poor souls like him kicking about. Anyway, once the plaster was off his leg, Bill turned round and looked at his new paw as if it was something that didn't belong to him. The vet told me I must massage the limb every day. I promised to do so, then I paid his bill, which staggered me somewhat and made me realize that it was as expensive for a dog to be ill as it was for a human being.

Outside, Bill continued to walk as he had been doing with his dot-and-carry-three step until, stopping abruptly, he looked round at his back leg and slowly stretched himself; then his leg went out, his head went up, his body stiffened, and he was off.

It happened so quickly I didn't know what had hit me. I was hanging on to the end of the lead and he was racing ahead like a greyhound after a rabbit. When we came to the open quay, men stopped working to watch our progress. We had passed the turning that I usually took for home. Then as quickly as he had started he stopped, and at a lamp post. Like a top spinning, I wound round it before I, too, stopped; then I leant against it, gasping, and all I could say was, "Oh, you bad dog. Oh, you bad dog."

A man approached us from along the quay. He had jumped up from a small boat, and I could see that he was shaking with laughter. And when he stood in front of me, he said, "Enjoy your trip, miss?" Then looking down at Bill, his grin spreading from ear to ear, he said, "I shouldn't be surprised to see you in the greyhound stadium shortly, lad." But then, his glee subsiding a little, he asked with some concern, "You all right, miss?"

"Yes; a little out of puff."

"I'd say. I thought you were going to take off. I've never seen anything so funny afore. You pay to go to the pictures, but what you see for free on this waterfront is nobody's business. If - " he started to shake again and spluttered, "If you could have seen yourself, lass, you would have died."

"I felt I was going to."

This seemed to add to his amusement. Bill, in the meantime, had been examining the lamp post from all angles, twisting his body back and forward in order to get the right position to leave his mark. I now pulled hard on his lead, saying, "Come on. Come on, Bill." And as the man repeated, "Bill? You call him, Bill? Well, he's well named," what seemed to be the last straw happened: I gave one sharp tug, and off came his collar.

If the man hadn't been there and eager to help, everything would have gone smoothly. I would have said, "Stay! Bill," and Bill would have stayed. But the man made a grab at him and Bill, likely remembering other men who had made grabs at him before he had come under my protection, took to his heels, crossed the road and scooted back in the direction from which we had just come.

I didn't stop to say anything to the man, but took to my heels. Did I hear him laughing? It didn't matter. I ran, yelling, "Bill! Bill! Come back! Bill!" When I saw him turn the corner into the road we should have taken on our way home, I thought, Good. Good. He's making for home. But when I got to the corner, there was no sign of him. The road was a long one, and I was sure he couldn't have reached the end of it. Then I remembered the butcher's shop.

When I arrived gasping at the door, there he was, sitting on the sawdust, looking up at the butcher. There were three customers in the shop and they were keeping well away from him. The butcher looked at me and said, "He's determined to be chopped up, this one."

As I grabbed him and thrust the collar over his head, he didn't even bother to rise to his feet; he just sat looking up at the butcher.

"What do you feed him on?" said the butcher.

"Dog food, tinned dog food."

"Huh! That dog's got sense; he knows what's best. Do you want a pound of scraps?"

"Oh, yes. Yes, please."

I got the pound of scraps, then handed the butcher the sixpence he had asked for, and now, tugging at Bill, I said, "Come on. Come on." But Bill just looked at me and turned his gaze once more on the butcher.

Without a smile on his face now, the butcher said, "He doesn't want meat, he wants chopping up. He's suicide bent, that dog." There was a deep chuckle in his throat and the three women, still keeping their distance, gave nervous sniggers.

"I wonder if a bone will do it?" He now turned to the bench behind him and, taking up a marrow bone about a foot long, he came round the block and said, "This what you want?" Whereupon Bill stood up and took one quick step towards the butcher who, taking two quick steps back, thrust the bone at me, saying, "It's all yours."

When I handed Bill the bone he took it quite gently from me; then turned his thick stumpy body about and led me from the shop. At the door, I pulled him to a temporary halt, saying over my shoulder, "Thank you. Thank you." And the butcher called after me, "You're welcome, but don't bring him back."

I wish I could remember all the remarks that were passed about us as we walked across the market place, Bill carrying that huge marrow bone and still doing his dot-and-carry-three walk and I almost slinking by his side.

At home, I tied him up in the yard on a long piece of rope and there he sat for the next two hours gnawing happily at that bone, after he had licked the marrow out of it as far as his tongue would reach.

After making myself a cup of tea, I sat down and reviewed the events of the past hour. I wished I had somebody to relate them to. It was too late in the afternoon to go to Gran's; and anyway, I'd wasted enough time today. I must get on with the typing. But wouldn't it be nice, I thought, if there was a man coming in for his tea and I could tell him what had happened. Yes, yes, it would have been very nice. . .

A man did come in for his tea and I didn't tell him what had happened, but the dog became the topic of our conversation and, in a way, the beginning of the bribery. Or would you call it blackmail? Whatever it was, it meant if I wanted to keep Bill and, too, something of my personal privacy, I had to part with money.

As soon as he sat down to his tea I knew there was something in the wind. Since May had gone, at least up till now, he hadn't grumbled at his meals, but, looking at the sausage, egg and chips I had cooked, he said, "Doesn't your mind go beyond fries?"

"I thought you liked sausage and eggs?"

To this he answered, "You can get too much even of a good thing if you have a repeat pattern every week: sausage and egg, bacon and egg, egg and chips, scrambled eggs, boiled eggs. And when I'm on, there's another thing I'm going to tell you: this kitchen smells of that dog. The whole house smells of him. Get rid of him."

The fork almost sprang out of my hand as my whole body jerked in the chair, and I said, "No, I'll not! I'll not get rid of Bill."

"Well, if you won't I will, by the simple process of leaving the back door open and letting him go. And he'll go straight back to where he came from, the dock front. Dogs, like people, always revert to their beginnings."

From between tight lips I said, "That's a pity."

"What do you mean?"

"I was just agreeing with you about people reverting."

His face reddened. The implication of my words seemed to have struck home. I knew nothing about his real early beginnings, only May's reference to the nice life they had led in Gosforth, which I surmised now must have been only a brief interlude.

Following the meal, he went upstairs and changed, and when he came down again he was ready for outdoors in a new suit, and over his arm was what looked like a new light overcoat. Well, he was in the trade, it wouldn't cost him all that much, I thought. Grudgingly, I had to admit that he looked very smart, and he surprised me when, going out of the door, he turned and looked at me saying, quietly, "Why do we always have to get off on the wrong foot?"

It was the nearest to an apology he had ever come. He didn't wait for an answer and went out.

I was surprised still further when, two hours later, he returned home. He came straight into the study where I was working, another unusual procedure, and, sitting down in the big leather chair that I understood had been my grandfather's favourite seat, he looked at me for a moment before he said, hesitantly, "I've got to talk to you."

I waited, not knowing what was coming. Here was a different man, likely the one May had known.

He said, still hesitantly, "I've been offered the chance of something big. You know, ours is a very good class shop and Mr Hempies has the idea of opening a branch in Durham or somewhere near, and . . . and if he does, that will mean he will go and manage that one most of the time as he lives out that way, and the management here will be going. . . Paul Richardson, he's been there longer than me and he's mostly over the cutters and the stitchers, but he's dying for the job. Well, I might as well come to the point, it means buying oneself in, sort of partnership like."

Oh, so this was it.

"You see with the money I got for the furniture and the bit I'd saved, all I can raise is two hundred and fifty five pounds. And from what I understand, well. . ." He uncrossed his knees, and then crossed them again the other way before ending, "I'd need a thousand." There was a long pause before he said, "What about it, Maisie?"

"I'm sorry," I replied. "You know what I did with my money; I haven't got it. All I've got is the bit I earn from my typing." And, I nearly added, the measly bit you give me for housekeeping, which was three pounds a week.

His face was straight and tight now as he said, "You can get it if you want to. She'll give it back to you."

"I . . . I couldn't ask her."

"Look." He suddenly sprang to his feet and was leaning forward now, his hands gripping the ends of the desk, his face close to mine. "It'll make all the difference to . . . to everything, to my way of life and to your way of life. Yes, to your way of life." And he nodded his head at me now. "Just think it over. I've got till the end of the month to make the decision." He straightened up and turned about, but took only one step before he stopped and looked down on Bill who was sitting by my side. And he held this position for some seconds and it spoke louder than any words he might have uttered concerning Bill's future if I didn't comply with his demands.

Two hours later I was on the point of sleep when the light flashed on, and he came to the bed and said, "Move over."

"No . . . please."

"Move over!"

When I didn't, he gripped my short arm and almost lifted me out of the bed. . .

Fifteen minutes later I was alone with my head buried in the pillow.

The following day I was sitting on Gran's couch and she was putting into words my thoughts of Howard.

"The bloody blackmailing swine. That's all it is, blackmail. Now what'll happen, lass, if you give in to him this time? There'll come another and another until he has the whole damn lot out of you."

"He won't. He won't."

"How can you say he won't when you're breakin' under it now? Seven hundred and fifty pounds! Eeh, my God!. . . Well, it's your money, and you seem determined to let him have it, but, lass, I would have some agreement in writing, mind, that he leaves you alone, an' the dog an' all."

That was an idea. But how could I do it? Ask him to sign a paper saying that he wasn't to come near my person for such and such a time, nor molest my dog? Yes, yes, I could do that. Yes, I could. I could type out a statement and get him to sign it. Why shouldn't I? And stipulate a year . . . no, two. . . Or three? No, I'd better just leave it at two. Two years is a long time; something could have happened by then. Yes, that's what I would do. I said to Gran. "You've given me an idea, Gran. I'll write out a statement and get him to sign it."

"Aye, and you can add that you'll expose him and take him to court if he doesn't keep his word to whatever you demand. By! I'm glad our Georgie isn't here, 'cos if he was Mr Howard Stickle would have to pick out his teeth from his guernsey. But, by the way, I forgot to tell you, he says he's comin' this way with a load a week come Tuesday. Eeh! I can't wait, lass. It's months since I clapped eyes on him."

"I haven't heard from him for ages. Did you get a letter?"

"No, you know he's hardly any hand at writing letters. He made an effort at first like, but that soon stopped. You know yourself the kind of thing he writes: 'I hope it leaves you as it finds me at present.' And what I know about our George, I've thought to meself when I've read that, oh, lad, those days are past for me."

She put her head back and let out a laugh, and I laughed with her. It was so seldom I got the opportunity to laugh with anyone these days. I used to laugh inside a lot when Hamilton got up to his antics, but Hamilton's antics these past weeks had been anything but funny. Most times, when I encountered him, he was lying down and looked very shaggy and had little to say, except as a sort of recrimination: Why can't you stand on your own feet? Or throw the dinner at him, right in his face?

Well, things like that weren't very helpful and wouldn't solve any problems, and I told him so. My salvation was: I had to become strong inside, self-reliant; I had to become somebody that could ride above people like Howard and Mrs McVitie next door who was always complaining about Bill, not that he barked, but that he howled.

I had told Howard he could have the money on one condition, and when he enquired what that was, I said, that he had to sign a note to the effect that he had received the money and on my terms.

"Well, let's have a look at your terms," he had said. And when he had read the sheet of paper I passed to him, his mouth fell into a gape. Then he used a common phrase, as common as Gran Carter ever used: "You're not so green as you're cabbage-looking," he said; and then added, "But you must have sense enough to know that this doesn't hold water; you are my wife."

"It'll hold water," I said quietly.

My tone caused his eyes to narrow, and he said, "That old witch put you up to this, didn't she? But anyway, what's her word?"

"It doesn't only rest with that old witch, as you call her, there's another who is aware of the transaction."

His face now took on a tight look as he said, "Which other? Who?"

"That's my business. I just want to impress upon you that this will hold, even though" - I paused - "it should come to the push and is taken to court."

"My God! As our May said to me, you hadn't been hoodwinked so much by us as us by you. But don't get too clever, because there's. . ."

"You were going to say ways and means, weren't you? You haven't got the cheque yet, Howard."

He drooped his head now as he muttered, "I can never understand why we go for each other like we do."

Instantly, I saw Hamilton: he looked huge and sleek and his lips were well back from his teeth as he said, The slimy bugger!

Eeh! dear, dear. I was getting as bad as Gran. I must stop myself using swear-words in my mind. I had never used one verbally in my life, not even a weak damn. It was very disturbing when I swore inside.

I said now, "Are you going to sign it?" And for an answer he took up a pen and wrote his name, in an almost illegible form, across the bottom of the page, and as I looked at it I said, "That's no good, Howard. That name could be anybody's. Sign it legibly."

I saw his whole body rear; but he snatched up the pen again and signed the paper clearly this time.

When he stood up, he held out his hand and said, "The cheque."

"I'll give it to you tomorrow," I said, "after I've lodged this in a safe place."

The following day, when I handed him the cheque, signed by Gran, he stood looking down at it as if slightly amazed. He did not say thank you, not even in a sarcastic tone, but turned round and went out.

Three days later he said to me, "I've got it; I'm manager. And Mr Hempies has asked me over for the week-end to . . . his place. He's a widower, you know, and getting on. You don't know what it might lead to."

Some days later, as I was walking down the street, Mrs Nelson came to her door and remarked on the weather; then she added, "I hear your husband's been made manager of Hempies'. It's a good position that. You're very lucky, you know. You're a very lucky girl to have a man like that."

I had Bill on the lead, and I let him tug me away without answering. . . . Lucky to have a man like that! Did anybody know what went on behind the closed doors in this terrace? Or, for that matter, behind all the doors in Fellburn and Newcastle and Sunderland, on and on down the river and over the whole country, over the whole world? Did anyone really know how people reacted to each other in their own homes? Everybody seemed to have a face that they put on for other people. Who would think, watching Mr Howard Stickle go out every morning in his smart tailored suit, carrying his brief-case - oh yes, he carried a briefcase now, as also he left home a quarter of an hour earlier and got a different bus into the middle of the town - who would have thought that he was a coarse, dirty, cruel individual, and that small mouth of his could utter words that were so vile they made you sick to listen to them. Very definitely, no one in this terrace.

Then Bill took ill; well, not exactly ill, but there appeared great wet patches on his coat. The hair disappeared and the skin became mattery. I washed these parts in disinfectant and put salve on. But to no avail;

they spread. So I took him to the P.D.S.A., because, there, sixpence on the plate would cover the advice I needed, whereas the fee from the vet's could run into shillings, and my shillings were very scarce these days. I couldn't stretch the three pounds Howard threw on the kitchen table every week to cover the groceries and the window cleaner and such like, let alone the bills, and so I had more often than not to supplement it with my earnings from the typing.

The P.D.S.A. attendant gave me a bottle of liquid and told me to apply it to the dog's coat.

If he had seen the result of the application he would never, I'm sure, have handed out another bottle of whatever it was, because the first dab of it on Bill's bare flesh nearly sent him berserk. He raced round the kitchen and tried to get out of the door; but, as I told him, it was for his own good, and so I clutched him tightly to me as I aimed to dab the stuff onto his writhing body. I didn't find out till long afterwards that I was applying a strong carbolic.

The patches got so large as to become evident to passers-by when we went out walking, and they shook their heads at this poor dog; in fact, a couple, strolling in the park, one day remarked, "You should have that animal put down. He must be in pain."

I couldn't bear the idea of putting Bill down. I'd do anything rather than put him down. He was my only contact, the only thing I could touch, hold, cuddle. And he liked being cuddled. With his head tucked into my shoulder, I would hold him and talk to him like I would to a child.

Then I had myself to cope with. I started to come out in spots; well, not quite spots, it was more like a rash. It started on my hands, covered my fingers, and there were bits on my forehead.

I visited the doctor again.

He looked at my hair, then said, "It's dandruff."

"Dandruff?" I was indignant. "It can't be dandruff, I wash my hair every week."

"All right, it isn't dandruff. If you know what it is, or isn't, why come seeking my advice? I've got a roomful of numskulls out there who *don't* know what's wrong with them, so you're wasting my time . . . I'll write you a prescription for ointment," he ended tartly.

I applied the ointment for a fortnight, but it only seemed to aggravate my rash and soon my whole body became unbearable; and when my face became covered and I could hardly see out of my eyes, there I was in the surgery again.

"God in heaven! What's happened to you?" he said.

"I don't know. It's all over me," I said.

"Been mixing with foreigners?" He peered at me.

"Mixing with foreigners?" My voice went high. I'd never mixed with anybody, never mind foreigners. "Why should you think I've been mixing with foreigners?" I said.

"Well," he barked at me, "for the simple reason I haven't seen a rash like this before." He tentatively turned my head to the side, then said again, "My God! You can't put a pin between them. Painful?"

"Yes, and very irritating. I want to scratch."

"You haven't been abroad? No, no, of course you haven't. Let me look at your arms. Take your clothes off."

I took my clothes off.

"In the name of goodness!" he said. "Well, well, what have we here? What have we here? Put your clothes on."

I put my clothes on; then I sat down and watched him pick out one book after another from his bookshelf. When he took out a very thick tome, he put it on the table to the side of me and as he flicked the pages I could see diagrams of people in all poses, and he kept talking at me: "You haven't been handling any foreign substance, or eating foreign foods like these package things?"

"No."

"And sure you haven't been in contact with anybody . . . well, I mean with somebody who's been abroad? There are carriers, you know."

"No, I've hardly been out of the house these last three weeks. Just to take Bill to the P.D.S.A. He's got mange, and his hair's dropped out and. . ."

His hand remained poised over a page. He turned his head very slowly towards me and stared at me for quite a long time; and then his fingers began flicking the pages over at a great rate. When he found what he apparently wanted, he stopped and began to read. After a moment he straightened up, ran his hands through his thick hair that seemed all a part of his face, and, his voice awe filled, he said, "You've got mange. Trust you. You've got mange, woman. There's only one in a million humans contract mange, but you would have to be that one. You've got mange."

"What!"

"I said, you've got mange."

"Mange?" I stood up. *"I've got mange?"*

I was feeling my face now, my fingers patting it.

"Well, you've just said you've been nursing your dog with mange, and his hair's dropped out. It's lucky for you that yours hasn't." He closed his eyes tightly, screwed them up, put his head back and held his brow for a moment before, his face returning to normal, he said, "Oh, Maisie, Maisie, what next?"

Yes, what next. "Well, there's one good thing," I said, "you can't put this down to wind, can you?"

I saw a flicker pass over his face, and, his thick hairy lips moving one over the other, he went back behind his desk and sat down, saying, "You don't believe about the wind, do you? That you can give yourself indigestion and all kind of stomach pains by swallowing wind."

"I'll believe anything after this. . . mange!"

He was now writing on a pad; then he said, "Sheep-dip."

"*What?*"

He straightened up, sighed, then drew the air back quickly into his lungs. "Maisie," he said, "you've got the unfortunate habit of using that word, 'what', and in such a way that must be irritating to anyone who's got to listen to it all the time. It's irritating to me, and I only hear it now and again, at least on a Monday morning. "

"*Well!*" I was bridling now. "Well!" I found myself almost glaring at him. And there was Hamilton in his usual position when in the surgery, with his feet on the back of the doctor's chair, nodding at me and encouraging me; and so I went on, "Wouldn't you say *what* if somebody was writing out a prescription for you to put on your face and your body and they said, 'Sheep-dip,' just like that. *Sheep-dip.*"

"Maisie," he said, "I suppose I'll have to explain to you. The book doesn't say sheep-dip, but this prescription does a similar job; mange is caused by a mite, and sheep-dip is used to cleanse sheep of vermin, and like them you should be dipped in it. I'm giving you a big bottle of it, at least the chemist will. Now, take it home and cover yourself from head to foot with it, and I mean exactly that. And don't wear any clothes for three days. And you'd better buy a distemper brush to put it on with."

"*Wh . . . at!*"

"*What!* You heard what I said, buy a distemper brush, a three inch one would do. And I repeat don't wear any clothes for three days, just a loose kimono or something like that. Then have a bath. And if you've done the job properly you'll be rid of your mange. If not, you'll have to start all over again. Now, do as I say and don't leave any parts bare." He paused. "And remember that. It's important."

"You're not joking? You expect me to do that?"

"Joking? woman. Have I time to joke" - he pointed to the door - "with that menagerie out there waiting to invade? Joking? Good gracious! girl, have some sense. I never joke."

As we stared at each other, there appeared on the screen of my mind a scene: I saw a farmyard, and in it a trough full of sheep-dip, and there I was, starkers, being prodded through it by grinning yokels. I took up the prescription from the desk, turned without another word and went out. I made for Gran's; she was looking after Bill.

"*Mange?*" Gran squealed. "Never! lass. God Almighty! What'll happen to you next? *Mange*. And all through that bloody beast. I'd get rid of him. I would, I'd get rid of him. You've never known a minute's peace since you got him."

"Gran," I said slowly, "I never knew what companionship was before I got him. And I can tell you this, if he was to get smallpox and leprosy I still wouldn't do away with him."

She looked at me for some seconds; then she said quietly, "I'm sorry, lass. I know what it must be like for you, loneliness, I mean. Here's me gets out and about, yet when I come back in the evenin' and I know our Georgie isn't comin' in half-bottled, or so bottled that he's popping his cork, I sit down here and I can tell you, lass, I feel very sorry for meself. So what in the name of God you must feel like, I don't know. Aw" - she went to pat Bill but her hand stayed some inches from him; then she laughed nervously as she laid it on his head, saying, "What am I frightened of, anyway? I've been sticking zinc ointment all over him since you left the house. My God, just fancy . . . if I got mange. Eeh! that would be a scream. It would that. It would cause a sensation at the club, and I bet I'd get lots of cheeky offers for them to come'n paint the stuff over me. But it makes me think, can you manage it by yourself? Will I do it for you?"

"And go home with my face plastered white?"

"Yes, there is that, I suppose. Well, get yourself off. And take your bloodhound with you. Eeh! just look at him. Isn't he a sight? Poor bugger. That stuff they gave you isn't doing him much good, is it?"

"No; and he's terrified of it: he's only got to see the bottle and he goes berserk."

"Well, lass, if the stuff the doctor's ordered you cures you, then it should cure him."

I smiled at her, saying, "You're right, Gran. You're right. I never thought about that."

"I've got a head on me shoulders, lass. I've got a head on me shoulders."

I left Gran laughing as usual, and when I got home I thought it best that I wait to apply the lotion until after I told Howard. . .

If I'd actually said leprosy, or smallpox, his reaction couldn't have been worse, for he backed from me; his mouth opened wider than I'd ever seen it, and he looked at me with his face screwed up as if there was emanating from me the most foul smell. And when he brought out the word "*Mange?*" it sounded unclean.

"Yes, mange," I answered brightly. "And I don't think it will be wise for me to cook for you for the next three or four days as I've got to apply an obnoxious liquid. I understand it's what they dip sheep in to rid them of vermin and such. Ticks, I think they call them." As I walked out of the kitchen he shouted after me "And don't you make my bed."

I turned and, the grin still on my face, I said, "Oh, I don't mind making your bed, Howard. I can do that even with the stuff on me."

"I've told you. Keep out of my room."

"Just as you wish."

"And out of the sitting-room."

Now the grin disappeared from my face as I turned and confronted him squarely, saying, "It is my sitting-room, Howard. Your bedroom, you may consider you own, as you may the bottle room, but I'll go where I like in the rest of the house, mange or no mange; and as you are very rarely in the sitting-room nowadays I don't think there's any fear of your catching anything from where I might sit."

"And I'll be in it less in the future."

"That suits me perfectly." I turned on my heel and made for the stairs, but stopped abruptly when I heard a yelp coming from the kitchen.

I was back; in that room as if I'd been shot from a gun. He was just about to leave by the back door, and Bill was standing holding one of his front paws up; and now, my voice almost a scream, I yelled at him, "You do that just once again, just once, and I'll go into the street and I'll yell out what kind of man you really are. Do you hear me? I mean it, mind."

He came back into the room and closed the door and, his voice low now, he said, "Sometimes I think you're not right in the head. Nobody's touched him."

"Look at him!" I pointed. "A dog can't lie, he's standing holding his paw up. I heard him yelp from the contact with your boot." And then I added, "No. No, I won't do what I've just said, go out in the street, but I'll sell this house over your head."

When I saw him smile, I felt a shiver go through me, and all my bravery seeped away at his next words: "There's only thirteen months to go," he said, and on that he turned and went out. . .

Three days later, I took a bath, and, like a miracle, my mange was gone. I was back in the surgery the following morning, and I started even before he could get a word in, saying, "I haven't come about myself. Look! I'm clear." I tapped my face. "It was as you said, it cleared the mange. But I want another prescription. I mean, will you give me another prescription because I'd like to wash Bill in it, to see if it'll do the same for him."

"Certainly. Certainly. My, my; I've never seen you so bright and breezy for years. I think it would be a good idea if you contract mange every month."

"Don't be silly. . . I'm sorry." I lowered my head, and when I looked up at him again he was grinning, and as he handed me the prescription he said, "Life going all right for you now, Maisie?"

My ephemeral happiness vanished and I answered, "If you're referring to what I think you're referring, no, just the same, but in a different way. I . . . I must tell you about it sometime."

"Do. Do. But wait till I'm on my holidays."

"I thought you were going to Spain for your holidays?"

"I am."

I saw what he meant and pulled my lips tight together while my eyes laughed at him. Then thanking him for the prescription, I made to go out, but I turned at the door and said quietly, "I've made up my mind I'm not going to have anything to do with you for a long time."

"Good. Good. Thank God for that." His voice could have been heard all over the surgery, and when I passed the receptionist she looked at me curiously and I returned her look with a dignified inclination of my head. . .

I duly washed Bill in the lotion, and to save him washing it off himself on the carpets I put his collar back on, fastened on the lead, and took him into the park, where I ran him in and out of the trees until the stuff dried into his coat.

Most of the regulars in the park took no notice. I knew I was known to them as "That young lass with the bull-terrier", and their opinions were, I felt, that both of us weren't representative of the standards of our particular breeds.

I left the stuff on Bill for five days for good measure; then I bathed him, and behold, his skin was clear. And in no time the hair started to grow on it again.

We had both come through a crisis, which had been funny in its way.

Chapter 3

Hamilton, I was finding, came and went on my horizon. There were days at a time when I wouldn't see hilt nor hair of him, and other days when he was jumping about me all over the place. On one of these days the front door bell rang and I opened it to see George standing there.

"*George! George!*"

"Hallo, hinny."

I threw my arms about him, and he pressed me to him, then held me away from him, saying now, "What's happened to you? There's not a pick on your bones."

"Come in. Come in. How long are you home for? Oh, it's good to see you." I hung on to his arm as we went into the sitting-room, and there he stood in the middle of the room and looked about him. Such was the expression on his face that I didn't speak for a moment or so.

"It's just the same," I said.

"Aye, pet, aye, it's just the same. But it seems a thousand years ago since I lived in it. In fact, I can't believe I ever lived here. I suppose it's the dumps I've been in since." He punched me gently on the shoulder; then, pulling me towards the couch, he said, "Come on, sit down and tell me the story of your life."

"I want the story of *your* life."

"Oh" - he pulled a face - "you'll hear it from me ma soon enough. She's up in arms."

"Why?"

He turned his head to the side. "I'm a naughty lad."

"I never knew you to be anything else." But my banter died away as I added seriously, "You're not in trouble, I mean, police or. . . ?"

"Oh, no." He tossed his head from side to side. "Anyway, that's a small trouble, nothin' to worry about compared to other troubles I get into." He now leant his face close to mine and whispered, "Women. Playing the field."

"Oh, you are a bad lad. But why should Gran be upset? She knows you."

"Oh, it's a long story. Can I have a sup tea?"

"I'll have to think about it. Come on." I caught at his hand. "Come on into the kitchen and tell me all about it."

I looked at him sitting at the kitchen table, and the years fell away. I was a girl again and he was there, a bulwark: coarse, loving and kind . . . common, beautifully common.

He said, "I met a lass down in Devon. She was a part-time barmaid, a really canny lass in her twenties. I got into the habit of callin' into the pub on me trips, and, like it is, we got to know each other and I got fond of her. Aye; aye, I did." He stretched his neck out of his collar, his chin knobbled and his lower lip pushed itself out as if in defence of his statement, and he went on, "Then . . . well, I must admit I got a bit of a shock, she had four bairns. Her man had walked out and left her a year earlier afore her last bairn was born, and she hadn't heard a thing from him except she heard tell in a roundabout way he had joined a ship and jumped it in Australia. Well, I thought, bugger me, four bairns. No, thank you, Georgie. You've been in an' out of women-trouble all your life, but this is a bit too much of a good thing. So I stopped callin' in. And some months went past; then be-damned if I didn't run into her and the four youngsters in the supermarket. You see, I'd taken a room in this town and was feedin' meself. Well, what could I do? I walked along with her an' the bairns an' she asked me into her house. House, I said; it was a flat . . . It still is a flat." His head bobbed up and down now. "Three rooms you couldn't swing a cat in, a six foot square they called a kitchen, and a similar place for the bathroom. But what impressed me right away was, it was clean, everything was spankin' clean and tidy. And the bairns were clean. The youngest about sixteen months old, and the oldest on five. Two boys and two girls, and what they were starved for more than anything was a father, and they picked on me right away." He now grinned at me. "And anyway, there I am, stepfather again. An' have been for the past six months, and if we could find out where her bloody man is and she could sue for divorce we'd be married. Aye, yes, you can raise your eyebrows. That's what me ma did; and she opened her mouth at the same time, and you can imagine what came out of it."

After I'd placed the cup of tea in front of him, I bent and kissed him on the side of the brow, and as I did so I whispered, "Lucky bairns."

"Aw" - he put his arm around me - "there'll never be another like you. You were always an understanding lass. I loved you, you know. I still do. Oh aye, I still do. Nobody'll take your place."

I knew a moment of deep jealousy: four other bairns had taken my place. How strange I thought, this man who was made to be a father of a large family without a child of his own, yet giving out love in abundance to any child that came under his care.

"You'd like her, Maisie." He pulled a face at me now. "She's not loud or brassy. I don't know why it is that people think that anybody who serves in a bar is bound to be loud and brassy. Anyway, she's just the opposite, she's quiet, even timid. She had a hell of a job gettin' used to bar life, but it was the only thing she could do, to help keep them. You know, she put me in mind of you when I first met her."

"Oh" - I turned my head away from him - "don't stretch it, George."

"I'm tellin' you the truth." He brought his lips tight together for a moment, then added, "Aye, I am. There's something quite akin to you about her."

"Then all I can say is, God help her."

"Don't be so bloody soft." Then leaning towards me, he said, "How's he treating you now?"

I could answer honestly, "At present, things are quiet;" the two years weren't up yet.

"Do you get on better with him?"

"We don't see much of each other. He's manager now, you know, and he's in with the boss and goes to his place most weekends."

"Oh, rising in the world. Doesn't he take you with him?"

"Now would he?"

"Look" - he half rose from his chair, then sat down again - "don't keep knockin' yourself, woman; you've got what lots of the lookers haven't got, personality and a sense of humour. Put you in a taproom of a pub and you'd go down like a bomb."

"Yes" - I nodded at him - "and the explosion would take everybody down with me. Don't be silly . . . put me in a pub! George, it's no good; you don't have to keep anything up with me. I know exactly what I am. I accepted it years ago. People around here think I'm lucky to be married. I don't agree with them on that point, but I know that's the local opinion, and would be a general opinion too, so stop waffling about me and making believe I'm the ugly duckling looking down in the water and imagining she sees a swan, only to find when she lifts her head she's in the middle of a nervous breakdown."

At this point we both started to laugh, and he came round the table and caught hold of me and we rocked together; and as I felt the strong nearness of him and smelt the mixture of sweat and tobacco and maleness, my tears almost stopped being tears of laughter.

Oh, if I could have only married someone like George. All right, he might have gone after other women, seeking a little excitement, but one thing I felt sure of, if he had been mine he would have come back to me; his heart was too kind to leave anybody lonely for long. I gazed up at him now and said softly, "I wish I was one of those four children."

"Aw, Maisie, fancy saying a thing like that." I saw his Adam's apple jerk up and down; then he turned away from me, saying, "How's the business going? Ma tells me you're doin' fine."

"Oh, I get plenty of bits and pieces, but I get bored typing them. I've had nothing interesting since I typed a novel for a woman, but that's nearly a year ago."

When he walked into the hall, I knew he was going, and I said, "How long are you here for?"

"Just overnight. I'll be away early in the mornin' . But I promised Ma to come back at least once a month."

"That's good. She misses you; she gets very lonely."

"Aye," he nodded, "so she told me. She didn't half rub it in. But as I said, I'm a big lad now." He put his hands out and laid them on my shoulders and he said softly, "Life's funny, Maisie, crazy, barmy, bloody hell one minute, bloody heaven the next, but all the time, barmy. Have you ever asked yourself why we're here? I have. Lately I have. It never used to trouble me at one time, but I woke up the other night and I thought, Georgie lad. here you are lying aside somebody else's missis an' workin' for his four bairns an' who's to know that he doesn't come back through that door some day and try to knock your bloody head off."

Once again we were leaning against each other. Then all of a sudden, he pushed me away and with an abrupt, "Be seeing you, lass," he went hurriedly out, leaving me staring through the open door at him. He didn't even turn at the gate and wave. When closed the front door, I stood with my back to it and my head bowed, and I cried for there went the man I loved. Always had, and always would.

Chapter 4

It was 1973 and, strangely, I look back to that year as a time I realized I took very little interest in outside affairs; the state of the country, the state of the world passed me by. I didn't get a daily newspaper, but I listened to the radio. Yet, good, bad, or indifferent, it made very little impression on me. My life seemed to be taken up with looking after Bill, doing the typing and cleaning the house, yet I know now that, threading all this and the thing that blotted out the concerns of the outside world, was my fear of Howard. At times I might stand up to him, but most of the time I avoided him so that there would be no conflict. Yet, I saw very little of him. I cooked his breakfast in the morning, but left him to eat it alone while I got on with other things. I found I couldn't sit at the table with him. Now that he had his main meal out at dinner-time, there was only the evening one to see to, and this I left ready for him and had my own on a tray in the study.

Week-ends were the best because he often now left home on a Friday night. Sometimes he returned on a Sunday evening, but very often I didn't see him until the Monday evening. Even when he went to stay with Mr Hempies, he must have spent some time with his bottle hunting, because often he would bring a bagful back and they would be all clean and ready for the shelves; at least I presumed so because he would take them straight upstairs; those bottles the children gathered for him he cleaned thoroughly in the kitchen sink.

As time went on I blessed Mr Hempies, at the same time wondering what kind of a man he must be to take such a liking for Howard. He must be old and very lonely I imagined. And also what idea he had of Howard's wife, the woman that never went anywhere with her husband.

If the neighbours knew that he was never at home at the week-ends,

I'm sure they weren't surprised, because when he had lived with May, he spent most of Saturday and Sunday bottle hunting; in fact, the children called him "the bottle man".

The two years' grace I had demanded in payment for the money I had given him had passed, and he had made no move towards me. Just in case, I kept my bedroom door locked.

Then one night I knew the time had come again. It started in the kitchen. I had left his tea ready. I had mashed the tea and was about to leave the kitchen when he came in and stood behind his chair, looking down at the table. I thought he was about to find fault with the meal, but he said, "Sit down. I want to talk to you."

I didn't sit down, I just stood and looked at him; then he said, "Well, please yourself," and he sat down.

"We've been getting on pretty well together lately, haven't we, not treading on each other's toes?" he said.

I made no response, and he went on, "And that's the way it should be, and could be. Well, I'll come to the point; it's no good beating around the bush with you, I know that. It's just this. I don't think it's fitting that a man in my position should take the bus to work every morning, nor have to go by bus and train to . . . to Durham and Mr Hempies. Everybody else who goes there has a car."

I put my head on one side and said, "Everybody? I thought he was a lonely old man and that you were his sole companion."

"I don't know where you got that idea. Of course, he's an old man, and he hasn't got any family. I mean . . . well, any close family, except a nephew. But he has lots of callers at times, and friends . . . well, they come and stay, like me. He looks upon me, I can say, more like a son. So what I need at the moment is about two hundred pounds. I've seen a car. It's second-hand, and I'd like to have it. I've been taking driving lessons."

When I still didn't make any response, he said, "Well?"

Then I spoke. "If Mr Hempies looks upon you as a son, then why doesn't he buy you a car?"

As he got to his feet the fear cork-screwed within me, then seemed to lodge in my throat as he glared at me, his face working.

"I'm trying to keep things on an even keel, but you don't want it, do you? Now, you've got that money stacked away and you don't spend it on yourself. What do you think you're going to do with it?"

"I could buy a car and *I* could take lessons."

Why did I say such things? Why couldn't I keep my mouth shut? I was making things worse.

"Yes, you could; then we would both have cars."

"I can't ask Gran for any more."

"You're not asking Gran for anything. Don't try to hoodwink me. Anyway, think about it, but don't waste too much time over it."

I turned from him and made for the door, and when I reached it his words stopped me as he said, "And as for locking your door, if I wanted to get in I could, I've had extra keys made. I think ahead, you see. I said, if I wanted to get in, but I don't, at least not unless you force my hand. As I've said before, there's more ways of killing a cat than drowning it. And there's always Bill, isn't there? Bill."

Bill was standing at my side now waiting for the door to be opened to leave with me, and as if the animal knew what Howard meant it turned its head and gave a low growl. And I think this rather staggered Howard for he stared at Bill somewhat in surprise. As I opened the door I said, "I've told you before and I'm telling you again, if you touch that dog it will be the last thing you'll ever do." And now, what frightened me more than anything else was, I knew that I meant what I said, and the consequences made me feel so sick that I could have vomited there and then.

In the study, Bill lay close to my feet and when I put my hand down on his bony head and stroked it, he turned and licked my arm, and his small round eyes seemed to send a message of love to me. The next minute, I found myself on the floor, my arms about him, rocking him as if he really were a child. And in a way he was, he was my child. . .

It was difficult to see Gran these days unless I went in the morning. But I seemed to be able to get through the typing better in the mornings. In the afternoons, she was either playing bingo or she was at one of the numerous clubs round about. It was the same in the evening. As she said to me, and so often, "Lass, I can't abide in the house, not since our Georgie went, 'cos there's nothin' to stay in for."

But on this occasion, accompanied by Bill, I went to her the next morning early, although I knew what she would say, before I got there.

"Lass, you're mad. You give into him like this an' he'll have every penny off you. Look, go to that solicitor's and tell him what's happenin'."

"I can't, Gran."

"Why not?"

"Well, I just can't. I'd have to tell him everything, and there's some things I can't talk about. How could I, to a strange man? And anyway, being a man, he would likely say, he's your husband."

"What about the doctor?"

"Oh, him! I'm always telling him one thing or another. He must be sick of the sight of me. And I can't say that I look forward to seeing him either."

Gran now went into the kitchen to make the inevitable cup of tea, and from there she shouted, "Something should be done with that fellow. And it worries me at times, 'cos I don't know what's gona be the end of it."

When she came back with the tea, she said, "Stall. Aye, that's what to do, stall. Tell him I'm away on me holidays and, of course, I've got the cheque book. An' that's that."

I smiled at her. "That's an idea," I said. "But he'll have it in the end."

"Well, stop him, you silly little bitch, an' go and blow the lot. Go on a world cruise, or something like that."

"What! By myself?" I laughed.

"No, I'll come along wi' you."

"I believe you would an' all."

Gran threw back her head now and laughed; then on a more serious note she said, "You never spend anything on yourself, do you? Just look at you. When is the last time you had a new rag? Or your hair done properly? Or went to one of them beauty parlours?"

"Oh, Gran." I felt sharply annoyed now, and she came back at me, yelling at the top of her voice, "Yes, you can say, oh Gran, like that, but needs must when the devil drives, they say. And you could do somethin' with your face. I know I'm speaking with me mouth wide open and there's not a kind word coming out of it, but it's the truth: you needn't look as plain-faced as you do. You never wear a bit of lipstick or a bit of colour. There's a place round Brampton Hill way that transforms people. Why, even old 'uns like me do up. There's a Mrs Maddison comes to the club every now an' then an' shows us how." And at this, she kissed me.

I sighed deeply; then said slowly, "Gran, I've got no desire to change. I know myself as I am and I live with myself."

"Aw, lass." She dropped down on the couch beside me, and, taking my hand, she said, "I wish I could do something for you. You've had a rotten deal all along."

I said, "You do do something for me, just being you, Gran."

At teatime that evening I spoke first. I said, "With regard to the money, I'm sorry, even if I would consent to give it to you, I can't, Gran's gone on holiday. She's gone down to George's in Devon. I don't know when she'll be back."

He stared at me for a long moment, then said, "Is that so?" And I said, "Yes, that's so," before walking out with my knees almost knocking together.

About half an hour later he came downstairs ready to play tennis. He was wearing white shorts, a white shirt, and a light grey coat.

I saw him go into the kitchen. He usually left by the front door. I went into the sitting-room and waited to hear him leave. But after ten minutes or so had elapsed and there had been no sound of the door closing, I imagined he had left by the back door.

Remembering that Bill was in the kitchen and that Howard could have left the back door and the back gate open, accidentally on purpose, I hurried out of the sitting-room, across the hall, and pushed open the kitchen door; then I let out a high-powered scream of pain as the tennis racket swished to both sides of me. As I staggered back against the dresser, Bill sprang from his basket, his teeth bared, and stood in front of me, growling at Howard who appeared greatly contrite, saying, "I'm sorry. I . . . I was just practising my strokes. I . . . I didn't expect the door to open."

I knew he was standing some distance from me, not daring to move because of the dog. I had my hands cupping my breasts; the double swish of the racket had caught both of them. I felt I was going to faint as everything swam round me. Then his voice penetrated my shaken senses, saying, "Call him off. I want to get out. Maisie, do you hear? Call him off!" As I opened my eyes, he said, "It was an accident. I didn't expect you to come barging in like that. Call him off, the dog."

I followed his nodding head and looked down on Bill, who was braced as if ready to spring. Slowly, I leant over and caught him by the collar, and the very fact of bending nearly brought me tumbling to the floor. Holding Bill with one hand, I groped with my short arm for a chair and sat down, while Howard, now opening the kitchen door into the hall, repeated, "It was an accident. How was I to know you were coming in."

Like hell it was! I heard Hamilton's voice as if from a far distance.

I felt sick. My breasts were never big, but they were shapely. Strangely, my body had grown very shapely: I had a thirty-two bust and a twenty-six waist and a thirty-six hip measurement. Now my breasts were paining as if they'd been punched, which indeed they had. He had caught one with the inside of the racket and the other with the outside as if he were changing from forward drive to backhand. Practising!

Practising. He had been waiting for me. He had likely been aiming for my face, but I'd put my arms up swiftly to protect myself, and my breasts had caught the blows. What kind of a man was he, anyway? A dangerous one. Oh yes, a mean dangerous one. A weakness in me said now, Let him have it all, every penny, and then he'll no more need to get at you.

Bill was at my side, his head pressed tight against my knees. And Hamilton was standing by the end of the table, his long face drooped towards me. That money is your only protection, he was saying. Without it, it could be your life next, with a man like that. Oh yes, you can shake your head, but after he's got all you've got money-wise, he'll start on the house and what's in it. And you'll be lucky if you escape. Stranger things have happened, and to stronger people than you.

After a while, I went upstairs and took a hot bath, and the pain eased somewhat. Then later, when I went to bed, I not only locked the door but stuck the back of a strong chair beneath the handle. . .

I put up with the pain for three days; then I went to Gran's to leave Bill with her while I went to the doctor's again. And all she could say on my relating the story of the tennis practice was, "My God, lass, what next? What next?"

Reaching the waiting-room I found myself sitting next to the "You here again?" woman; and that's what she said immediately to me, "You here again . . . nerves?" She nodded. "Your eyelid's at it. Well, you're lucky, in a way, because you can get over nerves, if you pull yourself together."

When my turn came to go into the surgery, he said, "What now?" It had become his usual form of address.

"It's my breasts," I said; "they're swollen and they're all lumps. "

"Your breasts, swollen and all lumps?"

"Yes."

"What have you done to make them like that?"

"I . . . I had an accident."

"To both of them at once?"

"Yes."

He looked at me steadily for a moment, then said, "Mmm. Well, let's have a look-see. Take your blouse off."

I went behind the screen and took my blouse off.

He examined me without uttering a word; then said, "Put your things on."

As I was getting dressed I heard him washing his hands at the sink; and now his voice came to me, saying, "You've got mastitis."

"What?"

"I said, you've got mastitis."

"Ma . . . stit . . . is?"

"Yes, mastitis. Cows get it in their udders."

"*Cows?*"

"Yes, that's what I said. They get it in their udders and they can't give milk. But you needn't worry on that score."

I came slowly out from behind the screen and, looking at him, I repeated, "*Cows?*"

"That's what I said, cows. They are females too, you know."

He now sat down at his desk and began to write. Presently, looking up at me, he said, "Anyway, you're luckier than the cows, you can wear a camp brassière."

"*What?*" I watched him now close his eyes and droop his head, and his voice seemed to come from way beneath the floor as he said, "Maisie. Maisie, I've told you before, will you please stop *what-ing* me!"

"Well, a thing like mastitis. You tell me cows get it, and now I've got to wear a . . . a what?"

He put his hand to his head and pressed his lips tight together, and I turned my head away, only to see Hamilton crouched in the corner of the room with his forelegs crossed, his head leaning against the wall, looking as if he was having cramp from laughing so much.

The doctor lifted his bearded face now and there was a touch of merriment in the back of his eyes as he said, "A what is a stiffish brassière, Maisie. It's for conditions such as you've got, mastitis. If you wear it, it will keep your breasts firm and stop them. . ." He didn't say wagging from side to side, but he moved his hand descriptively, and almost immediately I had a mental picture of a herd of cows, and me on all fours in the middle of them. We were all wearing camp brassières, and the only difference between us was that their udders were swinging one way and mine the other.

Why did I see the funny side of things even when I was in pain. There was a very odd side to me, I had to admit.

I leant my elbow on the table and covered my face with my hand, and he said to me, "Well now, what's funny?"

"Just that I've seen myself amidst a herd of cows all wearing camp brassières, and their udders were. . ." I moved my hand as he had done; then added, "but mine wouldn't work like that."

When he let out his rare roar of laughter I knew I'd be in for another funny look from the receptionist when later I passed through the waiting-room.

After a moment, his face became straight and he rose and came round the desk and, looking at me full in the face, he said, "How did you come by this business anyway?"

"I was hit with a tennis racket."

I saw small globules of moisture on the end of his moustache as he leant towards me, his eyes screwed up. "Come again," he said.

"I was hit with a tennis racket."

"On both breasts?"

"On both breasts."

"How come?"

"He was supposed to be practising, when I went into the kitchen."

"Supposed to be practising?"

"Yes. He did a back and forward drive. Bang! Bang!" I demonstrated. "I think he was aiming for my face, but missed."

He now turned his head to the side and pulled at his ear, as if he was thinking; then he said, "If somebody doesn't talk to him, the police certainly will one day. You're a fool of a girl for staying. You know that, Maisie. The house just isn't worth it."

"It's all I've got."

"Yes" - he nodded - "I can understand that. But still I feel something should be done. I've tried. I couldn't get through to him; he's too smooth, too crafty. You're sure it was no accident?"

"If he had just hit one side, yes, but not both. It was too neatly done."

He sighed now and said, "Well, go along, but take care. Come and see me next week." Bending towards me now, he added, "And I won't grumble at the sight of you."

"Very considerate of you." I nodded at him.

"Go on with you."

He opened the door for me, and I walked through the waiting-room as if I was a privileged person, and felt it, because I'm sure it wasn't very often, in fact, never to my knowledge, that he had opened the door for a patient.

No matter how rough and brusque his manner, I felt, underneath it, I had a friend and that he had been there for a long time.

Part Three

FULL BLOOM

Chapter 1

How did the years pass? How does any year pass? By months, weeks, days, minutes. And the days sometimes seem as long as the years. Yet looking back, I seemed to have kept myself busy. I must have, looking at the mass of writing I'd turned out, and apparently to no avail. Until one day, the one day that lies buried deep in the heart of everyone who has ever taken up a pen to tell a story.

I was now thirty years old and I had been married for twelve years. Had there been a time when I had never been married? Had there been a time when I hadn't shared this house with a man called Howard Stickle? A forty-year-old man who didn't seem to have aged at all in the last twelve years. He was still tall and fair; nothing about him seemed to have altered except perhaps his manner towards me, which at times made me imagine that I didn't exist, because he seemed to look beyond me; at times he would bump into me, almost knocking me off my feet, and never once with a word of apology. The last occasion he apologized was when he hit me with the tennis racket.

He had by now had all my money with the exception of a few pounds that I had saved from my typing. He had got his second-hand car; but that hadn't satisfied him. A year later, he'd had a better second-hand car; eighteen months later he had a new car. At one period he said he had been invited to go abroad with Mr Hempies for a fortnight and would need two hundred pounds to cover his expenses. I had stuck out at that, until I accidentally fell downstairs; the clips that held the brass rod had become loose. I became really frightened after that. My arms and legs were black and blue with the tumble and Doctor Kane had said, "Now you've got to do something. Nobody else can do it; it's up to you." And I knew it was up to me. But what proof had I? Because as Howard had made great play of knocking the clips back into the stairs, he had pointed out to me that there was woodworm in the treads.

It was three months ago he got the last of the money that was in Gran's care. She had given up offering me advice. However, once she surprised me by saying, "Do you care for the fellow?"

Care for him? The idea sounded preposterous, but she came back with, "Well, there's no other thing I can think of that'll make you stick with a man like that."

"It's my home," I had said.

"Well," she answered, "he'll have you out of it, in a box. You mark my words. And nobody'll be able to say a word against him, because, like a damn fool, you've kept your mouth shut all these years, and because you've kept yourself to yourself too much. You've got a funny name among the neighbours. Do you know that?"

Oh yes, I knew that. I also knew that Howard's standing with the neighbours was high.

It was also about three years ago that I started dropping into the church, the Catholic church, not for the services, but just going in and sitting quietly and looking at the side altar. It was very peaceful. Sometimes I had a word with Father Mackin. He was always jocular and very nice to me. It had been in my mind for some time to talk to him, in a form of confession, and tell him about my life, what I was going through, what I was afraid of. And I did just that. The result was rather surprising.

On this particular day I was very down. I hadn't seen Gran for over a week. By the way, George had now married his lady with the four children. There was Betty, now fourteen, John thirteen, Kitty twelve, and Gordon nearly eleven. They were nice children. I had met them a number of times and liked them. But George was no longer my George. He was the children's George and Dad, and his wife's George and husband. That was another pain I couldn't get rid of. Anyway, there I was this day sitting in the pew when the priest came out of the vestry, accompanied by a fat young woman and a young man who seemed little more than a boy. They stood in front of the main altar, the priest talking to them. It was when she turned round that I saw she was very pregnant. A few minutes later, after he had seen them out of the church, he came to my side and, after genuflecting, he sat down in a pew beside me, saying, "Well, now. Well, now, here we are again. Did you see that couple? They are going to be married."

It was jealousy of her condition that prompted the thought, not before time, and I had voiced the first two words when I stopped myself, and he put in, "Oh yes, yes, condemn. Not before time, you were going to say. Well, better late than never, I say."

As I said, I'd been feeling very low this day, but of a sudden my depression lifted when I saw Hamilton galloping up the aisle, dressed all in white, and on his hoofs four big navvy's boots. I lowered my head and made a slight choking sound. And now the priest's voice came to me, saying, "Some of us are luckier than others, and they get through life without making mistakes."

I lifted my head quickly, my face straight now. "Oh, Father," I said; "I . . . I wasn't laughing at them. You see, it's. . ." I turned my head to the side. "Well, how can I put it? It's a quirk I have."

"A quirk?" He leant towards me and repeated. "A quirk?"

"Well, that's the only way I can describe it. You see, even today when I'm feeling very down, sort of low and depressed, even at times like this I sometimes think of very funny things. Well, you see, it's like this, Father." I began to look from side to side before I went on, "I suppose I could tell you in a sort of confession like." There I was using the word like, the same as Gran did. "I suppose it's because I've always been rather alone. At one time I just used to natter to myself. You know, like people do."

He nodded at me now, a smile on his face as he said, "Yes, yes, I understand. We all natter to ourselves. But go on. Go on, my dear."

So I went on, and by the look on his face the next moment I think he wished I hadn't, because I could see his opinion of me taking rapid strides towards the asylum.

"Well, you see, Father, I talk to this horse."

His eyes became round.

"I . . . I call him Hamilton."

His mouth fell open.

"He appears quite real to me."

His eyebrows took on points.

"For instance, what made me laugh a moment ago was that the young lady changed into him and he galloped up the aisle all in white, with boots on."

His head moved slightly downward, his lips formed a kind of rosebud.

I became a little apprehensive and I said, "I'm . . . I'm not daft, or . . . well, anything like that, Father."

His head moved slowly from side to side.

"I suppose he's just a figment of my imagination, but it's very strange. When I want the truth about anything he gives me the right answers. I don't always pay heed to them. But on looking back, I wish I had."

His chin seemed to draw his face to the side now and his pointed eyebrows and round eyes, his puckered mouth, were joined by his nose, which was twitching, and the dreadful thing about it all was that there was Hamilton standing to the side, looking at him and shaking his head slowly as if he was sorry for the poor man and the position I'd put him in. But surely priests, I thought, were used to listening to all kinds of things, murders and such, but what I had just said seemed to be affecting him more than if I had confessed to something terrible.

His dog collar now jerked so quickly that it caught him under the chin and it seemed to affect the way he spoke. "Have you talked, well . . ." his voice went falsetto, "about this to anyone else . . . your doctor?"

"No . . . not my doctor."

He now joined his hands between his knees and bent over them and surveyed them for a time before he said, "Have you had a breakdown of any kind?"

"No, Father, no; but I've been troubled with nerves."

"Yes, yes, I can understand. Yes, troubled with nerves."

"Father" - I leaned towards him trying to look into his face - "I'm not bats."

He straightened up quickly, and now his voice quite loud, he said, "No, no, of course you're not. Who said you were? There's no suggestion of it, no, no. But about this horse. What did you say his name . . . you called him?"

"Hamilton."

"Hamilton. It's a very nice name, very nice name for a horse. And . . . and you say he acts the goat a bit?"

"He does a bit, and all at the wrong moments." I'd say he did at the wrong moments. "That's what I mean by this quirk in me seeing . . . well, I suppose the funny side of things. It's sort of like the bishop and the banana skin."

"Ho! Ho!" His head went back now and he laughed. "Yes, yes, the bishop and the banana skin . . . dignity defiled."

"Yes, yes" - I agreed with him - "it's always funnier with people like that who are . . . well, up to the eyebrows in God, so to speak."

Oh dear me, dear me, that had nothing to do with Hamilton. Now, why had I said that?

The priest's face was working again, but without the contortions of astonishment on it. Then I noticed the front of his tunic starting to bob, and I knew he was laughing inside. Presently, he said, "You are a funny girl, you know. I've heard a lot of descriptions about us but that's a new one on me, up to the eyebrows in God. By the way, do you go out to work? I mean, do you do anything other than . . . well, housework?"

"I do typing in my home: people's stories, you know, and articles; anything they want doing."

"You do? Well now, I should have thought you would have seen an opening in that line for yourself. Have you ever thought about writing? All these funny little things you think about, this horse business?"

"Oh yes, I've written lots about Hamilton. For years and years I've done bits on him."

"You have?" His voice was now high with surprise, and he went on, "Well now, well now, you should put all those bits together into a book. I could see it as a bestseller."

I smiled at him now in a patient sort of way. I must have typed dozens of stories for the members of the Writers' Circle and others over the past years, and the percentage of publications had been painfully small.

But it was at that moment that the priest's suggestion set something moving in my mind. I remember he set me to the church door and, looking down on me, he said, "You're not so troubled now, are you?"

"No Father," I answered, "if you can talk things out with someone it's half the battle." It was then he said, "Can't you talk to your husband about it . . . I mean, what troubles you?"

Looking at him fully in the face and because he was a priest and, I understood, had to keep things to himself, I said, simply, "He's my trouble, Father, if I had a good husband I wouldn't need Hamilton. . ."

I've seen him at intervals since that time and we've always had a laugh together. But, I remember, I went straight home that day and up into the attic and sat on the floor reading through the pile of bits and pieces I had written since the very first day I'd given Hamilton a name. And I found myself laughing out aloud at some of the things, and at others hardly being able to suppress my tears, such as, the page I had written the night George had left, and then again, my lacerated feelings after the first few days of my marriage. And the fears seemed to leap freshly from the scribbled lines as I read.

It was from then that my mind got to work on how to go about putting all these pieces into book form. I'd learned a great deal from the mistakes of others over the years and, up till now, without any thought of putting what I had learned to my own use in a big way. So it came about that I set out the plan of a story.

It didn't have any plot, so to speak. They were always going on about plots at the Writers' Circle. I had never been able to see why plots were so important. To my mind, if you got a couple of good

123

characters they made the story themselves; the environment you set them in created all the incidents. Hadn't I proof of that in myself? The fact that I was made as I was and had the good or bad fortune, however you looked at it now, to own this house, had attracted May and her brother to me, and in that setting, because of our diverse characters, the incidents had seemingly happened naturally; they hadn't been plotted. Yet, hadn't they? What about Howard?

But I found the arranging of all these bits and pieces much harder to do in actual fact than it had appeared in my mind, and as I could only type for myself at odd times, and then each day see what I'd done was safely deposited underneath the floor boards once again, it was nearly two years before I had completed the story of Hamilton.

When at last, I reread it through, to my surprise I realized I had been telling the story of my own life up to that time, and I also realized that the story hadn't turned out the way I had intended. What I had imagined to be screamingly funny parts had resulted in a sort of pathos. What I'd written as straight serious parts turned out to be amusing when read. There were times when I wrote about myself being deeply worried, but in some strange way they read as the funny bits.

But it was completed. Now, I asked myself, what to do with it? And up came the question of markets. The members of the Writers' Circle were always yammering on about markets. I suppose they were right up to a point, markets meant publishers. So I went to the reference library and got out the *Writers' & Artists' Yearbook*, and there they were in their hundreds. Which one was going to have the honour of reading this daft story? Because that's what it would be called, a daft story about a nondescript woman and a talking, laughing, sad at times, merry at others, mad galloping horse.

Needless to say, Hamilton came along with me that day, and after I had been pondering for some time which publisher to choose he put his left front hoof on the page. It looked very dainty at this moment, and didn't obliterate any of the print, and I saw it was pointing to Houseman and Rington, Ltd., 42 Chapman's Yard, London, WC2B 3AR.

"So that's it," I said to him.

That's the one, he answered.

Well, Houseman and Rington, get yourself fortified, because here we come.

The next day I took my manuscript, all neatly parcelled up together with an enclosed very short note, to Gran's.

It was half past nine in the morning and she said, "You're up afore your clothes are on, lass. What is it now?"

I showed her the parcel, saying, "It's a kind of book I've written. I'm sending it off, and it will likely come back. I've given this address, so I'm just telling you like" - there I went again; I was getting as bad as her - "that when it comes back you'll know what it is. Oh yes, and I'm calling myself Miriam Carter. "

"Does he know about it?" She laughingly pointed to Bill, and I said, "Yes, he knows all about it, every word, even as much as Hamilton."

The name had slipped out, and she screwed up her face at me and said, "Hamilton? Who's he, Hamilton?"

I knew my face was red, and I said, "I must tell you about him some day."

"A fellow you know?" Her expression became bright, and I said, "No, no." And at this she said, "Oh, it's all right, you needn't blush; I wouldn't blame you if you had three fellows on the side every night."

"Oh, Gran."

"Yes, oh Gran. So his name's Hamilton?"

"Yes, Gran." I said slowly. "But please don't get your hopes up; he's not that kind of a man."

"Well, what do you write about, lass . . . I mean, to make a book?"

"Oh -" I turned my head away from her and thought for a moment for a way to describe what I wrote. Then looking at her again, I smiled at her as I said, "You won't believe it, but I write funny bits."

"Funny bits?"

"Yes, funny bits. Anything that tickles my fancy, mostly about . . . Oh, I can't really explain. You can't explain humour, Gran, because people's tastes differ. What we laugh at, other people would think silly."

"Well, make me laugh. Go on, make me laugh."

"Oh, Gran."

"Don't say, oh, Gran. Make me laugh."

"I can't, not like that, not to order; it's got to come sort of offhand, spontaneous."

"Aye, well, you want to tell that to some of the comics we get in the club. Eeh! if I couldn't do better than them, I'd walk on water just to see if God was on my side."

At this Hamilton did a gallop round and round the kitchen. His mane was flying, his white tail was stuck up in the air, and I was flapping Gran on the shoulder with my good arm while my short one was tight around my waist to ease the pain of my laughter. Gran was laughing too, but more at me than what she had said, and I now spluttered, "That's it, you see, Gran, that's it."

"What's it? Just what I said there?"

"Yes, yes."

She wiped her face with her apron, then said, "Well then, lass, if that tickles your fancy, you're easily pleased."

"I'm not easily pleased, not in that way, Gran. You see, it isn't the content of humour but how it's said."

"Aye, an' it's how I say it, I suppose. Me common way."

"Exactly, Mrs Carter. " I stood up now and repeated, "Exactly," and we were laughing again.

And once more I said, Oh, thank God for Gran.

Chapter 2

A month had passed and no word.

Like the fool I was, I had expected a reply within a week; and every morning of the second week, there I was on Gran's doorstep well before ten o'clock. But there was no letter, and no parcel, and I think she got a little tired of seeing me.

She dampened my spirits well and truly one morning by telling me that there had been a programme on the wireless the previous night about people sending manuscripts to publishers and some of them received so many in a week, amounting to hundreds, that they never even looked at them . . . well, not after the first two pages, because they could tell straightaway if it was worth going on reading the stuff. When she had finished, she said, "I'm not trying to put you off, lass, but that's what they said." And I said, "Well, Gran, I hope I'm not in need of being cheered up when you do try to put me off."

I didn't go back for four days, and when I did, she was very sweet to me and apologized for telling me what she had heard on the wireless, and ended by saying, "Come on, lass, buck up and be a rabbit."

Then the third week passed, and the fourth week almost passed.

It was a Friday. I didn't go round to Gran's until nearly dinner-time, and I hardly got in the door when she yelled at me, "Where've you been?"

"What do you mean, where've I been?"

"You've practically got me out of bed durin' the last month, an' look!" She now took a long cream envelope from the mantelpiece and pushed it into my hand; then pointing to the heading on the top, she said, "It's from them people that you sent your story to, Houseman and Rington."

I stared down at the envelope. My stomach gave a leap and seemed to land between my breast bones. I turned the envelope over and fingered its good quality paper, only to give a start as Gran shouted, "Bugger me! lass, open the blasted thing. You've been waitin' for it long enough."

I opened it and read:

Dear Miss Carter,

    It is with great interest that we have read the manuscript of *Hamilton*. We find it most unusual and very amusing, and if you would care to call at our office at a time convenient to you we would be very pleased to discuss the possibility of publishing it.

    In the hope that we shall come to an amicable agreement.

        I am,

            Yours faithfully,

There followed a scribbled signature and a typed one underneath that read,

Bernard Houseman.

I sat down with a plop, then handed the letter to Gran. Then she very slowly sank down by my side, and we stared at each other. "Eeh! God, lass," she said, "you're gona have a book published. Eeh! . . . aw, hinny." She fell against me and we put our arms around each other and both of our faces were wet, but not through laughter. When we straightened up again, she said, "What is it about, really, hinny? I know you said it was funny, but is it a love story, or what?"

"It's about a horse, Gran."

"*A horse?*" Her face puckered.

I nodded at her now, swallowed, and said, "It's about a horse called Hamilton."

"What do you know about horses, lass? You've never been on one, have you?"

I bit on my lip as Hamilton kicked up his back legs and almost knocked the plant-stand near the window flying.

"It isn't that kind of a horse. Well, what I mean is, you see, it's a horse" - and I tapped my forehead - "that . . . well, I just think about; and I talk to him."

She turned her chin almost to her shoulder while keeping her eyes on me, and she said, "Did I hear aright, lass?"

"Gran" - I leant forward and took her hand - "it's a long story, but, you know, like children have imaginary playmates . . . well, it's like that."

"And you've got a'maginary horse?"

"Yes."

"At your age?"

I looked downwards because Hamilton was standing to the side of me now. His round eyes I knew were right on me as I admitted, "Yes, at my age."

"Eeh! God help us." Now her voice rose a couple of tones. "You mean to say, that's what the story's about and they're gona print it?"

"Well, it seems so."

"There's some funny people in the world."

"And there's one of them sitting here."

"You're not funny . . . well . . . aye you are. You've never been like other lasses. But then what chance did you have? My! I've just thought, wait till our Georgie hears about this. He'll be over the moon. He always said you had it up top. Aye, he did. He used to say, 'Ma, there's more in that one than meets the eye.' An' he was right. By God! he was right. You a writer an' goin' to London."

She stopped and stared at me, then she said, "*London*. Do you realize that, lass? It isn't like Gateshead or Newcastle. You can't walk round there in your bedroom slippers or lookin' as if you've been pulled through a hedge backwards."

"I don't go round in my bedroom slippers, Gran. . ."

"You know what I mean."

I knew what she meant.

"We'll have to do somethin'. Eeh! yes, we'll have to do somethin'."

"You mean, I'll have to do something with meself."

"Aye, yes, I suppose that's what I mean."

"Well, forget it, Gran. They are not interested in what I look like."

"Don't you believe it. Half the world gets by on appearances. If everybody got credit for what's up in their nappers, things would be topsy-turvy the day. I can tell you that."

She now rose from the couch and took a step backward towards the fire, and, her chin working from side to side, she said, "You'll have to have your hair done properly, and not frizzed this time. And you'll get yourself a new rig-out; I'm sick of the sight of you in that grey thing. You look grey all over. You want something in brown, warm browns. I know what, Mrs Maddison will know what to do with you."

"And who is Mrs Maddison?"

"Well, I mentioned her to you afore, she's a bit of everything. She's got one place Brampton Hill, and another in Bog's End. She's in the two camps. And she gives some of her time now and again in OAP's clubs, telling us how to make the best of our wrinkles." She laughed now, then added, "She's the right one."

"Gran" - I stood up and again took her hand - "don't try to work any more miracles, will you? You remember the last one you did on me?"

"This is different, lass. And Mrs Maddison is class, not like that other bitch. Now, let me get meself pulled together an' think. I'll go along an' see if she's at her low town one this afternoon an' if she'll see you in the mornin'. I'll tell her it's important. . ."

"Gran." I took hold of both her arms and, my face serious, I said, "I must ask you this, and you must promise me: I want no one to know about this. No one. Do you understand? Just you and me. "

"Aw, lass, you're missing a chance of a . .."

"Gran, if you don't promise me, I can tell you this, I won't go to London. I'll tell them to send it back. I don't want anybody to know. Nobody knows this Miriam Carter, and that's how I want it to be, because if it once got round it would reach Howard. And remember, he had every penny out of me before and he would do it again. He would, Gran."

"But, lass, all the excitement an' that."

"*Gran, promise me.* If it leaks out at all . . . *at all*, do you hear me? I'll stop its publication, that's if they really want to do it, because I've sworn that he gets nothing more out of me."

"What about our Georgie?"

"No, not Georgie. Nobody."

"But if you get rigged up, he's bound to see."

"I can come here and change and get back into me old duds before I go home again."

"Aw" - she bent her head - "you've taken all the stuffing out of me. I could see meself braggin' in the club and sayin' in an offhand way, 'Me granddaughter's a writer, one of them novelists.'" And she now put her hand on my cheek and said softly, "And I've always thought of you as me granddaughter, no step about it, just as our Georgie always thought of you as his. Eeh! he'd be over the moon."

"Gran."

"All right!" she bellowed now. "All right. As you say, 'tween you and me. But for how long?"

"I don't know, just as long as I say. And Gran, I feel so strongly about this that if you let on in any way at all, it will be the finish between us. I mean that."

Her expression became sad now as she said, "I believe you do, lass."

"Yes, I'm sorry, Gran, but I do. You see, I've gone through so much back there." I lifted my head towards the door. "I've had to pay him for every peaceful moment that I've had. I say peaceful, I don't think I've ever known any as long as he's been in the house, and I know if he thought I was getting something for this book, he'd have it. I've still got to pay odds and ends out of my typing money. Twelve years he's been in that house and he's still giving me a mere pittance."

"That's your fault. You should have done something, taken him to court."

"You can't take people to court unless you have proof, and he's too wily to give me that."

"Well, do you intend to go on living like this till the end of your days?"

"I don't know, Gran. I seem to be biding my time for something. I can't explain it to you."

"Perhaps your horse could."

At this we fell against each other and, as my body shook, I thought yet again, what would I have done all these years without Gran.

I liked Peg Maddison. She was small and dainty and business like . . . very kind. The following morning I sat in a cubby hole that she called her office in her Bog's End dress salon, and she looked me over; then she felt my head and said, "It's a good shape. You don't want a great fuss around it. Your hair wants to be short, taken behind your ears. You've got nice ears." She smiled at me.

"Won't that hair style make my face look smaller?" I said.

"No, just the opposite. It's ridiculous to think that a mass of hair makes the face larger, it doesn't, it acts the other way. Your face is small, but you've got good bone formation. You'll find as you get older your skin won't droop as much as most around the cheeks, because you're high cheek-boned. A little make-up on your eyes towards the corners" - her fingers lightly touched my skin - "and they'll be all right. I can do quite a bit for you, but I hope you don't mind me saying this, your best advantage is your figure." She now spread her hands and gripped my waist. "You want a smart rig-out, plain. Is it an evening or day do you're going to?"

"A day do."

"Well, a good suit, sort of semi-fitting. Don't wear anything slack; you want to show off anything you've got."

When I shook my head, she said seriously, "I'm stating facts."

"Yes, I know you are, but I don't feel they belong to me, particularly my figure. And how am I going to get a suit to fit this?" I lifted my short arm.

With a flick of her hand she dismissed this, saying, "Oh, any good class house will fix that. One of their cutters will do it in a few minutes. In fact I know a place where you'll get the very thing to suit you. It mightn't be exactly cheap, but it will be worth it. What do you say?"

What I said was, "Thank you," while thinking, Will I have enough money?

"Your grandmother won't know you when we're finished with you." She smiled now, then said, "Mrs Carter's a character, isn't she?"

"Yes, she is, but a nice one."

"Indeed, indeed. And I love going to the club and meeting all her cronies." She hunched her smart shoulders and made a face at me, and of a sudden I felt we were compatible. And so it proved, in the time ahead.

*

On the Monday, I phoned Houseman and Rington and asked if the following Friday would be convenient for my visit - I couldn't see myself getting rigged out and being made new in a shorter time - and the secretary informed me that Mr Houseman would be pleased to see me between twelve o'clock and one on that day. Would that be convenient?

From this distance I didn't think of the times of trains, or how long it would take me, but said, "Yes, yes, thank you."

And so it was arranged. . .

"That'll mean you'll have to get an early train up from Newcastle," said Gran. "And how are you going to explain leaving the house at that time to him?"

I'd thought about this. So I said to her, "We are going down to see Georgie."

"We are?"

"Yes. That's what I'm going to tell him. So I'm sleeping here on Thursday night because we are getting an early train."

"And we're just going down for the day?"

"Yes."

"I hope for your sake he doesn't start working things out because it's a long way to Devon and it would be like, hail and farewell."

"He doesn't know exactly where Georgie lives."

"For your own sake I think you had better tell him we're staying the night, and you can take the couch." She thumbed towards it. "'Cos

Georgie's bed'll be damp. It'll all be the same price."

"Yes, I could do that. Yes . . . that's what I'll do. It will be safest. "

"I'm not so sure. What if anybody should see you going off on your own?"

"Well, I hope by the time you and Mrs Maddison are finished with me, nobody will recognize me.". . .

It was on the Thursday evening, as he was going out for his weekly game of tennis, that I spoke to him. Endeavouring to keep my voice level and the excitement out of it, I said, "I'm going away for the day, tomorrow. Gran and I are going to see George. I'm . . . I'm sleeping at her place tonight, and we'll likely stay over at George's tomorrow night an' all. I'm . . . I'm leaving Bill with Gran's neighbour."

He turned and looked at me. Then his face going into an oily smile, he said, "Good. Good. Coming out, are we? Hair do an' all. But aren't you afraid to leave the house? I mightn't let you in when you come back. Or, just fancy." He poked his head towards me. "What if I had another woman installed when you returned? There's stranger things happen."

My voice deadly flat now, I said, "I wouldn't try it on. What I think you've overlooked for a long time and which it would be wise to consider, is that I have friends and all in influential positions: the medical profession" - I paused - "the legal profession -" I paused again, and then ended, "and in the Church. And they are all aware, in different ways, of the situation. "

I thought for a moment he was going to spring on me. His pale skin was suffused with colour; his eyes looked black; then from between his teeth he said, "By God! there'll come a day soon when you'll need all the help you can get. I can tell you that." And on this he went out, closing the door behind him, but, and this again added something deeply sinister to his action, closing it softly: the neighbours could never say that Mr Stickle banged the door in a temper.

Chapter 3

I didn't know the person who took a return ticket from Newcastle Central to London the following morning. I had come by taxi from Gran's.

There were lots of people milling about the station but very few on the London train. Never in my life had I been further than Durham in a train, and when it slowly moved out of the station I felt for a moment I would collapse, so churned up with excitement was I.

After a while, being alone in the compartment, I stood up and looked at myself in the mirror. Was that me? Was it really me? I took off my new hat. It was a reddish brown straw with a velvet band around it and a narrow brim, which was turned up at one side making it look perky. My hair was flat on my head; my ears were there for all to see; my large mouth was covered with a dusty pink lipstick, and I had green eye-shadow on my lids and black lines to the corners of them. I had practised this art for days past now. I was wearing a corduroy two-piece suit in a russet brown colour. Underneath was a silk blouse that buttoned decorously to the neck. It was a dusty pink shade. On my feet, I had brown court shoes with a three inch heel. I had never walked on such heels before, but I found them quite comfortable. I was comfortable all over. I couldn't believe it. I wanted to pat myself to make sure I was here, this was me. Although on again looking in the glass I realized it was still my face, it was now a face I could bear to look at, and I refused at this point to admit to myself there was the same old pattern under the make-up.

I now sat looking out of the window and for a moment I wished I had someone to talk to, to tell of my excitement. But there was no one, not even Hamilton. Now that was very strange, but since the reformation had begun on me I hadn't seen him. I'd talked to him a number of times, but he hadn't materialized. I wondered why.

When, sometime later, the door was pulled open, I started and looked at the attendant who smiled and said, "Would you like breakfast, madam?"

Breakfast? Breakfast on a train? I had ten pounds in my pocket. I'd borrowed that from Gran. "Yes, I would like breakfast. Thank you, yes."

"Whenever you're ready, madam."

The door closed. Whenever you're ready, madam. This was a different kind of life. This must happen every morning to somebody. That man would say, Would you like breakfast, madam? Would you like breakfast, sir?

I waited five minutes before I walked along the swaying train and entered the dining-car. Only one other passenger was seated at the tables, and he was at the far end reading a paper. I took the first seat I came to, and almost immediately the nice attendant came and hovered over me. "What would madam like: kippers? bacon, egg and sausages? boiled egg? poached egg?'

"I'll have bacon, egg and sausage, please."

"And to begin with, cereals? orange juice?"

"Yes, yes." I said yes to everything.

I'd never enjoyed a meal like it in my life. At one point, when the train was rocking, I couldn't get the cup of coffee to my lips and I started to shake inside with laughing.

Oh, Hamilton, Hamilton, what a beginning to a day. I looked along the car, expecting him to come galloping towards me and laughing his head off. But there was no sign of him. For a moment, I felt suddenly empty. . .

The train had filled up by now, and I sat in the compartment with five other people, and no one spoke to anyone. But that suited me; I wouldn't have known what to say anyway. Yet, I was bursting inside, shouting inside: I've written a book and it's going to be published; it's about me talking to a horse. At one point, I wondered what would have happened if I had yelled out in my excitement. Somebody would have undoubtedly pulled the communication cord and I would never have reached Houseman and Rington. . .

King's Cross station was a maze, which made me feel dizzy. Just follow the crowd, I told myself, and you'll get out of it. And I did. I'd thought I'd take a bus to the publishers. But where was it? And where would I get a bus?

I next found myself standing in a taxi queue, and when my turn came, and before I got in, I politely said to the taxi driver, "Do you know where 42 Chapman's Yard, is please?" And he answered just as politely but with a streak of something in it that I couldn't put a name to, except perhaps patience, "Miss, if I didn't, I wouldn't be sitting here.

Get in." He hadn't sounded nasty.

What had I expected from this address, Chapman's Yard? It didn't sound a very classy place, but here I was now, standing in a sort of courtyard of cobbled stones, and around it were a number of tall houses. They didn't look at all like offices, but each house, I noticed, had a big brass plate outside. I walked towards one. It said, thirty-two. I walked to the next one. It said, forty-two. It had jumped ten. But underneath the forty-two I read the magic name of Houseman and Rington, Publishers. I went through a glass door and into a small hall where, behind a glass panel, a young girl sat typing.

Catching her attention, I said, "I'm Miss Carter. I have an appointment."

"Oh, yes, he is expecting you." She smiled pleasantly. "Just go straight up. . . The top floor, first door. I'll let him know you've arrived."

Inside, the place was like an ordinary house. I went up four flights of stairs and the treads were brass bound and my high heels caught against them, click, click, click, click. On the fourth floor, there was a widish landing and off it went four doors. I made for the first one, knocked, and when a voice said, "Come in," I opened the door, and a man rose from behind a desk and came towards me, his hand outstretched, saying, "Miss Carter. I'm very pleased to meet you."

"How do you do?"

"Have you had a good journey?"

"Yes, very pleasant, thank you."

"Do take a seat. What would you like, a cup of coffee? Or would you rather wait and have a drink before lunch?"

A drink before lunch. They were going to give me lunch. "I'll . . . I'll wait. It isn't long since I had a coffee on the train."

"Well . . . well, now, I am so pleased to meet you at last."

It sounded as if he had been trying to get in contact with me for years. I looked him over. He was tall, well built, rather florid, sixty I would say, very well groomed, and once must have been very good looking.

He went behind the desk again, pressed a button, then spoke down to something on his desk, saying, "Tell Mr Rington and Mr Leviston to come in for a moment, will you, please?"

He turned to me now, saying, "These are the other directors. They would like to meet you; in fact, they must -" he poked his head forward as he added, "for they'll be working with you." There followed a short silence while we surveyed each other; then the door opened and Mr Houseman exclaimed, "Ah! Ah, Tom. Here is Miss Carter."

I saw that Mr Rington appeared a little younger than Mr Houseman and was of quite different stature, being of medium height and plump, with a longish face that bore a serious expression. As we shook hands he bent towards me in a courtly manner, saying, "I am most pleased to meet you, Miss Carter."

"How do you do?"

"Ah, here's Nardy." Mr Houseman turned again towards the door through which was entering a small man. Well, he was small in comparison with the other two. And he was younger; I guessed in his middle forties, because his hair was going grey above his ears. I didn't take much notice of his face at the time, only his eyes. They weren't all that large, but they seemed to cover his face. I suppose it was their kindly expression.

"Miss Carter." He held my hand and shook it up and down as he stared into my face, then said, "I'm delighted to meet you."

When we were all seated, Mr Houseman smiled towards me in a benign way and, indicating Mr Leviston, he said, "You'd better not take a dislike to him, at least not right away, because it's he you'll see the most of, he being your editor."

My editor. All this talk seemed to be floating around me. It wasn't really being addressed to me, but to a sort of dream self. My feet weren't on the ground; in fact the chair I was sitting on wasn't on the floor. Mr Houseman was speaking again, saying, "It was Nardy. By the way that is short for Leonard; but I don't know how Nardy came about, but Nardy it's always been." The three men were laughing now, and when Mr Rington put in, "It should have been Narky," there was more laughter; and I accompanied it by smiling widely. They seemed to be on very good terms, these three, and they were all so gentlemanly. The whole thing didn't seem real. And he went on, "It was Nardy who discovered you. He happened to glance through your manuscript, and that was that."

"I didn't only glance -" Mr Leviston was nodding at his partners now, and Mr Houseman answered, "No, from what you told us, you took it home and it kept you going till the early hours." He turned to me. "You have a keen sense of humour, Miss Carter. It's very evident in your work. Have you been writing long?"

"I . . . I've been scribbling for years, but nothing big like a book. It's my first effort."

"Really!" They were all nodding at me now, and Mr Houseman said, "Well, it certainly won't be your last. It's going to have a wide appeal, I think. Wouldn't you say so, Tom?"

"Yes, indeed, indeed. I thought it was very funny." Mr Rington's serious expression moved into a smile. "The part where Rosie gets the mange, well, I've never laughed so much for a long time. And the cows and their udders!"

"Oh, I thought the bit in the church with the priest capped that. Didn't you think so, Nardy?"

We were all looking at Mr Leviston now because he wasn't smiling, and his head was moving slowly from side to side, and after a long pause, he said, "Those bits were funny, in a way, yes, but I . . . I didn't find the book as a whole funny." He was now speaking directly to me. "I . .. I hope you don't mind my saying this, Miss Carter, but I found it a rather sad book, full of pathos."

I said nothing, but continued to look back at him.

"You surprise me, Nardy." There was a stiff note in Mr Houseman's voice now, and Mr Leviston turned to him quickly, saying, "Oh, some people may find it funny, Bernard, but what struck me forcibly was the pathos, the sadness of Rosie's life, so lonely, so isolated that she had to create a horse for companionship and a sort of protection against her husband. But of course -" he turned his eyes on to me again, saying softly now, "In Rosie, you have created a marvellous character. It isn't often one can make a heroine out of a girl who is a bit, shall we say, gormless. Well, she must have been to be taken in by that brute of a man, and then to stay with him all those years. But of course there was the pull of the property, and so many women stick by such men just to keep a roof over their heads." He now glanced towards Mr Houseman as he ended, "You have only to read the daily papers."

"Yes, you're right there, Nardy; and perhaps you're right as you very often are in your summing up."

Gormless! Must have been gormless to take on a man like that. But yes, yes, I had been gormless. I still was in a way. Did these gentlemen realize that I was sitting here with my mouth metaphorically so far open it had swallowed me. . .

"What . . . ? Oh, pardon."

Before Mr Houseman could repeat what he had been saying Mr Leviston put in on a laugh, "That's a habit that Rosie had in your story, saying what. It irritated the doctor. And you know, Miss Carter, it's recognized the author puts quite a bit of himself over in his first novel."

I looked at this kindly man because I recognized that he was a kindly man, and I answered him, "You're quite right, it is a bad habit of mine, saying what."

"Not at all. How many of us go through life saying pardon, or excuse me. . ."

"Or, come again." Mr Rington's face was bright now at his own quip, and once more there was laughter. But it was checked by Mr Houseman saying, "Well, time is going on and if you've got to get to the café, Nardy, you'll soon have to be going. So, Miss Carter" - he inclined his head towards me - "to business. Well now, we are prepared to offer you five hundred pounds advance on account of royalties on your novel, half to be paid on acceptance as now and the other half on publication. How does that appear to you?"

How did it appear to me? Five hundred pounds. I drew in a long breath prior to speaking, but no words came, and he went on, "Of course, there will be royalties. It all depends on how the book sells, and this kind of story, we think, will catch on. It could, if we are all very lucky, start a kind of series about Hamilton, because you make him more of a person than a horse; he is not just a talking animal in a Walt Disney film or a cartoon; I cannot describe exactly how I view Hamilton. So, what do you say, Miss Carter?"

What I said was simply, "Thank you."

"You'll accept that?"

"Yes, thank you."

"Then the royalties. Shall we say ten percent on the first five thousand, twelve and a half percent on the next five thousand, and fifteen thereafter?"

It sounded like double Dutch to me, but I inclined my head in acceptance.

"Well now -" he lay back in his chair and smiled at me, saying, "that's over. We'll draw up a contract and send it to you. Now for the best part of the business, at least I always think it is. Lunch at the café."

Lunch at a café. I was being taken to a café for lunch, not an hotel. Well, well. Mr Leviston now stood up, saying, "I'll be back in a moment," and inclining his head towards me, he left the room.

Now Mr Rington shook me by the hand, saying, "I hope this is the beginning of a long association, Miss Carter." I mumbled something, and he too left the room.

Then Mr Houseman, coming round the desk once more, said, 'We are always very excited when we spot new talent and of your particular type. And you know, Nardy is right, there is a great deal of pathos in your story. But then, the best stories in the world have been a mixture of humour and pathos. And by the way, I like your title. Titles are always very tricky things. We often have to discuss and discuss titles, because they are as important as the jackets. But you'll come to that later on. Yet, I don't think in this case we could have bettered *Hamilton*, just plain *Hamilton*. The only thing that might happen, as was pointed out at the committee meeting, is that it might be taken for Nelson's lady, but as someone else remarked, not with a galloping horse in a bridal gown and wearing boots on the dust jacket."

"Are you going to make that the cover?" My face and voice

expressed my surprise.

"Well, we're seriously thinking about it."

I laughed outright now; and at this moment Mr Leviston came back into the room. He was carrying a rolled umbrella and kid gloves. He looked very spruce and for a moment I felt dowdy, until I remembered that I had my new self on, right from my high heels to the top of my flat hair and, of course, my new hat with the cocky side. But that was another thing. Hardly any woman I'd seen in London so far was wearing a hat.

There was more handshaking, and then Mr Leviston led the way downstairs.

A taxi was waiting. "Café Royal, please," said Mr Leviston.

Café Royal! Not just an ordinary café.

"Do you know London at all, Miss Carter?" said Mr Leviston, when he was seated next to me.

"It is my first trip here."

"Really! Oh, then you have lots of surprises in store for you. But you can't hope to see them in an hour or two."

I was stunned into silence by the Café. It was evident that Mr Leviston was well known here. Before going into the dining-room, we sat in a sort of lounge and he asked me what I would like to drink. When I hesitated, he said, "Sherry, or a long drink? Pimms?"

Oh yes, I'd like a long drink, I thought, so I replied, "Yes, thank you, Pimms."

Pimms I found was very nice. It had fruit floating on the top. I'd never seen anything like it or tasted anything like it for a fruit drink. It took me some time to finish it, and when I did I felt warm inside, and for the first time in days, weeks, months, and, oh yes, years before that, I knew what it was to feel relaxed and to experience tenseness leaving my body. . .

In a long room that was all red plush, one of many waiters pulled out a chair for me to sit down. And I sat speechless, and felt even more so when I read the menu. Soup seemed the safest thing to start with. But *no, no*, this was a very, very, special day. *Cocktail de Crevettes?* That was a prawn cocktail. In plays on the television they usually started with prawn cocktails. Yes, I would have prawn cocktail. . . And what else?

Mr Leviston leant across the small table towards me from where he was sitting on what looked like a padded bench that went right along the room. Yet you couldn't call it a bench because everything was so elegant. And he said, "The duck is very nice."

"It is?"

"Yes, I can recommend it."

"Then I'll have the duck." I smiled at him.

He, too, ordered duck, but started with smoked salmon, which I saw to my surprise was a large, pinkish, wafer-thin piece of fish on an equally large plate.

When the wine waiter came, Mr Leviston said to me, "Do you prefer sweet or medium? Ladies don't often like a dry wine."

I felt sophisticated; I said, "Medium, please."

Steady, steady. I wasn't used to drink. What if it got hold of me and I passed out. Don't be silly. Don't be silly. You can have one glass; and it's different when you're eating with it, at least so I understand.

I had two glasses. When, a long time later, which time seemed to have been filled up with laughter, another waiter pushed a table towards us and began cooking pancakes which he then set alight with brandy, I knew that nothing more would surprise me. But something did.

The meal ended, the bill paid, our waiters all smiling, I stood up, and nearly toppled over. Mr Leviston, putting his hand out quickly, said, "It's the chair." And his voice dropped lower. "Ladies' vanity; high heels."

What a nice man he was. What a nice man. But there was something wrong with my legs and my head. Was I drunk? No, no, of course not. On two glasses of wine and a thing called Pimms and some brandy sauce! Could one get drunk on that?

"I will see you in the foyer." He took my arm and led me from the room. And did he point me in the way of the ladies? I'm not sure, but I found myself in that room being attended to by a very nice middle-aged woman. There was no one else there, and I sat on a chair and she bent over me, saying, "It's no good giving you a drink of water, it'll only make things worse."

"I feel dizzy," I told her.

"Well, love" - her face swam before me - "it appears to me you mightn't have had one over the eight but you've had two up to the seven." She sounded just like Gran, although her voice was different.

I nodded and smiled at her, saying candidly, "I'm not used to it."

"Lucky for you, love; you've got pleasures to come. Look, put your face under the tap; sluice it with cold water." She led me to the basins, and I sluiced my face; then said, regretfully, "All my make-up will be off now."

"Well, here's a bit more." She opened a drawer, full of cosmetics. "Take your pick."

Through slightly blurred vision I made up my lids, dabbed some powder on my cheeks, combed my hair, and put on my hat again; then turning, I thanked the lady of the ladies, as I thought of her afterwards, and after putting fifty pence on the plate, which seemed to me an extraordinary large tip but well worth it, I said good-bye to her and walked out a little steadier but still not right.

Mr Leviston was waiting for me in the foyer. He looked at me closely, took my arm and led me outside; and there I gulped strongly at the air and immediately felt worse. Turning, I looked at him fully and said, "I'm not used to it. I've . . . I've had too much to drink. I'm . . . I'm not used to it."

His soft smile looked to me the sweetest thing I'd ever seen on a face, and he said, "Miss Carter, how refreshing to hear you say that. You know" - his face came closer to mine, but seemed to melt to either side of me - "you are a refreshing person altogether. "

"I am?"

"Yes, yes, you are. And now I know why you wrote *Hamilton*."

"No, you don't." My voice sounded just like Gran's, and I saw the surprise on his face. I turned and walked somewhat unsteadily up the street, and he walked by my side, his hand through my arm. "I've got to get the train," I said now.

"What time does it go?"

"There's one something after five."

"Oh. Oh, well, it isn't three yet. We've got the afternoon for sightseeing."

I stopped and looked at him. "We have?"

"We have." He was laughing all over his face, and now I started to laugh. I opened my mouth wide and I laughed and passers-by turned and looked at me and they, too, started to laugh. And while I was laughing Mr Leviston hailed a taxi and we got in. And then we got out, and there was the river with boats on it, and Mr Leviston said, "A walk along the Embankment and a cup of strong tea and you'll be fine."

We walked and walked, and he talked. I cannot really remember all he said, but mostly I know he was describing London. Then he took me to a tea stall and ordered two cups of strong tea. I didn't like strong tea, but having drunk it I felt much steadier. Then we went back the road we had come, that was, through a churchyard, and we sat there.

There was silence between us for a time, and in it I grew ashamed. I had spoilt the day, made an ass of myself, I should have never taken that wine. I said as much. "I'm sorry," I said.

"What on earth for?" He had screwed round on the seat and was looking at me gently. "You're sorry because the wine went to your head? If you only knew how pleasant this outing has been, this lunch has been, for me. I mostly dine with people so pickled in wine that it hasn't touched their heads for years." He laughed now and added, "Oh, Miss Carter, don't be sorry for anything you do or say. It's so nice to meet someone who isn't putting on any literary side."

"Literary side?" I repeated.

"Just that, literary side. You meet all types in this business, and naturally they are all literary, but some . . . I'm going to whisper this -" he leant towards my ear and now he said, "I find some writers unbearable, arrogant, bigheaded, and egotistical. Some think that their first book is the only book that's ever been written, a worthwhile one that is; and God help us if it's successful, because then they imagine themselves little gods . . . and goddesses." He straightened up now and emphasized his last remark again with a deep obeisance of his head as he repeated, "Goddesses? Most of them are fakes."

I looked at him sadly as I said, "I'm a fake."

"You are?"

"Yes, I've . . . I've got to tell you this because it'll be about the cheque."

"The cheque?"

"Yes, the money that is going to be paid to me for the . . . the advanced royalties."

"Well, what about them?"

"Well, it'll be sent to me by cheque, won't it?"

"Yes."

"Well, I thought about this back in the office but I didn't know how to put it to Mr Houseman. I can put it to you though. Do you think I could have it paid in cash?"

"All in cash?" His expression didn't alter, although his tone showed that he was a little surprised by the suggestion.

"Yes, You see, Carter isn't my right name, nor is Miriam. It is my mother's name . . . well, by her second marriage to George Carter, who by the way is Dickie in the book, and his mother who is Mary in the book is my Gran, Hannah Carter. Do you follow?"

He blinked his eyelids rapidly, pursed his lips, then said, "Go on; I'm trying."

"Well, you see, I -" I turned away and looked across the flat headstones for a moment before bending my head and muttering, "I'm Rosie in the book." He was quiet for so long that I turned slowly and looked at him, and I'll always remember the expression that was on his face and what he said. "Oh, my dear," he murmured; "and to think that I said those things about her. . ."

"You were right. I was gullible. I still am, I suppose, but not so much. You see, looking as I did, as I do" - I pointed to my face - "I've just been made up for the occasion today. And . . . and with this" - I touched my short arm which I must say not one of the three men had seemed to notice, which proved them to be gentlemen indeed - "I thought he was my only chance and that nobody else would ever want to marry me. And I was lonely. But as I said in the story, it was the house he was after. He had a sister, but I haven't brought in May, because she died of leukaemia in my house, and towards the end she knew and admitted she had done wrong because it was she who manoeuvred us both into the marriage. "

"Is he as nasty as you make him out in the book?"

I looked away over the headstones again before I answered, "Much worse."

"And . . . and you've put up with this for years just because of your house?"

I turned and faced him again, saying now, "It isn't just a house, it's all I've got, and I was born there. And . . . and another thing, I hate the idea of him achieving his aim."

"And you really think it's worth it? He . . . he could have driven you mad. The horse business, was that through him?"

"Not really, no." I gave a small smile now. "I think he began first as a dog, when I was very young, then later on as a little girl friend, at least that's what I like to fancy, because I had the habit of talking to myself. There didn't seem to be anyone else to talk to. Then when I lost George, Dickie in the story, things were bad at home with my mother and I had to have someone . . . something, and so, Hamilton. But he really came into being through the doctor, when he told me I had horse sense. Anyway, now you know. Will you have to tell the others? Will it make any difference?"

"Well, I'll have to tell Bernard . . . Mr Houseman, and Tom too, and perhaps our financial director. But Bernard could explain to him that it was just a fad of yours, not wanting the money to go into the bank. But I think that Bernard, being the chairman of the company, should know. I'm sure we can work out something to meet your wishes. It will not make the slightest difference, though, your going under the name of Miriam Carter. There's one point, however. Would your husband recognize himself if he read it?"

"No, I don't think he would. But the doctor might. Yes, I'm sure he would."

"Anyway, you have set the story in the south country. Do you know that part at all about which you have written?"

"No, not a thing. I looked at a map and altered the names a bit. But I imagine one town is as much like another: there's a high end and a low end and a struggling middle."

He sat looking at me in silence for quite some time, and I had no words with which to break it. Then he said, "You know, I'll remember this day for a very long time as a day on which I met for the first time a remarkable young woman."

I gave an embarrassed laugh. "You know, in some way, Mr Leviston," I said, "you're like George, or Dickie. You're kind."

"Kind? Nonsense. I'm stating a fact, and from now on-" He suddenly leant forward and caught my hand and gripped it tightly as he shook it up and down, saying, "You must look upon yourself as a personality. Forget Rosie, forget Miriam. What is your real name by the way?"

"Mrs Stickle. . . It's an awful name. I was Maisie Rochester."

"Oh, that's a good name, Rochester. Got a ring about it, Maisie Rochester. Well from now on, I shall think of you as Maisie Rochester, a novelist who's going places."

"Oh, Mr Leviston." I was shaking his hand up and down as I said, "You know something? This has been the most wonderful day of my life. No matter what happens in the future, nothing will ever be able to surpass it or dim it. There's only one other desire I want in life and I doubt if I'll ever accomplish it. I have neither the strength nor the courage, but it doesn't matter."

"May I ask what your other desire is?"

For the first time in weeks I saw Hamilton. He came galloping across the headstones to stand right behind Mr Leviston, and I watched him place his right front hoof on his shoulder and rest his chin on the top of his head. I closed my eyes and muttered, "Oh, Hamilton."

"You want to achieve something with Hamilton?"

"No, no." I shook my head. Then, my eyes wide and tears of laughter dimming them now, I said, "Would you believe it if I told you Hamilton was standing right behind you with his right front . . . hoof on your shoulder, signifying to me that he considers you a very worthy man? Would you believe it?"

"Miss Rochester -" He was laughing now, too, his own eyes bright with moisture as he replied, "I'll believe anything you say. If Hamilton is embracing me, then please tell him I am honoured. But now, satisfy my curiosity and tell me of this other thing, this other desire you have to make your life complete."

"I want to hit my husband."

He looked at me. I looked at him. And Hamilton looked from one to the other. And then our laughter joined. We laughed so loudly that the noise seemed to re-echo from one headstone to another. And when two ladies, taking a stroll, stopped in front of us, and one of them admonished us with, "I would have thought you would have found some other place where you could express your hilarity," before walking on, like two children, we slunk up from the bench and Mr Leviston took my arm and, to quote a term, we went on our way rejoicing.

Chapter 4

During the months that followed, my life became so full of concealed excitement that I failed to notice yet another change in Howard's life style. I didn't seem to think it very strange that, having gone out practically every night during the past years, he now seemed to spend more evenings at home in his bottle room. After I had gone to bed I often heard him downstairs, but I was so full of my own affairs that it didn't seem to matter. For instance, I was corresponding regularly with Mr Leviston. He had done some editing on my book which, I understood, meant deleting bits here and there where I had repeated myself and tightening up, as he put it, loose threads.

I was to go up next week for a meeting with him, as he again so tactfully put it, to discuss whether I was in agreement or not with the alterations he had made. The next step would be the proofs.

They hoped the book would come out in the following spring. It seemed a long time to wait, but I understood that this was the usual procedure: the publishing of a book didn't come about overnight. I was also, at this time, well into another story of Hamilton; but most of this story, I must say, was wishful thinking. In it, Rosie had, on the grounds of cruelty, managed to get a divorce from her husband and was now doing a weekly column all about Hamilton in a national paper. I had found plenty of new escapades to lay at Hamilton's door; I took some of the characters from our terrace and a number from Gran's neighbours. I again brought in the doctor, and the priest, and, too, my kindly solicitor who, in this second edition, was fighting the case against the husband who was claiming damages for libel.

And so it was with some surprise and return of the never far submerged feeling of fear that I viewed Howard as he thrust open the study door and approached my little desk.

There, he stood looking down at me in silence for a full minute before, leaning over my typewriter, he said, "Carry on, Maisie. Carry on. I've nearly got you where I want you. It's taken time, but everything comes to him who waits." And on this he turned about and walked out, and I found that I was trembling from head to foot and that my good hand was clutching my throat.

When there penetrated my mind the sound of a little whirr to the side of me, I put out my short arm and switched off the small tape recorder I had acquired some time ago. I'd found this instrument very handy, especially when I was along at Gran's and she came out with something that would set me laughing. So that I shouldn't forget exactly what she had said, or the tales she related to me, I had bought this little pocket tape recorder. She didn't know for some long time that I was using it. Of course, when she moved a distance away into the kitchen, the voice on the tape almost disappeared.

When she eventually found out about it and I played her own voice back to her, she wouldn't believe it, and it was sometime after this before I could persuade her to talk naturally, and forget about the machine.

But now I ran the tape back some way, and there his voice came over to me, repeating the words, "I've nearly got you where I want you. It's taken time, but everything comes to him who waits." The words sounded as ominous on the tape as they had done when he voiced them.

But as I sat staring ahead of me, wondering what new scheme he had in his evil mind for me, it gradually came to me that I had a witness. At last I had a witness, a witness that couldn't lie.

I was shaking with excitement when I picked up the little recorder. Yes. Yes, I could put it in my blouse. I could stick it down the bib of my fancy house apron. I grabbed the little instrument and held it to my chest. It could be a life-saver, my life-saver. If this machine could register the things he said to me, and the way he said them, then I too might have the means of divorce in my hands. Oh, wonderful. Wonderful.

Then something happened the following day that seemed to make the use of the tape recorder quite unnecessary.

When I went round to Gran's I found another letter from Mr Leviston. The contents were intriguing. It started:

Dear Miss Carter - he continued to call me Miss
Carter - I have great news for you, but unfortunately I
may not divulge it. This pleasure, I'm afraid, must be left to Mr

Houseman; but I can say, you're on your way.

When I showed it to Gran, she said, "And what does all that mean, d'you think?"

"You've got as much idea as I have."

"He seems a nice man, that Mr Leviston."

"Yes, he is." And now I leant towards her as I said, "You've said that before and I've given you the same answer before: He seems a nice man, that Mr Leviston, and, Yes, he is. And that's that, Gran. He's a publisher. He's on the wrong side of forty, he's going grey, and I don't even know if he's married or not. I don't know anything about him only that he is, as I said, a nice man. What's the matter?"

She had turned from me and gone to the fireplace and, with one foot on the fender and her elbow on the low mantelpiece, she turned her head towards me and said, "I heard something in the club yesterday that I think's very fishy. You know Sarah Talbot? Well, you've heard me talk of her, the one that's had nine and they're all married and scattered round and hardly any of them want to know her now except the one that lives out Durham way. Remember?"

"Yes, yes, I remember."

"She's the one whose husband went to the races when she was in labour with her first bairn. He won a good bit an' he went on the spree, an' she didn't see him for days."

"That's the one?"

"Aye, that's her. Well now, Sarah's youngest lass Maggie was put to the trade in Hempies' down in the sewing-room, and she didn't like it. But anyway, she's married now and that's the one that Sarah visits, an' she tells me, Sarah does, that Bob, that's her son-in-law, took them all out, kids an' all, for a run. Well, apparently the car started to steam up, needed water, so Maggie said. I thought cars ran on petrol." She grinned now, then went on, "Anyway, Bob said to Maggie, 'Go and ask at that cottage for a can of water,' and off Maggie went. And Sarah said she followed her just to stretch her legs, and she reached Maggie just as the door opened, and who should open it in his shirt-sleeves?" She now stared at me, and I waited, and then she said, "Your husband."

"Howard?" I hardly heard my own whisper.

"Aye, Howard. Now our Maggie worked for him, so she wasn't mistaken. And as for Sarah, it was him who she had to see to get Maggie the job. Sarah said he lost his colour for a bit and he seemed unable to speak until Maggie said, 'Hello, Mr Stickle. We . . . we've run out of water, the car's boiling. Do you think you could oblige?'"

"Sarah said he grabbed the can from her, shut the door an' left them standing on the path; but he was back in a minute and he thrust the can at Maggie an' said, 'I'm visitin' a friend.'

"'Oh,' Maggie said, 'It's nice to get away from the town a bit.' And he said, 'Yes, it is. I always take the opportunity when I can.'

"Sarah said they had just got out of the gate and into the road when round the corner from a narrow side road came two young lads, about nine or ten, she would say. They come pedalling up an', jumpin' off their bikes, they propped them against the railings afore running through the gate, calling, 'Dad. Dad.' Now whether there was another man inside or whether your dear Howard has a family on the side, and has had all these years, I don't know, but it's up to you, lass, to find out."

I sat down on the couch, leant my elbow on the head of it, and rested my head in my hand. All these years, supposedly visiting his boss, Mr Hempies. All the money he had got out of me, all to keep another home going and the woman and children. . . Were they his?

"What are you going to do, lass?"

I lifted my head from my hands and it rocked on my shoulders; it seemed, at this moment, too big for my body. It was expanding, my mind was pushing it in all directions, because I was being filled with a blind anger. *Gullible?* That name didn't fit me; I was *mental*. Yes, that's what I was, and had been for years, *mental*. Why hadn't I gone to the shop? Why hadn't I insisted on being recognized as the wife of Mr Hempies's manager, just for once, just once? Why hadn't I asserted myself in some way, instead of staying in my prison, my privately owned prison, because that's what I had made my house into, a privately owned prison, with a gaoler who was determined to see me die in order to get it . . . and bring his woman there . . . and his children.

My God! I was standing on my feet now and I knew Gran had hold of me by the shoulders, and I was repeating aloud, "Twelve years. Twelve years. I'm insane, Gran. I'm insane. I should have known that no boss, however good, would invite his manager week after week after week, year after year. I'm insane. . ."

"Stop it, lass. Stop it. Now look, listen. Listen to me. You've got a way out. Go and have a look, see for yourself, then go to your solicitor. Now calm yourself. Come on, calm yourself. Sit yourself down again and I'll make a cup of tea and put a drop whisky in it."

"Saturday, Sunday. He won't be there till then, and I've got to go to London on Friday."

"Well, go to London on Friday; there's nothin' to stop you. In the meantime, I'll see Sarah and get her to ask their Maggie to see if their Bob will run you out from Durham next Sunday. Maggie'll fix it, I know, because she can't stand the sight of Stickle."

A minute or so later, when she brought me up a cup of tea that smelt strongly of whisky, I gulped at it; then I said, "I don't think I can go to London on Friday. I wouldn't be able to keep my mind on things."

"You're going to London on Friday. Strikes me things are moving in all directions and you're not going to miss any more chances in life. You're going to London on Friday."

I went to London on Friday, and Mr Houseman told me the good news: not only was a magazine considering the book for serialisation, but a paperback company wanted to do it, too. Wasn't that wonderful, he said.

Indeed, yes, yes, it was wonderful, I said.

There followed more small talk. And then I spent an hour with Mr Leviston in his office going over the alterations he had made on my manuscript.

I was again to be taken out to lunch and Mr Leviston told me that he had chosen a place that specialized in fish dishes. Did I like fish?

Yes, I said, I was very fond of fish.

It wasn't until sometime later, when we were sitting in the fish restaurant, that he suddenly stopped joking about what wine I should drink on this occasion, and, looking intently at me, he said, "Excuse my remarking on this, Miss Carter, but is there anything wrong?"

"No, no."

"You're quite happy with the arrangements Mr Houseman has made?"

"Oh, yes, yes. That's like a fairy tale; I just cannot believe any part of it. And . . . and you're all so kind, it's bewildering. No, it isn't anything to do with the book or. . ."

"But there is something?"

"Yes."

"Oh, well" - he sat back in his chair- "as long as you're satisfied with the business arrangements. I'm sorry if it appears that I'm probing, but your spontaneous gaiety seems lacking today.

My spontaneous gaiety. I never knew I had any gaiety in me. I saw the funny side of things, but . . . spontaneous gaiety. That was putting a fancy name to it. He was very kind, Mr Leviston. Of a sudden, I felt myself choking and I reached out and, picking up the wine glass, gulped at the wine.

From then on Mr Leviston seemed to do all the talking. Would I like to go to the National Gallery, or Madame Tussaud's? Or what about the Tower of London? The whole afternoon stretched before us.

I managed to say, "You're very kind, but I mustn't take up all your time. I really don't expect it, and I can go on my own now."

He put his head on one side and said in what I took to be mock sadness, "You don't want my company?"

"Oh, Mr Leviston." I bowed my head and shook it from side to side, and at this he said, "All right, it's the British Museum."

It was a lovely meal, but somehow I didn't enjoy it, as I had done on the other occasion, for all the time I was comparing this kind of living with what I had to put up with every day. Yet at the same time, I was wise enough to know that the three gentlemen I had met likely lived an ordinary family life away from the office, and that wining and dining clients was just part of the business. But above all, my thoughts were on that man back in Fellburn in the tailor's shop, who had for years treated me worse than a slave. Oh yes, much worse than any slave, for if in the old days they had been tortured it had been physically, but that man had almost maimed me mentally, while all the time he was living with another woman and supporting her on the money he had blackmailed out of me. And . . . a very sore point, those children could be his.

When, later, we were walking along the street, Mr Leviston remained quiet until we came to St. Paul's, Covent Garden, churchyard again, and here he did not say, "Let us sit down," but, stopping in front of me, he said, "Please don't consider it presumption on my part, Miss Carter, but I had so much pleasure from our first meeting and this has continued through your letters. You write a remarkably graphic letter, you know. So I feel that I have known you for quite some time; and then, of course, I have been going over your work and knowing it is partly your life story, so it is with genuine concern that I say to you, would you like to talk about what is troubling you?"

I didn't answer him for perhaps a full minute and then I said, "Yes, yes, I would. But I'm afraid, if I did, I . . I would start to cry, and make a fool of myself in the open." I glanced from side to side at the people passing to and fro.

He also seemed to take some time in speaking. Then of a sudden, he caught me by the arm and turned me round, saying, "Come on. Come on."

He now led me through Covent Garden, past the Opera House, and into a main thoroughfare. There he hailed a taxi and, pressing me into it, he gave the driver an address. Seated now, I looked at him for enlightenment but he said nothing, simply sat looking straight ahead. It was a good fifteen minutes later when the taxi stopped, in a street of tall houses, each with an iron balcony fronting the upper windows.

After paying the taxi he led me up three broad steps, the top one flanked by urns. He inserted a key in the beautifully polished brown door, then took my arm again and led me into a hall and into a lift, and when it stopped he once more took my arm and led me into a grey-panelled hallway. The floor was covered by a dull rose coloured carpet in which my feet seemed to sink. There was a marble hallstand against one wall and he placed his umbrella on it; then coming behind me, he said, "Let me have your coat. You'll find it warm in here."

Slowly I took off my coat, and as I adjusted the collar of my blouse he said, "And your hat." He was smiling at me now, so I took off my hat; then going before me, he pushed open a door and called loudly, "You there, Janet?"

At the same time he had thrust one arm behind him and caught hold of my hand and so led me into the most beautiful room I'd ever seen. It was large and high, and beyond the big window at the end I could see the iron balcony. I could just take in that the colour of the walls was grey and that the carpet continued from the hallway; but what stood out like sunshine was the drapes at the window and the upholstery of the big couch and easy chairs. The colour was like a citrus yellow and it gave the whole room an air of bright sunshine.

"There you are, Janet. And don't look so surprised to see me. What were you doing, guzzling tea as usual?"

"Oh, Mr Leonard, there's some time in this place to guzzle tea, with all the work to be done." As the woman spoke she was looking at me; and now Mr Leviston said, in a different tone, "This is Janet. And Janet, this is Miss Carter." And he pointed to the elderly woman, adding now, "Janet keeps me and my house in order, and has done for as long as I can remember."

Now clapping his hands together and his tone becoming light once more, he said, "Well, now introductions are over, what about it, Janet, a cup of your best?"

"Well, I'll see what I can do for you." Janet turned away smiling, and Mr Leviston took me up the room towards the window, saying, "It's right what I said, she's been here all my life. You wouldn't think she was sixty-seven, would you?"

"No, no."

"She's been in this house fifty years, except during those periods she was giving birth to one or other of her brood. She's had eight children."

"Never!"

"Yes." He nodded at me. "She came to work for my mother before I was born and as she will tell you, no doubt, before very long, it was later her daily chore to push me in my pram over there." We were now standing at the window, and he pointed to where in the middle of a square was a garden. "It wasn't railed round in those days," he said. "But now, all the residents who support it have keys to it, although you hardly ever see anyone in there except the gardener. But it's nice to look upon."

"It's lovely . . . it's a lovely view. And this room." I turned about. "I've never seen anything so beautiful."

"It is a nice room, isn't it? My mother designed it. It was her hobby, interior decorating. There are six other rooms like it, almost as large. As my father used to say, you could drive round the bed in a coach and pair. These were all bedrooms up here at one time when we owned the whole house."

"You owned the whole house?"

"Yes, but what could I do with a huge place like this? So I had it turned into three flats, although you could hardly call them flats. Now" - he motioned with his hand - "come and sit down. But before you say anything, I want to say my piece, and it's just this: I'm not in the habit of bringing young ladies - not even when they're authors - to my home. I may tell you you're the first author who has ever been here. I'm not" - he laughed now - "inferring that it's an honour, only I want you to know I don't make a habit of pushing young ladies into taxis and landing them in my apartments. In fact, if I told Bernard or Tom . . . Rington you know, that I had abducted you, they wouldn't believe me."

He was talking to put me at ease, and when Janet brought the tea in, he joked with her and she chaffed him back and for a moment I thought, here was another one who sounded like Gran, only more refined.

"Would you like to pour out? Or shall I?"

"You do it, please."

I drank my tea in silence, but my mind was working rapidly. I was bewildered by events and not a little surprised to find myself sitting in this beautiful room drinking tea with this kind man, who was a very surprising individual. Somehow I had imagined him to be married with a family; I never thought of him being a bachelor. Perhaps he was married and was separated from his wife. Perhaps he had been married and she had died. But that wasn't the point, the point was that he had brought me here so that I could tell him what was troubling me, and cry if I must.

I put my cup down and with my right hand I gripped the upper part of my short arm. I only just in time stopped myself from rocking backwards and forwards, but abruptly I started. "I . . .. I got a shock," I said, "I learned something about my husband and it upset me. Not that it hurt my feelings in the way it might have done if I cared for him. You understand?"

He said nothing, but inclined his head towards me.

"But, over the years he has -" I closed my eyes tightly and bowed my head now and my throat filled up; then with my head still bowed I said, "Like in the story, my mother left me the house and furniture, but what I didn't mention in the story was that she also left me over four thousand pounds, and after what he had put me through when we were married I determined he wouldn't get it and passed it all over in trust to Gran, my step-grandmother. But over the years he got every penny. It was the only way I could save myself from . . . his physical abuse or keep my dog. The first amount, seven hundred and fifty pounds, supposedly to enter in partnership with the owner of the shop. Anyway -" I gulped again and found difficulty in going on, but he remained silent, and after a moment I said, "And now, I have found out that all the time he must have been living with a woman. And . . . and there are children, so perhaps they are his. All these years he is supposed to have spent the week-ends at his employer's house." I raised my head now and, the tears streaming down my face, I muttered, "What . .. what hurts me is the fact that he has treated me like a brainless idiot, and also that at times I have been so paralysed with fear of him I wanted to fly away. But then I used to ask myself where I could fly to. Only to Gran's and her two little rooms, you see." I dried my eyes now. "I loved my house. It's nothing like this." I spread my hand out, my wet handkerchief dangling from it. "But it is nice and it's all I have. In those early days I couldn't see me ever holding down any kind of a post outside the house. I had this" - I patted my short arm - "and then, I was so painfully plain, still am. . ."

His hand came out now and caught my wrist but he still said nothing, and I went on, "And recently, he has something else hatching. He told me so. What it is I don't know. But this is the kind of thing that attacks one's nerves. Anyway, on Sunday I'm going to see this cottage where I'm told he lives, and I shall take matters from there."

"My dear Miss Carter." The tone of his voice almost caused the tears to flow again, and then he said, "It's incredible that you should have put up with this for so long, yet I understand your feelings about your home; I feel the same about this." He lifted his eyes to the moulded and painted ceiling. "I cannot imagine my feelings if someone tried to take it from me. . . He must be a demon of a man."

"I don't suppose you would think so if you met him, because . . . he appears to have a certain gentleness of manner. It's the salesman in him. And the irony of it is, the people in the terrace think he's quite a gentleman and that I have been more than lucky to have married him; in fact, I know they pitied him for having such a wife."

"Oh, Miss Car. . . No, I'm not going to call you Miss Carter any more, I'm not even going to ask your permission, I'm going to call you

Maisie."

I smiled weakly at him as I said, "That's an awful name too."

"Of course, it isn't. Maisie" - he seemed to roll his tongue around it - "sort of indicates jollity, and, you know, there's a lot of jollity in you. Your humour testifies to this."

Yes - I thought for a moment - I suppose my frolics with Hamilton could be put down to jollity, but at the present moment I felt anything but jolly, for I was beginning to feel foolish in having unburdened myself like this to a man who was . . . well, almost a stranger. . . Nonsense! I chided myself, for I don't think I've got to know anybody in my life, with the exception of George and Gran, as much as I have done Mr Leviston.

Now he was repeating his name, saying, "And no more Mr Leviston, everybody calls me Nardy. I'm not quite sure if I like that name or not, but I'm stuck with it. It was given to me by a very charming man. You see, James Houseman, Bernard's brother, started the business, the publishing business, and James *was* a very charming man. But he had a bad stammer, and when I joined the firm at eighteen - I never made university" - he smiled widely now - "I never had that kind of brain - James, who was a friend of my father, said, send the lad to us. And so the lad went to them, and I've been there ever since. But with regard to my name: James had a booming voice and you can imagine, with the stammer, how it sounded, and as my name was Leonard, he seemed to have some difficulty with it and he would shout, Le . . . n . . . nard . . . y, so in the end it sounded more like Nardy, and this stuck."

I was smiling at him now as I said, "It's a friendly name."

"Well, do you think you can be friendly and call me by it?"

Oh dear. I wasn't good at calling people by their Christian name.

"Try; it won't be too hard; you get used to it after a time." But now his tone changed to a serious note, and he went on, "If you confirm your suspicions on Sunday, you must go directly to a solicitor. You have one?"

"Yes, and he knows a little of the situation. I had to go to him to arrange about the money in the first place."

"Good. But about your fear of this man, can't you have someone in the house as a sort of companion for the present time, a friend?"

It took me a moment to admit that I had no friends to speak of. I said, "I know a number of people who go to the Writers' Circle. They are all acquaintances, but somehow . . . well, I suppose it's my fault, I don't seem to be able to make friends all that easily. I had one very close friend in my young days; she lived down the terrace. You know, I mentioned her in the book; I make her mother the High Church lady who didn't think I was a suitable companion for her daughter, rather obstructive in the marriage market. And that's true. I found out, and only in recent years, that that was why Katie's mother stopped our friendship: I would be a drawback to her meeting the right young men."

I watched him rise from the chair and walk to the window and stand there looking out; and this he did for a good few minutes before he said, "You know, Maisie, I hate to admit it, but there are lots of cruel people in the world. I have such a nature that I want to think everybody is nice, everything is rosy and comfortable. I was brought up in this house in the most happy atmosphere and it didn't serve me to any good purpose when I went out into the world. When I recognized the meanness, the cruelness, and the vindictiveness in human nature, I was for running back into this nest. But my mother was a very wise woman, she pushed me out. She even wouldn't let me live here; she made me set up in a flat on my own. Oh, that was an experience." He half turned, pulled a little face at me, then turning fully towards me, said, "You know, Maisie, I think it's the petty meanness that hurts one the most, the trickery, the chicanery that one meets in business. Not so much, I'm pleased to say, in our line, although it still goes on. Yet none of it seems to have the impact on me as does the small meannesses. I'm afraid that I allow these to grow out of all proportion in my mind. However, at this moment when I'm comparing my life with yours, I'm really ashamed that I allow such trivialities to worry me. But Maisie -" he took a step towards me and caught my hand and, bending his face down to mine, he said earnestly, "you really have the best years of your life before you, you are still so young. "

"I'm on thirty-one."

"Thirty-one!" His voice was scornful. "You could start anew from here and really live . . . and I mean really live, a happy successful life, because you've got a talent that you've only recently unearthed, and it will ripen and grow. Come on, now, up and at 'em!" As he pulled me to my feet he said, "Sunday is your turning point; you'll know where you're going from then on."

*

Sunday didn't turn out to be my turning point. I rode in the car with Mrs Talbot, her daughter Maggie, and Maggie's husband Bob, and we stopped some distance from the cottage and we saw nothing, no movement. When we got in the car again and passed it, two boys were kicking a ball on the grass patch that was edged by the railings. Bob stopped the car some distance away at the other side of the cottage;

then he said he would dander back as if he was out for a walk. Nobody would recognize him.

He was away almost fifteen minutes, and when he returned he said he had seen the woman. He reckoned she was about forty, and a blonde, but she had a head scarf on and a coat. He had skirted the back of the cottage by walking along the edge of a field, but he hadn't seen the sight of any man, and when he came back past it, the woman was playing football with the boys.

There was always another time, Bob said. He might be playing clever and sitting tight in the house. What about trying on a Saturday? He'd be pleased to run me out. I thanked him and said, "All right, next Saturday."

The following day, Monday, I wrote to Nardy, as I now thought of him, and told him what had transpired. By return of post he was brief and to the point: to keep trying, he said. His letters were not a bit like his conversation, because that wasn't stilted at all.

Towards the end of the week, I received another letter from him. This said that at a board meeting the previous day they had decided to bring the date of publication of the book forward and were going to do a rush job on it in order that it would be in the shops for Christmas. Wouldn't that be nice? he said.

Yes, it would be . . . or would have been if my mind hadn't been in a turmoil, for I knew Howard was brewing something.

But what?

I kept a close watch on Bill. Bill was aging fast and he hadn't been well of late. I'd had him to the vet's who said he had a little trouble with his kidneys. This had confirmed my suspicions that there was something wrong internally with him, because he didn't visit as many lamp-posts as usual, and when he deigned to stop at one his acquaintance with it was mostly half-hearted. I was so afraid that something might happen to him through Howard's hands or feet that I was now taking his basket up into the bedroom, but whereas at one time he would bound up the stairs after me now he would lumber laboriously, and I often had to assist him from half-way up.

I didn't know what I would do if anything happened to Bill, or when it happened to Bill, for the vet said he was old for a bull-terrier, nearing thirteen, he thought. I had Hamilton. Or did I? Hamilton seemed shy of me these days, standing in faraway corners, even sometimes turning his back on me. This would happen when he didn't seem to agree with my thinking. But Bill was a different matter. Bill was something I could hold . . . no not something, someone, for his love for me was a thing apart from any other feeling I had ever experienced. This ugly lumbersome piece of animal flesh had shown me more affection than anyone else in my life; yes, even than George.

So I was worried about Bill. If it had been possible I would have left him at Gran's, but he was too much of a handful for her. She said so openly. She didn't mind looking after him for a day, but I knew she was always relieved when I took him home. . .

I went with the Talbots to Durham the following Saturday, and the Saturday after that, and the Saturday after that, and the Sunday after that, but not one of us saw anything of Howard, not even of any man. We saw the children and the woman. They were always about the place, but no man was present. I later said to Gran, "Mrs Talbot must have made a mistake."

"Look lass," she said: "if Sarah made a mistake, Maggie didn't. She spoke to him and called him by his name. He's there but he's lying low. He's playin' a game with you. I'd bet me bottom dollar that he knows you're on to him."

"No, no, I don't think he does. . . And yet."

"What do you mean by, an' yet?" she said.

"Last night I was going upstairs just as he was about to come down, and he stopped and he pushed his face almost into mine and said, 'Ha, ha!'"

"Ha, ha?"

"Just that, ha, ha!"

"Well, if you want any proof, there you have it; he's laughing up his sleeve at you. If I were you, you know what I'd do? I'd take some of your money and put a private detective on to him. I would. I would that." . . .

I thought about this. I thought about it for days. And the days went into a few weeks, and then it was November, and it became bitterly cold and the heavy frosts in the morning lay like snow on the window panes.

It was partly through the frost that the climax came about, and I did it. I did what I had wanted to do for the past thirteen years. I did it . . .

During the past month my eyelid had begun to flicker and the corner of my mouth to twitch and I had once again been paying my weekly visits to the doctor. And on this Monday morning when I went into the surgery he glanced up from writing something on a pad and his look said, "Oh, you again." At least that's what I thought. I had come to the conclusion that in spite of his telling me I had a lot of horse sense, he thought that I really was stupid at bottom, or I wouldn't put up with the cause of my twitch.

His hands flat on the desk now, he sat back in his chair and said, "Well, what now?"

"I'm feeling awful," I said.

He sighed, dropped his head to the side and began, "Maisie, the cure's in your own hands. I've been telling you that for years. In fact, I'm tired of telling you, tired of seeing you. Do you know that?" He now poked his head across the table towards me, but there was a slight smile behind the whiskers which I noticed had gone grey half-way down the cheeks. It was as if he had put a false beard on, because I hadn't noticed the change in colour before. Likely too concerned about myself, I thought. He now asked quietly, "Any change? . . . I mean, with him?"

"Yes."

"In what way?"

"He's acting oddly, and I didn't tell you before but he threatened me. Some weeks ago he threatened me."

"What did he say?"

"I can't remember the exact words but it was to the effect that it wouldn't be long now, that he had something on me."

"He can get nothing on you, can he? You don't do anything that you shouldn't do?" It was a question.

"No."

"You don't sound so sure."

I longed at this moment to tell him about my book, and I felt if I had he would have been so pleased for me. But I couldn't, so what I said was, "I do a bit of writing."

"What kind of writing?"

"Oh, well -" I looked down at my hands as I muttered, "funny bits. Well, all kinds."

"You write funny bits?"

He was surprised.

"Yes -" I looked up at him now, and, my tone slightly arrogant, I said, "I write funny bits . . . about a horse."

His features became lost in the fuzz of his beard as he repeated, "Funny bits about a horse?"

"Yes." And when I said, "I talk to this horse; I've talked to him for years," he rose from the seat, then sat down again, and after a moment he half muttered, half growled, "Maisie, what are you telling me?"

"I'm telling you, Doctor, that I write funny bits of things about me talking to this horse and the antics he gets up to."

"Maisie. Maisie." He stared at me silently for some seconds, and then he said, "Do you leave these bits lying around?"

"No; I . . . well, I hide them in the attic under the floor boards."

"And you've been doing this for years?"

"Yes. I had to have someone to talk to and . . . and something to make me laugh, or else I would have gone insane."

I knew by his face I'd said the wrong word, and now he said, slowly, "Maisie, if that husband of yours gets his hands on those bits of writing, he'll try to prove just that. He's that kind of man."

"Yes, yes." It was as if a light had come into my mind clearing the fog. Had he discovered all that stuff under the floor boards? It could be, and . . . and that was what he was holding against me, thinking it would - I could hardly think the words myself- certify me insane. But no, no. I shook my head at the very thought. Lots of people talked to animals. . . Yes, but not in the same way as I talked to Hamilton. People talk to real animals. I talked to an imaginary horse, who had become so real to me that at times he wasn't a figment of my imagination at all; and this had definitely come over in my writing. That's why they had taken the book.

I felt sick.

"You're a very odd girl, you know, Maisie." He was staring at me; I answered him in the same vein: "In my experience I've found that I don't happen to be the only one," I said.

"Oh no, you're right there." He gave a small laugh. "But in this case, your oddness might give that husband of yours a very strong lever. Not that I can see it would be strong enough to do anything drastic, but say for instance he decided . . . or he took it further with the idea that you weren't capable of running the house unless you had treatment or some such. It's been done. Oh, it's been done. He would then have the house to himself, if only for a time. . ."

"And bring a woman in."

"Well, you said it."

"Yes, yes," - I nodded at him - "I said it. And . . . and I can see it now. Yes, I can see it now." I was on my feet and, leaning over the desk towards him, I blurted out, "The business of the cottage and him being recognized there, and his supposed staying with his boss at week-ends."

When I finished, he was round the desk, his hands on my shoulders pressing me down into the chair again. "Maisie," he said quietly, "what you've got to do is to go to a solicitor and tell him all this. Oh no, you needn't tell him about your horse, just what you found out about the cottage, and ask his advice. Myself, I know what I would do, but I'm not a legal man; and in this case, it's better that I keep my mouth shut, at least at present. Now, do as I tell you. You get yourself to a solicitor. You have one, haven't you? Do you like him?"

"Yes, he's a very nice man, thoughtful."

"Well, spill the beans to him. Go on, and do it this very morning. You will, won't you?"

"Yes, yes, thank you, Doctor." I stood up feeling a little calmer now and, strangely, for the first time I spoke in an ordinary way to him, not as if he was a doctor, and what I said was, "You know, you've been like a friend to me all these years. And there's something else I would like to be able to tell you, but I can't, not yet awhile. But when I can, you'll be the first to know."

"Something else? Now, come clean. Is it to do with . . . ?"

"No, no; nothing like that. It's one good thing that's happened to me, but because of Howard I'm frightened he'll get to know, and so I can't tell you what it is yet."

"You *are* a strange lass, Maisie."

"You said that before, Doctor. And you know something, some day you'll know just what I think about you."

He screwed up his eyes until they were almost lost in his hair then he shook his head gently while guiding me to the door, and with no further exchange of words I went out.

As he had advised, I went and saw my solicitor. His office was only a bus ride away in Gateshead. I told him not only about Howard's suspected double life, but why I had withdrawn the money bit by bit after putting it in security through Gran, and the fear that I had lived in for years.

"You've been a very foolish young woman," he said; "you should have made a stand right from the first, and I'm sure none of this would have happened." And to this I replied, "Oh yes, it would, Mr Pearson; you don't know my husband."

I arrived back home about half past twelve. It was freezing cold. I had to be careful in mounting the three steps to the front door because they were still slippery with the frost as the wintry sun hadn't got round to the front of the house yet. A cardboard box was lying to the side of the door. It was full of bottles, a dozen or so, I would say, in it and two or three lying across the top. Someone knowing of Howard's interest had left them there. The children very rarely left the bottles, they always knocked on the door and expected a copper for them.

I left the box where it was and went indoors. Bill heard me and set up a weak bark from the kitchen. I hadn't taken him to Gran's this morning as he didn't seem too well, and I'd had a job to get him to do his usual business. But now, after greeting me, he went to the back door, and I opened it and said to him, "Well, just go on round the yard." I had closed the front gate and the back gate was locked, so he couldn't get out. I always left the storehouse door open so that he could go in and take shelter if he wanted to. I had put a hessian bag there with some straw in it and covered it with a blanket, and often he would snuggle down in this.

I next made myself a cup of tea, and while drinking it, I opened two brown envelopes I'd found on the mat. They were articles from members of the Writers' Circle asking for them to be typed. I still had quite a bit of work to catch up on, but seemed disinclined to do it these days as I wanted to get on with my own book. Up to the past week or so, it had been going very well. I'd devised some quite funny pieces concerning Hamilton's reactions to my thinking.

After pouring myself out another cup of tea, I picked up the manuscripts and went into the study. The room was icy cold and, after switching on the electric fire, I had to hold my fingers over it before I could get them flexed in order to type. But then, with my hands on the keys, I found that my mind wouldn't work, either to do the request for typing or, yet, get on with my book: I was asking myself what would be the outcome of it all, would I ever have sufficient proof to get a divorce from Howard when I heard Bill bark, not ferociously like he used to do when anyone came in the gate, but nevertheless, he was barking.

I rose from the chair and had just reached the study door when I heard the key grating in the lock. That was Howard, and it was just on one o'clock. The shop closed between half past twelve and half past one for lunch, but he never came home for a meal.

Almost with a spring, I was sitting on my chair again in front of the typewriter, and two things happened almost immediately: I saw Hamilton standing near the window rearing upwards on his hind legs; at the same time my hand went out and I switched on the little tape recorder that was lying on the desk by the side of the typewriter. It was half hidden by the remains of a ream of typing paper.

The door opened and there he was. My heart was beating so rapidly that it was vibrating in my throat. I looked towards him as he neared the desk. And then he was leaning on it, his hands sprawled flat and his body bent towards me, and he began, "Well now, little Maisie, so you've been snooping around, eh? And what did you find, eh? Nothing. You just had to take the word of your friends, hadn't you? You've had nice little journeys out there on Saturdays and Sundays, haven't you, Maisie?"

My whole body was trembling. I took my hands off the keys because they were beginning to rattle, and he went on, "You think you've got me where you want me now, don't you? But what proof have you? None whatever. I was visiting a friend the day Maggie Talbot happened to come to the door. My friend's name is Mrs Ribber, and her two boys are called Ribber. No, Maisie, you've got nothing on me, but by God, I've got something on you. Something that, if it doesn't fix you for good, it'll prove you are in need of psychiatric treatment and should be put away for a time."

It was as if his voice was echoing words that I'd heard just a short time ago, and it went on echoing as he said, "And while you're away, I'll have to have someone to look after me, won't I? So I'll bring in a housekeeper, all very proper, and who better than Mrs Ribber and her two boys. And should you ever come out of wherever they send you, you'll have to have someone to carry on looking after you, won't you, Maisie? And Mrs Ribber will see to it, and I will see to it, for as long as you care to stay. Do you understand me, Maisie?"

I found my voice. It sounded cracked and it trembled as I said, "You can't do anything like that, as much as you would like to. I have my doctor and. . .."

"But has he seen these, Maisie?" He now thrust his hand into an inside pocket of his jacket and pulled out what I recognized to be discarded pieces of typing paper that I'd torn up and put in the waste paper-basket. I could see that they had been stuck together. Having learned from all the corrections that had to be done on the manuscript of the book that was shortly to come out, I now endeavoured to cut out all superfluous pieces of writing. One is apt to repeat oneself, often telling the same thing in two different ways, perhaps on the same page. So, with this in mind, I had scrapped numbers of sheets. But I always tore them up and threw them in the wastepaper basket under the desk, then every morning I meticulously emptied it. But I'd forgotten about the period between the time I went to bed and the next morning. And now I knew why he had, over the past months, spent so much time downstairs late at night. He must have selected some pieces and stuck them together, but left enough in the basket so I wouldn't notice anything different. He now waved the sheets in my face, saying, "This is just a sample. I've got dozens of them, telling about a woman who's so barmy she talks to a horse that crawls around this house, and gets on buses with her, and goes into the supermarket and stands on its hind legs in indignation when it sees women shop-lifting. Oh, Maisie, Maisie, what have you put into my hands, eh? Well now, can we come to terms, eh? Will I have to have you exposed and put away, at least for a time in order to bring my wife. . . And yes -" His jocular manner changed, and his hands slid over the table and knocked against the typing paper which pushed the tape recorder almost off the desk. I saved it with the side of my hand as he growled at me, "yes, my wife. And if you hadn't been mental you would have suspected something long ago. What did you think I got the seven hundred and fifty out of you for? To give to old Hempies in order to become manager? Huh! I wouldn't give that old sod the smoke that goes up the chimney. As for him inviting me for the week-ends there. . . Eeh! God, when you swallowed that, I realized you'd swallow anything. No, that money went to buy the cottage. And the rest of your four thousand to get my first car and add a bit on the the end of the house. Oh, anybody that wasn't mental would have seen through it years ago. But you are, aren't you? You're bats. You've not got one scrap of brain, except to copy what other people think, and any idiot can do that, any idiot." He now banged the typewriter with his doubled-up fist, then added, "And write down your madness. Well now, am I to expose you, or are you going to sit quiet and let me bring in her and the boys? It's up to you, because, let me tell you this, I'll have this house in the end. May persuaded me to marry you in order to get it and get it I will, because by God, I've bloody well worked for it. Just seeing you day after day has been a heavy mortgage. Now I'll give you till this evening to make up your mind, no longer, then I'm going to the doctor. And, by the way, for some time now I've taken the precaution to mention your oddities to him. I've also said you've denied me your bed for the past ten years or more. Huh! and by the way, I can tell you this, that you can thank my woman on that score, because without her, by God! I would have taken it out of your limbs. What I did to you in the beginning would have been nothing to what I would have done if I hadn't had her. Anyway, there it is."

He straightened up, stood looking at me with that dreadful expression on his face, then turned and walked out.

The door hadn't closed before I jumped up and followed him.

He was buttoning up his coat as he crossed the hall. I watched him pick up his cap - he was wearing a tweed cap these days - and open the front door. I was behind him now and there, through his legs, I saw Bill. Apparently, he had been wanting to come in and had come round to the front door. He had the clever habit of thudding his head against it; it was a form of knocking.

Howard became aware of me behind him as he looked on the dog who was now attempting to get past his legs and into the house. When his foot came out and he kicked Bill and sent him dithering and yelping across the top of the icy steps, the explosion happened. I think it would have come about in any case, but that was the match to the powder. I heard myself scream as, at the same time, I stooped down towards the box of bottles. The top one happened to be an old-fashioned brown stone ginger beer bottle. I caught it by the neck and in a lightning swing I brought it to the side of Howard's head. Before his scream had time to give itself an echo, I had used his tennis racket technique on him, and brought the bottle to the other side of his face. The blood was spurting in all directions now and the sight of it seemed to elate me, for as he fell backwards down the steps I stooped again for another bottle and threw it at him. It bounced off the back of his head, and he lay still now at the foot of the steps.

As if from a distance I heard a voice yelling as I threw another, then another: "Stop it! Stop it!" When the words, "She's killed him. She's killed him," came to me, some great cry burst soundlessly from me, yelling, "I hope I have. I hope I have."

I looked down into the box. There were no more bottles left; but there was a sea of faces on the pavement, and great narration in the street. People were looking up to me, with their mouths open. I stared back at them until, as if I had two bodies, one of them turned me about and gave me the impetus to dash indoors. Almost tripping over Bill in a headlong rush for the stairs, I made straight up them for the bottle room.

The window of this room faced the front of the house, and I thrust it right up. And then I started my onslaught. I gathered up the bottles in armsful, fat ones, thin ones, three-cornered ones, green ones, blue ones, black ones, red ones, ones with long necks, ones so small they were no bigger than my little finger, and one after the other I pelted them with all the force I was capable of, and so quick was I that it seemed for a time that Hamilton was bringing them to me. As I pelted them down the street I took a delight in seeing the people jumping here and there as if they were on hot bricks.

There were some vehicles in the street now but I couldn't make out exactly what they were because I didn't seem to be able to see clearly, and I was becoming very tired. The shelves were almost empty now. I was grabbing up the last of the bottles from a high shelf when two men appeared in the doorway. I recognized them as policemen. One had his helmet in his hand and his fingers to his brow and there was blood on his hand.

When the other said quietly, "Now missis. Now missis," I saw Hamilton for the first time. He was standing in the corner, his head half buried in an empty shelf, and as I looked at him, the elation seeped out of me. My vision cleared and I realized that the policeman's brow was cut, and a voice within me said, Oh I'm sorry, I didn't mean to hit you, but no words came.

"That's a good lass. Come on, you've done your stuff." It was the same policeman talking. He had a fatherly manner, and I went quietly with him down the stairs. "Have you got a coat, lass?" he said.

The injured policeman spoke for the first time. He had his helmet under his arm now and he pointed with his free hand, saying, "You might find one in there, it looks like a wardrobe."

The kindly policeman still had hold of my arm and he led me

towards the hall wardrobe and opened the door, and then he said, "Ah, yes, here's your coat."

He left loose of me and I put my coat on. As I did so Bill came and stood close to me, and the other policeman said, "What about her dog? They say she's here by herself." He spoke as if I couldn't hear him, and at this I stooped down quickly and with an effort lifted Bill up into my arms, which prompted the kindly policeman to say, "Put him down, hinny. Put him down now. He's a heavy beast. Put him down."

For answer I just stared at him, and the policeman who was again holding one hand to his brow, said, "Take him off her."

"You kiddin'?" The kindly policeman turned his head to the side. "Do you see what it is, it's a bull-terrier?"

"But she can hardly hold him."

The kind policeman's voice was very low now as he said, "The condition she's in, she could hold an elephant, lad. Let's get her to the station. Come on." He didn't take my arm now, but indicated that I should go to the door.

I obeyed him, and on the steps he said, "Mind how you go. Step over your handiwork, lass."

There was a crowd of people at both sides of the gate and they were silent as I passed through them. Then a voice from the back of the crowd came to me, saying, "Has she done him in?" And another voice said, "Had a damned good try by all accounts."

Bill nestled close to me in the car and his weight seemed to press the air and tension out of my body. I was quieter now inside, yet there was still that sense of elation and from somewhere like a voice re-echoing from down the years, the words, "I've done it. I've done it," kept floating around me.

When the policeman helped me out of the car and into the station, my mind seemed very clear. Everything and everyone seemed to stand out in sharp relief about me. Two men in mackintoshes who had got out of another car were now talking to the kind policeman; the other policeman was showing the cut in his forehead to a man who was standing behind a counter. The man listened in silence to the policeman; then he looked at me and, speaking as if I wasn't there, he said, "That little 'un?"

"That little 'un," the hurt policeman said.

"Well, you know what they say." The policeman behind the counter moved along it now to get a better view of me, then muttered, "Well, a stick of dynamite isn't very big after all."

Then my kind escort leant across the counter and said something to him, and he replied, "Aye, yes, I see what you mean. People grow like their dogs, and when that breed get their teeth in they don't let go."

Then looking towards me, he said, quietly, "Would you like to sit down, missis?"

I looked round, and then went and sat thankfully on the form that was placed against the wall, and once seated, I let Bill slide from my lap on to the floor.

Now the three policemen and the two men in mackintoshes were joined by a policewoman, and they all talked together for a moment; then my kind policeman, as I thought of him, said, "They say she's got a granny somewhere in Bog's End."

Almost on a bawl now, the man behind the counter seemed to yell, "Well, find her Gran;" only to subside again as he muttered, "Find her, wherever she is. And we'd better get the doctor in here an' all."

There was a general movement around the counter now, and the policewoman approached me. But she came to within only two steps of me, when Bill let out a low growl.

She stopped and looked at him, and then at me, and she said, "Would . . . would you like a cup of tea, dear?"

The voice inside me said, Yes, please, but I couldn't get it past my throat. I was finding this strange. There was a great deal of talking going on in my head but I couldn't give voice to it. I stared at her for some seconds, and she turned away.

One of the men in a mackintosh was now saying to the man behind the counter, "I've never seen so many broken bottles in me life." His voice sounded full of laughter, although his face was straight. "She kept 'em coming. She didn't mean to hit one of your lot, she just aimed for him, her man that was lying on the pathway. By! she must have had it in for him to turn like that. And yet, by the talk around of the neighbours, he was a quiet enough fellow. Very gentlemanly, they said. A bit of a sportsman, played tennis an' that. Manager of Hempies'; had been for years. Well, well, you never know, do you? But by! if it hadn't been so tragic, I would have laughed me head off. I didn't get there till nearly the end, but there they were, coming from that window, all shapes and sizes, the neighbours all under cover and the ambulance men dodging them as they tried to get him into the ambulance. It was as good as a play. As I said, if it hadn't been serious, I would have split me sides. . . And she hasn't said a word since?" They were looking at me now, and one policeman said, "I wonder what Doc will make of her when he comes? One bawl from him and she'll be on her feet, I'll bet."

How long did I sit on that bench? I don't know. It only seemed like a second before I saw Doctor Kane come through the door with his black bag. He was apologizing to one of the officers for being so long because he had been down to the quayside where a man had been hurt in a winch. And then he turned and looked at me, and all the hairs on his face spread out, his mouth opened wide, and I saw his tongue. It came out twice before he clamped his teeth shut. Then coming slowly towards me, he said, "What in the name of God! has happened to you?"

The kindly policeman was at his side now and he said, "Doctor, can you spare a minute, just a minute?" And my dear friend turned from me, because he was a dear friend. And I was so pleased to see him, yet I didn't show it. But he went with the kind policeman to the counter, and there he stood listening to the man behind the counter and the kind policeman and the one with the blood on his brow which by now had congealed. It didn't look a very big cut, not from where I was sitting. And all the while the conference was going on, the doctor kept turning and looking towards me, and the hairs kept moving on his face. Then I saw that he was talking, and the policeman was looking towards me, and their eyes were stretching.

When Doctor Kane eventually came over to the bench, he first bent down and patted Bill, saying, "Hello there, old fellow. Bet you never expected to be in the clink." Then sitting down beside me, he took hold of my hand and he said, "Well, you did something at last, Maisie; but you needn't have made it so drastic." He leant forward towards me now and, his face close to mine, he said, "Don't worry. Something had to happen. Just take everything quietly. But I'm afraid, Maisie, you'll have to stay here for a time. You understand that?"

Yes, yes, my mind was saying; definitely, yes, I understand that I have to stay in. . . I hesitated at the word, gaol. But that's where I was, I was in the police station and they would keep me here until somebody could take me out. He said now, quietly, "I'll bring your granny, and she'll take the dog. He likes staying with her, doesn't he?"

My eyes answered him, but still I said no word. He put up his hand and stroked my hair, and his touch brought a flood of tears. Like a spring bursting from a rock, they flowed out of my eyes and nose and mouth. Yet unlike a spring, they didn't make any gurgling sound, no sound at all. And the doctor got up and abruptly walked to the counter, and he said something to them, then went hastily out.

The three policemen and the policewoman all looked towards me. Their faces had a quiet look.

There followed a period during which different people came in. One lady had lost her cat; but the greatest commotion was when two policemen brought in an old lady who was singing, and when she tried to stop and speak to the policeman behind the counter, he yelled at her, "Get goin', Mary Ellen! Get goin'!" And she called back at him, "Okay, darling. Okay. See you at the 'sizes."

It was all very cheeky and I was beginning to feel very quiet inside, but then the door opened and in came Doctor Kane and Gran. It seemed that the doctor had to push Gran towards me, because she kept hesitating and looking at me as if she didn't recognize me. And when she eventually sat down beside me, her remark was typical: "God in heaven! lass," she said. "God in heaven! You needn't have gone and killed him."

Had I killed him? Well, that's what I'd wanted to do, wasn't it? When I lifted that first bottle I wanted to obliterate him like something that was festeringly evil.

"Say something, lass," she said.

I stared at her and my mind said, What can I say, Gran? It had to come. If only you could have heard him. I'm not a worm, Gran. I'm not a slug. I am a person. Mr Leviston knows I am a person. Mr Leviston is the first one who has ever recognized that I've got a mind. You're kind, Gran. You're a lovely woman, but you never recognized that I'd got a mind. And neither did George. You both loved me through pity. But Mr Leviston . . . well, he likes me. He likes my turn of phrase. He likes what goes on in my mind.

"Why won't she speak?" Gran had turned to the doctor now, and he said, "It's a kind of shock. She's retreated into herself because she can't stand any more."

"What'll they do with her?"

"Oh, they'll likely keep her here . . . well, until she's charged, and then she'll get bail. We'll have to arrange that some way."

"Keep her in the cells?"

"Yes, yes, in the cells." His whiskers were bristling now. "She's almost killed him. If he survives, he'll bring a case against her. By God! he will. He'll do his best. . ." He turned away now and, helping Gran up from the seat, he walked with her to the counter, his voice low, and although I couldn't hear with my ears the end of that sentence, my mind knew what it was: after this to have her put away. "Anyway -" His voice came to me now, saying, "the police will charge her. It's really their case."

Dear God. That would mean he would achieve his aims in the end. But then, there was the tape. What he said was on the tape. If I could tell the doctor about the tape. But I couldn't.

Gran and the doctor seemed to be a long time at the counter talking to the man behind it, and bits of the conversation drifted towards me, such as when the man behind the counter said, "She could have knocked his eye out." And the doctor answered, "Oh, it's only a scratch: a couple of stitches and that'll be all right."

"Nevertheless, the charge will be bodily harm, you know that yourself. And I've got to charge her in the normal way, dumb or not dumb as she makes out to be."

Of a sudden I felt tired; all I wanted to do was lie down, even on this form.

I was only dimly aware now of Gran coming and putting her arms around me and kissing me, then leading Bill away; and of the doctor, his hand once again on my hair, saying, "It's going to be all right, Maisie. Don't you worry; it's going to be all right. I'll see to it. Trust me. It's going to be all right."

When the policewoman took my arm, I went quietly with her, but when she put me in a small room and closed the heavy door, the tiredness for a moment left me and a great yell spiralled up, seemingly coming through the stone floor and up through my body and out through the top of my head. Yet I didn't make a sound. Instead, I lay down on the wooden bench that had a mattress on it and I drifted away into a kind of sleeping wakefulness in which the voice of the singing woman came through the wall and bottles of all kinds floated round the room. I started naming them: There went a big one. It hadn't any neck; that had broken off when it hit the ground. I could see the label: "Allsop's Indian Pale Ale". And there were his precious blues, some of them dark blue, some of them pale blue. Some of them with the word "Poison" raised in the glass. And, oh, there went a variety of the soda-water ones, the marbles all rattling in the necks. Funny, but few of those had broken. They were very solid bottles. 'Twas a pity I thought. And there went a row of little medicine ones, patent medicine ones: "Veno's Cough Cure", "Glycerine and Honey". And now the beer bottles started passing each other as if in a dance: "Guinness's Double Stout", "Guinness's Extra Strong Stout", "Australian Pale Ale". That was a funny one, why Australian? He had prized that one. Some of them were quite whole and bright and looked just as they did when he used to hold them up to the light after washing them in the kitchen sink. If he had only treated me as gently as he had done those bottles.

When the bottles started to mark time to the woman's singing voice coming through the wall, a hand came on my shoulder and I shrunk instinctively from it and crouched against the wall. But as a quiet voice said, "Sit up and have this drink," I opened my eyes, and there was the policewoman. And I sat up and I thankfully drank the mug of steaming tea.

"How are you feeling now?" she asked.

I looked at her and shook my head.

"I'll bring you another blanket," she said, and she did.

When she left me and the door clanged again, I shuddered, and the shudder told me I was back in my senses, for I seemed to have been out of them for some time. I drew in a long breath and looked about me.

This was terrible; I was in a cell. It doesn't matter, I told myself, you've done it. And I answered, Yes, yes, I've done it. But where was the exaltation I'd felt earlier on? I wanted someone, company, the doctor, Gran, anybody. I got up and started to walk about in the narrow confines, then sat down again, and as I did so, the door opened yet again and there entered the doctor and the solicitor. I almost threw myself upon Doctor Kane and he, gripping my hand, said, "There now. There now." And looking intently into my face, he said, "You feel better?"

I shook my head, and for the first time in what appeared to me years my voice came out of my mouth, and I said, "No. Terrible."

"Well, that's better than your dumb show anyway. Now, here, as you see, is Mr Pearson. I'm going to let him do the talking."

Mr Pearson now asked me to tell him exactly what had happened, and I was telling him when, half-way through, he stopped me and said, "You had a tape recorder running through all that he said?"

"Yes, at least I switched it on; unless in the excitement I ran it back and rubbed it off."

"Pray God that you didn't, then."

Yes - I nodded at him - pray God that I didn't.

When I had finished telling him all that had happened, I asked pathetically, "Will they let me go out now?"

The two men exchanged glances, and Mr Pearson said, "My dear Mrs Stickle, I have no doubt that your husband deserved everything you gave him, but as yet I don't know how serious his injuries are. I'll have to visit the hospital to find that out. Let's hope they are not as serious as some people seem to think. And then, don't forget, my dear, that you also left your mark on a policeman. "

I closed my eyes tightly and looked down and muttered, "I'm sorry about that; but" - my eyes opened as quickly as they had closed - "I'm not sorry about what I did to him . . . Howard, and never will be, not even if he dies. I'm only wondering now how I resisted doing it before. But . . . but when he kicked the dog, and he isn't well, Bill, that seemed the last straw."

"He kicked the dog?"

"Yes."

Mr Pearson turned now and looked at the doctor, saying, "I suppose I could get the key from the police to enter the house. You could come with me and pick up that tape because" - he turned now and looked at me - "if that conversation is recorded, it's going to be your main witness. No matter what the doctor or I might say, or your counsel, and you'll have to have a counsel, if your husband is condemned out of his own mouth, then that should carry great weight with the judge."

I felt sick from the pit of my stomach. I'd have to go to court, face a judge? Well, I wasn't stupid altogether; of course, I'd have to go to court and face a judge. I said on a gulp, "Will they let me out now . . . I mean, until the time comes?"

Mr Pearson pursed his lips for a moment. "I'm sorry, my dear," he said, "procedure is: you will have to go before the magistrates in the morning, and it depends on how you plead whether you get bail straightaway or not. If you plead not guilty, you'll be allowed out on bail, but if you plead guilty, I'm afraid you'll likely be kept . . . be kept in custody until your case comes up."

"But . . . but I am guilty. I did do it. I did hit him. Well!" My voice was shaking now, not with laughter, but at the silliness of his suggestion: guilty, or not guilty. Everybody knew I was guilty and I said so: "Everybody knows I did it. There was a big crowd there; they saw me."

"Yes, I know that. We all know that. But I'm telling you that you must plead not guilty if you want to get out of here and stay out until your trial."

Doctor Kane had hold of my hand and once more patted it as he said, "It's difficult to understand, but that's the law. Now tomorrow morning we'll be around here like a shot, and all you've got to do when you go before the magistrates and they ask if you're guilty or not guilty, you've just got to say, not guilty. Anyway, we'll go into the procedure more tomorrow morning. Now" - he got to his feet - "try to get a night's rest."

As they went to leave I caught hold of Doctor Kane's arm and said, "You will come? I mean. . ."

"Of course I'll come. I'll skip surgery. My lazy good-for-nothing partner can do some work for a change." He grinned, but it was a weak grin, an anxious grin; and I nodded at him, then at Mr Pearson, and they went out. The door clanged again and I put all my fingers in my mouth and bit down hard on my nails.

Chapter 5

I was in the street. There was the sky above me. It had never looked so wide, nor so high, nor had the air tasted so wonderful, it was going down my throat like the wine I'd had that time in London. I stood and looked about me as if in wonder, and the doctor was standing on one side of me and Mr Pearson on the other, and Mr Pearson patted my shoulder and smiled at me now as he said, "You did very well."

"I only said, not guilty."

"But you said it with some conviction."

"Did I?"

"Yes, you did."

"By the way, two hundred pounds. Who stood all that amount?"

"Never you mind." Doctor Kane now caught hold of my arm, saying, "I don't know about you, but I'm frozen standing here. The quicker we get to your granny's the better. And I hope she's got the teapot on the hob."

"You put up the money?"

"Yes." He now poked his head towards me. "And don't you go and scarper."

"Oh, Doctor Kane."

"Never mind, oh Doctor Kane." His voice was impatient. "Come on, get into the car. . . You following?"

Mr Pearson nodded, saying, "Yes, I'll come along; I'll have to see where I can find you." He now smiled kindly at me and walked back to his car.

As soon as we entered the door of Gran's house, and not without curtains being drawn aside in the street, Bill scrambled towards me, and Gran put her arms round me and, the tears running down her face, she said, "Doctor thought it better that I didn't come. Aw, lass, I've been worried sick in case you said the wrong thing and didn't get out."

"Don't let's have so much palaver, Hannah. What about that teapot?"

"Oh, aye, the teapot." She looked from one to the other as if in a daze, then went to the kitchen, only to return almost immediately to the doorway and ask the doctor, "How is he, Stickle?"

"Oh, he'll survive. But no thanks to this one here." He now looked at me and added, "You did a good job on him. And after listening to that tape" - he nodded at me now - "oh yes, we found it-" He glanced at the solicitor, then turned his gaze on me again as he went on, his voice quiet, "I don't blame you, nobody would."

"Where's the tape now?"

"I've got it." Mr Pearson held up his index finger. "And as the doctor just said, it's understandable, your reactions; but I must add, you are very lucky that you succeeded in taking down what he said, because without this evidence, had your husband produced the . . . well, writings about this horse that the doctor tells me here is a sort of" - he paused - "companion, he might have, after all, succeeded in his claims." As he finished speaking, Gran came out of the kitchen carrying four cups of tea on a painted tin tray, and just before she put it down on the table she glanced towards the window, saying, "There's a taxi just pulled up. That'll be another of 'em. They were swarmin' round here last night like flies on a midden. All the way here from Newcastle and Sunderland, they had come. At the finish, I clashed the door on their faces and told them to get the hell out of it. An' that's what I'll say to this one an' all."

She marched to the door now, and when I heard the voice say, "Are you Mrs Carter?" and Gran's reply, "Yes; and what of it?" I got up from the couch and pushed past Mr Pearson and the Doctor and went to the door; and there, pressing Gran aside, I looked at the visitor and said, "Oh, Nardy."

"Maisie." He held out his hand, and I looked about me in bewilderment back to the two men who were looking towards us down the passage, then to Gran, and I said, "Gran, this is Mr Leviston, you know, from London."

"Oh, aye. Aye." Gran's whole manner changed, and she now extended her hand, saying, "I'm pleased to see you, sir. Come in. Come in."

He came in, and in a fluster now I looked from the Doctor to Mr Pearson and said, "This is a . . . a friend of mine from London, Mr Leviston." Now I turned and looked at Nardy and added, "This is my solicitor, Mr Pearson."

The men shook hands, then stood looking at each other, and it was evident to me that the doctor was definitely wanting to know how I'd come by this friend from London, this well-dressed, city-looking, gent. Then as I was about to speak, Gran said, "Would you have a cup of tea, sir?"

"Yes, yes, Mrs Carter; that would be very acceptable." Once again the men looked at each other, and now I said to Nardy, "I'd better tell them."

And he answered, "As you wish, Maisie. As you wish."

I looked pointedly at the doctor as I said, "This is my publisher." I indicated Nardy with my hand, and when Doctor Kane's eyes became lost in his hair, as they were wont to do when he was puzzled, he said, "Your what?" And at this I said, without a smile because there wasn't a smile in me, "You've got that habit now. You heard alright, my publisher. I've written a book."

I saw him look at the solicitor, and they exchanged glances that, a few minutes earlier, if Nardy hadn't been present, would have read, Poor thing. It's a pity, but he was right. Yet, still their glances exchanged incredulity.

I think it was the first time in our acquaintance that I found the doctor absolutely stumped for words. It was Mr Pearson who said, "A book . . . you have written a book?"

"Yes, that's what I said, I've written a book. And it's to be published. . . . When?" I looked at Nardy, and he, now seeming to enjoy the situation, smiled from one to the other as he said, "It should be out in the first week of December."

The doctor now spoke. "A book about what?" he asked.

I looked directly at him as I replied, "Hamilton, the horse I told you about."

"Hamilton?"

"Yes, the horse."

"And you've made it into a book -" He cast a glance at Nardy now before he added, "that will sell?"

"We have every hope that it will romp, and keep pace with Hamilton himself."

Gran now brought all the attention upon herself by saying, "She's been tellin' me for ages about this horse that's been rompin' round me kitchen, an' I've said, well, it's a pity it couldn't be of some real use and leave some manure on me patch of garden."

"Oh, Gran." Once more I wanted to laugh, but I couldn't. I had the feeling deep inside me that I'd never laugh again, nor would I ever think anything funny again, Hamilton or no Hamilton. I felt that, since twelve o'clock yesterday, my whole personality had undergone a strange change. First, I felt much older, and adult with it. I knew that some people could reach seventy and never be adult, but now I felt adult. I felt that in a way, whatever lay in the future, I would be able to cope with it. But I added a proviso to this thought, and it was, as long as I had friends such as these to support me. Part of my whole being, I knew, was still in that cell in the police station, and the thought that I might have to return there created a blackness shutting off some section of my mind wherein lay my future.

"Maisie, it sounds trite, but you amaze me. You always have." I was looking at the doctor, and he went on, "There you've been, pestering me morning after Monday morning, with one thing and another, and all the time you've been living another life, because you must have been if you've written a book. So I'm going to ask you this, woman: why, if you are capable of writing a book that's going to be published, and it must have some quality if that's the case, because from what I've heard of publishers" - he glanced at Nardy - "they don't act like a charitable organisation; that being so, why the devil couldn't you take yourself in hand before now?"

I let a pause elapse before I answered him, and then I said, "When you read the book, you'll find out."

"We've got another situation here." We all looked at Mr Pearson now and watched him take a drink of tea from his cup, which from his veiled expression I didn't think he found palatable, as Gran's tea always looked like ink and she put very little milk in it, because that's the way she liked it herself. Then he went on, "You have written this book under a pseudonym, I presume?"

"Yes."

"And no one up till now has known about it except Mrs Carter" - he inclined his head towards Gran - "and your publishers?"

"Yes, that's right."

"Well, that being the case, if you want my advice, I would leave it like that until the case comes up. And of course, the timing of that will depend upon how quickly your husband recovers.
Anyway, it might not come up for months. In the meantime, your book will have come out and have been read. When you say it's about a horse, I presume it deals with your imagination, you just imagine you see this horse. Is that so?"

I paused before I answered, because I expected Hamilton to appear rearing on his hind legs in denial of his immaterialism, but there was no sign of him, so I said, "Yes, you could say that."

"Well, as this seems to be one of the main points on which your husband will press his case, which, putting it plainly, is that you are mentally unbalanced, and if it appears that this is carrying weight, and with some judges it certainly could do, even with the evidence of his conversation on the tape recorder, the fact that you've written this as a book could influence the proceedings. But then, we must remember, the real case concerns your attack on him."

As he pursed his lips in a jocular fashion I bowed my head, but it wasn't with any feeling of remorse because I felt not one tinge of regret at what I had done. I wasn't even interested in the extent of Howard's injuries. Yet when Doctor Kane said, "Anyway, what's twenty-seven stitches here and there between friends?" I looked up and at him, and he nodded back at me, adding, "It's a good job you spread those bottles around. If they'd hit the one place, things might have been serious." He now turned to Nardy and said, "I suppose you know all about it? Have you been to the police station?"

"Yes. I . . . I called there, naturally after I'd read the morning papers."

"But how did you get from London to here in this short time?"

"I flew up. Anyway, the news really didn't surprise me."

It seemed that both Doctor Kane and the solicitor spoke at once, and he repeated, "No, not after having read Maisie's story. It is intended, I think . . . at least you would say, wouldn't you, Maisie, that it is a funny book? Yet running through it is the story of a sadist and his treatment of his wife Rosie. That's the girl in the book. Anyway, I felt I came to know Mr Stickle very well before Rosie" - he now inclined his head towards me - "gets rid of him towards the end."

"Gets rid of him?" Doctor Kane poked his head forward. "You mean . . . you mean, actually?"

"No. Maisie was kind: she let Rosie divorce him, but not before Rosie's supposed brother has a go at him; and also Rosie's dog, which didn't happen to be a bull-terrier, but a small Highland terrier whose chief occupation was chasing rats; and he recognized a big rat when he saw one and so he went for Rosie's husband. There is a court case at the end of the story, too, where the man is trying to have the dog put down."

"Does he succeed?"

Nardy shook his head and smiled at Doctor Kane as he replied, "Of course not."

"And how, may I ask, does that story end?" Doctor Kane's face was straight now.

"Oh" - Nardy turned and smiled at me as he said - "Rosie achieves her heart's desire. She goes on a sea cruise, dressed up to the nines. And there begins the sequel . . . we hope."

"Well, well." The doctor got to his feet, adding now, "And we all lived happily ever after." Then looking down at me, he said, "I hope your own story turns out as well as the one you've written. Anyway, we'll do our best to see that it does. . . Do you want to go on a sea cruise?"

"No." I shook my head. "I'd be seasick; I heave when I cross the ferry."

As the doctor buttoned his coat I said to him, "Will it be all right if I go home?"

"No, it won't!" His words came from deep within his throat. "You'll have the place infested with reporters once they know you're there. What's more, you'll have to put up with the neighbours. You stay put, here with your granny for a few days." And he added, with a laugh, "The neighbours around this quarter will be more in sympathy with you, because if some of them had been with you, they would certainly have helped you with your pelting, imagining they were getting one back on their own men. Isn't that so?" He looked at Gran, and she said tartly, "If you say so."

Doctor Kane and Mr Pearson shook hands with Nardy, and the moment the door closed on them, Gran said, "Now that you've got company for a bit, I'll get out and do me shoppin'. That all right with you?"

"Yes, Gran."

I knew the shopping idea was a pretext; she wanted to leave me alone with Nardy so we could talk. She'd had her own ideas about him and me long before this morning, and as I said, it was no use telling her that, as I saw it, she was barking up the wrong tree.

Once we were alone, we sat quietly on the couch looking at each other. I broke the silence by muttering, "I'm not sorry."

"I'm not either. I'm glad."

"He kicked Bill. That was the breaking point. But I'd meant to do something, anyway, even before that. I didn't know what. And then there were the bottles right to my hand as if they had been placed there on purpose."

"Perhaps they had; God works in strange ways His miracles to perform."

"Oh" - I turned my head away - "I don't think anything I did could have been under the directive of God. I know now that I went mad, I did really, I went mad for a time. It seemed as if I was jealous of the bottles, because he was always tender with the bottles, washing them carefully, drying them, polishing them, arranging them in sizes and colours. . . What do you think will happen to me?"

He hitched himself towards me and caught my hands and, pressing them firmly, he said, "Nothing that cannot be overcome. You seem to have a very good man in your solicitor . . . and your doctor; well, he's just as you described him in the book. And when he says his piece, and that tape is played through. . . By the way, that was a brilliant idea." He nodded at me. "That, I'm sure, was God-inspired. And then the fact that you are a writer, and I, and everyone else in the office, think the book is going to be a great success. Well, when that is revealed, it should quash any ideas that your husband has with regard to your mental deficiency." He ended by pulling a face.

"Do you think he'll try to get back into the house?"

"No, I don't think there'll be a chance once the judge knows of the woman and the children . . . if they are his. Anyway, your solicitor saw to that side of it; his personal belongings have been sent to him."

"But . . . but what -" I found that I could hardly speak the words that I was thinking now, and when they did come out they were low and muttered, "But what if things don't go as you think they will and I'm sent to prison?"

"Maisie." He had lifted my two hands and was holding them against his chest, and slowly he said, "Look at me." And when I looked at him, he went on, "Whatever happens, do you hear? Whatever happens, just remember this, I am your friend . . . and more than a friend. You understand?"

I did and didn't, because what I thought his words meant conveyed something that was really beyond contemplating. This man, an educated man, well-born, because that much I had gathered from his house and his style of living, which was as natural to him as breathing, this man was suggesting. . . What was he suggesting? No, it was impossible. I wasn't going to dwell on that with all the rest of the things raging in my mind. He said he was a friend, more than a friend. That meant a dear friend, and that was enough, quite enough. *I wasn't going to bark up the wrong tree.*

The leading northern papers had carried headlines of my escapade. The Battle of the Bottles, it was called. They had described, each in a different way, my raining the bottles down on to a crowd in the street.

"The neighbours say the victim was a quiet, gentlemanly man." said one paper. Another heading was: "Little termagant wages bottle battle against husband". And the third one began, "Virago goes berserk with bottles. Husband in dangerous state in hospital. Policeman's head split open".

Then on Saturday morning came the local paper. Gran had gone out to the butcher's and she brought it back with her. She almost burst into the room and threw the paper at me, crying, "Read that! Read that!" She pointed to the right-hand corner and the last column on the front page. The headlines were: "A Reason for the Bottle Bashing". Then followed the words: "So far no one seems to have got to the bottom of why a wife should attack her quiet gentlemanly husband, a man who was well-known in the business centre of the town, but new light was thrown on the situation yesterday when a woman visited Mr Stickle in hospital. She was accompanied by two young boys who spontaneously addressed the patient as Dad. A reporter, who happened to be visiting a patient in an adjoining bed, took the matter up with the woman when she later left the hospital and she aggressively stated that she had lived with the man for over twelve years. Moreover, she had been engaged to him before he had married his present wife, whom she said, he found it difficult to live with because she was unbalanced."

There was more but I didn't read on. I looked up at Gran, and she said, "There's your divorce, lass. There's your divorce." And I said, "Yes, from an unbalanced woman."

"Oh" - she jerked her chin upwards - "that will be knocked on the head when the case comes up and they find out what this so-called unbalanced woman has done and is now the famous writer. . . "

"Oh, Gran! Gran!"

"Well, you will be. You know I don't read stuff like that, but when I read that copy you brought back, well, I was laughin' one minute and cryin' the next. It's that kind of a book, 'cos in a way it explains things, you know, like talkin' to yourself. I never realized that I've been talkin' to meself all me life. That's when I had nobody else to talk to. And that's just what you did. You had nobody to talk to, so you made up a horse. By the way" - she looked about her - "where's he got his big feet now?"

"I haven't seen him for days."

She seemed to recognize the sad note in my voice and she said, "Well, the quicker you get back in touch with him the better if you're goin' on writin' about him. Eeh" - she wagged her head - "didn't those men laugh when I said he should have left some manure for the garden. . . I think I could write a book meself." She turned about and took off her coat and the silly woolly hat with the red pom-pom, that from the back made her look like sixteen; more and more she was wearing younger type clothes, even going out in trousers. I often thought some young lads must have received a shock when they got round to her front.

As she went into the kitchen I said, "I've just made the tea." And to this she answered, "Good."

Then she called, "What d'you say, lass?"

And I called, "After reading this" - I tapped the paper - "I think it would be all right to go back home, because the neighbours might now be thinking a little differently and seeing things perhaps from my point of view."

She came to the kitchen door. "Well, it's up to you, lass. I know this place must be getting on your nerves, only being able to creep out at night with that fella." She pointed to Bill.

"You won't mind?"

"Don't be silly, lass. Anyway, once you're gone I'll be able to get out and to me bingo. I've never won anything this week. Well, I wouldn't, would I? 'cos I haven't been."

"Oh, Gran."

Two hours later, as I was about to leave, she said, "I'd better tell you that I wrote to our Georgie, telling him about it, 'cos I don't suppose they get our news down that end of the country, so don't be surprised if he's on the doorstep any day from Monday."

Funny that. I hadn't given George a thought in days. Was it possible that people once loved could take a back seat in your mind? I'd thought of George as my protector for years, whether he was with me or away from me. But now I thought of him no more, not in that way, because his place had been taken by Nardy.

Chapter 6

It was the day of publication. I received two telegrams, one from Mr Houseman and Mr Rington, and a separate one from Nardy saying simply, "Congratulations". Then followed two bouquets. The man who brought the flowers said, "Is it your birthday?" And I said, "Yes." I left the flowers as they were, all wrapped up, in a bucket of water. They were bringing no joy, for my heart was like lead.

I went back into the sitting-room where, before a big coal fire - I had discarded the electric one - on the rug lay Bill. On each of the past three days the vet had called, and he said there was nothing that could be done: Bill had kidney trouble. What was more, he was having hallucinations, when he would urge his weakened body to rise and go for something on the wall.

I knelt down beside him and stroked his dear head, and he turned his eyes towards me, and his tongue came out, but he couldn't lick me. "Oh, Bill. Bill. What am I going to do without you?" I was moaning aloud. At this moment I had nobody in the world but Bill. Gran, Nardy, the doctor, the solicitor, George, they didn't matter, only this animal which had been the only creature I had been able to hold tight to me during the past long years. I began to plead with him now, "Don't go, Bill. Oh, please don't go. Don't leave me."

And when I knew his breaths were numbered I crouched low down until my head was on a level with his, and his round dark eyes looked deep into mine and they were full of love. Slowly he lifted a fore paw - it was a form of shaking hands - and when his whole body jerked as if he was going to get up and run, I put my arms about him and he became still, so still, that his head fell on to the side of my arm.

I sat rocking him and crying, and Hamilton came and sat by my side. He had been with me all day, that is, as long as I was in the room with Bill. He never followed me out of it, but when I returned, there he would be sitting on his haunches, his head drooped, looking down on Bill. I looked at him now and cried brokenly, "There'll never be another Bill." And he answered, No, there'll never be another Bill. There might be a Simon, or a Sandy, or a Rover, but there'll never be another Bill.

"No! No!" I knew my voice was almost a yell. "I'll never have another. Do you hear? *Never. Never.*"

All right. All right, he said. Calm yourself, or you'll have Mrs Nelson in. She is very attentive these days.

"Yes, yes" - I nodded at him - "she's very attentive these days when I don't want her to be. If only she or one of the others had given me their attention or even noticed me eight or ten years ago, I wouldn't have had to rely on you so much, would I?"

No, no. He nodded at me. That's true; but there again you wouldn't have had a book out today, would you?

Oh, a book, a book. What did it matter? What did it matter? I'd lost Bill.

I was unaware that the back door had opened or that someone had come across the hall, until the sitting-room door opened and there stood Gran. She came towards me slowly, and I looked up to her through a blur and I said, "He's gone."

"Well, you knew he was going, lass. You knew it was coming."

"I can't bear it, not any more. I've had enough; I can't bear this, Gran."

"Lass -" She bent down to me as if she was going to take Bill from my arms as she said, "He's only a dog, lass. Now look at it like that, he's only a dog."

"*Shut up, Gran. Shut up.* He wasn't just a dog to me. He was the baby I lost; he was the husband I never had; he was the friend I never had. Don't you say he was just a dog, Gran. He had more consideration for me than anybody else in my life. "

"Aw, lass, that isn't fair. You're not thinkin' of me or Georgie when you're sayin' that. Well now, come on. Come on. Put him down."

"No, no, I'll not put him down."

I wasn't surprised when she walked straight out. When presently she came back, she said, "Let me hold him while you drink this cup of tea."

"No, no. I can manage."

But when I lifted my arm from him to take the cup, he slipped gently from my hold and on to the rug again.

I found myself gulping at the tea because it was the first drink I'd had that day.

During the following half-hour, Gran kept walking from the sitting-room into the hall and back, in and out, in and out. And then, when the bell rang, she hurried to the door, and the next minute there was Doctor Kane looking down on me. So that's what she had done. Well, what could he do for Bill? Nobody could do anything for Bill now. I said that to him. Looking up at him, I said, "You can't do anything for him."

"No, I know that, but I can do something for you. Come on, get to your feet."

"No, no."

"Maisie. Look, behave yourself." He was talking to me as if I was a child, and now he gripped me by the arm and hauled me up. Then pointing down to Bill, he said, "You've got two choices: one, he goes to the vet and they'll dispose of him; two, we bury him in the garden." And now his voice softened and he said, "In that way you can make a little grave and you can tend him every day. What is it to be, he goes to the vet?"

"*No! no! no!*"

"All right then, let's see about it."

I wrapped Bill in his rug and laid him in a large packing case I'd brought down from the attic. I put his rubber bone and his toys by his side, and when that was done, the doctor forced me to close the lid. He himself dug the hole at the bottom of the garden. I realized, even as I watched him, that he wasn't used to digging, but when I went to help, he thrust me aside. Although it was an icy cold day the sweat was dripping from his beard.

It took us all our time to lift the case down the garden, even with

Gran helping, and when it was in the hole and covered over, he had to pull me away back into the house.

Gran made more tea, and I sat staring into the fire, the tears raining unheeded down my face.

"So it's come," he said. He was holding out my book to me. That morning I had received the six free copies that I was told were allotted to every writer on publication. His voice held an excited note as he said, "It's a splendid cover, isn't it? A horse sitting at a table, its forelegs crossed on it-" and he chuckled as he added, "as if he was talking to you. And I suppose that's you sitting at the other side. It isn't unlike you, you know."

There was a pause, and now he was reading aloud from the back cover of the book.

"This is a funny book. It will make you laugh. But there are places where it may make you cry, because many will identify with the woman in this book who is so lost and lonely that she conjured up a horse and clothed it with flesh and bone until it became real. And this story tells what happened to Rosie and Hamilton. Take it to bed with you, but don't expect to sleep. "

Nardy had written that. They called it a blurb.

"Aren't you proud of yourself?"

I looked up at him and said simply, "It doesn't matter."

"Don't be silly, woman. Look, you'll get another dog. In fact I know where there's some pup. . ."

"*I don't want another dog. Bill wasn't just a dog.*"

"*Bill was a dog.*" He was shouting as loudly as I had done.

"All right he was a good companion, but nevertheless he was a dog . . . an animal. What you've got to do now, Maisie, is to concentrate on human beings."

"I've never found any worth concentrating on."

"Thank you." His voice dropped now, and when he added "Thank you very much," I put my hand to my head and stood up and whimpered, "I'm sorry. I'm sorry. I didn't mean that. But can't you see, I'm . . . I'm so distressed."

"Yes, yes." His voice was soothing now. "But you will soon have other things to think about that will certainly take your mind off Bill. I happened to meet Mr Pearson this morning and he thinks your case will come up early in the New Year, and you will be charged with grievous bodily harm, and from what I gather, your husband is going to sue you for everything that he can think of with regard to the damage you've done him. He's suffering headaches, impaired memory, loss of work, facial scarring, et cetera, et cetera. But, as I understand, you would have to take his cap off to see the evidence of the last. Anyway, as I see it, he knows he stands no chance of getting the house, but he does stand a chance of making you pay so much compensation that you would likely have to sell it. Now think on that."

I couldn't think on it, not then, I could only think of Bill lying out there in the cold ground.

I started to cry again, and he left me, saying, "It will do you no harm to cry it out."

But when the following day Gran came and found me still crying, there he was again, in the bedroom this time, and he stuck a needle into me and I went to sleep, and slept for two days, and when I eventually woke up fully I knew that tears would not bring Bill back, but that I would carry the weight of him in my memory forever.

Chapter 7

My case came up in February. It was to extend over two days and I returned home after the first day slightly stunned and very apprehensive.

Nardy was with me, as were George and the doctor, and no sooner had we got indoors than George demanded of Nardy, "What did she need a bloody counsel for? What did he do? When that swine was on the stand, he treated him as if he was defending him, not against him." And Nardy said quietly, "Wait until tomorrow; he'll spring a lot of surprises tomorrow."

"He'll bloody well need to. To my mind the defence and the prosecutin' counsels should change places 'cos that fellow Taggart had some force. . ."

"Wind."

George turned to the doctor, who repeated, "Wind. As Mr Leviston says, wait until tomorrow, and there'll be a lot of surprises all round; even you might get one."

"That'll be the day when anythin' surprises me, Doctor."

"And stranger things have happened, George. Well, I must be off."
He turned to me and stood looking at me for a moment quietly, before
he said, "This time tomorrow it'll be all in the past."

"One way or another," I said.

"Yes, as you say, Maisie, one way or another. But don't forget
Hamilton."

He now nodded towards Nardy, saying, "See you sometime
tomorrow. "

"Yes, Doctor."

George now turned to me and said, "Aye, what's this about this
thing called Hamilton? We got in court late, an' just heard the last bit
on it." Then changing his tone, George bent over me, saying, "I just had
to be here, Maisie. We set off last night. It was a hell of a journey. We
stopped for three hours on a lay-by, and the bairns were nearly frozen
in that van."

"Serves you damn well right." This was from Gran as, coming from
the dining-room, she passed us on her way to the kitchen. "Whoever
thought of packing four bairns into that thing in weather like this."

"Well, what did you expect me to do? Leave them there?"

"Yes, yes."

"Aw, Ma." He followed her now to the kitchen, saying, "I didn't
know how long I was gona be here. And Mary doesn't like to be left on
her own."

"Did you ever hear the like?" The voices faded away as I walked
with Nardy into the sitting-room, and there he smiled at me, saying,
"You get your characters dead on. He's exactly like you portrayed him
in the book."

"He won't recognize himself." I smiled wearily at him.

"Oh, I don't know. I think there's quite a bit of sense behind that
blustery manner, and a very big heart. The children, are they his?"

"No."

"Well, it's as I said, he's got a very big heart."

I looked at Nardy. He was so nice to look at: his eyes were always
kind and he had such a nice face. I said, "Thank you for coming up."

"Don't be silly. As if I could stay away. And Bernard will be here
tomorrow. He's delighted with the way the book's going, and that's
before there's any further publicity. The whole house is really on tiptoe,
and when there was an order came in last week for another two
hundred and fifty from one store I understand the packers yelled
hooray."

"They are all very kind."

"They are all very fond of you."

"Only perhaps because I'm . . . well" - I smiled deprecatingly at myself - "because I'm different from the usual type of novelist."

He was leaning forward as he said slowly, "And let me say that in some cases that's a very good thing, and right through the house, they are not slow to recognize it. As I've said before, first novels are often very heady medicine to some people. How's the second one going?"

"I'm stuck, and will be until . . . well, until I know what's going to happen. Nardy" - I caught hold of his hand now - "it's right what George said: Mr Collins didn't seem to make any impression on anyone, and when he started putting words into Howard's mouth, like him having compassion for me all these years and being very worried about my mental state, well, I couldn't . . . well really, I don't know what he's up to."

He now pressed my hand tightly, saying, "Maisie, if we knew what these fellows were up to, there wouldn't be any cases for defence counsels, the matter would be simple and we would defend ourselves. Some people try, and a few manage to come out on top. But it's a very tricky business. Counsels such as Mr Collins are devious men. They've got to be. They're actors: in fact, you could say they're con men because they con those in the stand to make liars of themselves, as you will find out tomorrow. I'm not in the least perturbed that our Mr Collins appeared to be a soft touch. And from what I've heard about him, he is a very clever defence counsel, and in this case the right man for the right job. You'll see, tomorrow. He'll make your husband eat the words that he has spoken today about his consideration for you; about the facts of his taking up with another woman mainly because you refused him your bed; how he tried to get you interested in outside games such as tennis. Oh my! Maisie" - he pulled a face at me now - "wait till tomorrow."

At this point Gran came bursting into the room, saying, "Well, there's a meal ready such as it is in the dining-room, lass." Then looking at Nardy, she said, "It'll likely be nothin' what you're used to, but the parts of you it doesn't fatten, it'll fill up. An' what do you think of that stupid bug . . . big lump of nothin' out there?" She jerked her head towards the door. "Bringing his woman and four bairns!"

I stopped her. "Don't call her his woman, Gran, it maddens him, she's his wife."

"Aye, well, here he is landed, as you say, with his wife and her four bairns. And where, may I ask, are they going to sleep the night? In that covered wagon that looks as if it had come out of the films, an' been half across America an' through the gold rush an' all? It's a wonder those bairns are alive, havin' slept in that."

"Well, Gran" - I was walking towards the door now - "as you say,

they can't sleep in that tonight. So where do you propose they should
sleep?"

"You tell me where I'm going to put six of 'em. I ask you. He said he
and the lads would sleep in the van if her and the lasses can sleep in
my place. But there's only a single bed in that back room. And,
anyway, it's never been used for years."

"Gran." I caught hold of her arm and endeavoured not to look at
Nardy who was standing behind her, his head bowed as he tried to
suppress his laughter. He had become very fond of Gran. "Gran," I
said slowly, "there are four empty rooms upstairs; they haven't been
put to use for a long time. They can all come here."

"You must be up the pole. Once you get them in, you'll never get
them out."

"That'll be nice because I like them, I like them all, especially Betty."
Betty was fifteen and seemed to have a sweet disposition. "And I could
do with some company. And, don't let us forget" - I bent my face down
towards hers now - "the house might need a caretaker for some time
from now on."

"Aw, lass" - she backed from me, her face trembling - "don't say
that. Just don't say it. If that happened it would put the tin hat on
everythin'. You've knocked the stuffing out of me for enjoyment over
the past weeks, but if you went along the line . . . oh, my God!" She
almost rushed into the hall now, her head wagging, saying, "I
shouldn't have this worry, not at my time of life."

Nardy, his head still bent, took my arm now, saying, "Come on, and
let us get through that which doesn't fatten but fills up."

I let myself be led towards the dining-room, thinking as I went. He's
wonderful; he can adapt to anyone and any place. But then, gentlemen
usually could. And for a moment a weight lifted from my heart and I
thought that, no matter what happened tomorrow, if I did go along the
line, as Gran had said, he'd be there when I came out.

Chapter 8

The court-room was crowded, but from where I sat in the dock I could see the whole court. There below me was my counsel, Mr Collins, and next to him sat Mr Pearson; in a balcony to the left were seated the doctor and Nardy and Mr Houseman, and behind them were George and Gran and Father Mackin; and seated at the end of a row was Mrs Maddison who only that morning had done my face up. That had been Gran's idea. And vaguely, seated at the back of the public gallery, I took in known faces from the terrace as I'd seen them last night from behind their curtains when I returned home after my counsel had got my bail extended.

The reports in the city papers last night had been relegated to inside pages. One such said: Husband emphatically denies ever being cruel to wife. Another: Patient husband had to recognize that she was mentally unstable when he discovered she was talking to a horse that wasn't there, and her instability was emphasized when she attacked him with his precious collection of bottles, cutting his head in several places.

The only report that seemed anywhere near the truth was: The policeman said the accused didn't actually hit him with a bottle; it bounced off the stone wall and struck his head while he was attending to the prostrate man.

Across the far side of the court sat Howard. He was quietly but sprucely dressed, as always. He had half turned towards me as I entered the dock, brought up from below by a policeman and, at first, his expression, I saw, was one of pained injury. Then, his eyes fully on me, his face underwent such a quick change one could imagine he had been prodded with a pin . . . or my elbow. And certainly, my appearance must have prodded him, for yesterday I had come into court drably dressed, wearing a grey coat, a grey felt hat, and no make-up. Now, this morning, I had on my London rig-out - this, on the advice of my counsel and a suggestion of Nardy's, and I knew I had literally turned the heads of those people who had been here yesterday.

When the judge entered we all stood up, and when we were seated his eyes came to rest on me, and I think it was a few seconds before he connected me with the accused who had come before him yesterday.

So the second day began. My heart was beating so rapidly at times that the noise of it seemed to shut out the voices and the legal jargon that was going on to the side of me. And when someone said, "Will Mrs Stickle take the stand?" the policeman had to assist me to rise, and guide me out of the dock and down the side of the court, past Howard and into the witness-box, where I seemed to be standing eye to eye with the judge.

The prosecuting counsel was a huge man. He had a round face and heavy-lidded eyes. He had the habit of moving one lip over the other before asking a question. "You are Mrs Maisie Stickle?" he said.

"Yes." Of course he knew I was Mrs Stickle. It seemed all a waste of time.

"And you live at 7, Wellenmore Terrace, Fellburn?"

"Yes."

"You have been married to Mr Howard Stickle for thirteen years?"

"Yes."

"How would you describe your married life?"

"Hell."

There was a slight rustling in the court; then everything went quiet.

"Would you deny that your husband swore yesterday, where you are standing now, that he was most kind and considerate towards you?"

"I would emphatically. He was never. . ."

"Please answer yes or no. I will repeat the question: Would you deny that yesterday your husband stood where you are standing now and under oath swore that he was most kind and considerate towards you?"

"No, I wouldn't deny that he stood here and said that, but I would deny that it was the truth and. . ."

"I would be obliged if you would answer yes or no, to my questions. "

"One could not answer yes or no to the way you phrased that question, sir.

I heard a lot of clearing of throats from the people sitting in the first two rows now.

Then the judge's voice broke in, saying, "The defendant has a point there, Mr Taggart, if you have time to analyse it."

And Mr Taggart replied, "I'm obliged to your lordship." Then he turned towards me again. His expression had altered slightly. I saw him draw in a sharp breath now before he said, "Is it true that you are in the habit of addressing a horse?"

"Yes."

"And that you have been doing it for some long while?"

"Yes."

"Do you not consider it an odd habit for a grown woman to converse with a horse . . . an imaginary horse?"

"Not when the horse is as sensible as Hamilton."

I felt a stir going through the court, but for some strange reason all fear had left me. Perhaps it was because there he actually was, sitting up on the bench next to the judge, leaning forward, his forefeet crossed in front of him, his whole attitude one of attention.

The counsel now took three steps away from me and picked up some papers from a table to the side, and I recognized them as the discarded sheets that Howard had stuck together and waved in my face. And he looked at me before he began to read, saying, "Would you consider this sensible conversation, or at least sensible talk? From what I gather you and the horse are in church and you go on to say here -" He now began to read: "Hamilton left the pew, genuflected deeply, walked up the altar steps and stood by Father Mackin, and before the priest had time to raise his hand, Hamilton gave the blessing, saying, 'As it was in the beginning, is *not* now and *never* shall be.'"

When the judge's hammer banged on the bench the laughter faded away and counsel stared up at me as his hand gently waved the patched sheets backward and forward.

Now I knew this was the opening that my counsel said would come and I took it. "Oh, that!" I said airily. "That was a funny part of the second book."

My answer brought counsel's eyes wide and there was almost a look of triumphant glee on his face. I could almost read his thoughts: I had won his case out of my own mouth.

He leant towards me. "You have written a book about the horse?"

"Yes, about the horse called Hamilton."

"Well, now. Well now. Correct me," he said, "if I'm mistaken. Isn't there a book already achieving some success with a title of that very name?"

I let a long pause elapse before I said, "Yes."

"And" - his thick lips moved one over the other before he went on - "you said you had written a book, a similar book about a similar horse?"

"No, about the same one."

"Now, now, Mrs Stickle."

"My name is not only Mrs Stickle, it is Miriam Carter."

"Oh. Oh, yes, I remember, that is the name of the author of the book about the horse called Hamilton. And you are Miriam Carter?"

"Yes, I am Miriam Carter."

There was a great stir in the court. I kept my eyes on the counsel, but I felt the rustling and the moving of people. Then the counsel left me for a moment and went to the bench and said something to the judge, and the judge looked towards me. Then he spoke to me and there was behind his question another question: Was I or was I not the person I was saying? Because I'm sure he was remembering me from yesterday and today I certainly didn't look like the Mrs Stickle of yesterday because she possibly could have been a little deranged in her mind. What he said to me was, "Have you any authority for that statement, Mrs Stickle, that you are the author of the book *Hamilton*?"

"Yes my Lord. My publishers are present, Mr Houseman and Mr Leviston."

I pointed, and all eyes turned on Mr Houseman and Nardy.

I saw my counsel go up to the bench now, where the prosecuting counsel was still standing, and he spoke to the judge who was leaning forward, and then to the prosecuting counsel, whom I noticed held the palm of his hand to the front of his wig for a moment. Then I saw him talk rapidly to my counsel before returning to me. And now the oily smooth look had gone entirely from his face. It was flushed and his lips were working at speed, and he began, "Well, it is established that you have written a book on what appears your pet hobby of talking to a horse, but as I see it, this only goes to prove that you were of a deceitful and unbalanced. . ."

My counsel was protesting strongly now, and the judge, speaking to the prosecuting counsel, said, "Objection sustained."

"Well, I shall rephrase my question." And he did, saying, "Was it the action of an ordinary thinking person to make out that she was a null, ill-treated, poor little woman, while at the same time having the intelligence to write a novel that seems set, to use the common term, to become a bestseller?"

"If, as you say, sir, it takes intelligence to write, then my intelligence goes back to when I was a child because I have always written bits and pieces, and all I did last year with my bits and pieces was to compile them."

He stared at me in hostility for a moment, then said, "And when your husband found out what you were doing, you became so enraged that you attacked him, not with your hands but with implements, glass implements, heavy bottles, and occasioned him such bodily harm that he will never again be the man he was."

"If that is the case, sir, there can be nothing but improvement."

"Madam. "

I turned to the judge who was speaking to me now. His face straight, he said, "Kindly endeavour to keep your answers brief."

The counsel was at me again. "Then you admit to attacking your husband?" he said.

"Objection." My counsel was standing again; and this time the judge said, "Objection overruled."

"Did you or did you not throw a number of bottles at your husband?"

"I did."

"With the intention of maiming him?"

"No."

"What then?"

Of a sudden my throat was tight, I was seeing back down the years, and my voice came out now as a sort of whimper as I said, "In retaliation for years of humiliation and fear, and because he kicked my dog who was ill, dying."

The counsel stepped back from me. He looked at me almost like Howard used to. I stood with my head bowed as I listened to him speaking to the jury, telling them they had been listening to a devious woman. Could anyone imagine looking at her and listening to her that she had been made null and was browbeaten? Wasn't the boot on the other foot? Hadn't they listened to her husband yesterday, a quiet sensitive man? And could they imagine him kicking a dying dog? They must not forget that here was a woman who used her imagination.

I was saying, Oh, my God. Oh, my God, inside myself when the voice of my counsel came to me, "Tell me, Mrs Stickle, what were you doing about a quarter to one on the day in question?"

I again swallowed deeply before I said, "Typing, in my study."

"What were you typing?"

"I was doing an article for a member of the Writers' Circle."

"What did you happen to have on your desk at the side of your typewriter?"

"A little tape recorder."

"And what did you use this tape recorder for?"

"For making notes."

"What kind of notes."

"Well, funny little things I might think of to put in my book, because I couldn't always remember them later."

"And you had just stopped typing and switched it on to record something when the door burst open?"

This was a piece of invention advised by my counsel.

"Yes."

"And your husband came into the room?"

"Yes."

"What did he say to you?"

"He . . . he told me how he was at last going to get my house, by making me out to be of unsound mind because he had found pieces of my writing in the wastepaper basket."

"Could you remember everything word for word?"

"No, but the tape was running and everything he said went down."

My counsel turned from me, and now he went to the table and picked up my tape recorder and, taking it to the bench, he spoke to the judge.

The prosecuting counsel was standing once again beside him and there seemed to be some slight argument. Then the judge said, "We will hear the tape."

At this my counsel said, "It isn't very loud, my lord, as it is only a pocket tape recorder, but I have brought an attachment that will make it much clearer. . . With your permission."

He went back to the table and opened his case; then returned to the bench and, placing my tape recorder on it, he attached a sort of amplifier to it.

Then my voice filled the court, saying, "If anything happens to Bill, I don't know what I'll do. Gran says I should get another dog straightaway, but I'll never have another dog. There'll never be another one like Bill. I've felt lost when I've had him, but that will be nothing to what I'll feel when he goes."

There was a silence now. Then as Howard's voice burst into the court-room, I saw him swivel round towards me and the look on his face was similar to that which it had held when he had first spurted the words at me.

"Well now, little Maisie, so you've been snooping around, eh? And what did you find, eh? Nothing. You just had to take the word of your friends, hadn't you? You've had nice little journeys out there on Saturdays and Sundays, haven't you, Maisie? You think you've got me where you want me now, don't you? But what proof have you? None whatever. I was visiting a friend the day Maggie Talbot happened to come to the door. My friend's name is Mrs Ribber, and her two boys are called Ribber. No, Maisie, you've got nothing on me, but by God, I've got something on you. Something that, if it doesn't fix you for good, it'll prove that you are in need of psychiatric treatment and should be put away for a time. And while you're away, I'll have to have someone to look after me, won't I? So I'll bring in a housekeeper, all very proper, and who better than Mrs Ribber and her two boys. And should you ever come out of wherever they send you, you'll have to have someone to carry on looking after you, won't you, Maisie? And Mrs Ribber will see to it, and I will see to it, for as long as you care to stay. Do you understand me, Maisie?"

"You can't do anything like that, as much as you would like to. I have my doctor and. . ."

"But has he seen these, Maisie? . . . This is just a sample. I've got dozens of them, telling about a woman who's so barmy she talks to a horse that crawls around this house and gets on buses with her and goes into the supermarket and stands on its hind legs in indignation when it sees women shop-lifting. Oh, Maisie, Maisie, what have you put into my hands, eh? Well now, can we come to terms, eh? Will I have to have you exposed and put away, at least for a time in order to bring my wife. . . And yes, she is my wife. And if you hadn't been mental you would have suspected something long ago. What did you think I got the seven hundred and fifty out of you for? To give to old Hempies in order to become manager? Huh! I wouldn't give that old sod the smoke that goes up the chimney. As for him inviting me for the weekends there. . . Eeh! God, when you swallowed that, I realized you'd swallow anything. No, that money went to buy the cottage. And the rest of your four thousand to get my first car and add a bit on to the end of the house. Oh, anybody that wasn't mental would have seen through it years ago. But you are, aren't you? You're bats. You've not got one scrap of brain, except to copy what other people think, and any idiot can do that, any idiot. And write down your madness. Well now, am I to expose you, or are you going to sit quiet and let me bring in her and the boys? It's up to you, because, let me tell you this, I'll have this house in the end. May persuaded me to marry you in order to get it and get it I will, because by God, I've bloody well worked for it. Just seeing you day after day has been a heavy mortgage. Now I'll give you till this evening to make up your mind, no longer, then I'm going to the doctor. And, by the way, for some time now I've taken the precaution to mention your oddities to him. I've also said you've denied me your bed for the past ten years or more. Huh! and by the way, I can tell you this, that you can thank my woman on that score, because without her, by God! I would have taken it out of your limbs. What I did to you in the beginning would have been nothing to what I would have done if I hadn't had her. Anyway, there it is."

When there sounded on the tape a little click which was the door closing, there was silence in the court. It was like the silence that follows a marvellous play or concert. Then the noise became almost deafening and the judge had to bang his hammer three times before the last voice faded away and he said, "Any more of this and the court will be cleared."

Now, he turned to me where I was standing, but standing with an effort for my legs felt like jelly, and in the complete silence he and I looked at each other. And then he began to speak, partly to me and partly it seemed to the jury. "I see before me," he said, "a woman who has been physically handicapped since she was a child. I see before me an intelligent woman, whose intelligence was battened down by circumstances of her life, and she became so lonely that she resorted to fantasy in order to gain a friend. And for a friend who does she pick but a noble animal, a horse." He paused here; then went on, "I think that if a priest was attempting to explain her choice of a friend in whom she could confide, he would, in my opinion, say that she had been really communicating with her spirit. Or on the other hand, if an atheist was endeavouring to explain it he would say she was communing with the 'I' in her . . . the 'I' that is in each one of us."

Again he paused, but his eyes never left my face; then he went on, "Now, if it was Rabindranath Tagore or - say - Sai Baba, either of these Indian mystics, they would undoubtedly put the name of soul to Hamilton, but with whatever name you care to explain her friend, she was I think . . . no, I am sure, communing with her better and wiser self. And who among us, except the utter fools, do not at some time have the sense to look deep inside ourselves and find that small spark which is really the core of all that is in us. This thing that never lies.

"So, as I see it, far from Hamilton being the evidence of a disordered mind, I would say he is proof of a deep spirituality, which" - he paused now and shook his head - "I'm afraid must for a short time have deserted her when she resorted to an old-fashioned ginger beer bottle as an implement of retaliation for what she says she had suffered from both the hands and the tongue of her husband for thirteen years. And her husband has just, for all to hear, endorsed her statement." He paused a long moment here and his eyes turned from me and moved to the jury, and he went on, "You will, I know, judge this woman as your minds direct, but I would point out to you . . . and the press, who will no doubt make tonight's headlines out of this case, that it is nothing new for the human mind to take an animal into its consciousness and to talk to it, because, while being unique, we are nevertheless lonely creatures at best, and I feel it was the deep awareness of this knowledge that prompted an eminent American doctor to write a book called, *Feeling Fine*. This book states it is a twenty-day programme of pleasure for a lifetime of health, and I can vouch that if you read it and follow the advice therein, you cannot but help feel better. By the way, the doctor author himself talks to a rabbit, called Corky, and in doing so, taps his inner wisdom. And, I may add at this point, this particular doctor is not considered to be mad. They don't usually give great lengths of television time in the U.S. to madmen. I myself enjoyed reading this book because it confirmed in my mind that I wasn't any different from the rest of youth when from five to fourteen years old I talked to a she-wolfhound.

"But when my father remarried, after being a widower for seven years, I didn't need my canine friend any more. And I don't think after this Mrs Stickle will have further need of Hamilton, except as a subject for her books."

Did he smile at her? The muscles of his face moved. But then I could hardly see him. Somebody said, "Stand down." Somebody else led me into the dock again. I knew the Doctor and Gran and George and Nardy and others were all looking towards me, yet I couldn't distinguish their faces.

The jury was out for only fifteen minutes. The man at the end stood up and when he was asked, "Do you find the accused, guilty or not guilty?" He said, "Not guilty, on all counts."

Again the judge's hammer banged on the bench. And now he was speaking to me, "Mrs Stickle," he said, "you have been found not guilty. But you did cause what's called an affray. May I suggest that in future you rely more on your spiritual self to guide your behaviour." And now he smiled quite broadly.

I had seen the devil in Howard when he stood looking at me over the desk that fateful day, fateful for him, but that look was nothing to the expression on his face as he turned and looked at me across the court-room before his solicitor took his arm and almost pulled him up the aisle.

Then Father Mackin pushed his way towards me, and he said, "I'm happy for you. Yes, I am, but there's no getting away from it, you are a dark horse." This caused general laughter, until he said, "As it was in the beginning, is not now, and never shall be. Well, there's a lot of truth in that, and more's the pity." Then almost whispering in my ear, he said, "We're very tolerant people, we R.C.'s, and we laugh at ourselves until we bust, but we don't take too kindly to it coming from the outside. So, why don't you bring your horse into our stable, eh?"

I laughed and he laughed as I was tugged away. He'd never let up, would Father Mackin. But I liked him. And after all, it was he who had sparked off the idea of making Hamilton into a book. I must tell him that next time I see him, I thought.

It was only through the efforts and protection of the men around me that I got through the crowd of reporters and clicking cameras outside the court-room. And then I was home. We were all home, and Gran was hugging me, and George's Mary was hugging me, and the children were jumping about, and everybody was talking and all seemingly at once. Then George's voice rose above the rest and he, with his big hands under my oxters, lifted me up off the floor, crying, "A bloody novelist of all things! I knew you had it in you. Eeh! But I couldn't believe it. Eeh, by! but I was proud of you. You showed 'em. By! you showed 'em."

"Shut up you! An' put her down. An' look," Gran cried; "get yourselves into the sitting-room. There's something in there to wet your whistles, and I'll bring the tea in in a minute."

And there was something in the sitting-room to wet the whistles: two bottles of whisky, a bottle of sherry, and a bottle of port. It crossed my mind that it wouldn't have gone to waste if I hadn't come home.

George did the honours and they all drank to me: The doctor, Mr Houseman, George and Nardy, Gran and Mary, and I still continued to cry even while I was smiling.

About half an hour later, Doctor Kane said he would have to go as he had a surgery and that fool of a partner of his would be killing the patients off two at a time. He was very fond of his partner, I knew that.

I walked with him to the door and I held his hands, and when he leant forward and his bushy face came close to mine, closer than ever it had been before, and he kissed me, I put my arms around him and said, "Thank you, my dear Doctor, thank you for giving me Hamilton."

"Oh my God!" He pushed me away from him. "Don't you lay the blame on me for him." Then he said softly, "You know what I would like to do?"

"No?"

"I'd like to bring the wife around later on if I may?"

"Oh, I'd love that. I've never met her. Oh, I'd love that."

"And you'll love her; she's a canny lass."

When he was gone, Mr Houseman followed, but not before telling me that my book would have runaway sales from now on. When Nardy said he would see him to the station, I was surprised, yet so pleased he wasn't returning to London until tomorrow. He said he had some unfinished business to attend to.

When they had gone, I said to George, Mary, and Gran, "Nardy's coming back, and you know what? The doctor's bringing his wife round tonight."

"Oh, my God!" said Gran, getting up. "The doctor's wife? Eeh! that'll mean we'll have to get somethin' in, bits and pieces to make sandwiches an' such." And at this she hurried out of the room, saying to Mary, "Come on, lass, get your coat on. We'll have to do a bit of shoppin'."

Left with George, we sat close together on the couch, and quietly now he said, "Well, it's over, lass. Your purgatory's over."

"Yes, George, my purgatory is over."

"You're puttin' in for a divorce?"

"That's already in hand."

"Well, with what's happened these last few days, it shouldn't take long. By the way, he's a nice fellow, that Nardy."

"Yes, he is."

"You like him, don't you?"

"Yes, I like him."

"He likes you."

I turned and looked at him as I said, "Yes, I know he likes me. But he's a bachelor of forty-five, and settled in his ways. Moreover, he's a gentleman. So, we both like each other and that is as far as it will go."

"You never know. No, you never know where a blister might light."

"Oh, George. I'll tell you whom I more than like."

"Who?"

"You."

"Aw, lass." He put his arms around me and hugged me.

He seemed to have his arms still around me at ten o'clock that night, when with the doctor and his wife Jane, Nardy, Gran and Mary, he sat singing, "Now Is The Hour", an old Gracie Fields song, and we were all joining in. It was past eleven o'clock and the drinks had been flowing from shortly after eight. We were all very merry. There had been another addition to the company earlier on, for my solicitor, Mr Pearson, called in. He had congratulated me, and everybody had congratulated him on his choice of counsel, and when he had left me an hour ago, there was no sign of the formal man I had come to know. Three large whiskies had, in George's words, slackened his face.

The doctor had added to the liquor store a bottle of brandy and a bottle of whisky, and Nardy had gone out with George and returned with bottles of beer and more spirits.

What not only I but the whole company had discovered in the last few hours was that Nardy had a beautiful tenor voice. Apparently, from what I remember him saying to the Doctor, he had been at a sort of choir school in his youth and had been weaned on the usual "O For The Wings Of A Dove".

George was now crying towards him, "Come on, let's have another one of them ballads! It's a night for sweetness an' light."

These last two words, sweetness and light, said in George's broad Geordie twang, sent the whole company roaring. And Gran, thumping her son on the side of the head, cried, "Did you ever! Him comin' out with things like that, sweetness an' light."

Nardy was on his feet now: standing with his back to the fire, his face was flushed, his eyes were bright. He had, I had noticed, drunk as much as anyone there, yet seemed the least affected by it. He didn't sway on his feet, nor was his voice fuddled, as was the doctor's when he cried, "'I Hear You Calling Me,' or 'Love, Could I Only Tell You?' They're lovely. They're lovely."

Before anyone could answer, Nardy said, "Let it be this one."

I hadn't drunk anything near the quantity that the others had imbibed because I was wanting to remember every detail of this night. I'd had two sherries and I was glad at this moment that the emotion that Nardy's voice created in me did not come about through spirits. His voice was clear and warm, the cadences rising and falling, and his eyes were fixed on me as he sang:

> "One day when we were young,
> One wonderful morning in May.
> You told me you loved me,
> When we were young one day."

My emotions became almost unbearable. If only he was younger and I was older. If only he did not look upon me just as a friend, a dear, dear, friend. If only I could see him in the same light and not as I did. If only . . . if only.

> "Remember, you loved me
> When we were young one day."

He was looking at me, his face soft, yet aglow. The tears were streaming down my face, but I was the only one who wasn't shouting his praise and clapping.

"'I Hear You Calling Me'." It was the doctor shouting again. "My mother used to sing that. Go on, Nardy." Everybody called him Nardy now. "Go on, Nardy," he said. "Go on, give us, 'I Hear you Calling Me'."

And so, still standing, he sang,

> "I hear you calling me.
> You called me when the moon had veiled her light
> Before I went from you into the night;
> I came, do you remember, back to you
> For one last kiss beneath the kind star's light."

The beauty and the sweetness and the sadness of his voice was too much. And as he finished drawing out those last four words, "I hear you call----ing me", I could bear it no longer and I went out of the room.

I had broken up the party and I was sorry. The Doctor and his wife came into the hall and he was saying now, "Look at the time. And there they'll be, in the morning, rows and rows of 'em. And where will I be? Stuck in the bathroom with my head under the tap. Isn't that so?" He leant, swaying, towards his wife, and she, putting one arm around his waist, said, "Yes, as you have been so many times before, dear."

And now the doctor turned to Nardy and said, "Where you staying? You staying here?"

"Oh, no, it's a full house here. No, I booked a room in the town."

"Well, come on, we'll take you there."

"I think it would be safer to walk."

"Who you insultin'?"

There was laughter now as the doctor's wife said, "I'll be driving. You'll be safe with me."

There followed the business of putting on coats and of wrapping up, then handshaking all round; and when Nardy took my hands, he bent towards me, saying, "Get yourself out first thing tomorrow and try to find some summer dresses. You'll need them."

"Need summer dresses -" I screwed my face up as I ended, "In February?"

"It won't be February where you're going, miss. It's all settled. At least it will be in the morning. Remember what Rosie did at the end of your book?"

Yes, of course I remembered what Rosie did at the end of my book. We had discussed it before. She went on a cruise.

I didn't answer him, and he said, "Well, that's where you are going shortly. We'll see that you get your passport in time. And Doctor Kane will jab you."

"What's this? What's this?" George and the doctor and Gran were all speaking at once. And Nardy, opening the front door, turned for a moment and looked at them as he said, "She's going on a month's cruise to the West Indies. Anyway, I'll be round in the morning."

When the door was closed again, George and Gran turned to me, saying, "What's this about a cruise?"

"You know as much about it as I do. And anyway" - I laughed - "I'm going on no cruise: I don't like the sea; I'm always seasick. But where I'm going now is to bed. Will you lock up, George?"

"Aye. Aye, I'll lock up. It's been a wonderful night, hasn't it? The best I remember. Eeh! they're a fine lot of people. And" - his voice dropped - "a wonderful day. Aye, lass, a wonderful day." He gave me a smacking kiss and I turned from him and called to Gran and Mary, "Good-night, Gran. Good-night, Mary." And they answered softly, "Good-night, lass."

Going on a sea cruise? Not me. What did he mean anyway, it was all fixed? Really!

The following morning Nardy was round at the house by half past nine. He showed no signs of a hangover; whereas George was suffering from a severe headache. "That's the bloody spirits," he had informed me when he staggered downstairs. "I should have stuck to beer. I've never felt like this in me life afore, even after I've had a skinful. Have I, Ma?"

"Of course you have," replied Gran. "There's times when you haven't seen daylight until the bars opened again."

Gran and George tactfully left me alone with Nardy in the sitting-room, and immediately I said to him, "I haven't got a hangover and I remember clearly your last words to me, that I had to buy a summer rig-out, dresses you said, for a cruise."

"Yes" - he nodded at me - "you're right. I haven't got a hangover either, and those were my very words: You're going on a cruise."

"Oh, no."

"Oh, yes, Maisie." He now pulled me down to the couch, saying, "From now on, for weeks ahead you will be eaten alive by reporters and all their kin: Smart ladies from magazines asking you to tell the world how you began to write; feminist women wanting your opinion on man and his subtleties. After yesterday's business you'd be eaten alive. Just go to the window now, my dear, and you'll see three men at different points along the railing bordering the field."

"No."

"Yes."

"But I've got no need to go on a cruise to get away from them; I can go on a holiday anywhere in England."

"Maisie, your picture has been splashed over all the morning papers. Every word that came over on the tape, every word that the judge said. And my word, he did say some words, didn't he?" He grinned at me now. "And all kindly. So you'd be recognized in any hotel the length and breadth of the country, unless you went and hid in the Welsh hills or in the depths of Cumbria. No; I thought about this some time ago, and I have a friend who runs a travel agency. I put the situation to him and they had a cancellation and he held it until last night to see how things went in court. And so my dear, you're booked on the *Oriana*, sorry! not the *QE2*, heading for Madeira and then the Caribbean islands. But in the meantime you'll be staying with a friend of mine in Carlisle."

"Oh, Nardy." I sat back against the end of the couch and, like a child now, I said, "But what will I do on board ship? I won't know anybody."

"Everybody knows everybody within the first few days on a cruise."

"Well, if that's the case, won't they know as much about me there as they would on dry land?"

"No, not really. People who are going on cruises are so taken up with excitement for days ahead that half of them haven't time to read the newspapers. And if the other half do and you're recognized, well, my dear, you've got to get used to being a celebrity, and making friends."

"Celebrity my foot. Here, I've got Gran, and perhaps George and his family because Gran tell me George doesn't want to go back to the West Country and is going to try and get a job here again. And then I have my trips to London." I now pulled a face at him. "But on board ship, how will I spend my days?"

"You'd be surprised."

I stood up and walked to the fire and, my forearm resting on the mantelpiece, I looked down into the flames, and his voice came to me quietly, saying, "You need a change. You need to get away from this house for a time and all the memories it contains. "

I knew he was right, I did need a change. And I needed to get away from this house. This house that was totally mine now had of a sudden taken on the appearance of a cage, a cage I had made for myself and was afraid to leave.

I turned towards him, saying, "I'd be terribly seasick."

"I'll see to that. I'll get some special pills."

"A month's time you say?"

"Yes, a month's time. You'll sail on Saturday. That's four weeks including today, so you'll have to get cracking."

"I'll have to close up the house."

"I'd thought about that. But you've just said that George would like to come back to the north again. Why not let them stay on here the time you're away, and he can look around. And these friends that you are going to, they're an old couple. Anne is my mother's cousin - you'll like her, and the house in the country."

"You think of everything, don't you?" I know my tone sounded a little terse, but then I was feeling a little terse, because this friend of mine, this dear, dear friend of mine was quite willing that I should go on a month's cruise and meet lots of other people. It signified something in my mind that I didn't like. Then he rose from the couch and came towards me and, holding my hands, he said, "I must tell you that after I get you settled at Anne's I won't be able to see you for a while, in fact, I don't think I shall be on the dock to wave you off."

"You won't?"

"No, I won't. You see" - he put his head to one side then bit his lip - "I . . . I have a little business. Well, not a little business; it's quite a big event in my life and it happens to fall on that same Saturday. But once I get back to town today I'll get cracking on those tickets and, of course, your passport. You'll have to fill in a form, but with a little prodding you should have it back well in time.

I stared at him. There was a big hurt inside me which all the good things that had happened to me of late couldn't soothe. I was soon to be divorced from that man; I had my house; I was acknowledged as a writer; but here was my dear friend telling me he couldn't come and see me off on a trip he had planned for me because he had other business on that day. When he took my hand and pressed it to his lips it meant nothing.

"Happy days, Maisie."

This created no response in me, and he went out of the room.

I knew he had gone into the kitchen to say good-bye to George, Gran and Mary. And I sat down and waited to hear him leave by the front door.

I looked at the clock. He had been in the kitchen over fifteen minutes.

I looked at the clock again. He had been in the kitchen over half an hour.

When at last I heard him leave, I turned and looked towards the door, and there walking through it, of all people or creatures or whatever he was, came Hamilton. And he was doing a slow waltz while singing,

> One day when we were young,
> One wonderful morning in May.
> You told me you loved me,
> When we were young one day.

I turned to the fire again and almost bitterly I said, "For God's sake, go away! Don't start that again. I don't need you any more. I've got Gran and George and Doctor and Mary and the children . . . and the neighbours are all nice to me, and I'm no longer looked upon as some sort of freak. And I'm shortly going on a cruise. Do you hear? a cruise!"

I turned to him as I asked the question; but he was gone, and I felt more lonely and rejected than ever I'd done when I'd lived with Howard.

Chapter 9

How did I manage to come here, sitting in a first-class cabin on the promenade deck of a ship loaded down with people all excited about going to islands where the sun shone all the time and the surrounding sea apparently hadn't any angry waves.

The weeks had passed like a flash. I hadn't gone to Nardy's friends as he had planned; something had made me perverse. It was, I think, all to do with his not coming to see me off after he had arranged to have me sent packing, as I now thought of the trip. I told him that George had offered to be my bodyguard, and would deal with reporters; and to this, all his reaction had been was to laugh and say, "Okay."

Gran and Mary had hustled me here and there, even to getting Peg Maddison to do a long job on me. I hoped her efforts would last during the cruise. She said they would if I followed her advice and applied the five layers as directed. I had found it a time-taking business, making up one's face. I was asking myself now, as I caught a glimpse of my slumped figure in the long mirror in the wardrobe to the side of me, if it was worth it. I guessed I must be the most dejected and reluctant holidaymaker on this ship.

Yet everybody, without exception, had been so kind, and they all praised Nardy for his brainwave, even Mr Pearson saying he thought it was a splendid idea: I had to go off and enjoy myself and not worry about a thing, and they would do their best to rattle my divorce through.

At times during these last few days I'd let my mind dwell on Howard, because the latest retribution he was suffering, I understood, was his dismissal from the shop. Mr Hempies apparently hadn't liked what he had said about him.

Did I feel sorry for him?

No . . . Oh no. I wasn't a fool any longer.

Looking back, I realized I hadn't believed in devils or evil, but my experience had taught me, and painfully, that there were people who were born evil. These people had two distinct personalities, and I felt now that Howard hadn't been alone within this category. I thought back to the days when I sat in the surgery waiting-room and heard snatches of conversation from weary women with regard to the lives they were being forced to lead, just a few words here and there, but so telling if you had the key, and I'd had the key.

I looked around my cabin and I had to admit it was lovely. And all those flowers. One bouquet had come from the doctor and his wife. Oh, he had been so kind. They had both come to Newcastle to see me off, and after I'd been hugged by Gran, Mary, George and the children, the doctor was the last to take my hands as I stood on the steps of the train, and what he said to me was, "I'm sorry, Maisie, I'll never see you sitting in the surgery again."

"Oh" - I managed to laugh - "don't be too sure."

"Well, I can be, at least on one point, it won't be for your old complaint. Now go and enjoy yourself. Life's going to open up for you." Then he reached up to me and his bushy whiskers were tickling my cheek as he whispered, "I'll take care of Hamilton for you; in fact, I'll adopt him."

Oh, the doctor. The doctor. What would I have done without him all these years; his concern, his understanding, all hidden behind that bushy hairy hedge and bullying manner.

When the train had gone round the curve as it went out of the station and I had seen the last of the waving hands, I sat back in that first-class compartment. Yes, Nardy had sent me, among other things, a first-class ticket to Southampton, and I felt more miserable than I'd ever done in my life before. And when eventually I reached the dock and, with the guidance of a porter and a steward, came on board, I think I was the only one on this trip without a friendly face to see me off or a hand to wave good-bye. There was a card attached to the bouquet from Mr Houseman and all in the publishing house wishing me a happy holiday. There was a card attached to another which read very characteristically: 'Live it up lass. George, Gran, Mary and the bairns'.

How does one live it up on one's own? Nardy said I would make a lot of friends on board, but in order to do so I would have to go out there and parade the decks, or go into the recreation room, or the saloon, or the dining-room. . . Well, I'd have to go into the dining-room, wouldn't I?

Oh, dear me. I got up and went to the window. There was the sea stretching away for miles, as yet looking quite smooth. Still standing looking out, my ear picked up the soft, soft hum that could have been the sound of the engines, and I thought for a moment, it will be all right if it keeps like this. But I knew it wouldn't. Anyway, I grabbed at the next thought, if I was seasick that would give me an excuse to stay tight put here in the cabin and be looked after by the steward. He was very nice. He told me he would be caring for me during the journey. He had said it in such a nice way, as if I was somebody special. I had just to ring if I wanted anything, anything at all.

Oh, my, what was I to do?

There came a tap on the door. That would be him.

"Come in," I said. And somebody came in and the door closed.

There he stood with his back to it. The shock was such that I grabbed at my ribs as I thought, Eeh no! It's all right conjuring up a horse, but not people that you miss. I don't think I could have been more surprised if I'd seen Howard standing there.

"Well aren't you going to say anything?"

He came slowly towards me and held out his hand, but I didn't take it. What I did was to flop down into a chair. Then, my voice a squeak, I said something silly: "What are you doing here?" And he answered, "I'm starting a long anticipated holiday in the West Indies. I haven't seen them for ten years."

My voice still a squeak: "Why . . . why had you to do it like this? Upsetting people. I mean . . . well, making me think. . . It wasn't nice; it wasn't fair."

He sat down beside me now, his hands on his knees. And he leant towards me as he said, "It mightn't have been nice for you, but it was fair. What do you think would have been said if I had announced that I was coming on holiday with you? Even if I'd accompanied you to Southampton? As I told you, your face is well-known over the country. Things being what they are, it will be replaced shortly by someone else who has caused a sensation. But there was bound to be reporters on the quay, and I think you've had all the publicity you can stand for a while. So here am I. Here we are. And you don't look very pleased to see me."

"Oh, Nardy; you are a funny man."

"Oh, my dear. Me . . . a funny man? Anyway, are you pleased to see me?"

"Do you need to ask?"

"No; but I do need to ask you something and tell you something, and I think I'd better tell you the something first. And it's just this, Maisie." He now brought my hand up to his cheek as he said softly, "I love you. I love you very much."

No one in my life had ever said they loved me; not one, not even George, and here was this man . . . this gentleman saying these words to me, and meaning them, for the essence of them was in his eyes. There came over me a feeling of emerging, as if I was being born again; I felt my body growing, swelling, pushing out, away beyond this cabin, this ship, this great sea. My mind was singing beautifully but in his voice:

> You told me you loved me,
> When we were young one day.

"Maisie." He was patting my cheek now. "Don't cry, my dear. Oh, please don't cry."

"I love you, Nardy. I've loved you for a long time," I said, as the tears ran from my chin. Then I muttered, "But how can you love me . . . me?" I thumbed myself in the chest. "You could have anybody; you're so . . . so. . . ."

"I don't want anybody, I only want you. I've only loved two women in my life."

My mouth fell open. He had loved before! Of course he had loved before. Don't be such a fool, woman! He's forty-five. Oh, you are a fool.

"We were engaged," he was saying. "It was in '65. A week before our wedding she had a car accident. She didn't die; she lived for eight years, and she never knew anyone again."

"Oh, Nardy."

"It's all in the past. I loved her, and I love you. And perhaps for the same reason" - he smiled softly - "she was a real person and had a great sense of humour . . . Will you marry me, Maisie?"

No words came. I simply threw myself into his arms and howled and howled his name over and over: "Oh! Nardy. Nardy. Oh! Nardy. Nardy."

When for the first time in my life I was really kissed I had the most odd and really ridiculous feeling: I felt beautiful.

Then to cap it all, there *He* came squeezing through the window, and he stood on his hind legs, his mane waving, and his white tail lashing from side to side.

We were standing, Nardy's arms around me, my arms around him when I said, "Will you take on Hamilton an' all?" And when he drew himself up and said in dignified tones, "Of course, I'll take on Hamilton; your people are my people," I answered through choking laughter, "That's a good thing, because he's prancing behind you now with mane and tail flying."

Again we fell against each other, and we laughed until we ached. Then holding me from him, he said, solemnly, "God bless Hamilton." And I said, "Amen to that. Oh yes, amen to that, because without Hamilton I'd never have met you."

GOODBYE
HAMILTON

Chapter 1

The sun was shining; it was a beautiful day; and I was going to be married for the second time. But with what a difference! The first time had been a more than quiet affair in the Registry Office, to a man who, I can truthfully say, tortured me for thirteen years, and who finally tried to prove me insane because I talked to an imaginary horse.

Well, yes, I did talk to an imaginary horse; I talked to him because I was lonely and lost. But I'm not lonely or lost any more. And strangely I haven't seen Hamilton, as I called him, since that day on the ship when Nardy declared his love for me. At times, I've felt he was still there lurking in the background, but he has never put in a real appearance.

It was eight o'clock on the morning of this very special day and I was sitting in the little study room of my house in Fellburn where I wrote *Hamilton*. I say, of my house, but it was to be mine no longer, not as a home, for I was to let my stepfather George Carter and his second wife and her children live here; I was to take up residence, as Nardy put it, in London.

Nardy's is a beautiful house; he was brought up in it, and he loved it in, strangely, the same way that I loved this house. Yet I had no reason to love this house, for I had suffered in it practically since the day I was born. Being of extreme plainness, and having a deformed arm, I was a trial to my mother, then easy prey for the man and his sister who coveted the house and what it held and who could only get it by his taking me on through marriage.

Yet it was the continuous hell experienced in my childhood, my youth, and my womanhood which created that one compensation, Hamilton.

That is not quite true, however, for in George my stepfather, that big ungainly loud-voiced individual, I had a champion; and in his mother also. Oh yes, indeed in Gran, for it was her rough humour that had saved me from utter despair more than once. And then I must not forget my flesh and blood companion, Bill, my bull terrier. How I loved that ugly animal.

And there was one more very important man who came into my life at that time, the doctor, Doctor Mike Kane, brusque, bearded, and grumpy. At first, I disliked him wholeheartedly, then grew to respect and love him. And it was really he who brought Hamilton into being. After my mother had almost disfigured me with her fists, then told him I'd received my injuries through falling downstairs, he had looked at me and said, "Come! Come! Tell me what happened; I'd always thought you had a lot of horse sense." And that term, horse sense, he frequently applied to me. And so, you could say, it was he who created Hamilton, that beautiful stallion with the white flowing mane and tail, and the wise eyes, and his love of the ridiculous, which, after all, amounted really to the essence of my own spirit and the hunger of my soul for love and companionship. . .

But all my friends would be round me today, not only the old ones but the new ones too. My! My! The number of people whom Nardy had brought from London had filled the main hotel in the town. Oh, and I must not forget all my neighbours in the Terrace. These people who had ignored me for years and thought I was the luckiest girl alive when Howard Stickle the assistant manager of a tailor's shop had deigned to look at me in the first place, then marry me. I knew that their opinion was that I should go down on my knees and thank God for such a break. And the odd thing about it was, they kept to that same opinion for years, right up to the day he was exposed in court as a sadist, a man who would stop at nothing to gain his ends, which were to bring into this house the woman he had been living with on the side for years, and the children he had given her. He had even gone as far as to consider murder: the stair rods hadn't become loose on their own.

But why did I stand such treatment? The simple answer is, this house. It was all I had in those days, that and my dog.

Still, that was all in the past, for on this day I was to be married to my Nardy. Nardy is an abbreviation of Leonard. It sounds silly, but I loved it, and him. Oh, yes, how I loved him.

At the thought, I put my good arm tightly around my waist and hugged myself; then sat back in the chair and closed my eyes. Was I really going to walk up the aisle of a church on the arm of George, and be married to my loved one by a minister? Yes, yes, I was.

The Reverend Hobson was a very understanding man. The two

previous ministers whom we had approached hadn't been so. I was a divorced woman, and being the innocent party cut no ice. Strangely, I didn't feel a woman at all. I felt a girl, and I was a girl, because I was in love for the first time in my life; I was really happy for the first time in my life.

Of course, Father Mackin had been round. He had looked at me ruefully, raised his eyebrows and said, "You are aware that me hands are tied?" and I had said, "Yes, Father, and I'm sorry." And he'd answered, "You're not a bit sorry," but he had smiled as he said it, and he wished me happiness. . . I like him. I like Father Mackin. . .

"Are you comin' for your breakfast, lass? They've nearly all finished. You don't want to collapse in the aisle, do you? If you do they'll have to stick you on that horse an' get you up there, eh?" Gran's laughter filled the room and the hallway where she stood with the door in her hand, her wrinkled ageless face abeam. She stepped further into the room as I rose from the desk, and her head on one side, she said, "We never hear of him these days, do we, your Hamilton?"

"No." I went up to her and took her hand and as we walked from the room, I said, "No, we don't, do we? But he's still there ready to gallop all over you, and don't you forget it." I pulled her arm tighter into my side and we looked at each other, and our exchanged glances held feelings we couldn't put into words.

George was crossing the hall, his big face red and shining. He thumbed over his shoulder while saying, "That lot in there pig, guts, hog, and artful, that's what they are. I've never seen so much grub shovelled away. You thought I could eat when I was a lad, but two of that four are females." And to this Gran answered as she now walked past him, "Well, you took them on."

I looked at George and shook my head, indicating that he should make no retort. Gran always got a dig in when she could about her only son's saddling himself with a woman who already had four bairns. Yet she was fond of Mary, at least they didn't quarrel. At the same time, though, she didn't look upon Mary's children as real grandchildren because they had not come through her son.

"She never lets up, does she?" George was bending down to me now, whispering, "One of these days I'll come back at her, I will. Where's Mary?'

"She's upstairs making the beds. And you must never do that, come back at her."

"No; I know. Anyway, lass" - his face went into a big beam - "it's come, your weddin' day." He caught hold of both my hands now and drew me towards him. And I looked up at this man, the only person who had brought any brightness into my childhood days. I had loved him dearly. I still did.

"And gettin' a grand fellow, the best in the world. The only thing is" - his voice changed and he straightened up - "what the hell am I goin' to look like in that grey rig-out eh? Me in tails! Oh my God!" He again thumbed towards the kitchen. "She nearly wet herself yesterday when I tried the gear on. But what'll happen when I'm goin' up that aisle with you? I tell you, she'll let you down: if she doesn't bellow she'll snigger."

"No, she won't. And let me tell you something, Georgie: you'll look splendid in grey tails and your topper."

"Eeh! God above. That topper! It's a good job we're not leavin' by Mam's street else they'd be rollin' in the gutters. I'm tellin' you, 'cos let's face it, Maisie, I'm not built for that kind of rig-out. I'm too bulky."

"You're not, you're just right, and you'll look the smartest man there."

"Oh aye. Well, if you say so, Maisie. But fancy" - he screwed up his face - "being able to hire togs like that. I wonder who had that suit on last?"

"Somebody with the itch, no doubt," I said, laughing.

"Aw! you." He pushed me in the shoulder, and when I staggered slightly his big hand gripped my arm and pulled me forward again. Then his voice low, he said, "There won't be much time for talkin' after this, but . . . but I just want to say again, thank you, Maisie, for lettin' us stay here. I never thought in my wildest dreams I'd ever come back to this house."

"It should have been yours really, Georgie, in the first place. You were her husband, she should have left it to you. And then that devil wouldn't have got his claws into me."

"Well, hair goes the way the wind blows, lass, an' if things hadn't worked out as they did, although they were hell for you, I doubt if you'd be standin' here the day. Nor me either." And his face going into a grin again, he said, "Talkin' of wind, on me long treks I had an assistant driver. He was an educated bloke. How he come to be on the road, I don't know, he never said, but he was always spouting poetry. And he used to say, 'The wind bloweth where it listeth, and thou hearest the sound thereof, but canst not tell whence it cometh, and whither it goeth.' And you can imagine what my reply was to that, can't you?"

"Yes, I can," I said, pushing him. "You've got a crude mind, Georgie Carter. You'd catch on to anything like that and remember it word perfect, wouldn't you!"

"Aye, I take after me mother. And I'll tell you another thing," he now said: "Nardy's Big Top friends, they think we're a lot of Geordie aborigines up here. I heard one of them say to his mate, 'You should hear him talk, not that you'll understand him, but you should hear him.' They meant me. I was talking to Jimmy Tyler in the pub last night. I'm tellin' you they think we've just been dug up, prehistoric like. By! lad, I laid it on thick just for them."

He was laughing, he wasn't upset by it all. He now left me and bounded up the stairs. And I went on into the kitchen where his four adopted children were still at the table eating, and on my entrance their chatter subsided. They were apt to be more subdued in my presence because Auntie Maisie was someone of importance, she had written a book and it was a best-seller. And because of it, she was going to marry a gentleman, her publisher indeed, and live in London, and had let them have this house and they had to behave themselves.

I had heard them being lectured in different ways by their mother, their stepfather, and their stepgrandmother, but they amounted to the same thing, they'd all be out on their necks if they didn't behave.

I smiled at them and said, "It'll soon be time for your getting ready," to which Betty, who was fifteen and the eldest, answered, "It's the first time I've ever been a bridesmaid, Auntie Maisie." Her voice and face looked serious. But when her brother John put in on a splutter, "And never the blushing bride. That was on the television the other night, a fellow was singin' it," Betty said, "Oh you!" and slapped out at him. But Gran shouted, "There's one thing I can promise you, me lad, if you don't finish that plate and scarper you'll never live to be a bridegroom."

"Perhaps he'll turn out to be a groom to Aunt Maisie's horse."

There was utter silence in the kitchen for a moment; then an explosion of laughter, and I looked at Gordon who was the youngest and who was blushing to the roots of his red hair, and I ruffled it, saying, "Well, he could do just that." And I asked him, "What would you be?" For answer he looked at his brother and, quietly, he said, "I'd be assistant groom to our John."

He had a nice nature had Gordon, he'd never hurt anyone knowingly. I liked all four children but I think I favoured Betty and Gordon above John and Kitty. Then we were all brought back from a hypothetical future to the present by Gran's shouting, "Well, you two grooms better get a brush in your hand and sweep up the muck from the horse by way of getting rid of those boxes in the backyard and tidying up the place."

"What, this mornin'?" It was a chorus from both boys and she yelled back at them, "Not this afternoon, or the morrow, but aye, this very mornin'. So get!"

I got, too. I left the war zone and went quickly up to my room. I looked at my bed with my beautiful blue voile dress laid on it and my cases standing at the foot of it and already packed. And for some strange reason I wanted to cry. Then going swiftly to the door, I turned the key and, throwing myself on my knees by the side of the bed, the bed in which I had never known a moment of love or happiness, I gave way to a bout of weeping. And as I knelt there, my hands holding my face, I felt a presence near me. It wasn't a human presence, and it wasn't a single presence either. Without raising my head I knew it was Hamilton and Bill standing there: Bill who had been flesh and blood, Hamilton who had been the creation of my lonely mind; they were both there and I took my hand away from my face and held it out towards them, and I felt a great peace overwhelm me and an assuredness that nothing ill would ever befall me again.

Such are the wishful illusions of the mind.

Chapter 2

Doctor Mike Kane held me at arm's length. Shaking his head slowly, he said, "This is how it should have been from the very first, Maisie, and_" his voice changing he growled at me, "don't you contradict me when I say you look beautiful, because at this moment you do look beautiful."

"I have no intention of contradicting you, Doctor. But I can say in return, I don't believe you, or, let me add, beauty is in the eye of the beholder, and from under that awful bristle of yours your vision is distorted." I put my hand up and pulled his beard. "But under there too is the man who changed the original ugly duckling. I know it is a policy for doctors not to get involved in their patients' lives. In their illnesses. . . Oh yes, they can muddle them up as much as they like: if they're not really bad when they go into the surgery they'll see all that is altered by the time they come out." My smile had softened my words, and I went on, "But right from the beginning you were concerned for me and, whatever else age makes me forget, I'll never forget that."

Slowly now he bent forward and kissed me, and I was buried for a moment in the bush of his face and my throat and heart were full.

"Well" - he looked down at himself- "it'll be a pearl-grey pageant coming out of the church. Anyway, girl" - his tone had changed again - "this is likely the last private word I'll have with you for the next month or so." And his voice suddenly rising, he cried, "Then after, I don't want to see you ever again, except when I'm invited up to London."

I said nothing, and he backed from me before turning and walking swiftly towards the door, there to turn again and add, "Only one thing I'll ask. Keep that damned horse out of the proceedings."

I laughed, then blinked my eyes rapidly, and the door closed again on the commotion in the hall and the to-and-froing down the front steps to the cars.

The door opened again and Gran came hurrying in, but then she almost stopped before continuing to walk towards me, saying, "Oh lass, I used to think you were as plain as a pikestaff and that what you had was all inside your head, but I take it all back. An' that little blue hat . . . Oh my!"

"Oh, Gran, be quiet!"

"Aye, I will, 'cos I'm near makin' a fool of meself. An' I won't come nearer you, 'cos if I do, there'll be buckets flowin', but I just want to tell you, it's . . . it's as if you were me own goin' to the church this very day, 'cos I love you like I've never loved anybody else, except me lad. God bless you, lass."

As she scurried from the room I put my hand tightly over my mouth. This was no good; I'd go up that aisle crying my eyes out.

There was the sound of cars moving away along the street. Then there were only the strange voices coming from the hall now, those of the caterers who were to serve light refreshments in the sitting-room for all the guests, that's if they were ever able to get in the house. Then Nardy and I would start on our honeymoon and our life together, and later, there was to be a dinner and dance in the hotel for the family and guests.

When the door finally opened, George stood there in all his glory. He didn't speak but came slowly towards me. There was no bright grin on his face either. Solemnly he offered me his arm and I, accepting his mood, took it and went from the room and through the hall, down the steps and through the crowd of spectators, some with cameras flashing, and into the white-ribboned Rolls-Royce.

I was amazed at the size of the crowd outside the church, but I was more amazed at the crowd inside; I glimpsed people standing at the back. The organ was pealing out "Here Comes The Bride", and I was walking by the side of my burly stepfather and all eyes were turning in our direction but mine could see only one man. There he was waiting for me at the bottom of the aisle. He looked beautiful today, too. Of course he always looked attractive, with his kind eyes and gentle manner and, above all, his lovely voice.

I was standing by his side now and we were gazing at each other. I had to take my eyes from him as I walked up the two steps to where the minister was waiting. Betty took my bouquet, George stood on one side of me, and Tommy Balfour, Nardy's best friend, stood to Nardy's side. And it was just as the minister began to speak that my heart lost a beat and I gasped audibly, for there, close to him, was standing the familiar figure of my old friend in all his glory: his coat had never shone so black, nor his tail and mane looked so purely white; his eyes were like two stars, and his lips were well back from his teeth, and his mouth was wide open. But that was not all. Inwardly I cried out against what I was seeing on the other side of the minister, for there was standing the most beautiful cream and brown mare. She was about half the size of Hamilton, but if you could ever put the word wondrous to a horse, this animal looked wondrous: her eyes were as soft as those of a seal, her nose was moist, her milk-chocolate mane was floating in the air as her head moved up and down as if in answer to something Hamilton was saying, for they were looking across the minister. But it was at Hamilton I inwardly cried, Now why are you here? It's all over and done with. And what he said was, We're happy for you. You wouldn't want this day to pass without seeing me, would you? Because, don't forget, I started it all. And anyway I wanted you to meet my mate. They call her Begonia.

I closed my eyes. I mustn't laugh. I mustn't laugh; I was being married; this was a serious moment.

"Leonard Murray Leviston, wilt thou have this woman to thy wedded wife, to live together. . ."

"I will."

"Maisie Rochester, wilt thou have this man to thy wedded husband, to live together after God's ordinance. . ."

They were still standing there, the pair of them, and I'll say this, they were behaving themselves.

". . . And, forsaking all other, keep thee only unto him, so long as ye both shall live?"

Oh dear. They were nodding their heads and smiling. Yes. "I will." . . .

The main ceremony was over but the minister was still talking, telling us about the sanctity of marriage. I couldn't listen to what he was saying for I was asking myself, was there some part of me really a bit barmy? because those two animals standing there still, one on each side of the minister, were as real to me as he was, if not more real. In fact, I was thinking that at times Hamilton talked more sense than this man was doing now.

By the time the minister led the way into the vestry, Hamilton and. . . How on earth had I given his mate the name of *Begonia*? What a name to give a horse, *Begonia!* But anyway, they had both disappeared and things were back to normal. Nardy was looking at me so lovingly and I felt so happy; I was, as Gran would say, like fit to burst. . .

Outside the church, amid the headstones and the flower beds, the crowd was milling about us. I had never been kissed so much in my life, and by women too: wives of Nardy's friends, smart ladies who while smiling at me were, I'm sure, thinking, Whatever in the name of heaven can he see in her! It's because she's become famous likely, with that book. . . And I knew that this was the opinion of most people, because, after all, take away the frills and the make-up, there was just me left underneath, and I was well aware of what my mirror presented to me. . .

It was almost an hour later before we all poured out of the cars and into the house. There, the champagne corks popped and speeches were made by various men, the one causing the greatest stir coming, of course, from George, who ended his by saying in his thick Geordie accent, "I'm her stepfather, but there's many a time, years ago, when I wished she had been a bit older and me a bit younger, and I would have changed all that," and the only one who took this in good part seemingly was Nardy, for he clapped Georgie on the back and said, "Well, I'm quite a bit older than you and I beat you to it."

Gran's response came later: "My God!" she said: "trust him to come out with something like that. The minister's wife, who had answered the call, nearly dropped it there and then an' with another three months to go by the looks of her." Gran could be relied upon always to cap her son. . .

Then came the goodbyes. And for the first time since it had all begun, we were alone together, in the car making for the station, and when he looked at me with that loving look, I said to him, "Did I act funny during the ceremony?"

"Funny?" He screwed up his face. "What do you mean, funny?"

"Did I act as if I was startled or something?"

He shook his head, then said, "No. But wait. Yes, I remember now:

you jerked a little as if you were going to lose your balance. It was just before I put the ring on your finger, and I thought, she doesn't want it." I leant towards him and he kissed me long and hard; then, still in his embrace, I said, "I was startled. I saw them."

"Them?" He drew his head slightly back from me.

"Yes. Hamilton."

"Oho! you did?" His face broadened into a smile. "That's a good omen. You haven't seen him for months and months; so you told me."

"I don't know so much about a good omen. I said them, didn't I?'

"Yes, yes, you did, Mrs Leviston."

Again he kissed me, then said, "Explain the plural."

"He has a mate. They call her Begonia."

His body shook us both as he said, "No! No! Not *Begonia*."

I nodded at him. "And they were standing one each side of the minister as large as life."

"Never!"

"I'm telling you. Now why should that be? I . . . I don't need him any more."

"Oh, come on, come on. You're in for a series. I told you that. But what is she like?"

I looked away from him, through the glass panel and over the chauffeur's head and out into the swiftly passing traffic, and I said softly, "She's beautiful: milk-chocolate brown with the most wonderful eyes in the world, and . . . and he loves her."

He pulled me round to him again and, softly now, he said, "Of course he's bound to, because she's you."

"Oh! Nardy."

"Oh! Maisie," he mimicked; then, his brow touching mine, he said, softly again, "My delightful, delightful Maisie. What have I ever done to deserve you? Never change. Tell me you'll never change."

I turned from him, lay back against the upholstered padding and asked myself seriously, Was this happening to me, really happening to me? Had I not slipped back into the fantasy world of Hamilton and become so much lost in it that it appeared real?

My question was answered when the car drew up outside the station and the door was pulled open by Tommy Balfour who helped me out into a crowd of grey-clad figures who, like a lot of hooting schoolboys, surrounded us and accompanied us onto the platform and, when the train arrived, brought heads out of carriages as they shouted and showered us with confetti. The minister had made it a strict condition that no confetti or ricewould be used outside the church. And when the train began to move out and some of Nardy's friends ran along the platform by the side of the carriage giving him advice, and I saw, among them, the face of one of the older members of the publishing house, I was made to think: Why should I imagine I was odd when middle-aged and elderly men acted like schoolboys out on a spree whenever the occasion warranted.

When at last they were out of sight and we sank back into the temporary privacy of the compartment, Nardy seemed to endorse my thoughts as he said, "And you imagine Hamilton is unusual. Did you see old Rington there skipping along like a two-year-old? I wouldn't like to see that lot after the dinner tonight. Anyway" - he put his arms about me - "we've given them an excuse to let their hair down. And you know it isn't very often our lot get the chance to do that. We're stiff-necks, at least they are, I'm not any more." He shook his head vigorously. "For who, I ask you, could remain a stiff-neck with Gran, Georgie, Mike, and above all, Hamilton."

My chin went up and I put in, "Not forgetting Begonia."

"No, Mrs Leviston, not forgetting Begonia. Oh, Begonia; I'm dying to meet Begonia. But very likely, now that you're a settled married woman there'll be very few occasions when they will visit you, only when you are stuck for some incidents in your new book."

"Yes I suppose so," I said.

But why, I asked myself at this precious moment, should I sound so unsure as to cross my fingers.

Chapter 3

I had lived in London for three months and I didn't know yet whether I liked it or not. I loved my new home. The citric yellow suite and the matching curtains at the windows in the drawing-room filled it with sunlight all hours of the day. Then there was the warmth and comfort of the rose-coloured carpet that went through the eight rooms of the top flat of the house where Nardy had been born, the whole of which he had at one time owned, but which, after the deaths of his parents, had become too large for his bachelor existence.

Nardy had turned one of the rooms at the end of the corridor into a study and sitting-room for me. In it I had a desk for my typewriter and plenty of space for books. But I often found it difficult to work there, and I would find myself sitting in the corner of the comfortable couch, going over what had happened yesterday or thinking about what was going to happen tonight when we'd be doing a show or a concert or accepting the invitations of Nardy's friends.

I considered he had a lot of friends, but he maintained he had three friends and a lot of acquaintances. Heading the three friends was Tommy Balfour who had been his best man. Tommy was publicity manager in the publishing house of Houseman and Rington where Nardy was editorial director. I had come to know Tommy well over the past weeks and, in a way, I felt sorry for him, because of what Nardy had told me about his mother. I'd met her only once and that was in the company of others, but I'd likely know more about her tomorrow because I was having tea with her. Then there was Alice and Andrew Freeman. Nardy had gone to school with Andrew; they were lifelong friends and I liked them, but only up to a point: I couldn't feel at home with them.

Since my marriage my appearance had worried me less and less. I had acquired something, but I can't find a name to put to it. It wasn't just confidence, for my mirror showed me the same face unfortunately as it had done all through the years, except that now it looked happy. And I was happy. I had never imagined such happiness. Every day I found something or someone to laugh at, and not least, Janet, Nardy's housekeeper, once nursemaid to him, and now maid of all work.

Mrs Janet Flood, to give her her correct title, was the first person to bring Hamilton back into my life, and of course Begonia with him.

I don't think Janet was over-happy with the situation when I first took up my position as mistress of the house, for she had seen to "her Mr Leonard" for years. On her half-day visits she had her own method of cleaning, and she made this very evident to the new wife; and also, she had her special times for stopping and having her cuppa.

It was during one of her cuppas that I broke through the "Good-morning, Mrs Leviston," or the "Good-morning, Mrs Leviston, ma'am," or simply, "Good-morning, ma'am." (It was as "Mrs Leviston, ma'am" that she was usually to address me for all our subsequent years together.) But on this particular morning, knowing it was the time for her cuppa, I ventured into the kitchen and said, tentatively, "Janet, do you mind if I join you? I feel a bit lost."

Metaphorically speaking, it was from that moment she took me to her bosom like a long-lost daughter. And for days afterwards I regaled Nardy with titbits about her family life that he had never heard before. But it was on that first morning that Hamilton galloped around the kitchen, and he was on his own. When I told him to let up, he pulled out a chair and sat next to Janet, nodding at her every word.

But the morning she gave me a run down on her family, Hamilton got up to such antics that I had a fit of coughing to cover my mirth. She had been sympathising with me losing my baby, then had ended, "But God has funny ways of working, for if your child had grown up to be like that man, you would sometime or other have tried to do him in an' all." My mouth had fallen slightly agape at this, and I was about to tell her that I hadn't intentionally tried to do my husband in, when I saw Hamilton sitting in the corner on his haunches and hugging himself with delight. Then Janet was saying, "People long for kids but if they only knew what was in store for them, not for the kids, but for them. Eight of them I've had, as you know, and there's our Max, Billy, and Joe, all divorced, the three eldest all divorced. Then our Maggie left her husband for another man and her three youngsters don't know which end of them's up, if you follow me. And what's gona happen to young ' Arry or 'Arold, as he insists on being called, God only knows, for he's a livin' terror. Only three and a half, and he's completely out of hand. But then can you blame him, poor little fella, because his dad's new piece hates his guts. Then there's our Hilda, she's single, at least in name 'cos she's going round with this fella in a band, with his hair standin' up straight as if he'd just got an electric shock. Then there's our Greg, Rodney, and May, they're still at home, 'cos they know where they're well off. Their dad's told them more than once to get the hell . . . well, to get out of it, 'cos they're livin' rent free. What they're payin' for their keep wouldn't cover one decent meal outside. But they know when they're on a good thing. They've got it both ways: Greg and Rodney have got their beer and broads outside, an' May's got her so-called boy friend. I tell you, Mrs Leviston, ma'am, shed no tears about not havin' a family. I had it all taken away after May was born, 'cos he said he wouldn't mind havin' a baker's dozen. I remember the night when he said that. I came back at him, in poetry like, sayin', 'If that's what you want, Henry Flood, put yourself out to stud.'"

And she leant back in the chair, her face wide with laughter, her hand tight across her mouth. I too was laughing my loudest, not only at Mrs Janet Flood, but at Hamilton, who was almost standing on his head, so doubled up was he with his mirth. But Begonia wasn't laughing, she too was bending forward, simply, apparently, to find out why her mate had taken up such a ridiculous position.

Begonia, I had found, hadn't a keen sense of humour. I remember putting this to Hamilton after I'd left the kitchen that morning and knowing that Janet and I had reached an understanding. And he replied, No, you're right, she hasn't as yet our sense of humour. But then she's only a two-year-old. But what she has got is a deep sense of compassion. If ever you were in trouble, you could lay your head upon her shoulder. I laughed, but noticed that he hadn't joined me; in fact, he had assumed an attitude of dignity and turned away.

But this evening I was attending the fire in the drawing-room when I heard Nardy's key in the lock, and as I scrambled to my feet and just missed knocking the tea-trolley over, I heard him say, "Wait there a moment," and I stopped in my tracks. He had brought someone home with him. Oh, dear, dear; this was the time of day I had come to love, when we had tea together and talked over the doings of the day. But who was it that he could say to, "Wait there a moment." That wasn't very polite, especially coming from Nardy, who was a gentleman of gentlemen where courtesy was concerned.

He entered the room, closed the door behind him, came quickly towards me, took me in his arms and kissed me; then, holding me at arm's length, he said, "I've brought someone to see you."

"Yes?" I nodded at him, then whispered, "But why leave them out in the hall?"

"Oh, he understands."

"He?"

"Yes. Come and sit down a minute."

He led me back to the couch and, taking my hands, he said, "I often think it must be lonely for you here during the day after Janet has gone, and if you had a companion. . ."

"A companion?" I put in quickly. "What kind of a companion?"

"Oh." He put his head on one side and squinted his eyes towards the ceiling as he said, "A little boy."

"*A little boy!*" The words came out of the top of my head. I didn't want any little boy . . . or a little girl. I'd given up the idea of children long ago. I liked George's children, but only for short periods at a time.

"Oh, Nardy." My voice was a whimper now. "How old is he?" I asked, for there was flashing through my mind the thought that it must be Janet's 'Arold.

"Just on two."

"What!" There it was again, that 'what' that had so annoyed Doctor Kane for years, but surely I could be excused and be allowed to show my amazement; and I was amazed that Nardy could plonk a two-year-old on me.

"Where . . . where are his parents? I mean. . ."

He shook his hands up and down. "They've had to go abroad; he's going to work in Canada, and they were going to put him into . . . well, a sort of home, but when I saw him I thought immediately that you would love him."

I withdrew my hands from his saying, "His parents were going to put him to a sort of home? What kind of parents are they?"

"Well, as far as I can gather they are pretty high class. There's blue blood there. Look, stay there; I'll let you judge for yourself."

He hurried from the room. I heard him talking again. I sat now with my hands tight between my knees telling myself that I had been a fool to hope that this way of life could go on indefinitely.

When the door opened again I slowly raised my head, then my mouth fell into a gape, and as Nardy came towards me carrying the two-year-old in his arms I got to my feet and cried, "Oh, you! you awful man," for there he was holding a beautiful white poodle.

Now I have never considered poodles to be dogs. And as for my choosing a poodle after having a bull-terrier for years, well, that was chalk after cheese indeed. But this fellow I saw wasn't one of those tiny things with bows on them, or the big ones cut into fantastic shapes. Yet he was big for a poodle.

His face was within two hands' distance from me now and he began to murmur, or was it grunt? And at this Nardy said, "He can talk. Proctor from the packing-room who owned him says he's got a

language all his own. His wife was heartbroken at having to leave
him."

"What do they call him?"

"Sandy."

"Sandy? And him pure white! Hello, Sandy."

I wasn't prepared for the tongue that covered my face from my chin
to my eyebrows, or the two feet that came out, and the next moment he
had one front leg round my neck and the two back were resting on my
hand as if it was a chair. It seemed such a natural position for him. His
nose now was almost touching mine, and again he gave me the benefit
of a free wash.

"Oh, Nardy, he's lovely."

"I thought you would like him. I saw him last week but I didn't say
anything just in case they pulled out from going at the last moment.
Proctor's wife really was in a state. They looked upon him as their
child. They'd had him since he was six weeks old. To make the break
Proctor brought him to the packing-room over a week ago. That's
where I really came across him. Of course everybody wanted to take
him, but Proctor went into each one's background as if he were head of
an adoption society. It became a bit of a joke. When I put my name
forward, the first thing he asked was, 'Have you ever had a dog?' And
I had to be truthful and say, no, but that my wife was well acquainted
with dogs. And the deed was done. Poor fellow." He now patted
Sandy's head. "He grieved terribly at first, howled all night, the
caretaker said. He used to sleep in Proctor's bedroom, sometimes on
the bed. What do you think about that?"

"I like it. Oh" - I put out my free hand - "thank you, Nardy.
Oh, thank you. But you know, you gave me a shock. I thought it was a
boy you were bringing in."

"A boy? A nipper? Oh, my goodness, no. I don't think I could stand
a child, not now. All right for a time to have a romp with, but too much
of a responsibility. No, I think we'll plump for Sandy."

And so Sandy became, not just my companion, but our companion.
Right from the beginning he was a strange dog. He did have a
language of his own and an independent spirit. He didn't like closed
doors, and he scratched them, or tried to rattle the knobs until the
doors opened. He jumped up at all newcomers and barked in greeting.
He did not like sleeping on the floor but chose the best chairs, on which
he would proceed to arrange the cushions to please himself. Above all,
he never seemed to be content until we were both together, when he
would sit on one lap and put his head on the other. And he loved to be
held in our joined arms when he would lick first one face and then the
other. And he seemed as wise as Hamilton, for he came to know my

moods and to act accordingly.

I had said to Hamilton, "Well, what do you think of the new addition?" He had pursed his lips. Well, he said, he'll never be another Bill, but he's all right in his own right, so to speak. And I repeated, "So to speak."

Christmas was upon us, our first Christmas together. Looking back over the year, it had been an eventful one. I had gone through a traumatic court case; I had become the author of a best-seller; I had filled the headlines of the newspapers for a few days, at least those in the north-east end of the country; I'd had a wonderful cruise with a wonderful man; I'd had a lovely wedding; now, I was firmly settled down and life was like a fairy tale, one that I had never read or even imagined. And here we were, sitting in front of the fire, Sandy stretched between us, discussing the holidays ahead.

"I had a letter from George this morning," I said; "a bit longer than the 'It leaves me at present' one." I laughed. He says, how about us going up for New Year."

"Fine, yes. Oh, I'd love that. A New Year in the north, yes."

"All right, I'll write and tell him."

"You know what?" said Nardy now. "I'd love Tommy to meet George and the family; really meet them, stay for a day or two. I get worried about him at times. That mother of his will be the finish of him. You haven't forgotten we're due there on Saturday, have you?"

"No, I haven't forgotten. But from what I've already glimpsed of her I'm not looking forward to our meeting. Anyway" - I laid my head upon his shoulder- "I might find her bark worse than her bite. I'll leave it to Hamilton to decide."

Nardy chuckled; then said, "How's he these days anyway? It's weeks since you mentioned him."

"Yes, it is, isn't it?" I said musingly. "I think he's deserted me for his new love."

"Well, you had better not let him get away altogether. Sales were down last month. Not on yours, fortunately, but we need another best-seller, so get going, woman. That horse has got to earn his keep."

I looked around for Hamilton but he was nowhere in sight.

The following morning Nardy wakened me with a cup of tea, and, seeing him already dressed for the office, I sat bolt upright, saying. "What time is it?"

"About twenty to nine."

"Why did you let me sleep all this time?"

"Why not? You haven't to go out into the bleak morning and it is a bleak morning, it's sleeting - and earn your living like I have. No, you can stay at home and make a pile by just scribbling on pieces of paper."

He had put down the cup on the bedside table and now had my face between his hands and was kissing me. I put my arms around his neck and said, "I'll work my fingers to the bone for you until the day I die.'

A few minutes later, when he came in to say goodbye to me, he whispered, "Janet's come. She said I'll get wringing. She's soaked through. She's a fool of a woman; she won't take the bus all the way. Practice of a lifetime, I suppose, still saving the pennies. She has no need now, but there it is, habit." He sat on the edge of the bed for a moment, saying, "And you know something, Mrs Leviston. I'm getting into the habit of not wanting to go to work in the morning; I'd much rather stay here with you. You know, there's not a thing to laugh about in that office."

"And there is here?"

"Oh, yes, yes. I've just got to look at you, my dear, and I want to giggle."

"Thank you very much, Mr Leviston, but I don't take that as a compliment."

"You should, my dear, you should; people who can make others laugh without trying should be given special honours, say -" He thought for a moment, then he went on, "DOB."

"What's DOB?"

"Dispeller of Blues."

"Oh! Nardy; if I'm capable of doing only that for you, then I'm happy."

"You're capable of doing a lot more than that for me, my dear." He held me tightly for a moment, then kissed me gently, and went out.

And once more I lay back on my pillows and wondered at my good fortune. And being me, I thought, it's too good to last.

I was on the point of getting up when Janet came into the room, saying without any preamble, "And that's where you want to stay today. I'm a bit late. That little beggar 'Arry. His dad landed him on me last night; his new piece can't put up with him. And you know something? Neither can I. He'd drive anybody up the wall. You'd think he was plugged in for the sparks seem to fly off him, he's so alive. I had to give him a beltin' before I could get out."

"Why don't you take the bus right to the corner, Janet?"

"What! and pay double for those three stops? Oh" - she now came quickly towards me - "What is it, Mrs Leviston?"

I had suddenly felt a severe pain in my left side, and it wasn't the first time I'd experienced it of late. "I keep getting a pain in my side," I said.

"Appendix?"

"No; it's on the left side, the appendix is on the right."

"Aye, yes, that's what they say. What can it be then? Perhaps it's wind."

I wanted to laugh and say, Could be your cabbage, for she wasn't a good hand at cooking greens. Instead I said, "Yes, very likely."

"Look, you stay where you are, I'll get you a hot water bottle and some hot milk."

By the time she had brought the hot water bottle and the hot milk the pain had gone entirely. And after thanking her, I smiled and said, "I'm a bit of a fraud; I can't feel anything now even when I press the part." And I demonstrated by pressing on my nightdress.

"Could just be wind then."

"Yes, yes, I think so."

It was about half an hour later, I should say, when I shouted, "Janet! Janet!" And when she rushed in she found me again doubled up, but in the middle of the bed this time.

"Oh my! Oh my! Something must be done. I'd better phone Mr Leonard."

"No, no," I gasped at her; "it could be nothing."

"You're not twisted up with pain like that for nothing. Look, who's your doctor?"

"I . . . I haven't one yet."

"Well, who's Mr Leonard's?"

I lay back on the pillow now, gasping, "I don't know. It's silly, but I don't know."

"I know what I'll do. There's a fellow round the corner in the terrace. He's got a plate up. Doctor somebody. Oh, what's his name? Double-barrelled I think. Morgan, Morgan, Morgan-Blythe. That's it, Morgan-Blythe. I'll get it out of the directory."

I didn't tell her not to bother, because by now I was more than a little perturbed. I could hear her voice from the hall, shrill as it always was when she was excited or upset. It had been like that the morning she came and told me that her May had brought home the fellow with the electric hair, with the intention of letting him sleep in her room, and Henry, Mr Flood, had thrown him out, literally by the neck. During all that morning her voice had been shrill.

She came back into the room, saying, "Who do these secretaries think they are anyway, God's missises? Wanted to know what ailed me or what ailed who, or where did we live, and so on. I told her, half a dozen steps to the end of the terrace and up the street, and to get him here pronto . . . or else."

"You didn't!'

"I did. Who are they anyroad? Jumped up little nothin's. They're not even nurses and they play at bein' doctors."

I said, "I feel a fool, Janet; the pain's gone now."

"You were no fool a minute ago. Shall I ring Mr Leonard?"

"No, no, Janet. Please, please don't. Anyway, wait until this man comes, the doctor, and see what he says."

It was almost an hour later when the bell from the downstairs hall rang and I knew he'd now be in the lift. I waited nervously and then there he was.

He was a big man, florid, and he didn't walk into the room, he bounced. I took a dislike to him immediately.

"Well! what's all this?"

"I don't know, that's why I sent for you."

He stared at me for a moment, before saying, "Is it? Is it then?" Then not finding an available table near to hand on which to put his bag, he threw it on top of the bed. "What's the trouble?"

"I . . . I have a pain."

"What kind of a pain?"

"It's very sharp. It's in my left side." I pointed.

"How long has it been going on?"

"I've felt twinges on and off for some time but, but it hasn't had any great effect until just a while ago."

"Well, what happened then?" He looked around for a chair, saw one at the far end of the room, brought it forward and sat down, crossed his legs, then stared at me as I said, "I was doubled up with pain."

"Well, we'd better have a look, hadn't we?"

He bounced to his feet now, and I pressed back the bedclothes, then made to lie down again when he said, "Well, let's have your nightie up."

I paused a moment while I thought, Oh, for my own dear Mike.

His hands were dead cold and my body jerked and he said, "That hurt?"

"No, it was your hand, it was like ice."

He gave me a sharp glance, then pressed his fingers into my right side, and while he did so I put in, "The pain is mostly on the left."

"Sympathetic. "

"What?"

"The pain was sympathetic."

Now I did start as he pressed his fingers hard into my right side. He straightened up, saying now, "Appendix."

"What?" There I went again: it was just like the time when I first went to Doctor Kane.

"You had better have it seen to."

"Immediately?"

"Well, that's up to you. If you've been feeling it, as you said, on and off for some time, it could go on grumbling for God knows how long. Then one day it might decide to burst. It's up to you. Could you go into hospital?"

"I could, but I don't want to, not before the holidays."

"What's your name again?"

"Leviston, Mrs Leviston."

He was sitting down now and, looking around him, he said, "Nice place you have here. What's your husband?"

"He's a publisher."

"Oh." He turned, slanted his gaze now to the bedside table and books there, and putting his hand out, he picked up one, looked at the title and said, "Huh! Tagore. You go in for cults?"

"Not that I know of."

He picked up another book and made a huffing sound before he said, "John Donne. My, my!" And as he dropped the book on to the table, he stretched his thick neck out and looked to where, on the far corner, *Hamilton* lay and, picking it up, he actually wagged it in his hand as he said, "Your choice of reading is catholic if nothing else. They'll print anything when they print that. Barmy. Clean barmy, that woman."

When, between tight lips, I said, "You think so?" Hamilton sprang on to the foot of the bed. He was standing straight on his hind legs, and by the side of him stood Begonia. She too was rearing.

"You ask me if I think so. Of course I think so. Did you read the court case at the beginning of the year? That judge was as barmy as she was, telling the jury that he too had imaginary friends." He rose to his feet now, snorting, "Lunatics! My sympathy was with her husband. No wonder he tried to get rid of her. But I can't understand, if your taste runs to philosophers and poets, how you can stand that tripe. . . What's the matter with you?"

He followed my gaze for I was looking at Hamilton who was now prancing round him. And I brought his head poking towards me when I answered, "I was looking at Hamilton. At this moment he's prancing round you, and if it were possible he would take pleasure in kicking your tactless ignorant hide down the stairs." And I grabbed the book out of his hand, turned it over and presented him with a portrait of myself.

He stared at it, then turned his head slowly and stared at me. And now, without taking his eyes from me, his hand went out to the bag at the bottom of the bed, and slowly he lifted it up. Then, still staring at me, his teeth ground together and his knobbled chin came out and his mouth opened as if he were about to speak. But apparently thinking better of it, he turned, then bounced out of the room as he had bounced in. And I drooped my head forward and the hot tears ran through my fingers.

I heard the front door bang. The next moment Janet entered the room and, seeing how I was affected, she came hurriedly to me and put her arms around me, saying, "There now. There now. Don't upset yourself about that one. And I had to go an' pick him! He didn't stop to put his hat and coat on. You were right about your horse. I wanted to kick him downstairs meself."

I lifted my head from her shoulder and she nodded at me, saying, "Well, I was standin' outside; I thought I might be wanted like. Who's he to say that you're daft, or anybody else who sees things. There's my 'Arry. He saw some things I can tell you three years gone before he went for his cure, and they weren't things like a nice horse that you can talk to and can make you laugh. No, he saw black-beetles crawling over the ceiling and over the bed and over me, in their tens of thousands, he said. He tore me nightie off one night trying to get rid of them. Not satisfied with that, he banged me all over trying to kill the things. By, I'll never forget that night. It took all the strength of our Greg and Rodney and Joe. Joe was at home that time. He had left his wife, or what was she, and there they were all struggling on me new carpet. It had been a toss up atween that or a spin drier, and. . ."

"Oh, Janet." I was wiping my face that had now spread into laughter, and I patted her cheek as I murmured, "You're very good for me."

She seemed slightly embarrassed now, for she pushed me back on the pillows, punched each side of them, pulled the coverlet up under my chin and said, "There now. Well, a good cup of coffee is what you want." Her face coming nearer to me now, she added, "Should I put a drop of brandy in it?"

"No thanks, Janet, just the coffee, strong."

"Just the coffee, strong." She nodded, as if disappointed. Then straightening up, she said, "'Tis 'pendicitis then?"

"Sort of, I suppose. What you call a grumbling one."

"Are you goin' into hospital?"

"No, I'm not. Not before the holidays anyway. And not afterwards if I can help it."

"But you couldn't put up with a pain like that for any length of time, now could you? You mightn't have any choice."

She nodded at me before turning about and leaving the room. And I thought, Yes, she's quite right. I mightn't have any choice.

I didn't get up, and so I was still in bed when Nardy rushed in at lunch-time, and my greeting to him was, "What do you want?"

"What's all this? is my answer to that question. Did that fellow upset you?"

"He did somewhat. Anyway, Janet shouldn't have told you. And well, yes he did. He was very rude, and the fact that I won my case seemed to infuriate him."

"Lie still," he said. "I'll be back shortly."

"Where are you going?"

"I'm just slipping out for a while."

"Nardy, please, don't take it any further. There's nothing you can do. He can simply say he wasn't insulting me."

"Lie still, my dear."

I lay still for a few moments, thinking that I hadn't told him I had a grumbling appendix; the complaint seemed to have been thrust into the background.

He was gone more than half an hour and when he came back he walked slowly into the room and sat on the side of the bed. Taking my hand, he said, "I don't think our friend will express his uninvited opinion in the future, or at least for a long time. It all depends on how long he can subdue that ego you so rightly detected."

"What did you do?"

"Oh, I just let him have it."

"What!"

He laughed and said, "Oh, no, my dear, not physically, in height and breadth he doubled me all over. No, there's a much better way to put a man like him in his place. The mention of the Medical Council, to which I told him I was writing, had a very subduing effect on his manner. I think he's got a thing about women. Anyway, you've got a grumbling appendix and it's making itself audible; you must see about it."

"Not until I must, and certainly not until after the holidays."

"Well, we'll see. If that pain gets bad, Christmas and New Year will have to be postponed until such times as you can eat and be merry. Now, I'm going to knock us up some lunch."

"Aren't you going back to the office?"

"No; I've already phoned them and told them I won't be in. Of course, the place will go to pot, me not being there during the next few hours, but that's life."

"Big head."

"You said it, Mrs Leviston."

Left alone again, I asked myself why I should have let that man upset me so much. For the first time in months I was now feeling tense, afraid, for he seemed to have dragged the past into this serene new life of mine. And now it was here, I felt I should never get rid of it, not really. And this was confirmed, because for the rest of the day I saw Hamilton, and once I spoke to him, saying, "Why can't I throw this off?" And his answer was, You should know enough by now to realize that you can never throw off the past. Everything that's happened in your life is still in it, locked away in boxes and docketed. And a fellow like him is a kind of key, and the lid's off and there you are, and the only way you can close it again is to ignore it.

"Ignore it?" I said. "How? How can you ignore things that man said to me, and what's more, what he thinks quite a lot of other people might think?"

Oh, sure; yes, you've got a certainty there. Only fools expect everybody to love them. You should know that, an' all, by now. And the same applies to tastes in reading. Don't forget one or two reviewers were very much of the same opinion as that fellow, although not quite so strong. Nevertheless, as one pointed out, there were people who had been in asylums for years and who had never even thought of talking to a horse. This is life, Maisie. Your cocoon of love now seems the whole of life but the world is going on all round it, and you'll be brought out into the cold reality of living sometime or other. Oh, I'm not suggesting that you'll be disappointed in Nardy; no, I think you're safe for life in that quarter, but he's not the entire universe.

"You're not very comforting," I said. I saw him turn his head away while keeping his eyes fixed on me and now he said slowly, You never took me on to be a comfort, not really; your honest judge and jury, that was more like it, wasn't it?

Yes, I suppose it was true. I watched him put out his front hoof and draw Begonia to him and turn her about, and together they walked out through the wall. And I repeated to myself: Your honest judge and jury.

Chapter 4

I had no sign of pain the following day, so we went to have tea with Tommy's mother.

Tommy lived in a suburban terraced house. It was one of these tall four-storey houses, one which still retained some of last century's elegance. And if the elegance hadn't rubbed off on to his mother, who had lived in the house since she was a child, the flavour of the last century had, for she sat in her very Victorian drawing-room, the very picture of a lady of that time. The only thing that was lacking in her attire was a lace cap. Her dress was long, almost to her ankles, and attached to it were white lace cuffs and a collar, and over all was a cashmere shawl. Her hair was grey and pulled tight back showing her ears, which were large and inclined to stick out. Her face was long, her eyes round and bright, and her mouth, when in repose, pouted slightly. Nardy said she had married late and Tommy was born when she was in her forties. Yet, even he did not know her exact age. But as Nardy pointed out, Tommy being thirty-eight, put her at one side or the other of eighty.

Well, she might have been eighty in looks and a hundred and eighty in her dress and manner, but her voice and eyes denied all this, for her voice was crisp and her eyes bright and piercing.

Tommy had greeted us at the front door after it had been opened by a woman in her sixties, whom Tommy then introduced as Bella, his mother's companion. I later learned that the companion was merely a complimentary title for poor Bella who had begun her life in an orphanage and who had for almost forty years now cooked, cleaned, and maided the mistress of the house. Bella had a round kindly face and her body was as thin as mine, for likely all the fat had been run off it early on. I'd heard about Bella and I shook her hand, saying how

pleased I was to meet her, at which her face had brightened, only for it
to redden as Tommy put his hand on her shoulder and said simply,
"My saviour." I guessed now that Tommy was the reason why poor
Bella had stuck to his mother all these years. To her, he was likely the
son she had been deprived of.

Anyway, here I was, standing in front of the regal lady and saying
politely, "How do you do, Mrs Balfour. I'm so pleased to meet you. But
I think we've brushed shoulders before, at Andrew's and . . ."

My voice was cut short by the voice now saying to me, "Rubbed
shoulders, did you say? You'd have to grow a bit, young woman."

"Mother."

"What?" The steely eyes were turned on Tommy.

Tommy made no answer. Then the voice said to me, "Well, sit down
and let me hear your version of it."

She was pointing to the sofa opposite her chair and I sat down and
found myself much nearer the floor. I'd heard of business men who
viewed applicants placed strategically in a lower seat on the opposite
side of the desk, and I felt very much in the same position at this
moment as the bird-like eyes riveted on me and the voice now said,
"An imaginary horse, I can't believe it."

"Mother, you haven't said hello to Nardy."

"Don't be silly." She cast her glance towards her son. "Do I say hello
to you every time you enter the room? And Nardy has surely been here
often enough not to expect a hello as if he were a stranger." On the last
words she looked at me again and now said, "Well, about this horse."

I stared back at her. There was something already rearing in me
against this woman's manner, and it took shape, for there he was
standing to the side of her chair on his two back legs with his head
thrust forward.

"Have you always seen things?"

"I don't quite follow you, Mrs Balfour. What do you mean by seeing
things?" My cool tone seemed to take her aback for a moment and her
chin, on which were showing long prominent hairs, jerked upwards.
"Well, by what you said in that book you'd imagined weird things
from a child, imaginary children and dogs."

"I didn't consider them weird; most children don't."

"Huh! Well, I never imagined such things. Did you, Nardy?"

"No, Mrs Balfour, no, not children or dogs; but I once imagined I had
a crocodile."

I turned my gaze on my husband. That was the first I'd heard about
the crocodile. And when he now turned his head slightly towards me
and smiled as if apologetically, I wanted to laugh. He had never
imagined seeing a crocodile. And Hamilton confirmed this by tossing

his head to the side and kicking his left front leg out as if dismissing the whole idea. It was then an imp got into me and I looked at Tommy and said, "Did you ever have an imaginary playmate, Tommy? A horse or a crocodile or a dog?'

Tommy looked at me for an embarrassingly long time, it seemed. Then he looked at Nardy, and then at Bella; he didn't look at his mother as he said, "No, I never imagined an animal, but I did imagine I had a companion. It was a little girl, and she stayed with me for a long time." He smiled now a wry smile as he ended, "But I could never get her to grow up."

"Don't talk such rot." Mrs Balfour's head was moving from side to side, and she added now, "Bring in the tea, Bella."

And as Bella went to obey, her mistress said, "There's one, thank goodness, who I'm sure never had any hallucinations."

Bella had reached the door before she turned, and her smile was tinged with bitterness as she said, "There you are wrong, Mrs Balfour; I did have what you call an hallucination. It was about a knight on a white horse, but he was always riding the wrong way." Her smile slipped away and she made a sound in her throat which I put down poetically to the knell tolling the death of lost hopes.

For a moment I was touched by the depth of sadness that must lie in Bella, created mostly, I should imagine, by her life spent under this old tyrant. And I asked myself, how had she come to give birth to such a nice fellow as Tommy. Nardy had told me that Tommy took after his father, who had died some twenty years ago but whom he remembered as being a quiet man with a strong sense of humour. And he must have had a sense of humour and a great patience to stick this woman. Perhaps, though, she hadn't always been as she was now. But I couldn't see her any different; some women were born like her, tyrants from birth, who yet managed to cloak their inordinate desire for power until they hooked some poor fellow, such as Tommy's father.

"You could have done a great deal of harm with that book, and I've already expressed my opinion to Nardy there, haven't I?"

"Yes, you have. But you remember I didn't agree with you."

"Besotted individuals are devoid of reason. But how on earth . . ." She pulled herself up short, and at this I bowed my head when I saw Hamilton do his famous kick in the back of the front and the spiteful old lady being lifted straight from her chair on the point of his hoof before sailing out through the front window opposite, over the iron railings that skirted the patch of garden and right into the middle of the road.

"You've got a cough. People with your fleshless frame often have."

I swallowed deeply, and while my eyelids blinked rapidly I looked at her and said, "I don't usually cough." Then I couldn't prevent myself from hitting back at this tactless and dominant being by smiling at her as I went on, "Quite candidly, I was choking. You see, I have this wicked sense of humour and your last words conjured up a situation that gave me a little episode for my next book."

"Episode, for your next book!" She was bridling now. "What have I said that was so amusing?"

"Well, really, it wasn't what you said that made it amusing, but my horse's reactions to your words, 'besotted individuals are devoid of reason', by which I think you meant that Nardy could not, to put it in ordinary words, see straight, or think straight where I was concerned."

Her mouth opened twice; her eyes widened; I watched the hairs on her chin jerk before she said, "You mean to say you are seeing that horse in my house, and it's having reactions?"

"Mrs Balfour," Nardy's voice broke in soothingly, "my wife is a bit of a tease." He cast a warning glance in my direction now. "Of course she's not seeing the horse here; it is . . . well, it is really a fictional character. We all know that, don't we, Tommy?"

There was not a little consternation in the room when Tommy didn't confirm Nardy's statement, but after a moment, during which he put his big head on one side and looked at me, he smiled and said, "I'd give my eye teeth to see Hamilton career round this room."

"*Tommy!*" The name vibrated like thunder over our heads, and the voice went on, "*Have you lost your senses?*"

Her son now stood up and said quietly, "Just about, Mother," then turned on his heel, saying, "I'll see what Bella's doing."

I watched the tall body sink back into the chair. The head was nodding now, and she addressed herself solely to Nardy as she said in, what for her, was a quiet voice, "Tell me, Nardy, have you noticed anything odd about Tommy lately?"

"Odd? No. Tommy odd? No. Of all my friends and acquaintances he's the least odd. I can say that with all truth. What makes you think . . . ?"

"He's been acting strange." She now leant forward and beckoned Nardy towards her; and he rose from his chair and went to her, and in a whisper, with each word perfectly clear to me, she said, "He was away all last week-end, and he wouldn't tell me where. That's the second time it's happened of late. He wasn't with you, because I rang, didn't I?"

"Yes, yes, you did."

"Have you any idea what's going on?"

"Nothing that I know of. I haven't seen any change in him."

I would have loved to butt in here and say, "That isn't strictly true, dear, because only a week or so ago, you said to me, Tommy's all on edge. It's that old witch of a mother of his; she's getting on his nerves."

"Perhaps he went to stay with a friend."

"I know all his friends. I rang round. No one had seen him."

"Well, did you ask him?"

"Of course I did, but he said he had been for a walk. Imagine it, not home Friday night, Saturday night, or Sunday night, and he had been for a walk. I'm worried . . . I'm worried, Nardy. Look, promise me you'll try to find out what's afoot." Her voice sank lower now: "I think he's got a woman somewhere: some common piece has got her claws into him, and he wouldn't dare bring her back here."

As the door opened Mrs Balfour leant back and pushed Nardy from her, and he resumed his seat, and Bella poured the tea and handed round her home-made scones and pastries which were very nice indeed, and I congratulated her on them. But such praise wasn't allowed to pass, and her mistress turned from carrying on a conversation with Nardy to say, "She has me to thank for that. She couldn't boil water when she came to me first."

"Well, Mother, she's had forty years to learn."

I looked at Tommy. He *was* changed. There *was* a change in him: he was standing up for himself. And so was Hamilton, for having now been joined by Begonia, he was tugging on one of Mrs Balfour's big ears while directing Begonia to pull harder on the other. And Begonia's lips were well back from her beautiful white teeth. And for the first time I recognized that she was really enjoying herself as the old lady's "cuddy's lugs", as Gran would have termed them, stretched further and further out across the room.

I closed my eyes for a moment as I told myself I must stop this, and I took a firm hold on myself as I glanced at Nardy. He was looking rather perturbed and, as I wouldn't have him worried for anything in the world, I made myself speak to the old dragon politely: "Do you spend Christmas at home, Mrs Balfour, or do you go away?"

"Why should I go away? What's a home for if not to spend Christmas in? Everyone makes for home at Christmas. I thought that was universally understood."

Still endeavouring to please, I said, "Oh, some folks, I understand, take the opportunity to turn it into a restful and entertaining holiday and book up in hotels."

"Well," she said, looking straight at me, "some people are odd; that is a well-known fact too," and I was aware of the meaning behind her words.

It was Tommy who broke in again, and what he said proved one thing conclusively, he had declared war on his mother: "I think that's a splendid idea, Maisie,-" he said; "a knees-up, Mother Brown, would do us all good."

That his mother was both astounded and somewhat upset was evident. And when Nardy looked at his watch and, turning to me, said, "If you want to keep that appointment, dear, I think we'd better be making our way," I fell in with it and said, "Oh, yes, yes. I'd almost forgotten." And I rose to my feet and, standing before the dragon, whose shoulder I now did come up to, I looked into those hard round eyes and, smiling, said, "Goodbye, Mrs Balfour. You must call on us sometime when you feel able."

She did not speak, merely inclined her head towards me.

Bella was clearing the tea things away and I said, "Goodbye, Bella. Pop in sometime when you are free, will you?" She stopped what she was doing and she smiled at me as she said, "I will, Mrs Leviston. Yes, I will. And thank you very much."

I had just passed through the door into the hall when Mrs Balfour's voice came clearly to me, saying, "What in the name of God did he see in her? an undersized giggling nincompoop."

Nardy was in the process of getting into his coat and Tommy had my coat over one arm and my hat in his other hand. They had both heard plainly what she had said. My head drooped slightly as I walked towards them. Tommy was definitely agitated and was about to say something when Nardy, helping me on with my coat, said, "We are going up to Fellburn for the New Year, what about joining us then?"

I turned, and Tommy handed my hat to me and as I looked at him I thought for an awful moment that he was about to cry; his face looked all twisted up. Then, he was saying, "Thanks, Nardy. I'll be glad to. Yes, I'll be glad to. When may I come?"

"Come up with us; we'll be going the day before New Year's Eve. And as the office isn't opening again until the following week, we'll be staying until about the third, won't we, dear?"

I could not answer for the moment but nodded.

"But would there be enough room?"

"We'll make room," said Nardy. . .

We had come by tube because the station was quite near; but now Nardy hailed a taxi, and when we were seated in it, he caught my hand and held it tightly. It was the wrong thing to do because the silent sympathy made me want to cry. . . What in the name of God did he see in her, an undersized giggling nincompoop. I didn't giggle. But as to the words undersized nincompoop, that was a good description of how I'd seen myself all those years ago, a plain little nothing, loved by only two people, and knowing that their emotion had been bred out of pity. But for some time now, ever since I had won the court case and proved that I had a mind, I had felt that I was looked upon at least as an intelligent human being, still small and plain with a deformed arm, nothing about me but becoming quite good company as a conversationalist, and particularly so with those people with whom I felt at home. But that woman, she was like a demon. And that was the word Nardy now used.

"She's a demon," he said. "How Tommy has stood by her all these years I just can't understand. But the worm is definitely turning. "

I knew he was ignoring her last remark but I couldn't let it pass, and so I said softly, "What in the name of God did you see in me?"

He drew me closer, saying now and just as softly, "Oh, Maisie, Maisie, you shouldn't even have to think about that. I fell, as you must know, when I witnessed your first reaction to strong drink in the Café Royal." He now put his arm about me and hugged me to him. . .

Once indoors and seated before the fire with the tea-trolley to the side of the couch and Sandy at our feet, I watched him lie back, join his hands behind his head and say, "I wonder if Tommy's got a woman. I heard years ago he was strong on one of the girls in the office, but I think she met his mother and that was that, as you can imagine." He slanted his eyes towards me, then said, "What a pity Bella is so much older. She's such a nice woman, Bella, and she's been slave to that individual all her life." Then looking at the ceiling, he said, "I would like to know where he got to last weekend."

"Why don't you ask him?"

"Oh, I couldn't do that." Then he added, "Do you wish you were going up to George's for Christmas as well?"

"No. No, of course not; I want to spend it here, in our own house."

"So do I."

It hadn't been strictly true what I had said, that I didn't want to go up to George's for Christmas; I had a great longing to be with them all, if only for a short time. Yet, Nardy, I knew, wanted our first Christmas together to be spent in his home. And it turned out to be a lovely time.

On Christmas morning he brought our tea and toast to bed and we laughed and talked for a while. And later, when I got up to dress, I had another twinge in my side. That was the third one during the last week, but it was really nothing, just a twinge. However, I knew that the time was near when I should have to do something about this twinge, but I prayed we should get the holiday over first.

I dressed and went leisurely into the drawing-room where we were going to open our Christmas presents, but I stopped half-way up the room, for there, added to the parcels around the foot of the tree, was one extremely large one. I turned and looked at Nardy, saying, "What's that?"

"What's what?"

"Don't be silly. That parcel. It wasn't there last night."

"No, it wasn't."

"I . . . I didn't see you bring it in. I . . ."

"I didn't bring it in, Father Christmas brought it down the chimney."

"Oh, you!" I pushed him and he said quietly, "Go and open it."

I opened it, and there disclosed something that delighted me on sight yet at the same time hit my conscience. And when I looked up at him, he said, "Oh, yes, yes I know what you think about animal cruelty, but those animals have been dead for years. Put it on, woman."

I lifted up the beautiful mink coat and held it to me for a moment; my hands, going over the skins, felt they were tracing silk. I put the coat on, then hurried out into the hall where there was a long mirror. The picture it gave me was like a transformation. It was longer than my usual coats, reaching down to just below my calves, and it had a large collar which, when I lifted it up at the back, almost formed a hood. Nardy was looking over my shoulder and there were tears in my eyes when I turned about and threw my arms around him, muttering, "It's beautiful. It's beautiful. I never imagined wearing anything like this."

"You suit it. It has two pockets."

"Has it?" I fumbled excitedly for the pockets. "For handkerchiefs," I said.

He preened. "Or invitation cards. At least, that's what the salesman pointed out to me." And he bowed.

I bowed back; then tugging him back into the drawing room, I said, "Come and see yours. They'll seem insignificant now."

He was delighted with his presents: a gold wristwatch, and a silk scarf with initialled handkerchiefs to match. And when I opened my smaller parcels I found in one a beautiful mauve silk negligee, in another a pair of calf gloves, and lastly, a charm bracelet, a beautiful thing in gold and platinum. Oh, I'd never known such a Christmas. And then there were Sandy's presents: a new collar and a tartan coat which, when we put it on him, he tried his best to take off, going as far as to roll around on the carpet on his back, and his antics caused us to laugh and to hug him.

I look back on it as a fairy-tale Christmas. We had a jolly time at the Freemans, and the day after they came to us when a number of the staff also called in for we had arranged to go to a pantomime. And when the Dame yelled, "Shall I beat Jack?" we yelled back with the children, "No!" And when she went on to say, "Yes, I will!" we all yelled, "No, you won't!" I was back in childhood, but one I had never experienced. Later, we went to a restaurant and had a lovely meal, and enjoyed the floor show. When we returned home that night I was indeed drunk with happiness.

Janet, who was on holiday, popped in the morning we were due to leave for Fellburn to pick up the key. She'd always had Christmas off, I understood, to see to her family.

She came in, her face red with the cold, but this morning her stockings weren't wet for she was sporting a pair of high legged fur-lined suede boots, and proudly she showed them off, saying, "They clubbed up and got them for me."

Clubbed up, I thought. How many of them did it take to buy her these boots?

"What else did you get?" I asked as we sat at opposite sides of the kitchen table drinking our coffee laced with brandy.

"Oh" - she put her head to one side - "the usual, you know: a couple of aprons, three tea-towels, a tea-cosy." Then giving a funny little laugh that wasn't really unhappy but full of understanding she said, "You know, you're no longer a mother after you've had eight, you're just somebody who works in the kitchen."

"Oh, Janet."

"Oh, yes, ma'am. Oh yes. You don't know."

"What did your husband buy you?"

"What did he buy me? Let's think." She put her head first to one side and then to the other while directing her gaze to the ceiling, then said, "He brought me in a bottle of whisky." Now closing her eyes and shaking her head, she said, "And I don't like whisky. What I do like is a glass of sherry; but I've never been able to stand whisky. He likes it though. Ho! Ho!"

Hamilton was now at one end of the table, his forelegs crossed on it, his face almost between us both, and he was enjoying himself. Yet, when Janet said, "You know, Mrs Leviston, ma'am, that man's never bought me a Christmas present in me life. All the years we've been together I've never had a Christmas present from him, not even a card. And some of the older ones take after him."

It was at this Hamilton drew his head and legs back and sat down on the chair. And as I forced myself to say, "But . . . but he's likely been a good father and seen to the children," she hesitated, then said, "My answer to that, ma'am, is that he works when he can get it. And when the two eldest were young he made them odds and ends; he was good with his hands, woodwork like. But he's never done anything like that for years." She stood up now, laughing. "His main occupation in life is to see how much he can put down his gullet afore fallin' over."

At this Hamilton couped his creels, head over heels he went. And Janet, laughing now, said, "My mother used to say a woman in my position had three choices, the same as she'd had: the first was, to walk out and to keep on walking; the second was, to do him in; and the third was, to commit suicide."

We were both laughing loudly now, and, as always when I laughed, Sandy joined in: he was racing round the table barking his head off.

When I said, "Oh, Janet, it's dreadful to laugh at calamities, really," she answered, "Well, as I found out, Mrs Leviston, ma'am, if you didn't laugh at times, you would do one or the other of those things. Yet, you know, it's funny, Rodney, who's the only thinkin' one of the lot, says if I was to peg out tomorrow his dad wouldn't be long after me, 'cos his stay would be gone. Funny that, when you come to think of it, because there's hardly half a dozen words pass between us in the twenty-four hours. And there I've been, lying side by side with him all these years, and the only time I seem to know he's there now is when he snores."

I didn't laugh because her words conveyed to me the sadness and futility of some people's lives. Yet, between them, she and her husband had produced eight individual people, and they in their turn were producing more. Strange, the source of the population, when you came to think about it.

Nardy came into the kitchen now, saying, "What was all that heeing and hawing about? Have I missed something?"

"Not much, Mr Leonard," Janet said, smiling at him; "we're just laughin' at life, sort of. Oh, and by the way" - she looked from one to the other of us now - "thanks very much for me envelope. That was very kind of you, more than kind. I'm goin' to give meself a real treat and buy a thick coat to go with these boots."

"Well, see that you do, and don't spend it on that family of yours. "

She nodded at Nardy now, saying, "I can assure you, Mr Leonard, I've spent me last on that lot. No, it's a coat that I'm goin' to have an' keep it for best."

"You'll do no such thing," said Nardy, wagging his finger at her now; "you'll wear it in the winter, weekdays and Sundays alike. It's a wonder you haven't caught pneumonia over the years."

"Funny that." She looked at me now. "I never seem to catch cold, everything else but not cold. Well, I'll away, and I'll pop over every day and see to things. And if you'll drop me a line to let me know when to expect you, I'll have the house all warm and a meal ready."

"Thank you, Janet. I'll do that."

After Janet had left, Nardy brought the cases from the bedroom, and I put on Sandy's coat. As I strapped it underneath his tummy I talked to him, saying, "Oh, you are a lovely boy," and he licked my face and made that murmuring sound that was really like a human being mumbling.

When Nardy helped me into my fur coat he pulled the collar up around my face, kissed me, then said, "You look marvellous."

"Oh, Nardy." I shook my head. It never made me feel good when he paid me such compliments. The clothes might look marvellous, but I knew that I myself could never lay claim to that description. Yet, a moment later when I pulled on my small hat, picked up Sandy and happened to look in the hall mirror, once again I could hardly believe what I saw. Such was the magic of clothes.

Sandy's whiteness stood out against the dark brown of the fur, and he was the one I thought looked marvellous, with his pompom head and moustaches and chin beard, and his long beautiful silken ears. There are poodles and poodles, but I've never seen one as beautiful as my Sandy.

Nardy looked at his watch, then said, "By the time we get downstairs the taxi should be there. I hope Tommy arrives on time, that's if he's been able to make his escape."

We needn't have worried. Tommy was at the station and was delighted to be coming with us. Nardy had booked three first-class seats and we laughed and talked during most of the journey. It was only during lunch that Tommy gave any indication of what Christmas had been like. When Nardy said, "How did you leave your mother? Does she know you're coming north?" it was some seconds before he answered, saying as he looked from one to the other of us, "Do me a favour, will you, my good friends? Don't mention my home to me during the next couple of days or the time, however long, I'm to spend with you. I want to forget that there is such a place as Seventeen The Crescent."

A slightly awkward silence followed; then we resumed our ordinary chat. And back in the compartment Tommy became quite amusing and surprisingly entertaining. Apparently, he was a great reader of poetry and could quote appropriate lines to fit any topic of conversation. . .

It was the middle of the afternoon when the train passed through Durham, and I had the strange and unusual feeling that I was home.

When we ran into Newcastle and the train ground to a halt and Nardy helped me down onto the platform, I put my head back and sniffed the air. And we all laughed as Sandy, who was in my arms, gave two short barks, and Tommy said, "He's hooting for Newcastle."

We were at the far end of the platform and our way to the barrier was momentarily blocked by some dignitary who had just alighted and was posing for a photographer.

By the time this little business was completed the platform was almost cleared. I was walking between the two men when I saw the lady reporter, as I thought of her, look back along the platform and point. Then she was hurrying towards us. Stopping dead in front of me, she said, "Miss Carter?"

At this point, Nardy's voice checked her, saying stiffly, "Mrs Leviston."

"Oh, yes, sir. I'm sorry, but I was thinking . . . well, of her pseudonym, writing, the book you know." She nodded now and, again looking at me, she said, "Have you come back for the holiday?"

"Yes, just for a few days."

She was walking sideways now as we moved on and she said, "You're looking very well, Mrs Leviston. And what a lovely poodle."

"Yes, he is, isn't he. His name is Sandy." I could afford to be pleasant, I was so happy. I felt her eyes travelling over my coat and knew naturally she would be thinking that's what a book does for you, whereas she herself was working for what she'd likely considered a mere pittance.

"Would you mind?" It was the photographer now, his camera held shoulder high. I glanced at Nardy and he smiled. I smiled too, held Sandy a little further up in my arms, bringing his face level with mine. There were a number of clicks and the photographer said, "Thank you very much. That'll be grand. A happy New Year to you." The journalist now added her voice to his saying, "Yes, a happy New Year to you." And we all answered, "The same to you. The same to you."

A minute or so later as Tommy helped me into the taxi and Nardy saw to the porter, I thought wryly, such is fame, for less than a couple of years ago I could have walked down that platform and caused less stir than a stray dog, a small grey creature, indistinguishable from the nonentities of life.

When, twenty minutes later and after a number of traffic hold-ups, the taxi drew up outside the terraced house where I was born and had lived until a few months ago, the front door opened before we had time to emerge, and there was George running down the steps, the children after him, and Gran and Mary standing in the doorway.

"Oh, it's lovely to see you, lass." I was smothered against the broad chest and enlarging stomach of George, then held at arm's length as he said, "In the name of God! what's that you're holdin'?"

Sandy answered with a bark; he didn't like being squeezed. And, too, at that moment Gran's voice bellowed from the door, "Let her in, you big noodle; she'll be froze out there."

I was almost carried into the hall, and here pandemonium reigned for at least five minutes, with Sandy jumping from one child to another, and the questions bouncing off my head, and hands being shaken, and Tommy being welcomed, and Gran and Mary, and the two girls Betty and Kitty oohing and aahing over my fur coat.

It seemed an age before we were settled in the sitting-room and the children shooed into the kitchen.

From the couch opposite the roaring fire I looked around the room. It was different. Still comfortable, but different, and smaller somehow. Yet it had always seemed a big room, having originally been two rooms. It was this room that had attracted Howard Stickle and his sister to the house and formed the basis of their design.

My reminiscing was swept away by Gran declaring. "How've you done it? You're different." Then looking at Nardy, she said, "What've you done to her? She's not our Maisie any more; she's a stylish piece."

At this I preened myself and, putting on a haughty tone, I said, "One rises in the world, Mrs Carter. Remember to whom you are talking."

"I'll remember" - she pushed her arm out towards me - "with me foot up your a. . ." She swallowed deeply; then on a choked laugh she said, "Backside."

Looking at Mary now, who had so far remained quiet, probably, I thought, because she was of a quiet nature and was probably, too, dominated by Gran who was inclined to rule the roost, I said, "How do you put up with the pair of them, Mary? It must be very trying." And I shook my head in sympathy while she smiled understandingly.

And George, taking up Gran's point, looked at his mother and, nodding, said, "You're right, Mam, you're right; she not the same. Got the mistress touch about her, unsettlin' our staff now, she is."

At this, Nardy said in a serious tone, "It is a bad habit she has acquired, George. She's done the same in my household, bringing everything down to one level."

I sat straight-faced for a moment; then reached out my hand to where Tommy had been sitting quietly at the end of the couch and said, "Will you be my friend, Tommy?" And he, gripping my hand, answered softly, "For life, Maisie, for life. When you find you can't stand any more, you just come to me."

I nearly said, "And your mother," and threw my head up and choked with my inward laughter.

The phone rang and Mary went to answer it. She was back within a minute or so, saying, "It's the doctor. He wanted to know if you'd arrived. He'll be around after surgery."

"Oh, it'll be lovely seeing him again," I said. "And you know what? I'm going to try and persuade him to take up a practice in London." And laughing now at the memory, I told them of my experiences with the bouncing doctor and of his opinion of Hamilton's author.

"Insolent bugger!" said George.

It was two hours later when Mike arrived. There he was at the door, those clinical but kindly eyes peering out from the bush of hair around his face, his arms stretched out towards me, and I actually ran into them.

"Oh, it's good to see you." There were tears in my eyes and tears in my voice, and I knew at this moment that he was another person that I loved, for he knew more about me than did anybody else in this room, yes, even Nardy.

"You look marvellous." He was holding me at arm's length. "What have you done to yourself?"

"It's the dress. It was very expensive."

"Nonsense." He twisted me about, put his arm around my shoulder and led me back into the sitting-room and into the babble of voices. I cannot recall what we talked about, only that the conversation was jocular and general; and it wasn't until an hour later that Gran said to him, "Will you stay and have a bite, Doctor?" But he rose to his feet, saying, "No; thanks all the same, I've got to get back. Anyway, I'm on call, but I'll be seeing you all. I'll come and be your first foot."

"That's the idea," I said: "a dark hairy man."

"Watch it! horse dealer," he said and slapped me gently on the cheek. Then arm in arm we went from the room, and in the comparative quiet of the hall, he looked at me and said, "All right?"

"Fine. Wonderful."

"I'm so glad. You know that, don't you?"

"Yes, Mike; yes, I know that." - It was only on very rare occasions that I used his Christian name - "The only dim light on my horizon is that you and the family seem so far away at times."

"You don't like living in London?"

"I don't dislike it, but I only like it because Nardy's there."

"By the way," he now said, his tone becoming professional; "referring to the story of your doctor that you described so vividly. Apart from his stinking opinion of your ability, his diagnosis was likely right, and I think I should have a look at you. Have you had any more twinges?"

"One or two, but nothing to speak of."

"Come, come. Have you had any real pain there?"

I looked away from him for a moment and said, "Yes, the day before yesterday. But I wanted to come up here so I didn't mention it to Nardy."

"Well now, look" - he dug me in the chest with his finger "the first real twinge, and I mean real twinge, you have, get on that phone."

"Very well, Doctor Kane. But I'm not going to have any real twinges until this holiday is over. Above everything else, I want Tommy to enjoy himself. I must tell you about him and his mother sometime. I had an afternoon with her that really beat that doctor."

"No."

"Yes. I think he's ready for jumping off somewhere. She's a real case."

The kitchen door opened now and Sandy came pelting into the hall and, with one swoop, jumped into my arms; and the doctor patted his head, saying, "My! he is a good-looking gent, isn't he? I heard you'd an addition to the family. I like poodles. I've never understood why they call them pets because they're the most intelligent of dogs. Oh, you are a fine fellow."

Sandy leant forward and licked the hairy chin, eliciting from Mike the retort, "Give over, man. Give over. Sloppy individual." Then pressing my shoulder, he added, "I'll be away. Take care now. I'll be seeing you soon."

"Bye-bye."

I opened the door and waited until he had run down the steps and was in his car; then I waved to him. When I turned into the hall again, Mary was ushering the children from upstairs kitchenwards, saying, "Now, make the most of it, because that's your tea and supper combined. Then to your rooms with you." And now looking towards me, she said, "It's all ready in the dining-room, I'm bringing it in. Will you tell them?"

I told them, and we all sat down to a meal which in a way was like the children's, a combination of tea and supper, but one which we all thoroughly enjoyed.

New Year's Eve, the house was filled with bustle: Mary and Gran cooking, the children running errands, George stocking up with liquid refreshment; and when Tommy expressed a wish to go out shopping Nardy took him into Newcastle, and they returned with their arms full of fancy boxes of sweets, chocolates, pastries, and bunches of flowers. It was Tommy's way of saying thank you.

As was usual, for the welcoming of the New Year in the real North Country style, the dining-room table, sideboard, and every available space, was laden with food and drink. But around eleven o'clock when everybody was changing their clothes as if for a ceremony, I found myself alone in the drawing-room with Tommy. We were sitting on the couch and he was bending forward towards the roaring fire, his elbows on his knees, his joined hands hanging between them. "You know something, Maisie?" he said quietly. "I don't think I've ever felt so relaxed and so at home in my life as I have done since I arrived here yesterday. I know everybody is in festive mood and out to see a good time is had by all, but it isn't just that, it's . . . well, I felt it when I came up for your wedding. Mainly, I suppose, it's George and Gran. They have something." He turned his head and glanced at me, then asked, "What is it?"

I thought for a moment before saying, "I suppose it's because they want so little out of life, Tommy: a good fire, a cupboard full of food, a drink, a meet-up at the local at the week-end. That's their life. As long as they've got the necessities of it and a little bit extra now and again, something to look forward to, they're happy. They're free from ambition. I think that's where the happiness lies, because you know, Tommy, once you start to allow your thinking to move away from that which is necessary to carry you through the ordinary day, happiness, such as theirs, is impossible."

"But you're happy." He straightened himself up and faced me.

"Yes, I am, very happy, Tommy. But it's an off-shoot; it doesn't seem permanent, and I'm daily afraid of losing the feeling. I can't get it as yet to mix with the main stream of my thinking which for years was governed by fear, fear of my mother, then of Stickle. Life with Nardy has not really got through to me yet. I might as well tell you that I wake up at nights in a sweat, fearing that something will happen and I shall find myself back to where I once was, consumed with fear and hate. Hate's a dreadful thing, Tommy. It eats you up."

I was sorry I had made that last remark, for he turned from me and looked into the fire again and, his voice a mutter, he said, "You're telling me. I've never loved my mother. I feared her, too, when I was young. The fear is still with me but in a different way. Do you know something, Maisie?" He swung round again and leaned towards me and, his voice just above a whisper, he said, "For a long time now I've wished her dead, but of late I've been terrified of what I might do to her if I was forced to spend another full weekend with her. Do you know where I went on that missing week-end?"

I shook my head.

"I went down to Brighton. I booked an hotel room, and, like a bloody fool, I stayed mostly in it, except for a walk along the promenade. I think the proprietor expected to find I'd hanged myself or taken an overdose. He seemed glad to see me go on the Monday morning."

"Oh, Tommy. Why didn't you come to us?"

He straightened up; gave a short, sharp laugh, and said, "Bella told me that Mother thought I was with you and Nardy and that she was for coming round; but then, if she had, it would have proved that she wasn't as bad on her feet as she makes out to be in order to be waited on hand and foot."

"Why haven't you married and got away?"

He lay back in the corner of the couch, saying now, "I was in love with a girl in the office and she with me. But she was frank: she said, she just couldn't stand Mother, and in those days, it meant we would have had to live at home. It was about the time she was deciding to be a semi-invalid. And then later on, I was engaged to another girl when dear Mama had a heart attack. But when that didn't part Evelyn and me, something else did, something I never understood for years: Evelyn went off to South Africa quite suddenly; she married her cousin out there. It was like a story in a novelette: she sent the ring back in a letter, saying she was so sorry but she found it was a mistake. I saw her again about six years ago. She had come back on a holiday - her parents lived not far away - she was still married and had three children, but wasn't very happy. And she told me then why she had gone off like that: Mother had insinuated that there was some kind of lunacy on my father's side and that I had spasms every now and again."

My eyes wide, my mouth half-open, I said, "Never!" And he nodded slowly and said, "But yes. I think I nearly did go a bit mad at that stage, and I confronted Mother with it. She denied, of course, the implication with regard to myself but reminded me that my Uncle Henry had epileptic fits and would disappear for short spells."

"You should leave her, Tommy."

"I know that."

"Tommy." I put out my hand and caught his as I said, "You must take a flat and, not just a flat, a girl friend."

His reaction to this suggestion was to place his hand on top of mine and to stare at me for a moment before saying, "When will you be free?"

"Oh, Tommy." I pulled my hand sharply away from his and said seriously, "There are some fine women about, lonely women, just waiting for someone like you to say, hello there. They'd jump at the chance."

"Yes, I suppose they might." He got to his feet now and went to the side of the fire and leant his elbow on the mantelshelf, and after a moment he said quietly, "Yes, I suppose there's a woman somewhere who wouldn't mind linking up with me. But life plays dirty tricks on you. Something happens and you find you can't tolerate even the thought of such a thing."

Into the silence that fell between us there penetrated the bustle in the house and a commotion in the hall; then young Gordon rushed in, waving a paper and crying, "Auntie! Auntie! Look! You're in the paper, in the Evening Chronicle. Front page, look."

He held the paper before me, and yes, there I saw this fur-clad

251

individual holding a white poodle in her arms. She was smiling. . . That wasn't me, was it? But yes it was: there was Nardy at one side of me and Tommy at the other. As I took the paper from Gordon, George came into the room, yelling, "Let's have a look!"

He had a look; then put his arm around me and said, "Film star. That's what you look like, bloody film star. And look what it says:

Mrs Leviston, better known as Miriam Carter, the successful novelist, has returned to her old home to spend New Year with her friends, Mr & Mrs George Carter. She was accompanied by her husband.

Now what d'you think of that, eh? Her friends Mr & Mrs George Carter. That'll show the lot of'em round about. I can't wait to hear the chatter."

Gordon now grinned at me and, his head nodding shyly, he said, "You look smashin', like me dad said; like a film star."

"Oh, Gordon." I ruffled his thick hair. "You've never seen a film star."

"Oh, yes, I have, on the telly and at the pictures. They all wear fur coats in the winter."

Mary, Gran, and Nardy now came into the room, followed by the other children, and there was a series of "Oohs" and "Aahs" and "Would you believe it," with Gran putting the cap on it all in her inimitable way by saying, "It doesn't look a bit like you, lass." And when George bawled at her, "Oh, that's you, Ma, as tactful as a billy-goat with its head down," she bawled back at him, "She knows I didn't mean it that way; people dressed in fur coats like that are generally empty-headed upstarts, or those no better than they should be, 'specially if they are posin' with dogs an'. . ."

Her voice was drowned with the laughter. Even the children were saying, "Oh! Gran. Gran."

And to this she responded with "Oh, to hell with the lot of you! I want a drink; let battle begin."

It was at this very moment that the battle inside me did begin: the pain shot through my side like a knife. I opened my mouth and gasped aloud, but it was drowned by the hubbub in the room. Dropping down quickly into a chair I lay back and gripped the arms, crying inside myself, "No, no. Not now, not at this moment." The pain eased a little and I looked around. Everybody was dressed in his best: the children, Mary, George, Gran, and of course, Nardy and Tommy, who always looked as if they were dressed in their best. We were all ready to greet the New Year; and this I felt sure was going to be wonderful for all of us, including Tommy. Something must happen to bring Tommy some happiness, for he had become so dear to both Nardy and me.

"Oh! Oo . . . h!" My legs stiffened against the pain. Nardy was at my side now, anxiously enquiring, "What is it?"

I gulped in my throat and said, "Nothing, just a twinge."

"A twinge? Come along, tell me the truth, this is no time for being heroic. You're in pain?"

I put my hand on his and gripped it tight, and I felt my nails going into his flesh as another pain racked me. When it was gone I muttered, "It'll pass. It's just the kind of. . ." I was about to say "spasm", when I was brought double. And now, there was Tommy, and Gran, and George, and Mary all about me, and I heard Nardy say, "It's the appendix. I knew this would happen. She should have had it seen to weeks ago."

"I'll phone the doctor."

As George went to move away I managed to hold up my hand and cry, "No! No! Please. It'll go."

"Phone him." Nardy's tone was definite, and his voice seemed to be the last clear one I heard until I saw, through a haze of pain, Mike's face hovering above me, and him saying, "There now, it's all right. Everything's arranged; you're going to be all right."

I remembered feeling the cold air on my face as I was carried outside, then the floating feeling as I was lifted onto a trolley. The last I remembered was being in an enclosed room and someone lifting my arm and saying, "You're going to sleep. You'll be all right, you're going to sleep."

I was told later they had just got it in time. Another hour or so and things would have gone pretty badly with me. As it was, they had not only taken my appendix out, but also removed quite a lot of adhesions from lower down in the bowel. Two for the price of one.

Two for the price of one.

Two for the price of one.

The words were repeated as someone tapped my face and a voice said, "Come on, my dear, your husband's tired of waiting for you to wake up."

Slowly I opened my eyes, and there was Nardy's face above me. And as my muzzy mind said, "Oh, my love, my love," I opened my mouth wide and groaned. They hadn't taken it out, I knew they hadn't taken it out. This pain was awful. "Oh, Nardy, Nardy."

"It's all right, my dear, it's all over."

"Oh, I can't bear this, it's dreadful."

Someone was messing about with my arm again. I turned my head and looked at the nurse as she stuck a needle in. I looked up into her face, but it was Begonia, and I spoke her name, saying, "Thank you, Begonia." And the last thing I heard at this time was her voice saying, "She called me Begonia and my name's Betty."

Chapter 5

After the first two days I had a string of visitors. Everybody was very cheerful, and I had to beg George and Gran not to make me laugh. About the fourth or fifth day I noticed the change in my visitors: their merriment was forced; they didn't stay long. I said to Nardy, "Is anything wrong at home?" And he said, "Now what could be wrong."

I said to Tommy, "Something's the matter with George and Gran. What is it?"

"Nothing that I know of," he said. "You're a bit low; and of course you're bound to be, aren't you? After what you've gone through.'

On the seventh day I said to Nardy, "I want to go home; I'm quite up to it." And to this he answered brusquely, "You're certainly not up to it, and you're certainly not coming home until the doctor gives the word. You've hardly been on your feet yet. Now look, I'm leaving tonight for home. I'll go to the office in the morning, collect some work, and I'll be back by tomorrow evening; and in the meantime, you be a good girl and do what you're told." His voice changed as he added, "I do miss you, dear. It isn't life when you're not there."

How comforting were those words, how warming to my heart.

The following afternoon I had only one visitor, Mary. She said Gran had developed a cold. I looked into her face; her eyes looked slightly swollen. I said, "Have you caught a cold too, Mary?"

"Yes, yes, I've got a bit of it," she said. "It's . . . it's gone right through the children."

The following evening, Nardy came and brought a message from Janet. Apparently, she said she was missing me, and would I hurry home. And to this I said, "I want to hurry home. Look, I am up." And I went to pull myself from the chair, but he pressed me back, saying, "Yes, I know you are, dear. Just give it one or two more days. Do this for me, will you?"

"Nardy."

"Yes, my love?"

"There's something wrong somewhere. Mary said Gran's got a cold, and George didn't come in last night. Is it the children? Has something happened to one of the children?"

"No, no, they're as healthy and noisy as ever. I left them squabbling amongst themselves in the kitchen."

I jerked at the chair. "Gran's ill. Something's happened to Gran.

"Woman! Nothing's happened to Gran. She's her old, loud, brash self. Well" - he paused - "not quite that, she's . . . as Mary said, she's got this cold."

"She's in bed?"

"No, no, she's not in bed, but . . . but you know what a cold's like, streaming eyes, runny nose. She would have passed it onto you if she had come."

I went through them all in my mind. Gran, George. *George*. I put my hand out and gripped Nardy's. "It's George. He wasn't in last night; he . . . he. . ."

"Oh, my lord! woman. I left George not half an hour ago. The only thing I can tell that has happened to George in the last day or two is that his vocabulary has extended somewhat. I thought he had used every swear-word in the book, but he's added a few more."

"Why? What's made him do that?" My tone was testy, and he spread out his hand and said, "The bus I suppose, the passengers."

I was puzzled. I was quick to pick up an atmosphere. There was something wrong with one of them and the rest were troubled. But who? I looked at Nardy and noticed that his face looked white and slightly drawn. I mentioned this. "You're tired," I said. "You look pale."

"Well, I've had a long day. I dashed to the office, and was held up there giving one and the other the news. They all send their love, especially Tommy. I had to make another dash for the train, laden down with manuscripts that I don't want to read. The sun was shining when I left London; when I got out at Newcastle the sleet nearly blinded me. I dumped my burden in the hall, said hello and goodbye to them all, and here I am. Of course I look pale. I'm a poor harassed man, because I've got a wife who's let her imagination run wild again. By the way, where's Hamilton?"

I smiled wryly. "It's funny, but I haven't seen him for days. I saw

Begonia once, at least I think I did, but that's all. They've deserted me."

He shook his head. "I don't like that. I want another book."

"That's all you think about, books, and the money you can make out of me."

"Yes, of course. Why do you think I married you?" And this quip he softened by putting his arms around me and kissing me.

The bell went for the visitors, but he had no need to take note of it because I was alone in a side ward. Yet he looked at his watch and said, "I think I'd better be making a move. Mary said she'd . . . well, she'd have a meal ready about half-past eight, and I am a little weary and not very good company."

I nodded, saying, "Yes, yes, dear; and . . . and get early to bed."

We said goodbye, and as I saw the door close on him I became filled with a feeling of panic. He had never left before nine o'clock on other evenings; in fact, one night he was still here when night staff brought the milk round, and the nurse had laughingly said to him, "We've got an empty bed next door. We could push it in, sir, if you like." And in the same vein he had answered, "That's a splendid idea. I'll give you a hand." But tonight it was just turned eight o'clock and it seemed he couldn't get away quickly enough. What was the matter? Gran, George, Mary, they were all right. He himself was all right. There was nobody else, only. . . Like a flash of lightning Hamilton appeared before me. He stood stiff and straight, his great eyes looking into mine. I said to him, "Sandy." And he moved his head twice.

I had a phone in my room. I got through to the receptionist and gave her the house number. It was Mary's voice that came to me, saying, "Fellburn 29476."

"Mary."

"Is that . . . is that you, Maisie?"

"Yes. Mary, where's Sandy?"

"S . . . Sandy, he's" - there was a pause - "in the sitting-room."

"Mary, are you telling me the truth?"

There was a pause, and then she said, "Yes, Maisie, I'm telling you the truth. Sandy is in the sitting-room at this minute."

I heaved a great sigh, then said again, "Mary." And again, she said, "Yes, Maisie?" And now I put it to her, "Tell me what's wrong. There's something gone wrong, I can feel it."

"We . . . we are all right, Maisie. Everybody's all right now."

"What do you mean, now?" There was a longer pause.

"I . . . I suppose I should have told you that Gran was a bit off-colour, but she's perfectly all right now."

"Then why couldn't somebody just say that instead of all this mystery? Has she had the doctor?"

"No, nothing like that. And she'll be in tomorrow."

"She will?"

"Yes, yes, you'll see her for yourself."

"Oh, that's a relief. Good-night, dear."

"Good-night, Maisie."

I sat down on the side of the bed. Hamilton was still with me. He had been standing by the phone. I looked at him and said ruefully, "The quicker I get my imagination on something practical, the better."

His expression didn't change: he neither agreed nor disagreed with me. But I nodded at him and said, "Doctors or no doctors, I'm going home tomorrow."

The following morning around nine o'clock there was a bit of a commotion outside my door. But then there was always commotion in the corridor, comings and goings. In any case, the kitchen was almost opposite, and there was the clatter of trays and crockery for most part of the day. But this was a different commotion. The handle of the door moved and I heard the nurse say, "She's not seeing anyone. I've told you before."

"And I've told you before that she knows me. I . . . I did a piece about her at Christmas."

"I've got my instructions, no reporters. As for knowing her" - her voice sank - "everybody in the town knows her."

"But I told you."

"I don't care what you told me. Now am I to bring the sister?" The voice dropped lower again and I moved towards the door and heard the last words, "She's had an operation. It was quite a big affair. She hasn't got to be troubled."

"She'll be troubled enough when she finds out."

The opening of the door nearly knocked me on my back and the nurse said, "Now what you up to?" To this I replied, "What will upset me when I find out?"

"Oh, nothing, it's . . . it's . . . Look, Mrs Leviston; now don't agitate yourself. Come and sit down."

"I'm not sitting down, nurse, I'm going home."

"Oh, Mrs Leviston."

"And stop saying, Oh, Mrs Leviston, nurse." I caught hold of her arm. "Nurse," I said again quietly, "I'm worried, and feeling like I do, I . . . I won't get any better sitting in this room trying to find out what I should know, and nobody will tell me. It's been going on for days; I've sensed it. And now I know that something is wrong. That reporter knows. You know. Well, I'm not going to press you to tell me, I'm going home. Would you mind, please, asking sister to come in."

"Oh, Mrs Leviston."

I forced a smile and said, "Oh, nurse."

Sister was some time in making her appearance; but before that I got on the phone again. It was young Betty who answered, and I said quietly. "Tell Uncle Nardy I want to speak to him."

"Yes, Auntie."

"What is it, dear? What's the matter?"

"The matter is, whether you come to fetch me or I make the journey myself, I'm coming home this morning."

"You're . . . you're not. You must see the doctor. . ."

"Doctor, or no doctor, Nardy, I'm coming home. Would you please bring my clothes. If you don't then I shall discharge myself, order a taxi, and get into it in my dressing-gown. I mean this." And I banged the phone down. . .

Half an hour later there was Nardy, the doctor, and the sister, all saying in their different ways, "This is very unwise of you."

I thanked the staff; and had one little surprise when my generous tip to be distributed among them was refused. It was a rule that all such remuneration was forbidden.

You live and learn, I thought. Fancy that in this commercialized, money-grabbing age.

Nardy held my hand tightly in the taxi, but we hardly exchanged two words.

I was going up the front steps; the door opened, and there was Gran and Mary and George and the four children. Tommy, I thought. Oh, Tommy! I turned to Nardy, saying, "It's Tommy!" and the word ended on a high note, almost a squeal.

"Tommy's all right," he answered quietly. "He's as fit as a fiddle. At least he was when I left him yesterday except that he had threatened to do his mother in. But he laughed as he said it, so I hope he won't do anything until we get back."

I was being held by Gran. I looked into her face. It was swollen, her eyes were red. The children weren't jolly. As usual George held me and said, "Hello, love. Glad to see you back."

I was relieved of my coat and hat and led like an invalid into the sitting-room. The rest followed. There was a trolley set, and on a little side-table the electric coffee-maker that I'd bought Mary for Christmas was bubbling gently away.

I had a cup of coffee; then I lay against the back of the couch and looked from one to the other and said simply, "What is it?"

When I saw the tears well up in Gran's eyes and she bowed her head, my voice was almost a yell as I cried again, "What's happened? What is it?" Then I was sitting bolt upright. "Sandy! I knew it. He's gone. He's dead."

"No, no, no." There were hands patting my shoulders. "No, no. He's in the kitchen."

I relaxed and my throat had a piteous sound even to myself as I said simply, "Please."

Nardy now looked at George and said, "You had better start at the beginning."

I watched George rub his hand over his mouth and chin two or three times before he said, "Well, it was like this, Maisie. The bairns took the dog out. Yes, yes, yes" - he wagged his finger - "it's to do with the dog, but rest your mind, he's there in the kitchen. But listen. As I said, they took him out, on the same walk as you used to take Bill, through the park and into the copse. There, they took the lead off and threw the ball for him; then they chased him and he chased them, in and out of the trees. You know the game he plays. Well, as they said, there they were, the three of them, John, Kitty, and Gordon, racing round when they realized they were just racing after each other and the dog wasn't there. Now, there was nobody else in the copse, not that they could see, and after all it isn't that big, you can almost see from one end to the other of it when the trees are bare as they are now, except at the far end where the holly's entangled. And as they said an' all, coming through the park, the only people they met out with dogs was a woman with an Afghan hound, you know the one, and the fellow from the bottom of the terrace with his bull terrier, an' two young lads pushing bikes. Anyway, they couldn't find him, and it was on dark, John even climbed over the wire fence at the side of the copse, you know, the railway cutting. And he went along the line, and even under the footbridge, which is damned dangerous, 'cos the line curves there and the train could have been on him. Anyway, they came back here in a terrible state. We were all in a state." He glanced from one to the other. "It was black dark by now, but we all went out again looking, every one of us. We knocked on all the doors in the council estate but nobody had seen a white poodle. We went to the police station and they said they would look into it. And when Mam, here, didn't take much to their casual approach about a dog being lost and did a bit of yelling, as is usual, the one behind the counter became sarcastic and said, 'There's an accident, madam, on the main road to Bog's End: an oil lorry's overturned, a car's been set on fire, two people are known already to be dead, but we'll stop our enquiry if you insist and see to your dog.' That's what he said, didn't he, Mam?"

Gran merely nodded and George went on, "By! lad, I gave him the length of me tongue. Anyway, it's wonderful what a name can do. I told him who the dog belonged to, an' first thing next mornin' there was a copper on the doorstep taking particulars. And speak as you find, from then on they did everything in their power to be helpful. But there was no sign of Sandy. That night there was a big advert in the local paper offering a hundred pounds for his return. Nardy thought of that." He nodded towards Nardy. "And you wouldn't believe it" - a small smile touched his lips - "we had all kinds of dogs brought to the door, didn't we? Mary there" - he thumbed towards her- "she could tell you a tale about the kids that brought a poor little, distempered-white mongrel. But even now we can't laugh about anything, because it was one hell of a time. As Mam there said, knowing how you went on about Bill, what you would do when you found out about Sandy was past thinking about. Anyway, four full days passed and we were practically giving up hope when the bell rang one night. It was around ten o'clock, and I went to the door."

He stopped and stared at me and I stared back at him, waiting, telling myself that Sandy was in the kitchen, what more was there to know? I watched him wetting his lips; then he began again, but slower now. "There was nobody at the front door when I opened it, but there on the step was a bundle. It was wrapped up and I didn't know what it was. But I stepped over it and looked along the street. And in the light of the last lamp I saw two figures running, one what looked like a woman, the other a child. Anyway, I stooped down and I picked up the bundle. My God! Maisie, the shock will be with me till me dyin' day. It's no good keeping it from you any more, you'll see the result of it for yourself in a minute. It . . . it was Sandy I was looking at, what was left of him."

"Don't go on . . . don't go on, George. Don't go on." Nardy had put his hand out towards George and his other arm was around me. " She'll see soon enough for herself. Now, my dear" - he jerked me tightly to him - "he's alive and getting better every day and, given time, he'll look like himself once more. Just think of that."

"Will I bring the basket in?" Mary's voice was small, and Nardy said, "Yes, please, Mary."

I didn't speak; I just waited, and a few minutes later Mary placed the basket at my feet, and I stared down on the thing lying there, which on the sight of me stumbled to its feet and spoke its welcoming sound. I thought my whole being would burst asunder in the agony of pity. This skeleton was my Sandy, because that's what he was, just a skeleton: there was no hair left on his ears, it had been hacked off close to his head; his head had been shaved and apparently with a blunt razor, for the healing scars were evident; his body showed tufts of hair here and there, but in between them was revealed the bare skin, again with scars on it; the tail had no pom-pom, it was a piece of bone sticking out.

Gran was kneeling by the basket now, gently stroking one of the tufts of hair. Her face was awash, as was Mary's, and it was she who whispered brokenly, "He's eatin' again though, and . . . and he barked this morning. He must have known you were comin'."

George, now on his hunkers, put his finger under the chin of my poor little beast and said, "He'll be as right as rain, won't you, laddie? Won't you?" Then looking at me, he said, "The one who did this wants crucifying. That's the word, he wants crucifying. To tie a poor beast's mouth up with tape so he couldn't bark, or eat, or drink. . ."

"George!" Nardy's voice was firm. Then Gran said, "Look. Look, he wants to get on your knee."

I stared down into the hairless face. Only the eyes were recognisable, and they were looking at me and in them was a deep plea. I put out my arms and drew him upwards, and when his nose found its way into the old position under my chin I couldn't bear any more: I let out a cry that ended in a long wail, and when my tears ran onto his face he licked my cheek. Then Gran said, "Here, give him to me. Put him in his basket." And I gulped, I gasped, and cried, "No, no."

George's voice came to me now, saying, "He'll get along like a house on fire from now on. And when you feel a bit rested, lass, you'll have to look through all the postcards and letters that were sent to you in sympathy like, after the R.S.P.C.A. had put his picture in the paper. Eeh! that inspector said he had never seen anything like it in his life. One thing I do know, when we can prove the maniac who did this, all I can say is, God help him.'

It was the words "when we can prove", as if the maniac was already known to George, that brought Hamilton into view. He was standing to the side of me. His eyes looked red; there was steam coming from his nostrils and hanging in the air as if encased in frost; and he was repeating a name in my mind. And of a sudden I wanted to be sick. I pushed Sandy into Gran's arms, and as I made to rise from the couch, I felt the hands come out to help me. I thrust them aside, put my own hand over my mouth and stumbled from the room as quickly as I could. . .

It was some hours later when Gran and I found ourselves alone. I had gone to bed early, and here she was sitting by the bedside. Presumably she had come up to say good-night. "Feeling better, lass?" she said.

"Yes, Gran. I'm glad to be home." And to this she said, "Well, the best thing I think you can do as soon as you're able to travel is to get yourself away back home, to your real home now. You've had enough of this end to last you a lifetime."

"Gran.

"Aye, lass."

"Have you any idea who did this?"

She blinked her eyes rapidly, wetted her lips, then said, "Well, you might know we've talked this over so often, you could have walked from John O'Groats to Land's End and our ideas haven't changed, at least, that is Georgie's and mine; the others are not in the picture like we are, not even Nardy. But the only one who could really wish you ill, and you know it, is Stickle. And there's something I didn't know until this business came up. He's living now not three streets away from us, in the new council estate. He must have had to sell the cottage. I made a few enquiries here and there and he's been out of work this past year, until recently. He's now driving a taxi, part-time. For Corbett's you know; they have that big garage opposite the supermarket in Bower Street that runs off the market square. I say, I made enquiries. I'm telling a lie, I got this from John. Apparently, Stickle's two lads go to the same school now and, funny, but he's chummed up with this Neil, that's the younger one. This happened after he had a fight with the older one, because . . . what d'you think? The lad Ronnie, so he's called, tackled John, saying he was living in their house . . . this house" - Gran now pointed down to the floor - "and this was his dad's house, Stickle's you know. That was the time John came home with a black eye, and apparently the younger lad, Neil, had a black eye an' all because he had tried to help John. It seems that the brothers don't get on. Then, now this is what made us think" - she now leant forward and caught my hand - "it was the day after the dog had been brought back that the young lad, Neil, asked John if the dog was all right, and John wanted to know how he knew about the dog. And the lad became flustered and said, it was in the papers. And of course it was in the papers . . . the next night. But this was the first day back at school in the afternoon. Anyway, Georgie passed this on to the police and they went round there. It's one of these districts where you're not allowed to keep animals. There was a bit of a shed in the garden, but there was no sign of a dog having been kept in it. But, as our Georgie said, there are plenty of cupboards in the house and if a poor dog's mouth was tied up with sticky tape, as Sandy's was. . ."

When I closed my eyes tightly, imagining what Sandy had gone through during those three or four days, Gran said, "I'm sorry, lass, I'm sorry. I shouldn't jabber, but I think you should be put in the picture an' know where you stand. That man'll never forgive you till the day he dies. And our Georgie swears it's him, an' that he'll get him one day. I hope to God he doesn't, lass, I do, I hope to God he doesn't, 'cos he'll do for him. He swears it must have been the wife and the young lad who brought the dog back. I understand she used to be a spritely piece, quite good looking, but they say she looks a null individual now. And Mary Pratt - you know, the Pratts who lived below us - well, her daughter's got one of the new council houses only three doors from Stickle's and from what she can gather there's hell to pay goes on there every now and again. But he still goes out dressed up like the tailor's dummy that he once was, and when anybody speaks to him butter wouldn't melt in his mouth, so it's said. Oh, he's an actor that one, and the devil's been his tutor. And, you know, he still has the sympathy of some folks. That's because you've got on and your name's countrywide now. Some folks cannot bear the thought of anybody moving upwards and being able to change their style of living."

"Oh, Gran." I patted her hand gently. "I'm still myself. As for moving up..."

"I know that, lass, I know, but it's them papers. And of course, you've got to admit your mind's not like everybody else's. Now is it?" She punched me gently. "And there's them that wishes they had a mind like it an' could make money hand over fist..."

I again closed my eyes. This was life, ordinary life. I was back in it again.

The following morning, quite early, Mike popped in. He sat on the side of the bed and said, "Well now, Mrs Hamilton-cum-Leviston-cum-Carter, how goes it?"

"Sadly I'm afraid, Doctor."

"Yes, it couldn't be otherwise but sadly. What you've got to realize, my dear, is besides the nice people in this world, such as Nardy, and George, Gran, Mary, and me and Jane, of course, there are fiends, demons " his teeth ground together for a moment before he went on, "maniacs, lunatics. But it isn't the lunatics or the maniacs you've got to look out for, it's the fiends and the demons, for they are usually classed as sane. They carry around with them the appearance of normality. They do all the things that every ordinary person does, but there is in them one extra brain cell, as it were, and this brews such evil that makes the minds of us ordinary folks boggle. Howard Stickle is an example, my dear."

There was a constriction in my throat. I felt fear sweep over me, it was as if my blood had suddenly been heated to an unbearable temperature. I gasped and gripped the hands that were now holding mine, and then muttered, "You too ... you think?"

"Yes, I think. Who else would want to harm you? You had thirteen years experience of him."

Yes, yes, I had thirteen years experience of him. As I nodded to myself, there was Hamilton standing by the doctor's side, towering over him. I raised my eyes and looked at him and as I did so the atmosphere was lightened slightly by the doctor exclaiming, "Don't tell me he's standing up there again? You know how I used to go for you for looking over my head."

"Yes, yes. And yes he is standing up there. He's confirming all you say."

"I had a word with Gran," he said. "She told you last night you should get back into the big city as soon as possible, and I'm with her in that. You are too near the source of disaster here and you want to rest. You went through a pretty hectic time, you know. Do you realize that? You should have taken notice of my fellow worker in London and had it done there and then."

"Perhaps you're right; and if I had I should have saved poor Sandy from that torture."

"Oh, I don't know so much about that; there'd be other times. You've got to remember that: there will still be other times, as long as he lives."

"What else can he do, except try to kill me?"

"Oh, I don't think he'll go that far, not openly anyway. That kind of individual thinks too much of his own skin, and at bottom his type are afraid of prison."

I smiled wryly as I said, "That's comforting."

He laughed; then, standing up, he placed his hand on my head and, his voice soft, he said, "I've heard it said that no one should be called upon to pay the price demanded of success. And you know there's something in that. Anyway, it stems back to the old saying that everything has to be paid for. But in your case, my dear, you paid even before your success. Life isn't really fair. But then it never is, is it?" His tone changing, he thumbed at himself, saying, "Look at me. If I had my due I should be up in Harley Street raking in the shekels, and being addressed as Mister Kane, instead of having to see to a lot of barmy old girls every morning, expecting me to give them pills to keep them alive, and in the afternoon clinic handling a bunch of young ones, their stomachs sticking out a mile, some of them telling me they don't know how it happened, or that they never wanted it to happen, with here and there, oh yes, here and there, one in her forties telling me that God has answered her prayers and provided her with a miracle. Eeh, the Immaculate Conceptions I've examined. Lass, you wouldn't believe it." He was sounding just like George, and I lay back in the pillows holding my short forearm tight against the wound of my stomach, and I was laughing while at the same time the tears were running down my face.

Dear, dear, dear, Doctor. Was there anyone like him anywhere?

Tommy came up on Friday night. He stayed over the week-end and returned with us on the Monday. He and Nardy saw to the luggage. I cradled Sandy, like a baby, in my arms during all the journey. He was wrapped in a small white fleecy blanket, and no one queried but that he was a child, for he lay so quietly under the influence of a pill the vet had given him. And not until I sat in that sun-coloured drawing-room, with Sandy lying in his basket to the side of the fireplace and Nardy hovering on one side of me and our dear friend Tommy on the other, did the dreadful feeling of fear gradually slip away from me. And I promised myself it would be a long, long time before I ever visited Fellburn again. . . . But as the weeks went by I had a longing to see Gran and Georgie, so it was arranged that they should come down to us for the week-end. I must have been excited at the prospect, for it was only when thinking of the practicalities to cover the week-end that I remembered Tommy's mother; and quickly I turned to Nardy and said, "Oh dear! Oh dear! Oh dear!"

"What is it now?"

"She's coming to tea on Saturday, isn't she, Mrs Balfour?"

"Yes." And then he put his hand over his mouth and repeated my words, "Oh dear! Oh dear! Oh dear! And George and Gran are coming on Friday." Our foreheads touched and we repeated, together this time, "Oh dear! Oh dear! Oh dear!"

Nardy picked them up at the station; and when they entered the hall I was smothered in George's great arms, then hugged tightly to Gran, while Sandy raced round us barking his head off in excitement. Gran picked him up and kissed him as she cried, "He's his old self again. Thank God. Thank God."

I took her hat and coat, then led them into the drawing-room and there they both stood speechless and gaped.

Characteristically coming from the heart, George said, "Bugger me! but this is some place." And Gran muttered, "Eeh! lass, I never dreamed. You described it, but I never dreamed. It's so lovely, beautiful."

"Never mind all the eulogies," said Nardy; "sit yourselves down. What do you feel like, George? A drink, something hard? . . . or tea, or coffee, or what have you?"

Before George had time to answer, Gran looked at Nardy and said, "Eeh! lad, I'd like a drop."

"It's a drop you'll have, Gran."

As Nardy went out of the room, I cried at them, feeling a little embarrassed but nevertheless pleased, "Well, sit down, sit down; it's the same price."

They sat down, but continued to look about them. Then in a voice that was slightly tinged with awe, George asked, "D'you live in here all the time, lass?"

"Well, where else do you think we live?"

"Well, what I mean is, this room, is it just for special occasions?"

"This is our sitting-room, George; and we also eat in here most days. We usually have our tea in here and often a bite at night before the fire."

"And does that Janet woman keep all this clean?" Gran was nodding her head from side to side now.

"Yes, she does, Gran, and has done for years. She has a routine and gets through marvellously. I told you about her; I told you she's very like yourself."

"What! Like me, an' livin' in a place like this half her time. Don't be daft."

"The place has nothing to do with her character. She's as daft as you at times, I mean the way she looks at things. You'll see her in the morning. She doesn't usually come in on a Saturday, but she's . . . obliging, that's what she says. 'I'll oblige you, Mrs Leviston, ma'am. I'll oblige you. Happy to do so, Mrs Leviston, ma'am.' "

They laughed; then George said, "Come and sit down aside us." He pointed to the space in the middle of the couch, and when I was seated, he went on, "How are you really?"

"I'm fine, fine."

They looked about the room again and Gran said, "Could be the Ritz."

"Aye, it could be that," said George; then glancing sideways at me, he whispered, "She told them in the street we're being taken to the Ritz for lunch."

"She didn't!"

"She did."

"Well, you're not."

"I know that," said Gran now; "and I wouldn't go if I was assed."

"Well, you're not bein' assed."

Gran now leant in front of me and looked at George, saying, "She's turned snooty."

And George, smiling his big grinning smile, said, "Oh, I knew what would happen once she come down here among the toffs. I said to you, didn't I, all southerners are snooty."

"Well, there's a snooty one coming tonight; you can tell him what you think about southerners."

"One of your publishers?"

I shook my head at George and said simply, "Tommy."

"Oh." They both laughed. "He's different, Tommy. He's the exception is Tommy."

"He might be; but I've got a surprise for you, Gran: you're going to meet his mother tomorrow."

"That stuck-up old bitch that you told me about?"

"Yes, the stuck-up old bitch that I told you about. Now she will be a match for you."

"Well, we'll have to wait and see, won't we?"

"Yes, you will, Gran."

Later we had a meal in the dining-room which brought forth more "Oohs" and "Aahs", but not as many as when Gran saw our bedroom. There, she did an unusual thing, for she sat down in the blue quilted rest chair and she cried. Her hands covering her face, she cried. And I put my arms about her and said, "What is it? What is it, my dear? Are you all right? Have you got a pain?"

"No, no." She pushed me roughly, muttering, "I'm just overcome. I've never been in a place like this; and for the moment I can't imagine you livin' in it all the time. I thought your own house, back in Fellburn, was what you call . . . well, the pinnacle of grandeur like, but this. Eeh! lass." She gripped my hands now. "I'm happy for you. I am. I am. As I said to Georgie just a little while ago back there in the room, this is a sort of payment for what you'd had to go through for years. By the way, I saw him t'other day. He was openin' the door of the taxi to let a passenger out. It was near the market. And when she handed him the money he bowed to her. He looked as oily as ever, that's until he saw me. He had just closed the door when we came abreast and he was about to go round the back of the car when he stopped, and he glared at me. My God! I'm tellin' you, Maisie, that fella's full of evil. If he could have struck me down dead he would have done. You know what I thought? I wouldn't know a minute's peace if you ever came back there."

"Don't worry, Gran, I've no intention of going back there. But you must come more often and see us."

Little did I know at that moment that it would be she herself who would take me back there. . .

It was about seven o'clock when Tommy came, and there were more hearty greetings and laughter and drinks, and by half-past nine we were all very merry.

I had discovered it took only two sherries to make me merry. I would talk twenty to the dozen on those two sherries, but strangely, should I take another I would become quiet, or were I unwise enough to take a different drink, all I should want then would be to sleep.

Tommy had caused a great deal of laughter: he had told uproarious tales about his early days when he was trying to court and his mother was determined to stop him. They were uproarious, yet if I hadn't had my two sherries I would have been looking for a deeper meaning into why he should be recalling them again.

Gran, spluttering with laughter, was saying, "And what did your ma do to the second one?"

"She sniffed at her."

We were all laughing hilariously now.

"Sniffed at her, like this?" Georgie cleared his nostrils at one draught, and Tommy shook his head and, the tears running from his eyes, said, "No, no, not like that, Geordie man; she did it with her whole face, like this." He now raised his eyebrows, at the same time curling his lip upwards, the action in itself showed utter disdain, then looked down his nose, gave a slight hitch to an imaginary bust and said in a voice that was an exact imitation of his mother's, "You dye your hair?"

We actually fell about. But then quite suddenly, his voice taking on a sad note, he caught hold of Gran's hand and said, "With Christina Rossetti, I said goodbye to my love:

Remember me when I am gone away,
Gone far away into the silent land;
When you can no more hold me by the hand,
Nor I half turn to go, yet turning stay.
Remember me when no more day by day
You tell me of our future that you planned:
Only remember me; you understand
It will be late to counsel then or pray.
Yet if you should forget me for a while
And afterwards remember, do not grieve:
For if the darkness and corruption leave
A vestige of the thoughts that once I had,
Better by far you should forget and smile
Than that you should remember and be sad."

We laughed no more. He had let go of Gran's hand, and she was nodding at him now, and, her tone quiet for her, she said, "Aye, that was nice, Tommy, that was nice. Not the kind I understand, but it sounded nice."

He was lying back on the couch, his head turned towards me now, and I took his hand and to my embarrassment and not a little to my amazement, he quoted directly to me,

"When do I see thee most, beloved one?
When in the light the spirits of mine eyes
Before thy face, their altar, solemnize
The worship of that Love through thee made known?"

He stopped now and stared at me. I withdrew my hand from his grasp,
and he, giving a deep laugh and turning to Gran, leaned towards her
and cried,

"Oh love, my love! if I no more should see
Thyself, nor on the earth the shadow of thee,
Nor image of thine eyes in any spring. . ."

"Look here! lad," Gran's voice broke in, and it had a flat sound to it
now as she said, "If I understood half of what you're spoutin' I would
clap. But now you be yourself an' talk plain English."

And at this, Tommy lay back into the corner of the couch and,
looking up towards the ceiling, he cried, "Dante Gabriel Rossetti. Plain
English, she says, plain English." Then suddenly bending towards
Gran again, he said, "Bugger me eyes! if you're not right, woman. "

During the latter performance I had noted that Nardy didn't laugh;
and now getting to his feet, he looked down on Tommy and said, "A
cup of black coffee; then it's home for you."

"Can't I stay here?"

The words sounded like a plea from a small boy. And I saw Nardy
glance towards me, then purse his lips and say,

"You could, but I don't think the bed has been aired."

"That won't matter. I never catch cold. May I stay?"

"Of course, of course." Nardy's voice seemed over loud. Then he
added, "But don't forget your mother's coming to tea tomorrow. What
will you do about that?"

"Go along in the morning and fetch her, and hear her say -" He now
struck a pose, pulled himself up straight, joined his hands across his
chest, and exclaimed, "You've been with that woman again. Now if
this doesn't stop, I'll . . . yes, I'll cut you out of my will." He dropped
the pose and, nodding at us and his face unsmiling now, he said,
"That's what she said last week, that she was going to cut me out of her
will. I've kept that house going for years, and now she's going to cut
me out of her will. Oh, Nardy" - he put his hand up to Nardy and
gripped his wrist - "I nearly hit her, I did. Honest to God, I nearly hit
her." Then he laughed, and spluttered as he said, "Do you remember
Babs, in the office, big Babs? Well, we were as close as damn it, weren't

we, about making a go of it. And there was Babs. She had sat through one of those teas; she had listened to Mother's veiled insults; and when she was about to leave and I went to get her coat and hat, she stood up to say goodbye, and Mother looked at her and said, 'Are you a virgin?' . . . Bella told me this. That's what she said: 'Are you a virgin?' And Babs stared back at her for a moment; then throwing her head up - you remember how she used to do that before she laughed, Nardy? And like Hamilton" - he was now looking at me - "aye, just like your Hamilton, Maisie, up would go her head. And that night she looked down on Mother and said, 'Me a virgin, Mrs Balfour? How could I possibly be after keeping company with your son for the past six months, and him known as the office rape!'"

As if of one mind none of us laughed at this, but we stared at him as he went on, quietly now, "In the hall Babs said, 'Goodbye, Tommy, and it is goodbye.'"

"Come on, come on, on your feet, and to bed." Nardy had got hold of his arm and now tugged him up. And he went from the room without saying good-night to any of us. And when the door had closed on them, George looked at me and said, "Hell's bells! It got past being funny that. What d'you say, Maisie?"

"Yes, it's got past being funny, George."

"D'you know somethin'?" We both looked at Gran, and she said, "The state that fella's in, he could do for her."

Something of that kind had passed through my own mind, and not just tonight.

Then George said, "Is she really as bad as he makes out?"

"I should say worse when you've got to live with her. Yet, in a way, I suppose" - I stopped for a moment before I expressed my next thought, which I questioned even as I put it into words - "it's . . . it's likely because she loves him in her own way, she doesn't want to lose him."

But did love belittle the object that it loved, as that woman belittled her son? As I had said to myself before, there are all kinds of love. Look how I had mourned after Bill, my dog, as I had never mourned after my mother. Yet I had loved her, or at least: I had wanted to love her.

Gran now said something that was very telling. Getting to her feet and taking a deep breath, she said, "At one time I used to envy people with money an' education an' think, oh, if only we'd had money I could have had that big lout there educated" - she stabbed her finger towards George - "because, believe it or not, they said he was quite bright at school. I used to imagine that once you had education an' money, life would run on roller-skates. By lad, you live an' learn, don't you?"

"Aye, Mrs Carter, you live an' learn." And George too, got to his feet and, taking her arm, he said, "I never knew you wanted that for me." And to this, she answered, "There's lots of things you don't know, lad, and in this minute, after what I've heard the night I'm glad that you don't. Well, here's one off to bed. Good-night, lass." She leaned towards me and I kissed her. Then George hugged me, saying as he did so, "It's been a smashing night, Maisie, a smashing night."

I did not immediately gather up the coffee cups, but I sat down on the couch again, and there was Hamilton sitting with his two front legs resting over the end of it. And he looked at me and he repeated, A smashing night, so why aren't you laughing now?

I'm a bit worried over Tommy, I said.

Yes, Tommy. He nodded his big head and his expression was odd. I didn't know whether he was vexed or pleased. And then he said, You've got to think seriously about Tommy. He's making this his second home.

Well, what's wrong in that? He's Nardy's best friend, always has been, and he's mine now.

There are friends and friends. Nardy didn't like him spouting that poetry tonight.

Don't be silly, you're imagining things.

Huh! Huh! His big lip left his teeth and he said, That's funny coming from you.

It might be, but I'm not so vain, or mad, as to think that another. . . I couldn't go on. And at that moment the door opened and Nardy entered the room, and I looked at him as he made straight for the coffee cups and gathered them up and put them on the tray.

"Is he all right?"

"For the moment." His answer was brief.

"I'm . . . I'm worried about him, Nardy."

"You're not the only one."

The cups stacked on the trolley, he now came and sat down beside me and, taking my hand in both of his, he looked at me for some seconds before he said quietly, "Don't become too sorry for him, Maisie."

I looked to the side, and there was Hamilton, his big head nodding slowly, and with him was Begonia, but she was shaking her head from side to side. She wasn't looking at me but at her mate, and there was a look of indignation in her whole attitude. And there was indignation in my tone as I said, "What do you mean, Nardy, don't get too sorry for him?"

"Just what I say, don't get too sorry for him. You must have guessed how he feels about you."

"Oh Nardy." I went to pull my hand away from his, but he held on to it, saying now, "Don't play about. You must have realized it."

"I don't, I didn't, I mean. . ."

"What do you mean, dear?"

"Well, I felt a bit embarrassed tonight when he was spouting his love poems, but . . . but he was tight."

"Yes, he was tight tonight, but he's been solid and sober at other times when he's spouted his love poems. I'm just putting you on your guard."

"But Nardy" - I shook my head - "How could you imagine, I mean that. . . Well" - I swallowed deeply - "I think it's a miracle that you love me, but that I could . . . well. . ." I searched for a word, and there he was at the bottom of the couch, his big head wagging, giving it to me. And I brought it out on a stammer, "A . . . attract anyone else, me of all people, because . . . oh Nardy, I love you so much, so very, very much, and right deep in my heart I'm so full of gratitude to you; you have given me a new way of life. And to think you would imagine that I would, or could dare. . ."

"I don't imagine that you would or could dare or do anything in that direction, my dearest. But you know, you are of a sympathetic nature, you hold out friendship with both hands, because, let's face it, you were deprived of it for so long, it's like a new wine to you, and . . . and Tommy has drunk deeply of it lately. He's hardly ever away from this house."

"But he's your friend. I welcomed him as your friend. You've told me you've been close for years, and he's told me that if it hadn't been for your friendship he just doesn't know how he would have got through at times. Nardy, you could be mistaken, you must be mistaken. Oh, I hope you are, because it will mean I'll have to . . . well, be stiff with him."

"There's no need to be stiff with him, my dear; I only want you to be on your guard. As Gran would say, keep your weather-eye open. I love you, my dear, I love you as I never imagined loving anyone again, and . . . and I'm jealous."

I closed my eyes. Was I Maisie Rochester who had known she would never be married, who had recognized her plainness and her overall lack of attraction, even without her deformed arm? Could this still be Maisie Rochester who for thirteen years had been married to a sadist and who had gained the love of a wonderful man and was now being told that he was jealous because another man was in love with her? No, no; it couldn't happen to her. Come off it.

"What did you say?"

"I didn't speak."

"Yes, you did."

I gave a small laugh. "It was Hamilton. He said, come off it."

"Oh" - he looked about him - "I agree with you, Hamilton; false modesty on her part."

"Oh, it wasn't that, it was just that ... that ... well, I couldn't think that these things were happening to me, or could ever happen to me, you in particular, darling." I now took his face between my hands and said, "Nardy, this I promise you, I shall love you till the day I die and never, never willingly cause you one moment's worry or regret."

"Oh, my dear, my dear." He held me gently in his arms. And as I looked over his shoulder, there they were, standing side by side and, strangely, their heads were hanging. That was odd, I thought. What had I said to make them look so sad? I had just made a vow that I would love my beloved until the day I died.

*

Mrs Balfour was sitting in very much the same position that Tommy had depicted her the previous night: she was seated in a straight-backed chair, her hands folded across her stomach. She had been seated like this for the last hour, and like a judge, or a better description would be the prosecuting counsel, she had been firing questions alternately at Gran and George. She was now looking at George. "I understand you drive a bus," she said.

"Yes, I drive a bus, missis."

"Couldn't you find a better occupation than that?"

"There is no better occupation than that, missis. As me ma says" - he thumbed towards Gran - "it's like life: it stops and starts; people get on an' get off, some you remember an' some you don't; some are nice an' some are real bug ... nasty. You'd like to run over the nasty ones" - he grinned widely now - "but there seems to be a law against it. A pity, I think."

Mrs Balfour pulled her chin inwards before saying now, "You have four children to support?"

"I have that, missis."

"But they're not your children?"

His expression changed and, gruffly now, he said, "They're my children all right, missis, and I'm their father."

"Oh. Oh, I was given to understand. . ."

"Aye, you were given to understand all right: their father scarpered and left them, and I married a woman with four bairns. But she's me wife and they are me children."

They stared at each other for a moment, and I was about to break in when the lady turned her attention on Gran, asking abruptly now, "Do you get on with your daughter-in-law, Mrs Carter?"

"Aye. Why shouldn't I?"

"Well" - there was a tight smile on the lady's face - "mother's don't often get on with their daughters-in-law."

"It all depends on who the mother is an' who the daughter-in-law is. D'you think you could get on with your daughter-in-law?"

"I don't happen to have a daughter-in-law."

"No, I know that, but say if you suddenly had."

"What do you mean, if I suddenly had?"

"Just that." Gran grinned at the lady now. "Say Tommy took it into his head to get married. There would be nothin' unusual about that, now would there? He could do it any minute."

I saw the skin tighten on the bony face, the wrinkles seemed to smooth out, the eyes narrowed and the voice came thinly through her teeth now as she said, "I don't think there's any possibility of my son marrying, and therefore the question of my becoming a mother-in-law has no point."

"Huh! You never know where a blister might light."

"What did you say?"

"I said, you never know where a blister might light. I'd better translate that for you, eh? You never know what men will do, especially 'round your Tommy's age. They get a sort of itch then, if they haven't had it afore. Now there's our Georgie. He always had the itch, born with it, weren't you, lad?"

To this George replied, "Just as you say, Ma, just as you say. But you're right." Pressing home his mother's point, and enjoying it, he now looked at our visitor and said, "Blisters can grow into boils, and then there's nothin' for it but a hot poultice. And the only equivalent to a hot poultice in this case is a bedmate. Come on, Ma." He got to his feet. "Tommy's in the kitchen supposedly nattering to Janet. I don't trust him an inch."

"Nor me," said Gran, and they both almost skipped out of the room. And when Nardy, who had been choking inwardly all this time, rose and said, "Will you excuse me for a moment? I think it's about time we were called in to tea. It's to be a north-country one." And he smiled at Mrs Balfour. And there I was left with her, and she stared at me hard before she spoke. "How do you put up with that pair, Mrs Leviston?" she said.

"What exactly do you mean, Mrs Balfour?"

"I . . . I shouldn't think that I have to explain what I mean, they are both uncouth. I have never met anyone like them before. Common isn't the word."

"You're right, common isn't the word, Mrs Balfour, and definitely not uncouth. I think the word you're really looking for is real. They are real people, uneducated, yes, but they both have wisdom that no education could have supplied."

"Well, well, they certainly have an advocate in you, Mrs Leviston."

"Yes, they have, because they were the only people in my young days to give me love and bring me any kind of happiness."

"What about your mother? I understand you were sixteen or more when she died."

"Oh, my mother." I nodded at her. "My mother was not common; my mother was refined, a lady you could say, even though a pseudo one, and she was vain and cruel without any real love in her."

"Really! I don't think it befits you to speak of the dead like that, Mrs Leviston."

I rose to my feet, and looking at her straight in the face now, I said, "Nor do I think it befits you to speak of the living and those who are my friends so disparagingly. Shall we go into tea?"

I saw her face working, her pale blue lips moving over one another as if she were already champing on food. Then, as I made to walk away, she said, "A moment, Mrs Leviston. I'm" - now I recognized she had to make an effort to go on - "I'm sorry if I've upset you, but before we go in there is something private I should like to discuss with you if you can give me another moment. "

I stepped back and faced her again.

"It's . . . it's about Tommy. I . . . I'm very worried about him."

"Really? Why are you worried about him?"

I watched her fingers as they began to pick at the material of her dress; it was as if she was removing insects from it. "It's . . . it's concerning a woman."

"A woman?"

"Yes. I wonder if you can . . . well, help me? Do you know who she is?"

"The woman?"

"Yes, the woman."

"No." I shook my head. "I know of no woman that Tommy is . . . well, associated with. How should I? We . . . we only see him now and again."

"That . . . that makes it worse." The picking went on and she looked to the side. "I . . . I understand that he often comes over here in the evenings. Bella seemed to think so. But . . . but he has, for some time now, spent week-ends away from home."

"Really?"

"Yes." She nodded at me. "And that suggests only one thing, you must admit."

"I wouldn't know."

Her voice was sharp now as she said, "Well, you wouldn't expect a man to spend week-ends on his own, now would you?"

I could have said, Yes. In Tommy's case, yes. Instead, I said, "Well, hardly."

"Well, there you are then. And . . . and you don't know who she is?"

"No."

"He hasn't given you any indication, a name, a place?"

"I'm afraid not."

"If he had told Nardy, would Nardy have confided in you?"

I thought for a moment before I let myself say, "I'm not so sure. They have been friends for years; he . . . he might be honouring a trust."

"Yes, yes, of course. May I ask you something?"

"Yes."

"Would you . . . well, I mean, would you do something for me?"

"That all depends if it's possible."

"Oh, it's quite possible. All I'm asking is that you . . . probe a little and . . . and let me know . . . if. . ."

I held up my hand. "Please don't go on, Mrs Balfour. I have no intention of probing into your son's private affairs. And if he were to confide in me, then it would be as a friend and, as such, a confidence. Shall we go into tea now?"

The look on her face was almost vicious. She pulled herself to her feet and I opened the door for her, and with a step very firm for one supposedly crippled with arthritis, she passed through.

Seeing Tommy approaching from the direction of the kitchen with Gran on his arm, and laughing together, she called in strident tones, "We cannot stay long. I am not feeling too well."

"That is a pity, Mother. It would have been nice if we could have made a night of it, wouldn't it, Gran?" He now turned and looked at Gran, and she, slapping him on the back, answered, "It would that, lad. It would that."

Hurriedly now, I led our guest into the dining-room, fearing that she would faint before she reached there, for all the colour had drained from her face.

Immediately the meal was over, she donned her coat. She had not removed her hat at all. And when we closed the door on her and Tommy, Nardy let out a long-drawn breath, saying, "God help him when he gets home."

I endorsed this in my mind, and I was also glad this evening was already taken care of: seats had been booked for four at the theatre later on; and afterwards a table was reserved in one of Nardy's favourite restaurants. Tomorrow, too, had been planned. We were to show Gran and George London. And on Monday they would be returning to Fellburn.

Why should I feel guilty at the thought that I should be glad to have the house to myself again? This was something new.

I went into the kitchen to thank Janet for her big effort in making such a splendid tea.

"Oh, that's all right," she said. "I'm glad you enjoyed it. But she's a tartar, that one, isn't she? How in the name of God does Mr Tommy stand her!" Then leaning forward to me and whispering, she said, "I bet she found her match in Gran, eh, ma'am?"

"She did, Janet, she did. And with George, too. But she found them very common . . . uncouth."

"She said that?"

"Yes, she did."

"Well, give me the common and uncouth any day. What do you say?"

"I say with you, Janet, yes, any day."

I liked Janet more the longer we were together. In a way she had taken Gran's place in this new world. But strangely, I had the idea that Gran hadn't quite taken to her.

Chapter 6

The weeks slid by. Nardy worked in the office, I worked on my book. He was nearly always in by half-past five. We would have tea; then talk. Some evenings, we would just sit by the fire; then go to bed and love; or we might go out to a play, or to Covent Garden Opera House. He was educating me in the world of music and art. He loved the opera, I wasn't so keen on it; my choice was the ballet. Life was good.

But there was still Tommy. He had become very quiet of late, and he wasn't dropping in so often. And even after a drink or two he had ceased to spout his poetry. Then one night came the climax.

It was a Friday evening. Autumn was setting in: the leaves in the garden opposite had turned to bronze and gold. I often sat by the window in the drawing-room looking down into the garden and thinking what a pity I never saw anyone strolling in it. All the residents in the square had keys to it, but I had yet to see anyone using one. The only human figure was that of the old gardener pottering about. I likened the garden to a jewel encased in an iron cage. Why didn't they take the railings down and let people walk among the beautiful shrubs . . . and leave their orange peel, and the beer cans, and their ice-cream cartons. I looked to the side. Hamilton was looking out of the window and I nodded at him, saying, "Yes, you're right."

I know I am, he said. People in the main are dirty. Some of them live like pigs. Remember Mrs Purdy?

I remembered Mrs Purdy, a distant relative of Nardy's we went down to Hampshire to visit. She lived in what you would call a manor-house, and it stank.

"Why" - I asked Hamilton - "do some women consider housework beneath them?"

And to this he answered, Because at one time only menials did housework and you could engage servants by the dozen for next to nothing; but now the servants have cars and can drive into the country and leave their litter scattered about, so following the example of their betters in bygone days. But they have no servants to rake it all up after them.

"You're being cynical." I smiled at him, and, his lip going up from his teeth, he smiled back and said, You could say we are. Anyway, here's your beloved coming.

I kissed my beloved, my beloved kissed me; then we sat down together on the couch and I poured out the tea that was set on the low trolley. And then I asked the usual question, "How's it gone?"

"It's been an unusual day," he said. "I took a new author out to lunch at the Café Royal."

"Oh," I said smiling. "Man or woman?"

"A man. And I thought of the day I took you there and of how different it all was, because this fellow . . . oh my God!" He closed his eyes for a moment and turned his head to the side. "The ego of some men. You know something? This book of his is the best that has ever been written by anyone."

"Is it so good?"

"No, it's not. I think it's quite mediocre. It's only the sex that's got it through. That's the trouble now, they think they've only to lay that on thick and they're there. And it is on thick, and the book will sell. Oh, yes, it'll sell. But there he was dictating about what would happen when it went into paperbacks and then into a film."

"No."

"Oh, yes, yes. And I couldn't get rid of him after lunch; I didn't get back to the office until nearly four, and then one of the clerks told me there had been two calls from Tommy's. Huh!" He laughed here. "Likely his mother wanted to know where he was going to spend the week-end. Perhaps he had told her he was making it a long one, because he was off to Eastbourne earlier today to see an author, a man who's writing his autobiography. Aren't they all!"

It was at this point the phone rang and I stayed him, saying, "I'll get it."

The phone was on a table to the side of the window, and I picked it up and a voice said, "Is that you, Mrs Leviston?"

"Yes, yes, Bella." I recognized her voice.

"Oh, Mrs Leviston, is . . . is Mr Leviston there?"

"Yes, yes, he's here, Bella. Is there anything wrong?"

"She's dead . . . she's dead, Mrs Leviston."

"*Wh . . . at!*" My voice ended on a screech that brought Nardy to my side. I gazed at him in horror, and I put my hand over the mouthpiece as I said, "She's dead."

As he whispered, "Oh, my God!" I spoke into the phone again, saying, "What . . . what happened?"

"It . . . it was around three o'clock."

She seemed to be gasping for breath now and I said, "Where's Tommy?"

"He's here, Mrs Leviston. Will you come around?"

"Yes, yes, right away, right away." And I banged down the phone before picking it up again to order a taxi. . .

Twenty minutes later we entered the house. Tommy met us in the hall. His face looked ashen. He didn't speak but after looking from one to the other of us he turned and we followed him into the dining-room. And now, sitting at the table and joining his hands together, he bowed his head over them, saying, "I feel terrible, terrible."

"What happened?" Nardy was standing by him, his hand on his shoulder. And now he raised his head and looked up at Nardy and muttered, "You know I . . . I went down to Eastbourne. Well, Bella phoned the office and they gave her the address; but I'd left by then, and when I got back, there she was."

Now Nardy had him by the shoulder shaking him and saying, "Well, what happened?"

"I don't know, except what Bella said. About two o'clock she had a sort of seizure and . . . and she rang for the doctor for her. And when he came, he said it was a heart attack and he would get her into hospital. But as he was examining her she just . . . well, she went."

Both Nardy and I groped for chairs and sat down, and as if of one mind we both put our elbows on the table and held our heads in our hands for a moment. The relief was making me sick, as I'm sure it was Nardy.

Tommy was shaking his head. "I . . . I feel awful, man, dreadful. The times . . . oh, the times " he now wagged his head slowly from shoulder to shoulder, his eyes screwed up tight as he went on, "I've wanted her dead. I've prayed I'd come home and find her dead. I've prayed she would have a heart attack. And then, only this morning, she said, "Where are you going?" and I said, "I'm going down to Eastbourne for the week-end. What are you going to make out of that, Mother?" I had no intention of staying away for the week-end, not now, not any more, for it didn't do any good. But . . . but that must have finished her."

"No. No, of course it didn't." Nardy's voice was harsh now. "She must have had a bad heart for years."

"Well, that was something I didn't know. But, oh God! Nardy, I feel weighed down." He now looked at me, saying, "I should feel free - shouldn't I, Maisie? - like you did after you got rid of Stickle, but I don't. I feel . . . well, I feel trapped inside myself. I'll never get over this feeling of guilt, because instead of hating her, I should have tried to understand her needs of me, and . .. and shown her some love, but I didn't. I didn't."

I rose now and went round and put a hand on his shoulder as I said, "She didn't show you any, not real love. You mustn't blame yourself for that."

"I think I'll blame myself till the day I die. When I saw her lying there she looked so . . . so helpless, and so very, very old, pityingly vulnerable. Oh, my God!" He again drooped his head on to his hands, and I said, "Believe me, Tommy, this feeling will pass. I had something similar when my mother went. It will pass, I tell you, it will pass. Anyway, I think the best thing you can do, and Bella too, is to come and sleep at our place for the next day or two. When will they take her away?"

"In the morning."

"Well, then, both of you. . ."

"No, no. Thanks all the same, Maisie. I've got to stay here, at least until she is finally put away. Then I'll know what I'm going to do. This . . . this house has been a drag on me for years. I'll . . . I'll likely sell it, and . . . and settle Bella some place. And then we'll see. Thanks for coming." He looked from one to the other; then getting to his feet, he squared his shoulders and said. "You two have borne the brunt of my moaning for a long time now. I'm sorry I burdened you with it. I must have been a proper pain in the neck at times. Well, it's all over. The only person I'll have to moan about now is myself and my conscience." He held up his hands as Nardy was about to say something, and he went on, "It's no use. I know myself too well, Nardy. I'm a coward. If I hadn't been I would have made a break years ago, before things got on top of me. It wouldn't have upset her half as much then. But then again" - he shrugged his shoulders "I couldn't have done that as I was her only support. That's been part of the trouble. You see, when my father died he was almost bankrupt: she hadn't a penny after he went, and she liked this house. And, of course, I had to have a home. So, what was more natural than that I should keep it going. And that's been part of the resentment. You see, I felt trapped from the beginning: were I to marry I couldn't run two homes, my wife would have to come here." He smiled now, a wan sad smile, "You get the picture? At least you've had it for a long time now. But don't worry." He held out his hands to both of us. "I'll be all right. I've been blessed in one way, I've got you two, and always will have, I hope."

Chapter 7

It was the day after the funeral, a Wednesday; she had been buried on the Tuesday. Apart from the heads of the office and Nardy and myself and Bella, there were no other mourners at the funeral.

Nardy had returned to the office. Tommy was to see the solicitor with regard to his mother's will. That's how things stood, until six o'clock that evening.

We had finished tea and I'd washed up and I was about to go and change because we were going to the opera when the lift bell rang. Nardy and I were both in the hall. He went and opened the door and in walked Tommy. Or did he race in? or jump in? I'm not quite sure.

There was the strangest look upon his face. Was it full of glee, or was it devilish? His large grey eyes looked almost black and, spreading his arms out towards us both in an exaggerated dramatic way, he said, "My friends. My friends." Then noticing the look on Nardy's face, he dropped his arms to his sides and, his voice changing, he said, "I'm not drunk, I'm solid and sober, but you see before you, dear friends, a man so full of hate that he'll have to live ten lifetimes before it's burnt out of him."

"What's the matter with you? What's happened?" Nardy's voice was terse.

"May I sit down and have a drink *now*?"

I turned to go to the drawing-room and Tommy followed me. Nardy went into the dining room to get the drink. When I sat down, Tommy, bending over me, said slowly, "You've got your Hamilton, Maisie, I've got the devil."

"Oh! Tommy. Tommy, what is it? What on earth's happened?"

Nardy was entering the room with a tray, and Tommy called, "Make it neat, Nardy, and a double."

He threw off his whisky in two gulps; then sat down on the couch and drew in a long shuddering breath before looking up at us and saying, "You also see before you a rich man."

We exchanged a glance, Nardy and I, both thinking the same thing, he had become deranged in some way. And he, picking up our thoughts, said, "Sit down, Nardy, sit down. You'll need to sit before I'm finished. And I'm not barmy, I haven't gone round the bend. But it wouldn't surprise me at all if I did. I've been with my solicitor all afternoon" - he nodded at Nardy "and I expected him to say, 'Well, Mr Balfour, there's little to talk about. Your mother's will is very straightforward. The house was in her name, as you know, and of the thousand pounds that her aunt left her, she has, as you know, taken the interest every year. But apart from that, I don't think there's anything further to discuss.' That's what I expected him to say. But what did he do? He invited me to sit down. He smiled at me, and then said, 'Your mother was a very strange lady, Mr Balfour.' I could have been flippant and said, you're telling me, but I remained mute, until he said, 'Right from the beginning she wanted this matter kept strictly private. No one was to know anything about it until she died. Then I'm afraid, if you had been married -' he then poked his head towards me and said, 'You are not married, are you?' And to this I replied, 'No, I am not married, sir.' And so he went on, 'Well then, the estate won't go to the animals so I can say now that everything appears to be straightforward, seeing that you have no brothers or sisters to make their claim on the estate.'"

Tommy stopped here, wetted his lips, then again exchanged a glance with us both and said, "I repeated, 'Estate?' and the dear old fellow nodded and said with emphasis, 'Yes, estate.' At this I smiled and said, 'A terrace house and a few pounds.' And then you know what he said?"

We waited while he stared at us, swallowed deeply, then put his hand to his throat and stroked it as if trying to push his Adam's apple down his gullet. And then he went on, "He said, 'I wouldn't consider seventy-five thousand pounds and four considerable properties to come under the heading of a few pounds.' And he smiled as he said it; and I stared at him, and I couldn't speak for a time, then I said, 'What?' And he repeated, 'Seventy-five thousand pounds. And there are the four properties, here in London, let as offices at present, but worth not less than one hundred thousand pounds each.'"

We were both speechless. We continued to gaze at him and he at us, until he went on, "It was fifteen years ago that her aunt died. She lived in Devon. I'd only met her once. I was a young fellow at the time, in my twenties, and I thought Mother and she could be sisters, they were so alike. Well, when she died, Mother went down to see to her affairs. She had always, I think, imagined her to be slightly hard up. And thinking about it now, she very likely got the idea of the games she played with me from her dear aunt, for the solicitor tells me that she was surprised to be left the four houses and amazed at the sum of money, which then was about fifty thousand pounds, apparently the aunt had played with stocks and shares. What Mother had expected, so I understand, was the cottage and the furniture, which then would have been worth about fifteen hundred pounds. I remember she stayed down there for four or five weeks, and it was such a nice respite for Bella and, of course, for me too. Oh, yes, me too. Then when she returned. . ." He stopped and, wetting his lips, he looked from side to side; then pointing to a chair, he said, "I can see her as if she were there now, sitting in the chair with her arms folded across her stomach, telling me that the aunt had left her the little house and that she had sold it and she was richer by a thousand pounds. But she had put it in the bank and had decided each year that the interest would buy her a winter or a summer outfit, and in that way it would ease my purse. Those were the very words she used, ease my purse."

He was silent now. We were all silent. We just couldn't take it in. That dreadful woman to hang on to him all these years, to plead poverty so he wouldn't leave her.

He now asked quietly, "Can you believe it?"

"No. No." Nardy's voice was small. "It's diabolical."

"Yes, that's the word, diabolical, because every month it's taken nearly all my pay cheque to keep things going: Bella had to be paid, as small as her wage was, she had to be paid. Poor Bella.

What she's gone through too." His head dropped back on his shoulders now and he said, "I've always wanted a car, but I've told myself again and again I'd never be able to afford one. Yet, all these years I could have had a car, couldn't I?" He looked at me now and said, "Couldn't I, Maisie? I could have had a car . . . two cars, three cars. And I could have taken her out and about. Can you see the reasoning in it? Oh!" He closed his eyes tight and clenched his fists now and shook them in front of his face as he said, "Why am I asking such a bloody silly question? Of course, anybody can see the reasoning of it: with a car I'd be able to drive away, wouldn't I, with a girl beside me? And with money like that I would have had half a dozen, no, a dozen suits and shirts to match. Aye, shirts to match instead of Bella having to turn the cuffs, which she has done for years." His head was wagging now. "Yes, Bella's turned the cuffs of my shirts for years."

He got abruptly to his feet and in silence we watched him stamping up and down behind the couch. Twice he went the length of the room and we didn't move. And then he stopped and, leaning over the couch towards us, he cried, "I wish I had killed her. I do, I wish I had killed her. I would willingly spend the next ten years in a cell for the pleasure of having killed her."

"Stop it! Stop it!" Nardy was on his feet now. "That's no way to talk. You would have never killed her."

"Oh, you don't know, Nardy. What do you know about it, really? You only saw the rehearsals, you didn't see the real acts. You didn't have to sit with her night after night and listen to her. If I wanted to read, she wanted to know why I didn't talk, and if I talked she would always slap me down as if I was a little boy, saying, 'Don't talk such tommy-rot. Poetry!' she used to say. 'No real man reads poetry.' When I pointed out Keats, Browning, Byron, and the rest, her answer was, 'They weren't real men, they were perverts.' It's many a long day since I talked poetry in that house. You know what she did once? She turfed nearly all the books out of my room and gave them to somebody who was collecting for a jumble sale, among them an early edition of Keats, and an edition of Shelley's poems arranged by Stopford Brooke." He pointed his finger into Nardy's chest, saying, "Macmillan published it. And then there was. . ."

"All right, all right. I know about that, you told me. But now it's over. Come and sit down and listen to me. As you said, you're rich, and you've still got a long life before you."

"What, at thirty-nine?"

"Yes, at thirty-nine. Don't be ridiculous. Sit down there." Nardy pushed him back onto the couch. "Now, the main thing for you to do is to come back to work, at least for a few weeks, if not for good. In the meantime, buy that car, learn to drive, get yourself out and about. You once said to me, how wonderful it would be to do a world tour. Well, do your world tour. But first give yourself time to think."

"Oh, I've given myself time to think. I've walked for miles before I came here. You know that? When I went back and told Bella, she couldn't believe it. She just couldn't. In fact, she thought I was crazy, like you two did." He gave a wry smile now. "In fact, I'm asking myself, am I not crazy? Anyway, crazy or not, I'm selling that house, and I can't think of the thousands that'll bring in these days. Huh!" He laughed. "Talking in thousands now when for years I've taken the tube because I couldn't afford to run to taxis. Anyway, Bella's got a hankering after Brighton. She's spent her one week's holiday a year there for some time past, and so I'm going to buy a flat and she can move into it. It will be a place for me to go at the week-ends when I'm at a loose end. Anyway, I'm giving her ten thousand. If anybody's earned it for a lifetime's work, she has."

"That's good of you."

He looked at Nardy, saying now in a bitter tone, "No, it isn't. I'm doing it mainly to get one back on her; she'd go stark staring mad if she thought that Bella was getting a cut of her cake."

"You're not doing it to spite her." I spoke for the first time. "Well, you're telling yourself you are, but you are really doing it out of the goodness of your heart."

"Maisie" - he slowly shook his head - "there's no goodness in my heart at the present moment. I disliked her. I loathed her at times, but I knew nothing about hate, real hate like that which is in me now. I tell you, I could. . ."

"No more of that!" Nardy was shouting at him. "And get it out of your mind; in fact, make yourself laugh about it."

"What!"

For a moment I thought Tommy was going to go for Nardy physically, for he bent towards him and his voice was a yell as he cried, "Laugh at what I've gone through since I was a lad? Laugh?" He now thumbed towards me, saying, "Maisie wouldn't tell me to laugh, Nardy, for she knows what it is to live with a sadist."

I got to my feet and went towards him and, taking his hand, I said, "Yes, I do, I do, Tommy; but I also know that the sadist wins if you let hate of him corrode you. I went mad for a time under such treatment. And just lately, when Sandy there" - I pointed to where the dog was lying curled up in his favourite place, hugging the fire - "was tortured, and I felt there was only one person who would have done it, there was in me for a time the feeling that if I came near Stickle I would make sure I had a knife in my hand, and I would tear the flesh from him bit by bit as he had done from that poor little beast. Then I knew that the only sane thing to do was to put distance between the perpetrator of evil and myself. Well now, Tommy, there's a great deal of distance between your perpetrator and yourself, and, as Nardy said, you have a long life before you. Get that car, then do a world tour, then get married."

He was staring down into my face and he repeated, "Get the car, do a world tour, then get married. Thank you, Maisie, I'll think about it. But now, I'll make myself scarce because I've just remembered this is the big night at the opera. You've had tickets for it for some time."

"Oh, that doesn't matter; you stay where you are and I'll make a . . ."

"You'll do no such thing. I'm off." He stood up and buttoned his coat. Then laughing a laugh that was threaded with bitterness, he said, "You see the beginnings of the new man. But I'll tell you what you can do, at the week-end you can come and help me choose the car."

"We'll do that, we'll do it with pleasure." Nardy was walking up the room with him. I didn't follow, and at the door Tommy turned and said, "Be seeing you, Maisie."

"Yes, Tommy, yes."

I stood where I was until I heard the outer door close, and then Nardy came back into the room. And when he reached me, we looked at each other for a moment but didn't speak. I stooped down and picked Sandy up into my arms and he snuggled his head into my neck. And it was then I said, "She would have left it all to the animals, and she wouldn't even let him have a dog, or a cat when he was a boy. She was a fiend."

"She was that all right. But you know something, dear?"

"What?"

"I feel more worried about him now than I was before, because he will go on hating her."

"Time will tell," I said. Then looking at the clock, I added, "We'd be late, wouldn't we?" And he nodded and said, "Yes, we'd be late. But what does it matter? I don't think I could enjoy even the singing of angels at this moment." Then reaching out his arm, he said, "Come and sit down and let us thank the gods that we are what we are and we have each other."

And as I sat down, still holding Sandy, I added, "And Sandy."

"Yes, of course, Sandy."

"And Hamilton."

"Oh, yes, Hamilton."

"And Begonia."

He smiled but he didn't laugh.

Tommy had come into a fortune, but it seemed to have put a damper on all merriment.

Tommy got his car. He took driving lessons, a crash course, and passed first time. He sold the terraced house, bought the flat in Brighton, and Bella, hardly able to believe that this was happening to her, went to live there, and found herself a part-time job in relieving a nurse who was looking after an invalid, a woman, the antithesis of her previous mistress. She kept her week-ends free so that she could be in the flat and see to Tommy, should he care to come down. So life for her had fallen into what she termed, a fairy-tale pattern.

Tommy said he wouldn't dream of leaving Houseman's, but he intended to ask for an extended leave in order that he could realize his dream of doing a world tour. He had it all mapped out.

Chapter 8

It was again a week before Christmas, and both Nardy and I were in a dilemma. Gran had been unwell for some time. It had started with a cold. It had developed into pneumonia, and Mary kept saying that Gran wished she could see me. Remembering the events of last New Year, I was afraid to go back to Fellburn. So we talked it over and we came to the decision that we would go up for just a couple of days and see Gran, and if she was on the mend we would come straight back.

Also there was another tangent we had to sort out. Tommy had bought a host of presents for the children, all kinds of things. He seemed bent on spending. Shortly after he had come into the money, he had presented me with a diamond brooch and matching earrings, and Nardy with a magnificent pair of gold cuff links. More than once Nardy had warned him that the rate at which his money was going would soon see him back to where he had been. But Tommy had laughed and said in an airy fashion, "Why, since I sold one of those houses to that advertising firm, I'm not even making a hole in the interest on the money. And who've I got to spend it on but my friends? And as charming as dear Housey is and our friend Rington, do you know they never once invited me to dinner at their homes. . . Oh yes, you were, you were" - he had nodded to Nardy - "but never me. No, my friends are few, but they're of the best quality."

He could say the nicest things, could Tommy. But here we were, and Nardy was saying, "Well, as he was coming to us for the holidays the best thing for it is to let him come up with us. But I'm not going in that car; he's a madman behind that wheel. You'd think he'd been driving in Le Mans races for years. No, let him go up his way and we'll go by train as usual."

And so it was arranged.

I phoned Mary and told her we'd be up the next day, but not to expect us to stay very long, especially not over Christmas. And also to prepare for an invasion by Tommy.

So, once again we were getting off the train in Newcastle station, and I was carrying Sandy in my arms and was dressed in my fur coat and hat, but fortunately there were no photographers and journalists there today. Our luggage was light, only two cases, one filled with presents, the other with our night clothes and toiletries.

We had to stand for a few minutes in a queue for a taxi. Then one drew up. The driver turned his head towards us and the constriction in my throat, at the sight of him, caused me to grip Sandy so close that he yelped. And in the same instant, Nardy, who had bent down towards the driver, clutched my arm, pulled me back onto the pavement, and almost dragged me along to where the next cab was approaching. He himself was gasping as he gave this driver our address. Then when we were seated, he gripped my hand, saying, "It's all right. It's all right. Stop shivering; nothing can happen. He wouldn't dare attempt anything. There's nothing he can do. And we'll get back home as soon as possible. Now stop it, stop shivering."

But I couldn't stop shivering. And for the first time in weeks I saw Hamilton. He was crouched on the opposite seat, and seemingly filled with the same fear that was coursing through me. When Nardy said, "We will go back tonight, we'll get the midnight train," Hamilton immediately made a great obeisance with his head. And when I could force myself to speak, I said, "We must wait and see how she is."

When we reached the house the children swarmed over us, and Mary greeted us warmly. George wasn't in. She said he was along with his mother. And yes, Gran was pretty low. What was the matter?

Wasn't I well?

The children were scattered back to the kitchen with Sandy while we went into the old sitting-room where Mary had tea ready, and I said simply, "We . . . we came face to face with Stickle. We almost got into his cab."

"Oh my! Oh, my goodness! No wonder you're looking white. Still, I'm sure he knows you're on to him. He wouldn't dare start anything."

"He'd better not," Nardy said grimly. Then he asked,

"Do you hear anything of him?"

"Yes, now and again. His lad seems determined to pal up with our Gordon."

"Does the boy mention his father?"

"No, never, Gordon says; but there're signs that the man has been at him now and again, for Gordon once said Neil had a split lip; and another time he said he couldn't hold his pen. Anyway, don't you worry, nothing's going to happen. He wouldn't dare."

"That man would dare anything, Mary. Oh, the look on his face when he recognized me. For a split second there was that oily smile of the yes, sir, yes, madam, look, the tailor's shop smile. And then that awful look of hate enveloped it."

As I warmed myself at the fire I thought about hate. It was a dreadful thing, hate. Look how it had changed Tommy. Thinking back, I realized that all my life I had been in touch with hate. I recalled the trunk in the attic upstairs in this very house, and it was still there, and my mother's wedding-gown was still in it, meticulously slashed to a hundred and one pieces. I remembered the night I first saw it and glimpsed a little the rage that must have consumed her to make her cut that gown into ribbons and then lay it out piece by piece to fit its original shape before doubling it in half and putting it in the trunk.

Once hate becomes alive it is difficult to kill. I had tried with regard to Stickle, but there it was, churning in me now, yet almost obliterated by my fear.

Nardy pulled at my arm and brought me out of my reverie, saying, "Come on, let's get along to Gran's while there's still some light."

There was more bustle. I went into the kitchen where the children were going mad with Sandy and, picking him up, I said, "I'm putting him in our bedroom. Now, please, don't let him out no matter how much noise he makes. Play with him up there, but you won't, will you, let him out?"

Mary, coming behind me, said, "I'll see to that now. Don't worry. Do you want me to call a taxi?"

"No, we'll walk." I looked at Nardy, and repeated, "We'll walk, yes?" He nodded, and a few minutes later we set out.

Our entry into Gran's street didn't go unnoticed, and people called to me, saying, "Why, hello there, Maisie. How are you? By! you're lookin' bonny."

It was the usual greeting when people meant to be kind.

George opened the door to us, and I was once more lost in his bear-hugging embrace. But there was no great laughter issuing from his lips today and after he had shaken hands firmly with Nardy I said to him, "How is she?" And he pursed his wide lips and wrinkled his nose before saying, "She hasn't been too good, Maisie, not too good. But she's turned the corner now. It's funny to see her lying there without a bellow in her. Just thought lately, if anything were to happen to her, life would lose its spring, at least for me, because I haven't been meself since she took to that bed."

"That's natural." I patted his arm. "Anyway, here, take my coat, and" - I stabbed my finger at him - "don't leave it lying on the couch for the cat to curl up on." I was aiming to be cheerful because I could see that there was a great change in him. And yes, I thought, the spring would go out of all our lives if anything happened to Gran, Gran whom I had loved first because she, like her son, was common, and through her I had imagined that everything nice in this world must be common.

We went upstairs and I opened the bedroom door and I saw her expression change. But, oh dear me, how she had altered. She did look ill, really ill.

When I bent over and kissed her she lifted one weak hand and patted my cheek. I had to keep the tears from my voice as I said, "I can't leave you for a minute, can I? Why can't you look after yourself? I'm tired of trailing after you." It was the same way in which she would have greeted me had our positions been reversed. And she smiled, a pale, wan smile; then her mouth dropped in at the corner and her voice came as a croak when she said, "It's because you went away."

"Well, here I am back, and I want you out of that bed."

"I'll be all right. . . The bucket."

I looked round the room for the bucket, and she lifted her hand wearily again and smiled as she said, "The bucket was hanging " she drew in a deep breath, then went on, "on the knob of the bed . . . the bucket, but I wouldn't kick it."

"Oh. Oh, Gran." It was too much. The tears spilled over from my eyes, and I turned away and Nardy took my place and I heard her say, "Ah, lad, lad." Then, after a moment when I turned to the bed again, she looked at me and said, "Sandy?"

"He's back in the house. They're all looking after him."

"That fella?" She was again aiming to smile.

I glanced at Nardy, then looked at her again and said, "Which fellow, dear?"

She closed her eyes and showed a slight return of her impatience before she brought out, "Ham . . . il . . . ton."

"Oh, him. Oh, he's here all right." I looked towards the bottom of the bed. "He's standing there with his girl-friend Begonia."

Her smile widened and she made a sound like, "Aha."

"He's going to make an honest woman of her, they're going to be married."

I put my hand out and squeezed Nardy's as I saw the bedclothes shake. She was laughing inside. And when Nardy, bending towards her, said, "Tommy's riding down on her," she made a croaking sound. Then as suddenly, her expression changed, and, turning away from the bed, I said quickly, "We're tiring her." It was partly an excuse for myself to get out of the room for I felt that I would howl audibly.

A minute later, down in the passage, George was opening the door to the doctor, and once again I was enveloped in a bear hug, and it could have been a bear because his face was more hairy than ever. Yet, I noticed when he held me at arm's length that it was mostly grey now. He, too, seemed to have changed so very much in a year. Yet, his voice was as I remembered it, and his compliments were as caustic as ever. "You haven't altered much," he said. "I thought they went in for high living up in London; you're getting scraggier."

"I'm in the fashion," I replied.

Taking off his hat and coat now, he said, "You've seen her?"

"Yes."

"She's had a rough passage."

"Is she all right now? I mean, is she over it?"

"I should think so. She'll have to go steady. . . . How long are you staying?"

"Well" - I hesitated, then looked at Nardy - "only for a couple of days."

"Not for the holidays?"

"Not . . . not this time."

He didn't ask the reason why but just nodded his head; then going towards the stairs, he said, "I'll be seeing you; I'll call in at the house after surgery."

In the kitchen I said to George, "Can I help you?" and he replied, "Aye, yes. Get yourself back to the house and have something to eat. Once the meal's over, Mary'll come and relieve me. Go on, now."

I wanted to protest, but Nardy put in, "Do as George says."

So we went back to the house and had a meal. Then, just as she was about to leave for Gran's, Mary said, "What with one thing and another

I haven't been able to do much turning around regarding beds. But John is sleeping up in the attic because Betty wanted a room to herself. You know what they're like. But there's another single up there. Do you think Tommy would mind . . . ?"

"Not a bit of it," Nardy put in now; "he'll be in his element. He'll think he's camping out with the boys."

"Oh, there's only John sleeps there; I don't let Gordon go up, because there would be skull and hair flyin'. Those two . . . funny, but they're at each other's throats most of the time, yet, let anyone else go for either of them and there they are like close buddies."

Just as she finished speaking there came the sound of screeching brakes outside the front door, and Nardy said, "He's arrived."

We opened the door and there, grabbing up parcels from the boot, was Tommy. As I stood with the others waiting for him to bounce up the steps I thought, Of all that could happen in a year! for Tommy, of all others, seemed to have changed out of all recognition.

As soon as he entered the house the children's squeals and high laughter filled the place and his greeting to Nardy, Mary and me was lost under it.

Some short time later I opened the sitting-room door and there was Tommy sitting on the hearthrug, Sandy lying across his knees, and John, Kitty and Gordon squatting near him; only Betty was standing. But they all turned as Nardy and I entered the room, and Tommy, rising to his feet and for the first time, mentioned Gran, saying, "How did you find her?" He seemed to have forgotten that Gran was our main reason for being here.

"Pretty bad, but doctor says she's turned the corner," I said.

"Good, good." He nodded. Then, looking at Nardy and his expression changing, he almost cried, "Five hours, twenty-three minutes, with only one stop! How about that, laddie?"

"You're a maniac."

"I never went over sixty. . . Well, just now and then to pass something. You could have saved your railway fare."

"I've got a whole neck, that's something to be thankful for."

Tommy, now casting his eyes over the children and nodding towards Nardy, said, "He's old, crotchety."

"So am I. Come on you lot!" It was George coming into the room. "Scram!"

"Aw, Dad, you're back." It was a chorus from the three younger ones, and he replied, "Never mind, Aw Dad, you're back. I'll give you two seconds to get off your hunkers before I skelp your lugs for you."

Rising to her feet, Kitty looked at John and Gordon, and, the three of them nodding together, said, "Promises, promises."

With raised hand, George advanced on them crying, "I'll carry out me promises on your bare backsides if you don't get." And laughing, they ran from the room.

In this moment I felt happy for George: here he was with his four adopted children and loving them as he had once loved me when I was small; and I could sense that his affection was returned fourfold.

After George had marshalled them out of the room and we were left alone with Tommy, we both looked at him as he sat on the couch, his long legs sprawled out. And when he didn't speak, I said, "Tired?"

"No, not really." He looked, first to the right and then to the left. "Somehow it's all changed," he said; "I suppose it's because Gran isn't here."

I didn't answer, for a moment thinking that he was right. But then, Gran didn't live here. Yet she had been here when he last visited. However, I realized he was right, for, to me, even were Gran here, the house wasn't the same, which was natural for it was occupied by a family now, and their different way of life had changed the atmosphere.

Nardy was saying to Tommy, "When are you starting on your run around the world?" And Tommy answered, "Oh, sometime in March." Then he looked at me and said, "Can you imagine longing for something all your life, then when you get it you don't want it."

"Not really," I said as I thought, I've wanted to be loved all my life, and now I'm being loved I want to go on being loved. I have never wanted it to lessen, this feeling that has existed between Nardy and me, because I know he has been and is happy. That I had the power to make him happy always appears to me a miracle and not a small one.

Tommy was still looking at me as he said, "I don't want to go on the damn tour. I realize now that I would much rather take her ladyship - this was the name he had given to his car - and run around the country, and perhaps take her over to France."

"Oh, you'll enjoy it once you get going. And what an experience to do a world tour. I wouldn't mind it myself, would you, Nardy?"

Nardy shrugged his shoulders and pursed his lips before answering, "I hate flying and I cannot see myself being months on a boat. Rough weather and I don't agree, do we?" And he smiled at me as he recalled our cruise together before we were married.

Tommy now straightened himself up abruptly on the couch and, bending forward, placed his elbows on his knees, and with his hands dangling between them he looked down at them as he said quietly, "I've had a kind of funny feeling on me of late that something was about to happen. It's made me wonder about the damned tour. Keeps niggling at me. I'm not given to that kind of thinking. It worries me."

Nardy rose hastily to his feet, saying, "Which all goes to prove, laddie, that you're in need of a holiday. Now come on, let's go along to Gran's again."

As we walked down the room, I thought it was strange that Tommy should be troubled by premonitions, for he wasn't really the type. But then a little of his fear rubbed off on to me as my thoughts ran ahead. Enough! Enough! He can't do anything. He wouldn't dare.

Then as we entered the hall I saw Hamilton in the far distance. He looked solemn, sad, and his outline wasn't clear. Begonia was with him, and I watched him turn her about while she still looked over her shoulder at me with those compassionate eyes of hers, and I thought, Gran is going to die.

Chapter 9

The following day, I spent the morning and all afternoon with Gran, and she definitely seemed stronger. As George said, she had turned the corner at a gallop since I had come. At one stage in the afternoon when we had the room to ourselves, she held my hand and she said, "I'm goin' to make it now, lass. I thought me number was up, and that's why I trailed you all the way here. I'm sorry."

"Oh, stop your jabbering." I used her tone. "I've been wanting to come for months, but . . . but you know why I didn't."

"Aye. Aye, lass." She moved her head slowly. "He's still about." She drew in a long breath, then said, "I heard at the club that he'd been taken on full-time with Morgans Motors, the taxis, you know. But he's not liked among the fellas, plays the big 'I am' too much." Then after a moment, she said something that brought the fear of him galloping back. "It must rankle enough to drive him mad," she said, "to know how you've got on, being famous like and married to a gentleman, and your name in the papers through your books. It was in last week again, saying you had done another best-seller." Once more she gasped, then ended, "By! it must burn him up." . . .

My staying with Gran all day had afforded Mary a break, but Tommy had now brought her in the car. She was to stay the night. Apparently he had had the children out nearly all afternoon and they'd had a rare time.

Before leaving, I told Gran I'd be round in the morning first thing and that the last thing I was going to do before we got the train was to slip in to see the doctor.

I made her laugh: "I've a good mind to go to the surgery and wait me turn," I said. "You can imagine what he'd say when I walked in, can't you? And what's more, I'd likely meet my old friend there, you know, the one who used to greet me with, "You here again? It's your nerves."" At this, she caught my hand and said, "You know something, lass? Love must agree with you, 'cos you could end up being quite canny-lookin'!"

"Go on with you!" I flapped my hand at her. "I thought all you've had was pneumonia, not softening of the brain."

Nardy hadn't come with Tommy. Being a good cook, he was seeing to the meal tonight. And so, for the first time I found myself alone in the car with Tommy, and he, with his hand on the starter turned to me and put my thoughts into words, saying, "You know, it's the first time you've sat there."

"Don't be silly," I said; "I've been in this scary thing a number of times."

"Not sitting there in the passenger seat." He started the car and almost in the one motion turned quickly out from the kerb, and I said, "Oh, Tommy, for goodness sake, drive carefully."

"You're safe with me, madam."

"I don't know so much."

"No?" He glanced at me. I made no answer to this, but loudly I said, "Look, there are traffic lights ahead."

His laughter filled the car and his only answer was, "Oh, Maisie."

At one point I glanced at the window and then turned sharply to him as I said, "We're going through the market place."

"Yes, I know."

"But why? This is the long way round."

"Oh, I didn't know it was the longer way round. I just thought it was another route. The children showed me."

"Tommy."

"Yes, Maisie?"

"Please drive a little slower, and go straight home."

"Anything for you, Maisie."

It was as we were nearing the terrace that he said, "Let's elope, Maisie. What about it, eh? Let's go straight on."

This should have come over as something funny, but it didn't, and Nardy's words came back to me: Don't get too fond of Tommy. And now my voice took on the tone of a jocular reply as I said, "I'll elope you! if you don't pull this contraption up slowly and not jerk my stomach into my mouth. Whoever taught you to drive wants to take lessons."

A minute later he was helping me out of the car, and there was laughter on his face as, bowing towards me, he said, "That'll be one pound seventy-five pence, ma'am."

I went to push him, but he caught hold of my hand, and like that he ran me up the steps and pushed open the door, to enter the hall hand in hand and to see Nardy crossing it. He had on a white apron and he was carrying a dish. He looked at us, and it was some seconds before he said, "You're back then."

"Only just," I said. "He's as mad as a hatter." I now jerked my head back towards Tommy. "He shouldn't be allowed on the road."

"How did you find Gran?" I was walking into the dining-room with Nardy now, and I answered, "Oh, much better, really much better." He placed the dish in the middle of the table, then turned towards me, and swiftly I put my arms about him and said, "I love you. The more I see of other men, the more I love you."

"That's comforting."

My arms still about him and aiming to take that look out of his eyes, I went on, "You know what Gran said, she said that love suited me, so much_" I gave an embarrassed laugh before finishing, "I would one day end up being quite canny-looking."

"You've always been canny-looking to me, much more, beautiful. It's got nothing to do with how you look, it's the whole of you."

We were in as tight an embrace as my shortened arm would allow when a voice from the doorway said, "Oh. Oh, I'm sorry."

We turned to see Tommy standing there, and I, purposely making my voice airy, said, "Oh, that's all right, Tommy. There's nothing to be sorry over. I was merely telling my husband how much I loved him and, as Gran would say, how I'm the luckiest lass in the lane." And I smiled at Nardy, who was now taking off his apron, then walked past Tommy who was still standing n the doorway, and as he looked down on me I noticed the pain in his eyes.

It was ridiculous. Here I was in this house where I had spent an agonizing childhood, a torture-filled marriage, and now there were two men who . . . loved me. I could hardly make the claim to myself when I knew I had been the most fortunate of creatures in finding Nardy, but now that Tommy, too, should have an affection for me seemed beyond belief. As I was constantly reminding myself, I was still me, and no matter what they said, I was a plain woman.

*

If it hadn't been for the children's chatter and George's usual raw remarks dinner would have been a very strained affair.

After it was over and the dishes washed and the breakfast set for the next morning, we had a game of Monopoly in the kitchen with the children.

It was close on ten when they went to bed, and after a drink in the sitting-room, Tommy admitted to being tired and he, too, said good-night. Then Nardy took Sandy out to do his last little bit of business, and when he returned he laughed as he said, "He got it over quickly because it's enough to freeze you out there." I said good-night to George and as usual his good-night made me breathless. He then shook Nardy's hand as if for a long farewell, as he was wont to do each night, and we went up to bed, Sandy bouncing before us and straight into a blanket-lined basket.

It was as we were lying enfolded in each other's arms that Nardy said to me, "What happened in the car?"

"Happened in the car? What do you mean?"

"Well, you came bouncing in together like two children who had been up to mischief."

"Oh, Nardy, that was Tommy, Tommy's way. He . . . when I got out of the car, he said, 'That will be one pound seventy-five pence, ma'am,' and as I went to push him he caught my hand and ran me in. Nardy, Nardy" - I took his face between my hands - "all this should be the other way about. It's I who should be afraid of your being interested in anybody else. Don't you see?"

"Not really, dear, because big fellows like Tommy always arouse the mother instinct in women. They start by being sorry for them."

"Well, I have no mother instinct except towards you. Oh, good gracious me!" I now flounced from him, making the bed bounce, and, my tone changing, I said, "I can't believe this." Then rising on my elbow I looked down on him and said, "Mr Leviston, stop this nonsense at once. I want to hear no more of it, ever."

In answer, he smiled gently, saying, "Lie down, Mrs Leviston, I want to put my arms around you. But before you do, would you mind switching off the light? Thank you."

In the darkness we lay close, laughing now and loving before we both fell into a deep sleep. . .

Sandy was inclined to night sickness, especially should he have been given titbits of anything fishy. At home I could control his titbits, but it was impossible to stop the children taking pieces off their plates and holding them in their fingers and wagging them under the table. It was a kind of a game to see which one of them could attract him first.

Sandy was a very intelligent animal. Whenever he was about to be sick he would endeavour to wake us, not by barking but by a series of sounds that was very akin to muffled language, and was always accompanied by a paw scratching not too gently on whatever part of your anatomy he could reach.

I was usually the one whom he managed to waken first. And I was aware that his talking was penetrating my sleep. Yet in this state I must be dreaming because I couldn't feel a paw scratching my arm or my neck.

Gradually I came out of sleep and into the awareness that he wasn't just talking, but was whining. I leant over the side of the bed and put my hand towards his basket. It was empty. I next groped for the light and switched it on, and there I saw him standing by the door. And when I said, "What is it, dear?" He didn't move far from it but began to bark.

Most poodles have a yapping bark but not our boy. He has a hard shrill bark that one would have credited would come only from a larger animal.

I got out of bed and tiptoed towards the door, whispering now, "What is it? What is it, dear?" Yet, as I stood bending over him I was conscious of something strange, and when my mind put into my sleepy brain a name that I could attach to this oddness, I became suddenly wide awake, and at the same instant pulled open the door, only to scream, "Oh, my God!" and bang it closed again. I now stood bent double, half-choked with smoke; then I was screaming, "Nardy! Nardy!"

"What is it?" He was sitting up.

"Fire! Fire!"

"What? No!"

I threw his dressing-gown at him and got into mine; then I grabbed up Sandy and once again I was at the door. But Nardy pulled me back, saying, "Stay where you are." He pulled open the door, then turned his back towards the hallway and coughed before thrusting me further into the room yelling, "Stay there! Shut the door!" And then he was gone.

Presently. I heard cries and muffled screams coming from the landing. I rushed now to the window and, pulling it open, I put my head out into the frost-filled night and screamed, "Fire! Fire!"

This bedroom window was at the back of the house and, looking down, I could see the whole of the yard and part of the garden illuminated with a warm red glow.

In panic now, and still clutching Sandy who had his forelegs tight around my throat, I rushed across the room and opened the door, only to see, through the smoke, that the same red glow was coming from the direction of the stairs.

The next thing I knew I was knocked to the floor. Automatically, I let go of Sandy, but his legs clutched my neck and he seemed to dangle from me, assisting the smoke to choke me as someone pulled me forward.

Now I knew we were in the bathroom and that there were others packed there. As a wet towel was thrown over my head I managed to gasp, "Nardy!" And George's voice, like a far distant croak, came at me, saying, "He's here. Now do as I say. Follow me, right down. Come on. Betty is behind you, then Gordon, then Kitty with Nardy."

I didn't ask where John and Tommy were. George seemed to be in charge; they must be all right.

Just before George pulled me forward out of the bathroom I managed to open the top of my dressing-gown and stick Sandy's back legs down inside of it to where he had the support of the cord around my waist. But his forelegs were still round my neck.

We were now on our hands and knees crawling towards the landing. Then I knew a moment of real terror when I saw not only the bannisters of the stairs blazing but also the carpet itself. But I was being pulled upright as in turn was Betty, and then we seemed to be all dancing from one flaming tread to another until we reached the great blaze of the hall. Here it seemed that all hell was let loose and everything more that was to happen happened at once. Water sprayed onto us; my face was speared with stinging jets; hands were reaching out and pulling us towards the door. At the same time there was a crash behind us and I turned to see the lower part of the stairs fall inwards and Nardy and Kitty, whom he seemed to be holding in his arms, disappear from view. Yet, not entirely. Nardy's head was sticking upwards above the tread of the stairs, but Kitty must have fallen through into the cupboard below. In this instant, I remembered Howard Stickle saying that there was dry rot in the stairs. This was when he had loosened all the stair rods in an effort to finish me off that way.

As I gave a muffled scream someone lifted me bodily and carried me outside and into the cold night and a great bustle of noise. And when I was stood on my feet I strained to go back towards the house, but the fireman's arms were tight around me. Then Betty and Gordon were clinging to me, and Sandy was whining like a child.

When I heard a voice above the melee shouting, "Get them into the ambulance, I cried, "No! No!" And now I almost tore Sandy's legs from my neck and pulled him up from the dressing-gown and thrust him into Betty's arms; then I clawed at the man who tried to restrain me, crying now, "My husband! My husband!" And his voice came as soft as a woman's, saying, "There now. There now. Look, they're coming out." And there was George on one side of Nardy and the fireman on the other and behind them another fireman, and, lying across his arms, was Kitty.

I flew to Nardy and was about to put my arms around him when George, his face ashen and his hair singed to his scalp, said quietly, "Leave him be, Maisie. Leave him be."

Something in his voice made me step back and my tortured gaze went over my husband's body. His face looked all right, but then I saw that the lower part of his dressing-gown was a charred mass and his pyjamas seemed to be sticking to his skin.

As for Kitty, her body was quite inert and what must have been her nylon nightdress was like a black veil from her neck downwards.

As one in a nightmare, I watched them both being laid on stretchers and put into the ambulance, and as the door closed on them I rushed to get in, but was held back by George. For a moment I was standing pressed close to him. He had only one arm around me and for the first time I noticed that the other was hanging limp by his side. He now pulled his arm from me and clasped his brow, and his voice sounded almost a whimper as, his head jerking upwards, he cried, "Oh Christ! I thought they were out. I yelled up the stairs. I thought they were out."

I, too, now gazed upwards in horror to where, hanging out of the fanlight in the roof of the attic, was the figure of John. There was a great commotion all about us. I had been unaware until then of all the people huddled in groups with coats over their nightwear. But as the turntable ladder passed the top of the now blazing windows and swung close to the jagged hole in the roof, everyone became quiet. We watched the fireman put his arms out towards John, but the boy appeared too terrified to grasp the man's hand; then it seemed that he was tossed from the window, and he was clutched in the fireman's arms. Hastily now the ladder was pulled away and the man descended. And now George was holding John in one arm and trying to still his loud crying. Then once again the ladder was being hoisted towards the roof; but there was no one now at the gap to take the fireman's outstretched hand. And I cried inside myself, Oh no! No! Tommy! Please! please! Don't give up.

The next minute we could see the fireman lean forward from the ladder, to which he was attached by some form of lead, and grip the sides of the fanlight window and then disappear from view, and in doing so he lifted the silence from the crowd in the sound of a concerted moan, and a voice near me said feelingly, "Silly bugger. Stupid bugger. Fanlights are hell to get out of."

Then suddenly the moan changed into a drawn out "O . . . oh!" as the fireman's head reappeared through the gap. Then silence again as the man obviously struggled to help Tommy upwards. He seemed to straddle the intervening distance between the window and the ladder with his feet while pulling Tommy's bulky figure forward.

When they both became still I realized the fireman was giving himself and Tommy time to breathe.

The ladder swung away from the roof and billowing smoke. And within a minute or so the two men had reached the street. The fireman was still on his feet, although he stood bent over while he coughed the smoke from his lungs. But not so Tommy, for his tall body had concertinaed: his head was sunk deep in his shoulders, and his knees were pulled upwards. Once again a stretcher was brought, and the next minute he, too, was whisked away in an ambulance.

Of a sudden I thought I was going to faint. It was only George's voice that checked me and beat me to it, for he said quietly, "Maisie, look after them, will you?" And thrusting John into my arms, he himself toppled over on to the road, and as if from a distance I heard an ambulance man saying, "No wonder, look at that hand."

I looked at the hand that one of the men was laying gently across George's chest. It was black and it looked as if the fingers were burnt to the bone, and two of them were hanging at a funny angle.

There came a blankness in my mind. I don't remember Mary arriving; I only heard her say, "Oh my God!" before she got into the ambulance with George. I then recall myself being bundled into an ambulance with the children, and we were all crying. . .

What followed in those early hours is confusion. At one point I must have fainted; but by daylight the following morning the children and I were back at Gran's.

It was sometime later in the morning when the doctor appeared. "You all right?" he said.

I couldn't say yes, I just moved my head, then I muttered, "I'm . . . I'm about to go to the hospital."

"I've just come from there." He looked to where the children were standing and he went towards them, saying now, "It's all right, it's all right."

"Dad and Tommy?" It was John asking the question, and the doctor said, "Your dad's fine. It's just his hand. And Tommy, he'll be home shortly."

It was Betty who now said, "And Kitty, Doctor?" And at this he paused before answering, "She'll be fine." Then he put his hand on my elbow and, pushing me towards the door, said, "Get into the car. I'll be with you in a minute. I'm just going to have a word with Gran. How's she taken it?"

"Not very well. It hasn't done her any good."

"No, I shouldn't think it has."

It was a full ten minutes later when he himself got into the car, and we had gone some little distance when he growled, "By God! somebody'll pay for this."

It was then I gave voice and put a name to the feeling that had been raging behind a shield in my mind since I had stood in the road and watched the flames coming out of every window in my old home.

"*Stickle.*"

"Who else? It seems it must have been set off in three different places, so I'm told. The sitting-room window was open. If there's any justice he'll do a long stretch for this."

The sitting-room window! I thought back to the time when he had mislaid his key and I happened to be at Gran's, and he had got in by the sitting-room window. He had said afterwards that a different sneck should be put on it as anybody could get in by slipping a knife underneath it as he had done. I had done nothing about it because at that time if a burglar had got into the house he wouldn't have frightened me half as much as my then husband had done.

As I whimpered, "He's determined to get me," there appeared on the front of the windscreen, as if he were seated on the bonnet of the car, the face of Hamilton. He looked like a wild horse might: his eyes were blazing; there was smoke coming out of his nostrils; his lips were right back from his teeth. And as I stared at him I knew that some part of me was in rebellion, while yet another part was sick with fear.

When he turned and galloped away into the darkness I said, "Nardy. How bad is he?"

"His legs are no pretty sight. They had put him under when I left. But . . . but the child, Kitty, she's in a bad way."

There was a catch in my throat as I said, "Really bad? I mean. . . "

"Yes, really bad. Her slippers must have had plastic soles and her nightie was made of that inflammable material. Damn and blast it! Like Nardy, her legs got it. But it was the smoke almost did for her; and Tommy had a bellyful of it, too. By what I've heard he owes his life to a fireman who must have risked his own neck to get him out of the attic. And Tommy had risked his own to push the boy out. God! why didn't you poison that fellow when you had the chance."

Yes, why hadn't I? But such a thing had never crossed my mind; until I tried to finish him off by raining his own collection of bottles on him.

In the hospital a nurse led me towards a bed; not the same one I had last seen Nardy in; this one was covered with a plastic cage.

I looked down on him. His face was lint-white; his arms were lying stretched down by his sides. There was some sort of shield over the lower part of his body. As I whispered his name the nurse said, "He's asleep, dear. He'll be like that for a while." And so I sat down and kept my eyes on that beloved face. . .

A short time elapsed, then Mike came to my side, saying, "Come away now." Then he added, "George is out too."

I followed his pointing finger and I saw a face in the bed opposite. I could hardly recognize George; I had forgotten that his hair had been burnt off. One arm was stretched out and covered with bandages.

I now looked around for Kitty, and when I couldn't see her, I said, "Where is she . . . Kitty?"

"In another ward." Mike nodded at me, and the nurse put in, "She's in intensive care."

Intensive care. What did that mean? Near death? Oh no! Oh no! Mary would go mad, George would go mad, and all through me. It was only me that Stickle wanted to get rid of. Or was it? Or was it everyone that was living in the house he had coveted for years?. . .

"Here, drink this. Drink it up."

I didn't recall being taken from the ward and seated in an anteroom. But, looking up into Mike's face, I said, "I'll kill him." And he answered soberly, "Well, if you don't, somebody will or should."

Chapter 10

The next three days are hazy in my mind. The only thing that stands out clearly is, later that first day, sitting by Nardy's bed and, when he opened his eyes and whispered my name, I could not even speak his. Although the nurse had said he was heavily sedated and was, as yet, in no pain, nevertheless, the pain seemed to be expressed in every line of his face.

George had had two fingers amputated; but fortunately, so the nurse had said earlier, the working part of his hand had been saved. But they were still fighting for Kitty's life.

I had been to the bank and made arrangements about money, and had then bought clothes for myself and the children. But wherever I went I was escorted by a plain-clothes policeman, while a uniformed one was on duty outside Gran's house because we were being continually harassed by reporters.

It was now known that the fire must have been started deliberately; but what I couldn't understand was that Stickle apparently wasn't the culprit.

After Mike had spoken to the police, they had gone to Stickle's house, only to find him in bed and hardly able to move with back trouble. And confirmation had come from his own doctor who had said he had been called in two days beforehand. Moreover, I learned that they were troubled in another way for the younger boy had gone missing. This I read in the local paper.

Who then had done this ghastly thing? Paraffin or petrol rags must have been pushed through the letter box, whilst the kitchen window had been forced and oil-soaked rags thrown in there as well. The perpetrator must have actually got into the sitting-room and soaked the couch with oil.

Now that suspicion had lifted from Stickle I was presented with the thought that perhaps some of George's workmates had it in for him, reasoning that when an ordinary man like George prospers it can arouse jealousy among his associates: George now lived in a very nice house, or had done; moreover, he had a car and had been able to take his family, including his mother, on a fortnight's holiday. Could the devil who had done this be one of George's associates? I put this question to Mike, and he said, "Could be. Could be. But I would have bet my bottom dollar it was the work of Stickle. The dog business last year, too. Yet old Howell says he attended him the second day you were here, in fact the very afternoon before the fire. He said the man was in dire pain, and he's still not up. And what's more, apparently he's very worried about his boy who went missing that same night and hasn't been seen since. . . Could it have been his boy?"

We looked at each other.

I was again sitting beside Nardy who was still in a very painful and critical condition, but he could talk a little. And I almost burst into tears when he turned his eyes on me, saying, "Maisie, smile. Come on, do."

"Oh, Nardy."

"Go on, smile. I'm all right, so smile."

My eyes misted. I smiled; then he said, "That's better." After a moment he asked, "How is Kitty really?"

"She's . . . she's holding her own. George is with her nearly all the time, and Mary."

"Gran?"

My smile widened as I answered, "It's amazing, but she's got her fighting spirit back again. And her voice. She's sitting up and letting everybody know it. The shock had the opposite effect on her to what was expected."

"Tommy?"

"He's all right," I said. "He went back yesterday, you know."

"Yes, I know." He moved his head. "But he didn't look . . . he didn't look right."

No, Tommy didn't look right. He had suffered no physical injury, only taken in a lot of smoke, but he was oddly quiet as if he were still under shock. If I hadn't been so worried about Nardy and Kitty I should have been more worried about Tommy. But Kitty was fighting for her life, and my dear, dear beloved Nardy had just missed losing his, and there lay before him weeks of pain and treatment before he would be himself again, if ever.

I sat with my beloved until he went to sleep. Then I went along the corridor to where Kitty lay in the intensive care unit. I looked through the door and saw George sitting there, his bandaged hand lying across his chest, his face turned towards the cot, and I knew I mustn't go in, my emotions were too near the surface. If not the sight of that child, then the look on his face would be too much for me. I went out into the sleet-driven night, and was fortunate to see a taxi at the gate letting down some passengers. Within a few minutes I was at Gran's, and the minute I entered the house I knew there was something further wrong. Mary was there and she was seeing to Gordon, dabbing at his eye.

"What is it? What's happened?"

She looked up at me from where she was kneeling on the mat before the fire, Gordon in front of her, and she said, "It's that Stickle boy, the older one, he collared him and punched him. He imagines Gordon knows where the young one is, the one that is lost, he even said he was hiding him here. Can you imagine it?"

I bent down towards Gordon and asked quietly, "What did he actually say to you, Gordon?"

"He . . . he said that if I didn't tell him where Neil was, it would be all the worse for him when they did find him, his father would skin him alive because Neil was a liar."

"Why did he say that?"

"I . . . I don't know, Auntie, except that he thought Neil had told me something and it was a lie."

When I sat down on the couch Hamilton appeared to the side of the fireplace and was throwing his head from side to side. But I actually shook mine at him as I dismissed the thought that Stickle could have set fire to the house: he had been attended by a doctor, hadn't he, who had verified not only that his back was bad but also that he was practically unable to move on the night of the fire.

However, even as I now silently protested, Hamilton's head kept bouncing up and down until his mane streaked out from behind him as if driven there by a strong wind.

"What is it, Maisie?" Mary was holding my hand, and I closed my eyes for a moment, saying, "Nothing, nothing, Mary; I was just thinking."

"You look tired."

"I'm certainly not the only one" - I smiled weakly at her" you must be worn out."

"Oh, I don't mind being worn out. I wouldn't mind anything as long as I felt that Kitty was. . ." She stopped and closed her eyes tightly, and Betty, suddenly bursting into tears, flung her arms around her, crying, "Oh, Mam, Mam," and in broken tones, Mary soothed her, saying, "She'll be all right. Don't worry, dear, she'll be all right. They're doing everything possible, and your Dad's with her." Mary now turned her head and looked down at me saying, "It's odd, isn't it? but the nurses say she cries if, when she wakes up, he's not sitting there. I've never known a man who loves children so much."

I, too, had never known a man who loved children so much.

"Well now. Well now." Mary's voice became brisk. "Let's have something to eat. Come on, Betty; you see to the table. And by the way" - she looked at me again - "we've got to do something, Maisie, about where you ought to sleep. That couch" - she thumbed to where I was sitting - "would break anybody's back. But in the meantime, will you go upstairs and sit with Gran for a bit and we'll call you down as soon as the meal's ready. She'll want to know how Nardy is. And tell her . . . tell her that Kitty's all right. You know what to say."

As I rose from the couch I thought it was strange how Mary had somehow come into her own in this crisis. She was no longer in the background. She had the whole situation in hand.

As I made towards the stairs there came a knock on the door, and John said, "I'll see who it is, Mam." But Mary caught his arm and whispered, "If it's one of them reporters, tell them there's nothing to say."

I was about to go up the stairs when John opened the door, and there, in the dim light, I saw the figure of a policeman and another plain-clothes man standing by his side. Going quickly towards them now, I recognized the policeman who had been on duty outside up till yesterday, and he said, "Good-evening, Mrs Leviston. I . . . I wonder if you'd come down to the station with us? There has . . . well, there has been some developments."

"Yes, yes, of course." I paused, then looked to where Mary was coming along the passage and I called to her, "I'm to go to the station, Mary; something seems to have come up."

Within a couple of minutes or so I had my hat and coat on again and was seated in the back of the police car. As it started up I leant forward and said, "What is it? I mean, is it some news from the hospital?" There was a tremble in my voice, and the policeman turned his head towards me, saying, "No, not . . . not that, Mrs Leviston." He hesitated, then said, "It'll be explained to you by the sergeant."

I sat back and remained quiet. But when I actually entered the station I felt a shiver pass through my body: the last time prior to entering this room I had left a cell and was about to appear at the magistrates' court.

"Will you come this way, please?" Another policeman was leading me along a passage. He opened a door and there, rising from a table was a sergeant, together with a woman officer and a person I imagined to be a plain-clothes officer. But sitting at the other side of the table was a boy, who looked to be eleven or twelve years old. He was thin and had a white peaked face and eyes that held a deep fear. Before anyone

307

spoke I knew that this was Stickle's son, the one who had gone
missing. On the table before him was an empty tea-cup and a plate
with biscuits on it.

"Will you please take a seat, Mrs Leviston?" It was the sergeant
speaking.

As I sat down I kept my eyes fixed on the boy, and his were tight on
me, and I saw he was afraid of me.

The sergeant was speaking again. "This is Neil, Mrs Leviston. I think
you should hear what he's got to say." He now looked at the boy and
said, "You tell Mrs Leviston what you told us. And don't worry, your
father or no one else is going to touch you ever again. And Mrs
Leviston will not be angry with you, will you, Mrs Leviston?"

I said, "No, no," and waited.

The boy had his hands in front of him on the table and began to nip
his finger ends one after the other as if he were pulling off a tight glove.
Then his head jerked backwards and he gulped in his throat, and again
the sergeant said to him, "It's all right now, it's all right. You have my
word for it: I said no one will lay a hand on you in future, and I meant
it. Now go on; tell Mrs Leviston all you know."

The boy brought his head forward and he stared at me for some
seconds before, his voice coming like a croak out of a dry throat, he
said, "My da set fire to your house."

I remained perfectly still. Although Hamilton was going mad at the
other end of the room, galloping backwards and forwards in the
restricted space, I did not look towards him but kept my gaze fixed on
the boy.

"He . . . he said his back was bad. They sent me to bed early on. My
mam had . . . had gone to Middlesbrough. My grandad had died, she
had gone to the funeral. Da said his back was bad and he couldn't get
out of bed and Ronnie went and phoned for the doctor." The boy
gulped again, looked at the sergeant, and when the sergeant nodded at
him, he turned his gaze once more on me and said, "I . . . I went to
watch the football match, but it was too cold and I came home and
went in the back way and sat in the kitchen near the stove to warm me
hands, and . .. and then I . . . well" - he looked upwards - "heard the
chain being pulled, and I knew it wasn't our Ronnie because I had
passed him in the yard, he said he was going for a message on his bike.
I went to the bottom of the stairs and I heard me da's bedroom door
closing. And I thought it was funny because I knew he had told the
doctor he couldn't go to the lav, and the doctor had told our Ronnie
that he could get a loan of one of them bedpans from the Red Cross."
He sniffed now; then rubbed his nose with the side of his forefinger
before going on, "Later on like, I had a bad head. I often get bad

headaches an' me mam gives me a pill. She keeps them in her room, and I asked our Ronnie if I could have one, and he went into the bedroom and he brought a pill down. But it wasn't like one of the ones me mam gives me, these were just round hard ones, this was one of those long ones with powder inside. It was like one of her sleeping pills, but he said it was all right, it was for headaches and to go and take it. So I went into the back an' got a cup of water, but I don't know why, but I didn't take the pill, I pushed it down the sink. Then after I had gone to bed, our Ronnie bent over me and I made on I was asleep and . . . anyway. . ."

He started to pull on his fingers again and once more he looked at the sergeant, and once more the sergeant nodded at him; and then he began again: "I heard our Ronnie come into the room again, and I knew he was putting his coat on. Then I heard me da's door open; then the stairs creaked and I knew they had both gone down. Our bedroom window looks on to the yard and we are near the end of the block and there's a lamp there and it gives a little bit of light, and I saw them comin' out of the shed. Me da was dressed and he was carrying a case and he went out of the back door. But our Ronnie didn't, so . . . so I got back into bed again quick."

He stopped again and looked down at his hands which had become still on the table, and the sergeant asked quietly, "Can't you recall what time it was?"

"No, 'cos I think I went to sleep for a little bit before our Ronnie came back into the room and took his coat off. But I don't know how long."

"Do you think it would be after twelve o'clock?"

"I don't know."

"It doesn't matter. Go on."

And he went on.

"I became sort of frightened, I don't know why. I kept wishing me mam was back and I wished we had never come back. We had left the house afore an' gone to live in Middlesbrough with me granda. Then he was taken to the hospital and his council house was given to somebody else, so we came back. And . . . and " He was gulping now, and the policeman bent towards him and said, "Would you like another cup of tea?"

The boy shook his head, then, speaking more quickly now, he said, "I heard them coming up the stairs. But they didn't go into the bedroom. There's a chair on the landing that you can stand on and get into the loft, and I heard the hatch being pushed back. An' then after that I heard the bath being run. It was then the door opened and I knew that our Ronnie was standing over me. I. . ."

The boy was staring at me now with pleading in his eyes and, his voice still coming in a rush and as if he was appealing to me for understanding, he said, "I nearly screamed like I do in a nightmare, and I think I would have but he went away, and . . . and they were a long time in the bathroom. Then . . . then he came to bed, and he was soon asleep. And I must have gone to sleep. But it was the next morning when I went down into the yard to get some coal for the fire, Mrs Dixon from next door, she came to the fence and asked me how me da was. And when I said he was gettin' better she laughed and said he would be when he hears his lady wife's house was burnt down last night. That's what she said, his lady wife. And then she said something about him gettin' his own back."

I watched the boy now close his eyes and draw in a long shuddering breath before he added, "I was sick. I . . . I went in the lav and I was sick. Then I went into the shed. He always keeps two petrol cans in there, full, in case it's his turn on nights and he needs more petrol. One of them was empty and he hadn't been on night call for a long time. And our paraffin can was empty an' all. It . . . it was then I knew I had to find me mam, and I got on a bus for Middlesbrough. But I got off half-way 'cos I knew if I'd found her she'd take me back there, an' me da would knock the daylights out of me, an' our Ronnie would an' all. So . . . so I just kept on."

He stopped, and there was silence in that bare room. Hamilton had ceased his prancing. He was standing behind the boy, and I said to him, Strange, isn't it, that a man like Stickle can have a son like this who holds no part of him. He was likely all his mother. I put my hand out and laid it on his joined fingers that had formed into a tight fist, and I said, quietly, "Thank you for telling me. And don't worry; as the sergeant says, no one will hurt you in the future."

I rose from the table and went out, and the sergeant followed me.

He led me into an office and, after offering me a chair, he sat down at his desk and said, "Now we've got to prove the boy's words, and I've no doubt in my mind that we shall. Also what the boy didn't tell you is that it was his father who tortured your dog, and it was him and his mother who brought it back. They really meant to take it and bury it, but they thought that with attention it might still live. Apparently the man struck them both when he knew what they had done. It was after that she left him. It's amazing" - he shook his head - "to look at him, and I remember him well when he was in court before, you would think that butter wouldn't melt in his mouth. Well, let's hope, for his sake, that the child doesn't die, for I understand she's in a bad way. And your husband too."

"What do you do next?"

"Well, our next step, I think, is to get a search warrant for the house. Of course, he'll be in bed with his bad back, but it's under the roof we must look to find that case."

"When will you make the search, do you think?"

"Within the next hour, I hope. We shall contact the boy's mother again. After the boy went missing we contacted her in Middlesbrough. She felt that the boy would make for there. We asked her to keep in touch, but we haven't heard from her since yesterday morning. The boy himself was found just outside the town in an old disused barn. He must have been lying there for a couple of days. The two policemen who found him, or really it was their dog who smelt him out, said he was ravenous."

"What will happen to the boy?"

"Oh well, we'll arrange to keep him away from that house, while Stickle is still there anyway. Then there is the elder son to be dealt with. He's obviously had a hand in it too. Now I'll get one of the men to run you back home, Mrs Leviston."

As I rose to my feet I said to him, "No matter what time of the night it is, would you get word to me about what you find . . . in the roof, and also let me know that he's in custody?"

"I'll do that. Yes, I'll do that, Mrs Leviston."

When I arrived back at Gran's I took Mary aside and I told her briefly what had transpired. She gaped at me open-mouthed.

"My God! My God!" she said; then putting her hand to her mouth, she muttered, "If my Kitty were to die he could be brought up for murder, but things being what they are, they would bring it in as manslaughter. But it would be murder, wouldn't it?" Her voice suddenly rose, "Murder!"

I took her by the shoulders, saying, "Sh! Sh! Gran'll hear you."

She became still within my hold and, looking into my face, she said, "Strange, isn't it, Maisie, that all this has come out of kindness, your kindness. If you hadn't given us that house to live in, this wouldn't have happened to us."

I knew she didn't mean to stab me in the heart but her words had done just that. In this moment I felt responsible for Kitty, and Nardy, and George, George who might find it difficult to drive a bus again.

As I turned away she said, "I didn't mean to upset you, Maisie. Don't take me wrong."

Then she rushed past me as she heard George's key turn in the front door, and a moment later, when he entered the kitchen, I could see by his face he was relieved. And when they all gathered round him and, his voice thick, he said, "She'll make it," Mary dropped her head towards him and he put his good arm around her and Betty, and he

311

looked at the two boys and me, then he said. "What d'you think?"

We remained silent. Then he went on, "She was awake, really awake and she said, "Hello, Popeye.""

At this the boys sniffed, then giggled.

And George went on, "And I looked down on her and said, "Hello Olive Oil.""

His chin knobbled as he made an effort to keep back his tears. Then, almost roughly, he pushed Mary from him, saving, "Stop your bubblin', woman, and get me something to eat; I'm as hungry as a horse." And on this, for the first time in days, he laughed as he turned to me, saying, "You'd better look out for yours. How is he anyway? Still kickin' his heels up?"

My smile was tentative as I replied, "He's up and down, you could say." Then I added, "May I see you a minute?" I walked towards the kitchen again and he followed me.

Quietly, I told him what had transpired at the police station; and during the telling he gripped the top of his head with one hand while staring down at the other bandaged one, and then, from between his teeth, he said, "If he gets off with this I'll swing for the bugger. I will, Maisie. I tell you I will."

I didn't hear anything from the police until the following morning at eight o'clock. It was from the sergeant himself, who was accompanied by a plain-clothes man.

Only Mary and I were up, and in the kitchen, without any preamble, the sergeant said, "We've got him. Of course, he raised a fuss, couldn't get out of bed." He gave a tight smile as he added, "We helped him up. That was after we had examined the loft. There was a case there that reeked of petrol. There were two empty bottles in it; one had definitely held petrol, the other paraffin. One was rolled in part of a towel, likely to make sure they wouldn't jingle as he carried the case. I can see why he had it up in the attic because if he had put it in the dustbin, the smell might have aroused the dustman's curiosity, for he would be more likely to open the case. Then his son, the elder one, who's a bit of a bully-boy, almost gave him away by shouting, "It was me da's house anyway." We took him along, too and, like all bullies, he broke down after a time and confirmed his younger brother's statement."

"His wife?" I asked.

"Oh, she was there all the time, and strangely she never said one word. We interviewed her, but it was plain she knew nothing whatever about it. As her young son said, she was at her father's funeral the day it happened."

It was Mary who asked now, "When will he be tried?" And the sergeant said, "Oh, I couldn't put a date to that yet. But don't worry, I can't see him getting bail. I can't see anybody coming forward to stand for him if it was asked for."

Later that day, as I sat beside Nardy, I broke the news to him, and surprisingly he said, "There was never a doubt in my mind but it was him. A man like that would have worked out every detail. I . . . I knew he had from the first. But anyway, my dear, you're safe now."

I held his hand and looked down into his grey face as I asked, "How's the pain?"

"Bearable. They're very good. Oh, so very good. But . . . but I wish we were home, at least, for your sake. It must be very crowded at Gran's."

"Oh, I don't mind, dear."

"Why don't you go into an hotel in the city for the time being?"

"Oh, I couldn't do that, it would upset them. Don't worry about me. My goodness! I'm the least of your worries."

We became silent for a while, and then, as if making conversation, he said, "How's the weather? I can't see anything from here."

"Oh, it's grey, and damp, and cold, yet you forget about it when you come into the hospital; all the wards look gay."

"Yes" - he moved his head slowly - "they always say that hospitals are the happiest places at Christmas. The nurses are so cheerful. That one over there at the desk, she's always got a smile. She calls me laddie."

I looked towards where the nurse was standing, and then looking down on him again, I said, "She's very pretty. Now don't you pay her too much attention."

As he closed his eyes for a moment, I thought of the trite things one says in place of words that are spurting upwards from the painful emotion tearing at your innards: chatting about the weather, the Christmas decoration, and the pretty nurses. I felt of a sudden I was quite alone: Nardy was there, but he wasn't still with me; I was back in the days when I had only Bill my bull terrier, George and Gran on one side, and the doctor as a bulwark against insanity.

That reminded me. I must call in at the evening surgery when on my way home and tell him the latest news.

"Have you heard from Tommy?"

"Yes," I said, "I heard from him yesterday. He's coming up at New Year. He said he was writing to you. You haven't had a letter yet?"

He smiled weakly, then he asked, "Did you give Janet her Christmas box before we left?"

"Yes, yes." My throat was full, and I was, in a way, grateful to the

Scottish nurse who appeared at the bedside with a glass in one hand and a spatula in the other with pills on it, saying, "Now then, laddie, open your mouth and close your eyes and see what God'll send you."

It was a long time since I had heard those words. Gran used to say them to me as she popped a sweet into my mouth. "Open your mouth and close your eyes and see what God'll send you." It was too much. I heard myself laughing, and the nurse turned to me and said, "Is that a new one to you?"

I put my hand over my mouth for, standing by the bedside between me and the nurse, was Begonia. She put up a front leg on to my arm, saying, I'd go now; they'll be wanting to do his treatment, that's why they've given him the pills.

When I put my lips gently on Nardy's, they trembled, and his hand came onto the back of my head and held my face close to his for a moment. Then, his kind eyes looking into mine, he said, "Don't worry; we'll get through. The main thing is, Kitty's making it. Go on now. Go and see your prehistoric bushman, he'll do you good."

I could say nothing, not one word, not even a goodbye. I walked out of the hospital. It was dark now, and I was grateful for it, for the tears were streaming down my face.

The doctor held his surgery from five till half-past six. It was almost half-past when I got off the bus, hurried up the street, and pushed the door open into that room that I knew so well. There was only one patient left waiting to be seen, and who should it be but You *again*, the woman who always greeted me with those words, "You here again? It's your nerves, I suppose?" And yes, I was greeted by those very words.

Half-rising from the seat, and a smile on her thin face, the woman said, "You here again?" Only this time she didn't add, "It's your nerves?" at least not in that way. What she did say was, "I heard your house was burnt down. As I said to our Susie, you are an unlucky sod. First you had a pig of a man, then that to happen. It's enough to give anybody nerves. And you wrote a funny book, didn't you, about things you imagined seeing when you were in a breakdown?"

I reared, Hamilton reared, and Begonia stood on her dignity. "Yes," I said, "I wrote a funny book, but it . . . it wasn't because I was in a breakdown."

"No?"

"No."

"Oh, I thought it was. Our Susie read it. She said it was like what fellows see when they've got the D.T.s. White elephants going up the wall, and ants crawling all over them."

I was back in the old life, sitting here on a Monday morning, waiting my turn, looking around at all the weary faces, and, should I be unfortunate, seated next to this particular woman listening to her complaints, which always began: "It's the neck of me bladder, you know. He can do nothin' about it." And sometimes she would add, "I don't know why I come." But here she was, still coming.

Miss Price, one of the secretaries, was standing in front of me now, surprise on her face, and her manner and voice so changed from the old days as she said, "Oh, Mrs Leviston, shall I tell the doctor you're here?"

"No, don't bother, Miss Price, I can wait."

At that moment his door opened and the patient came out and my "neck of the bladder" acquaintance rose, nodded at me, saying, "Be seein' you then" - she seemed sure of this - then went into the surgery.

"How are you, Mrs Leviston? I was so sorry to hear about the trouble. Were you injured in any way?"

"No, no, Miss Price; fortunately not."

She bent nearer to me now, a prim smile on her face as she said, "I've read your book. I think it's very funny. I bought a second one for my mother's Christmas box. I wonder if you'd autograph it for me sometime, Mrs Leviston?"

"Yes, certainly, I'd be pleased to."

Life was funny, wasn't it. This particular secretary never, as I remember, gave me a civil word all the years I was Mrs Stickle and a regular customer here. To her I was just one of those nerve-ridden individuals who wasted the doctor's time. Odd how a little bit of fame could alter a person's attitude towards you. I hadn't liked Miss Price then and I didn't like her now.

A few minutes later the lady with the weak bladder came out of the surgery and she waved to me and I waved back. Then I went in and was greeted immediately with, "What the devil are you doing here?"

"I've come for a bottle and a note."

"How long have you been sitting out there?" He thumbed towards the door.

"Not long."

"Why didn't you go to the house and see Jane?" His head jerked in the other direction now, and to this I replied, "I wanted to see you alone for a few minutes. Did you know that it was Stickle?"

"Yes. Well, I knew it all along," he said, nodding his head the while; then he added, "Sit yourself down. . . Yes, I was along at the station this morning; I heard it all. God! I hope he gets his deserts. If ever there was a fiend on this earth, he's it. How are you feeling?"

I sighed before I answered, "I just don't know," but then contradicted myself by adding quickly, "Yes, I do. I feel I've gone back years, and it was confirmed a few minutes ago when I met up with your last patient. We always seemed to come on the same day; she reminded me."

He gave a laugh now. "Oh, you mean Water Lily."

"Water Lily?" I felt my stomach shake. "Is that what you call her?"

"Yes. She's had trouble with her inner tubes for years. They're all right now, but she won't have it. It's nerves with her really."

When the high laughter erupted from me he rose quickly and came round the desk, saying, "Now, now, what is it?"

The tears were running down my face. I was laughing and crying at the same time, and he put his arms around me and held me for a moment until the paroxysm passed.

Wiping my face, I looked at him and said, "Nerves? You saying she's got nerves? For years she's accused me of visiting you simply because I had nerves. She hadn't nerves, it was the neck of her bladder. It was always the neck of her bladder."

We were both laughing now. "Come round and have a drink," he said. "I've got one call out tonight so far, then we'll have a bite."

"No thanks, they'll be expecting me back."

He shook his bushy head, then said, "It must be a tight squeeze round there, and you haven't been used to tight squeezes this last year or so living in your lap of luxury up in the wicked city. Come and spend a couple of days with us in the New Year; I'm sure Nardy would be happy to know you're having a change."

"Yes, yes, he would. I'll try to arrange it without hurting feelings."

"Do that."

He stared at me now; then placing his hands on my shoulders, he said, "You know it's going to be a long job with Nardy, don't you?"

"I've . .. I've sort of guessed that."

"They'll make a good job of his legs in the end, but it's going to take time. You can't replace large areas of skin all at once."

"No, I suppose not."

"Anyway" - he grinned at me now - "he's going to be all right. And the child too. Oh, it was touch and go with her, and I'm afraid she's in for a long spell an' all. It'll be worse for her in the long run being a girl, because she'll be scarred up to her chest. Still, she's alive. And George'll get by; he's got the main part of his hand, and that's something. And Tommy? Have you heard anything from him?"

"Yes, I had a letter, but he didn't say how he was feeling."

"The smoke nearly finished him off. If it hadn't been for that fireman he certainly would have been a goner. And the experience has left its mark on him. I had a talk with him before he left. All his bounce had gone, hadn't it? He was always so cheery."

"Yes." I nodded.

"Sure you won't come in and have a drink?"

"No thanks, Mike, not tonight, but I'll likely take you up on your other invitation."

"Good. Good."

He was leading me towards the door when he stopped and said, "You know, Maisie, it's funny to see you back in this room again. I often think of the old days and they're not all that far away. And you know something? I can tell you now, I got to look forward to your coming; there was something about you that was different." He leant his hairy face down to me as he added, "I didn't know it was because you were accompanied by a blooming great horse." He chuckled now, then said, "How is he by the way?"

"Oh," I replied, "I don't see him so often, not since he took a wife."

"*Never! A wife? Never!*"

"Oh, yes. Why shouldn't he? I took a husband."

"Well, yes, there's something in that. Freud would be able to supply the answer there. Or would it be Jung? What do you call her?"

"Begonia."

"Be . . . go . . . nia." His face was twisted up so much in disbelief that the hair seemed to have taken over so that even his eyes were invisible for a moment.

"It's a nice name."

"For a horse?"

"She's a mare . . . naturally, and she's definitely a lady, smallish, cream chocolate-coloured, with lovely soft eyes."

I was swung round and pushed in the back and through the door into the waiting room and past a surprised Miss Price. And then I was in the street and he was saying, in no soft voice, "I refuse to certify you, you'll have to get somebody else. But it will have to be done." And I went on my way really laughing for once and wondering what Miss Price would be making of that.

The lonely feeling had gone. Strange how that man could bring comfort to me, reassurance and the will to persevere. I asked myself again: What would I have done without his help all those dreary years?

My mood was changing, telling me that I should be thankful that Nardy had escaped with his life, that Kitty was getting better, that Tommy was alive, and there was still George. And this is what decided me to go into the church. It was only two streets out of my way.

When I entered I could see that the confessions were over, and there were only three people altogether there, a mother and small child kneeling before the crib, and a woman lighting some candles.

I knelt down at the end of a row facing the side altar in the very place where I had knelt once before and startled poor Father Mackin when in a sort of confession I told him there was a horse dressed in bridal white galloping up the aisle. Poor man. I could recall the look on his face.

I sat back in the pew; I hadn't said a prayer. I was now looking towards the high altar, but no words of thanksgiving entered my mind. But I wasn't surprised when I saw my two friends kneeling side by side on the actual altar steps. Hamilton's coat was gleaming like the back of a seal. His white mane was hanging gently downwards and touching that of Begonia's. She always wore hers to the left. Her cream skin seemed to ripple softly in the candlelight. In another moment I may have dropped off to sleep, such was the feeling of peace, but a voice aroused me, saying quietly, "Well! well! 'tis you."

"Yes. Yes, Father, 'tis me." I went to rise from the pew but his hand on my shoulder pressed me back; and then he sat down beside me, asking softly now, "How are you?"

"Not too bad, Father."

"What a thing to happen. God forgive him. It was in the evening paper. The man's mad; but I doubt if he'll do you any more damage after this. . . How is your husband, and the child?"

"They both seem to be getting along nicely."

"That's good. That's good. I'm due to visit tomorrow; I'll look in on them." He sighed now, then said, "The things that happen. And you were so settled in your new life, and your book selling like wildfire." He smiled now. "By the way" - he leant towards me - "does he still keep you company? You know . . . you know who."

"Oh, yes, Father." I nodded solemnly at him. "In fact" - I pointed towards the altar - "they've both been kneeling there."

He turned his head and looked towards the altar as if he were expecting to see them; then looking at me again, he whispered, "Both? Another one?"

"Yes. Oh, you wouldn't know because that book isn't out yet, but he's married."

He pulled his scraggy chin into his neck, turned his head slightly to the side while keeping his eyes on me and said, "You're joking?"

"No, no, Father, I'm not."

"He's married?" He sounded like Mike in his disbelief.

"Yes, and very happily."

"Glory be to God! You're still seeing things then?"

"Oh yes, Father." I now saw his cassock shake, then his voice rumbled in his throat, and again he was leaning towards me, asking now, "Is she in or is she *out*?"

"Oh, I'm sorry to say, Father, I think she's out."

"Oh, she would be. Connected with you, she would be." His lips were tight together now, yet the rest of his face was smiling, and the words were whispered as he said, "What denomination?"

"Presbyterian, I think, Father."

"Oh, my God!" Then, his voice altering, he asked, "But how d'you know?"

"I . . . I think it's the look on her face."

"Oh, do they look different, the Presbyterians?"

I thought for a moment, then whispered, "Yes, I think they do, Father."

"Ah" - he straightened up - "you're still a queer girl, marriage hasn't altered you. You know something? I remember the day you told me that the big fellow, Hamilton, was just behind me."

"Father -" It was I who now leant towards him and said very softly and slowly, "he's there again now."

I watched his head move swiftly from side to side, and then he said, "No kiddin'?"

"No kiddin', Father. They're both there. She's to your right hand and says she's very glad to make your acquaintance; she'd heard a lot about you."

"Really?" His eyebrows were moving up into peaks. And now he asked in a stage whisper, "And his nibs? What has he got to say?"

I paused a moment, and then I said gently, "He seems to think you're wasted in this job, Father. He thinks you would have made it on the stage, been a wow, in fact."

I watched the smile spread over his face and he nodded at me as he whispered, "He's nearer the truth than he knows - do you know that? - 'cos that was what I wanted to be in me mad youth. I saw meself holding audiences spellbound. Then the dear Lord took a hand and said He had an audience already made for me. But you know something?" He paused; then his lips twisting into a wry smile, he said, "I've never yet been able to have a spellbound one. There's an old fellow sits there Sunday after Sunday" - he pointed to the middle aisle - "and as soon as I open me mouth he closes his eyes. I tell you, the minute I start he goes to sleep. And I kid meself the fellow works night-shift, because me pride won't let me accept that what I've got to say would put anybody to sleep, not week after week, anyway."

"Oh! Father." My stomach was shaking. "I think God made a mistake in dragging you in."

"No, no." He shook his head vigorously. "No, no; He never makes a mistake. He knew what He was doing: I was so puffed up with self-importance. In those days I thought I was funny, I wanted to make the world laugh, and pride is a great sin and He saved me from that.

Anyway " his grin widening and his whispering becoming almost inaudible, he went on, "He's allowing me a little compensation in me old age because we're starting an amateur theatrical group along at the club and they've asked me to direct. What d'you think of that for kindness? Of course, I've only got another two years to go. You know, I'm nearly on me time."

I looked at him gently, saying, "Well, you don't look it, Father; and you'll be greatly missed."

"Oh, I look it all right: the mirror never lies, and this" - he tapped his ear now - "I'm having to have a hearing aid. I can see me father getting on his hind legs in his grave because there he was, ninety-three when he died, and he had half of his own teeth left, his eyes were as good as a pair of binoculars, and his hearing . . . oh, he could hear your thoughts, could me father. And now look at me: false teeth I've had for the last twenty years, glasses for even longer, and now a hearing aid; the next thing will be a wheelchair. Anyway" - he looked at his watch - "I've got to see a couple in the vestry, they'll be here any minute now, I'll have to be away. But how long are you staying in town?"

"That depends, Father, on how soon my husband can be moved."

"Then we may be bumping into each other again?"

"Yes, Father."

"Would . . . would you like to kneel with me and say a bit prayer?"

"Yes, Father." So, side by side we knelt down, and now I did pray: I said, "Thank you, God, for two kind men, for the doctor and this dear old priest, who have brought me back on to an even keel."

The hand came on my shoulder, the voice said quietly, "Good-night and God bless you."

"Good-night, Father."

"Pop in anytime you feel the need."

"I will, Father."

He stepped out of the pew, then stepped back again, and there was a deep twinkle in his eye as he put his head close to mine, saying, "I hope your friends haven't left their visiting card on the altar steps."

And to this I answered quietly and soberly, "No, Father, I'm sure they haven't, they're both house-trained."

He pushed me gently; then I watched him walk towards the vestry before I rose from my knees and went out of the church and into the dark street. But my spirit was light, and I felt I had the strength to face the future, which in the weeks ahead would be a pain-filled testing time for Nardy, not forgetting the same painful experience that would have to be endured by Kitty, and for myself, the facing of Howard Stickle once again across a court-room.

Chapter 11

It was the second week in February, a Tuesday, eleven o'clock in the morning, and I was back in that court-room as if I'd never left it, the only difference being, Stickle's and my places were reversed. It was the second day of the hearing. As on that first occasion two years ago, it seemed that Stickle might even get the better of me. For yesterday his doctor had stood in the witness-box and confirmed that the man had had a bad back and to his mind was in extreme pain. No, he said, he hadn't examined him for the simple reason that the man was unable to turn on to his side; nor had he visited him the following day - there was an influenza epidemic and he had extra calls to make.

When questioned by Mr Collins - yes, it was the same counsel who had defended me but was now appearing for the prosecution - he had hummed and ha'ed and then admitted that he had not thought the man's condition warranted a further visit from him on that particular day.

When I had left the court last night I felt that the doctor's statement could or might, in a way, leave the case open to doubt, in spite of what the younger boy had said and the older boy had admitted. For Stickle's defending counsel had claimed that the older boy had been bullied into making a statement and the younger one was a highly strung emotional child with a strong imagination and given to drawing attention to himself, and endeavoured to substantiate this supposition by stating that the accused had admitted having very little love for the younger boy, and that he had thrashed him on occasions for his lying; and further, that any disharmony in the house between him and his second wife had been caused by her defence of the boy.

When I said to Mr Pearson, my solicitor, that there seemed to be a possibility that Stickle would wangle out of this through his defending counsel, he said to me, as he had done once before, "Wait and see. Remember Mr Collins."

Yes, I remembered Mr Collins. He seemed to be a slow starter.

The court-room was packed to capacity. I was sitting next to Mr Pearson; on his right sat Tommy, on my left sat George; behind us sat Mike and the veterinary surgeon. Behind them was Gran, Mary, Betty, and Father Mackin.

Mr Collins was now referring to the incident of the dog, and as his words revived the horror of my first sight of Sandy, I was for turning and glaring at the man in the box. It was only the fact that he had never taken his eyes off me all yesterday, nor yet this morning, that prevented me from doing so. When he had entered the dock yesterday morning, a policeman on each side of him, I knew that his well-brushed appearance, his sleeked hair, his long pale face, would have elicited in many minds in the court-room disbelief that such a man was capable of torturing a dog, let alone setting fire to a house in the hope it would kill one in particular of its inhabitants. But in the witness-box his mien altered somewhat when Mr Collins asked, "Do you deny this?"

"Yes, I do." The words came from deep within Stickle's throat. "It . . . it was Neil that did it. He's . . . he's like that with animals. A bit wrong in the head."

"You say your son is wrong in the head? Mental?"

From under my shaded gaze I saw Stickle wag his head from side to side before he muttered, "Not quite mental, but he's been recommended to see a psychiatrist by the school doctor."

"Yes, I understand that too, but I suggest this was because of your treatment of him."

"That's a lie!" It was almost a bellow.

"Everything's a lie in your estimation, Mr Stickle. You seem to be the only honest person in this court. Well, we'll leave the case of the dog and come to what, but for the grace of God, one might say, could be making you stand now facing not only a charge of arson, with intent to cause grievous bodily harm, but also a charge of murder on two counts. Two of the victims of your hate, a man and a child, are still in hospital and it is only by a miracle, I understand, that the child is still alive. As for Mr Leviston, it will be a long, long time before he is able to walk."

"I didn't do it. I was in bed. I couldn't move."

"Oh, you couldn't move? Well, the police have given evidence that once they got you out of bed and on your feet, you moved with some defiance; you even resisted arrest."

"It was the shock."

"Oh, then" - Mr Collins smiled - "if that's the case we must recommend to the Medical Council that all people with bad backs should be given a shock, and the employers in the country will be so grateful for the reduction in absenteeism for there will be a swarm of men returning to work." Then, his mood altering like lightning, he went on quickly, "I suggest, Mr Stickle, you had nothing more wrong with your back than I have. What you did was premeditated: you knew how to get into your former home; you knew that your former wife was there. Your insane hate of her prompted you to plan carefully, but not carefully enough: you took an ordinary attaché-case, stuffed it with rags, filled two bottles, one with petrol and one with paraffin and went out into the night; and your presence on the street would cause no local comment because you were a taxi driver and on night call. And had you been stopped . . . well, you were on your way to your employer's garage to pick up a car. You reached the house, you quietly forced open the windows and it only took a matter of minutes to soak those rags and throw them into the room, and push the rest through the letter-box. You knew there were other people in that house besides your first wife, and you hated them too because they were living in the house that you had coveted, then plotted and planned to possess. . ."

"Objection, my Lord."

"Objection overruled."

I now had my head up, my eyes wide, and I saw Stickle glance towards the judge. He too was the same man who had presided over the earlier case. Mr Collins was going on. "Being frustrated in that, you could not bear the thought of your down-trodden former wife not only rising to fame through her literary efforts, and marrying a gentleman of no small means, but also that she dared to come back to this town and stay in the house that you and your son had openly declared should be yours. It was too much to bear; you must put her out of the way for good and all. . ."

"Objection, my Lord."

The judge now warned Mr Collins in a half-hearted tone that he must not allow his feelings to cloud his judgement.

"Yes, my Lord." Mr Collins inclined his head towards the bench, then returned to the attack.

"You are a conceited man, Mr Stickle. And to put it into common phraseology, a two-faced one. Oh, definitely that I would say, for your demeanour suggests mildness, but all the while it is covering up a raging ferocity of hate, which has spread to cover all those connected with your first wife. You are a Jekyll and Hyde, Mr Stickle. Years ago your sister preyed on a young lonely girl in order to secure, for you, an excellent home. . ."

"You leave my sister out of this!"

Stickle's attitude had undergone such a change that it brought a stir in the court. Gone was the meek, placid-looking man. Someone had dared to say a disparaging word about the only person that, I'm sure, he had ever loved.

"Mr Stickle, please."

"Don't you 'Mr Stickle, please' me, stick to the point. You've been doing it all along. My sister was worth a thousand of her, and she didn't do any pushing. That's the one that did the pushing." His finger was now pointing at me, his eyes spurting hate. "She was man mad, she would have taken anybody. She looked nothing, she was nothing. A barmy cripple."

The judge's hammer rapped on the bench. When it did not subdue the high murmur in the court, it rapped louder. The jurors had their heads bent towards each other and the voice of the judge rang out, "I shall have this court cleared unless I have silence. And I must warn the accused to control himself."

He had silence and in it, my breath seeming to stick in my throat, I stared at Stickle. He was gripping the sides of the witness-box and bending over it; there was saliva running out of the corner of his mouth. I could see the beads of sweat on his brow and it was just as Mr Collins was about to resume that Stickle's voice, addressed to me only, yelled, "Yes, I did it, and I'd do it again. Just give me the chance and I'll get you yet. By God! I will. I'll-get-you-yet." The last words were spaced, then were followed by, "You crippled undersized, barmy sod, you!"

My head drooped onto my chest. I was dimly aware of the bustle that ensued, of the policemen hauling Stickle back into the dock, of the judge's hammer banging loudly on the bench again, of Mr Collins and the defending counsel standing below the judge, talking earnestly, of George's arm around my shoulder, of Tommy taking the vacant seat and holding my hand. I heard my own voice as if from a long distance whimpering, "I want to go home."

"Stay put. Stay put. It won't be long now." It was Mike's voice from behind.

I saw the legs moving away from below the judge's bench. I heard the bustle slowly subside, and a silence again came on the court. But all the while I kept my head down, my mind yelling at me, You undersized, crippled, barmy sod, you! I was aware now of Gran's voice repeating, "Oh, lass. Oh, lass," and somebody saying, "Sh! Sh!"

The judge was speaking. It came to me he had been speaking for some time. My mind seemed to have gone blank. I became aware of his words now: "When you were last in this court, I can recall being surprised, nay, amazed, that a man of your appearance and demeanour could stand proved of subjecting your wife to mental cruelty, sadistic mental cruelty, for thirteen years. I can still allow myself some surprise that, and I have confirmation here" - he now looked down at the desk and picked up a paper - "to the effect that you have been examined by two psychiatrists who find that your mental state is normal. So therefore I must come to the conclusion already stated by the prosecuting counsel that you are of a Jekyll and Hyde nature and part of that nature can deceive onlookers into imagining that they are dealing with a very ordinary person, a quiet-natured, even refined man. Yet, I'm sure that there are those who from time to time must have questioned this quiet nature, when it was known that your former wife left you, that your younger son appeared at school with facial disfigurement and bodily bruising which was supposed to have come from fighting with his brother. Yet, people can still be forgiven for still seeing you as this ordinary man. But Howard Stickle, it has been proved in this court today that you are anything but an ordinary man. The setting fire to your previous home with the intention of at least injuring if not killing your former wife, and without a thought of the other occupants of that house, four of them children. That act was an act of viciousness beyond ordinary conception. You, Howard Stickle, have admitted your guilt. It is now up to the jury to decide whether your admission comes from a sane or unbalanced individual."

There were more words but they were forming a fuzz in my mind. Someone handed me a glass of water. I sipped at it. A voice said, "Do you want to go outside?" I shook my head.

A short time elapsed. There was a buzz of voices about me. I felt I was going to collapse because there, holding me up on one side was Hamilton and on the other, Begonia, and they were saying, Hang on, hang on. It won't be long. It can't be long. Then a voice broke in on theirs, saying, "Here they come."

"Do you find the prisoner guilty, or not guilty?"

"Guilty on all charges."

The glass was at my mouth again. I took another sip of water, then I was looking upwards. My head didn't seem to belong to my body, it wanted to roll from side to side, it seemed so heavy. I was looking at the judge and he was addressing Stickle. I felt a great sigh escape from the bottom of my stomach, spiral up through my chest, my throat, and out of my mouth at his words: "I sentence you to twelve years imprisonment. To my mind it is a just sentence for the acts you have perpetrated. I see you as a cruel, calculating, and wicked man, and for the safety of your former wife and those connected with her, it is wise to see that you are put in a position where you can offer them no further harm. And let us hope by the time your sentence expires you will have rid yourself of the fearful hate that has consumed you and brought you to the position you are in today."

He had hardly finished speaking when a scream vibrated through the court, and Stickle, held now on each side by the two policemen, was glaring in my direction as he yelled, "What's twelve years? I have a son, he'll see to you, you bloody, barmy. . ."

His voice could still be heard as he was dragged down the steps to the cells below.

It was too much. As Hamilton put his foreleg around me I let myself go. . .

I came to in what, I suppose, was one of the offices at the back of the court. I kept my eyes closed for some time and was aware of low voices murmuring. I wasn't interested in anything they were saying until I heard someone say, "The boy. His case will come up tomorrow. He'll likely be sent to a special home. Sergeant Green says that since he broke down and spilled the beans he's been different again. It was the father's influence, I think, that brought out the worst in him. He's expressed a wish to go home to his mother, but I don't think she's very anxious to have him. That's another one the verdict will have pleased because by all accounts she, too, has gone through the hoop with that fellow."

"She wasn't in court?"

"No."

"Mind, I didn't think he would get that, twelve years. I imagined the old boy would give him five or perhaps seven at the most, but twelve! Of course, he would remember the last time he was in court when butter wouldn't melt in his mouth. And then, it was arson, and you can get life for that."

"Are you all right, lass?" It was Gran's voice. "Come on, sit up and have this cup of tea. It's all over. You're all right now. Come on."

There were hands under my shoulders and I was brought upright on the leather couch. The room seemed full of men. I turned my head and looked at the man who had helped me up. It was Mike, and he repeated Gran's words, "It's over now, lass," he said.

I made no movement, not even to blink, I just stared at him, for Stickle's hate was still ringing in my ears and his words, "What's twelve years?" And I shuddered as I thought that the verdict might have taken a different turn had not the counsel brought up his sister May's name. Strange, May had been the instigator of all that had happened, because, yes, she had manoeuvred me into marriage with Howard because of her one desire to give him the security of a good house and a wife with a bit of money. But it was the mention of her name that had condemned him. Strange, strange. . .

There was no celebration after this case as there had been after the previous one, when we had all gone back to the house, and the drink had flowed, and Nardy had sung. He had sung to me, telling me of his love before he had actually voiced it. And we had all sung. It had been a wonderful night. But this time there was no drink except tea, and we sat crowded in Gran's kitchen, just the family and Tommy: the rest had gone their ways. I kept saying, "I must go to the hospital. I must tell Nardy." And one after the other they said, "There's plenty of time. Rest yourself. 'Tisn't every day you pass out." This hadn't even raised a titter.

Mary had made a scratch meal, but I couldn't eat anything, neither could Tommy. And after a short while George said, "You won't be satisfied until you go, will you? So I think you'd better get yourself away." He looked at Tommy and Tommy said, "Yes, you're right, George."

And so I was sitting alone in the car again with Tommy. He had come up yesterday especially for the case, but prior to that I hadn't seen him for a month. I knew he wrote to Nardy, and I felt peeved at times that he didn't come up at the week-end to see him. But Nardy had made excuses for him, saying that he was seeing to his work as well as his own, as they hadn't taken on anyone else. But I still thought he could have made the journey for his life now seemed to be spent racing around in this car.

We drew up in the car park next to the hospital and as he took out the keys and was about to get out, I put my hand on his sleeve and said, "What is it, Tommy?"

"What do you mean, what is it, Maisie?"

"Aren't you well?"

"Yes, I'm well, that's as well . . . as the doctor would say, as can be expected. We've all been through a difficult time. Perhaps you remember."

This wasn't the Tommy I knew, and I said, harshly, "Tommy, please don't take that attitude with me." And at this he lay back in the seat and drooped his head forward for a moment before he said, "I'm sorry, Maisie, but, I don't feel myself these days." He gave a shaky laugh now and glanced at me as he went on, "I don't read poetry any more: I don't spout it to myself as I'm getting dressed; I don't quote it at people on every possible occasion. The hate of my mother and her duplicity over all those years to keep me tied to her apron strings has deepened tenfold. And that's only the beginning of it."

I had my hand on his now, saying softly, "You are the same Tommy. This is all the result of shock. We are all undergoing it in one way or another, and we are all, yes, we are all worried about you, and especially so is Nardy. You are his best friend. He thinks the world of you." I didn't know whether this was absolutely true now but I was making myself say it.

He withdrew his hand from mine and, bringing himself upright in the seat, he said, "Nardy. I . . . I want you to break something to him, because I'll find it difficult to tell him, but I'm leaving the firm, really leaving, not just taking the sabbatical to do the tour."

"What!" The question came from high in my head. "I . . . I understand that you are for promotion when Mr Rington goes at the end of the year."

"Yes, I understand that too, but it's come too late. Anyway, I've told God the Father" - this was Tommy's nickname for Mr Houseman - "and all being well, I'll be off permanently at Easter, that's if they can find a replacement." He now showed a bit of his old self when he dug his thumb into his chest, saying, "Of course it will be difficult to find anyone to replace me." Then he went on, "June, at the latest."

My voice was very small when I said, "What are you going to do?"

"Oh" - his reply was airy - "I've got it all planned out. I'm not just going to do a world tour, I'm going to discover the world.

I'm going to travel. I'm sick of London. I'm sick of the whole country. Everything's changed. Oh, this is not a new thought. You see, I used to set my judgement by the House of Houseman and the people who worked there. In the main, we were all . . . well, sort of gentlemen, you know what I mean, at least on the surface. Our attitude to one another, our manners. We still opened doors for secretaries; we still bid each other good morning; and bloody was about as far as we went in language, at least while on the premises. But all that's changed."

I looked through the windscreen at the flashing lights of cars coming and going in the darkening twilight, and after a moment I said, "That to me is a poor excuse for opting out, which is only another name for running away."

"Perhaps you're right. Perhaps the main trouble is I'm immature, I need to grow up. But I'll have to get going, won't I?"

His hand on the door handle again, he asked, "When do you think you'll be coming home, back to town?"

"I don't really know but I'm going to see the doctor to find out when it will be safe for Nardy to be moved. The graftings could surely be done in London."

"And when will you be up again?" I asked him.

"Likely at the week-end." He was smiling at me now. "By the way,

Hamilton hasn't got a spare friend he could let me have? I need someone to talk at at times."

I smiled back at him as I replied, "I'll see what I can do. But there's one thing you must remember, Tommy, you must never talk at a horse, you must talk to him."

"O.K. I'll remember that."

We parted smiling, but I didn't see Hamilton galloping before me, nor yet Begonia. But half-way up the hospital corridor my step slowed, and it came to me that Tommy was desperately lonely, and I said to myself: He should be married. Yes, he should get married. And I earnestly hoped that he would. . .

Nardy looked much brighter. He put both hands out towards me in greeting, and he was the first to speak, saying, "I know all about it."

"You can't. I've just come from there. Well, I mean, I went back with Gran and them, but. . ."

"Sister was off duty. She was in the court. She came back bursting with it."

Of a sudden I was grateful to the sister, for I would have found it painful, even to describe in a little Stickle's intense hate of me. The fact that I could arouse such hate in a human being both worried and frightened me.

Nardy was saying, "It's all over. He's been put where he won't trouble you for a long time, and he'll likely find plenty inside to work out his hate on. Oh, my dear, you look so tired."

"I'm not tired. I don't do anything to make me tired, but -" I paused, then drew one of his hands tight against my breast as I added, "I'd love to be home. Wouldn't you?"

"Two minds but a single thought. I saw the specialist yesterday. He says two or three weeks. Let them have another go at me. They're all so very good, marvellous, and I'm feeling better every day." He asked now, "Has Tommy gone down to see Kitty?"

I shook my head, "No, no, he hasn't; he's going straight back to town."

"Without coming in?" There was a hurt note in his voice and his expression was a puzzled one. "He purposely didn't come in," I said, "because he had something to tell you and he couldn't bring himself to it."

He waited, staring straight at me, and when I said, "He's leaving the firm," he made a small noise in his throat, then said, "No!" and added, "Well, I'm not really surprised."

"He's in a very odd mental state, has been since that night," I said. "I can't get to the bottom of it. He told me just a little while ago that he doesn't read poetry any more, nor spout it, and that he is disillusioned with the firm and the country and everything."

Nardy turned his head and looked towards the man in the opposite bed who was in an even worse state than himself, having being scalded when a boiler burst, and he said, quietly, "But that isn't like Tommy." And looking at me again, he asked quietly, "Is that all you gathered?"

"What do you mean, dear, is that all I gathered?"

"Well, he didn't confide in you personally about anything?"

"No, no, not at all."

"He's been avoiding me."

"Oh, no."

"Oh, yes. Do you know that the last time he was here he didn't stay five minutes, and I know that he made two visits to Kitty. I wouldn't have known he had been in again only one of the nurses told me what great fun he had caused in her ward. He had them all singing? K . . . K . . . Katie. Beautiful Katie. And then George and Mary came on the scene and it ended up more like a party."

All of a sudden his head jerked upwards and he said, "Well, if that's the way he wants it, let him have it."

"Oh, but Nardy, he thinks the world of you."

There I was again saying something I was doubting in my own mind. And Nardy said, his tone serious now, "What does that really mean, Maisie, when somebody thinks the world of you? If they think the world of you like I do of you, and you of me, they want to see the person they think the world of as often as possible. Friendship, you know, can be as strong as love." Then his mood changing, he made an effort to lean towards me as he said, "Come along, don't look like that. You see the man over there, the second from the end? He's got a pet phrase: There's nowt so funny as folk. His family come in and they talk round his bed and he never opens his mouth until they go, and then he looks down the ward, his face one big grin, and he says, 'There's nowt so funny as folk.' His wife brings him sweets; she talks all the time. His grandchildren come in and eat the sweets. His daughter brings him fruit, and his son-in-law practically goes through that. He's got a grandson who comes in in full motor-bike kit, stands at the bottom of the bed and shouts as if his grandfather was sailing up the Tyne, 'Hello, codger!' "

I was smiling now, even laughing, and I said, "You'll have to write a book about your experiences here."

"No, I'll just tell them to you, and you put it in. By the way, where's Hamilton?" He turned his head slowly and looked about him, then added, "And his dear wife?"

My voice was quiet as I replied, "Strangely, I haven't seen either of them for some time except for a moment or two in the court."

"Oh, come now, come, you've got to get hold of him again. Put a halter on him; he's our jam on the bread." He gripped my hand now and in a whisper he said, "Bring Hamilton back. You're always happier when he's about; you're more yourself."

I didn't answer. I just looked at my dear, dear husband who was telling me that I appeared much more sane when I conjured up a horse and his mate and gave them life form.

I noted that he hadn't alluded to Stickle's last throw at me: You crippled, undersized, barmy sod, you! But then perhaps the sister had been thoughtful.

Chapter 12

I didn't write to Janet to tell her that I would be going down because I knew she would scurry around cleaning places that didn't need cleaning. So when I put my key in the door and stepped into the hall I was amazed to hear a childish voice coming from the direction of the kitchen.

I had got the first train down this morning with the intention of getting the business done with regard to Nardy's future treatment. I had a letter from the hospital doctor which was to be given to the doctor with whom I had made an appointment over the phone. I pushed from my mind the suspicion that the hospital doctor had written this letter with some reluctance. Anyway I was aiming to return north tonight, because somehow I couldn't let a day pass without seeing Nardy. So here I was, at a quarter to one, and evidently Janet was still here and she had a child with her, likely the grandchild she had spoken of.

Not to startle her, I called loudly, "Janet! It's me."

A very surprised woman looked at me from the kitchen door at the far end of the hall, and as she did so she thrust her foot backwards and

I heard a small shrill voice say, "Oh, gag!" or something that sounded like that.

"I didn't expect you." Janet reached out and pulled the kitchen door closed after her, then came towards me, saying, "Are you all right? What's happened? Why are you. . . ?"

I held up my hand now, flapping it at her, saying, "I've just popped down, Janet. I'm . . . I'm seeing a doctor this afternoon about Nardy. I want to bring him home as soon as possible."

Whatever she was going to say next was stilled as she turned her face to the side to where a small boy was emerging from the kitchen. He was bent over, rubbing his shins, and he said, "You bloody well kicked me, Gag."

I watched Janet close her eyes for a moment, then, stretching out a hand, grab the little fellow and thrust him back into the kitchen; and, before closing the door on him, she growled, "You stay put. Don't move. Do you hear?"

Then as I took my hat and coat off she came up to me again, saying, "Sorry, ma'am, Mrs Leviston. It's a long story. But I'll get you a cup of tea first." She was definitely flustered.

"Don't bother with tea, Janet. Let's go and sit down and have a sherry, I'm needing it, and by the look of you" - I smiled now "so are you."

I went into the drawing-room, but stopped just within the doorway. I hadn't forgotten what this room looked like, but on the sight of it, at this moment, it appeared like heaven, all gold and blue. Turning to Janet, I said, "Oh, it looks wonderful. You've got no idea how wonderful it is just to see it again." And I put my hand out to her and patted her arm as I added, "It's just as if I had left it yesterday. Go on, bring the sherry in."

A few minutes later I was seated on the couch and Janet was perched on the edge of the chair opposite me. I had briefly given her my news concerning Nardy and Kitty, and the rest of the family, and she tut-tutted here and there, the while shaking her head. Yet, all the time I knew that what she had to tell me of her own troubles seemed naturally much more important at the moment. And, to bring the matter up, I said, "Who is our visitor? Where does he come in?"

She sighed now and seemed to slip further back onto the chair before she said, "He's me grandson, ma'am, you know, the one I told you about, one of our Maggie's lot. Oh, I've had a time of it, I can tell you. I told you, ma'am, she went off and left the three of them with Jimmy, that's their dad, but she saw them every weekend. They were like Yo-yos: first with their dad and his new fancy piece, and then with our Maggie and her bit. Anyway, ma'am, to cut a long story short, our

Maggie scarpered." She nodded her head at me now. "Yes, she did it again from the fellow she left Jimmy for, she went off with another one. And where to? As far as I can gather, Australia. And Jimmy's piece finding them on her hands all the time wouldn't have it, and she threatens to walk out on him, and Jimmy's at his wits end an' for putting the lot of them into care. But my Harry got on his hind legs and said they had to come home, I had to take them; and there was I with Greg, Rodney and May still clinging to me skirt tails. And Max, who I told you was divorced, well he's out of work and he landed. Well, I can tell you, ma'am, I nearly went round the bend. But I was just saved by Hilda. You know, she's single but she's got a boy friend, and she's got a bit of a flat, and they're a couple, dyed hair, the lot. But I must say she turned up trumps and said she'd take Doris and Gloria - Doris is eight and Gloria's nine - for a time. But there was no way she would have young 'Arry" - Janet now thumbed towards the drawing-room door - "because he's a holy terror. But in a way it's understandable, for he's been passed from dog to devil and he's listened to so much he doesn't know right from wrong, I mean with regard to talkin' like. Well, as you've just heard, ma'am, it comes out as often as God Bless You with him. Anyway, for the last few weeks he's been mostly with his grandad, his dad's father, and that man should be locked up. Well, he is for a time because he's now been put in a home. So there you are, ma'am. It was either staying at home to look after him, because nobody else will take the responsibility of him, or bringin' him along of me."

"Well, don't let that worry you, Janet. If you don't mind bringing him, I certainly won't mind his being here, and I'm sure neither will Nardy."

"Oh, you don't know what you're sayin', ma'am. He never stops talkin' and askin' questions. But I wouldn't care if it's in ordinary English. Oh! I'm ashamed to me boots at times. And I wouldn't take him in a bus, not to save me life."

"You don't walk all this way with him?"

"I do, ma'am." She made a deep obeisance with her head. "You haven't heard him. He's got one tone, and that's loud. And if people don't look at him when he starts, they look at me and they tut-tut-tut. Mind, at times I feel like turning on them I do; I'd like to hear their language when they're behind their own doors. And the trouble is he picks up everything so quickly. He's bright, more than bright for his age, and he comes out with things like an old man at times. But of course, that's his grandad. And I don't get any help from the lads at home: they encourage him; they think it's funny. Yet, ask one of them to stay in and look after him, an' they leave greased lightning standing'."

"Come on, Janet." I rose to my feet. "Let me go and meet the culprit properly." I smiled widely at her, but she did not return the smile.

"You'll have to be prepared, ma'am, an' not be shocked," she said.

"It will take a lot of language to shock me, Janet." My tone and face were serious now. "I had a husband once who, from almost the day we were married, sprayed me every night with the most vile language, and I mean vile language, not just swearing."

"That a fact, ma'am?"

"Yes, it's a fact, Janet. And that man got his deserts a few days ago, twelve years."

"Yes, yes, I know that, I read it. But to think he treated you like that. For meself, I don't mind swearin', but I can't stand dirt."

I understood what she meant only too well: I couldn't stand dirt either.

When I entered the kitchen and really looked at Harold Stoddart for the first time, a sort of gurgle spiralled up from my stomach and stuck somewhere at the top of my breast bone. He was what you call, podgy. He had round dark eyes in a round face, topped by a mass of fair hair. But this combination didn't make him look like a cherub, anything but.

"Hello there," I said.

He made no reply, just fixed those dark round eyes on me, until Janet said, "Say hello to the lady, young 'Arry."

The eyes were turned from me and took on a glare as he looked at his grandmother and said, "I've told you, Gag, 'tain't 'Arry, 'tis 'Arold." Then looking at me again, he stated, "I'm 'Arold, like 'Ark the 'Arold Angels Sing, that 'Arold."

"That's not Harold," I now stated, holding the young man's eye; "That's Hark The Herald Angels Sing."

"Same."

"No it isn't."

"Bloody well is."

"'Arry."

"Well, 'tis."

"You behave yourself, d'you hear?" Janet was bending over him. "Or you know what you'll get."

"Smacked arse." The round face went into a wide grin now. Then he almost fell on that same part of his anatomy as Janet's hand slapped him lightly across the ear. And now the small face twisted up, the lips trembled as he said, "Oh, Gag, that 'urt."

It was obvious, however, that there was no resentment in the child's statement; but Janet, for her part, was visibly disturbed. And I came to her rescue by saying, "Can you knock me up a poached egg or something quickly, Janet? I've got an appointment with the doctor at half-past two. But in the meantime this young man and I will go into the drawing-room and have a talk."

As Janet groaned I held out my hand, and to my surprise it was instantly taken. Together, we walked across the hall and entered the drawing-room. But immediately we crossed the threshold my young companion said, "She won't let me in 'ere, Gag won't."

"Well, I can understand that."

"What? What d'yer say?"

"I said, I can understand your grandmother not letting you come into this room because there's a lot of ornaments that you could easily knock over. Come and sit down." I led him to the couch. And when he went to climb on it I said, "No, not with your feet, sit down." And I lifted him up and plonked him on the edge of the couch, his feet sticking out before him.

I did not sit down by his side, but took the chair that Janet had vacated earlier, so that we were facing each other. And I was about to speak when my young visitor said, "This your 'ouse?"

"Yes, this is my house."

"All on it?"

"Yes, all on . . . of it. "

He now let his gaze range round the room as far as his head could see over the end of the couch. Then he made an exclamation, I don't know whether of condemnation or admiration: "Bloody hell!" he said.

"*Harold!*"

"Yes?"

"Do you know that you are swearing?"

The round eyes gazed fixedly into mine. Then he said, "What d'yer mean?"

"I mean that you were using bad words."

"What bad words?"

"Those that you've just said, when you were looking around this room and you were surprised by the colours and the size of it."

His eyes were screwed up, and I saw that he was thinking. And now, when that loud, toneless voice said, "You mean bloody hell?" I managed to say calmly, "Yes, that's what I mean. Those are swear-words."

"Swear-words?"

"Yes, swear-words, not nice, not for little boys to use."

"Uncle Max uses 'em, an' Uncle Greg, an' Grandad Stodd, he uses 'em all the time . . . swear-words."

"Well, they are grown up, you are just a little boy."

"I ain't. I'm four-an'-'alf, comin' up five. . . . You the woman wots got an 'orse?"

I swallowed deeply now, closed my eyes for a second, and knew what I would see when I opened them, and there he was, hanging over the back of the couch, his whole big black sleek body shaking with laughter, while Begonia stood at the head of the couch gazing solemnly down on this precocious mite.

I tried to ignore the pair of them and, looking at Harold again, I said, "Yes, I'm the lady who has a horse."

"Wot ain't there, like?"

When I made no comment on this, Harold added for my information, "You're the lady wot sees things, an' gets a barra' money for it. Are you barmy?"

I refused to look over the back of the couch. I kept my eyes fixed on this terrible infant and said, "No, I am not barmy. What makes you think I am?"

I watched him trying to think up an answer. His fixed gaze left my face, he looked at his fingernails, then began to pick them, using the thumb and the nail of the index finger of his left hand to clean the nails of his right. Then, lowering his gaze, he looked at his feet sticking out before him, and then he made another statement: "Grandad Stodd says; all the buggers around our way are barmy."

What could I do? My head drooped; I covered my eyes as much as I could with my outstretched hand; I coughed, took a handkerchief from the pocket of my dress, and blew my nose; and, when his voice came at me, asking, "You got the flu?" I shook my head while I continued to blow my nose.

When I uncovered my eyes and relieved my nose of rubbing it with my handkerchief, my companion asked, "You feel better now?"

"Yes. Yes, thank you."

"I'm goin' to school soon."

As I saw Hamilton now cover his eyes with one of his front hoofs and mutter, God help them! I said, "That will be nice. But you must· learn not to swear before you go to school."

"Why?"

"Because . . . because little boys don't swear at school."

I almost did hear a snort coming from behind the couch as I went on, "They'll be punished if they do."

"You mean they'll get their ear 'oles banged?"

"Yes. Well, not exactly." Oh dear me. I looked towards the drawing-room door and almost said aloud, Oh, Janet, hurry up! for this little fellow was getting beyond me. And when, hitching himself towards the end of the couch and placing his feet on the carpet, he poked his head forward and in a voice that was for once a tone lower, which I imagined was his type of whisper, he said, "I know a lot of other words

Grandad Stodd told me. D'yer want to hear 'em?"

"No . . . not particularly. What I mean is. . ."

He was by the side of my chair now. His whisper still loud, he went on, "Grandad Stodd said they were special like an' . . . an' I had to keep 'em till I got to school."

"He did? Well, I think. . ." I was about to say, your Grandfather Stodd is a very nasty old man, when the small hand came up and gripped the collar of my dress, which caused me to bend my head towards him, and there he was, his face close to mine, a wicked grin on it: "If I tell yer can I come back 'ere again?" he said.

Well, I thought, I might as well hear the worst, so I nodded slightly. Then the small mouth was close to my ear and a puff of his breath crept over my cheek before he brought out the words, "Goal stones!"

My head swung round, our noses almost scraped in the passing, and I could see glee registered on his face at the amazement on mine. And now I whispered back at him, almost choking as I did so, "Gall-stones?" His eyes stretched, his upper lip aimed to reach his chin, his nose poked forward, and he repeated, " Goal stones."

Now the imp in myself asked quietly, "Do you know any more like that . . . that Grandad Stodd said?"

He had hold of my ear now and his breath was once again fanning my cheek, and the next dreadful words which came from his small mouth were, "Bedpan an' 'abit shirt."

My face was screwed up tight. Whoever Grandad Stodd was, he had a sense of humour, and he was a man who realized that gall-stones and bedpans and habit shirt, whatever that was, wouldn't shock the teachers as much as bloody and bugger might.

I was saved from another confidence by Janet coming into the room carrying a tray. After placing it on the table, she came towards us and, noticing my wet face, she looked from me to her grandson, then back to me. And after a moment she said, "Has he behaved himself, ma'am?"

"Oh, yes, yes," I said hastily; "he's been a very good boy. And if he remains a good boy" - I had one eye on him now - "and doesn't swear so much, you know, using those big naughty words, then you may bring him into this room when I'm away."

"Can I, ma'am?"

Janet realising the situation, played up, adding now, "But I'll have to tell you if he keeps using them, won't I, ma'am?"

"Oh, yes, yes." I nodded emphatically at her now. Then we both looked down on the subject of our exchange when it said, "Will you tell me Uncle Max an' Uncle Greg, Gag, they got to stop an' all? And Grandad 'Arry, will you tell him an' all? 'cos he's always sayin' soddid. Is soddid a swear. . . ?"

Janet took him swiftly from the room, the child's feet hardly touching the ground, and I dropped on to the couch and laid my head back and looked at Hamilton doing cartwheels the whole length of the room, while Begonia still stood at the end of the couch, smiling, the while she endeavoured not to. When at last Hamilton stopped and sat on his haunches in front of me, he said, Won't Nardy enjoy him? And I, nodding at him, replied, "Oh, yes, yes, he will."

Chapter 13

It was early May when I finally brought Nardy home. The sun was shining, the trees were in their first coat of light green. The parks and window boxes were full of wallflowers, and tulips. We had come by ambulance from Newcastle. Although Nardy could now sit in a wheelchair and walk a few steps with aid, a train journey would have been out of the question. And here he was, being pushed out of the lift and into the hallway. And there was Janet waiting.

She remained still, looking at him for a moment; then swiftly coming towards him, she held out both her hands and when he gripped them and pulled her down to him and kissed her, she burst into a flood of tears, saying, "Oh, Mr Leonard. Oh, Mr Leonard."

"Would you mind?" I said to the ambulance men, and pointed to our hall door. And when they had pushed Nardy's chair through and into the drawing-room, both men stopped for a moment before pushing the chair further towards the couch. And when Nardy was seated on it, one of the men looked around him. Then bending towards Nardy, he said, "I can see how you wanted to be back, sir."

Nardy said nothing; he only smiled at the men, laid his head back against the couch and let his eyes roam round the room.

I thanked the ambulance men warmly. We had got to know each

other on the long journey, especially the one who had sat by the bed all the way. And my heart went out to him because, not only had he read *Hamilton*, but he had been able to quote from it, in particular the bits in the doctor's surgery. Apparently his wife had already endorsed that it was exactly as I had described.

They were both surprised at and very grateful for the tip they received and they shook my hand and wished me all the luck in the world.

When I once again entered the drawing-room, Nardy extended his hand towards me, and I hurried to him. I sat down beside him; and his arm about me, he laid his head on my shoulder and said simply, "Thank God!"

I too thanked Him for having my dear one back home safe, if not sound, for now I was carrying a fresh burden.

This morning the doctor had asked to see me before we left the hospital and, after a polite exchange, he had said, "I have written to Doctor Bell concerning your husband, Mrs Leviston, and I think you, too, should be put in the picture. You may have been wondering why we haven't continued the graftings these last few weeks. Well, we didn't think it wise owing to the condition of your husband's heart."

At these words, a steel hammer seemed to have leapt up and hit my ribs, and the pain made me dumb. I just stared at the man, waiting for his next words. "It will no doubt improve with time, rest, and care. The main thing in his case is rest, at least for the present. He will naturally have to have therapy to get his joints moving again. Fortunately these are all intact. Doctor Bell will no doubt arrange for a therapist to visit him."

In a small voice I had asked now, "Does my husband know of his condition?"

And to this the doctor had answered, "Yes, he knows. But it was his wish that you shouldn't be informed. However, I made no promise to him one way or the other, but I felt you should know the situation, and how, in the future, he should be treated. He needs rest, but not inertia. The quicker he can walk unaided, the better, for gentle exercise will aid and strengthen his limbs."

He then ended, "It will be up to you whether you let him know that you are aware of this or not. But my advice would be, at the moment, to pretend ignorance, for it would be of no help if he knew you were worried more than you have been."

So here I was chatting away about the future and where we were going as soon as he was able to travel.

The door opened and Janet came in with the tea-trolley, and she stood in front of us and smiled, a warm welcoming smile, as she said,

"Oh, I'm glad to see you both sitting there again. Oh, I am. It does me heart good."

I put my hand out towards her, asking now, "Where is he?"

"In the kitchen. I've practically had to strap him down."

"Fetch him in."

"You're sure? You'd better have a cup of tea first, 'cos mind, I'm tellin' you, ma'am, he -" she pressed her lips together, and her eyelids were blinking hiding the laughter there as she ended, "he hasn't improved."

I wanted to say, "Good, good," because I had told Nardy so much about the little fellow which had made him laugh until he had begged me to stop, and the fact that the child might have improved would, I thought, have made Nardy imagine that I had created someone else to join my little menagerie.

It was Nardy now who answered for me, saying, "I'm glad to hear that. Give us five minutes, then fetch him in."

During the five minutes which stretched to ten we had two cups of tea each, and a sandwich, then the door opened and Janet came in leading Harold by the hand, and on first sight he appeared a different child. The last time I had seen him he had been wearing patched jeans and a scruffed little jacket, over which part of a none too clean shirt collar had probed. But coming towards us now was a smart little fellow in bright blue jeans and a white tee-shirt.

When Janet relinquished his hand, he stood in front of us looking from one to the other; then he stumbled sideways as Janet's hand pushed him none too gently, saying, "Mind what I told you. Behave yourself."

I watched him slant his eyes up at his grandmother, then he emitted a long drawn out, "Oo . . . h!" as she left the room.

"Hello, Harold."

Harold did not answer me; he was looking at Nardy. Now Nardy said, "Hello Harold." And to this Harold deigned to reply, "Hello."

There was silence now between the three of us, and the questioning seemed to be carried on by our eyes because, first, Harold would lift his gaze from Nardy, look at me, then look back at Nardy again; and I would look at Harold, then look at Nardy, then look back at Harold once more.

"Have you been a good boy?"

There was no answer, but a definite nodding of his head. Harold wasn't acting to form. It seemed to be that Nardy's presence was stilling his tongue. Then I found I was mistaken, for what the young man now said, addressing himself directly to Nardy, was, "You the fella as got burnt?"

I heard Nardy swallow. "Yes," he said, "I'm the fella as got burnt."

"All over?"

"No, no, not quite."

"I got burnt once."

"You did?"

"Aye, I did."

"Where were you burnt?"

"On me arse." He started, while at the same time I started, and Nardy started, and our joined glances went swiftly towards the door as if we expected to see his grandmother flying up the room, her hand uplifted. After a moment I heard my own voice, mock stern now, saying, "You didn't mean that, did you, Harold? You meant your bottom?"

He looked at me, the expression on his face telling me that he definitely wasn't going to sink as low as that, for he emitted one word, "Backside."

Then switching his gaze to Nardy again, he said, "You want to see?"

I daren't look at Nardy, but his voice sounded steady as he said, "Yes. Yes, I'd like to see where you were burnt."

I watched the small hands deftly now unbuttoning the straps that kept his jeans up and when they were dropped around his ankles, he shuffled forward, turned round, at the same time pulling down a tiny pair of clean underpants. And there, across one small bare buttock, about four inches by two, almost covering the whole pad of flesh, was a scar that proved the extent of a bad burn.

"Dear, dear! you have been burnt, haven't you?"

"Yes. An' if I sit like this" - he now bent over and pushed his bottom out - "I can see it in the glass."

As I had once done, I saw Nardy cover his eyes with his hand; then he made a strange sound before he asked, "How did you manage to get burnt like that?"

The small pants were being pulled up, then the jeans, and these were safely buttoned before the answer came, "I sat on the bloody fire bar."

There seemed to be pandemonium in the room. I was coughing hard, Nardy was bent forward, his hand still over his eyes; Hamilton was racing round the lot of us, and not alone now, but dragging Begonia with him.

When I found my voice I said, "How on earth did you manage to get burnt by a fire bar?"

"Grandad Stodd showed me. He used to lift up 'is shirt at night, like this" - he now demonstrated, bending over again and holding up an imaginary shirt away from his hips - "to warm his a . . . backside."

I realized that was a good effort and, trying to keep my face straight, I said, "And you followed suit?"

He hesitated a moment before answering, his eyes screwed up again in a manner with which, in the future, I was to become well acquainted whenever he tried to understand the meaning of some word or saying. Now, seeming to get my gist, he said, "Well I stood on the fender, an' it was slippy an' I fell backward, an' . .. an' I raised hell. Grandad Stodd said they heard me down at the fish market. An' I kept on when I was in the hospital; I raised the bloody place. An' you know what?" He now transferred his gaze from Nardy's tortured expression to mine, and he moved a step nearer to me and, poking his head forward and his face going into a smile, he said again, "You know what?" And I shook my head as I said, "No: what?"

I watched him press his lips tight together before he said in what to him was his whisper, "The nurse, she kissed me when I was comin' out."

"*Never!*" I shook my head as if in disbelief.

And now indignantly and loudly, he cried, "She did! An' she said, if I would like to sit on any more bars she would see to me. She did. Why you holdin' hands?"

Our fingers parted as if a spring had released them; then Nardy said, "Because we are fond of each other, we like holding hands."

He stared at Nardy for some time, then moved from one foot to the other before he spoke again: "Me mum went off with a bloke," he said.

What could you say to that? We said nothing. And he went on, "An' me dad's bit, she doesn't like me." He shook his head vigorously now. And when I was forced to say, "Oh, I'm sure you are mistaken, Harold," his voice came back at me in an almost screaming bark as he yelled, "No, I'm not mis . . . mistakin'. She clouted me, not like Gag does, like that!" He used his hand to demonstrate by banging himself on the ear. "She hit me with the dog's lead." Then he added in almost the same breath," Gag says you've got a dog. Where is it?"

"A friend of ours is bringing it down by car from the north. I . . . I think you'll like it. His name is Sandy."

"Will you bring it round to Gag's?"

My eyes widened in surprise as I said, "No, no; you'll see it here."

"I won't, 'cos . . . 'cos this is me finish."

"Your finish?"

"Yes. I'm not comin' back any more, Gran says, 'cos . . . 'cos of you." He was now nodding at Nardy. "'Cos . . . 'cos you bein' an old man, you want to be quiet."

"He's not an old man." I indignantly spoke up in Nardy's defence. But my opponent, looking my husband over from top to bottom, stated flatly, "He is an' all."

Nardy was nodding at him now: "Yes, yes, of course I am, but that doesn't mean you can't come here to see me."

"Yer mean I can? Can I?"

"Yes, of course."

"Every day?" He was looking at me now and I nodded and said, "Yes, except the week-ends when your grandmother doesn't come."

He now glanced towards the door again and, his voice dropping; he emitted, "God Almighty!"

"What's wrong?"

He was appealing to me now: "Will . . . will yer tell her that you asked me, else she'll bash me ear 'ole for me?"

"Yes, I'll tell her. And Harold. . ."

He waited, and while pulling myself to the end of the couch I put out my hand and caught his and said, "What you have just said. . ."

"What?"

"The" - I stopped, looked down, and was aware of Nardy moving restlessly to the side of me - "the expression you used about . . . about God."

"Oh, God? Like on a Sunday night on the telly?"

"Yes, like on a Sunday night on the telly."

"Gag looks at that 'cos she says it clears the house."

Puzzled, I bent my head towards him and repeated, "Clears the house?"

"Yes, 'cos me Uncle Greg and Rodney and me Auntie May, they go out and sit in the kitchen. But I sit with Gag . . . well, 'cos, she makes me. But . . . but I don't mind, I don't, 'cos I sit on her knee then an' sometimes I fall asleep."

His eyes roaming round the room, he now made a statement: "I'd like to live in this house," he said.

"I'm sure you would, I'm sure you would." My voice was brisk; and giving him now a slight pat on the bottom, I said, "Go and tell your grandma that we'd like some more hot water."

He didn't move, but, instead, asked, "An' will I tell 'er I can come every day 'cos you say so?"

"Yes." I looked at Nardy, and he endorsed this. "Yes, yes, of course."

With this he darted down the room, and I saw Hamilton, still holding on to Begonia, dancing after him.

"Amazing."

I nodded at Nardy, saying, "Yes, isn't he just."

"How old did you say he was?"

"Five now, I think."

"He's bright. He thinks; you can see his mind working. But what will he end up like among that lot? Poor Janet. You cannot imagine her breeding that crew, can you? I wonder whom he takes after?"

"Well, evidently not his mother, and by all Janet's accounts his father's a very ordinary individual."

"Anyway," he laughed now, "he's picked up a wonderful vocabulary. I don't think I've laughed so much since I first met Gran and George. Yet" - he turned and looked at me - "you know what you said when you left me the other night? It's made me think."

"What was that?"

"Well, I imagined you were a bit tired of the constant wisecracking of George and Gran. And, if you remember, you said, everything should be doled out in small amounts, except love and peace of mind."

"Did I say that?"

"Of course, you did. You know you did."

"Well, yes, I suppose it's true, because" - I started to chuckle now - "fancy having Harold for twenty-four hours of the day."

"Oh, yes, just fancy. Still, I think I'm going to see him as a diversion in the future, during the times I get bored with you."

As I put my arms about him and we kissed, a long, soft, tender kiss, I tried to thrust to the back of my mind the knowledge of his condition that I now carried with me.

A couple of hours later Tommy arrived with Sandy. I had become a little worried when he didn't show up about the same time as us, but, as he said, he had taken it slowly because of Sandy's nerves.

Sandy's greeting of me was as if we had been parted for weeks; and he greeted Nardy the same. And Tommy, looking at the dog kissing first one and then the other of us, remarked, "What it is to be loved."

At this I made Sandy behave.

Tommy refused tea but accepted whisky. He was drinking more of late, I noted. And as he stood sipping his drink, he looked round the room, saying, "One can see how you wanted to be back. I'd forgotten what this room looked like."

I noted that he had never asked Nardy how he was feeling, or how he had stood the journey. Tommy was indeed changed; he created a feeling of uneasiness in me.

I was glad when he got up to go.

I opened the door for him and crossed the hall to the lift with him, and we stood looking at each other for a moment while he said, "This time next week I'll be on my way."

"Really?"

"Yes, really. It's all fixed, passport, route, the lot. At least the route is until I get overseas; then who knows?"

"Have you any idea where you're actually aiming for once you arrive?"

"No, none whatever. My idea is to get lost, and perhaps in getting lost" - he paused - "I'll find myself."

"Oh, Tommy." I had the desire to put my hands out and take his, but I resisted, because I was afraid of what the result might be. Yet, I kept telling myself that his change of personality was not due in any way to a feeling he might have for me, because supposedly he'd felt like this before the fire, and it hadn't caused him to act in this strange way.

"Bye-bye, Maisie."

"Bye-bye, Tommy. You will look in before you go?"

"Yes, if I can manage it."

"Tommy!" He was inside the lift and my voice was loud now. "You've got to say goodbye to Nardy. What's the matter with you anyway?"

He stared at me before saying again, "Bye-bye, Maisie." Then the lift doors closed on him and I was left standing listening to the soft hum as it descended to the ground floor. I felt angry. What was the matter with the man anyway? Nardy was his best friend and he had, in a way, put up with him for years listening to his tirades against his mother.

I actually shook my body as if throwing something off. I had enough on my plate without worrying about him. He was going, apparently out of our lives, to get lost. Well, let him get lost, and the sooner the better.

It was the following Thursday night when Tommy came to say goodbye. The shadow of his old self seemed to have returned and he sat with us and talked normally. He showed us two routes: one did seem to cover the world, taking in Nepal and the foothills of the Himalayas before plunging back into the crowds of Singapore and later Hong Kong. Another plan showed a less sophisticated route. Here he thought of walking through the Rockies, after realizing a childhood dream of crossing Canada via the C.P.R.

When we had our last drink together, he held his glass up towards Nardy, saying, "Here's to you taking the stairs instead of the lift."

I helped Nardy to his feet and there they stood looking at each other. Nardy put out his hand and Tommy took it. They gripped tight while Nardy said, "You will keep in touch, won't you? Let us know where you are."

"Yes, I promise, if it's only by cards. Goodbye, Nardy. Thanks for everything, right back down the years."

I saw that Nardy was too full to make any reply, and, as I looked at them, I had the most dreadful feeling of foreboding; it looked as if they were saying goodbye for ever. I turned from them and went hastily down the room and into the hall. And when, a few minutes later, Tommy joined me, I was wiping my eyes; and then, there before me, stood the old Tommy.

"Oh, Maisie, Maisie, don't please. I beg of you, don't. Look, I'm not going away forever; I'll be back in your lives before . . . before you know I've gone."

I looked up at him and said quietly, "Nardy is in a bad way, Tommy. Before we left the hospital the doctor told me that his heart had been affected, so much so that they hadn't done any more grafting. I . . . I suppose they were afraid to use the anaesthetic. And he was examined yesterday by our new doctor, a Doctor Bell, and he confirmed this. But, as he said, taking it easy and with care and attention - he's having therapy every other day - it will likely strengthen."

I put out my hand and touched Tommy's arm, saying, "What is it? What's the matter?" for he had put his hand to his brow, shading his eye, like I did when wanting to hide a smile from young Harold. But Tommy wasn't trying to hide a smile; his mouth was open and he was drawing in a long, shuddering breath.

"Are you all right?" I asked.

He took his hand away, blinked at me, wet his lips, then said, "Yes, yes, Maisie;" and then he added, "No, no; I'm not all right." He stood with his arm outstretched and his finger on the lift button for a moment before he burst out, "Why had you to happen to me?"
The lift door slowly closed itself across my open-mouthed amazed gaze.

Why had you to happen to me?

It was me then that had brought about the change in him. But why had he been so affected by what I had told him about Nardy?
I walked into the hall. There was a half-moon table set between the dining-room and kitchen doors. It had a mirror above it. I leant my hands on the table for support and bowed my head and, like that, I thanked God that Tommy had gone out of our lives. When I lifted up my face, there I was looking at myself. And at this moment the image was no different to what it had been three or four years ago: the hair was brown and straight, the face was heart-shaped, the eyes were round, the nose straight, the mouth wide. Reading these features as a description, they should have made, if not a beautiful face, then a bonny face, a homely face; but their combination resulted in none of these, I was plain. That was the name for me, plain. Perhaps in my eyes I had one asset, they were kindly. Another could be my voice. But given those, what was there about me that could sever a lifetime

friendship that had existed between two men? What was it about me that had attracted either of them?

The reflection in the mirror was shaking its head: it didn't know. And behind it now, the rest of the glass was taken up by Hamilton. I looked at him and he said, You'll never get the answer to that question. If you could put your finger on what creates love, you'd be Solomon's first wife. And in your case you could ask yourself, too, why that same face could create so much hate, not only from Stickle, but from your mother.

I turned away. There was a deep sickness in my stomach.

Chapter 14

The weeks followed pleasantly. The therapist was getting good results: Nardy was able to walk unaided around the flat. But as I watched him I was amazed at how he could bear to move his scarred legs. At my first sight of them, I had been shocked: the left leg was burnt up to his thigh; the scars on the right leg ended just above his knee, but below the knee, down one side as far as the calf, the skin seemed to have been stuck on the bone; the other side had been built up from the skin taken from the thigh of the same leg. This had left sickly white patches here and there that appeared like burns themselves. And I was made to wonder how he had ever survived; and also how poor little Kitty had survived.

And now, according to the letters from Mary, she was doing splendidly, still having graftings but being allowed home in between times. But even with the letters from Fellburn they all now seemed a part of another life, a dim, fast receding life. The only life I was experiencing was the daily routine in these very pleasant rooms, the companionship of Nardy, and the lighter amusing intervals provided by Harold.

Strange, but there were many days when I blessed Harold, for he relieved Nardy's growing boredom.

Nardy had work sent from the office, but the doing of it didn't seem to fill his day, not even with the time spent with the therapist, nor yet, I had to admit, his time spent with me. He missed his daily ride or walk to the office, he missed the companionship of all those who worked there. Although from Mr Houseman down, they visited him from time to time, their visits only seemed to leave him more low and depressed. Now and again he expressed the wish to go out and we hired a car and drove into the country. We would get out and walk for a little way or perhaps have dinner at an inn, but lately the journey itself seemed to tire him.

Then one day, there was presented to me a way to alleviate his periods of boredom.

The heath was only five minutes walk from the house and, at least once a day, in all weathers, I would take Sandy there to do his "necessaries" and give him a bit of play with a ball.

On this day when I went to put on his lead, he was, as usual, in the kitchen having a game with Harold. They were wrestling on the rug, and when I said, "Come along, up with you, you scamp," and caught hold of Harold's arm and pulled him to his feet, he said, "You gonna take him out?"

"Yes."

"But him, the caretaker" - he stabbed his finger towards the floor - "he takes him round the block first thing, don't he?"

"Yes, but that's different; he doesn't get a run then."

"Can I come along o' you?"

This was a new tactic.

Just at that moment Janet entered the room, a duster in her hand, and her grandson ran towards her, saying, "She . . . Mrs Nardy " We were Mr and Mrs Nardy to him now; no clips along the ear could get him to call us anything else. His attempts at Leviston had resulted in verbal gymnastics, so Mr and Mrs Nardy we were. And now he was going on, "She says I can go with her to the heath."

Knowing her grandson better than anyone and, too, noting the expression on my face, Janet looked down on her daily cross, saying, "She never said any such thing, did she?"

He stared back at her, silent now, and her reaction was to bring her hand across his ear as she said, "I've told you about lies. You come out with any more of your smarties an' it won't be a clip along the ear you'll get."

What made me say it? "I asked him, Janet."

"You did?" Her voice was high. I nodded and, looking to where the child was holding his ear, I said to him, "Go and get your coat; there's a wind blowing this morning."

He didn't run from the room but walked out slowly.

Turning to Janet, I said, "Janet, you know you shouldn't hit him across the ears like that, you'll make him deaf."

"Oh" - she jerked her chin upwards - "it'll take a lot to make that one deaf. I wish I could, and dumb. I thought I would have been rid of him at least for part of the day. I went to the school yesterday afternoon, and what d'you think he said, the teacher? He can't take him in until September, nearly four months ahead. My God!" She ran her fingers round the hem of the duster. Then more to herself than to me, she said, "If it was only him I had to put up with. Our house is gettin' like a menagerie. I told you about Joe comin' back, didn't I?" She was looking at me now. "Well, last week our Bill turned up, on the dole. Couldn't pay his board, he said. No, I said to him, that would interfere with your beer money, wouldn't it? Eeh!" She shook her head. "To think what we lived on when we were first married. They each go through that much every night at the pub, and then they grumble. Then I'm havin' trouble with the one next door 'cos of the noise, 'cos when they come in three sheets to the wind it's like hell let loose. I don't blame her in a way, but now she's threatening to go to the council, 'cos I'm takin' in lodgers, she says. You know what, ma'am, I hope she does; it'll get rid of some of them, 'cos when I tell them to scarper they look at me and say, 'Mum, where else can I go, if I can't come home?' Eeh!" She glanced towards the door. "I suppose I shouldn't take it out on that little 'un, but he's just one more sack on me back."

"I'm sorry, Janet, I really am. And then you have all this work to do. . ."

"Oh, ma'am, don't pity me 'cos of that. If I hadn't this house to come to, I really would go round the bend." And now she smiled and nodded at me as she finished, "That's what I said to them last week: if it wasn't for Mr and Mrs Leviston, I'd take a carving knife one night an' go round and finish you all off."

I bit on my lip and said, "You didn't!"

"I did." Her eyes were wide now, her lips were pursed, her head was bobbing. "Me very words. And y'know" - her voice became serious - "you can get to such a pitch you would do anything to sort of clear your mind."

The kitchen door opened and her grandson stood there. He was holding his hand out and he looked at me as he said, "I've brought me new cap."

"Oh, that is a nice one. I haven't seen that before. It matches your coat. Put it on."

He put it on, and I held my head to one side as I said, "Oh, you do look smart. Well, we'll be off, shall we?" Janet and I exchanged looks; then I took up Sandy's lead and we went out.

Once we reached the street, I felt my hand gripped, and there we went, like a little family across the road, down past the public garden still railed round and locked, through the suburb and on to the heath.

The wind was blowing, the air was fresh. I took off my head scarf and ran my fingers through my hair, drawing in one deep breath after another. I walked slowly, watching Harold throw the ball and Sandy scampering after it, then bring it back to him.

Harold would yell, "Sit!" and Sandy would obey. Then Harold would throw the ball again. But the procedure was interrupted: Sandy didn't run after the ball; his head went up, he sniffed, sniffed again, then turning, he looked to where, far away in the distance were the figures of a woman and a dog. They weren't coming towards us but were walking parallel with us.

One second Sandy was there, the next he was off, and I was yelling, "Sandy! Sandy! Stay! Come back!"

Harold made an exclamation which I didn't catch; then we were both running in the direction Sandy had taken.

We were still some distance away when we saw his meeting up with what I could see now was another poodle, much smaller than he. I saw the woman stoop down and pick up her dog; and then she did what I considered a very kind thing. She came walking in our direction.

My running stopped. I stood panting; then checked Harold, caught his hand and together we walked to where Sandy was alternately running round and jumping up at the woman while barking his head off.

"Oh, thank you. I'm so sorry."

"It's all right." The owner of the small black poodle smiled; then looking down on the culprit, she said, "He's a fine fellow, isn't he? He just wanted to make the acquaintance of. . ."

Her words were cut off by a statement issuing from the mouth of a little boy who, bending down, now grabbed Sandy's collar while exclaiming loudly, "He's not a fine fella, he's a naughty little bugger."

Our new acquaintance had a refined voice; she looked a refined person altogether. Her gaze remained on the child who had coupled naughty with bugger in one breath. Her eyes met mine; then they covered me from head to foot. She likely noted that I was wearing a well-cut, seemingly expensive fine woollen two-piece. My shoes, too, were smart. I was wearing a gold wrist-watch and three rings, two of them heavily stoned. Yet, here was this person, because in the woman's mind I must have been registered as just a person, whose little boy came out with the word bugger as natural as he had done naughty. Children, and she would know, learn by copying.

"Good-morning."

My "Good-morning, and thank you," was a mere trickle of a

whisper. I felt ashamed and ashamed of feeling ashamed. I wanted to run after her and say, "He doesn't belong to me. He's the grandson of my help." Snob. I looked down to where Harold was grinning up at me while holding on to Sandy's collar. I bent down and clipped on the lead; then, taking Harold's hand, I led him to a grassy patch and, pressing him down none too gently on to it, I sat down by his side, and as he was about to speak, I heard myself suddenly yell, "Shut up!"

My voice even startled Sandy, and Harold's round eyes narrowed while his mouth widened.

"Do you know what you said there?" I demanded.

"What?"

"Don't you 'what' me. You know what you said to the dog just a moment ago."

I watched him think; then he said, "I told him he was naughty."

"Yes, but you used another word."

I could see light dawning, and his voice in his usual whisper brought out, "Bugger?"

"Yes, that was the word, bugger. Now, you've been told before, haven't you, that these are bad words, at least for a little boy to use." His eyes were blinking, his mouth was closed, and I went on, "Now, I'm going to put this straight to you, Harold. I know you're just turned five, but you are not stupid. In fact, you are far from stupid. You know you've been told not to use those words, haven't you?"

Still there was no response.

"Well, now I'm going to tell you something: either you stop using those words and at once, or you don't come to my house any more. Now have you got that?"

Still no response. And now I watched his lower lip begin to tremble; then his mouth opened and he said, in a real whisper this time, "Everybody . . . everybody says 'em. They says 'em. Talks. I . . . I can't help it, 'cos . . . well. . ."

I turned my head away and looked over the heath. Of course the child couldn't help it. As I'd thought earlier, everyone learns by copying. What he needed was other words to copy. But he wouldn't be going to school until September when very likely he'd add to somebody's vocabulary while extending his own in the same direction. I looked at him again. His lip was still trembling, but I saw that he was being comforted, for there to his side, and looking not much bigger than himself, stood Begonia. Hamilton was present too, but he was some distance away, as if just acting as a spectator. Begonia was nuzzling the fair hair. Then, turning her liquid gaze on me, she said, French. Nardy speaks French like a native, doesn't he? This child, here, likes words. Haven't you noticed how he tries to repeat words, bringing in those that he's heard you or Nardy say? Didn't he only yesterday cause laughter by trying to repeat secondary? Get Nardy to take him on: half an hour or so in the mornings with, *Le livre est sur la table*; or, *Ouvrez la porte. Fermez la fenêtre*. And Nardy would like that, I know he would. You were looking for something different to alleviate his boredom. He enjoys the boy as he is, but just think, if he could extract a foreign language from these small lips instead of crude swearwords, what an achievement that would be! He wouldn't feel so useless. And that's what's troubling him at present, he feels useless.

It was the only conversation I had had with Begonia, and when I nodded at her, she went on softly: And you know something more? The child is lost for love. Clips across the ears don't express affection. He has lost his mother, he has lost his father; he's in a house full of men who, to put it mildly, are rough types. What is more, and what adds to the rejection of his parents is that the woman his father has taken up with must hate him. From what you have been given to understand, the ultimatum was, either he goes or. . . She went. Maisie, you have a piece of gold here covered in clay; it's up to you to strip it until its colour matches your room.

I smiled widely and warmly at Begonia and thanked her for opening my eyes. She said I was welcome. And as she turned away from the child, there was Hamilton. He had come much closer and was waiting for her. He looked at her with pride, then nodded to me, as much as to say, You see, you can't do without one or the other of us.

The next minute they were blocked from my view. I hadn't seen the child rise from the grass, but there he was standing in front of me, his face on a level with mine. What really possessed me at that moment I don't know, perhaps it was the thought of giving Nardy a new interest, anyway; I leant forward and kissed him gently.

I wasn't prepared for what followed. The next instant his arms were about my neck, and he was kissing me in much the same way as Sandy was wont to do, but with a difference, for he was crying loudly while talking all the time: "You let me stay in our 'ouse, Mrs Nardy. I like you, Mrs Nardy. I want to stay with you, Mrs Nardy, an' Mr Nardy. I won't swear. I won't. I love you, Mrs Nardy. . ."

"Sh! Sh! Quiet now."

"Don't tell Gag on me, will you? Will you? Don't tell Gag on me."

"Sh! Sh! now. It's all right. No, I won't tell Gag. No, I won't, my dear." Good gracious! There I was crying myself now. "Come on. Come on." I groped for a handkerchief, which was difficult because Sandy, his paws resting on my shoulder, was now licking our faces alternately.

Finding the handkerchief, I wiped the child's face, then wiped mine.

He was quiet now, but he didn't leave loose of me; instead he put his arms underneath mine and laid his head on my breast and curled the rest of his body into my lap. I supported him with my short arm while balancing myself with my other by pressing it on to the grass because I was finding it difficult to sit upright. Then I found my body rocking slightly and, as I looked down on his face lying on my breast, I had a strange thought: I had a child . . . I had a child.

Chapter 15

"What! Teach Childe Harold French when his English is mostly Saxon?"

"He would hang on to strange words and forget the others, and he'd learn English and grammar as he went along."

Nardy surveyed me through narrowed eyes. I became embarrassed in the silence, and I couldn't say to him, I'm thinking it might help you. Then, following on his first response and the look on his face that my suggestion had evoked, he surprised me now by putting his head back and laughing, as he said, "You know something, Maisie? God is a funny fella."

It was my turn to screw up my eyes and say, "What?"

"I said God is a funny fella. Half consciously you appeal to Him . . . well, in your thinking you say, Show me a way out. Show me how to ease this situation; and when you give up, saying, What's the good? Let things take their course, I can do nothing more, in through the back door walks the answer."

"What are you talking about?"

"What you were talking about, teaching Childe Harold French. Anyway, tell me what brought this on. You come bursting in as if you had just drunk the elixir of life."

So I told him what happened. And he laughed as he said, "For once I think the word naughty was linked up with something meaningful because, you know, that word used to irritate me when in the office. Someone would say, "It's very naughty of him," when the person being spoken of had probably done something really bad, even criminal. It's like nice. That annoys me too. I've discovered if people are really jealous of a possession or of someone else, they'll say, it, or he, or she is ve . . . ry nice."

The last two words were uttered in a refined squeak. And at this I dropped down to his side, laughing, put my arms about him and said, "Oh, Nardy. You know, at times you are very funny, but awfully nice."

"I am?"

"Yes, you are."

"Well, well." He mockingly preened himself, then added, "And all without the aid of a horse. But that's another word, awfully. How can anyone be awfully nice?"

I gave him a push, and as I rose I said, "One thing I've learned about you, you're secretly conceited about your knowledge of English. Anyway, I'm off now to tell Janet you are about to take on her very small rough diamond and polish it, with the result that every one of his family will want to claim acquaintance with him, he being the only one who can speak a foreign language."

I stopped when I reached the door and, looking back at him, I said, "You know, there's some truth in that, isn't there? If that boy ever did turn out to be educationally superior to them all, they would be the first to claim acquaintance with him, and recall the fun they'd had with him when he was a child. Even Janet would bring back the times she had almost deafened him with her hand across his ear."

Nardy nodded at me. "Wise old owl," he said. "But I think you had better tell Janet to sit down before you give her the news." . . .

Nardy was right. Janet looked at me across the kitchen table as if she were thinking that what some people thought about me was actually true. And in a small voice, she said, "French?"

"Yes, French."

"Teach him French?" Her voice still small, she was thumbing to where Harold was lying on the rug, his arms around Sandy. They were facing each other and they presented an angelic picture. And I looked down on them for a moment, then I said, "He'll pick it up, and quickly."

"Huh! ma'am, you mean to say that Mr Leonard is for this?"

"Yes, wholeheartedly."

She turned from the table and went to the oven; bending down, she opened the door and lifted out a casserole dish. Placing it on the table, she said, "Well, never again will I say, nothin' surprises me. But just wait till I tell my lot about this. That'll crease them; they won't straighten up for days."

"Well, we'll see. But whenever Harold is in this house, the notice will go up, *Ici on parle français.*"

"What?" She was half smiling, her face screwed up now.

"I said, French is spoken here."

"Oh, Mrs Leviston, ma'am." She suddenly sat down on the chair, put her elbows on the table, cupped her face in her hands and, from the look on it, I didn't know whether she was about to laugh or cry. But the remark from her grandson tilted the balance.

Harold was now lying on his back, aiming to push away Sandy's licking tongue from his face, and our future French student said, "Stop it! you silly sod."

No reprimand was forthcoming from his grandmother, and I, like her now, suddenly sat down on a chair, and our heads were almost touching across the table as we groaned with our laughter.

Chapter 16

On August Saturday, George and Gran paid us a flying visit. They came down on day return tickets. It was good to see them, but guilt struck me when I knew they weren't aiming to stay the week-end.

They said Kitty was getting along splendidly, but they didn't seem to have the same opinion of Nardy. They made great play of his being able to walk, but when Gran got me alone, she said, "What's wrong with him? He looks peaked."

"He's confined to the house too much," I said.

One thing I found odd: they didn't laugh about Nardy's pupil. Of course, they had when I had first described how he interspersed his speech with swear-words - this they could recognize and so understand - but when I told them Nardy spoke French to him for an hour every morning and that it was amazing how the child had taken to it, they both stared at me, then looked at each other. And Gran said a strange thing: "You adopting him?" she asked.

"Adopting Harold?" I laughed out loud. "Of course not! He's got a family, seven uncles and aunts, a mother and a stepmother, sort of, and his own father. Adopt him? No, of course not!"

"Doesn't he go to school?" Gran asked.

"He starts next month."

"What about the French then?" said George.

"Oh, Nardy is going to take him at the week-ends and whenever he can come around at night."

"My, my!" Gran shook her head. "Some people are lucky."

Yes, I had to admit I was glad when they left; only to lie awake far into the night trying to work out the change in pattern of the emotions that life cut out for you and apparently without your consent. And Gran had been right, Nardy did look peaked.

And it wasn't for the want of fresh air. Nardy was changing. In some subtle way he was changing right before my eyes. He was more quiet. I would find him sitting staring at me, and if I asked, "What is it, dear?" he'd come out with some little compliment, such as, "I love you."

One day he said that he wished he didn't.

"What is it, dear?" I had said, and he had taken my face between his hands and replied, "Sometimes I feel sick at heart because I love you and I wish I didn't." . . .

Then there was Tommy. As promised he had sent us cards from various places across Canada. And when on one of them was written, "Still looking," Nardy had said, "What does he mean, still looking? And I said, "I think he's looking for himself," to which Nardy had replied, "Well, there's one thing I know for sure, he won't find it out there." . . .

So life went on. We had visitors. The Freemans called regularly. They were always very nice to me, but I never seemed to get close to Alice. Although she accepted me, kissed me warmly, I felt that, like all Nardy's friends, she, at bottom, couldn't understand what it was about me that had attracted their charming friend to this small plain girl . . . or woman.

Bernard Houseman and his wife came. Now, I knew where I stood with Mrs Sarah Houseman, for her manner towards me had always indicated that I was of an inferior class.

But one week-end we had a visitor who did warm my heart. Mike came and he brought with him all the warmth, understanding, and kindness that I needed. Until we had a quiet talk I hadn't realized the effort it was taking for me to keep up the easy-going normal attitude that indicated everything in the garden was lovely. I said to him, "Tell me, is he in a really bad way?"

He had answered, "I haven't examined him myself, but I can only go on what two highly experienced men have said. His heart's in a poor condition. And apparently it wasn't caused by the fire, only exacerbated by it. What has come to light is that his father died from a heart attack when he was fifty-two and an uncle in the same way. So Nardy's condition could be partly congenital, which obviously wouldn't have mattered so much if it hadn't been for the fire and the physical strain the burns have put on his system. But," he had ended cheerfully, "there's no need for you to despair, nor to worry yourself more skinny than you are. Given a quiet life, a bit of exercise, no undue worries, and he could be attending your funeral in your eighties."

I think the highlight of Mike's visit was his introduction to Harold.

"So this is our little linguistic genius," he had said, bending over the minute but wide-eyed figure.

When Harold made no reply, Mike went on, "I hear you can speak three languages: English, French, and your own."

Still no reply.

A little push from Nardy's hand brought Harold's face towards him, and when Nardy said, "Well, what have you to say to the doctor?"

Harold waited some further seconds before he replied, "He's hairy . . . like Flannagan's dog. It's got long hair." And he made a dramatic gesture with his hand from his small shoulder down his body and outwards to describe the length of the hair on Flannagan's dog.

Nardy and I both cried together, "Harold!" And Harold looked at Mike who had straightened up, turned about and was walking towards the window. An elbow was sticking out, indicating that he had his hand across the lower part of his face, and his shoulders were slightly hunched.

"Now you see what you've done," Nardy's voice was stern. "You've upset the doctor."

"Haven't."

"Oh, yes you have."

"No, I haven't; he's too big."

Nardy's puzzled glance was on me. There were times when he couldn't follow his pupil's thinking; but it was plain to me that anybody as big as Mike could not possibly be upset by anyone as small as himself. Get angry with him, swear at him, box his ears, kick his backside, as his uncles did, but not get upset by him.

This line of thought brought Hamilton on the scene. It seemed that it was he who swung Mike round to face his opponent again and then walked by his side until Mike was once more towering over

Childe Harold.

"So, I'm like Flannagan's dog, am I? What kind of a dog is it?"

Harold appeared slightly puzzled for a moment, then answered, "He's a dog."

"You said that, but what type? Is he like Sandy there, a poodle? or a . . .?'

"No, silly, he's not like Sandy, he's a scruffy bug . . . he's a scruffy dog."

"Oh, my goodness." I hung my head.

"So, I'm like a long-haired scruffy dog, am I?'

"Well -" Harold looked from Nardy to me and, noting that we weren't pleased with him and the latent diplomat coming to the fore, he now said, "Bumps is all right. He once caught some burglars at night. They was takin' the wheels off me Uncle Rod's banger. 'Twas outside the front door."

Nardy, Mike, and I kept our faces straight but our eyelids were blinking rapidly. "So they call the dog, Bumps," Mike said. "Why give it a name like that?"

"Eh?"

"I said, why do they call Flannagan's dog, Bumps?"

Harold thought, then said, "'Cos of Bumps-A-Daisy'." And without further prompting he went on to explain: "'Cos he's big, I s'pose, an' gets in the way of Mrs Flannagan's feet, and she says she'll make a mat of him after she's cut him up, and so the lads bump him out of her way."

I could imagine how the lads bumped the poor dog out of the way, likely with their feet. Anyway, that session ended with Mike lifting Harold high in the air and shaking him while Harold laughed a high glee-filled laugh.

And I held the picture in my mind for a long time afterwards.

Chapter 17

I remember the day when I first registered the fact that Nardy was fading away before my eyes. Harold was in the picture that day too.

It was a Saturday morning in November. Harold had been at school since September, so he came only on a Saturday morning for his "is he on" lesson, as he called it. But during the half-term holiday he came every morning with Janet.

It was amazing how the child had progressed with this new language, while still dropping his aitches in the English one and occasionally falling back on his flowery one.

Nardy had not dressed this morning, but remained in his dressing-gown, which was unusual because he was meticulous about his attire. So much so, that I laughingly put it to him one day: "You feel undressed, don't you, when you are not wearing a collar and tie?" And good-humouredly he had come back at me with, "Yes; especially at night in bed." But this morning he said, "I feel a bit lazy today, dear; I hope our young genius doesn't object to my dressing-gown."

"Our young genius wouldn't object to your being stark naked as long as he was with you," I assured him, to which he answered, "Tut-tut!"

After depositing her grandson, Janet usually did some odd shopping for me while I went to my study and left the tutor and his pupil together. But I'd been in the room only about twenty minutes when the door opened and in rushed Harold, gabbling, "Mr Nardy, 'e's got a pain. 'E's 'oldin'. . ."

I didn't hear the rest of what he had to say for I had scrambled out of the room and into the dining-room where the lessons usually took place, and there was Nardy, bent over the table, one arm tight around his chest.

GOODBYE HAMILTON

"What is it, dear?" Even as I said the words I was chiding myself for asking the road I knew.

He couldn't answer for a moment; then he said, "A . . . a bit of a pain."

"Sit quiet. Don't move." I rushed out of the room again and grabbed up the phone and dialled the doctor. . .

Doctor Bell lived a five minutes car ride from us. He arrived in less than ten minutes. Luckily he had just finished surgery.

He did not examine Nardy, but said brightly, "We'll have to get you into hospital, laddie."

Nardy, making a great effort to speak, said, "No . . . no hospital . . . bed."

When the doctor began to speak again, saying, "Well now," Nardy slowly raised his hand from his chest and, looking up and after a pause, he managed to repeat, "Bed."

"Stay still for a moment then."

As the doctor hurried out of the room I followed him, and in the hallway he said, "I've got something in the car that might help, but the place for him is hospital. He's in a very bad way. You understand that, don't you?"

"Yes, yes, doctor, I understand that. And he knows he is, too, but he wants to stay at home."

He made an impatient movement with his head, then hurried out. A few minutes later he was back and, after getting Nardy to swallow some pills, he gave him an injection, saying, "This'll help."

Between us, we got him into the bedroom and into bed, and all the while I'd been conscious of a spectator in the form of Harold.

Just as the doctor left Janet returned, and she became so distressed that I had to plead with her, saying, "Janet! Janet! I need help. Don't, please, don't give way like that."

"Oh, I'm sorry, I'm sorry, ma'am. I really am. I'll be all right. But . . . but I've seen it comin', the change in him. You see, he, I've got to say it, he's been like me own because I've pushed him along since he was a bairn. I love him, I do, I do."

"I know you do. I know you do, Janet, but you've got to help me. He . . . he should be in hospital. . ." I didn't finish and voice my thoughts, but said, "Do you think you could spare me a few hours this afternoon if the family . . . ?"

"Blast the family. They can look after themselves, today and tomorrow and as long as I'm needed here. It'll do them good."

A sniff and a choking sound, coming from the side of us, caused us both to look at the boy. The tears were running down his face. Then, coming to me, he clutched my hand and said, "'E'll get better, Mr

Nardy, won't 'e?"

"Yes, yes, of course he'll get better." I put my hand on his hair. "Of course he will. Of course he will. Be a good boy now;" then hurried out and into the bedroom.

Standing near the bed I looked down on my dear one. His face had taken on a blue tinge but his breathing was easy. He was asleep; the injection had done its work.

Sometime later Janet said, "I'll take this one home" - she thumbed towards Harold - "and tell my lot what they can get on with." And Harold said, "Don't want to go, Gag."

"It doesn't matter what you want, young man, it's what you're goin' to get. Come on, get your coat on."

"But I want to stay, Gag. I want to stay with Mrs. . ."

"You heard me."

"Janet." She looked at me. "Let him stay."

"You've got enough on your plate without. . ."

"Please, Janet, let him stay."

"Well, if you say so, ma'am; but mind" - she had turned to her grandson again, her fingers wagging - "you make a noise an' open your mouth when you shouldn't an' I'll put me foot in it when I come back, because I'll know, I'll know."

The door had hardly closed on her when the child came to me and I almost wailed aloud my misery and foreboding when he held out his arms and I lifted him up and he cuddled my neck tightly while his face was pressed close to mine and he never uttered a word. It was then that my two friends appeared, one on each side of us: Hamilton's whole demeanour was grave; Begonia's eyes were large and soft and full of understanding, and it was she who said, It is strange - isn't it? - from where you derive comfort in times of need.

The doctor called every day for a week. Nardy took his pills three times a day. If he felt further pain he didn't show it. He lay relaxed and quiet but ever ready to hold my hand when I neared the bed.

Janet had slept in one of the spare rooms for six nights, but I had insisted she went home on the Friday, because I am sure, in spite of her protestations, she had been worrying about how they were getting on at home. But when she arrived on the Saturday she wasn't accompanied by Harold, and I felt a keen sense of disappointment. And so, apparently, did Nardy, for although there was no possibility of a lesson taking place, I felt he was disappointed at not seeing the boy. And he voiced this when I was sitting by the bedside and we were having a coffee: "Saturday mornings don't seem the same without

Childe Harold, do they?" he said.

"No." I smiled. "He always made us aware that it was Saturday morning, if nothing else."

"You like the boy, don't you?"

"Yes." My reply was quiet and I nodded at him, saying, "And you do too, don't you?"

"Oh, yes, yes, I like him. I'd like to think he'd be given a chance to be something later on. He's got it up top, you know, that child. It's amazing how he picks things up. He's learnt more French in two months than I did in a year when I began. And his pronunciation is amazing, seeing that sometimes he's as broad in all ways as a Billingsgate porter."

I was sipping at my coffee when he said, quietly, "Would you like to adopt him?"

"*What?*"

He chuckled now as he said, "That's how you must have sounded in the surgery to Mike with your Wh-at! every Monday morning. You know, you do sound funny when you say it like that."

"I'm not the only one that sounds funny. You did say would I like to adopt him?"

"Yes, that's what I said."

I was silent for a moment before I answered in the same way as I had done Gran, "And him with a father, a mother and a half, a grandmother, and, as far as I can count, seven uncles and aunts. And you saying, adopt him."

"Well," his voice was sober now, "as far as I can see it, dear, between his father and his mother and a half, and his seven uncles and aunts, his future is going to stand a very thin chance. He'll end up either driving a lorry, or working in a warehouse, or some such. And he'll become popular because of his quick mind, colourful vocabulary. And that will be about the limit of his career."

"But . . . but, my dear, they'd never agree to that."

"You don't know what they would agree to until you put the question to them."

I remained quiet for a moment, and then I said, "I don't think I could stand him running around this flat seven days a week; and he would upset you; it would be too much of a good thing."

He put down his cup and his hand came out and sought mine. "My dear, let's face facts. Now, now, don't get agitated." He shook my hand. "There's bound to come a time when he won't irritate me, let's put it like that."

"*Nardy, Nardy, please,* I won't listen to you."

"All right, my dear, don't listen to me, only think about it." His blue lips stretched into a broad smile as he ended, "Consult Hamilton. Yes, that's what to do, consult Hamilton, and, of course, his good lady."

"Oh, Nardy." I pulled my hand away from his, picked up the coffee cups and put them on to the tray, shaking visibly as I did so while I said, "I don't need to consult anyone. And, I am not going in for adoption. So get that out of your head, Mr Leviston." And on that I left the room, and I arrived in the kitchen at a run where, dropping the tray on to the table, I flopped into a chair and held my face in my hands. But I daren't cry, because I knew that once I gave way to the despair that was in me there would be a deluge that I should be unable to control.

At about half-past three the following day I heard the ring from the downstairs hall, and as I went to open the door I was thinking it could be Bernard Houseman and his wife or the Freemans, or someone else from the office. But to my utter amazement, there, stepping out of the lift was the tiny form of Harold.

"What on earth!" I looked beyond him, then asked, "Where is your . . . ?"

"I came meself." He had walked past me and, after closing the door quickly, I grabbed at his collar, swung him round and said, "You came on your own? It's nearly dark. Do . . . do they know?"

"No. They were asleep."

Asleep. Of course, after a Sunday dinner and likely their usual swig of beer, the men, like those in the north, would be taking their Sunday afternoon nap. But surely not Janet.

"Your . . . your grandmother?"

His brief reply gave me the picture.

"It's all right," he assured me airily now; "I know me way. I get on the bus for school, but comin' this way I didn't get off at Gag's corner, I come all the way. I have enough money." He put his hand in his anorak pocket now and held out his palm upwards towards me and on which lay three ten pence pieces and one penny piece.

I looked around me as if searching for someone to tell me what to do with this child, and then, my eye catching the telephone, I said, "I must phone your grandmother," or at least, I thought, the shop on the corner who would get in touch with her. She had given me the number in case I should want her in an emergency. I rushed to the telephone table, but he was there by my side, his hand on my wrist, pleading now, "Please, Mrs Nardy, don't get Gag to come. She'll only belt me. She belted me yesterday 'cos I followed 'er to the bus."

"But Harold" - I leant over him - "they'll be worried to death when they find you're gone."

"They won't 'cos I was out to play."

"But they would expect you in - well . . . for your tea."

"Mrs Nardy." His voice was quiet, unusually quiet for him, its tone a deep plea. "I . . . I want to stay 'ere 'side of you an' . . . an' Mr Nardy. I . . . I won't make any noise. I'll sit quiet in the kitchen with Sandy, an' I can wash up." He nodded his head. "I wash up for Gag, an' I take the ashes out." He looked around and, seeming to remember there were no ashes here to be taken out, he ended lamely, "I can do things."

I straightened up, closed my eyes tightly, bit on my lip, then said, "Go in the kitchen. Keep quiet; I'll be there in a minute."

I got on the phone to the shop. I asked if they could please get a message to Mrs Flood, and to ask her to phone me. They weren't very enthusiastic, it being Sunday, but they said they would. I went into Nardy and, standing by the bed, I said, "We've got a visitor."

"Yes, who?"

"Childe Harold. He's come on his own."

"No."

"But yes. What am I to do?"

His smile slowly widened and he said, "I suppose you've phoned Janet?"

"Yes. Well, I mean when the shop people get to her."

"If they do and she phones, tell her he's going to stay here tonight and there's no need for her to worry."

"Oh, Nardy."

"Oh, Maisie," he mimicked. "Funny isn't it; the adoption's on the other foot now so to speak."

Adoption. Adoption.

The phone rang and I went to the side table. I could hear Janet's voice but she talked so quickly I couldn't understand what she was saying. And so I put in, "Janet, it's all right, he's quite safe, he's here, and he's going to stay the night."

"What! What did you say, ma'am?"

"I said, Harold's here. He was very naughty to leave as he did, but it's perfectly all right. He's going to stay the night."

"Oh, my God! ma'am. You mean, Harold, he's . . . he's come all the way there himself?"

"Well, what did you think I was saying?"

She said something now to which I could not refer: she had thought that Nardy must be worse or dead. And then she cried, "He just went out to play down at the Flannagans. I saw him running round mad, with their dog. Then I just sat down and looked at the telly. Oh, God in heaven! what's to be done with that boy? I'm so sorry. I'll come. . ."

"You won't, Janet, you just won't. Now, do as I say, stop worrying.

He won't be a nuisance. He's as good as gold. I'll get him up in the morning and if you get here a little earlier with his school things, you'll get him there in time."

"Oh, ma'am." There was a long sigh; then, "I won't be able to keep me hands off him."

"You will, Janet, you will, or I'll never forgive you. I'm going to say it now, but I've said it before, you must stop hitting him, especially across the ears. And another thing I can tell you, Mr Leonard is very pleased that he is here. When the doorbell rang, he thought it was some boring individual from the office, but he brightened up considerably when he knew it was his Saturday morning friend. Now I'll see you in the morning. Don't worry. Bye-bye."

As I put the phone down, Nardy said, "You can't only write tales, you can tell them. Well, go and bring him in. And you're right, I shall be pleased to see him." And he was.

The boy sat quietly by the bedside for the next hour, regaling Nardy with stories of the exploits of Flannagan's dog, and of Mr Flannagan who apparently went to confession on a Saturday night and then got drunk but was always steady enough on a Sunday morning to go to Mass. And apparently Harold's Uncle Max could do Mr Flannagan, as Harold said, like as if he was on the telly, like. And when he ended solemnly, "'E makes game 'e's in church, 'e does, an' says,

'Please Father I want to say me prayers
'Cos I kicked me wife up the apples and pears.'"

It was too much. Choking, I almost hauled him out of the room because I was afraid of the result of Nardy's laughter, for he was holding himself as if in pain.

In the kitchen, the entertainer said to me, "I never said nothin' well, not swears or anythin'. I just said about Mr Flannagan. . ."

"It's all right. It's all right." My eyes were blinking back the water. "But you see, Mr Nardy isn't very well, as you know, and if he laughs too much it might bring on a pain."

"Oh . . . you're not vexed then?"

"No, I'm not vexed."

I made the mistake again of bending down and kissing him; and once more I was enveloped in a choking hug.

Adoption! Adoption!

I shall pass over the Monday morning and the meeting between Janet and her grandson, because I knew how difficult it was for her to keep her hands off him, when he greeted her with, "I didn't cause an uproar,

Gag. Ask Mrs Nardy."

It was on the Wednesday morning that we got a surprise, an actual letter from Tommy. We'd had a few cards but this was the first real correspondence. Nardy said, "You open it. Read it out."

The letter was short; it didn't even cover a full page. It told us that he had been laid up with a bug, but a couple he had met, a Mr and Mrs Atkins, had been kind enough to let him stay with them. The letter finished by saying, he just wanted to wish us a happy Christmas, and he didn't know where his next stop of call would be but that he intended to go to the Rockies.

After reading the letter I remarked sarcastically, "Brief and to the point, very unlike Tommy," then handed it over to Nardy; and, he scanning it, said, "It's his new friends' private notepaper. There's an address on the envelope."

When I said, "Well, I don't think I'll be writing back," he made no comment.

I felt bitter against Tommy these days: of all Nardy's friends and acquaintances, it was he that Nardy would like to see pop in each day. But no, he had to go off to find himself. Well, I hoped when he did find himself, he wouldn't be disappointed with what he saw.

Either Gran, or Mary, or George, phoned every day; and it was strange, but when Gran asked if she should come down and, to use her own words, give me a hand, I had replied quickly, no, there was no need for that; everything was under control. Why was it that I couldn't bear the thought of either her, George, or Mary living with me day in, day out? I knew I still loved George and Gran and that at one time I should have been pleased to spend any hour of the day with either of them.

The thought conjured up Hamilton and Begonia. I was surprised to see them for they hadn't put in an appearance for some time now. Hamilton looked at me while pursing his great lips, and he said, Well, don't let that worry you. You've grown up, you've moved away, not only to another place, but inside your head. You know that piece in the Bible about, When you are a child you act as a child, but when you are a man. . .

I waved him to a stop. I knew all about the piece from the Bible, but I couldn't see that when one matured one's feelings towards those once loved could change, or should change. Yet, I wondered if my estranged feelings had started with the refusal by Mary and George to take up my offer of a new house; they said they had already made arrangements to go into a council house. And Gran had backed them up. It was she who with her non-tact said they thought that none of what had happened would have taken place, at least not to them, if they'd had a place of their own.

It was on the Saturday night when I was lying by Nardy's side that he said, "Maisie, let's talk."

I did not say what about, because his words had heightened the dread that seemed to be gathering speed these last few days.

And then my feelings became almost unbearable when reaching out my hand to turn out the light, he said, "Leave it. I want to look at you."

Over the great lump in my throat I brought out the words, "Nardy, please, don't tire yourself. Go to sleep."

"I'm past being tired, dear, and I'm not going to sleep until I have to."

What did he mean by that? "Oh, God!" I said to myself. "Don't let him talk to me about when. . ."

"You know, dear, you've given me the happiest period of my life. It's been short compared to the rest of it, but I'd give up the whole just to experience one day with you. Please, please, dear, don't cry. Now Maisie" - he was patting my cheek - "don't, I beg of you, give way like that, because I have things to say."

He went on talking, but I hardly heard his words because even my ears seemed to be blocked by my emotions and withheld tears. Yet they were alive to the cry in my head: Don't leave me, Nardy! Don't leave me! What would I do without him? He was my way of life, this new wonderful way of life. I couldn't go back, not even to those days between the freedom from Stickle and my marriage. I was still in limbo then, not believing anything good could happen to me. I now visualized the years stretching ahead with only Hamilton, and he getting larger and larger in my consciousness, because inside, I was a lonely creature; my real being wandered in arid places to where I had been thrust as a child by my mother. As any other normal human being, I needed hands to hold mine; I needed kind words; I needed friendship; but above all, I needed love and the feel of a body close to me.

He had hold of my chin, shaking it, "You're not listening."

"I am."

"What did I say last?"

When I was silent, he said, "There you are. Maisie! Maisie! Maisie!" He again shook my face. "You must listen. Don't close your mind to facts, it isn't like you. And it is a fact that I won't be much longer with you. . ."

"*Oh. Nardy. Nardy.*"

'No, no. Now stop it. Listen."

"I won't listen." I pulled my face away from his hand. "People with bad hearts can go on living for years and years, if they want to. That's the point, if they *want* to. You're not putting up a fight; you're letting go. I've seen you, you're letting go. Yes you are. Yes you are." I heard my voice getting higher and higher.

"My dear, be quiet. Now be quiet. I know people with bad hearts can live for years, but mine isn't only a bad heart. I've never gone over my medical history with you. I had scarlet fever as a child; it left me with a weakness then. I thought I had outgrown it."

"But they can do anything today, they can give people new hearts."

"Yes, I know that. But in this case . . . my case, there is the complication that is no use going into, and ... and the fire didn't help."

I half buried my face in the pillow as I muttered, "Stickle, and through him, me. If it hadn't been for me. . ."

"Don't be silly, woman. You could say, if you hadn't been born, or if I hadn't been born, we wouldn't have met. These things happen. But, look at me."

Through a thick mist I looked into his dear, dear face and those kindly eyes, and I listened to him as he said, "There are one or two things I want you to promise me that you'll do. First of all, try to adopt the child. If it had been possible I myself would have taken this matter up, because I should like to see that boy make something of himself. The second thing is, you must keep on writing. Not about Hamilton, no; write about people; you have a very good insight into people. And, lastly, and this to my mind is the most important, you must not let yourself be lonely, you must marry again."

I actually did spring away from him almost out of the bed, and I said one word: "*Nardy.*"

"Yes, my dear?" His tone was gentle, even had a thread of amusement in it.

"You can say that to me?"

"Yes, yes, I can say that to you."

"Well, Mr Leviston, which of the line of suitors would you suggest I take? Because there's dozens of men out there breaking their necks to . . . to. . ."

He caught my hand and gently drew me towards him again. "You know, my dear, that's your fault. It's been practically inbred in you, you undervalue yourself. Oh" - he made an impatient movement - "forget about looks. You can't live with looks, they fade, it's the personality that counts, it never fades, it grows, it deepens."

"Nardy" - my voice was low now - "are you thinking of Tommy?"

He made a sound in his throat like a choked cough; then he said, "Well, I won't say he wasn't in my mind."

"Well, I think you'll have to scratch him off the list, dear, because all Tommy wanted, if he only knew it, was another mother."

"Don't we all. That's why I took you."

"Please, please be serious."

"I was never more, my darling, never more. But apart from Tommy, you will find that your horizon won't be devoid of males, for one reason, you are a name now."

"And they'll want me only for my money, which they would find is surprisingly little."

"Not with my not so small estate attached to it."

I knew that Nardy owned this part of the house. I also knew that his mother had left him another property further into the city. I had seen it. It wasn't a very prepossessing place, a tallish house let off into four offices. And as if picking my thoughts, he said, "That little city block is worth a small fortune at today's prices. So you'll be quite a warm lady. Then there will be the pension."

"*Nardy. Please.* I beg of you. I've never had any money, not real money, so it doesn't really matter what. . ."

"Don't be silly. And don't say money doesn't matter. You only say money doesn't matter when you have plenty of it. If you were left alone without money it would matter, and very much."

He was right; as usual he was right.

As I went to put my arms around him my toe accidentally rubbed against a bad part of his leg, and when he winced I said, "Oh my dear, have I hurt you?"

"You've never hurt me, or anybody in your life," he said. And at this and with tears running down my face, I spluttered, "You've forgotten I went to jail once for trying to knock somebody off." And at this, he too, laughed gently. Then we lay close and quiet and I died and died again until we went to sleep. Who went first I don't know. I only know that the next morning I woke with a start, fearing at what I should find on the pillow beside me. But he was asleep and still with me.

Chapter 18

Nardy died at the beginning of the second week before Christmas.

I awoke this morning and he was no longer with me; he had gone. How long I lay beside him with my arms holding him, I don't know; I only know that Janet came in and found me like that and pulled me from the bed. Strangely, I hadn't cried, and all that day, and the next, and the next, I didn't cry. When I phoned Mike that morning, he said, "Keep your pecker up, girl. I'll be with you shortly. Just remember this: You've had love and happiness not known to many. Like everything precious, such things are either small or short."

When I phoned George, his response was characteristic. "God, no!" he said. "I'll bring Gran down."

He brought Gran down the following day, and it was from the moment she entered the flat, or rather the kitchen, that the feeling of harmony left the place, because she became violently jealous of Janet, and Janet had never taken to her. But I took little notice of it at the time, although when she said openly, while looking down on Harold, "That child shouldn't be in the house," I had to say openly to her, "Nardy would want him here to be with me, Gran. In fact, it was his wish." She took real umbrage, hardly speaking for the rest of the day.

Nardy was cremated. Although the weather was really awful, there was an amazing number of people in the chapel. It is strange, but immediately after Janet had pulled me from him until his coffin had disappeared I had felt I had lost him, he had gone forever; but when I came out of the chapel, it was as if he were near me, his spirit was almost tangible. At one point, when someone was shaking my hand and offering their condolences, I saw him standing with Hamilton and Begonia and, strangely, my mother. Their faces looked bright, even happy as they looked towards me, seemingly over the shoulder of the man who would keep talking until George took me by the elbow and led me to the car, in which Janet and Gran were already seated.

Much to Gran's chagrin, I had insisted on Janet riding with us. As I had explained to Gran, Janet had practically brought Nardy up; she had been with him since he was born. Gran, I recall, had said nothing, only given me a very odd look. Her feelings were to be expressed to me later.

Mike had been unable to get to the funeral. One of his partners was off sick and there was an epidemic of colds and flu keeping him busy most of the day and quite a part of the night. But he arrived at eight o'clock that night, having flown down.

All the friends and sympathizers had left. There were only Janet, Gran, and I in the house, and, of course, Harold. When I look back, the sense of that boy at that time amazes me even now, for he did exactly what he was told. He remained quiet, but whenever he was near me he took my hand and held it firmly, and never uttered a word.

However, it wasn't until I saw Mike's hairy face that the built-up emotions in me were set free and, held in his arms, I went into a paroxysm of weeping as I had once done when I had lost Bill. But now, I hadn't only lost a dog, this time I had lost my love, my stay, that wonderful man who had told a small plain partially deformed woman that he loved her.

Mike let me cry for a while; and then, in that voice of his I remembered from the surgery days, he said, "Now that's enough. Come on. That's enough. Life's out there; it's got to be seen to. Now, you either stop or I give you the needle, and that'll put you to sleep for the next twenty-four hours. What about it?"

Presently I choked to a standstill and, sitting on the couch, my head on his shoulder, I whimpered, "What am I going to do, Mike?" and he answered practically, "What all women in your position have to do, or go under: face up to the fact that your life has changed, the pattern has altered; you've got to start, as it were, cutting out a different frock."

It was later that evening when I was sitting, dull and slumped, that he said, "I like that little fellow. Nardy wanted you to adopt him, didn't he?"

I was brought from my lethargy and my eyes widened as I said, "He told you?"

"Oh, yes; I had a letter from him a few weeks ago."

"You did?" The surprise in my voice made him repeat, "Yes, I did. Is there anything strange about that?"

Yes, there was, because Nardy hadn't told me he had written. I couldn't remember posting a letter in Nardy's handwriting to Mike. I would have remarked on it at the time had I done so.

"So, what about it? There's little chance of you having any of your own, you know, after that bad do you had. You must think about it."

"Oh." I shook my head. "It's impossible. I told Nardy. He's got a houseful of uncles and aunts, and a mix-up of his parents, and a grandmother. . ."

"And the whole bunch would likely jump at the chance of your taking him on."

"I can't see it that way, not . . . not at the moment."

"Well, leave it. But it's a good idea. And don't forget, it was Nardy's wish." Then he said, "What's up with Gran? She's not her usual breezy self."

"She's jealous of Janet, I think."

"Oh. Oh, I see." Mike nodded. "Of course, she would be. She looks upon you as her own bit of property, and she's too old to let go. Women are queer cattle. Do you intend to go on living here?"

"Oh, yes, yes."

"You wouldn't think about coming back to Fellburn?"

"No, no. Never."

"What will you do with yourself then? Have you made any really close friends?"

I hadn't to think for an answer, but again said, "No. No, I haven't."

"Then, you're going to find life very bare, my dear."

"I'll get through."

After a moment's pause he put his arm round my shoulder, saying, "Yes, yes, of course you will."

Mike's departure the following day left the house empty of male influence, except for the boy in the kitchen. And it was to be deprived still further, before very long, of female influence this time.

At about eleven o'clock of the morning of the day before Christmas Eve I was sitting in the drawing-room staring at the fire, thinking of our first Christmas together, and the house all decorated. And my tears were about to spring from my eyes again when the door opened and Janet came in. She had a cup of coffee on a tray, and after placing it on a side table, she looked down at me and said, "Ma'am, I'm sorry to say this, but that kitchen isn't big enough for the two of us, I mean for Mrs Carter and me. I'm upset as it is. I'm missin' Mr Nardy, you know that ma'am, but somehow, she just won't fit in. She keeps going for the lad. Oh, I know I go for him, but there's different ways of goin' for a child. And he understands me. Anyway, ma'am, until she's gone I'll cut me hours down to two in the morn. . ."

"Well! you won't have long to wait if that's the case. I know when I'm not wanted."

Neither of us had heard Gran come into the room. In full war cry, she now approached us, and when I held up my hand, pleading, "Gran; this is not the time. . ." she interrupted, "There'll never be a better! Who does some people think they are any road? Here's me, knowin' you all your life."

"Gran!" I actually screamed the name, at the same time getting to my feet. "I can't stand this," I said; "I can't. I can't."

I watched Janet bow her head, then turn and hurry from the room. And there we were, Gran and I, facing each other. And now, my voice calmer, I said, "What's the matter with you, Gran? Here I am, in this state of not knowing what I'm going to do without Nardy, and you acting like . . . like. . ."

"Like what, lass? Like what?" Her voice was harsh.

And mine was equally harsh now as I replied, "Well, not like yourself, the understanding woman that I've always known."

"Well, when we're gettin' down to home truths, you're not like yourself either, an' haven't been since you came to live up in this quarter. You've grown away from us."

"That's not fair; I've done no such thing. But . . . but we've all changed since the fire."

Quite suddenly I saw the stiffness go out of her body, and she let out a deep sigh, saying, "Aye, since the fire. Perhaps you're right, nothin's been the same." Then her voice taking on the edge of its former tone, she said, "But there I was, dashing up here to look after you an' see to things, an' what do I find? Her runnin' the place; an' that lad. He's a cheeky little bugger and wants puttin' in his place. And that's all I've tried to do. What there's about him you can take to, God alone knows."

At a different time I could have laughed and replied, Because he's a male replica of yourself, Gran. Instead, I said, "I've already explained to you that Janet has been in this house since Nardy was a baby, and she's been very good and helped to look after him . . . and . . . and obliging me. . ."

"Oh yes, that's her favourite word; I'm obligin'. That maddens me; you would think she was doin' it for nothin'. She gets a good enough screw I bet, besides rollin' in it, I would say, with eight of 'em. "

"She isn't rolling in it, Gran. The eight of them, I think, are without exception all hanging on to her. . . You've never tried to get to know her."

"An' I don't want to. She's a different kind from me. All them down here are."

"That's prejudice, Gran."

"Aye, well, you can put what name you like to it. It's always been the same an' it always will, the north and the south are like two different countries. As somebody said in the club the other night, we're nearer to the Germans than we are to the southerners. An' I think he was right."

I had a retort to make to this, but I stilled my tongue as I thought, Yes, perhaps, she's right, for, as long as there were people with closed minds like herself, the north and the south would be at variance. And which side was at fault? More so us, I thought, we northerners, for we were insular, we were afraid to move away from the known. And there was a thread of bumptiousness running through our genes to cover up our feelings of inadequacy. The result was, I'm as good as thee, lad. And everybody who tried to rise above the norm, was an upstart.

But yet Gran was right in one way, I had changed. My outlook and opinions now weren't those I held three years ago, even apart from the tyranny I'd undergone under Stickle.

I looked at Gran now. Her head was bowed and the tears were oozing from under her lashes. Quickly I went to her and put my arms about her, saying, "Don't . . . don't cry, please."

She sniffed, wiped her eyes, then said, "I feel ashamed of meself, lass. I shouldn't have gone on like this. But to tell you the truth, I'm missin' the bairns an' one thing an' another."

Again I thought, how odd human nature was. Gone from her was the idea that the bairns just belonged to Mary and had no connection with her son: they were her bairns now, she was their gran. And the one thing and another that she referred to was her bingo, and her club nights. She had been told how sorely she had been missed at the club during her illness, and I could well imagine it: she was a voice there; she could be amusing; she was the one who could start up a sing-song; she was the one to get things going. I had never thought up to this moment about the contrast between her life in Fellburn and that which she was experiencing in this house. If I had, I should have imagined that she would have looked upon the sojourn with me as a holiday, even under the present circumstances. But no, she had been bred in the north. She had lived there all her life; she was a woman of the north, and of her particular class, let's face it, of her particular class, in which she was happy. Take her, and any other like her, out of it, and what happened? Conflict, unhappiness. To put it in her own words, A fish out of water.

"Would you like to go home, Gran? Now, now" - I patted her cheek - "I'm all right here. You haven't got to worry about me. I've got to face up to my kind of life, and it's to be lived in this house where all the memories of Nardy are. I've got to get used to being on my own some time or other; and . . . and I'll have my work. . ."

What was I talking about, having my work? I didn't think I'd ever put pencil to paper again; there was no incentive. As for my imaginary friends? They had vanished as surely as Nardy had done. My mind had, as it were, become merely a receptacle for pain and a new kind of loneliness. While I was married to Stickle, I longed to be alone; only when I was alone did I have any peace. But after my life was joined to Nardy's, I was alone when I wasn't with him: there was always the fact that he would be in for tea, that we would lie side by side through the night, that we'd have the week-ends together. Now what stretched before me? I didn't know. I couldn't visualize how time would be filled.

"What did you say, Gran?"

"I said, lass, are you sure you wouldn't mind if I went home?"

"No, of course not. And you would like to be there for the holidays, wouldn't you?"

"Aw, lass, I couldn't leave you by yourself here on Christmas Day."

"Now look, don't you worry. Alice Freeman is determined to yank me off for Christmas, and for as long as I'd like to stay afterwards. I've had invitations, too, from here and there. So I've got a choice. Now look, I'll send a telegram off, and I'll put you on the afternoon train."

"Oh, no, lass, I couldn't leave you like that, not at a minute's notice."

"Well, if you don't go today, you won't be able to get on a seat on the train tomorrow."

"I feel I'm desertin' you, lass."

"Don't be silly. I'll feel more content myself if I know that you're back with the family."

I watched her face lighten and she put her hand out and gripped my arm, saying, "You wouldn't come back with me, would you? You needn't fear anything now, and. . ."

"No, Gran, no. I know I needn't fear anything, but it will be a long time before I can face up to going north again. The house business has been completed. As you know I'm not having it rebuilt, and those on either side have been compensated for what damage was done to their property. . ." My voice trailed off, and she said, "I understand, I understand." She now put her arms around me and we kissed. And when she muttered brokenly, "I'm sorry. I'm sorry," I pressed her away from me, saying, "Now, now stop it, and go and get your things packed, and I'll see about that telegram."

When she left the room I sat down and after letting out a long, long, drawn breath I almost said, "Thank God!" only to chastise myself: How could I feel so relieved that she was going; I was fond of Mary and the children, but I loved her and George, they were woven into my life. She was right, I had changed. Indeed, indeed, I had changed. I had changed because I had met a man like Nardy, and he had shown me another side to living.

Oh, Nardy, Nardy. How am I going to bear life without you?

Chapter 19

It was Christmas Day and I was alone. I couldn't take in the fact that I was alone. I had been awake since five o'clock. I got out of bed at seven and made myself a cup of coffee, and I switched on the radio, to hear a sanctimonious voice saying, "All over the country, and in many parts of the world, children are excitedly examining their Christmas presents. Fathers are testing model trains they've given to their sons; mothers are oohing and aahing over dolls they've presented to their daughters; some so-called lucky wives are examining diamond pendants, their husbands exclaiming over hand-made silk shirts, the cuffs linked with ruby studs. At the other end of the spectrum, a man is saying, "Ta," for a pair of nylon socks, while his wife is trying on a fancy apron. But on this morning, even if only for a short time, there is, in the main, giving and taking and love. . ."

I switched off, went and had a hot bath, got dressed, then asked myself what I was going to do? I would not allow myself to dwell on the happenings of that first Christmas morning together because, had I done so, I was afraid that I would throw myself on the floor and beat the carpet with my clenched fists whilst demanding of God why He had recompensed me for my life of torture only, with the taste still full in my mouth, to cry, "Enough! You were never made for happiness."

Having walked from the drawing-room into the dining-room, from there into my study, then into the spare bedrooms, one after another, I found myself back in the drawing-room. I did not sit down, I looked out of the window. The day was grey and cold. But what did the weather matter? I would go out. I would go for a walk, perhaps go into a church and hear a service. . . No, no; because, there, I would likely break down. No, I would just walk, walk, with Sandy who, with the intelligence of the poodle breed, sensed sorrow in me and was as lost as I was.

We went out and we walked. By lunchtime I was home again.

I was used to London by now. I was used to the streets around this district, but I'd hardly encountered a dozen people in all the time I had been out. I had shut my eyes to the Christmas trees in windows and my ears to the sound of laughter coming from behind doors. And now, still fully dressed, I stood in the hallway and asked myself what I was going to do. I could phone Alice Freeman. Hadn't she pressed me to spend Christmas with them. But I had said that Gran was with me and I'd be all right. Bernard Houseman, too, had invited me to their place, but I had refused. As I stood there the phone rang, and I ran towards it. I don't know whom I was expecting, but when I heard Mike's voice I couldn't answer for a moment. He hadn't said, "A Happy Christmas," he had just said, "How are you?"

His voice came again, saying, "Are you there, Maisie? Are you there?"

"Yes, Mike, yes, I'm here."

"What's this I hear?" he said. "That Gran's come back? I was in the hospital this morning. I looked in on Kitty; they were all there."

The lump in my throat threatened to choke me.

"Are you all right?"

"Yes, yes. Mike, I'm all right."

"Is anyone with you?"

I looked first to the right then to the left, then said, "Yes, yes, Janet and the boy."

"Well, I suppose that's enough; you wouldn't want company at this time. But look, Jane and I are going to slip down early in the New Year. We'll stay over the week-end if you'll have us."

"Of course, of course, Mike. I'd . . . I'd love to see you."

"Well, I must be off now. I'll phone again later. Take care of yourself."

"I will, Mike. I will. Thanks for phoning."

They were all there. His words had conjured up Kitty's bed and the whole family around her. I closed my eyes tight while exclaiming aloud, "I should have been with them. I should have gone with Gran. I can't stand this. But I didn't want Gran's company, did I? nor George's, nor Mary's, nor the children's. Then what did I want? Who did I want?

I wanted Nardy.

Nardy's gone. Face up to it, Nardy's gone.

He's not; he's here, all about me. I spread my arms wide. Then, suddenly gritting my teeth, I said, "Stop it! Stop it!"

I turned to the phone again. Now I was dialling the shop at the corner of Janet's street. I knew they wouldn't be open, but they would go and ask Janet to get on the phone.

It was almost twenty minutes later and I was still sitting in the hall in my hat and coat when the phone rang again, and Janet's voice came over, saying, "Ma'am, are you all right? What is it?"

"Janet."

"Yes, yes, ma'am, I'm here. What is it?"

"Janet. I'm on my own."

"Oh God! What! On your own? I thought you were going to Mrs Freeman's?"

I had told Janet this, because she said that she would come in on Christmas Day if I was alone.

"I . . . I didn't go, Janet. Janet, do you think that Harold would like to come along this afternoon?"

"Yes. Why yes, of course. He'd come this minute if I let him."

"I . . . I don't want to disturb your day, or the child's."

"You certainly won't be disturbing his day. But look, I'll tell you what. I'm in the middle now of gettin' their dinner, but I'll get one of the lads to bring him along. Do . . . do you want him to stay the night?"

"Yes, please, Janet. As long as he would like to. Perhaps over the holidays."

"You're lettin' yourself in for something mind 'cos he'll want to bring some of his toys."

"Oh, of course, I understand that, about his toys. And as for letting myself in for something, Janet. Oh, Janet, I'm so lonely."

"Oh my God! I shouldn't have taken any notice of you. I should have come along. This lot could have fended for themselves."

"No, no, please; if one of your sons would bring him, that would be wonderful, lovely."

"Are you cookin' your dinner?"

"I . . . I'm not hungry, Janet."

"Oh, God in heaven! Christmas Day and no dinner!"

"Oh, there's plenty in the fridge, you know there is, and there are the pies and things you made the other morning."

"Well, get somethin' into you. And there's soup in the freezer. Now see you get somethin'. I'll send him along right away."

"Thank you, Janet. Thank you.'

I took my hat and coat off now and went into the kitchen. Harold was always hungry. I . . . . I would have to prepare something, cold or otherwise. . .

*

It was an hour later when the bell from the hall rang. I went out and I met the lift. As soon as it came to a stop, he was there, wearing a very nice new cap and coat; but in contrast he had on his feet, a pair of black and white sneakers, also new, something like you would have seen one of the gangsters wearing in an old film. I guessed these had come from one of his uncles, the one with the sense of humour. His arms were full of parcels, as were those of the young man who was standing awkwardly behind him. Before I had time to say hello, Harold made the introduction.

"This is - er - Uncle Rod, Mrs Nardy."

I smiled at the broad-shouldered, square-faced young man, and he smiled at me, saying, "How do?"

"Come in. Come in." I marshalled them across the inner hall and into the drawing-room; and there, Harold, dropping his parcels on to a chair, again turned to his uncle, saying, "This is it, like what I told yer."

"Nice. Nice." The young man's head was nodding as he turned it from one shoulder to the other, and he now added, "Yes, nice, very nice." Then, his tone changing, he looked down on his nephew and, in a voice very like his mother's, he said, "You're lucky, son. You know that? You're lucky."

"Would . . . would you like a drink?"

"No, thank you, ma'am. If it's all the same to you, I'll be makin' me way back. It's Mum, you see . . . loses her hair if we're not all in for the dinner."

"Yer goin' to the pub?"

The young man looked sideways down on Harold now, saying almost under his breath, "You watch it. Mind your tongue."

"Well, are yer?"

I couldn't find words to save the young man further embarrassment, when Harold, turning to me, said, "Gag says they're never out of the pub an' they've all got bellies like poisoned pups. . . D'yer want to see what I got for Christmas?"

"In a minute. In a minute. Take your coat and hat off and go into the kitchen and put your slippers on."

I could see from the young man's face that he had great difficulty, not only in restraining his tongue, but his hand. And when his nephew, looking now at me, and then at his feet, said, "I'm not gonna take these off; me Uncle Max give 'em me," Janet was reincarnated in her son when he almost bawled, "Do what the lady says, an' get 'em off! Go on, or else."

Harold went, but with a backward glance and a grin at his uncle, who now turned to me, saying in a tone that spelt his bewilderment, "You sure you want him to stay, missis?"

"Yes, I'm sure."

"Huh!" His head was shaking again. "It's funny. It's as Mum says, you can manage him, but you're about the only one that can. He's a holy terror. An' him learnin' to speak French. That nearly killed the lot of us." His voice trailed off now, his head drooped and he said, "I'm sorry, missis, about . . . about your loss. All me life I've heard me mum talk about Mr Leonard. He was a fine man. Well, missis." He moved from one foot to the other, and I said, "Yes, he was a fine man, and your mother was very fond of him."

He nodded, then muttered, "Well, I'll be off now. You're sure you'll be all right?"

"Yes, I'll be all right. Thank you. And thank you for bringing the boy."

"It was a pleasure, missis, it was a pleasure. And as the youngster's always said, this room's like a queen's palace."

"He says that?"

"Oh aye; he's always talkin' about Mrs Nardy's queen's palace."

He had reached the lift when he said, "I forgot to tell you, Mum'll be along later."

"Thank you. Goodbye."

"Goodbye, Mrs Nard . . . Leviston. It's been a pleasure meetin' you. Goodbye.". . .

I now went into the kitchen, but Harold wasn't there. I went into the drawing-room, and there he was sitting on the rug before the fire with his slippers on, his Christmas parcels spread around him and Sandy lying amidst them. He was in the process of winding up an object that looked half animal and half human. But he got to his feet when I entered the room, and when I sat down in the chair he came and stood by my side and, looking up into my face, he said, quietly, "Yer were all on your tod. weren't yer?"

I pressed my lips together to try to stop their trembling. I widened my eyes. I sniffed audibly and when, his voice still low, he said, "I liked Mr Nardy. I liked him a lot," it was too much. My head drooped, the tears blinded me, and when I felt him climbing onto my knee and his arms go tightly around my neck, I knew that here was the answer, Nardy's answer, to my lonely cry. This child had to be mine.

Chapter 20

The weeks passed into months. It was May again. I looked back and asked myself how I had come through this time. But since taking on the care of Harold, which included making arrangements for him to attend a small private school, my days had been pretty well occupied; but my nights had remained, for the most part, wide-eyed and sleepless . . . and lonely. I did not now have even the comfort of Hamilton and his Begonia. It would have been as puzzling to a psychiatrist, as it was to myself, that bereft of what the psychiatrist would have termed hallucination, I was dull, I lacked initiative, and was apparently very normal, whereas, generally whenever these two appeared on the screen of my mind I was happy and full of quirky humour, or at least alive to life.

Definitely, I think that Harold could be given credit for saving me from a breakdown. Not that my new charge had been an amenable subject. My main trouble had been and still was getting him to understand that it wasn't always funny to repeat the sayings of his uncles. And this matter had come to a climax today.

Harold had dutifully brought me a letter from Miss Casey, the lady who had turned her private house into a school for middle-class children between the ages of five and eight. I had explained my situation to Miss Casey when I first proposed sending Harold into her care. And she smilingly said she understood. Her first report of him had come at the end of a month, when she proudly stated that she had only twice heard him use a swear-word. And she was very pleased to inform me that he was above average intelligence for his age. And his grasp of elementary French was amazing in one so young and from his background. That was the first month.

The second month his report was not so glowing. It seemed it was difficult to get him to concentrate on any subject for very long.

Now here I was reading her letter, and the third month hadn't expired yet, there being another week still to go, and the gist of the letter was that Miss Casey thought it would be better if my charge could attend a more ordinary school where his language would not be so noticeable. It was distressing to state, she went on, but she'd had complaints from three parents whose children had surprised them with their knowledge of other than standard English. She had to admit that all the words didn't come under the heading of swearing but were, nevertheless, words that the parents did not approve of their children repeating. I took Harold into my study. I had found it was a better place to talk to him. The drawing-room somehow altered my attitude towards him and his towards me, for there, he would curl up on the couch and beguile me with a smile or some funny remark, mostly about Miss Casey, or Miss Dawn, a wizened lady to whom you could only apply the word spinster, for she seemed to have dropped out of the middle of the last century. She was, I understood, a poor relation of Miss Casey. But in the study, which I have said was also a sitting-room, I kept him from the couch and made him stand to the side of the desk while I sat in the leather chair behind it.

"Well, now, what's all this about?" I wagged the letter in the air.

"That?" He pointed. "It's a letter."

"I know it's a letter, and it's from Miss Casey, and it's about you."

"'Bout me?"

"Yes, about you, and your language."

"What lang-gage?"

"Your swearing."

"I never. Well" - he turned his head to the side - "just a little bit, 'cos Piggy Caplin said I didn't know no more."

I sighed. "And of course you did know some more?"

"Just them bits Grandad Stodd said."

"Gall-stones?"

He shook his head.

"What then?"

"Anty . . . mackassas."

"What?" I screwed up my face, and he repeated loudly and slowly, "Anty . . . mackassas. Gag used to put 'em on chairs like."

"Oh, antimacassars." I didn't smile, not outwardly. "Is that all you said?"

Again he looked away.

"Come on," I said. "Come on; let's have it."

He pursed his lips, then brought out, "Sylvia Watson said that was nothin'; she knew a bigger one. Her mother had it in hospital."

"Well, what did she get in hospital? What word was that?"

"Histry." I saw him thinking, then he added, "Rectory. Histryrectory."

At this I closed my eyes as if I was shocked. I put my elbow on the table, and leant my head on my hand. Hysterectomy. I kept my hand tight against my cheek as he went on now, "Nigel Broadhurst, he said it was nothin' an' all, an' that you wouldn't have to go to a hospital to get it, you would have to go to a church. And he should know 'cos his grandad's a parson like, an' wears a collar backside front, not like the Salvation Army crew. "

I took my hand away from my face and said, solemnly, "And you didn't swear, not real swearing?

"No, no, Mrs Nardy, I didn't, not . . . not today."

"Oh. Did you yesterday, then? Or the day before?"

I watched him thinking again, and he said, "I don't know, but Sylvia did. She swore today, she did, Sylvia Watson."

"What did she say?"

"Well" - his head wagged - "she pushed me an' said I was always swankin' 'bout me words, an' she didn't believe there was an anty-mackassa. And when I said there was, she said, 'Oh, you an' your anty . . . bloody . . . mack . . . assa.' So, she said it, not me. And Miss Dawn came out and put her hands over her ears. She didn't say anythin' to Sylvia, but she slapped my hands." He held out his hands now; then brightly, he added, "But it didn't hurt, not like when Gag wallops me. . . But it was her not me wot said it . . . Sylvia. An' she didn't belt her."

Anty . . . bloody . . . mack . . . assar. Children learn quickly. And Miss Sylvia Watson was apparently another one of the bright ones. What was I to do with him? The children at Primary school really did seem to proclaim the truth of all the good things that I had heard went on there. But I was worried that he would have to follow that by going to the nearest Comprehensive. I'd heard some of the boys as they scampered along the road, and their language was akin to that which Stickle had used on me. And as yet, Harold's had not got beyond damn, bloody, bugger, and that word I couldn't stand, which was sod.

I said, "Go and wash your hands and have your tea."

He didn't move. "You mad at me or summit?"

His English hadn't improved either under Miss Casey's tuition.

"Something, not summit."

"You still gonna 'dopt me then?"

"It all depends on what your father says and on how you yourself improve."

He moved nearer to me, put his hand gently on my knee now, looked up into my face and said, "I . . . I don't want to go back to Gag's,

I don't . . . I won't. I won't go. . . I won't, Mrs Nardy."

Now his lips were trembling, and I took his hand and said, "Don't worry, you're not going back to your gran's. But don't forget what I've told you before, your gran's a fine woman, it is only that she has that large family hanging round the house that makes her impatient."

He blinked his eyes, moved one lip over the other, then said brightly, "Will I bring you a sup tea?"

"A cup of tea. Where did you get sup tea from?"

"Your gran says sup tea."

And Gran was here for only a day or two.

I was about to say, "Yes, I'll have a cup of tea," when the bell rang.

Rising to my feet, I said, "Go on, have your tea, and take Sandy with you. I'll see who that is.". . .

I opened the door into the outer hall just as the lift stopped. The door gates swung open and out stepped a tall man. He was very thin; his skin was tanned to a dark brown; only his eyes and voice were recognisable. He moved into the hall and stared at me, and I caught my breath and said softly, "Tommy."

"Hello, Maisie."

Even his voice seemed to have changed. It had a rusty sound like that of someone unused to speaking.

I backed from him, pushed open the door into the inner hall, closed it after him, then held my hands out for his hat and the light coat he was wearing.

We exchanged no words as we went towards the drawing-room, but I saw him smooth his hair back and noted that it must have been cut recently.

In the drawing-room he did not pause as I might have expected and make a remark about the room as he had done once before, but he followed me to the middle of the room, and when I pointed to the armchair, he sat down. And I sat on the couch, but towards the edge of it. He was the first to open the conversation, and he did so by saying, "You all alone?"

"No . . . well, not really. I have Harold with me. You know, the little fellow. And there's Sandy. They're in the kitchen."

"How've you been?"

"Oh . . . well, you know." I spread out my hands. Then I asked, "When did you hear about Nardy?"

I watched him ease himself further back into the chair, then cross his long legs before looking from one hand to the other where they were resting on the arms of the chair; then he said, "I think I knew about it the day I received his letter. Although, I didn't get confirmation of it until I got yours about six weeks later."

"Nardy . . . Nardy had written to you?"

"Yes, yes, he wrote to me."

Nardy had never said anything about writing to him either.

"You were travelling then?"

"In a way, yes. I'd come down from the Rockies and was in Calgary. Then I went back again."

The old bitterness against him returned. He went back up again without writing a note of condolence after hearing that his one and only real friend had died. I asked with not a little sarcasm in my tone, "Did you find yourself up there? That's what you were looking for, wasn't it?"

He didn't answer for some seconds, but kept his eyes on me; then, his lips going into a twisted smile, he said, "Yes, Maisie, you could say I found myself, but I didn't much like the look of me. Maisie" - he brought his body forward towards me "don't hold bitterness against me; Nardy didn't, and he should have."

"Yes, he should have." I was nodding at him now. "You, his so-called . . . life-long friend, could walk out on him when he most needed you. Oh, yes, he had me, but you were in his life long before I came, and you walked out of it with never a care towards. . ."

"Don't say that!" His manner changed abruptly, and I saw him now as I had seen him the night he had stood in this room and told us of his mother's duplicity. "Who are you to condemn? You know nothing about it. While being the centre of it and the cause of it, you still know nothing about it."

This new tone and manner was like a physical onslaught: I sat back in the couch pressing my back tight against it as he went on, "I loved Nardy like a brother, but that love turned into an intense hate. I became eaten up with it. I . . . I. . ." Suddenly his back straightened, his eyes closed and his teeth clamping down onto his lower lip drained the blood from it.

The drawing-room door opened abruptly and Harold came running in, and stopped half-way up the room when he caught sight of the visitor. Then, his steps slow, he approached us, and I, at this moment thankful for his presence, was about to say, "You remember Mr Balfour?" when Harold said, "Hello."

But it was with an effort I saw Tommy reply with, "Hello."

Scrutinizing the visitor, Harold said, "By! your face is brown."

"Yes, yes, I've been in the sun quite . . . quite a lot."

Harold now turned from Tommy and, coming to me, held out his hand, saying, "Yer'd better come, 'e's done it on the mat again, all that yellow stuff. I told him yer'd scud his backside."

He had picked up the word scud from Gran: during her short stay here she'd often said in his presence that such a punishment should be meted out to him.

I rose, saying to Tommy, "Would you excuse me a minute?" And Harold ran before me out of the room, crying loudly, " 'E's had fish. Yer told me yer weren't goin' to giv 'im any more fish, the little bug . . . beggar." We were in the hall now and this imp of a boy turned his head up to me and smiled his impish smile as much as to say, "There, you see, I didn't say it."

Sandy greeted me with wagging tail and lolling tongue, but I demanded sternly, "What have you been up to now, you naughty boy?" And his friend answered for him, "'Tisn't 'is fault if yer stuff 'im with fish. Uncle Max can't take fish, 'cos it's oily, he spews. . ."

"He's sick."

"Who?"

"Your Uncle Max."

As I wiped up the bile with a wet disinfectant-soaked cloth, my charge stood by my shoulder as I knelt on the floor, his head level with mine; and his eyes looking into mine, he said, "Sick, not spewed."

"That's right."

"Sandy was sick."

"Yes, Sandy was sick." As I rose from my knees I saw that look on his face which meant he was trying to work out why the same word should not be applied to a man vomiting as to a dog. And being unable to do this, he dismissed it and asked, "Is 'e goin' to stay?"

"Who?"

"'Im, Mr Wotsisname." He thumbed towards the door.

"Mr Balfour?"

"Yes, 'im. Is 'e goin' to stay?"

"No. He's just calling."

"'E's big."

"Yes, he's big."

"Can I come back in with yer?"

"No, you can't. What I want you to do now is to put those things away off the table, and then get out your books, and I'll be with you shortly."

"Can I take 'em into yer study?"

"No, you can't. You stay here with Sandy until I come back."

"Tripe."

"*Harold.*"

"I only said, tripe. Gag gets it from the butchers an' she puts taters on it."

This was no time to go into the culinary effects created by Janet with tripe and the effect of the word on the ear when used to take the place of yet an even more telling adjective.

In the drawing-room once more, I said to Tommy, "He's a bit of a handful, but very lovable."

"Yes, I can imagine that. You couldn't be lonely where he was."

I confirmed this point by saying, "He's been a comfort to me of late, and before Nardy went we discussed adopting him."

"Adopting him?"

"Yes." I nodded. "It was Nardy's wish, and mine too. The matter is under discussion at the moment."

He sat back in his chair, his head drooping once again. Then, as if coming to a decision, he muttered, "I've got to talk to you, Maisie. I . . . I mean really talk, not just this polite jargon. I . . . I must tell you why I acted as I did." His head jerked up now as he said, "May I sit beside you? I . . . I won't need to look at your face then."

In a small voice I answered, "Yes. Yes, of course, Tommy."

He pulled himself up, then sat down on the couch my short arm's length from me, and, leaning forward once again, he put his elbows on his knees and joined his hands together before he began to talk. And his first words startled me. "I am a potential murderer, at least in my mind. You see, Maisie, just shortly after I met you, I fell in love with you. I could never understand when in the office why anyone should question the reason Nardy would want to marry you. To me, at first, you were the antithesis of my mother: you were kind; you were loving; you had a sense of humour. One forgot, when in your presence, that you were small, or that you had a deformed arm, and, as you have so often stated yourself, had no claim to beauty. I thought then the feeling I had for you was bound up with that which I held for Nardy. But later, I realized that I was kidding myself. You will remember I made this house almost a second home for a time, presumably to get out of my mother's presence, but really it was to be in yours. But -" His whole body now seemed to heave as he drew in a long breath; then as it subsided, he went on. "But my feelings for you weren't the reason I went away. It was because I was consumed with guilt. The fire did it. That fire didn't burn me physically, but it did mentally and spiritually. It ripped the skin off my hidden thoughts. In that smoked-filled attic, when I felt I was going to die, I thought, well, it was the best way out; it would save me being a traitor to my friend. This mightn't have been conscious thinking but I know now it was there. Then when I came out alive and heard that Nardy was in a bad way, one thought filled my mind. . ."

His head drooped further now towards his joined hands, and when he spoke, although his words were weighed with pain, they shocked me, for they were: "I waited for him to die. I wanted him to die. I willed him to die. . . Don't move away from me, Maisie, please, because I moved away from myself so much at that time I became a different human being, and the remorse will remain with me forever."

I hadn't moved away from him. Although I was shocked by his words, there had erupted in me a feeling of pity for him. Yet at the same time there was also the feeling of amazement that I, who was exactly as he had described me a few minutes earlier and who knew myself to be unprepossessing, could have in me something that had the power to drive a man such as Tommy to such lengths. It wasn't real; it didn't seem possible. In a way, it was like *Beauty And The Beast* in reverse.

He went on talking: "The feeling became strongest when I visited him in hospital. Each time after seeing him I got in that car and drove hell for leather, looking for an accident to happen. One day, I remember, after almost crashing into a car I stopped and got out and upbraided the fellow for his careless driving. I remember the man being almost speechless because I had come straight out of a side road and almost into him broadside on. And there were three children in his car. I think the man was in shock or he might have felled me for the things I said to him. The police sorted it out. After that I went to a psychiatrist. I remember he smiled and said I was still in shock from the fire; that this would pass, and to carry on my work as normally as possible. He said the love for this woman that I had which was driving me to act as I was doing towards my life-long friend was equivalent to a teenage crush. He ended by saying I was suffering a breakdown. I only paid him the visit. Then -" he turned his head now and looked at me, and after a second's pause he said, "my thinking took another twist. I began to hate you for being the cause of breaking up my life-long friendship with Nardy and for this dreadful desire to see him dead that was eating me up. I had to get away. So I went, but still refusing to believe I was in a breakdown which had the seeds of its beginnings in Mother's death."

He was looking at his hands again. His voice slow now, he said, "I kept a diary for a time about the places I stopped at or passed through, and then I let it go. What did it matter? It was after arriving in Calgary that things changed. I was feeling ropey. Then I met this couple. They invited me to their home. I stayed for a week. It wasn't that they had taken a liking to me, I think it was simply because I was British; they were that sort of people. It was just before I left them that I sent you the note on their headed paper. I wouldn't face up to the fact that I wanted to hear how things were at this end. Anyway, I started on my travels again and came across a family in a place they called a home and in which I'm sure you would hesitate to leave Sandy. There were seven of them and all in one room including a father and mother, grandmother, and great-grandfather, the son, and his wife, and their child. And we all slept on wooden boards. But what was in that room besides all those people was peace, a kind of peace that I cannot explain. It was through talking with the son that I came to myself. I worked with my hands for the first time in my life, really worked, grubbing the earth. I've promised to go back, and I will sometime. One day he asked me a question: 'Are you better now?' he said, and I answered simply, 'Almost.' It was odd, for I'd never mentioned that I was ill, physically or in my mind. Anyway, the following week I picked up your letter. But still I did not hurry back. I purposely made my way slowly. The feeling of guilt had gone but the remorse still checked my step."

He now turned and looked at me again. I knew this, but I wasn't looking at him, I was looking at Nardy's photograph that stood on a side table. He was smiling at me. And now at each side of the table, I saw my two friends standing, but as in a mist. Lately, since Harold had come, if I saw them at all, it was through a mist. Yet, even as I looked at them, Hamilton's form took on a more defined outline, and slowly he came towards me. And as he passed me, his eyes still on me, I turned my head and saw him put his front hoof on Tommy's shoulder. And there was Tommy now holding a letter out to me. "Would you like to read that?" he said.

I took it and opened it, and saw Nardy's handwriting. It began:

"My dear friend,
    We won't go into the why's and wherefore's but time is running out. So let me say that, although I don't understand your attitude over the past weeks, I do understand the reason that lies at the bottom of it. When I am gone, Tommy, Maisie is going to be lost. I loved her dearly and she loved me in return. But death is death and life without companionship or love, I should imagine, is worse than death. I don't think she will fall into your arms right away, she is not that kind, but give her your friendship and company, and time will tell. My affection for you has never lessened, Tommy. You were my friend. You will always be my friend. Until we meet wherever the Gods direct.

Yours,
Nardy."

It was like the day I lost Bill. A cry tore its way through my throat, the tears sprang from my eyes, nose, and mouth. Tommy's arms were around me, his voice was pleading, "Oh, Maisie, Maisie, don't, don't. Please. I'm sorry. I shouldn't have shown you that, but I wanted you to know. Oh, please, please, dear. Maisie, I wouldn't upset you for the world."

Then I knew there were other arms about me and claws pawing at me, for Harold was standing on the couch and Sandy was jumping up at my side, and Harold's voice penetrated my crying as he yelled, "Yer done this, mister! I'll bloody well get me Uncle Max at yer."

Slowly, but forcibly, I disentangled myself from the hands and the paws. Pushing both Tommy and Harold away, I leant back on the couch and when Tommy handed me his handkerchief, I dried my face. And as I did so, my champion demanded, "Did 'e 'it yer?"

I told myself not to laugh for I would become hysterical. But I shook my head, then glanced at Tommy and said, "No, he didn't hit me." Then I added, "He is Mr Nardy's friend." But I had to turn my head away because I could not bear to see the look in Tommy's eyes, for I saw that he, too, at any moment might burst into tears.

When I handed Tommy his handkerchief back, he took my hand and held it firmly. Then, as if not to be outdone, Childe Harold caught my other hand. And there we sat linked for a moment in silence, and in it I saw Hamilton and Begonia emerge from the mist once again, their coats shining brightly, their manes flying, their tails outstretched. Slowly, they came towards me, stopped for a second and looked at me, then walked through me and were gone.

I closed my eyes.

One life had ended. Another was to begin.

HAROLD

Part One

THE MOHICAN

Chapter 1

"Why do you want to adopt him?"

I stared at James Stoddart, the father of Harold, and I wanted to say, "Because I love him," but found that I couldn't use the word, not in front of this horde of the boy's uncles and aunts, and his grandmother and grandfather, not forgetting the outsider who was present. And to my dismay I heard myself sniff before I replied, "Because I am fond of him."

"You wouldn't like to adopt me, Mrs Leviston, now would you?" The big man grinned at me, and as the titter went round the room his mother, my dear Janet, yelled, "You, Max Flood! I warned you now, didn't I?"

"Oh, Mum. Mrs Nardy . . . I mean Mrs Leviston understands it was only a joke. Don't you, Mrs Leviston?"

"Yes." I smiled at him. "It was only a joke." Then endeavouring to bring a little lightness into the proceedings, I added, "I might have considered the proposition if you had been smaller," only to put my foot in it through my nervousness by adding, "But no doubt I'll be adopting some part of you because, you being his favourite uncle, Harold has picked up many of your sayings," which brought forth from the others a chorus of protests.

"You're not his favourite uncle."

"Who said you're his favourite uncle? I've seen to him time and time again."

"Who took him to the Zoo last week?"

"*Shut up! Shut up!* the lot of you."

All eyes now turned towards Janet, and I was amazed yet again at

how this slender woman in her sixties was able to cope with this crowd
of big lumbersome men and their attendant girl friends . . . so called.

Janet had become very dear to me over the past three years we had
been together. I think she had resented me a little at first when I
became the wife of her dear Mr Nardy. This, of course, was natural for
had she not attended him since he was a baby, and later, after his
mother died, become his housekeeper, although only part-time, for she
still had her own growing horde to attend to. Max was the eldest,
followed by Billy and Joe; the three of them, each over thirty and
divorced. Then came Maggie, Harold's mother who three years ago
had left her husband Jimmy Stoddart for another man, only to leave
this man for yet another and go off with him to Australia. She was the
only one of the family not here today. Greg, and Rodney, and Hilda
had followed at yearly intervals. May, the youngest, was smart: she
was well dressed. She had acquired a flat of her own, I understood, and
was now a receptionist in a small hotel. To use her mother's words, she
had made it, the only one of the lot of them to have done so.

But of all the family, it was Hilda and her boy friend who had held
my attention mostly since I had come into the house. Janet had
described them to me from time to time. Her description, however, was
but a pale shadow of the reality: Hilda's hair, which hung below her
shoulders, was of three distinct colours, green, blue, and yellow; she
had a long thin face, her eyes seemingly enlarged with coal-black
make-up, and her mouth with scarlet lipstick; her fingers were almost
hidden under rings all studded with large glass stones. She was
wearing a tight, very low-necked purple sweater, but the cleavage of
her breasts was covered by strings of beads. Her skirt was of a shiny
material that reached just to her knees. She wore ankle warmers,
apparently hand-knitted and of indescribable colours, and on her feet
she had heavy brogues. That was Hilda, and she was well out of her
teens.

Her boy friend was more easy to describe, he was simply the last of
the Mohicans. No one could mistake him for anything else: not only
did the ridge of his hair running across the crown of his head speak his
name loud and clear, but also his whole attire was pure Mohican
Indian. I had been really startled by his appearance and amazed at the
lack of self-consciousness that enabled him to walk abroad looking as
he did. But now I was in for another surprise.

All Janet's family talked with a cockney twang, and, with the
exception of May, were no respecters of aspirates. But when the
Mohican opened his mouth his voice was clear, his tone crisp and his
words very much to the point: he was saying to Jimmy Stoddart, "Why
all this caffuffle about why Mrs Leviston wants to adopt Harold. It's no

longer the case of *why* she would want to adopt him, it's more likely, *why* has she adopted him? The deed's done, it's all signed and sealed." He turned towards me now and the two painted marks on his cheeks spread as he smiled and added, "It isn't everyone that's taken for love, is it, Mrs Leviston?"

The voice was so incongruous with his get-up that I could find nothing to say at the moment; but it would have been cut off anyway for Jimmy Stoddart had risen to his feet and, with arm outstretched and finger pointing, he was crying, "Who's askin' you to butt in, you weirdy git! This is a family affair, and what my son does is no. . ."

"That's another point, isn't it, Mr Stoddart: he's no longer your son; you signed him away this morning." The Mohican's voice was quiet and cool.

The very next moment I yelled or yelped as a small vase flew past my face, headed straight for the Mohican, and splintered against the wall just behind his head. In that instant I noticed the expression on the Mohican's face: it wasn't fear, it looked like rage as if he could have been a real Indian, and on the attack.

But now there was pandemonium in the room. Janet was shouting, "You get out of here, Jimmy Stoddart. And the less I see of you the better."

The men were all on their feet, except Mr Flood, who had been seated near the fire and was still seated there and still smoking, having lit one cigarette from the other, and seemingly oblivious of the commotion.

"I'll go when I'm ready." Jimmy Stoddart was standing near the sitting-room door. He was a tall man, well built and what you might call good-looking in a flashy kind of way. His hair was dark and thick and had certainly been under the hairdresser's hands, as the waves above his ears testified. And ignoring Max, who was lumbering up to him and saying threateningly, "I'd get goin' when the goin's good, mate," he stepped to one side and, looking directly across the room at me, he shouted, "I want to know when I can see 'im."

"You never bothered seein' 'im much before." It was the bedecked Hilda now speaking for the first time since I'd come into the room and her voice, unlike her boy friend's, had certainly no refinement in it.

I answered the man, saying, "You know the agreement, you may see him every other Saturday and have him for a week-end once a month."

"I know that. But which week-end? This week-end? Next week-end?"

"Let it be the last week-end in the month."

He made no comment on this but stood still for a moment, and as he looked at me I was reminded of my first husband, Howard Stickle, who was now serving a twelve year sentence for having tried to kill me by burning me to death. In the attempt he was successful only in burning my husband and so bringing him to a premature death, burning the fingers off my stepfather, and horribly disfiguring the daughter of his second wife. It came to me that there was more than one Stickle in the world.

"To hell with you! What are you anyway, the lot of you? Scum. "

There was a surge towards the figure going out, but Janet blocked the way, her voice rising above the melée as she cried, *"Stop it! Leave him alone.* Enough! My God! What has this house come to?" Then pushing Rodney and Billy aside, she made her way towards me and her face was crumpled in distress as she said, "Ma'am, what can I say? The first time in my house and you meet a lot of hooligans."

"Janet. Janet, please, don't distress yourself. They're not . . . I . . . I mean it's natural. Look! Give me a cup of tea, will you?"

Janet sniffed, then laughed and said, "Oh, Mrs Leviston, ma'am, a cup of tea? Yes, of course, of course. I'll put the kettle on."

As she hurried from the room her family awkwardly took their seats again, and as was usual on these occasions a silence enveloped us all.

It was the Mohican who broke it and surprised me yet again by turning to me and saying, "Where do you intend to send him to school - later on I mean?"

All eyes were on me as I answered. "I . . . I don't rightly know. He should be all right where he is for a good while yet."

"Don't ever send him to a boarding school." His voice was flat sounding, his face looked stiff, and I replied, "No, no; I wouldn't dream of doing that."

"Good."

What a strange individual. I recalled Janet telling me a little of what she knew about him. Apparently he had been to a boarding school, spending most of his holidays there, too, with his housemaster, because his parents were travelling. When he was fifteen they were divorced. He remained at school until he was seventeen when, although he could have gone on further, he opted out. It was even rumoured he had been in the police force and was thrown out.

What a shame, I thought, because I could detect something warm and kindly about him. But yet, what was I thinking? Warm and kindly! He had been brought up two months ago for having caused actual bodily harm.

When he turned from me I looked down the room towards Max, who had been the one with most to say, and asked, "By the way, where is the young man in question?"

"Oh, along at the Flannagans, saying goodbye to the dog I think. The dog's missed 'im, yer know." And Max grinned at me, causing his features to take on an impish look as he ended, "Yer see, the kid's boots ain't as big as the others."

"Don't exaggerate, Max, nobody kicks the dog."

"What do yer know of it, May, yer never 'ere."

"I was brought up with their other dog, remember, and stopped you from kicking him."

"I never kicked 'im." Max now turned his still grinning face towards me, adding, "I would never kick a dog."

Looking straight at him, I replied soberly, "I've only your word for it." And at this there was a titter round the room and as he was saying, "Oh, Mrs Leviston," Janet came in with a tray on which was a teapot, a jug of milk, and four cups.

I wondered at the four cups until, glancing round the room, she said, "If you lot want tea you know where the water an' the tea caddy is," and proceeded to pour out the tea.

Having handed me mine, she passed one on to May and one to Hilda; then, taking one herself, she sat down and, looking at her son Billy, who was sitting to the left of her, she jerked her head as she said, "Go on, fetch him in. But I don't think you'll have to go far, he's waitin' outside the back door. I told him to stay there until he was sent for."

Again a silence fell on the room, until there appeared in the doorway, standing by the side of his uncle, the reason for my sitting in the midst of Janet's family. My adoptive son was not yet seven years old. He wasn't tall for his age, more broad than tall, of his Uncle Max's build. He had fair hair, a round face in which were two deep brown bright eyes. His mouth was well shaped and always ready to smile.

As he wound his way through the family towards me, one and another of his uncles giving him either a dig or a wink, he said nothing until he was standing in front of me and, because he always came straight to the point, he asked, "Are we goin' now?"

"'E can't get away quick enough. What d'yer think of that? Are we goin' now?"

"That's the last we'll see of 'im; too big for his boots already."

The laughing comments came from different quarters of the room, but the child took no notice, he just looked into my face, then made a statement, "Mr Tommy'll be waitin'."

"Oh, d'yer hear that, Mr Tommy'll be waitin'. 'E's got a smashin' car, not like our bangers, lads." His Uncle Joe was nodding from one to the other in assumed indignation, and when they all took it up, my new son turned on them and bawled, "Shut yer gobs, you lot!"

"*Harold!*" My tone was sharp; and Janet's accompanied mine but with more to say: "We'll have none of that," she said. "I'm still your gran an' I've still got a hand an' you've still got ears, an' they'll meet up in a minute."

"Oh, Gag." He turned to her. "Well, you should stop 'em."

"Yes" - Janet nodded at him now - "yes, I should stop 'em, I should have stopped 'em years ago."

I rose to my feet; the Mohican rose too, but except for Janet the others remained seated. That the oddest looking male individual should have such manners and also be considered by the rest of this family as a weirdy was odd in itself.

"Goodbye." I looked from one to the other, and each of them nodded, but only Max and Joe answered; Mr Flood didn't even nod.

In the little hallway I straightened Harold's cap, tucked his scarf inside his coat, told him to put his gloves on, then turned to Janet, saying quietly, "Thank you, Janet. I'll . . . I'll see you on Monday then."

For a moment she seemed overcome with emotion. She looked down on her grandson, then muttered, "You behave yourself mind. I'll be 'earin' about it, everything you do, mind. Do you hear me?"

"Yes, Gag." Impulsively now he put his arms up and she bent towards him, and he kissed her on the cheek. This was followed by a push that almost overbalanced him, but he laughed and gripped my hand and took me towards the front door that was being held open by the Mohican. Hilda was by his side now, and she, to my surprise, caught my arm and, after glancing at the Mohican, she said softly, "Yer can see why I like 'im, can't yer, Mrs Leviston? 'Cos 'e's a gentleman. 'E's the only gentleman I've ever met. As the sayin' is, never judge a bull by the ring through its nose. . ."

It was her turn to be nearly knocked on her back, and the cry, "Hilda!" certainly did sound as if it had come from the throat of an Indian Chief.

The Mohican was definitely embarrassed, but I smiled at him and said, "I don't know your name."

"John Drake."

"Goodbye, John," I said now. "It's been nice meeting you."

I gave one last look at Janet, then walked away down the street, my son by my side. And that's how I thought of this child, my son, not adopted, he was mine. And he wanted to be mine. That was the most important thing, he wanted to be mine.

Before we reached the end of the short street I knew that the family were no longer seated in the sitting-room but that most of them were on the front pavement. And they weren't alone, because other doors were open and other people were standing on their steps. And as if Harold knew this was happening, he swung round and waved, and I, looking over my shoulder, saw a number of hands lifted in reply.

We were now in another street, in another life, both of us. I looked down at him and he looked up at me, and we smiled at each other but did not speak; my hand, though, tightened on his and he walked closer to me. . .

Tommy was waiting for us in the car park. He had wanted to bring us to the house but I'd said no. The fact of him sitting outside in the flash Jaguar would certainly not have enamoured either him or me to the Flood family. He was now coming towards us. He was a tall man, six foot two, and his height always dwarfed me still further. As Gran Carter said, we looked like Mutt and Jeff, who, apparently, were two strip-cartoon figures from her childhood. He was thin and attractive, in fact quite good looking, and he was in love with me. . . God alone knew why, for I wasn't even what you would call attractively plain, and I had a withered left arm. In my favour, it could be said I had a sense of humour, and I was supposed to be a good conversationalist, and I was given credit for some kind of a mind because I wrote books, weird books in the opinion of some folk, about a woman, me, talking to an imaginary horse, which horse took on a wife. That being so, I suppose some people would have agreed with the description my first husband screamed at me in the court-room less than two years ago just before he had been sentenced: "Yes, I did it, and I'd do it again. Just give me the chance and I'll get you yet. By God! I will. I'll . . . get . . . you yet . . . you crippled undersized, barmy sod you!"

Tommy, towering over Harold, smiled down at him as he said, "Well now, young feller-me-lad, how does it feel to have a mother?"

"Just the same."

"Oh, it can't be the same," persisted Tommy; "she's not Mrs Nardy any more, she's your mother."

"She's still Mrs Nardy." Harold looked up at me and ended, "Aren't you?"

"Yes. Yes, Harold, I'm still Mrs Nardy."

Harold now ran towards the car and, opening the door, climbed onto the back seat.

When Tommy had settled me by his side and we were driving out of the car park, he said, "Well, Mrs Nardy," and I was aware of the stressed title, "What about celebrating? A slap-up tea somewhere?"

Immediately Harold's head was poked between us. "With cream buns?"

"With cream buns, as many as you can eat."

"Certainly not!" I said. "All right, we'll go to tea but only one cream bun." And I lifted my hand and tweaked Harold's nose; and he grinned at me, saying, "In that swanky place where the men are all dolled up as if they had pokers up their ar . . . ?" The head was slightly withdrawn and the voice was lower as it ended, "I mean, stiff shirts like."

Tommy was making a strange noise in his throat. I kept my eyes straight ahead and my voice level as I replied, "Yes, we'll go to that restaurant again."

When Tommy remarked in an aside, "One for effort," I replied primly, "Yes, yes indeed."

It was two hours later, as we were entering the hall of my home and making our way towards the lift carrying on a conversation that had begun in the car, that we met Captain and Mrs Beckingtree-Holland. They were stepping out of the lift as Tommy said, "You must be able to get a baby-sitter somewhere. . . Oh." He raised his hat and stood aside as the delicate-looking lady paused and divided a thin smile between us. She was wearing a well-worn fur coat, and above her china-doll face her white hair curled upwards about her ears onto a small matching fur hat. The man accompanying her had a military bearing. He wore a three-quarter length moleskin-coloured coat. He had a knotted silk scarf on his neck and a cap on his head which he raised as he passed us, at the same time extending towards me a slight bow.

They, I guessed, were the temporary occupants of the flat below ours.

The whole of this house had once belonged to my second husband, Leonard Leviston, but being too big for him he had turned it into three very spacious flats. There was a basement flat too in which the caretaker lived. He it was who kindly took my dear poodle Sandy for walks whenever possible.

We hadn't seen much of Mr and Mrs Stretton, the owners of the first floor flat as both he and she seemed to be connected with work at some ministry, and we very rarely met except in the hallway. But a fortnight ago Mr Stretton had told me he had been transferred to Germany for a year and that a distant relative of his wife was coming to look after the place until they came back. So here were Captain and Mrs Beckingtree-Holland. I didn't know their name at this time, I wasn't to know it until the next morning.

As we stepped out of the lift into our hallway, Harold confronted us both, saying flatly, "I don't want a baby-sitter; I can look after myself."

I glanced impatiently at Tommy. He'd no right to bring up the matter in front of the boy, but he had for some time been wanting to see *Noises Off* at the Savoy Theatre, and naturally he wanted me to go with him. He had suggested leaving the boy with Janet, but this would have meant an erosion of my efforts to improve my charge, for once

Harold was back in the company of his uncles for any length of time he reverted rapidly to their ways. The boy had been living with me now for some months, in fact, ever since Nardy died, shortly before last Christmas.

I pushed Harold before me into the inner hall, saying, "Get your things off and put your slippers on," and turning towards where he had flung his coat on a chair, I cried, "Hang it up! I've told you."

Good gracious! I was acting like a mother already. And an impatient one too. And so, smiling at him, I added, "And go and see Sandy in the kitchen; he's barking his head off. That's a good boy." And I turned towards the drawing-room, Tommy following.

It was rarely I entered this room without feeling a sense of wonderment and pleasure. I switched on the electric fire and then sat down on the couch opposite and looked to where Tommy was now standing near the mantelpiece gazing at the artificial logs that were beginning to glow, and I said to him, "Don't be annoyed, Tommy; you see how I'm fixed."

Slowly he came towards me and, sitting down beside me, he took my hand and said, "I could never be annoyed with you, Maisie, never, no matter what you said."

"Don't be silly." I pushed his hand away. "I can look back and remember times when you bawled at me."

"Oh, that was in another era, another life, when I never imagined that one day I'd sit here holding your hand." He again caught hold of my hand. "And you know, Maisie, if you never give me any more than this I'll be satisfied."

Of a sudden he jerked his whole body away from me, saying, "Why am I such a damn liar? I still go on pretending. The fact is I'm not satisfied with what you give me, I want more of you - you know I do - I want the lot. What I don't want is to put my hat and coat on and say, 'Good-night, Maisie.'" He lowered his head, then asked quietly, "Are you still thinking of Nardy?"

I too was looking down as I answered truthfully, "Yes; yes, I still think of him every day. And I still miss him."

"How long do you think you'll continue to feel like this? Oh" - he made an impatient movement by flinging out his hand - "I don't mean that you should forget him, you know that, but life must be lived, and Nardy, above all people, knew that. He said it in his letter to me, didn't he? He knew what I was feeling. He knew why I went away last year like a sick animal searching for some dark place to die in. He sensed my hate of him, the hate that had turned from love because of you. But he didn't hold it against me, he was my friend. My God! yes, he was a friend, always had been, and I had to go and play the dirty on him by wanting to be rid of him so I could have you." He turned and glanced at me, and there was bitterness in his voice when he added, "Things like that shouldn't happen. I blamed you for its happening, but you were as helpless as I was. It's your nature to be kind and comforting. I think that's what I fell in love with, your nature: you were so different from anyone I'd ever come across; after years with my mother you appeared like an oasis in the desert."

It was seldom now he mentioned his mother, a cruel, selfish, powerful, scheming woman who had kept him tied to her apron strings through supposed poverty for years. He'd had to work to support her in the middle-class way she'd been accustomed to, only to find, with her death, that he had become a rich man, for she had been sitting on a fortune for years, money left to her by an aunt. Twice she had stopped him from marrying; and long before her death there had been murder in his heart towards her. After she died he became consumed with hate, then embroiled in my affairs even to the extent of his being almost burned alive in that flaming house.

I liked Tommy . . . very much, but did I love him?

I look back on my life through sixteen loveless years with my mother, then twelve years of marriage to a sadist, the culmination of which led to a police cell; then divorce, followed by marriage to my editor Leonard Leviston and my meeting with his friend and publishing colleague, Tommy Balfour. Tommy had thrown up his job and gone off on a trip to Canada before Nardy, as my second husband was always known, had died; but since his return to England he had been invited to rejoin his old firm and was now a director and in effect my publisher.

Again I asked myself if I loved him.

I was saved from giving myself an answer by the opening of the door and Harold rushing in accompanied by Sandy, my beautiful big white poodle, who jumped up into my arms and licked my face. As I pushed him away, exclaiming, "Oh Sandy! Give over," Harold said, "I've put the kettle on and I've washed me hands, they were sticky." He turned them over for my inspection, then added, "You'll have to wash me gloves, 'cos they'll be sticky an' all inside."

"I'll see to them."

"You goin' home now?"

The straight gaze was directed towards Tommy, and Tommy, his eyes widening, his tone full of mock indignation, said, "Does that mean you want to be rid of me?"

"We . . . ll" - the word was drawn out; Harold was nothing if not honest - "you've been with us a long time, all 'safternoon."

"I took you to tea, didn't I?"

"Yes."

"Well, don't you think I should be shown some courtesy by being allowed to stay a little with my friend?"

He glanced towards me.

I fully expected my boy to speak the truth again, and he did, but in a rather diplomatic fashion: "Well, if she wants you to," he said, and looked directly at me.

I made no reply to this; but Tommy said, "You make quite a good cup of tea. If you'll give me a cup, then I'll think about going."

"Will yer?"

"Yes. Yes, I will."

At this Harold ran from the room, and Tommy, glancing at me, said, "You know something? I don't think he's cottoned on to me."

"Oh yes he has, he likes you. He talks about you when you aren't here."

"If it's in a similar vein to that of the last exchange it'll be no compliment, and if I know anything about that young gentleman, he'll make that tea, pour it straight out, and it'll be here within seconds, and just one cup, you'll see."

"He's just a child. He's had a rough upbringing. He's learning."

"He's a very old child." Tommy's face was solemn now, his voice flat.

And I agreed with him in my mind: yes, Harold was an old child. Since his mother left him when he was three years old, he'd passed through the testing care of his father's girlfriends to the stern and ear-slapping guidance of my dear Janet and the colourful vocabulary of his five uncles and his Grandfather Flood, not to mention his Grandfather Stoddart with whom he had lived for a time. And so of course he was an old child. But he was a loving child and a child that needed loving, and he was my child. Yes, from now on he was really my child, and he must be my first consideration. There was no question mark in my mind about loving him.

Chapter 2

It was on the Sunday morning, and we were both ready to goto church. Yes, we were going to church. I felt duty bound tosee that from now on he attended church.

A month ago I'd been lucky enough to get him into a church school which was quite near. It was a small primary school. I had always thought it was a Roman Catholic school, and so no thought of sending him there had entered my head, for one stipulation of the adoption made by his father was that he would remain Church of England; not that the father followed any denomination, he had merely wanted to stress his authority and this seemed to be one of the easier ways of doing so.

But having discovered the school was C.O.E. I approached the headmaster. I told him the circumstances through which I'd come into the possession of a son and he was so understanding that I took a liking to the man straightaway. Of course, there was the unspoken agreement that Harold would become a practising Christian. So here we were ready to attend not only the main church service but also the short children's one that would follow.

It had been evident from the beginning that Harold did not take to either the main service or the children's service. He had summed up his first visit with one word, "Tripe." The second visit had elicited a longer comment, "'Cos I don't know what he's talkin' about." The third visit had resulted in a question.

"If God's everywhere why doesn't somebody see him sometime?"

. . . Good question. And also, if he was up in heaven why didn't we see his feet when he was walking about in the sky? Answer that one.

We were about to walk across the hall when the lift opened and out stepped Mrs Beckingtree-Holland.

"Good-morning," she said.

"Good-morning."

"Oh, I've come at a wrong time; I see you are about to leave."

"No, no; I have a moment or two. Can I help you in any way?"

"Oh" - the doll-like head moved from side to side - "it was just the remark I overheard you make, or your friend make, when we got out of the lift yesterday."

I narrowed my eyes at her and waited.

"About a baby-sitter." She now looked at Harold, and as he stared back at her, I gripped his hand, warning him not to speak. If he had it would have been, "I don't want a baby-sitter, 'cos I ain't no baby."

"Oh?"

"Would it be possible to speak to you in private?"

I was flustered for a moment, then said, "Yes, yes. Now you stay there, Harold; I won't be a moment. Come in, Mrs . . . er?"

"Beckingtree-Holland. "

"Mrs Holland."

In the inner hall she said, "This is a very delicate matter. You see, I . . . I like to occupy my time and . . . er, I . . . well, where it is necessary I give lessons in deportment, and of course oblige people like yourselves by sitting with their children should they wish to go out in the evening."

"Yes, yes, of course. I understand."

And I did understand. This delicate, refined lady-like person wanted payment for her obliging. Well, wasn't it natural that she should? Yet, a person of her appearance and definite position. . . What position? She gave it to me the next moment by saying, "The Captain, my husband, had to leave the service because of his health. He has a small pension, added to which we had naturally our savings. But as you yourself know things have changed and what at one time afforded us a most pleasant way of living scarcely affords us existence now. It is rather humiliating, but nevertheless -" She shrugged her thin shoulders. "Well, that is the situation."

I wetted my lips, searched quickly for the right words, then said, "I'd be pleased to avail myself of your services from time to time, Mrs Beckingtree-Holland."

I sounded as correct as she.

"That is nice of you. Then I won't keep you any longer. Are you going out for a walk?"

"We are going to church."

"Oh, to church. How civilized."

We returned to the hall to find the lift had gone, and so had Harold. I glanced at her and she at me. The red light showed it had reached the ground floor. I pressed the button and as the lift ascended my companion said, "I suppose he is what is known as a handful."

"He is a boy." My voice was stiff now.

"Yes, yes, of course. Well, I'm sure we'll enjoy looking after him. My husband will teach him to play chess. He is a very good chess player."

"That would be nice." The gates opened and there was Harold. I did not say, "You should not have done that, Harold;" I just stepped in, Mrs Beckingtree-Holland followed and we descended to the next floor where Mrs Beckingtree-Holland got out, smiled, inclined her head towards me and disappeared as the lift went down to the ground floor.

"You shouldn't have done that, Harold."

"I don't like standin' about."

"You'll have to learn to stand about."

"Why?"

"Don't start that this morning. And hold your head up and walk straight." He did as he was bid, and we made our way to church.

The service was, as usual, dull. The parson was a nice man but nice men can be boring when let loose in a pulpit. The children's service proved to be much better and very enlightening to me, because for the first time I heard my boy sing.

"Good King Wencelas looked out on the Feast of Stephen, Where the snow lay round about deep, and crisp, and even."

There he was in the front row singing his head off and the sound that came from his throat was unbelievable.

"Away In a Manger" followed; then, "Once In David's Royal City"; and Harold Leviston, as he was now, sang all the carols word perfect.

The service over, the headmaster, who was also the Sunday School teacher, came up to me and said, "He's got a fine voice."

"I didn't know he could sing."

"You didn't? Well, well. I told the choirmaster about him and he would like him in the choir."

I, too, now said, "Well, well."

As we walked back home Harold was unusually quiet. This often happened when he was waiting for me to put him on the spot about some misdemeanour. But this wasn't a misdemeanour.

"Why didn't you tell me you could sing?"

"You never arst."

"Asked."

"A . . . sked. Well, you never did."

"But why should I have to ask you? You haven't to be given permission to sing."

It was some seconds before he answered, "'Cos they said me voice was funny, like a girl's. Me Uncle Max used to do me, make game like, an' it sounded funny, so I stopped."

"Don't say 'like' in the middle of a sentence. I've told you, like is a word that has its own meaning."

"Like what?"

"Harold."

He was, to use his own words, having me on. He had done so before. Oh! those uncles, especially Max, the jolly one, the one who could supposedly, by the boy's past accounts, take off all the television characters.

I said, "It was very wrong of your Uncle Max; you've got a nice voice and you must go on singing. And you must practise; you heard what the headmaster said, you can get into the church choir."

"*I don't want that.*" The statement was very emphatic.

"Why not?"

"They're cissies; they wear long frocks an' they sing like this:" he pulled his mouth into an elongated "O". Then laughing, he said, "I did sing once in the kitchen, but Sandy started to howl an' I had to roll on the floor with him to stop him."

Laughing at the memory, he leant his head towards me and I pressed him to my side. Then he darted off, taking leaps along the pavement and punching the air as he went. It was an expression of joy. I laughed out aloud and the sound that I made was also an expression of joy.

Chapter 3

Christmas had come and gone. It had been a traumatic time; Harrods had been bombed. Only an hour before the explosion I had been shopping in the store, accompanied by Harold. I was visibly shaken when I heard the news, policemen and policewomen dead, others terribly wounded. Good will to men.

For the remainder of the week London was on its toes but defiant: as it was said, if the blitz didn't get them down there was little chance of the I.R.A. accomplishing it. Yet, there was no doubt about it, there was an underlying fear that no place was safe. But such is the tenacity of Londoners, the first day of the sales there they were, a little late because most of them couldn't come into the city by car, but they came by bus and train from all parts.

During the holidays Tommy and I had taken Harold to a pantomime. And twice within the last twelve days, our neighbours had baby sat for us and Tommy had taken me to see two shows. Unlike Nardy's his taste didn't run to opera.

I couldn't quite get over the fact that the baby-sitters were definitely, as Gran would have put it, of the class, but the lady, I had found, had no qualms about discussing terms: £2.50 an hour with light refreshments being left. She had suggested the necessity for the latter in a very polite way, but it was nevertheless definite.

The first evening we were out six hours. When I handed her the two ten-pound notes, she did not say, "You'll want some change," but smiled sweetly, murmuring "Thank you so much;" and the Captain had made noises in his throat, causing me to wonder for a moment if he too wanted payment. I later recalled exactly what he had said to me about Harold that first evening. "Interesting little chap, isn't he? Certainly of the rough and tumble, cockney to the marrow and with all their wiles. I don't envy your job of chipping off the rough edges."

I didn't care very much for the Captain, nor did I care much for his wife, yet at the same time I felt sorry for them both, that people of their standing could find themselves in such a plight. I also remembered his remarks as he was leaving after the second baby-sitting session. "You have very good taste, Mrs Leviston." I didn't bother to tell him that nothing in the flat was of my choosing except one or two pieces of furniture that I'd brought from my old home.

Tommy found the couple very amusing. They were, he said, of the type that sometimes visited the publishing house practically demanding that their memoirs should be published. They would often put themselves over as the only people who had travelled through the jungles of Africa, or across Russia, or lived in India during the time of the White Raj.

The couple must also have amused Harold, for after that first evening of being "baby-sat" he, following in his Uncle Max's footsteps, "did" the Captain and even his genteel wife. And I had great difficulty in chastising him, for when attempting her voice he minced towards Sandy and, bending over him and patting his head, he said in a voice that was quite a good imitation of the lady's, "And now, little boy, it's to beddie-beds," and then prancing about and in a voice very much like that of his Uncle Max's ordinary tone, he had ended, "Up the apples and pears!"

"That's enough of that!" I said, but I was crying with laughing, and when he flung himself against me I hugged him.

It was Friday. I didn't like Fridays: all unpleasant things seemed to happen to me on a Friday. But Friday apart I'd had an unpleasant week, at least at nights, for on three occasions I had woken up with dreadful pains in my stomach and a queer ill feeling; yet in the morning the pain had gone, as had the feeling.

But this particular Friday was the last in the month and tomorrow Harold's father would be calling to take him for the week-end. It would be his fourth such visit. The more I saw of the man the less I liked him; and, strangely, this seemed to be shared by his son, for on his return from the very first outing Harold said he didn't want to go out with his father again.

The arrangement was that Harold would see his father on both the Saturday and Sunday, but that he would sleep here because his father's girl friend had always objected to him; and, anyway, Harold's two older sisters, Doris and Gloria, were now back with their father, and consequently they were short of room.

Friday too was the day I phoned Gran in Fellburn. This should have given me a great deal of pleasure: we should have laughed and joked as we used to, but since her visit following Nardy's death, when she became jealous of Janet and had caused a scene, things had changed between us. She would give me her news about the family, and I would give her mine, but we didn't laugh together any more. Even when at odd I times I spoke to her son, my stepfather George, it wasn't the same: he still said, "Hello Pet," or "How's my best girl?" But I was no longer his best girl, and of course I understood that, for he had, with his second marriage, adopted a family of four. The only one who remained the same over the distance of time was Mike, Doctor Kane, the man who really created Hamilton the imaginary horse that had been my friend during those lonely years. My weekly visits to Mike's surgery had been as a lifebelt to me over that long dark period, and I thank God that at least he had remained the same. . .

Mr Brown, the caretaker, had been up to take Sandy for his first walk, and after he had given me the run-down on the weather outside he asked if I would be kind enough to stop the young man, as he called Harold, from ringing his emergency bell every time he passed through the hall.

Oh, I didn't know Harold had been doing this, I said; I would certainly see to it. And I did.

"What's this I hear about your ringing Mr Brown's bell?"

"Me?"

"Stop that; you know what I mean."

There was a shrug of the shoulders, pursing of the lips, a sidelong glance up at me before he said, "It's only a bit of fun."

"It's no fun having Mr Brown running up those stone steps every time you happen to pass through the hall. One of these days when there is really something wrong he won't bother to come, he'll think it's you playing up again. Now it's got to stop. Understand?"

"All right," he said, and then sighed before making the statement: "I don't 'ate 'im; 'e's hall right, 'e does bug me though."

"Oh well, I'm sure he'll be glad to know you don't hate him, but he'd be more pleased if you restrained the urge to press the button."

He now laughed up into my face and put his hand out and pushed me gently in the waist, saying, "You know, you sound funny when you talk like that."

I pressed my lips together, then blinked before I said, "I had no intention of appearing funny, and you know it."

Another sigh. "Yes, hall right."

"All right."

He grinned, "As you said, hall right."

I drew in a long breath, "Keep your scarf tucked in and your cap on straight and don't lose your gloves today. Now where are you going?" I said as he darted from me towards the kitchen.

"Just to say so long to Sandy."

A minute later he was back, saying, "'E's lazy; 'e won't get out of 'is basket."

"It's because he's tired; he's had his walk," I said.

"I'm tired an' all."

"Go on with you." I pushed him into the outer hall, opened the lift doors; then bending down I kissed him, and, his arms coming round my neck, he hugged me to him for a moment. Then having to have the last word, he stepped into the lift, saying, "Look, you've knocked me cap for six."

"Be a good boy now, won't you?"

"Yes, all right," he said, and as his grinning face disappeared from my view I sighed happily and turned back into the house, the while thinking, He's learning, and quickly.

This period in the morning between Harold going to school and Janet's arriving seemed the loneliest time of the day; even more so than at night after Tommy had gone, for there was never an evening passed but he called in; and although very often he stayed too long, I had to admit I was glad of his company. But he having gone, I would go straight to bed and pray that I could sleep, only of late to be woken up by this weird pain.

I thought of the pain now and did what I had promised myself to do in the middle of last night: I went to the phone and as I was a private patient I asked if I could make an appointment to see my doctor that morning. When this was arranged, it being Friday morning, I phoned Gran.

I always found myself hesitating before ringing her number these days, wondering what her attitude would be. However, there was the number ringing.

"Hello, Gran."

"Hello, there."

"How are you?"

"Oh, not too bad."

There was a pause, then she said, "I've got news for you, you're in the papers again."

"What?"

"You're in the papers again."

"How?"

"Stickle."

The very name caused my heart to thump against my ribs. "What do you mean, Gran? Explain." My voice was sharp.

"Well, there seems to have been a fight in the prison: he went for another man; the fellow's in hospital."

"Well, what have I got to do with that?"

"Well, you were his wife, weren't you? And there it is in block letters: Husband of local author."

"He's no longer my husband. They know that, you know that; why do you say it like that, Gran? It's as if you were enjoying it."

"Now look here, lass, don't forget who you're talkin' to. I'm tellin' you what's in the paper. Anyway, you're out of it now, aren't you? You don't have to put up with it."

She spoke as if she was at the receiving end of something, and then in the next moment her explanation came: "I could hardly get through the club door last night afore there they were. 'Stickle's at it again,' they said, as if he was a damn relation."

I held the phone away from my face and looked at it as if looking at her, and my mind was saying, You were glad to be classed a relation when Nardy was alive. You used to make skits about my being married to a nob and preening yourself because you were connected with me. Why did people change? What made them act as they did? It was the same emotion, I suppose, as that which made me react as I did the next instant by bringing up a topic that I knew irritated her and which I had refrained from mentioning over the past weeks.

"I didn't tell you that the adoption had gone through, did I?"

There was a short silence before she said, "No you didn't. But all I can say in that direction is, you've made a rod for your own back."

I felt the colour rising to my face and my irritation boiled over as I cried into the phone, "Why don't you like him, Gran? What's the matter with you?"

"There's nothing the matter with me, lass. And you ask why I don't like him. Well, I'll tell you why, and our George thinks the same, an' Mary an' all, and it's this way, if you want to adopt a bairn it should have been somebody decent, not a raw-mouthed little cockney."

I glared at the mouthpiece, then banged it down onto the stand, and marched away into the bedroom, slammed the door, then attempted to make the bed as if I were attacking it, throwing the clothes here and there. But all of a sudden I stopped, sat down in a chair, drooped my head and began to cry, all the time whimpering, "Oh, Nardy. Nardy."

If Nardy had been there he would have had an explanation of why Gran felt like this: he would have soothed my ruffled feathers; and although I thought I knew perfectly well why she felt like this, his soft voice would have put a different light on her attitude, explaining once again the tangents of our complex personalities.

But Nardy wasn't here.

After a while I got up and finished making the bed, more gently now, and when, a short time later, I left the bedroom I suddenly wished that it was evening and I could see Tommy and I could talk to him about it. Such were the vagaries of my own nature. . .

Janet had hardly got in the door and said, "Morning, Mrs Leviston, ma'am. Nippy isn't it?" before I could see she was bursting with news of some kind. She took off her hat and coat, stooped down to lift up Sandy who was barking a welcome at her before making her way to the kitchen.

I stood at one side of the kitchen table, she at the other and she nodded at me before she said, "She's left him."

"Who? Hilda, the Mohican, I mean John?"

Janet smiled now, saying, "That's a good name for him; different from what some of the boys call him. Big Chief Bloody Nuisance, that's what my 'Arry calls him, 'cos he says he's never away from the door. But then that isn't true, 'cos he goes off and we never see him for days. Neither does Hilda. We don't know where he goes. But no, it wasn't him, it's the other one, Jimmy, Jimmy Stoddart the father." She nodded to the side as if Harold were present.

My mouth widened into an "Oh!" before I said, "The woman's left him?"

"Flat. Apparently she was only sticking because she thought she was going to have the baby, but since the miscarriage she's acted different like. She thought young 'Arold was a nuisance, but then she found the two girls were almost as bad. It was the way she treated them: May's good; they behave themselves with her because they want to stay there. So the bold boy's on his own now, and that serves him right. But being who he is he won't be like that long if I know anything about it. From what I can gather from his piece's cousin who knows Hilda, the woman thought that with Maggie coming back from Australia with that bloke and wanting to marry him and askin' for a divorce. That shook me, mind, Maggie wantin' to marry again. Anyway, Jimmy's piece thought the bloke would marry Maggie. But it seems he told her she was barking up the wrong tree. And I'll tell you this, ma'am, if Maggie hadn't had marriage in her mind again I don't think she would have agreed to the adoption; likely the bloke, whoever he is, didn't want to take on the responsibility of a ready-made family. Anyway, has the person in question" - she pulled a face here - "been behaving himself?"

I pulled a face back at her as I said, "Only in part. He's been ringing Mr Brown's emergency bell again."

"Ooh! the little devil. But then that's a boy, any boy would do that. But it's his language that worries me an' what he'll get up to at that school, it being connected with the church like. . . Well, I'll make a cup of tea and then we'll get started."

"By the way, Janet," I said, "I'll be popping out; I've made an appointment with Doctor Bell, he's seeing me at eleven o'clock."

"You had that pain again?"

"Yes, a little. It's beginning to worry me."

"Well, the best thing you can do is to see him. Put your mind at rest anyway. One thing you're certain of, it isn't your appendix this time."

It was just over an hour later when I left the house and as I stepped out of the front door I was met by the astonishing sight of the Mohican. It was astonishing for he looked more like an Indian Chief than ever. I stammered, "Hel . . . hello, John," and he replied in that surprisingly well-bred tone of his, "Good-morning, Mrs Leviston. No doubt you're surprised to see me."

"N . . . no. No," I stammered again; "not at all." He laughed gently now and leant back against the iron rail that bordered the steps to the basement and as he did so I looked past him down the street to where stood two more Indians. Well, they weren't quite Indians, and I couldn't really see from this distance whom they represented, but it certainly wasn't anyone in the British Isles.

"I just wanted to leave a message for Hilda with her mother. I've . . . well, unexpectedly got to go off for a few days. I didn't know till just a little while ago, and . . . and I don't want to go to the factory." And the marks on his cheeks spread again as he added, "She doesn't like it very much: she's with it herself, but they still kid her."

I nodded at him, saying, "I can understand that;" then pointedly I asked, "Why have you to go off at a moment's notice?"

"Oh," he said; then turned to look down the street to where his two friends had moved somewhat nearer, and I could now make out they were on the other side from the Indians, more like something left over from Custer's last stand, in fringed leather gear.

And as if remembering my question, the Mohican said slowly, "Well, we just feel the urge, you know, to move, to get away, to do something different." As he finished he stood up straight and, leaning slightly towards me, he said, "I'd like to talk to you sometime, Mrs Leviston; I think you'd understand."

For my part, at that moment I was thinking I couldn't understand the reason for his get-up, let alone his desire to do something different, when two heads appeared coming up the area steps. They were those of Mr Brown and his policeman son, and no sooner had the young policeman spotted the Mohican than defences were up on all sides.

"What do you want here?" demanded Mr Brown.

"Is he pestering you, ma'am?" This from the young policeman; and now a bark from the Mohican as he swung round, yelling, "No! I wasn't pestering her, copper." He spat out the last name. "I was just having a word with. . ."

"I know what you lot are just having. Now get yourself away and quick if you don't want any trouble. Now I'm. . ."

"Officer" - my voice sounded cool, icy, even to myself - "this young man happens to be a -" I paused on the word "friend", but I'd no sooner got it out than the Mohican put in, "Mrs Leviston's being kind in calling me friend. I'm not a friend of hers but a friend to the daughter of her daily, and I wanted to leave a message for her. That's why I've dared to walk on the pavement in this part of town. Now what d'you make of that?"

Both Mr Brown and his son looked at me, and I said quietly now, "He's right." Then turning towards the young fellow, I said, "Go on up and see her. It's the top floor."

He made no move for a moment but glared at the policeman. Then bending to the side towards where his two companions had come within earshot, he yelled, "I'm under surveillance," and had just turned back to the door when it opened again and out stepped the Captain and his wife. Then an odd thing happened, and I wasn't imagining it: on the sight of them there passed over the Mohican's face a look of surprise; then he turned his head quickly away and his gaze fell on to the policeman, and I thought, Ah, someone from his past, he recognized him; but although there was little chance of he himself having been recognized, the next moment, with head down, he almost slithered past the couple and entered the hall, and the Captain, looking at Mr Brown, said, "Where's he off to?"

It was I who answered him: "He's going up to my flat with a message, Captain," I said.

"Well, well." He looked from Mr Brown to the policeman, then to the two American civil war relics passing us now, and when one of them snorted like a pig, he cried, "Scum! Scum! They should be put into the army. . . Perverts. I would shoot the lot of them, horsewhip them."

What caused my silly mind to make me enquire, "Put them in the army before or after shooting them, Captain?"

What?"

And stupidly I still persisted: "Would you horsewhip them before you shot them or after, or. . ." My voice trailed off as he shifted his piercing gaze from me to his wife, then to Mr Brown, then to the policeman, and because he seemed lost for a reply I now said, "If you'll excuse me," and edging my way between Mr Brown and his son I walked away down the street.

When I crossed over the road towards the private gardens that fronted the terrace I knew that the four people I had just left were now deep in conversation, the while their eyes were following my progress.

Each of the tenants had a private key to the gardens and for only the third time since I'd lived here I used mine this morning and went in. The trees were bare, the shrubs and bushes heavy with hoar-frost and overall there was a silence. It was strange, as I had found before, how once you passed through the gate you were in a different world. I looked down on this garden from the drawing-room window every day, but you had to walk in it to feel its presence, and it had a presence all of its own. Now, as I passed round the shrubbery into the rose arbour where the bushes looked like bits of small dead twigs sticking out of the earth, I promised myself that I would come here more often.

Under the designed overhang of a stone wall was a wooden bench. The front of the seat still showed the frost clinging to it, but nevertheless I sat down, then drew a few deep cold breaths and looked across one of the beds to where a cherub's head protruded from a wall, its mouth agape but with no water pouring from it now. The head reminded me somewhat of Harold, and I should have felt heartened by the fact, but I didn't.

It was Friday again all right. It had started with Gran as it usually did; and then this morning there was Janet with her news that Harold's father was, as one would say, a freelance now, and why this should trouble me I didn't know. Yet it did. Then that scene with the Mohican. As my mind touched on that I thought, I don't like that Captain. As for the young policeman, he was, I thought, just doing his duty as he saw it, and I had to admit that the Mohican did look very out of place in this part of town. Yet London was free and open to all. If he had just been walking up the street likely there would have been no open opposition to him; it was the fact that he stopped outside a house and he was talking to a woman, perhaps begging, even on the point of mugging her. Yes, I could see the policeman's point of view.

Oh dear me! what more today? What would that doctor say after he had examined me? Well, I must get up and on my way to find out. Yet, I was reluctant to leave this spot, although the cold was beginning to penetrate even my fur coat. I recalled other times when I had sat on a park bench, but always at these times I had had Hamilton for company. He would lean his hooves on the back of the bench while giving me advice. As if now expecting him to appear I looked from side to side, but there was no sign of him: my mind had apparently sent him to regions beyond recall. Harold had taken his place; and Tommy too. Oh yes, Tommy too. What was I going to do about Tommy? And again the question arose: Did I love him? If I was comparing the feeling I had for him with that which I held for Nardy, no I didn't love him. Yet, were he to go out of my life now I should miss him greatly. So what did I feel for him? Affection? Yes, a quite deep affection, but it wasn't love. It was more than a year now since Nardy had gone from me and the pain of his loss was still with me, not so sharp, but nevertheless there.

If you're going to the doctor's you had better get on your way.

I got abruptly to my feet: it was as if Hamilton had spoken. But then, what had Hamilton been but my inner self; I might not see him any more but his voice remained. . .

Doctor Bell had finished his ordinary surgery. He greeted me kindly. What was my trouble?

I told him.

"Ah, well, we must see what it's all about, mustn't we? Just go behind the screen and the nurse will attend to you."

Mike had never had a nurse in attendance. What Mike had said and would still say was, "Get your clothes off." His manner had been rough at times, oh very rough, but he never treated me as a child.

The nurse appeared from somewhere behind the screen, smiled sweetly at me and without a word began to help me undress, making me feel very like a cross between the child suggested by the doctor and a geriatric.

Doctor Bell came in, smiled benignly, and rubbed his hands together as he said, "It's a cold morning." They were still cold when they touched my flesh.

After prodding and probing for a time, he said, "You say you feel the pain mostly in the stomach?"

"Yes; mostly; but in other places too, in my chest."

He sat me up and tapped my back; told me to say ah; told me to take a deep breath. Then he tried the reflexes of my legs; asked a few more questions, then left me to the ministrations of the nurse again.

Later, seated at one side of his desk I was again reminded of Mike and my regular Monday morning visits to his surgery and his acid tones and his bristling beard, but only by comparison with this doctor who, in a very quiet voice, said, "As far as I can ascertain, Mrs Leviston, I can find nothing wrong." He coughed, leant back in his chair, put his fingertips together and then said, "You are no doubt still feeling the loss of your husband, yes?"

"Oh, yes, yes, I still miss him very much."

"Well, my dear, I think that there might lie the problem of your movable pains."

I stiffened. "You think I'm imagining them?"

"No, no, not at all, they're very real to you, but as far as I can gather they have no organic source: you haven't any lumps or tender spots, your chest is sound, your heart is very good. What you likely need is just a tonic, and I shall give you a prescription for that." He leant forward now and began to write. Having finished, he got to his feet, came round the desk, handed me the slip of paper and, reverting to his fatherly manner, bent over me and said, "Now if we don't feel any better in a week or so, drop in again and see me, eh?"

I allowed a short silence to fall between us before, looking him straight in the face, I said, "I'll do that."

A certain amount of indignation caused me to walk briskly home. He thought I was imagining the pain. Likely, he had read my first book, *Hamilton*, and come to the conclusion that if I could think up a horse with which I held conversations then it would be quite easy for me to create a few pains here and there.

As soon as I got in the house Janet greeted me with, "There's been a phone call from the school. And what did you think of Big Chief Workshy having the nerve to call here? I gave him the length of me tongue. He's off again. And I ask you, Mrs Leviston, ma'am, where does he get the money? Of course, he's on the dole but that doesn't pay for his flittin' 'ere and there. I said to him. . ."

"Who was it phoned from the school, Janet?"

"It was a man. I think it could have been the headmaster 'cos . . . well, he spoke nice, pleasant like."

I almost grabbed up the phone, and when I heard the school secretary's voice at the other end I asked her to put me through to Mr Binn.

"Oh, good-morning, Mrs Leviston."

"Good-morning. . . You wanted to speak to me?"

"Yes. I wondered, if you had the time, could you pop in sometime today?"

"What's wrong? Is anything wrong?"

"Oh no, no, no, nothing serious."

I wanted to ask now, Is it to do with Harold? Of course it was to do with Harold. He had been up to something. Or perhaps not; perhaps it was to do with the choir. I understood the choirboys were in need of new cassocks; perhaps it was something to do with that. My voice had a light tone to it as I said, "I could come straightaway."

"There is no rush; whatever time suits you."

"Very well." I put the phone back on its stand and turned to where Janet stood near the kitchen door as she asked, "He's in trouble?"

"No, no. As far as I can gather, no. I think it must be something to do with his going into the choir."

She turned away laughing now, saying, "Good Lord! Him in the choir. God help 'em!"

"He's got a lovely little voice."

"Yes, I know that, Mrs Leviston, ma'am, but it's what 'e says with it or sings with it."

"Oh, Janet."

"You can say it like that, ma'am, but you'll never make an angel out of him."

"I don't want to make an angel out of him; anything but; I like him as he is."

She laughed again. "As I said to Hilda last night when she was on about her Indian Chief, there's no accountin' for tastes."

When I left the kitchen Sandy followed me into the study and I picked him up and when he nestled his head into my neck I walked the floor with him, rocking him gently as I would have a child. He liked this, and as I walked I talked to him: "Funny about Janet's attitude to Harold, isn't it? She's expecting the worst. But then, so do they all. They see him as a rip, a living terror. Why is it that I see him as a little boy who needs love and gives it? I wonder what the headmaster really wants to talk about?" I looked at the clock. It was just turned twelve. They'd be at lunch now, and anyway Janet would have mine ready in a very short time.

I stopped my prancing and dropped Sandy to the floor, which he didn't take to very well, so he went and curled himself up in the corner of the couch. Then I sat down at my typewriter, telling myself that I must get down to work, back into the routine I had got out of recently for if I didn't keep on with this present book I'd lose the theme.

My good intentions lasted for only twenty minutes; then Janet called me to lunch, after which I got dressed for outdoors again, not in my fur coat and hat this time, but more soberly and ordinarily as befitted the mother of a little boy. . .

Mr Binn seemed pleased to see me. "Do take a seat, Mrs Leviston," he said.

But he himself did not take the seat behind his desk; instead, he sat perched casually on the edge of it, seemingly to create an atmosphere that was light and easy. Yet he was reluctant to begin the conversation, so I said, "Is it about Harold going into the choir you wish to see me?"

"No, I'm afraid not, Mrs Leviston." His words came out on a kind of stuttering laugh. "Quite the reverse I would say."

I suddenly became cold inside. Oh! dear God, don't let them tell me that Harold has been coming out with language again. He had promised me.

"Oh, don't look so concerned; it's not all that serious, it's just something that . . . well, we'll have to nip in the bud, so to speak."

"What has he done?"

"Oh, it isn't what he does, as I think you might know, it's what he says."

"Swearing?"

"No, I wouldn't say swearing. But you know . . . well, I don't need to tell you he's a bright little boy, in fact his teacher says he's amazing for his age, and he's got an imagination. Moreover he's a bit of a comic actor, besides being something of a rhymester. And this is the point in question at the moment, so if you could help us to curb his leanings in this direction things would go along more smoothly. You understand?"

"Offensive rhymes?"

"Well" - again a shaky laugh - "not exactly offensive, more crude I would say. You know what children are."

No, I didn't; I only knew what Harold was, and I'd heard some of his rhymes.

"You know how. children get hold of a name. Look at mine for instance, Binn, my nickname's" - he leant towards me - "Dusty, or Three-two-one. You know, the television game."

Yes, yes, I knew the television game. But I waited, wanting to say, "Get on with it."

Mr Binn got on with it. "A lot of children do this, you know, but Harold has become quite an expert at it. Candidly I was going to speak to you some time ago but I thought it would fade away, children have phases, you know, but then two things have happened this week. A little girl, she's a spoilt little thing I must admit, but she went home crying because the boys were chanting after her: it was a combined chorus of three or four of them, and our composer had gone to the trouble of printing it out so that his confederates could learn the words by heart." He now reached back on to the desk and passed me a piece of paper, saying, "There's more to come, I'm afraid." The smile was still on his face.

I looked at the writing on the paper. Yes, this certainly was Harold's hand, and I read: "Millie Stott has two bots that she sits on a lot, so she gets spots on her bot, Millie Stott, silly clot. "

What could I say? It was so silly, so childish. There was only one thing I was thankful for: he had used bot instead of bum or, even worse still, arse. I looked at the headmaster and when he said, "Silly, isn't it?" I nodded. Then his tone altering, he said, "Yes, it's silly to us but to a little girl being followed by three or four boys chanting that in the street, you can understand she would arrive home crying. It resulted, of course, in a visit from her mother; but I'm afraid that is not all."

I bit my lip, and when for the moment he didn't continue to speak I felt like actually shouting, "Well, let's have it!"

"You have met Miss Scottie?"

"Yes."

"Well, I can tell you straight away, she is quite fond of Harold, but she has to chastise him very often. One of Miss Scottie's main endeavours is to instil good manners into her pupils, so every morning she insists that they stand up and greet her with 'Good-morning, Miss Scottie.' And yesterday morning she was a little late going to her class and as she approached it she heard chanting, and there was the bold Harold conducting a chant which went: "Good-morning, Miss Scottie. If you hit us again with the ruler you'll end up in the cooler"."

He laughed outright now, saying again, "Sounds so silly, doesn't it? But as you can imagine it's very difficult to keep discipline against an opponent like Master Harold. From what I understand about the matter, she had tapped his hand with his ruler some time before when she found him eating chewing-gum.

I drew in a deep breath. Chewing-gum. I'd forbidden him to buy chewing-gum after I'd found it stuck on the corner of his dressing-table and then between the leaves of a book.

But Mr Binn now came off the edge of the desk and faced me. "There is something slightly more serious, innocent in a way, yet with repercussions that I am afraid could bring many parents about my ears, especially, as you know, that this is a Church School."

I felt sick.

"As you know I had hopes of Mr Stevens taking him into the choir, and yesterday afternoon he called to see Miss Dixon. She was taking the singing class. Harold was present. As Mr Stevens wished to discuss

something with Miss Dixon they walked into the corridor. I happened
to come along at that moment and the three of us stood talking until we
heard giggles, then smothered laughter coming from the music room. I
myself glanced through the window and saw a small figure doing
what I suppose would be called a turn for the rest of the class." He
paused here. "I can still smile at his impression of Mr Frankie Vaughan
doing his act. The small figure was leaning back, his legs kicking out,
he was waving an imaginary straw hat and he was singing -" He
stopped.

My voice was harsh now as I said, "I'm waiting for the worst; you'd
better finish."

"Well" - he paused - "you know his signature tune, 'Give me the
moonlight, give me the girl, and leave the rest to me'?"

"Yes, I know that."

"Well -" I watched him wet his lips before he said, "add to those
lines -" Again he paused; then slowly he brought out the words, "And
I'll put a bun in your oven straight after tea."

If Gran and George had been here they'd have howled with laughter;
if Nardy had been here he would have covered his eyes and choked;
but there was only me, and I certainly didn't laugh. I didn't smile. I
turned my head to the side and looked through a tall window to where
the children were stampeding into the schoolyard.

"You can understand my situation?"

I looked back at him and muttered, "Yes. What . . . what do you
intend to do?"

"Well, really, I'm going to leave that to you. The little fellow has no
idea of the implication of his rhyme."

"It wouldn't be his rhyme," I put in quickly; "it's what he's heard his
uncles say, at least one of them who considers himself a mimic."

"Oh? I'm sorry this situation has arisen, but, you see, this is a Church
School and . . . and we have standards. Oh, I know children say
naughty things, but I'm afraid our dear little Harold is a connoisseur in
that direction. Anyway, do you think you can help him curb his
exuberance?"

"I'll try. I have, so far, succeeded in stopping him swearing. At least I
think I have."

"Well that's good; so we'll leave the matter in abeyance for a time,
shall we?"

"Thank you."

He opened the door for me, saying kindly now, "Try not to worry
too much about the matter; we shall do our best at this end. We do
know the circumstances of your taking him under your wing and I can
assure you we will help to turn him into a good Christian individual."

I did not even wish him goodbye. I walked along the corridor, passing scampering children. A good Christian individual, Harold. Anyway, where was he?

I was in the schoolyard now, and for a moment I felt like Janet: when I got hold of him I'd box his ears right and left. . . No, I wouldn't; that had never done any good. . . There he was, near the gate talking to two boys of his own age.

"Harold!"

He turned round towards me, "Oh. Hello. I didn't know you were 'ere. Why'd yer come? I can go 'ome on me own. . . This is me muvver." The last statement was made to his two companions, and under other circumstances I would have felt a surge of pride for he usually had difficulty in calling me mother, except when it was preceded by Mrs Nardy.

"He's Robbie Tennant and 'im's John Rankin." He was stabbing his finger toward each boy now. "They're me friends."

The boys stared at me; one sniffed, the other said, "'Allo, missis" which made me realize just how quickly Harold's speech reverted when he was among his schoolmates; and I had been congratulating myself on the way he had seemingly responded to my correcting his speech.

"Come along," I said. Harold now grabbed my hand and walked from his friends without more ado.

It wasn't until we had entered the house that it dawned upon him I hadn't spoken all the way from the school, and, stopping his chattering, he looked up at me, saying, "What's the matter?"

"I'll tell you what's the matter when you get your hat and coat off and come into the study."

Within seconds he had followed me along the corridor and into the room. When I sat down on the couch and he went to sit beside me I pulled him upwards and made him stand in front of me. And after a moment of staring at him I said, "You've done it again, haven't you?"

"What, me?"

"Yes, you."

"I've never swored, I mean sweared . . . I've never sweared at school. I never 'ave."

"You may not have sworn but you have written silly things, and encouraged the other children to say them, and said objectionable things."

"Object . . . what object . . . able things?"

"We'll come to that part in a moment."

I reached out to my bag on the table, opened it, then handed him the piece of paper that the headmaster had given to me.

"Who wrote that?"

He looked at it, then looked at me and said, "It was only in fun. "

"I see nothing funny about it. It is crude and rude. And what is more, you intended to hurt the little girl. I'm ashamed of you, going along the street bawling that out at a little girl."

"She's not a little girl, an' she's daft." He was bristling now.

"And I suppose Miss Scottie is daft too?"

"No, she's not, she's all right."

"Then why did you make silly rhymes up about her?"

He moved from one foot to the other, pushed out his lips, looked to the side, then said, "Well, she hit me on the knuckles with the ruler and it hurt."

"You must have been doing something wrong for her to do that."

"I wasn't. I was only -" He stopped, then stood staring at me, and I moved my head twice as I ended for him, "Only sticking chewing-gum on the lid of your desk and soiling the books with it. What did I tell you about chewing-gum?"

"I never bought it."

"Don't lie to me, Harold, else I'll become angry with you."

"I'm not lyin' to yer." There it was again; that's because he was angry. "I don't tell lies. I don't."

That had been true up till now; I'd never found him out in a lie.

"I didn't buy it. Millie Stott gave me a stick."

"Oh" - I raised my eyebrows - "Millie Stott. That's the little girl you don't like, the one you made the rhyme up about, isn't it?"

"Yes."

"Then if you don't like her why did you take the chewing-gum from her? You shouldn't accept gifts from people you don't like."

"I didn't take it, she pushed it into my pocket. And I don't like her, she's soppy. She wants to be me girl friend."

"Your . . . your girl . . . friend?"

He wriggled self-consciously, and even as I said, "I can't understand why a sweet little girl would want you for a boy friend," I knew I could understand perfectly well the attraction of this tough little individual; but up till now I had dealt with the simple things, now I had to tackle the more serious bit.

"About this imitation of yours, when you were doing Frankie Vaughan."

"I can do him as good as Uncle Max." His face was bright.

"Maybe, but you don't sing the right words."

"*I do.*"

"*You don't.*"

"*I do, Mrs Nardy, I do*: Give me the moonlight, give me the girl and leave the rest to me. . ." He was standing still, but his body was moving with the words when I stopped him here, saying, "Yes, that's what Frankie Vaughan sings, but not the next line."

"What?" He screwed up his face. "And I'll put a bun in your oven straight after tea. Not that line?"

"Definitely not that line."

"*He does! Frankie Vaughan does.*"

"*He doesn't!*" My voice was a bawl now, matching his. "Your Uncle Max made that line up and it's not nice, in fact it's very nasty."

He put his head on one side and looked at me as if he was sorry for me because I didn't know what I was talking about. Then he said, quietly for him, "But Gag puts buns in the oven every Sunday mornin' before she puts the meat in, and we have 'em for tea, and there's never any left, and she goes on about it."

I closed my eyes for a moment against the transient innocence of the young. Then I said softly, "The buns that Janet . . . I mean your grandmother puts in the oven are not the same as those referred to in the line that your Uncle Max sings. Do you understand?" I asked while knowing at the same time that he didn't understand. And he shook his head before asking quietly, "They're not Sunday buns?"

"No, they're not Sunday buns."

"What kind of buns then?"

Oh! dear me, where did I go from here? Could I say to this small boy that the bun he was singing about referred to a baby? No, I couldn't, for his mind, being as alert as it was, would certainly go ferreting further were I to attempt to explain, so I said, "It's just a word that refers to something else that isn't nice, nasty."

He stared at me in perplexity for a moment. "Like swearin'?" he said.

I paused before saying, "Yes, yes, in a way, but more so . . . nasty. "

"Than swearin'?"

"Yes, than swearing."

"And you don't want me to say it any more?"

"I'd be happy if you didn't."

"But I can still do Frankie Vaughan?"

"Oh yes, you may still do Frankie Vaughan."

He smiled now. That was that for him, the chastisement was over, and immediately he leant towards me, his finger crooked, his head poked out. His voice had changed and he said, "Here a minute. Here a minute; there's more. I had a letter from me mother."

"My mother," I said.

"*Me* mother," he said, as he went through the motion of pulling out the imaginary letter. And it was such a good imitation of Jimmy

Cricket that I burst out laughing, pulled him towards me and hugged him, and he, putting his arms around my waist, hugged me in return. Then pushing him abruptly from me, I said, "I want you to promise me something, really promise me."

His face was bright, his eyes were shining, he said nothing, but waited.

"I want you to promise you'll not make up any more rhymes about the children at school or the teachers. Promise?"

He nodded readily, saying, "All right, all right, I'll promise. Stick me finger in me eye, spit and swear I hope to die."

"What?"

"That's what we say when we promise, and if we break it we'll drop down dead."

"Oh, I see. Well, before you decide to drop down dead I think we had better have some tea, hadn't we?"

"Yes." He jumped away and made for the door. "What have we got?"

"Go into the kitchen and see."

We had just finished our meal when the bell rang and I stopped Harold from dashing into the hall by saying sharply, "Stay put!"

When I entered the outer hall I was surprised to see Tommy stepping out of the lift.

I greeted him with, "You're early."

"I've been seeing an author, quite near." He came towards me and, bending, he kissed me on the cheek. As he was taking off his overcoat Harold appeared in the kitchen doorway. "Hello," he said. "Want a cup of tea?"

"Oh, that would be splendid. Please."

"O.K." Harold disappeared, and as we walked towards the drawing-room Tommy said, "He seems to be in good form."

"Good form? Wait till you hear."

As I related Harold's school performance Tommy laughed, and when I came to the Frankie Vaughan piece he lay back on the couch and bellowed until the tears ran down his cheeks.

"That boy will go far," he said; "but you've taken on a handful," and after passing a handkerchief over his face he remarked nonchalantly, "and I think you need a hand with him. What do you say?"

"Oh, Tommy."

Quickly now his mood changed, and, gripping me by the shoulders, he pulled me round to him, saying, "Don't say 'Oh Tommy', in that way. It's over a year now since Nardy went. He understood the situation, you know he did, and he wouldn't want you to go on living alone. Oh, Maisie, apart from loving you and needing you, I want to look after you. You've had so many rough rides, I want to smooth the path ahead."

"I didn't have a rough ride with Nardy, it was a magnificent ride. I. . ."

"You know what I mean. But now . . . tell me truthfully now, how do you feel about me? How have you come to feel about me over the past year? Tell me."

I looked at him; then looked away and said quietly, "I'm very fond of you, I've grown more fond of you, but . . . but, Tommy, I can't say I love you, not like I did Nardy."

"I don't expect you to love me as you did Nardy. There are all ways of loving, all kinds of love; I'd be content with your affection, content with anything as long as I can stay near you."

I looked back into his eyes. There must have been an amazed expression in mine that was reflected in my voice as I said, "I can never understand it, I never will until the day I die, how men like Nardy and you could love someone like me. I sometimes think it's as if you were both under some spell that has changed your sight, and you see me as entirely different from what I am, as someone tall, slim, beautiful, gracious. . ."

He laughed gently now, saying, "No, our sight was not affected, my dear; we see you as someone small, plain but petite, but with a something that neither of us could define: character is an inadequate word; you have a natural drawing power and something that created in us a tenderness. . ."

Again I said, "Oh! Tommy," interrupting his flow of words and in doing so bending slightly towards him and lifting my hand with the intention of placing it on his cheek. But the action was fatal; it had the same result as when I was dealing with Harold: Tommy's arms came round me and for the first time his mouth fell hard on mine, and to my surprise I let it remain there, and I knew that I would not have withdrawn from him but for a voice saying gruffly, "I brought your tea."

I pulled myself from Tommy's embrace and there, over the end of the couch, I saw Harold standing in the middle of the room, a cup and saucer in his hand. Making my voice sound ordinary, I said, "Well, fetch it here."

He approached slowly and the cup rattled in the saucer and the tea spilled over as he handed it to Tommy, who said quietly, "Thank you, Harold."

Now my boy turned and confronted me.

"He was kissin' you."

I drew in a deep breath, saying "Yes, yes, he was kissing me."

"What for?"

This I wasn't called upon to answer because Tommy put in quietly, "Because I like her very much, like you do, I love her."

"You don't."

"Oh, but I do."

"Not like me you don't. Bloody well you don't, not like me."

"Harold!"

"Well, he doesn't. He's a big silly bugger all 'cos he's got a swanky car. Gag says he's a bloody mani . . . nac in it. Why'd you let him?"

"Harold!" My voice was loud. "That is enough. Go in the kitchen and give Sandy his tea."

"Won't. I'm goin' 'ome." And as he marched away I went to rise from the couch, but Tommy's hand stayed me. "Let him go," he said; "it was a natural reaction, he'll get over it."

"Will he? You don't know him. Oh dear me." I leant back and put my hand to my brow. "This has been the most irritating kind of day, right from early morning when I phoned Gran." I made to rise again, and again Tommy stayed me, saying, "Don't; he's likely packing his case." He smiled now. "He'll cool off, you'll see." Then he added, "One of the reasons I came round early was to ask you if you'd like to see Pack of Lies at the Lyric. Judi Dench and Michael Williams are in it."

"Oh, I couldn't, not tonight, Tommy."

"Yes, you could. This is the very night to do it, to leave him with the Captain and his lady. He'll miss you and likely run into your arms when you come back. And you did say he goes off with his father tomorrow, and I know that's not pleasing him. Now, is it? Well, that should show him on which side his bread's buttered. Don't worry, my dear." Again he put his arm around me and, looking into my face, he said, "I've kissed you, really kissed you, short but sweet" - he smiled - "but it's a beginning. What say you?"

I now did put my hand on his cheek and said quietly, "Let it go from here then."

"As you wish."

"I must go and see what he's up to."

"Go on then" - he pushed me from the couch- "you're like a little hen with her first chick."

A little hen with her first chick. Yes, he was right.

And he had been right too about packing the case, because there Harold was, in his bedroom, all his underwear from the top drawer of the chest thrown on the bed. He must have just pulled open the second drawer as I entered the room and was about to take out shirts.

"What are you doing?" I asked quietly.

"I'm goin' away, like I said."

"Oh? Where are you going to?"

He swung round. "I'm goin' back to Gag's. I told you."

"Oh, I'm sure she'll be pleased to hear that. Well, if that's the case I'd better go and phone her and prepare her." I had reached the door when he said, "You don't like me any more."

"Don't be silly." I looked back at him over my shoulder.

"You were kissin' him."

"Yes, of course. And I kiss you, don't I?"

"You shouldn't kiss him; he's a bloody big goof; I'll kick his shins." Three or four shirts were sent flying across the bed.

I was immediately at his side. Gripping him by the shoulders, I shook him hard. "Stop acting like a stupid little boy. And you know I could never let you go back to Gran's. And you know I love you more than anything in the world."

"More than 'im?"

"In a different way."

"What different way?"

"I can't explain; you'll understand when you're older. But I do love you, Harold, and I want you, and I don't want you to go back to Gran's. I'd miss you so, so much."

His lips trembled, his eyes blinked, as I said, "If you love me you wouldn't hurt me by saying you want to go back to Gran's."

"I do, I do love you." His arms were round my neck and he was gabbling unintelligibly now as the tears rained down his face, and I, stroking his hair and holding him tightly, soothed him, saying, "There now. There now. It's all over. And you know something? Mr Tommy likes you very much. He thinks you're a very bright boy and will grow up very clever. He was talking the other day about teaching you to swim, really swim. He's a great swimmer."

"Don't want to swim. Don't like him."

I pressed him from me, dried his face, and said, "Harold, you must not tell lies, you do like him. You told me you do."

"Is he gona live here?"

"Not for a long time, not until you're older."

"How older?"

"Oh." I thought as I moved my head from one side to the other, then said, "Oh, a year, perhaps two."

This long length of time seemed to satisfy him.

"And will he sleep with you like Grandad does with Gag?"

I made myself consider for a moment before I said, "Well, yes, perhaps."

He gave a shake to his shoulder as he turned from me, saying, "I'd be growed up by then in a year or two."

"Yes, of course you will. I tell you what: I'll put your things away again if you go and tell Mr Tommy that you're sorry."

"I can put me own things away."

He now grabbed up some of his underwear from the bed and as he did so I saw a pound note lying on the counterpane.

As yet I gave him only fifty pence for his pocket money at the weekend besides ten pence each day for some sweets. I asked him now, "Where did you get that from?"

He picked up the note and, taking it to the drawer, he pushed it down the side, saying, "Somebody gave it to me."

"Who?"

"I'm not to tell."

I stared at him. If his uncles had given him the money then he would have no compulsion crying aloud their generosity. It was likely his father. But why had he said not to tell? I let the matter pass, but now reverted to a little diplomacy that I found worked with him. "Would you mind, Harold," I asked, "if I went out to see a show with Mr Tommy tonight?"

Never in his short but wide-awake life had he been deferred to, had anything been requested of him, or his opinion been asked. On the contrary he had been ordered to do this or that and told what would happen to him if he didn't do it. In consequence, I'd found he'd become quite amenable when deferred to. But I also saw, on this occasion, that his permission was being granted very much against his will, for after flinging some more of his underwear into the drawer, which I immediately straightened, he said, "I don't care."

"Thank you." I now sat on the edge of the bed and pulled him towards me and, with my face on a level with his, I said softly, "I love you very much, the best in the world. Always remember that." I didn't attempt to kiss him as I didn't want any more tearful embraces, not at this moment, but, pushing him gently away, I said, "Go on, tell Mr Tommy you're sorry you swore at him."

Head down, he left the room, and a minute or so later I followed him, but outside the drawing-room door, which was half open, I stopped, arrested by his voice saying, "She says you can't sleep in her bed, not like Mr Nardy, not for two years anyway. "

"She did, did she? Not for two years?" Behind Tommy's serious tone there was a note of laughter. There followed a short silence and I was prevented from pushing the door further open by Harold's voice saying now, "She's my muvver."

"Yes, I know she is. You're lucky to have a mother; I haven't got a mother."

"You're too big to have a muvver." Oh! that word again.

"I'm not, what about all your uncles? They have a mother."

"I didn't mean big, I mean old."

"I'm not that old."

"Yes, you are. Anyway, all muvvers die when you grow old, or they leave you before you're five."

"They do?"

"Yes."

I felt I'd better make my appearance at this stage because Tommy would not be able to work out if mothers died because they were old, or because their sons were getting old, or why they left you before you were five. That last had a deep significance: his mother had left him when he was three.

I went in brightly, saying, "You know, Tommy, Harold and I hadn't quite finished our tea when you arrived and the cup he brought you must be cold now, so let's go into the kitchen and brew up again, eh? And Harold will give you a piece of his ginger cake. It's a very special ginger cake, it came in a tin from Fortnum and Mason's."

Harold turned and hurried from the room, whether at the thought of having another piece of ginger cake or the fact that he was still feeling upset I didn't know, but Tommy stopped me following him by catching my arm and, bending his long length down to me, whispering, "I understand there's been a discussion about my going into your bed."

I slapped at him and walked off, and as he followed me he laughed, and it had a very pleasant sound, a relieved sound. . .

At seven o'clock the Captain and his lady entered the flat. As usual he was all muscle and voice, she all dignity. And tonight she was wearing a long dated evening dress and a small silk shoulder cape that had seen better days.

"Well, well, well, here we are again."

The Captain was at his jolliest. "And where's my proteg_, the future chess champion. Oh, there you are, feller-me-lad. And already for bed. My! My!"

Harold had come from the passageway; he was dressed in his pyjamas and dressing-gown. I looked towards him, saying, "Say good-evening to the Captain and Mrs Beckingtree-Holland." Oh that name. . .

Harold now approached the Captain and, looking up at him, he said, "I'm not goin' to play chess any more, I want to play rummy."

"Rummy? Well, well. All right, sir, all right, rummy it shall be. I used to be a dab hand at rummy too. What are we going to play for tonight, pennies or pounds or liquorice allsorts?" He now put his head back and laughed and his lady wife, turning to me, said, "It's a very wild night, you're going to be buffeted. But then, of course" - her eyes slid to Tommy - "you have the car. How fortunate." Her gaze rested on me again. "About what time shall we expect you back?"

"About eleven I think. And . . . and I have left some cold salmon in the fridge and the usual accessories. There's a small gâteau, too."

"How nice. How nice."

I went towards Harold now and, bending down, I kissed him on the cheek, saying, "Be a good boy and go to bed at half-past eight. You will, won't you?"

He gave a small nod of his head but said nothing. I turned from him and amid nods and goodbyes we went out.

In the lift I laughed gently as I said, "You know, I feel that I've just left some strict parents and they were allowing me out for the first time." And Tommy, putting his arm around me, added, "And with a man." And for the second time he kissed me on the lips and I felt strangely happy. It was the first time I had actually felt this way since I had lost Nardy and I told myself it wasn't such a bad Friday after all. But that was only until the middle of the second half of the play when I was seized again by this awful pain in my stomach and chest and had to grip his hand tightly until it subsided.

Chapter 4

Saturday morning found me tired and listless. I had gone to bed about twelve o'clock last night, only to be wakened up at half-past with the pain again. It stayed longer than usual this time and left me wide awake wondering what on earth it could be, and I decided when the weather cleared a bit, for they had been having it very rough in the north, I'd make a trip back there and see Mike and get his opinion.

So I had almost to drag myself from the bed at eight o'clock because there was only an hour before Harold's father would appear on the scene, and I wanted the child ready; I did not want that man waiting about.

Harold took a lot of rousing. "Come on," I said; "that's a good boy; your father will be here shortly."

"I don't want to go."

"But you said he was going to take you to the pictures."

"I don't want to go to the pictures with him."

"Get up," I said abruptly. "Get washed. Do your teeth, then come and have your breakfast."

When later he entered the kitchen and Sandy ran to him to give him his morning greeting by standing on his hind legs and licking his face, for the first time in their acquaintance he was pushed aside while his playmate said, "Stop it! you soppy date."

"Do you want flakes or rice crispies?"

"I don't want nothin'."

Angrily I swung him round. "Now look here! I'm having no more of this nonsense. You're going out with your father and you're going to behave yourself. He has a right to see you. That was the arrangement. If you try to alter those arrangements you mightn't like it. Do you understand what I mean?"

He understood all right because he sat down at the table without another word. . .

By nine o'clock he was waiting in the hallway muffled up against the weather. And by five past when his father had not arrived I said, "Go and sit in the drawing-room where it's warm." He went, still not saying anything, and I went into the kitchen and began to wash the breakfast things.

When I next looked at the clock it was quarter past nine. Drying my hands, I now made my way to the drawing-room, but did not find Harold sitting before the fire with Sandy, who was now curled up on the hearthrug; instead, he was standing before one of the two china cabinets. The door was open and he was handling a miniature chest of drawers, pulling the drawers in and out.

"Harold! Haven't I told you about touching those pieces. You may look at them but I've told you not to take them out."

In his haste to put the piece back on the shelf he toppled another over and I snapped at him, "See what you've done!"

"I was only lookin'."

"You weren't looking, you were handling them."

As I closed the glass door of the cabinet I thought, I must clean them again.

Since coming into this house I had followed Nardy's method of twice a year polishing or washing the collection. There were over three hundred pieces in the two cabinets and not one more than six inches high. Nardy's father had been a collector of miniatures, and I understood there were some priceless pieces amongst them, especially the miniature silver tea service and the silver and gold Louis suite. This little set was a delight to look at as it was upholstered in green silk tapestry. There was also the copy of an Egyptian coffee jug, two inches high and of a beautiful design in silver, with a filigree lid.

The cabinet doors were never locked; in fact, there was only one key which, the cabinets being of different designs, did not fit both locks. Whilst going through Nardy's desk after his death I had found a catalogue of the collection.

When I turned from the cabinet Harold was standing on the hearthrug, and he looked at me and cried, "You're in a tizz, aren't you?"

"No, I'm not in a tizz, but you're in a temper . . . *aren't you?*"

He now dropped onto his hunkers and began to stroke Sandy as he muttered, "It's cold out, awful."

"I thought you were tough," I said quietly. When he turned his eyes up towards me and with a look almost of disdain at my stupid response, I was saved from saying anything further by the sound of the bell ringing, and I cried, "Here he is! Come on." And I took hold of his hand and tugged him down the room, across the inner hall and into the lift hall, just in time to see his father stepping from the cage. The man was smartly dressed if somewhat showy. He greeted us by saying, "All ready and waitin'." Then looking directly at me, he said, "It isn't very nice weather for taking a day out, more fitting to sit by the fireside. What d'you say?"

What I said was, "Harold is ready and waiting as you can see."

"Oh, I can see that." He put out his hand and screwed Harold's cap around, only for the child to jerk himself away and straighten his cap again.

"I'm a bit late but I can stick it on the other end, I suppose."

"Yes, if you wish, but as you say the weather is rough and I don't suppose you want him to stay out longer than four o'clock."

"Well" - he shrugged his shoulders - "it all depends on what we decide to do, isn't it, laddie?" He now looked down on Harold who stared back at him without speaking. Then looking beyond me to the inner hall he said, "It's bitter out. The first thing we'll do is to go and have a hot drink, I think."

I did not take up the suggestion but said somewhat tartly, "Well, that will fill in some of your time."

He gave me a hard stare before swinging round towards the lift again, saying to Harold, "Come on you!"

Harold, pausing for a moment, looked at me; and I bent down to him, saying, "Be a good boy. I'll see you later," and gave him a little push towards where his father was waiting, his hand now hovering over the lift button.

Looking at the child through the grid, I thought for a moment he was about to cry. I smiled at him and waved; then he was gone from my sight, and I turned and walked into the hall, where I stood looking around for a moment.

The place felt empty; in fact, it screamed emptiness. I felt I had to talk to someone and so, remembering my resolution in the night to contact Mike, I rang his number, forgetting that he would likely be in the midst of surgery at this time. Miss Price answered the phone, her polite tone enquiring who I was and what I wanted, and when I told her my name she said, "Oh, you, Mrs Leviston. Oh, I'll tell the doctor. He's got a patient with him but I'll tell him. Just hang on. Just hang on." It was another two minutes before I heard Mike's voice saying, "Well, hello there."

"Hello, Mike."

"How are you?"

"I don't really know, in a bit of a quandary."

"What's wrong?"

"As I said I don't really know. I . . . I've been having strange pains."

"Have you seen Doctor Bell?"

"Yes, but he seems to think I'm imagining them."

"What makes you think that?"

"His attitude. You know I'm very good at picking up the aura of doctors."

"Don't be cheeky. Where's your pain?"

After I had tried to describe the pain he said, "And you don't feel it so much in the daytime?"

"No. That's strange; I feel tired in the daytime, not well, but no pain."

"How early does the pain start?"

"Oh, sometimes around six, or seven."

"And it's never after two in the morning?"

"Well, as far as I can recall, no."

"I'm afraid your Doctor Bell could be right then."

"Oh, Mike."

"Never mind, Oh, Mike. Now if it keeps on you go to him again and ask for a thorough examination."

"What kind of an examination?"

"Well, how do I know unless I examined you. Get a hospital examination, there's a method now of putting a light inside, they can see everything."

"How nice for them."

"And for you if they find out nothing's wrong."

"Except with my mind."

"Could be. Could be."

"You're very comforting, I must say. Anyway, I thought of coming up to see you."

"I would like nothing better than to see you, but before you come you go to your own doctor and ask him for an examination. Now do you hear me?"

"All right. But I must say you haven't been much comfort."

"I never was."

I did not answer for a moment, then I said softly, "You know that's not true. Anyway, how's Jane?"

"Thinking about getting a divorce as she never sees me."

"I don't blame her."

"Anyway, there's one thing you can be thankful for, you're not at this end of the country at the moment, there's hardly a chimney left on any of the houses, and I've had three in this morning almost decapitated with slates. The roads are blocked, there's been a blizzard raging for the last two days. But I suppose living in your sunny south you've listened to it complacently on the news."

"Sunny South ended, it's enough to freeze you here this morning.

But nevertheless, snowbound or not, I wish I was up there at this moment."

"How's Tommy?"

"He's very well."

"Still paying attention."

"Yes."

"Why don't you marry him?"

"Oh, don't start that, Mike, I've got enough on my plate at the moment."

"What, sorry you adopted the barrow-boy?"

"No, I'm not sorry I adopted the barrow-boy. And he's no barrow-boy, he's an intelligent boy who will surprise everybody shortly."

"Well, from what I saw of him that wouldn't surprise me. I must go now; I've got another lunatic outside ready to attack me."

"Sorry I kept you, Mike, but I just wanted to talk to you."

"I understand, lass. I'm always here, and the phone's handy, ring whenever you like. 'Bye now."

"Goodbye, Mike."

I leant my elbows on the telephone table and dropped my face onto my hands. I was fortunate to have someone like Mike, oh yes, very fortunate. And I'd do what he said about an examination and that light because I was becoming worried about the way I was feeling.

Chapter 5

It was towards the end of February and I'd had the examination and I had known it. It had been preceded by a wash-out which almost knocked me out completely. Within two hours I was in the theatre, no anaesthetic, and the light certainly showed the doctor what was inside me, and I let him know it by the yell I gave. Then followed a barium test. What was left of me after that Tommy almost carried to the car; and I remained in bed the following day.

The result of the examination was there was nothing really wrong, perhaps a slight touch of diverticulitis, sort of a loose or weak bowel, so I was given to understand, which at odd times might cause pain, but nothing like the pains I described.

So Doctor Bell had sat back in his chair, put his fingertips together once more and said, "What more can I say? You're healthy." He had paused before adding, "Physically, you're healthy."

"Then I'm imagining this?" I said.

"Well, if you'd like to put it that way, Mrs Leviston. . . Is there anything worrying you?"

"Not a thing." And I could say this for Harold had seemingly reformed at school: I'd had a very good report from Mr Binn last week concerning him. No, I could say there was nothing worrying me.

"Perhaps," he said, "you should go away for a rest, a holiday."

I didn't want to go away for a holiday, at least not yet, and I told him so.

What I did was to go back home, look in the mirror and say, "What's the matter with you?" Then glancing from side to side, I said, "Hamilton, where are you? Please tell me what's the matter with me." But Hamilton did not appear.

Then one Saturday morning about the middle of March I found something to worry about. I found another four pound notes, this time in one of Harold's drawers. I waited for him to return from taking Sandy down the road and immediately, even practically before he had his coat off, I pulled him into the bedroom, opened the drawer, took out the notes and said, "Where did you get these other notes from?" He didn't answer for a moment, then said quietly, "From the same place what I got the first one from."

"Don't be cheeky, Harold; I asked you a question: who gave them to you?"

"I promised not to tell."

"You are going to tell me. You won't go out of this house again until you do tell me, nor will you get anything to eat. You'll stay in this room until you do tell me, and I'll stay with you."

He backed from me now and dropped down onto the edge of his bed. Then, his head down, he muttered something.

I bent over him: "What did you say? Who?"

"The Captain."

"*The Captain?*"

"Yes, *the Captain*. He gave them to me after we played cards, or chess, even when I didn't win, he said not to let on."

I stared down into the boy's angry countenance. I knew that the Captain did not like Harold - all his hail fellow well met was a pose - he, I think, considered him on the same level as the Mohican, scum, and it puzzled him why I should want to adopt such a child. So why should he want to give him money? Especially when they were so hard up that his wife had to baby-sit.

A few minutes later I slipped a coat on and went right down in the lift, rang the Captain's bell, then came up again onto the first floor, to be greeted by them both standing in the hallway, with a surprised look on their faces, and the lady greeted me, saying in her high-falutin voice, "We wondered who it was; we so seldom get visitors. But come in, my dear, come in. What can we do for you? Do you need us this evening?"

"No, no, it isn't about that I've come; I wanted to ask the Captain something."

"Go ahead then, lady, go ahead, ask." He was smiling.

"When you give Harold money why do you ask him not to tell me?"

I watched him turn his head and look at his wife, and she at him, before they both turned back to me when he said, 'Me, give Harold money?"

"Yes, five separate pounds."

"Huh! Huh!"

Now he was huh-ing towards his wife: "Did you hear that, me dear? Me giving five pounds away! Oh, Mrs Leviston" - he was addressing me again - "would I allow my wife to go baby-sitting in order to supplement our income if I had it in my power to give away five pounds to a little boy?"

I was sick to the pit of my stomach and my voice was small as I said, "You didn't?"

"No, of course I didn't." He again looked at his wife who was staring at him. Then she looked at me and said, "He said that the Captain had given him this money, really?"

"Yes."

Her face took on a sad expression and she bit on her lip; then she asked, "Where else do you think he might have got the money?"

Before I could make any comments the Captain said, "What about his father? That fellow seems to be pretty warm, the little I've seen of him, the way he comes swaggering in here."

"Yes" - I nodded - "it could be his father."

"Oh" - the Captain jerked his chin upwards - "it's amazing where boys get money from: they do exchanges, sell bits of things. I shouldn't let it worry you. Then of course there's his family, you must remember that, East Enders, a rough crowd, and some of those barrow-boys have money to burn. That's likely where it came from."

"But why would he say that you gave it to him?"

The answer came from his wife. "I suppose the child is looking for

9

respectability," she said.

There was no way to answer this; it was a statement that would have to be gone in to, argued over. When I muttered, "Thank you very much. I hope you don't mind my coming down," they both exclaimed, "Oh, no! not at all." And as they accompanied me to the door the lady said, "I will use the old phrase of making hay while the sun shines, my dear, so if you want to go out in the evenings I would take advantage of us over the next week or so; you see, my relative is returning sooner than she expected. Her husband is being transferred back. She had fully understood they would be away for a year. We'll be sorry to leave, it has been so pleasant here."

I merely nodded, then turned from them and went towards the door, accompanied by the Captain. As he saw me into the lift he said, "Not to worry, children get up to all kinds of tricks, especially those from the quarter from which your ward sprang. You've got to expect it."

I actually did feel sick, so much so that I could have retched. After I had closed my door I stood gripping the knob for a moment while staring at the blankness of it. I was up against something I had never considered possible. My charge had always appeared frank but now he had been proved a liar, and more, and facing up to this fact was what being a mother entailed. All the laughter, fun and games he had brought into my life sank beneath this latter vice, because stealing was a vice, acquired as the Captain had just intimated because Harold had been bred in the lowest end of the city; he had been brought up in a rough atmosphere. But enough of that! what was I talking about? There was not a more honest person on this earth than Janet, and her family might be rough-cast but each one of them, I'm sure, would have been the first to pull Harold up for lying . . . or stealing by trading.

I turned from the door. What was I thinking about? I'm sure Harold wouldn't steal; he was too straightforward, he. . .

He was a liar. Hadn't he told me that the Captain had given him this money? Was that not a barefaced lie?

Indignation now carried me forward at a rush into his room. He was still on the edge of the bed, but lying on his elbow now. "Stand up!"

He stood up, but not quickly.

"You told me the Captain had given you that money, didn't you?"

"Yes." His head was up, he was looking straight at me.

"You were lying."

"*What?*"

"Never mind, what, you heard what I said, you were lying."

"*No, I bloody well wasn't!*"

"Don't you dare swear at me."

He stepped back from me, crying loudly now. "I bloody well wasn't lying. He did give it me, five times he give it me."

"Harold." It was almost a scream. "I have just spoken to the Captain. He said he never gave you any money, and why should he when his wife and he have to baby-sit with you to earn extra money, so he can't afford to give pound notes away."

I watched him dash round the bottom of the bed, stare at me from the other side; then, bending over, he punched his fists into the counterpane, and screaming now, he cried, "Bugger! bloody hell! Hell! Hell! Hell!"

I wrenched him upwards and shook him almost fiercely. When his head stopped wagging, I said, "Don't you dare use that language in here!"

The tears spurting from his eyes, he cried back at me, "I will! I will! He did, he did give it me. He's a rotten bloody liar. If he says he didn't, bloody, bloody, bloody liar!"

"Stop it! Stop it this minute."

My own heart was racing, thumping against my ribs like a hammer. I pushed him away from me and I sank onto the edge of the bed and from there I stared at him. His face was screwed up, the tears were raining down his cheeks. I could swear that he was telling the truth. But the Captain?

The bell rang. I pulled myself up from the bed, saying, "Stay there!" only to be thrown the answer, "Won't. Goin' to Gag's. Gag'll believe me. Goin' to Gag's."

"You will stay there!"

Just in case he should carry out his threat I took the key from the inside of the door and locked it, and as I did so his fist battered on it and he yelled, "I'm goin' to Gag's. I'm goin' to Gag's."

I almost fell into Tommy's arms as he entered the hall.

"What is it? What is it, dear?".

Spluttering and almost crying myself now, I gave him a brief outline of what had happened.

He did not interrupt me, and after I had finished he still remained silent for a while. Then looking along the corridor, he said, "I'll have a word with him."

"You'll have to turn the key; I've locked the door."

I went into the kitchen now and sat down by the table. Why had this to happen? Why? Things would never be the same between us again, trust had been broken. And he wanted to go back to his grandmother's, not to his father I had noticed. Once outside I was sure he would make straight for Janet's. I'd . . . I'd better phone her and explain, I thought. Oh dear God! what next? I went into the hall again, got through to the corner shop and asked if they would be kind enough to ask Mrs Flood to come to the phone. I would hang on.

It was almost four minutes later when I heard Janet's voice say, "What is it? What's wrong? what's wrong, ma'am?"

"There's a little trouble, Janet. I'll . . . I'll try and be as brief as I can."

I finished with, "Once he's outside he'll make straight for you. I don't know what I'm going to do, Janet."

"Mrs Leviston, ma'am, I'll say this before I see him or hear anything more, if he said that man gave him the money I'd swear on my last penny that he did. There's one thing about that child, he has every fault under the sun, but not lying; he always took a pride in standing up and facing things. I'll be round as quick as I can."

"I'm sorry, Janet."

I don't think she heard because the phone was banged down.

As I rose from the chair Tommy came into the hall. He took my arm and led me into the drawing-room and there he said, "That boy's telling the truth. And I'll tell you something; I've never cared for the Captain; there's something . . . well, I don't know what it is, but I've met a number of his type, too much surface talk. I'll believe Harold any day before him, and I think you had better go and tell him you think the same."

"He won't listen to me now."

"Yes, he will. Tell him you're sorry."

When I entered the bedroom he was standing looking out of the window. I stood behind him and put my hand on his shoulder, only to have it shrugged off.

"I'm sorry, Harold."

He turned about. His eyes were swollen and still wet and his lips were trembling as he said, "You seen him again and he said he did?"

"No, I haven't seen him again, but I believe you. I do really."

"Because Mr Tommy told you to."

"No, not because Mr Tommy told me to, but because I know now I should have believed you right from the first; you wouldn't lie to me."

"Why . . . why didn't you say that before?"

"I don't know, I'm sorry."

"And you shook me, and 'urt me shoulders."

"Yes, I know, and I'm sorry for that too." I bent down until our faces were on a level and said softly, "You don't want to go to Gag's do you? You won't leave me and go to Gag's?"

He was silent for a moment. Then his face twisted, his arms came out and round my neck, and I hugged him close to me, so thankful that I said a prayer, which was unusual for me: Thank you, God. Oh, thank you, for I knew in this moment if I had lost this child Doctor Bell would have been right in his diagnosis, for my mind would really have skipped.

I was sorry now that I had phoned Janet for she'd come scampering round and the whole thing would be gone over again. Standing up now, I said, "Wash your face and then come and have a drink."

I stroked his hair back from his brow, and as I made for the door, he said, "Mr Tommy said he'd take me to a football match 'safternoon. Can I?"

"Yes, yes, of course. That'll be nice. Yes." I smiled at him.

Tommy wasn't in the drawing-room. I found him in the kitchen making some coffee. He turned from the stove, saying, "All right?"

"Yes, yes, I think so. Good move of yours to take him to the football match."

"Don't worry. Come and sit down." He pressed me on to a chair.

"I did a silly thing, I phoned Janet, she'll be round here any minute now. I was afraid he would run to her; he said he would."

"Oh dear. Well anyway, she'll find everything back to normal."

"I think that'll take some time."

We both looked towards the door now as the lift bell rang and I said, "That can't be her already. I . . . I hope it isn't the Captain. What'll I do if. . . ?"

"Go and see who it is." He pressed me gently forward.

And a minute later when I opened the door into the outer hall I was amazed to see the Mohican coming towards me from the lift.

He was smiling. Today he had two marks on each cheek and they seemed to form deep ruts in his face making him look almost an old man. "I'm deputising," he said. "I've . . . I've come in place of Mum."

"Oh. Oh, come in."

Inside the hall he stood for a moment, his glance flickering here and there as if he was appraising what he saw.

"We're in the kitchen just about to have coffee."

He followed me, his shoes, the uppers of which had been made to appear like moccasins, padding softly.

Tommy could not altogether hide his astonishment as he turned from the stove and saw the Indian. I had described the Mohican to him but my description did not live up to the flesh. I made the introduction fumbling somewhat: "This is Mr . . . John Drake, and this is Tommy . . . Mr Balfour." My short arm went out one way, my normal arm the other; then I said, "Sit down. Sit down, John."

"Thank you." He sat down at the corner of the table, and as he did so Tommy asked him, "Black or white?" A moment later I pushed the sugar basin towards him, saying, "Sugar?"

"No thanks." He smiled at me. I noticed his eyes again: they were deep brown nice eyes. Why on earth had he let himself go like this? Oh, what did it matter. Why had he come? That's what I wanted to know. And right away he gave me the answer to my unspoken question.

"If Harold said that the Captain . . . so-called, gave him that money, he was telling the truth."

"How would you know? And why do you say 'so-called'?"

"Because if he's ever been a captain it would have been in the Salvation Army. But then, of course, they wouldn't have had him." The furrows in his face deepened.

"Do you know him?" This came from Tommy.

"Oh yes, I know him."

"How on earth do you?"

The Mohican smiled a small tight smile now as he said, "Oh, me and my kind get around and mingle quite frequently with him and his sort."

"He isn't what he appears to be then?"

"Not by a long chalk. Oh no, not by a long chalk, Mrs Leviston."

I liked the way he spoke my name. "But he sounds educated," I said.

"Oh yes, you're right there: Public School; at least until he was thrown out. And you must give him credit for trying; I don't think there's an occupation at which he hasn't tried his hand, at least not one that would befit a scion of the upper class."

"How do you know all these things?" Tommy's voice was stiff.

"As I said, I get around."

"I should like a different answer to that."

There was no smile on the Mohican's face now as he replied, "You might like but it all depends on how much I want to give." And he stared at Tommy in evident hostility. Then looking at me he said, "Holland is a con man. I recognized him the other morning down in the hall although I hadn't seen him for almost two years when he came out after doing a stretch for embezzlement. Beckingtree is his wife's maiden name. She's as bad as him. They muscled in to our gang up in Harrogate; they thought we'd act as go-betweens, you know, passing on bits of stolen stuff, but our lot wasn't in on that kind of thing. If we were looking for trouble we only had to have a drag or dress up like this." He gave a slight grin now as he swept his fingers over his leather tunic, which caused the rows of spiked trinkets hanging from his neck to jangle. "We may do lots of things that offend the public eye -" he now turned his gaze towards Tommy before looking back at me and ending, "but nicking isn't one of them, at least -" his head went up now and he laughed deeply as he ended, "not from friends anyway."

"But why should he give Harold money then say he didn't?"

"That's got to be worked out, Mrs Leviston. To my mind he wants to lay something on the boy. What did he say to you when you went down to him?"

I told him practically what the Captain, so-called, had said.

"Huh! There you have got a clue in the suggestion that the lad might have been doing an exchange. Have you missed anything lately around the house?"

"No, no." I shook my head; then after a pause I said, "Well, nothing that is evident. There are a lot of specimens in the china cabinets." I half rose from the chair now, leant on the table and looked at Tommy and he said, "Let's go and see."

As we went towards the kitchen door, it opened and there stood Harold, his mouth agape, his face bright. "Hello, Johnny," he said.

"Hello, boyo," said the Mohican.

"What you doin' 'ere?"

"Well, well." The Mohican glanced at me. "I drop in to say hello to everybody and to see you in particular and I'm asked what I'm doing here. He has no manners, Mrs Leviston."

"He's very pleased to see you, John."

"Well, I wish he would show it."

Tommy pushed past us rather impatiently now, and we all followed him into the drawing-room; but there for the second time since entering the house the Mohican gazed about him. Then looking down at Harold, he said, "You weren't wrong, were you? You're a lucky fellow. Do you want a lodger? I'll sleep under your bed."

Harold pushed him and laughed, saying, "You'd smell."

"Oh boyo, no." The Mohican's voice was serious now. "That's one thing I don't do is smell. I have a bath every day; come hell or high water I wash. No, I don't smell."

Tommy's voice again cut in impatiently, saying, "Have a look here, Maisie." He had opened the first door of one of the cabinets. "At a glance, can you see anything missing?"

I scanned the shelves, then shook my head, saying, "No, but all the things are catalogued."

He walked from me down the room to the other cabinet, and once more I was standing looking at the shelves. Then I said, "Oh."

"You miss something?"

"One of the chairs to the little suite." I picked up the remaining one. "There were two of these."

"Have another look. What else?"

I looked again. "The silver miniature case, it used to lie in the corner; Nardy said his grandfather had got it from a general. He used to carry it in his pocket when he went into battle; it held the picture of his wife. And . . . and" - my voice was high now as I pointed to the back of the shelf - "the beautiful Egyptian coffee jug! It was only so high." I demonstrated with my fingers.

"Make sure it isn't on one of the other shelves."

"It couldn't be." I turned to Tommy. "They've always been on the same shelf and I've never altered Nardy's arrangement, nor he his father's."

I turned now swiftly and looked down on Harold, saying, "Did you ever see the Captain come near the china cabinets?"

He shook his head. "No; we just played cards or chess."

"He'd be much too clever to let anyone see him taking an interest in the china cabinets, or anything else in the house. He's no amateur is the Captain," said the Mohican. He now looked down on Harold, saying, "I could do with another cup of that coffee. May he go and get me one, Mrs Leviston? Or don't you let him pour out?"

"Oh, he can pour out, and he can make tea or coffee as good as the next. Go along, Harold, and get John a cup of coffee."

Whether Harold knew he was being dismissed or not, he didn't hesitate but left the room. And now the Mohican, looking at me, said, "I know what you'd like to do, go down and demand that they return these things. But by this time they will have been exchanged for a tenth of their value. And you'll have to be careful here because he would come back on the boy; you see you did go to him and ask if he had given the boy money. It would be only his word against the boy's. And as he said, boys are apt to do deals in exchange, and these things in here would look like little trinkets to any boy."

"Well, you seem to have the whole business in hand, what do you suggest?" Tommy's voice sounded curt, which made me want to turn on him and say, "You're judging him by his clothes, he's a nice boy." Oh, what a term that is. But he was nice; I sensed it. It would not have surprised me had the Mohican taken umbrage at the tone, but he contained his immediate feelings and said, "There are a number of shops he could have taken the stuff to, one in particular that I know of. The fellow deals with small bits like this. Could you make little drawings of the things missing?"

"Yes, yes I could, especially of the chair."

He asked now, "Have you a jewel-case or anything like that?"

"I haven't got a case but there are two trays fitted into the dressing-table drawer: one is fitted to hold rings, the other, brooches and suchlike, and I've got three or four little boxes with jewellery in them, pieces that my husband bought me."

"When did you last look at them?"

"Oh, I use the ring tray practically every day; as for the others I may not have opened the boxes . . . oh, perhaps for weeks."

"Would you like to go and have a look?"

I left the room, and in the hall I passed Harold bearing the requested cup of coffee. It was white, but I made no comment; only to say, "Mind you don't spill it."

In my bedroom I pulled open the top drawer of the dressing table and counted my rings. There were seven. Then I looked at the oddments on the brooch tray. As far as I could remember there was nothing missing from that. Now I picked up the first of the four boxes and in it there lay a gold-leaf spray of lily of the valley. It was a delicate thing. I recalled the day Nardy had given it to me. I closed the lid slowly on it and picked up the biggest box of the three. In it should have been a platinum and gold filigree brooch holding three small rubies and two diamonds representing the hearts and flowers in the centre of the exquisite work.

I closed my eyes tightly. My teeth were clenched together. I had the desire to rush from the room, spring into that lift, dash into that flat and accuse those two dirty thieves. Everything within me was racing. I quickly opened other boxes. One held a gold chain and pendant, the other was empty.

I entered the drawing-room, gasping now as if I had been running. I was about to burst out with my news when I saw Harold gazing at me. With an effort I held back and, looking at the Mohican, I said, "Was your coffee all right?"

"Yes, fine." I had noticed that the cup was empty and realized that neither the Mohican nor Tommy would ask in front of Harold what I had found. I did not realize though that I was beating my chest with the flat of my hand until Harold said, "What you doin' that for?"

"What?"

"Hittin' yourself?"

"Oh, I have a slight pain. I think I've got a bit of cold."

"I must be off," the Mohican said; "I have places to visit and things to see. I have far to go, being Thursday's child."

Then turning to me he said, "Could you get me that piece of paper?"

"Oh, yes, yes." I went out and into my study and there made rough outline drawings of the things that were missing, including the two brooches. When I returned to the hall both Tommy and the Mohican were standing there, and Tommy, while motioning towards the drawing-room door, said, "I've told him to stay by the fire."

The Mohican said, "Well?"

"Two brooches, one very valuable." And I handed him the paper and pointed, "It's like that, diamonds and rubies." Then I added, "I can't believe it: she was so ladylike, so sweet, so friendly."

Both Tommy and I now stared at him as, striking a pose, he said,

> "False friend, wilt thou smile or weep
> When my life is laid asleep?
> Little cares for a smile or a tear,
> The clay-cold corpse upon the bier!
> Farewell! Heigho!
> What is this whispers low?
> There is a snake in thy smile, my dear;
> And bitter poison within thy tear."

Tommy, who is a connoisseur of poetry, and who at one time before he became embittered against his mother, would declaim it whenever the opportunity occurred, stared at the Mohican and said, "The Dirge of Beatrice".

"Correct. You like Shelley?"

It was a moment before Tommy answered, "With others, yes."

"Don't look so surprised." The Mohican was smiling broadly. "Besides pot, we have our other pleasures." And he turned to me, saying, "Goodbye, Mrs Leviston. We'll be in touch, and shortly I hope."

I made no reply to this but opened the door and followed him to the lift, and there I said quietly, "Thanks, John."

"You are very welcome, Mrs Leviston," he said, just as quietly.

When I returned to the hall Tommy shook his head and said, "I can't understand him, nor that lot at all."

"He's a nice fellow underneath."

"Yes, perhaps, but why let himself go like that?"

"Perhaps he doesn't consider it letting himself go."

Drawing closer to me now, he put his arm around my shoulder and asked, "What are you going to say when they" - he thumbed towards the floor -" phone up and ask about baby-sitting?"

"I'll say I'm not well, or some such excuse."

"Then that will mean no more trips for us, unless you get another baby-sitter."

I glanced up at him as I replied, "There's always the Mohican."

"Oh. Oh, you couldn't have him."

I drew myself from his embrace. "I could, you know. Definitely I could. There's much more in him than meets the eye."

"You're right there; there would have to be."

"They are not all alike."

"Then why is it they all act in the same way?"

"Oh Tommy." I visibly drooped before him. "Don't start an argument, or even a discussion. I feel absolutely done in."

"I'm sorry, but all this proves to me one thing: I should be here all the time, then I'd be able to take him off your hands."

"I don't want him taken off my hands," and I pushed him from me; "that's the last thing I want done for me. I love him, Tommy, I need him. You'll always have to understand that."

He stared at me hard for a moment, then said, "Please, Maisie, don't make him into a greater opponent than Nardy; I couldn't stand it."

Chapter 6

All the week-end I was fuming inside: I wanted to get on the phone and scream down at that thieving pair below, or better still, phone the police because, as the Mohican had said, they had a record, at least he had. But, as the Mohican had also said, you have to furnish the police with more than the present suspicion concerning five pound notes and the missing pieces. And what is more, I'd had that dreadful pain in the night. I'd woken up in a sweat at about half past twelve, and my anger was intensified then by the thought of the suggestion that this excruciating pain was a figment of my imagination. And then on Sunday I hadn't had the comfort of Tommy: he had gone down to Brighton to visit Bella, a very nice oldish woman who had been a servant to his mother for years, a slave would have been a more appropriate title, and whom he had set up in a flat in a place of her choice when his mother's secret fortune had come to light.

So on this Monday morning I was glad to see Janet, at least in one way; in another, of course, I had a lot of explaining to do with regard to my frantic phone call. That she was upset was evident, and there was the same thought in her mind as to what I should have done about my neighbours, for she said, "I told Johnny that you should have sent for the police there and then 'cos, little scamp that he is, he would never take anything that didn't belong to him. There's been a box in the kitchen for years where I leave the milk an' the paper money, an' me purse has lain about an' all, and that child has never touched a penny."

Her indignation was evident all the morning.

It was in the afternoon that something went wrong with the tank in the roof above the bathroom: it would make a dreadful thumping noise every time taps were turned on or the cistern emptied. It was a modern cistern and easy to get at. I'd taken the top off to see if the ballcock had stuck, but that was all right.

Mr Brown's brother-in-law was a plumber and he usually saw to anything that went wrong in the flats, but because I didn't want to disturb the caretaker's teatime I left going down to see him until well after six o'clock.

Harold was sitting at the kitchen table, drawing. Sandy sat at his feet. I said to him, "I'm just going down to see Mr Brown about that noise, I won't be a minute."

He looked up at me, saying, "O.K."

He seemed to have forgotten Saturday's business, and yet not quite, because before going to school this morning, he had said, "He's not comin' up here again is he, the Captain?" And I had replied, "No," then added, "You'll remember what I asked you earlier on, won't you, not to say a word to anyone about the Captain?" and he had merely nodded.

It had been raining so I took a light mack from the hall wardrobe, then went down in the lift, and I had just opened the door into the street when to my amazement I saw Jimmy Stoddart coming towards me. He wasn't dressed as he usually was, with collar and tie, when he called on a Saturday to take Harold out, but was wearing corduroy trousers, a sweater and a loose jacket. His attire was casual, befitting his stance and manner of greeting: 'On your way out then?'

"No, I was just going down to see the caretaker." And I motioned towards the area steps. "Something's gone wrong in the tank, it's making a noise." I gave a little smile.

"Oh, perhaps I can 'elp there. I can turn my 'and to anything on the job. 'Ave to at times."

"Thank you all the same, but there is a resident plumber." This was stretching it a bit but I didn't want this man upstairs. "Is . . . is anything wrong?"

"No, nothing from my point of view except that tomorrow we are bein' moved down to Kent on a job an' I may not make it at the week-end, so I thought that I could take 'im out tonight."

"Oh, it's getting on and it would mean his being out in the dark and . . ."

His chin jerked up and he laughed, saying, "Well, I think I'd be able to protect 'im in the dark, what d'you say?" Then bending towards me he added, "Both of you in the dark. What about you comin' along?

pictures or some such."

I pressed myself back against the stanchion of the door and all I could think to say at that moment was, *"Mr Stoddart."*

"Oh! oh! Come off it now, you sound like somebody in one of them Victorian plays on the telly, shocked at the suitor's approach." He let out a laugh and he seemed pleased with his description of my attitude for he went on, "That's just how you sounded. It was funny."

"Well, it didn't sound funny to me, and I consider it presumption on your part. . ."

"What?" His voice was loud. *"Presumption?* My God! you are livin' in a play, aren't you? Know your place, man, know your place." Now his face was poking into mine as he said, "You want to realize there's no class these days: Jack's as good as his master an' I'm as good as you any day in the week; you're only where you are by chance. Oh" - he drew his head back from me - "you're a writer so-called. They say anybody goin' round the bend could write what you've done."

"Let me pass, Mr Stoddart."

His hand now came out and pressed flat against the wall to the side of the door, his sleeve almost touching my face, and he said, "I will when I'm ready. You've played the 'igh and mighty with me from the start. An' I'll tell you something now: I'm damned sorry I let the boy go. And if what I 'ear's true I could contest it on immoral grounds . . . you an' the big fella. An' you know what? You've got a bloody nerve to refuse any invitation 'cos who'd pick up with you 'cept for what you've got."

As my hand caught him a resounding slap on the face, in return I received a blow that knocked me dizzy. But the screeching of brakes penetrated the ringing in my ears. I was trying to keep my head still by holding it and my eyes were closed, but when I opened them there were two figures punching it out on the pavement, and Mr Brown yelling, "Give over! Stop it!"

I saw Tommy's fist land on Stoddart's jaw, causing the man to reel for a moment; but then he seemed to be battering Tommy's head first one side and then the other.

I staggered forward, screaming, "Stop it! Stop it!"

Mr Brown seemed to have disappeared, and for a moment I wondered why. Then my mind cried at me, Oh, no! No! Not the police. Not the police.

Stoddart now had Tommy bent back over the bonnet of the car. Tommy was no fighting man; he had been in an office all his life except for his trip abroad last year. I saw him now bring his knee up and Stoddart stagger back for a moment, then I put my hand tightly over my mouth as, locked together, they fell onto the roadway.

I was aware that we had a small crowd gathering, but when from out of the hall door the Captain stepped demanding, "What's this? What's this?" I turned on him like a tigress, screaming, "Shut up you! It's got nothing to do with you. You dare sp . . . speak to . . . to me."

Later, when I had time to think, I was to realize that it was on the sound of a police car that the Captain had disappeared indoors and not because of my manner towards him.

Now I watched in horror as two policemen wrenched the combatants apart and dragged them to their feet. There was blood streaming from both their faces and it was obvious that Tommy was in a very bad way because he could hardly stand but that Stoddart was still aggressive because he went to throw off the policeman's hold. And when the policeman said, "We'll have none of that. Now come on. Come on," Stoddart turned on him and there issued from his lips a spate of words that I hadn't heard since my first husband had spat them at me almost every night during the early part of our marriage.

The next minute two of the policemen were bundling Stoddart into the back of the car; and one policeman following him in, leaving the other to pull Tommy from where he was leaning against his own car and to thrust him into the front seat of the police car.

Then they were gone and the street was quiet. Nobody had spoken to me until Mr Brown, taking my arm, led me back into the hall, saying, "What started that, Mrs Leviston?"

I stammered now as I said, "It . . . it was the boy's father. He . . . he was insulting."

Then pulling myself from his hold I said, "I must go; they'll be at the station. I must see to Tommy . . . Mr Balfour, but I must lock up. I'll take the boy with me."

"I'll see to the boy when you bring him down; you can't take him to the station."

"Oh, thank you, thank you, Mr Brown." I now dashed into the lift and when, a minute later, I ran into the kitchen crying, "Come on, get your coat on," Harold slid from the chair saying, "What? Where we goin'?"

"You're going down to Mr Brown's."

"Mr Brown's? What for?"

"Look, all I can tell you at the moment" - I was bending over him now holding him by the shoulders - "Mr Tommy has had a slight accident and he's been taken to the . . . hospital. I've got to go and see him."

"He's bashed up his car?"

"No, no; the car's all right."

"Was he knocked down?"

"Yes. Yes."

"Where?"

"Never mind. Never mind. Come on; get your coat on."

"Can I take Sandy?"

"No. No, close the door."

I now dragged him into the hall, leaving him there whilst I ran to his room for his coat; then as I thrust it onto him his questions came at me: "Where did he have the accident? You've just gone down, how do you know?"

I pressed my lips tightly together before I said, "It happened in the street as he was getting out of his car." The last thing I wanted him to know was that his father was implicated.

When I reached the basement flat Mrs Brown greeted me with, "Don't worry, he'll be all right."

"Which hospital do you think they are likely to take him to? There's Beeside or Crunch Road."

Hospital. The poor woman seemed stumped for a moment; but luckily, light dawning on her, she said, "Oh, yes, yes, of course, the hospital . . . Beeside, I should think."

"Be a good boy." I touched Harold's head. He looked at me intently for a moment then turned away, and I ran up the area steps.

Beeside Police Station was the nearest, five minutes walk away, four if I verged on a run.

I verged on a run, and didn't stop until I was outside the door of the police station. But there I stopped, my jaws locked tight: I hated police stations, I was petrified of them. I pushed the door open into a small hall, then another door into a large room. The desk ran down one side. Two policemen stood behind it, and a man in a light mackintosh was leaning rather nonchalantly on the counter. They had been talking, but they stopped and looked towards me as I approached.

"What can I do for you, miss?"

No one ever took me for a missis. "I'm . . . I'm Mrs Leviston. I . . . I would like to enquire if two men, one of them my friend, were brought here a little while ago?"

"We get lots of men brought here, miss. What are their names and why were they brought in?"

I stiffened and my tone conveyed my feelings as I said, "His name is Mr Thomas Balfour. He is a director of Rington and Houseman the publishers. He was attacked by a man named James Stoddart. Now if they have been brought in here I don't suppose they have escaped your notice and my name happens to be *Mrs Leviston*."

The two policemen behind the counter were standing straight now, as was the man in the raincoat. The policemen exchanged glances; then the one in charge, adopting a manner similar to my own, replied, "No, it didn't exactly escape our notice, *Mrs Leviston*, that the men in question were brought in. I can inform you that they are now in the cells awaiting attention from the doctor after being charged with causing an affray and avoiding arrest."

"Mr Balfour did not avoid arrest, it was Stoddart, Mr Stoddart."

"Well, ma'am, Mr Balfour will be capable of explaining for himself."

"May I see him?"

"I'm afraid you can't, not at the moment." He had taken pleasure in saying this and he was about to go on when the man in the raincoat moved nearer along the counter and caused me to turn on him as he said, "Haven't I seen you before, Mrs Leviston?"

"I don't know, have you?"

His eyes travelled over me and rested for a moment on my short arm. Then his tone smooth and oily, he said, "Aren't you Miss Miriam Carter, the writer?"

I glanced from him back to the two policemen who were now giving me their full attention, before I answered, "Yes, I am Miriam Carter also."

"I thought you were. I was at the trial up north when your . . . your er -' He looked towards the policeman before ending, "your first husband was sentenced."

"You must have found it very interesting."

I knew I was assuming the wrong attitude with these men but I couldn't help it, and I recognized too late that this man was a reporter of sorts and that I'd got his back up, as I had that of the policeman, and the fact that I was a writer would do nothing to soften their attitudes towards me. The reporter's manner had been rather deferential up till now but when he said, "Is he your boy friend then, this Mr Balfour?" I exclaimed, "How dare you!"

Oh my goodness, I did sound as if I was in a Victorian play. But heedlessly I went on, only now using the vernacular of the writer and making matters worse by saying, "The connotation of boy friend that you assume in this case is wrong; Mr Balfour is my friend and he was the friend of my husband."

"Which one?"

I looked from him to the policemen as if asking for help, for of a sudden I felt like a pricked balloon and I knew I was about to cry: it was as if I was doing battle against three opponents and I knew I wasn't strong enough. I couldn't stop my lips from trembling or my eyes from blinking. I turned and went hastily from the room, out into the hallway, and there I stood for a moment with my hand pressed over my eyes before going into the street.

I did not run now but walked slowly and I had gone no more than a dozen steps when I heard someone coming behind me. I half turned to see the other policeman, the one who hadn't spoken, approaching. He was a tall man, over six foot, and he bent down to me and said quietly, "Don't worry, Mrs Leviston, it's nothing serious, just a squabble. He'll be out in the morning. He will have to go before the magistrate of course, and he'll get a small fine. It's always happening." He smiled now as he went on, "The other one will likely get more than your friend because he had a tussle with the uniform." He pointed to his chest.

The tears were sticking in my throat: I could bear the kindness less than I had the aggressiveness; and now they rolled down my cheeks as I muttered, "That man, he was a reporter, wasn't he?"

"Yes. They're always around scraping up the dirt. But I shouldn't worry, he's got nothing to go on. Anyway, go home now and think no more about it. They'll both appear in court at Crunch Road round about eleven in the morning. It all depends on how many cases there are. By the way -" His long length came down even further as he ended, "I enjoyed your book. My wife got it from the library, but the horse business tickled my fancy so I read it. And I remember thinking that the judge was right in what he said at the end about us feeling lonely at times and needing something to fill the gap and what better than an imaginary animal."

There were nice policemen. This man was kind; yet he certainly hadn't looked it back in the station. I said, "Thank you. Thank you so much."

"You'll be all right." He patted me now on the shoulder as a father might but he could only have been in his mid-twenties.

"Goodbye," I said.

"Goodbye, Mrs Leviston," he replied.

Head down, I cried all the way back to the house. I couldn't stop myself; and I began to wish that the policeman hadn't been so kind. I went upstairs and washed my face and straightened my hair before going down to collect Harold.

"How are things?" said Mr Brown.

"All right," I replied, forcing myself to smile because Harold's gaze was intent on me.

"Was he badly hurt?"

"No, no, not badly. He'll be coming out in the morning."

"Oh, that's nice," said Mrs Brown. "And he's been a good boy," and she chucked Harold under the chin.

After thanking them both I left without having asked Mr Brown to see to the cistern. Bangs in the roof could wait.

Once we were out of the flat and had entered the hall Harold turned to me and said, "It was me dad, wasn't it, Uncle Tommy was fightin'?"

My mouth fell into a gape. "Where . . . where did you hear that?"

"I heard them talkin' in the other room, Mr and Mrs Brown."

"You were listening?"

"Yes, I was listening, 'cos they were actin' funny. Why were they fightin'?"

I took off my coat and without further words led the way into the drawing-room, ignoring as I did so Sandy's barking coming from the kitchen.

When we were both seated before the fire I did not look at him but, bending forward, I joined my hands tightly together on my knee and said, "Do you like your father, Harold?"

No answer came for a moment, and then he said, "Not very much." Then after a pause, "No; I don't like him at all. Never 'ave. I liked me mum but she went orf. But that was a long time ago."

Yes it was: four years and more was a long time to a child.

"Then you won't be sorry if you miss going out with him tonight?"

"Out with 'im tonight? No, no, I won't."

"Well, that's what he came for, to take you out, because he's going away to work for a time and he wouldn't be here at the week-end. And . . . and he wanted to come up and when I put him off he became -" How could I explain to him how his father had become fresh. I used the word he would understand and said, "Nasty tempered, and he said something to me that wasn't nice and . . . and I slapped him."

"*You did?*" The tone was almost joyous. I turned and looked at him. He was grinning at me.

"Where did you 'it 'im?"

I too grinned as I said, "Across the face."

"An' what did he do then?"

My grin disappeared. "He hit me back."

"He did?" He slipped from the couch now and stood in front of me, gripping my hands. "He hit you back, me dad?"

"Yes. I . . . I suppose it was reaction."

"When me Uncle Max knows that he'll knock his bloody head clean off."

"Harold!" And I had begun to think he had so improved during these months he had been with me. He pulled his chin into his chest, saying now flatly, "Well, he would. An' the others too; they don't like me dad. Gag doesn't neither; she'd swipe his ears for him if she knew he'd hit you. But did me dad push Uncle Tommy under a car?"

"No; Mr Tommy wasn't pushed under a car at all. He saw what was happening as he got out of the car and that's what started the fight."

"And now they're both in the clink?" His eyes were bright; he was enjoying this.

"Yes," I said, "they're both in the clink."

"Bloody hell! Well, sorry, but . . . but I'm glad Mr Tommy hit me dad, 'cos me dad hit you." He reached out now and put his arms around my neck and as he clung to me and I held him tightly there penetrated the room Sandy's yelping bark, which caused my adoptive son to press back from me and say lightly, "Listen to that little bugger barking his bloody head orf."

His mouth in a wide gape, he stared at me and his nose twitched, his eyes blinked and his fingers jerked in mine before he brought out, "Well, it's 'cos I'm excited. They always come out when I'm excited, but they'll go orf, they'll go orf. Anyway, listen to him." And he pulled himself from my hands, backed two or three steps, then scampered from the room.

I lay back on the couch. They always come out when I'm excited. I would have to hope and pray, wouldn't I, that in future he wouldn't get excited and that they'd . . . go orf. That's another thing I must see to, that *orf*.

What a night. What a week-end. And what a life.

Yes, what a life for a nondescript person such as I knew myself to be: my days should have been mundane, my life should be running smoothly, uneventfully. Even my efforts over the past months to educate had ended up with "Listen to that little bugger barking his bloody head orf!"

Chapter 7

I was in the outer hall ready to leave the flat on the Tuesday morning to go to the court when the bell rang and Tommy stepped out of the lift. His normally long lean-looking face was swollen, at least one side of it: one eye was black and puffed almost level with his nose; the lower lip seemed to be at least twice its size and it had evidently been stitched, and as he walked with a slight limp towards me I backed from him, saying, "Oh! Tommy. Tommy. I . . . I was just on my way to . . . to the court."

"I'm . . . just . . . on my . . . way . . . from . . . it." His words were spaced and he spoke out of the corner of his mouth.

"I'm sorry, so sorry." I held out my hand and took his and led him back into the flat. Janet was in the drawing-room dusting and she turned on our entry, saying, "Oh my God! Mr Tommy. Oh my God!"

"And . . . mine too . . . and . . . mine too, Janet. But . . . please don't say . . . anything that will make me . . . want . . . to laugh."

"Oh! Mr Tommy! Ooh! when the lads get a hold of him it won't only be his face that'll get it, I'm tellin' you. . . . What did you get?"

She was asking all the questions, so I let her go on, and Tommy answered, "Fined ten pounds and . . . and bound over to keep . . . the peace."

"And him?"

"Fifty pounds and bound over . . . longer . . . term."

"They should have jugged him. Who does he think he is darin' to make a pass!"

I had given Janet all the details; I couldn't have given her any reason for slapping the man otherwise.

"I knew he was up to something, dressing as he has never done before, rag-bag he used to be. But the nerve of it, him thinkin' he could get his foot in here. If I ever come across him again I'll spit in his eye."

I tried to stop the flow: looking at Tommy, I said, "What would you like, coffee or something stronger?"

"Stronger."

"Will you bring the decanter, Janet, please?"

"Yes, will do."

"And bring the sherry, too," I called after her.

A minute or so later I had poured Tommy out a stiff measure of whisky and Janet and myself sherries. Tommy did not hold up his glass, nor did I, but Janet, raising hers, said, "Here's hoping he falls off the scaffoldin' and breaks his blasted neck."

"Oh! Janet. Don't." Tommy's hand was raised in protest; then, looking at me, he said, "I'll swear to you this moment, Maisie, that I'll never do a wrong thing in my life . . . ever, nothing that will ever get me into a . . . a cell again. Last night covered a whole eternity." He drew in a sharp breath and put his hand to his ribs, then said, "God Almighty! I don't know how they stand it. It's a . . . wonder . . . the prisons aren't turned into . . . lunatic asylums."

"Are your ribs paining?"

"Yes, two cracked ones. They say they can't do anything, that they heal themselves. Your son-in-law punches well . . . with his feet, Janet."

"Mr Tommy, you'll do me a favour if you'll not connect that man with me again when you're referrin' to him. He's out of our lives now and he stays out. Well, he will be when our Maggie gets her divorce, or he gets it from her, one or t'other. Oh, my goodness!" She threw off the rest of her sherry, put the glass down on the tray, then said to me, "I'll make a shepherd's pie. That'll slide down, 'cos he won't be able to chew with that mouth."

As she left the room I sat down on the couch beside Tommy and, taking his hand, I said, "Thank God for Janet and Harold . . . and you, my dear, for I don't know what would have happened if you hadn't come on the scene. And yet, if you hadn't you wouldn't have been in this state, nor have spent the night in a cell. *Oh, I am sorry.*"

"All in a good cause. It would be . . . gallant to say, I would do the same again, but not until . . . I get over this lot. So don't go slapping anybody else, will you . . . dear.'

"Oh, Tommy." I gently touched his swollen face, then said, "How are you going to do business looking like that?"

"Oh, I'll be a sort of hero, don't you know. By the way, I phoned God the Father" - he was referring to Mr Houseman the head of the publishing firm - "and the old boy came trotting along last night around ten o'clock and demanded to see me. He'd even managed to get hold of our solicitor and bring him along. It was after the doctor had been and declared I wasn't hospital . . . material. He was very concerned. He's a good old stick. He said I had done the right thing and thought it was real sporting of you to slap that fellow's face. I saw you do it, you know. I nearly ruined my brakes pulling up so . . . so quickly. Anyway, they would have got me out on bail, but the police doctor had said I was best left where I was overnight. Then I think the solicitor advised me to plead guilty this morning as that would . . . give the best chance of keeping your name out of it .. . and the way things went I reckon he - or somebody must have got Stoddart to do the same. Maisie" - his words were coming slower now - "do you think I could lie down for a while, I'm feeling ropy."

"Of course, of course. Come on, get up."

I took his arm and led him, as if he were an old man, from the room and into my bedroom. But there he stopped, saying, "Oh, no, no; the other room where I used to kip."

"That hasn't been aired for some time. Look; take your outer things off and get underneath the eiderdown and have a sleep; you'll feel the better for it."

"Thanks, my dear. Thanks."

As I left the room I thought it strange that Tommy should be lying in my bed where he had wanted to lie for such a long time, but not under these present circumstances.

When Janet left at two o'clock Tommy was still asleep. He didn't waken until four when his face seemed more swollen than ever and he had a splitting headache. I took him in a strong cup of tea and when he said, "I must get up and away," I replied, "Don't be silly. And look; if you go back to the flat, who's going to see to you?"

"But I can't stay here all night, what I mean is. . ."

"I know what you mean. But I've a chaperon haven't I. He's in the kitchen now demanding to come in and see you. What is more, and of which I was indirectly reminded in the police station last night, we are now living in nineteen eighty-four. So you'll stay put for tonight. By the way, could you drink some soup? I'm afraid Janet's shepherd's pie has got a little dry."

"Nothing, thank you, dear; another cup of tea and a couple of aspirins."

I let Harold bring the tray which, on seeing Tommy's face, he almost let fall. I took it from him, placed it on the side-table, put another pillow behind Tommy's head, then said as I handed him the cup of tea and the aspirins, "It's rather hot, be careful." And all the while Harold, struck into silence and mouth agape, surveyed the result of his father's work. Then as Tommy was about to take a sip from the cup, Harold exclaimed, 'Me dad did that to you?"

Tommy swallowed painfully before answering, "Yes, Harold, this is your father's handiwork."

"Does it 'urt?"

"Yes, yes, quite a bit; he's got very hard hands, has your father."

"What's his face look like?"

"Well, from what I saw of him this morning, pretty much like mine, but I didn't look closely."

"Me Uncle Max'll sort him out. I'm glad you hit him 'cos he hit Mrs Nardy. I'm not goin' with him again on a Saturday . . . I'll tell him."

"Come on, dear; Tommy wants to rest." And I took the cup from Tommy, put it onto the tray, which I then handed to Harold, saying, "Take it into the kitchen; I'll be there in a minute."

When the door had closed on him I turned to Tommy and said, "It looks as if there'll be trouble in that direction. Anyway, I don't think anything more can happen at the moment." Then I added, "Oh, by the way, I've got some steak. Janet went out and got it. That's the cure for black eyes; I'll bring it in."

I'd said nothing more could happen. I should have kept my mouth shut. It was about half past six when Gran rang. Her voice was high as she almost shouted, "That you, Maisie?"

"Yes, yes, of course, Gran. Anything wrong?"

"Nothing this end, but I see you've done it again."

"Done what again?"

"Got yourself into the papers. My God! lass, you're the one for notoriety."

"What do you mean, I'm the one for . . . ?"

"Well, haven't you seen the evenin' paper?"

"No, I haven't."

"Well, you should get it. I don't know what it'll be at yon end, it's headlines here. Our name must be mud."

I drew my head back from the phone and waited, and her voice came again, "You there?"

"Yes, of course I'm here waiting for your bad news that you appear determined and delighted to tell me."

"By God, lass, no, I'm not delighted to tell you this: two more men squabbling over you in the street, their faces bashed to bits, an' the heading 'Local Authoress hits headlines again. Mrs Leviston, better known as Mrs Stickle, wife of the man serving twelve years for trying to burn her to death, also sports another name, Miriam Carter, under which she writes about her life with a talking horse.' Then it goes on about a brawl atween the father of the boy you have adopted - I knew that would bring no good, I've said so all along - and a publisher by the name of Mr Thomas Balfour. Apparently Tommy saw you slapping the father of the child and him punching you back and so he joined in. My

God! girl, what are you up to now?"

"Goodbye, Gran." I banged the phone down and flopped into a chair near the telephone table. That was a woman who had loved me, and I had loved her. What changed people? One time she would have laughed and been proud of my name mentioned in the paper, no matter what the circumstances.

I pulled myself up from the chair, took my coat from the wardrobe, went into the kitchen and said to Harold, "I'm just going to slip along to the paper shop."

"I'll go for you."

"No, no; you stay with Sandy; he misses you when you go out and he doesn't see you all day. I . . . I won't be a minute or so. "

The paper shop was three streets away and just about to close. I bought two evening papers: the London one and another I'd not seen before which seemed more suburban in origin. When I returned home, I went into the drawing-room and opened the first one. I scanned the pages, but could find nothing and certainly not the headlines Gran had sounded off about. Then I turned to the other, and there in a sort of gossip column feature was that reporter's handiwork.

Talk about bitchiness among women! After revealing I was better known as author Miriam Carter, the writer claimed that "in an interview" Mrs Leviston had denied publisher Thomas Balfour was her boy friend, at least not as generally understood today, merely a close friend. How close she hadn't specified. Then he went on to say that Stoddart had stated after leaving court that he was unwarrantably attacked by Mrs Leviston's friend because the said friend thought he had struck Mrs Leviston when all he had done was try to evade a second blow from her, provoked by nothing more than his inviting her to accompany him and his son, whom she had recently adopted, out for the evening.

I put the pad of my thumb in my mouth and bit on it till I could stand the hurt no longer. Then my eyes returned to the end of the piece, and there I saw myself described as: "a small woman, in looks and stature reminiscent of the late Edith Piaf, but not - one ventures to think - with quite the same personality. And yet, it would seem men are prepared to fight over her!"

I would see my solicitor. I knew Edith Piaf had been a wonderful singer with a strong personality, but she had died twenty years ago when I was still at school and photographs I'd seen suggested she had been oldish and a little wizened woman.

Well, wasn't I a little plain woman? I felt sick, so sick and alone I wanted someone to hang on to, to clutch at, to hold me. Life was getting me down and strangely not by catastrophes but by niggling occurrences which were sapping me both physically and mentally, the former definitely through that pain in my stomach. . .

I did not tell Tommy of the newspaper report for he, too, I knew, was very low: his ribs were paining, his head was throbbing, his mouth seemed more swollen than ever. When I had insisted he must stay the night he hadn't protested over much. He had said it was the first time since his schooldays that he had been in a scrap and he was definitely out of practice.

It was just after eight o'clock when the phone rang again and I welcomed the sound of Mike's voice. "How are you?" he said.

"Pretty ropy at the moment," I answered.

"Gran was in the surgery tonight."

"Oh yes?" I knew what was coming.

"Don't worry your head about that report; you've got to get used to that kind of thing."

"What, have two men fighting over me?"

"Oh, Maisie, the things that happen to you. Elizabeth Taylor will soon have to look to her laurels with this kind of competition."

"Mike, don't joke about this."

"You've got to joke about it, you've got to laugh about it, girl. Anyway, I haven't phoned up about that. I'm attending a conference in Brighton at the week-end, Friday till Monday, and it was my intention to look in. Besides wanting to see your funny face again, I'd thought we'd have a talk about this strange disease of yours. I'm not happy about the sound of it; it's gone on too long. You still getting the pain?"

"Yes, I am, and it was bad last night."

"Aggravated by worry, I suppose."

"It needs no aggravation, Mike. When I'm feeling perfectly all right it hits me, and it's getting me down. I'm . . . I'm so glad you're coming, Mike. When I said I was coming up to see you I fully expected to, but now . . . well, I don't think I could stand the journey; I feel so weak at times. Oh, I'll be glad to see you, Mike. I wish you were here at this moment; I want a shoulder to cry on."

"Where's Tommy?"

"In my bed, *Doctor Kane*, at this moment."

"You don't say!"

"I do say. I also say that the poor fellow's in a bit of a mess."

"My! my! Anyway, I must be off now, I've got some calls to make because I'm the only doctor in Fellburn, or in the whole of the county for that matter."

"You are?"

"Yes, I'm positive of it, because during my nights on call the phone never stops ringing."

"You've got two partners, what about them?"

"Oh, they're no good. I tell you, I'm the only real doctor about, so I must away." Then his jocular tone changing, he said, "Goodbye, dear. Keep your pecker up, and when things get bad just remember that people are sinking all around you but you are on a raft."

People sinking all around you but you are on a raft.

That was telling me there were many worse off than myself. At one time Hamilton would have put in an appearance and I would have nodded at him and said, "Remember that and be thankful, you're on a raft." But there was no Hamilton now. I might be on a raft, but it was a straw one.

Chapter 8

It had been an eventful week. I had to call the doctor in to see to Tommy.

Doctor Bell had apparently read the evening paper, so he did not raise his eyebrows at finding in my bed a man whom he had never seen before when visiting the house. Anyway, he said Tommy should stay where he was for the next two or three days as he was running a slight temperature.

Following this I scampered about: I went to Tommy's flat and brought him back some night clothes, besides another suit and accessories.

It was a weird feeling to see that big fellow lying in my bed. Nardy had been of medium height and slim, my own height hadn't been dwarfed by his, but Tommy's six foot two made me feel like a pygmy at times, especially when we were outside and must appear like father and child, at least from the back.

So busy had I been looking after Tommy that the affair concerning our neighbours sank a little into the background, though never for a moment actually forgotten, for whenever I heard the phone ring, or the lift bell, I was ready for battle, thinking it might be the Captain being barefaced enough to call. And at times I would feel irritable at the thought that I'd let the Mohican persuade me to hold my hand.

By the Thursday I was glad that Tommy was out of bed dressed and sitting in the drawing-room because I myself was feeling far from well. Strangely, I did not feel this odd pain during the day, but every night now it either stopped me from going to sleep or woke me up, and its effects were staying with me now long after it was gone.

One thing I was pleased about: since the fight, the child's attitude towards Tommy had changed. It seemed that he was pleased Tommy had hit his father, when it should have been the other way round. Perhaps I felt that Tommy too was seeing the boy in a different light for he had smiled as he said, "He's a taking little imp, isn't he? And there's no doubt that he's been brought up among a bunch of men."

It was on the Friday evening when Tommy was almost ready to go - Mr Brown had brought his car round from the garage - when the lift bell rang, and, bracing myself once again to meet the Captain, I went into the outer hall. But it was the Mohican who appeared. He was looking slightly different for the marks on his cheeks were vertical now and there was a sort of star on his brow.

"Good-evening, Mrs Leviston."

"Good-evening . . . John."

His gaze left me and looked towards Tommy who was standing at the inner door. "Good-evening, Mr Balfour."

"Hello there," said Tommy quietly.

I still could not associate the Mohican's voice with his get-up and I had no doubt he could change it to fit the company.

"Feeling better?" he asked Tommy as he passed him, and to this Tommy answered, "Somewhat."

"It must have been a good fight. How many rounds did you last?"

I saw that Tommy wasn't amused and so I broke in, saying, "Have you any news?"

"Yes. Yes, I have news, unless I find it isn't news to you that your neighbours have flitted."

"Flitted? Gone?"

"Flitted, gone, yes."

"When?"

"Oh, as far back as Tuesday. They must have seen the red light."

I let out a long irritated breath as I said, "I should have got the police straightaway; they couldn't have implicated the child." And as Tommy, looking at the Mohican, said, "That's that then; we've seen the last of them and their hoard."

"Not necessarily; I know where they are and are likely to stay put for a time. As for the hoard, well, it's likely been spread around and, as often is the case unless it's sold abroad right away, it will be kept dark for a time and brought out later. They even have the nerve to bring the stuff back into the country and sell it. And it's legal. Funny business."

"You know where they are, I mean those two?"

"Yes, Mrs Leviston; they've returned to the bed-sit that they lived in before they got the chance to take up residence here."

His use of words somehow indicated the educated man behind that dreadful gear. Why? Why? There were drop-outs of all kinds, but the Mohican's kind was particularly sad to me.

"How did you find out?"

"Oh, I get about. And I'm not alone." He grinned at me now. "We're a kind of club, you know we Cowboys and Indians. Oh yes, we have a lot of Cowboys among us; in fact, there's a place down in Kent where they play at riding the range."

"You're referring to a different set of men." Tommy's tone was cold, but the Mohican's was even more icy as he retorted, "Don't you believe it! Because they come back on a Monday and take up a job they're deemed respectable, but they're the same as us under the skin."

"At least, as you say, they take up a job, but how do your kind exist? Where do you get the money from for your" - he paused and flapped his hand up and down - "rig-outs and pot and . . . ?"

"Tommy! Please."

"Oh, it's all right, Mrs Leviston, don't you worry." The Mohican was wagging his finger at me. "It was a natural follow-up question. Well, sir" - he had turned to Tommy again - "some of us exist on the dole alone, and that is the word, exist; others amongst us get a little extra aid from the establishment; and further there are those like myself who run messages."

Tommy's eyes narrowed, and I gaped a little at the Mohican while he inclined his head from one to the other of us as he smiled and said, "Yes, run messages. It's amazing what you learn running messages and who you run messages for. It's amazing how some people are interested in what other people are up to."

"Private detective?"

His head went back and he laughed. "Oh, Mrs Leviston, don't get romantic. Me a private detective?" Then still smiling he said, "No, I'm not a private detective, I'm a real Indian: I'm always on the alert; the only thing I don't use is smoke signals." He turned now and looked at Tommy, saying, "There's other work in the world besides sitting on a stool, and although those like me dress a bit way-out, we're not all thugs and druggers. Well" - he shrugged now - "not on the hard stuff anyway."

Oh, Mohican, why? Why? Not on the hard stuff. I felt so sad for him.

"Anyway" - he was addressing me again - "I thought I'd better let you know in case you hadn't already found out. Another thing is, it's a good job that the single gentleman in the bottom flat has been away in Barbados these last few months or he might have been rifled too. But they wouldn't break in; that isn't their style."

Not a little surprised, I said, "You seem to know more about the goings on in this house than I do myself, John."

"Oh, I only had that information a few minutes ago. Mr Brown spoke to me in the hall . . . and *civilly*. Fancy that." He grimaced which made the lines on his face seemingly become alive, like worms wriggling up to his eyebrows. "Now I must away to run some more messages." He glanced at Tommy, and to my surprise Tommy said, "Can I drive you anywhere?"

The Mohican stared at him for a full thirty seconds before he said quietly, "Thank you very much for the offer; there's nothing better I would enjoy than to get into your car. I've always liked Jags. But it would be slightly incongruous, don't you think, me in this gear and you looking the city gent, at least by your rig at the moment. Why, we would get our name up."

Tommy was forced to smile, then said, "Well, I made the offer."

"And it was very kind of you and I'm grateful, but if any of the gang saw me spinning along in that I'd be under suspicion of leading a double life."

"Well, aren't you?"

Again the Mohican paused before he answered, "Yes, I suppose so in a way. Yes; none of us are what we seem, there's always the inner man trying to get out. And -" Turning to me and smiling widely, he said, "And mine has certainly got out, hasn't it, Mrs Leviston?"

"Oh, John."

"Mrs Leviston, when you say, Oh, John, like that, I could dash downstairs - in the lift of course - rush to the nearest second-hand shop and swap this lot for a suit."

"Go along with you!"

"That's a point: one of us has got to go first; we can't both go out in that street together, can we? Can we, Mr Balfour?"

"I don't mind."

"I do, so I won't embarrass you. Goodbye. But by the way, where's Harold?"

"In his room. He can't have heard you, or else he'd have been out."

"Well, goodbye," he said and turned away.

We stood watching him cross the hall and enter the lift, and as this disappeared from view Tommy said, "Waste, utter waste of a life."

"Yes, I suppose so."

"Well now, here I go."

When the green light appeared he pressed the button; then turning to me, he said, "Except for the pain in my eye, my lip, and my ribs, this has been the happiest four days of my life."

"Oh Tommy," My voice was small.

Seeming to bend over me now, he said and in just as low a voice as mine, "I never thought I could love you more than I did, but having lived with you for four days . . . not nights" - he pulled a little face - "you're even more dear to me."

When he kissed me hard on the mouth I did not draw back.

"Take care," he said. "See you tomorrow." And as he stepped into the lift he said softly, "You'll have some explaining to do; we're being watched."

"What! Oh, dear!"

When a moment later I turned towards the hall door, there he was, his face tight, and before I had a chance to close the door he had reached up, his handkerchief in his hand, and rubbed it across my lips.

I stood back from him, saying, "What was that for?"

"'Cos you always do that after Sandy kisses you."

"Yes, but Sandy is a dog and, as I've told you, you shouldn't let him kiss you on the mouth."

"You let him kiss you on the mouth."

"I let you kiss me."

"That's 'cos you love me."

I evaded taking up the inference and said wearily, "I thought we'd been over all this and that you liked Mr Tommy."

He shrugged his shoulders and half turned away, saying, "He's all right, but he shouldn't kiss you like that. Anyway, he's too big, he fills up the house. I like the Indian. He's been. I like him. "

My expression must have shown my surprise. "If you knew the Mohican was here why didn't you come and see him?" I said.

"'Cos I was makin' something with gum and it was sticky. It's for a present." He glanced sideways at me. "It's a secret."

"Oh."

"One day I'm gona have a rig like the Indian 'cos I like him."

He now ran from me making war-cry noises with his hand across his mouth, and as I stood for a moment watching him I thought, Over my dead body you will. And yet I liked the Indian too. There was something about him, something beneath that weird rig-out that got to you. It had got to me anyway.

But why should the fact disturb me?

Chapter 9

I waited with impatience for the sight of Mike on Monday morning and when I eventually saw him I fell unrestrainedly into his arms and cried before I said a word.

"Well! well! This is a welcome, isn't it, being drowned before I get to the door."

"Oh, Mike, I'm so pleased to see you."

He held me from him, then said, "Well, I'm not so pleased to see you, not by the look of you. You hadn't much flesh on you a while ago but you're just skin and bone. Where's it gone to?"

"You tell me."

"Hello there, Janet." He turned from me as Janet came out of the kitchen carrying the coffee tray. "Hello, Doctor," she replied. "You're just in time; you must have smelt it."

"Not as it is, Janet; it's got to have a stiffener in it before it gets up my nose."

A moment or so later I said to Janet, "Fetch the brandy, will you, please, and a glass? I'm going to measure it."

"Don't you bother with the glass, Janet."

And so the chaffing went on until, left alone, we sat looking at each other on the couch before, leaning back, he spread his arms along it saying, "Well, come on now, start at the beginning, at least of that pain."

Strangely, when I tried to trace the pain back to when I first had it I couldn't actually pin-point the time, except to say, "I think I had a twinge when Nardy was still in hospital back home" - I still referred to Fellburn as home - "but whenever I had such a pain we put it down to Gran's cooking, all fries and plenty of fat. I think I first felt it as a real pain when Nardy was home here and I saw him fading away. I thought then it was the result of worry, and I didn't take much notice of it. Then after he died and it seemed to increase I naturally put it down to my missing him, and at that time if it hadn't been for Harold I would certainly, I feel sure, have snapped. But lately it seems to have intensified."

"Describe it," he said.

"I can't really, except to say it starts like a sharp stab, then turns into a grinding cramp."

"Whereabouts?"

"That's another thing, it's nearly always in my middle, first to one side then the other."

When he sighed I felt apprehensive and said quickly, "I'm not imagining this, Mike. Don't do a Doctor Bell on me, please."

"I'm not doing a Doctor Bell or anybody else on you, girl. You have a pain and there's evidence of it in that the flesh is dropping off you, because even after Nardy went you weren't like this. You say it's always at night that you feel it?"

"Yes, yes; but I seem to have a reaction to it during the day, more so of late, I feel so tired. Oh, Mike" - I caught at his hand and, my voice breaking now, I whimpered something that I had promised myself not to say, "There are times in the night when I feel I'm going to die."

He made no reply to this but sat looking at me; then he rubbed his hand round the thick grey bush of his face before he said, "You're not my patient now, but who's to know? Get your things off and I'll give you the once over."

It was like being back in the surgery again on a Monday morning, but I didn't smile as I rose from the couch. I went quickly down the room and into the bedroom.

I was lying waiting when he came in. . .

What did I expect from his examination? I don't know, but I thought, He's doing the same things as Doctor Bell did. But then he examined my throat and ears, and when he had finished he sat on the side of the bed and said, "From the outside, as far as I can see, there's nothing wrong; and you've had barium tests and the inside examined; and quite candidly, Maisie, apart from splitting you open I can't see what more can be done, at least to your body."

"*Oh! Mike. Oh! Mike*, don't tell me I'm going barmy."

"I'm not telling you you're going barmy, dear, but what I will tell you is, there may be something deep in your mind that is worrying you, and I think Doctor Bell was right when he suggested you might do worse than see a psychiatrist."

I turned my head away from him and covered my eyes, saying, "Mike, there's nothing in my mind that hasn't been cleared out."

"That's what you think. Remember Hamilton. Where is he, by the way?"

"Gone."

"Ah! Ah!"

I pulled myself up in the bed now, hugging the sheet around me. "Mike, for God's sake don't suggest that because I've lost Hamilton and Nardy I've replaced them with one hell of a pain."

His laughter shook the bed. "You know who you sounded like there? Your charge. You only needed to add, What the bloody hell do you mean by suggesting . . . et cetera, et cetera! Learning goes both ways. But listen to me." He reached and gripped my wrists and shook them. "Something's causing this pain, something's causing you to look all skin and bone and eyes. Even at your worst, on your weekly visits I never remember you with great dark shadows under your eyes. Whatever's troubling you, and I fear" - he nodded at me now - "yes, I fear, there's something in your mind that is troubling you, I say now, and firmly, do as Doctor Bell advised, go and see a brain char and have it swept out. He'll be the best one to advise you on that point. And don't be afraid; these fellows are just ordinary blokes who get paid for keeping their mouths shut and listening." He smiled now as he punched my cheek gently, adding, "Come on, come on. I'm sure there's nothing wrong with you that can't be sorted out. But that's the thing, it's got to be sorted out. Come on, get dressed, and I'll take you out to lunch in one of your fancy restaurants. That's if I can rise to it."

"Expensive week-end?"

"No, no, that was all free, compliments of a drug company. My! my! the liquor that some people get through. I'm not averse to moistening my gums, but at these do's I can see the reason for some doctors' early demise. Still, we have one life and we can do what we like with it, and who am I to criticize. I was so sozzled myself last night, my last thought when I was in bed was, I hope I'm not on call. . . Go on, jump to it!"

I didn't exactly jump to it, but a half an hour later we left the house. We took a taxi into the centre of London and to Brown's Hotel, because Nardy used to like Brown's. He had been not an infrequent visitor there because certain American publishers made it their headquarters while in London.

It was over lunch that I regaled Mike with the story of my neighbours and the description of the Mohican. But it was when I came to describe Harold's progress at school and in a quiet voice recited: "Give me the moonlight, give me the girl, and leave the rest to me, and I'll put a bun in your oven straight after tea," that he choked. His mouth was full of ice-cream sundae one minute, the next, this was sprayed across the table, to the indignant looks of our near neighbour. And when I wiped a narrow streak of ice-cream from my coat he muttered, "Oh, Maisie, Maisie, I'm sorry, but -" The tears were running out of his eyes now, and he dabbed at them with his handkerchief. Then taking his napkin he also dabbed at his glass and the tablecloth and the condiment set, and as he was doing so a waiter came up to us and, smiling broadly, he said, "Don't worry, sir, don't worry. As I always say, a good laugh saves a visit to a doctor."

At this Mike's head went back again and there issued from his beard a deep rumbling sound, while I, in my turn, almost spluttered now, as looking up at the waiter, I said, "He is a doctor."

"Oh my! Oh my!" The waiter too was laughing now.

Altogether it was a most enjoyable lunch and we lingered over it with coffee and liqueurs and the hovering attention of the nice waiter.

Mike's train was due out at six o'clock, and since he had expressed a wish to meet up again with my "stick for her own back", Gran's description of Harold apparently, we took a taxi back home, and it was as I led the way to the house door that it opened and out stepped the Mohican.

Although I had already and fairly fully described him to Mike, his reactions were nevertheless similar to those of Tommy on first viewing the young fellow. His make-up was slightly different today: the white streaks were running from his cheek-bones to his ears; there were strange marks on his brow, and his lower lip looked scarlet.

"Hello, Mrs Leviston. I'm glad I caught you."

"Hello, John. By the way, this is my friend, Doctor Kane."

"How do you do, sir."

Mike made no response to the greeting, he just stared; and even when the Mohican added, "I've heard Mrs Flood speak of you," Mike did not make any reply.

Turning to me, the Mohican said, "I've been tipped off about one of the missing pieces, at least I'm pretty sure it must be from your description, it's the little coffee jug. But if I'm right, and as I told you last week, it'll be kept under wraps for a while yet. I know it's not the usual shop, and I'll have to keep nosing around - with a little help from my friends! - until a certain individual risks putting it out on sale. That's when I can arrange to take you along, or" - his face stretched, and the lines with it - "direct you where to identify it. Trust me, and I promise to let you know the moment I've got something definite. Now I must be off again. Goodbye, Mrs Leviston." He now turned to Mike, adding, "Goodbye, Doctor. And don't worry about the numbness my appearance has caused, it will wear off: it falls into the same category as shock; a strong cup of tea helps."

I saw Mike stiffen, and I put my hand out quickly and caught, his arm, saying, "Come on, come on."

It wasn't until we were in the drawing-room again that, turning to me and his voice serious, he said, "I may have been worried about that odd pain you have when I came in before, but now I'm much more worried about your acquaintance with that individual. Now Maisie. . . Be quiet!" He wagged his finger at me. "Let me have my say. About these stolen things. It's the police you've got to go to, not the likes of that . . . because that lot are twisted, their minds are warped, and more so his kind because, going by his voice, he's had a decent upbringing, and apparently he's got a mind that works if his tongue's anything to go by. But it's working, like all of his kin, in the wrong direction, sustained by drugs."

"Mike, Mike, I don't think. . ." If I could have gone on and said, I don't think he's connected with drugs, it wouldn't have been absolutely true, but Mike's finger was still stabbing at me as he said, "And don't you say, you don't think he's on drugs, that get-up is the first indication of it."

Now I did put in, "Oh, Mike, no, don't go by his clothes, please. There are lots of youngsters dressed like that and they are not on drugs. I'm sure of it."

"You can be sure of nothing with that lot, Maisie; you've had no experience of them. You want to see some of the poor creatures who are inveigled into that life fighting withdrawal symptoms, screaming like tortured wild animals, willing that you should cut off their hand if only you give them some of the poison. And that fellow, he's got brains and has the makings of a pusher. Oh, they're very suave fellows the pushers. And he's right in the middle of his own set, I suppose, if in fact, not leading it. I tell you, Maisie, break off all connections with him. Cut your losses with regards to the silver and your miniatures, it will be worth it in the end."

"Mike" - my voice was loud now - "are you suggesting he'll get me on drugs?"

"No, I'm not suggesting it, but as you've mentioned it, it could be a possibility."

"*Oh, Mike.*"

"Never mind, *oh Mike*, in that tone of voice; you know nothing about what goes on in his kind of life. I wish I could take you down to the police cells one night, that would open your eyes. And tell me this, has he got a job, at least one that you know of?"

No, he hadn't, not as far as I knew, and he made those odd trips away. Oh, I hoped Mike wasn't right because . . . yes, as I had admitted to myself before, I liked the Mohican; there was something about him. . . . Yes, there was something about him, and likely this is what got other people. Perhaps Mike was right after all.

I swept the thought away by saying, "He's Janet's daughter's boy friend. As far as I know he's on the dole." Then my attitude and voice softening, I said, "Oh, Mike, I know you're concerned and I'll take heed of what you say, I'll be careful and I'll try to find out more about him."

"Don't do any such thing, Maisie, just drop him."

"But, Mike, it's very rarely I see him. I haven't met up with him more than four times altogether."

"Well, all I can say is his manner seemed very familiar for four times, even his Mrs Leviston had a touch of familiarity about it."

I laughed now, saying, "Come on; sit down, and draw in those bristles from your beard, you look like a porcupine. Anyway, I've always wanted to ask you, how does Jane put up with that forest on your face?"

His jocular manner returning, he said, "She likes it: she buries herself in it at night, it keeps her warm."

I was about to leave him to go and make the tea when the lift bell rang. Turning, I said, "That'll be the boyo."

A minute later Harold came barging into the hall, crying, "I gorra star."

"You've *got* a star. Is that what you said?"

"Yes, yes, I gorra star for writin'."

"You *got* a star. "

"Oh, you, I . . . got . . . a . . . star."

"That's better. We've got a visitor."

"Who?"

"Come and see." I took his hand, and when we entered the drawing-room and he saw Mike sitting on the couch he smiled and walked slowly towards him.

"Well, say hello to Doctor Kane."

My charge did not say, Hello, or, Hello Doctor Kane, but, his smile turning into a grin and casting a sidelong glance up at me, a mischievous wicked look that always preceded some cheeky remark he was about to make, he said,

"Flannagan's dog!"

For the second time that afternoon Mike let out a bellow. I too laughed because during the conversation that had ensued after their first meeting Harold had likened Mike to Flannagan's dog.

When the laughter died down, Mike said, "I've had my beard trimmed this week, let me tell you, sir."

"It still looks raggy."

Mike now looked at me, saying, "Apparently the education of this young man hasn't reached the social graces yet. Anyway" he held out his hand towards Harold - "come and sit down here and tell me what you've been up to at that school of yours. And in the meantime, Mrs Leviston, you can go out and make that cup of tea."

I left the room smiling; but as I prepared the tea my thoughts kept dwelling on the Mohican. I knew Mike was right in most of what he said, and I wondered why I should be so concerned that the Mohican should not be involved in the drug racket. Surely, if he had been, I told myself, the men in Janet's family would have found out something about him before now. And as for Janet herself, she would not have let her daughter bring him into the house. Yet, what had Janet said to me a while ago? They make their own friends these days and if you say anything against them you don't see them or their friends. That's the pass families have come to in this day and age.

As I entered the room Mike was saying, "Oh, I know a funnier rhyme than that. I used to say it when I was a boy. It went like this:

There was a bloomin' spuggy
Went up a bloomin' spout,
And then the bloomin' rain came down
And washed that bloomin' spuggy out.
Up came the bloomin' sun and dried up the bloomin' rain,
And then that bloomin' spuggy
Went up the bloomin' spout again."

It was years since I'd heard that one, and as Mike finished the last line in a rush as it was meant to be said, Harold lay back on the couch, drew up his knees and rocked himself while laughing hilariously.

Suddenly stopping, he said, "What's a spuggy?"

"A sparrow."

"A sparrow. Cor! we call sparrows spadgers. And I know a funny one, me Uncle Max sings it."

"Harold!" There was a reprimand in my tone, and he looked up at me, saying, "It's all right, there's no swearin' in it."

"I'm not worried so much about the swearing . . . at least, I am and everything else your Uncle Max sings."

"Me Uncle Max's funny."

"It all depends on what you call funny."

"Come on, come on," said Mike, "let's hear it, what your Uncle Max says."

"Now Mike!"

"Oh, woman, be quiet! We are boys together. Come on, Harold, let's hear your Uncle Max's funny one."

"Can I?" His face was bright, his eyes shining as he appealed to me.

"If there's no swearing in it."

"No, there's no swearin' in it."

"You're sure?"

"Yes, it goes to 'Rule Britannia'."

I started to pour the tea before I said, "All right, go on."

So he began in that surprising, beautifully clear voice. Now he sang:

> "Rule Britannia,
> Eat kippers when they're ripe,
> Fish . . . ish never, never, nev . . . ver
> shall be tripe."

I saw Mike's stomach wobbling; then before I had time to make any comment on the silliness of the words, Harold went into the next part. The tune changing, he sang:

> "Alway . . . ays, wear . . . ear your bikini in the sun,
> And pa . . . a . . . a . . . a . . . anties too . . . oo . . . oo . . . oo . . . oo!
> And be a goo . . . ood girl, now come, come, co . . . ome, come,
> Else you'll get bli . . . i . . . i . . . isters on your bum!"

Mike had turned his face away from the vocalist, but I hadn't.

"I don't think that's funny, Harold; it's silly."

"'Tisn't. There's a lot more, an' Uncle Max says. . ."

"I don't want to hear any more of what your Uncle Max says."

His eyes blinking, Mike now turned to Harold, saying, "You've got a fine voice there, young fellow."

"I know, an' I'm goin' in the choir with it."

"God help the choir." Mike's words were muffled in laughter, and Harold said, "What did you say?"

"I said, Good for the choir. . . Is your Uncle Max in the choir?"

Now it was Harold's turn to throw himself into a paroxysm of laughter, and when it was over and looking at Mike, he said, "No, silly, me Uncle Max sings in the pub."

"Yes, of course he would. Of course he would. As you said, it's silly of me."

When I handed Mike a cup of tea he said, "I envy you, you know; he's doing the same for you as you did for me on those far gone Monday mornings."

"You think so?" My voice was flat.

"Sure of it."

Harold was quick to take the conversation up, asking Mike now, "What did yer do for her on Monday mornin's?"

"Oh, I gave her a dose of castor oil and watered her horse."

When Harold now punched him in the arm, saying, "You're funnin'," I cried at him, "Don't do that! Harold."

"Well, he's funnin'."

"So are you."

"I know another. . ."

"We don't want to hear any more, Harold, at least none of your Uncle Max's compositions. Now sit up straight and have your tea unless you want to have it in the kitchen."

"No, I don't want to have it in the kitchen, but can I bring Sandy in? I haven't seen him."

"No you may not bring Sandy in."

"Aw!" This protest came from Mike, and I drew in a long deep breath, and when he said, "I wouldn't mind going into the kitchen and having my tea with Sandy," I said harshly, "Doctor Kane!"

"Yes, Mrs Leviston?"

Harold looked from one to the other, and when I said, "Go on . . . fetch him in," he sprang from the couch and ran down the room.

I looked sternly at Mike. "I wouldn't want to attempt to bring up that boy if you were in the house all the time."

"You know something, Maisie? As long as you've got him I'm not really going to worry about you, with your mysterious pains in the stomach and your questionable Indians."

From the moment Harold came bouncing back into the room accompanied by the equally bouncing Sandy our conversation became general. And when at half past five Mike left to catch his train his last words to me were, "See Doctor Bell as soon as you can about that other business, eh?"

"As you say, Doctor. As you say."

On the Tuesday morning I saw Doctor Bell. He was pleased at my decision. He rang up immediately and tried to make an early appointment for me, but the earliest I could get, apparently, was a week come Wednesday, eight days time.

And it should happen that I didn't go to see the psychiatrist.

Chapter 10

It was on the Thursday night about eleven o'clock, only a short while before I'd said goodbye to Tommy and he had put his arms around me and said, "Maisie, I'm worried about you. Look, until you make up your mind to marry me. . . And you will, you will one of these days, I know you will. You must. I couldn't feel about you the way I do without a little of it rubbing off on you, and then coming back to me. So, until then, what about me coming and staying here? Just to be near you. It's '84; nobody cares a damn what people do. And the time is going on; the older one gets the quicker it goes, and a day not spent near you is a day lost. What do you say?"

What I had said was, and gently, that I couldn't and that he was to give me a little more time. And I had added, "Let me get this pain business cleared up first; I don't want to take you as a night nurse." I had laughed but he hadn't.

After locking up I had looked in on Harold who had been asleep these past two hours. He was lying curled up in a ball and looked almost angelic. But he was no cherub, was Harold. I then went to bed, but I did not go straight to sleep, I lay awake waiting for the pain to start, but it didn't, and I was about to fall off to sleep when I experienced the most strange sensation: I was choking; it was as if I was dreaming I was choking. I turned from side to side and tried to throw something off, I didn't know what, I knew only that I was choking. I tried to cry out but no sound came, like in a dream when you are calling for help, when your voice is but a squeak. . .

I remembered no more, until I woke up hours later. I looked at the clock. It was twenty-past six. I'd had a good night's rest, an unbroken night.

I rose slowly from the bed, but feeling somewhat strange. I had no way of explaining the feeling, only that I wasn't worrying that this was Friday and tomorrow was the day when Jimmy Stoddart would call for his son. I would meet that obstacle when it arose, I told myself.

I had made a pot of tea and taken it into the drawing-room, switched on the electric fire, sat down and finished a second cup of tea. Only then did I question how I felt. And I could give myself no explanation why the night past was the only night for months that I hadn't been racked more or less with that pain. . . .

The day passed pleasantly, and when Tommy called late afternoon and said I looked better - did I feel better? - and I said, yes, strangely I did, he stayed only a short while because he had been invited out to dinner at the Housemans and, as he said, you couldn't refuse an invitation to be present at the table of God.

Alone, only one thing was worrying me: Gran hadn't phoned, nor when I had phoned her had there been any reply, and I had tried several times during the day.

When about seven o'clock the phone rang, there she was, and her first words to me were, "Have you seen the papers then?"

"No, I haven't seen the papers, Gran."

"You're in them again."

I held the mouthpiece back from me as if I were staring at her and in doing so missed something that she was saying. Then her voice came loud and clear - she always shouted on the phone - "I've just got in. I've been on a trip to Seahouses with the club, and there it was staring me in the face."

I waited, then said, "What was?"

"Stickle. "

"Stickle?"

"Yes. You remember him . . . Stickle."

"Don't be funny, Gran, please."

"I'm not being funny but you said it as if his name was new to you. Well, he won't trouble you any more, he's committed suicide."

If I'd heard the news of someone I'd dearly loved I could have understood my groping for a chair and sitting down and gasping as if for breath as I'd done in the early hours of this morning.

"What did you say, Gran?" My voice was small.

"It's in the papers, he's committed suicide."

Stickle would never commit suicide; he thought too much of himself. "You must have got it wrong, Gran."

Her words were lost in the shout she gave. Again I held the phone away from me, and when once more I could distinguish her words she was saying, "Headlines two inches deep and there underneath: Former husband of local writer, serving twelve years, et cetera, et cetera."

"All right, Gran, all right. But," I asked quietly now, "how could he hang himself in prison?"

"Don't ask me, it just says he was found hanged in a wash-place."

"In a wash-place?"

"That's what it says."

"Well, in a wash-place there would be bound to be somebody about."

"What's the matter with you, lass? Does it matter where he did it as long as he's gone? That's what I say, 'cos the way that fellow was made, twelve years would have been nothing to him, he would have had you in the end, of that I'm certain, and you know it inside yourself. . . I've got to go now; I promised to go down to Mary's. It's John's birthday, if you remembered."

When I was silent the voice came at me, "No, of course you wouldn't, you've got other interests now."

"Oh, Gran, why can't you let up?"

"Good-night, lass."

The phone went dead and I sank back into the chair. Yes, I'd forgotten John's birthday. But what did that matter against this other news? Suddenly I shivered violently, then shook my head again, remembering that strange choking feeling last night. . . It couldn't be possible, it couldn't. I didn't believe in things like that.

I hastily pulled myself up from the chair. The phone rang again.

"Maisie."

"Oh, hello, Mike."

"I have news for you."

"I think I've just heard it; Gran's been on the phone."

"Oh, yes she would. Now listen, dear. I've . . . I've got something to tell you, but I can't go into it over the phone. It's private, so I'm popping down tomorrow. It's my week-end off, I'll get the early train. I'll see you somewhere around twelve. . . Are you there?"

"Yes, Mike, I'm here. I'm bewildered."

"You'll be more so, dear, when you've heard my news. No more now; we're going to a show in Newcastle and Jane is waiting. See you tomorrow then, dear. Good-night."

Again the phone was put down abruptly.

I must have been walking like someone drunk across the hall because Harold, coming from his room with an exercise book in his hand, said, "You feelin' dizzy? You got a headache?"

I looked down at him but didn't seem to see him for a moment; then I blinked, saying, "Yes, a bad one."

"Will I make you a cup of tea?"

"Would you, dear?"

"Yes. But look" - he handed me the exercise book - "I've got to do that sum an' I've done it twice an' I've got different answers, an' I've done it on the computer. Will you look at it?"

"Yes, dear, yes." I took the book from him and he ran into the kitchen.

Sandy had been by his side, but now he didn't turn and go with him but followed me into the drawing-room. And when I sat on the couch he jumped into my arms and cuddled his head into my neck and I sat rocking him, and with each movement my mind jerked at the thought: It couldn't be. It couldn't be. Hate wasn't that strong.

Once again I was roused by the phone ringing. Slowly I rose and put Sandy on the floor. What now? Reporters?

When I lifted the phone I was relieved to hear Janet's voice saying, "That you, Mrs Leviston, eh?"

I wondered whom she expected, and I managed to say lightly, "Yes, Janet; who would you think it would be?"

She laughed, saying, "Well, your voice sounded different somehow."

Yes, it would sound different.

"Anything the matter, Janet?"

"No; I only thought I'd better tell you, you won't be seein' his nibs tomorrow, Stoddart. You'll never believe it, but he's gone down to have a talk with Maggie; he's goin' to try and stop the divorce. He wants to get back with her, so I hear. Oh, I hope she gives him his answer. But you never know, not with Maggie. And I understand her belly's full . . . well, she's pregnant again, so I wonder what he'll do when he sees that? Hie back I suppose as if the devil was after him, for he was never a one to stand his own responsibilities, let alone some other bloke's. Anyway, I thought I would tell you you're let off the hook tomorrow."

"Thank goodness for that, Janet."

"You all right?"

"Yes, yes, I'm all right, Janet."

"How's his nibs?"

"Splendid, acting like an angel."

"Huh!" I heard her laugh; "that'll be the day. Well, see you on Monday."

"Yes, Janet, see you on Monday. Good-night."

I'd had a peaceful night and had woken with a light feeling as if something had been drained from me. What, I didn't know, but I eagerly looked forward to Mike's arrival.

When he did come he didn't greet me with any jocular comment, but after being greeted by Harold and Sandy he said in an aside, "Can you get rid of the terror for the next ten minutes or so?" And this I did by going into the kitchen and setting the percolator going and telling

Harold to watch it and in the meantime to set a tray properly, and asking if he was capable of doing me a slice of toast as I'd had no breakfast.

In the drawing-room, Mike was sitting near the window that overlooked the gardens, and when I was seated he nodded towards them, saying, "Nice view," and I said, "Yes; it's a lovely garden, it's a pity it's not used more." Then looking at him, I asked, "What is it, Mike?" And in answer he asked a question, "How do you feel?"

I paused for a while before I replied, "You know, I can't really tell you: it's as if I was getting over an illness."

"Did you have any pain last night?"

"No; no, I didn't, nor the night before, Thursday night, although I had a most weird feeling around midnight. Why do you ask?"

"Well" - he let out a sigh - "what I'm going to tell you is off the cuff. It won't appear in the papers, I feel sure of that. Some things are better kept quiet, because both the papers and the television are accountable, in my opinion, for half the trouble that the young get up to. You only grow from babyhood to youth and then to man by copying. You see something on the telly tonight or read it in the papers, and you bet your life somebody takes it as a pattern tomorrow. Not that what I'm going to tell you is really new in that way, because there are groups at it here and there, but very much underground."

"What are you saying, Mike?"

"I'm saying this: you've been the victim over the past year, at least since Stickle started his time, if not before, but definitely since he started his time, of deep, deep hate thought."

I shuddered, and he said, "Yes, the result in your case was your pain."

"No." I could hardly hear the word myself, but he nodded as he repeated, "Yes. Definitely, yes. You see, it's this way. I happened to be working on a case with the prison doctor. I was called in as the second opinion. It was the morning after Stickle was found and I don't think. . . This is really off the cuff, mind, and you must never mention it to anyone, nor the rest of what I'm going to say. Now I don't think he hanged himself, not he, he wasn't that kind of fellow, he was hanged by some other inmates, not yet known. Never will be, I should imagine. Apparently he could never have done it himself; he was attached to the pipe above the cistern and his feet were only a few inches from the ground. I don't think he was quite dead when the warder found him, but he died all right. It seems he was hated by his fellow prisoners, especially by the friends of the man he'd had a fight with earlier on. Anyway, he had a hobby. It was modelling. He worked with clay and, I understand, turned out some quite good birds and animals. Two men he had shared a cell with said he could even work in the dark, but what he modelled in the dark wasn't animals or birds, it was a figure of you. When his things were examined there was part of a torso that hadn't been squashed up into a ball - he had likely been interrupted - and it was studded with matchsticks."

His hands were on my shoulders and he was saying now, "It's all right, it's all right, it's over, finished, ended. He'll hurt you no more. So come on, come on." He patted my cheeks quite hard. He waited; then he sat back on the chair and said, "This kind of thing isn't unknown, but I've never known it be so effective before, except we do know now of witch doctors willing men of their tribes to die, and they die. I've not much use for the God put over by the church, or the devil either, but what I do know is, there is evil in the world and in so many cases it proves to be stronger than good; as it has in your case, because I'm sure if it had gone on it would have affected your mind, even if it hadn't finished your body off first. You know, you are not all that robust and the human frame can stand up to only so much battering."

I laid my head back against the chair and said quietly now, "He must have got inside me because I know this, the moment he died I was choking. I didn't have any pain in my stomach or anywhere else but I knew I was choking. And then I went to sleep, and on Thursday morning when I woke up I had a strange feeling. Looking back now it was as if I had been released from something."

"You've been released all right. But now I must insist again, that you must not pass this on, not to Tommy or anyone else, because this part of the business hasn't been made public for reasons I've already made plain to you. Doctor Harper only told me because we're old friends and medically connected. Of course, through time it might leak out if there's talk, but by that time, should the papers get hold of anything, they will see that the recipient of Stickle's hate is alive and well and thriving."

"Shall we have a drink?" I asked quietly; "I feel I need it."

"Why not? And why not lunch somewhere? But not at Brown's again; two posh lunches in a week is beyond me."

"I'd love to, Mike, but I have my charge."

"Well, we'll take him along."

"Would you?"

"Why not? We'll make it his day an' all."

"You wouldn't like to go and see the new James Bond film, would you? Apparently that's where his father was going to take him today but he had other business."

"Why not? Why not? I've never been to the pictures for years." He rose from the chair and pulled me upwards, saying, "It's all in the past.

Remember that. It's a new life ahead of you; nothing worse can ever happen to you."

Not being God, Mike did not know my fate and what lay before me.

Chapter 11

During the following weeks I felt myself a new woman. I seemed to walk on air; a great weight had been lifted from my mind. The pain had vanished with Stickle's death, I'd cancelled my appointment with the psychiatrist, and Doctor Bell had confessed himself amazed by the sudden and sustained change in me. With each new week I couldn't get into my study quickly enough to start writing. And when Janet heard me singing about the flat, she said, "You won the pools, Mrs Leviston, ma'am?"

"Kind of," I said; and the reply puzzled her.

Now, incredibly it seemed, we were in August. Harold had broken up for the school holidays, and I had let him go off to spend a few days with one of his new friends. The Mohican had been largely silent, apart from occasional rather cryptic messages to the effect that he was still keeping watch; and then later on this Thursday afternoon he phoned me, his voice sounding very adult as he said, "Mrs Leviston, this is the Indian Chief."

"Oh, hello John." My voice was light, though tinged with surprise.

"I'm sorry this has all taken so long, but do you think you could meet me tomorrow morning? At last I can take you to the shop where the coffee jug is; now on offer, I may say as a solid silver antique with filigree lid and inner container. Did you know it had an inner container?"

"No, no, I didn't."

"Well, at that size, it's a work of art to have an inner container. Priced at one hundred and twenty-five pounds. Cheap at that, I should say, because at Sotheby's it would likely go for two or three times that price."

"Really?"

"Yes. Yes."

Why was I thinking that the person on the other end of the phone was dressed as an ordinary human being to match his voice?

"Can you manage it?"

"Yes. But where shall I meet you?"

"I'll be outside Liverpool Street station, the main entrance. I won't ask you to come and speak to me because I don't think you'd feel comfortable walking with me, would you?"

I stammered as I replied, "I . . . I wouldn't mind, John, knowing that under that make-up you're no Indian."

"Thank you once again, Mrs Leviston. Anyway, if you'll just follow me, I think it'll be better. It's about five minutes walk from there. I'll stand outside the shop and you can go in. Pretend you're looking for something. Don't remark on the jug or anything else you might see that's yours. Just take note. When you come out of the shop, there's a turning about twenty yards further down. It's a quiet part. Go up there. I'll be waiting. . . And, Mrs Leviston."

"Yes, John?"

"There's something else. In case there are people about and I can't have a word with you: I've . . I've got to go off for a few days, you know on a jaunt again, itchy feet; I wonder if you'd tell Mum to tell Hilda. . ."

"Why can't you tell her yourself, John?"

"Well, I won't be back tonight, and as I said, I don't like going to the factory. If you would tell Mum in the morning. . ."

"Won't Hilda worry?"

"Oh, I don't think Hilda worries very much, Mrs Leviston, she takes life as it comes. Anyway, will I see you in the morning because it's the only chance I'll have of showing you the shop?"

My voice was curt now as I said, "Couldn't you just tell me the name of it?"

There was a long pause before he said, "Yes, yes I could, but I . . . I wanted to have a word with you, as Mum would say, private like, if that's at all possible. You see I. . . Well, how can I put it? I feel you're on my side and I thought if . . . well, if I could explain something. . ."

I cut off his hesitant words by saying, "I'll be there."

"Fine, fine. Good-night, Mrs Leviston."

I didn't reply but put the phone down.

Why didn't I tell Tommy that I was going to meet the Mohican in the morning? I spent almost four hours with him later on, so why didn't I tell him? Because I knew that he would do everything in his power to stop me, or make it his business to come along with me, and somehow I knew that the Mohican wouldn't like that. . .

Next morning, when I gave Janet the message for her daughter, she put her hands on her hips and wagged her head as she said, "That's just like him, isn't it? He never turned up last night. Our Hilda came round about ten. I was gettin' ready for bed. Had anybody seen him? she asked. Nobody had. Joe was there and he went for her and said she was a blood . . . bloomin' fool and she wanted her head looked at; he was just playin' fast and loose with her. And what did he get up to on his jaunts? And when Joe said that he was likely on drugs, she went for him and said he wasn't. But to my mind she protested too quickly an' too loudly. Then I went for her, and I told her if I thought for half a minute she was on the stuff she wouldn't dare put her face in that door again ever. And you know what, Mrs Leviston, ma'am? She did what I've never seen her do in me life, she started to cry. She said she loved him; no matter what he was, she loved him. Ooh! I tell you there was a scene, and at that time at night. And of course after she left, an' when one after the other of them came in, Joe had to give them the whole tale over again. And there they were, the lot of them, havin' a committee meetin' about it, and they ended up all being of one mind, there was something fishy about the Indian. And as their dad went up to bed he said to Greg, 'You're chatty with that young market bobby, aren't you? Tell him what you think; it can do no harm and it'll put us in the clear if anything does come out about him.'"

Self-preservation, I thought. But they were right to try to find out what took the Mohican away on these trips of his.

A short while later I said to Janet, "I've got to go out to see my solicitor. I should be back before you leave."

"I'll keep something hot for you," she said.

"Thanks, Janet."

I had put on a grey costume and wore a head scarf as there was a high wind blowing. I took the bus to Liverpool Street station, and walked over to the main entrance; and from there I saw, in the distance, the Mohican. He was standing on the kerb looking as if he was waiting for an opening in the traffic to cross the road. He looked first one way then the other. Then it appeared as if he had decided not to cross over but to walk straight on: he turned away and sauntered along the road; and I followed.

A short time later I followed him across a road; and whilst he was waiting to cross a second, I came up almost behind him. But when I reached the other side I let him get ahead. I had never been in this part of town before. It wasn't a business district, and it certainly wasn't spruce.

I was now following him down a street that had a number of shops on one side only; on the opposite side the buildings looked like warehouses. I saw the Mohican stop in front of a shop window, then move on. By the time I reached the shop he had turned the corner he had spoken about.

I stood looking into the shop window. In the front were displayed two old guns in cases, behind them two naval swords, while round about was a conglomeration of brass and pewter and copper articles, urns and jugs and vases. There was a whole set of green plates, perhaps thirty pieces in all. To the side of the window there were three plates on stands. Two were Coalport, similar to those of my dinner service, and they were priced at thirty-five pounds each. Next to them was a smaller plate, the tag said Dresden. It had a tiny crack in the top but it was marked forty-five pounds. But standing between that and the Coalport was the miniature silver coffee jug. And yes, there it was priced at one hundred and twenty-five pounds. And further along the shelf lay the portrait locket that the General had carried in the breast pocket of his uniform. It was open, and pinned to the faded blue velvet interior was a tag, which read: Solid silver nineteenth century miniature locket. £140.

I didn't go into the shop; I felt I shouldn't be able to act as an ordinary customer. As I turned away from the window a big black car drew up at the kerb and the driver looked towards the window, as did one of the two men in the back. At least that's what I thought at the time. I walked quickly down the street to a turning which brought me into a broad thoroughfare at the far end of which was another street parallel to the one I had just walked down, and about half-way along it stood the Mohican talking to another man as oddly dressed as himself.

As I approached them I realized they were arguing, and I had almost reached them when I saw the man grab the Mohican by the throat, but seemingly in an instant the Mohican twisted free and at the same time he yelled something at me. What it was, I couldn't make out, but I must have taken it as a cry for help, for I screamed at the man, "Leave him alone!" And at this, the man swung round and made a grab at me.

What followed happened so quickly that even now I cannot explain it except that there was the black car again and three men pouring out of it, two of them going to the assistance of the Mohican's assailant and trying now to drag John into the car, whilst the third one, a huge individual with a nose that seemed spread right across his face, grabbed me and held me tightly against him with his hand across my mouth to stop my screaming. And all the time my dominant feeling was one of amazement that the Mohican could continue to kick and twist and punch at his assailants. But then the man who was dressed similarly to the Mohican stuck the knife into him.

When I saw the Mohican slide to the ground with the blood spurting from his neck my heart seemed to bleed too as my mind yelled, "Oh, no. No!" and one of the men cried, "You blasted fool!" and the man throwing the knife down whined back, "He would have grassed anyway."

"Not until he talked, you bloody idiot!" the man growled. Then turning to his companion, he said, "Come on! Let's get goin', and pronto!"

"What about this 'un, she's in on it?" my assailant yelled.

"Throw her in the back."

And that's what he did, he literally picked me up as if I were a feather and threw me onto the floor of the car, where I lay stunned for a moment until I felt his feet on me, and then I let out a high piercing scream which was half smothered by the grinding brakes of the car.

A voice above me said, "Shut her up!"

The next moment a hand came on my face and grabbed my nose. I opened my mouth naturally to yell again, and something was stuffed into it, almost choking me.

The voice above me said something again which I couldn't make out, but I soon knew when I was roughly turned over onto my face with the ease of someone lifting a shopping basket. And when my arms were wrenched behind my back my whole being screamed out, but silently, with the agony. When my ankles, too, were tied I was lying in such a position that I felt I couldn't bear it and prayed to lose consciousness. I didn't; I was kept awake through fear, petrifying fear. Tommy was right, they'd all been right, the Mohican had not been what he seemed, and now he had paid for it. Oh, the poor Mohican.

And me, what would they do to me? I had no doubt in my mind that these were dreadful men and that because I had seen their faces they would never let me go. And there was Harold. Oh Harold, Harold. Oh my dear Harold. And Tommy. Strange, but Tommy was fated not to have me. Dear God, why did these things happen to me. Why had I to get mixed up with such men, me of all people?

I must have lost consciousness for I didn't remember being carried from the car or arriving in this room or wherever I was for I was lying on a bed or a couch. It was soft and for a moment I didn't feel any pain; but just for a moment, for when I tried to move I experienced the feeling through my flesh and bones that I could only put down to being crucified. The last thing I could recall was being kicked. I had wriggled on the floor of the car and the boot had come into my side.

I was aware of the people talking. They were quite near. I kept my eyes closed. It was a woman's voice that got through to me first. She was arguing, shouting. Or was she pleading? She was calling someone Bunty. I couldn't imagine any of those men being called such a silly name as Bunty, but she was saying, "Now you won't do anything here with her, Bunty, will you? Promise me?"

"Be quiet! Be quiet!"

"I'll not be quiet. This is my place and so far I've been with you all along the line. But not that. And even if you did, you've still got to get rid of her. And what then? I tell you, Bunty, I'm havin' no Benson affair here, not above me shop. I couldn't stand it. I couldn't live here after."

"Will you shut up, Liz!"

"No, I won't shut up, I won't."

"I don't want to have to make you."

"Now don't you start with that on me, Bunty. I'm warnin' you, I'm no green kid, you should know that."

"It could be done quietly, Liz, with the needle."

That was a different voice, and now the woman's voice came again, louder now. "You shut up, Trucker," she said, "else you'll find that nose spread to your ears, I'm tellin' you. Give her the needle, you say, and then what? Little parcels goin' out of the door? You're a bastard. You always have been, always will be. If I had my way. . ."

A third voice entered into the conversation now, a soft voice. It said, "Couldn't you get her to promise to keep her mouth shut? Put her on the stuff . . . keep her for a time . . . 'noculate her like?"

There was dead silence. I strained my ears, thinking they had closed the door or gone. I moved my head to the side. Then the first man's voice said quite quietly, "Danny, when this load goes through I'm goin' to see to it that you go to a shrinker; he'll open up that bloody head of yours and insert a new brain, a monkey's will do because it'll be better than the one you've got."

"You're funny, Bunty." There was the high voice again; it was almost like a woman's. "I was only thinkin'."

"Well, don't!" It was a bawl from the man now. Then the woman's voice came in, saying, "And about this lot? When are you goin' to get it out of the store-room?"

"All in good time, Liz."

"Never mind about good time. I spew every time I see a copper pass the window."

"Well, you'll have to go on spewin' because I can't let it go all at once; I don't know what that bloody Indian was up to."

"He and Patsy took the last lot to Liverpool, didn't they?"

"Yes, they did. But why was Patsy picked up at the customs later? He's made that trip to Ireland fifty times before. Could he have been a police nark, the Indian?"

"No, Danny, no" - it was the first man talking now - "I've had him watched. Anyway, he's disposed of too many lots himself. No, he was featherin' his nest, startin' the game on his own, thinkin' he was a big boy because he had a bit of education. They always come a cropper that lot. And now he won't need his education any more."

"I'm not interested in what's happened to the Indian" - it was the woman again- "I'm only wantin' to know what you're goin' to do about her. But whatever it is you're not doin' it here."

"Why don't you give her the needle and walk her over the cliff?"

"Just like that: give her the needle and walk her over the cliff." It was the voice of the big man now, the one that had held me, the one with the flat nose.

Again there was a silence, longer this time; then the man I had come to think of as the ringleader, the one who was associated with the girl called Liz and whom she called Bunty, said, "I take it back, Danny, about havin' your head seen to. Why don't we give her the needle and walk her over the cliff? Now, now, now, that's a very . . . good . . . idea."

The last words brought Harold vividly to mind for they were mimicking Max Bygraves, and again my mind leapt away from my present situation and cried, Oh, Harold. Harold. Then, Tommy, Tommy. And I felt I was choking and I wanted to be sick.

I was brought back to the voices again by the man Trucker saying, "Beachy Head, Eastbourne."

Then the thin voice, "No, not Beachy Head; that bloody sloping green gives me the jitters. Hastings, that's it. You can take the car a good way along towards the cliff top there, up Fairlight way you know. Then what would be wrong to see a young girl . . . well, if you don't look at her face, her build gives you that idea, walking along with her mother and father, say."

"No, you don't! You bloody well don't get me on anything like that. Oh, no! Have another think, Bunty. Mother and father indeed! If you're doin' that kind of dirty work you're doin' it without me."

The man's voice held no offence as he said, "Well, she could be walkin' along with two friends, her father and her brother, me or Trucker or Danny there."

"Not me, Bunty, I'll be sittin' in the car waitin'. You know."

"Yes, yes, I know, Danny, you've got a weak stomach. Something will have to be done about it, and soon."

"Well, that's settled then. She has the needle and she thinks she's out for a trip to the seaside."

The woman's voice came to me again, asking now, "What has she to do with this business anyway?"

"Quite a bit I should say," came the reply, "on the sideline with the Indian. She lives in a posh house, and he's been there visitin'. We got the tip off The Tiger who used to go round with him. He said the Indian's girl friend's ma worked for the dame. She was supposed to be a writer, but it was a cover up. She's a bit of a hard case by all accounts: tried to do her first man in with a bottle or two on his head, but she got off; then he tries to murder her, supposedly, and he was doing twelve years for it when not long ago he hanged himself in stir; at least, that's what they said. And on top of that, about the same time I reckon, she had two blokes fightin' over her; she's adopted a boy and the kid's old man went for her boy friend. Oh, I don't think we need cry over her demise. Anyway, that's settled, so come on there, Liz, I need a drink."

"You can get it yourself. I've got a shop to see to and Jessie's got as much brain as Danny there when she's left to herself. By the way, you're sure nobody saw you comin' in the back way?"

"Does anybody ever see us comin' in the back way?"

"Yes, they do. I had to explain to old Nosey Wheatley across the lane last week when the car blocked her doorway that you were a rep, and that you'd got a ticket for parkin' too long in the front."

"Well, she would see nothin' today. We used some black polythene to carry the lady inside. If Ma Wheatley remarks on it, it's a dressmaker's dummy."

I was going to be sick; I was choking; I heaved and with the reaction my knees came up, and I opened my eyes. The next minute I was hoicked into a sitting position which racked my bones and brought from me a shuddering muffled groan.

I did not at first take in my surroundings, only the face hanging above mine. It was thin, as was the hair above it, and its owner said, "We're awake then, are we?" and he straightened up as the woman spoke again, saying, "If you want her to do any walkin' you'd better untie her else you'll really have to carry her like the dressmaker's dummy."

The man moved back from me now, saying, "Take her coat off, Trucker."

I looked toward the man with the flat nose. He too was stepping back, saying, "Not me; that short arm of hers gives me the creeps. Had a job to pull them together. There's things I don't mind 'andlin', but not that."

"God Almighty! Did you ever hear anything like it, coming from that mouth? I'll have two Dannys on my hands shortly."

The man called Danny, the youngest of the three I now noted, said brightly, "I'll do it. I don't mind strippin'."

"There's no strippin', just untie her and get her coat off."

"What about the gag?"

"Leave that; we don't want her screamin'." It was the woman's voice now.

"What if she takes it out?"

"Don't worry. It'll be some minutes before she can use her arms. By that time she won't want to."

He was quite right about the time it would take me to use my arms. I screamed aloud inside when the rope was taken off my wrists and I tried to bring my limbs forward.

The man with the thin face came towards me. He wrenched my good arm forward, pushed up the sleeve of my blouse, and when I saw what he was going to do I suddenly became convulsed and managed to half rise from the couch before he knocked me back.

When the needle was rammed into my flesh I remembered thinking, Oh, dear God, let me die now. And when a voice said, "Hold her still, you fool!" the man called Danny sat with a plop on my lap, winding me for a moment, and when my head hit the back of the wooden rim of the couch I went limp and dizzy. Then, as if I was going into sleep with my eyes open, everything inside me settled into a quiet acceptance, and when the gag was taken from my mouth I can remember saying, "Water."

The figures had moved away from me. I was looking down a room which was part sitting-room and part kitchen-cum-diner. There was a trellis-work some way along the room with a plant entwined in it. I saw the back of the woman and I heard a tap being turned on; then I saw her hand a glass to one of the men, but she herself didn't turn round. From the back she looked smart: she was wearing a blue summer dress, and her hair was a light blonde and dressed high on top of her head. I heard her say, "I'm goin' down now; keep it quiet." Then she disappeared from my view.

When I saw the glass of water being held before my face I went to lift my hand to take it, but, as in a slow motion picture, it didn't reach it. The man put the glass to my lips and I gulped on the water and choked, and gulped again and choked; and it dribbled down my chin and onto my neck, but I did nothing about it.

I sat on that couch a long, long time and it was an equally long, long time before I could make myself utter the word, "Lava. . . tory."

When the flat-nosed man pointed to a door, a voice barked him down, saying, "Bloody fool! There's a window in there."

"Well, what can she do now?"

"You never know."

I watched the man now walk over to a phone attached to the wall and speak into it, and after a few minutes the woman entered the room. She came straight towards me. Her eyes were downcast, almost completely hidden by her false eyelashes; she was heavily made-up and I could see that she wasn't young . . . well, she was older than me, around forty I would have said. She took hold of my hand and when I was on my feet I swayed and would have fallen had she not steadied me.

Whilst walking to the far door I seemed to be picking my feet quite high from the floor; and yes, there was the window. I recall that all the time I was in the bathroom the woman leant her back against the door while continuing to look at me, and every now and again she would move her head from side to side. I can't remember her leading me out nor what happened afterwards, except that someone gave me a cup of tea and offered me a biscuit from a plate, and that as I looked at the plate I thought of Harold, not with any regret but just with a sadness because I knew I would never see him again. Yet, all the while there was a great unrest in me: I was dimly aware that some part of me was fighting to get out, it was wanting to scream, but I knew that I couldn't supply the energy.

One after another the men went out, but the one that seemed to penetrate my lethargy and reach that tearing part of me in which there was fear, was the man called Danny, the young one. Once he sat close beside me on the couch and the fear almost got control when he started to fondle me, until a voice seemed to come from nowhere, yelling at him, "Out of that, you!" And I was surprised it was the woman's voice because it was so loud and angry-sounding. She went on talking rapidly at the man who was now saying, "Oh, Liz. Oh, Liz, it was only a bit of fun." And then she said, "If it's the last thing I do I'll see that Bunty kicks your arse out of here. It's in the loony-bin you should be, you perverted little bastard."

Yet all the while she was upbraiding him he kept smiling at her. I recall she did not leave the room until her boy friend came back, and then she spat words at him, too, and he seemed to be trying to placate her. But when she had gone he said nothing by way of a reprimand to the man Danny.

As time went on the lethargic feeling seemed to weaken and that part of me that was screaming got stronger. Once, it forced me to my feet and I was stumbling towards a window when there was a shout and I was hurled bodily back to the couch.

"That wasn't stiff enough, boss."

"We want her to walk, don't we?"

Although I struggled with them I knew I had as much chance as a fly had against a swatter. The needle stabbed me again and once more my inward yelling gradually receded.

It seemed that I'd sat on that couch for a lifetime watching the comings and goings before the woman helped me into my coat. When she had buttoned it I saw her bow her head and mutter, "Christ Almighty!" And then she turned on the men, her voice a hiss now and hardly audible: "This is the last," she said; "I'm finished, through. And as for you two, don't put your faces in here again or else you'll find yourselves takin' a long jump, and it'll be quicker than any you dish out for I'll shoot you both, I'll promise you that. And you, *big boss*, can have the job of disposing of the bodies. You're good at that. Now get her out of here before I do something I'll be sorry for an' so will you."

When they drew me down the room I walked slowly but steadily with them; then on down the stairs, and as we reached the bottom it was the flat-nosed man who said, "She's another one that'll have to be seen to if you ask me anything."

"You shut your trap. You lay a hand on her and by God! I'll finish you off meself. An' that goes for you too." He turned to the younger man. "Now I'm warnin' you. I'm also warnin' you she meant what she said, so it's up to me to save your skins and get somebody else to come back and do the loading."

They now sat me in the back seat of the car, my body crushed tightly between them; and then the car was backed out of the yard and we were away.

It seemed a long time before we reached the country, at least before I glimpsed green fields and hedges.

When the flat-nosed man, for the second time, took a drink from a bottle the man Bunty said, "Cold feet, Trucker?" and Trucker, looking across at me laughed and said, "You know me, Bunty. I always wear woollen socks."

The shaking of his body penetrated mine and seemed to force a crack within my mind that held the fear, and when I wriggled the Trucker man said, "She's laughin' at it," and the other answered, "I wouldn't reckon on it." Then he leant towards the driver asking now, "Will we get there before it wears off, Danny?"

"Yes, plenty of time, and it'll be on dark," the young man answered.

"It'll be a good two hours before it's dark."

"But we're not half-way there yet, are we? And anyway" - the young man laughed now - "we can sit and look at the view. That's what people do in their cars along the seafront there, they sit and look at the view, 'cept when they go to sleep." His head came back and he laughed again, and his boss said harshly, "We're not bloody well goin' into Hastings."

"No, you're right there, you're right there. Fairlight it is now. But you won't have to leave it too late else you won't find your own way back; the top of that cliff has as many scallops as a cockleshell."

The big man now laughed while the other said, "Thanks for the warnin'. Very kind of you."

"You're welcome. You're welcome, boss."

The note of jollity in the car seemed underlined with threats. My mind, although still muzzy, suggested I wasn't the only one in danger: any one of these men could do for the other what they were about to do for me, and without compunction. It came to me dimly that they were together simply because of the need of each other for whatever work they did, and my mind began to grope as to why I was here: what brought me here? Who brought me here? And the dim answer was, the Mohican. If I hadn't met the Mohican I wouldn't be in this situation. But then, as minds do, mine took me back to how and when I'd met the Mohican. It was because I was sitting in Janet's living-room meeting her family for the first time. And why was I sitting there? I had adopted her grandson. So if I hadn't adopted her grandson I wouldn't have met the Mohican. But the mind then took another leap. I wouldn't have adopted Harold if it hadn't been that I was acquainted with Janet, and Janet, in desperation, had brought the boy to work with her. Yet that hadn't made me adopt him. No; Janet had worked for Nardy and his parents for years. Back further: If I hadn't written a story called *Hamilton* and had it accepted by a publishing house called Rington and Houseman of which Mr Leviston was an editor, I would never have met Janet. Then back further still: Why had I written a book about a horse that had become my companion during the lonely years married to a sadistic man called Howard Stickle? And why had I married him? Why? Because I'd thought he'd be the only man ever to want to marry me. But he hadn't wanted to marry me, he had wanted to marry my house and the bit of money I had.

Where did things begin and how did they end? They ended here sitting in a car bowling towards some cliffs over which I was to be thrown. Death was the end. All life was planned. This was the end of my plan. But I'd be with Nardy. Yes, I'd be with Nardy. Yet, why was it I didn't want to go to Nardy? Not yet anyway, not yet.

"We'll have to stop for petrol."

"God Almighty! I thought you had filled up."

"I had, but that was yesterday. Trottin' round the town eats it, you know that."

The car stopped. The driver got out. He was now talking to two men on the forecourt; I could see them through the windscreen. A while later one of the men came to the half-open window and, looking in, said, "Lovely evening, sir."

"Yes, very nice. A bit too warm for me though."

"Oh, it won't last long. It never does, not in England."

The man was looking at me. I tried to lift my hand towards him. It was a slow movement, but it only got a few inches away from my knee when the big man took it and patted it.

The face was withdrawn from the window, and the voice said, "Good-evening, sir," as the driver got back into the car, and the flat-nosed man said, "Did you see that, Bunty? She lifted her hand. She should have another jab."

"Don't be a fool; she's got to walk, hasn't she? You don't want to support a drunken woman along the cliffs, do you?". . .When they eventually helped me out of the car I drew in a long breath. There was the smell of the sea. The last time I'd smelt it was the Saturday Tommy had run us down to Hastings and we had walked from one end of the long promenade to the other, ending up in the old town where we'd watched Harold enjoying himself in the small funfair. Afterwards we'd all played clock-golf, then stood at a stall and ate a plate of whelks. It had been a lovely day. But that had happened in another life.

When they began to walk me away from the car I glanced back. There were lights appearing in houses inland from the cliff and quite near was the sound of waves lashing against the rocks. A wind had come up and my hair was blowing into my eyes.

When a dog came bounding towards us I filled my throat with a cry, but it was muted. I wanted to call, "Sandy!" but it was a labrador and it did not even pause but went straight on past us. Then its owner appeared and when he said, "Good-evening," my whole body jerked from the arms linked with mine and my mouth opened and my head went back, but my hair was again in my eyes. I lifted my hand towards the man but it was grabbed and shaken playfully while one of them answered the man's greeting. Then they both laughed quite loudly as if we were enjoying a joke.

We walked on, until suddenly I was pulled behind some gorse bushes and thrust onto the ground.

The door to full consciousness was gradually opening: I could hear the thunder of the waves more clearly now as they battered the rocks; there was a great rushing feeling inside me.

One voice said to the other, "Go and saunter to the edge."

"What?"

"You heard. Have a decko right an' left."

"But you can hardly see now."

"Oh, God above!"

I knew one of them had stepped from the gorse and I began to pray and I knew in this moment that no matter who we are or what we have previously thought about there being a God or no God, in the knowledge of approaching eternity we turn to whatever is there and speak in the only way we know. And I said, "Our Father, who art in heaven, hallowed be Thy name, Thy Kingdom come, Thy will be done on earth as it is in heaven."

My mind stopped the prayer at this point for there, standing before me, was Nardy and with him was Hamilton, and it was Hamilton who said, It's all right. It's all right; it just takes a second.

And it only took a second because, having been led forward to the edge of the cliff, I flew into the air and it swept through my body as if pumped by a fire hose. There was a great roaring. It was the voice of God and it deafened me. Then all was still.

Part Two

TOMMY

Chapter 1

How many times can one die? Dozens of times. Hundreds of times. Dying was good, it was peaceful; it was when you were brought back to life, that's when the pain started. Life wasn't good. Life was this dreadful feeling of being dragged up from great black depths, up, up, through mud and water, up, up, past screaming voices, until you could stand no more, and you died again.

Every time I was dragged back to life I prayed to die, and I died.

It became more painful when there were longer intervals between the dying. I had once read that some people had been dead for so many seconds and when questioned about what they had experienced they had said, "Nothing, it was a mere blank;" and I knew this to be true, because when I died again and again there was nothing.

There was one period of living that I hated more than the others when this voice would come at me asking me questions, until God stopped it. And God had the voice of a woman. But this time the voice said, "I've got to ask; it's important. And look; she's opened her eyes."

Were my eyes open? I didn't know; everything was misty and I couldn't think of anything but the torture that they were applying to my body. That must be the man with the needle. He kept sticking it in me, and even up my nose and down my throat. But the voice kept on. It was saying, "Mrs Leviston. Mrs Leviston. "

I thought dimly that it sounded like the Mohican's voice, but the Mohican was dead. I knew that; I had seen him just before I died; he was dead.

"Mrs Leviston. Mrs Leviston. Can you remember where they took you, dear?

"Look, sister" - the voice had changed now - "I've got to get this information out of her, it's imperative. It's weeks now."

"It may be, but she's not fit yet, she's not fully round. Oh, you lot!"

"Yes, I know, us lot."

"Mrs Leviston. Mrs Leviston. Can you remember where they took you?"

Could I remember where they took me? Who took me? I'm going to die. I want to die. I can't stand any more. There's nothing that will make me stand any more.

"Mrs Leviston. Mrs Leviston."

Then another voice: "This is Tommy, Maisie darling. Can you hear me?"

"Tommy."

"She said Tommy, so she's round. Mrs Leviston. Mrs Leviston."

Why was Tommy calling me Mrs Leviston?

"Can you give us an idea where they took you in that black car?"

In the black car? Yes, I had been in a black car. And I went to Liz. Yes, Liz, in the dress shop, boutique.

"Liz?"

"Yes. Yes, Liz. Go on. Go on. Oh, please, Mrs Leviston."

"Boutique . . . dresses, Liz, stiff hair . . . boutique . . ."

"My God! Yes, yes, that little dress shop. It's called, Liz's. Yes, yes, Bainsworthy Place. Oh, Mrs Leviston, you're wonderful. I always knew you were wonderful, and brave and kind. . . I'll be back shortly, Tommy."

"Can you manage? Will you be all right? Are you fit enough?"

"Fit enough for this."

How nice of the man to say, "Mrs Leviston I always knew you were wonderful." I'd never been wonderful. Yet Nardy had thought so, and Tommy thought so. But I want to die; I'm so tired of all this I just want to die. And my head, my head, my head.

As I sank into the blackness again a woman's voice said, "Let her be. Let her be; it'll be longer next time."

Chapter 2

How many times can one die? Why did I still keep asking myself that question? One time when I had been returned to life I knew I was being wheeled into a room full of glaring lights, and I died again.

I was in great pain after I became alive that time, but from then I never died fully again. And the day I realized there'd be no more dying, at least not yet anyway, I really woke up and for a moment thought I was back in the drawing-room because this place, where I was, was full of yellow light. And then I saw two white-robed figures, one on each side of me. Their hands were around me and both together they said, "One, two, three, up we come!" and I groaned aloud and cried, "Oh. Oh. Oh."

But they took no notice of my moans and said, "There you are; there's a bonny girl for you."

I looked from one to the other. Their faces were bright.

"Good-morning, Mrs Leviston."

My mind said good-morning, but I didn't voice it. "What's happened?" I said. Was that my voice? I could hardly hear it, it was only a squeak.

They laughed now and one of them, striking a pose, said, "One of these days . . . *I'll tell you a story.*"

A streak of fear ran through me. That was Max Bygraves again, and a man had said those words. But . . . but I was alive, I wasn't dead. I spoke again, "I'm alive."

"Of course you're alive."

"Where am I?"

"Now where do you think? You're in hospital."

"Where?"

"In London, of course."

"But . . . but how?"

"Now don't ask so many questions all at once, save your breath to meet all these visitors that you'll be having. To tell you the truth" - a smiling face came down to mine - "I'm sick of them tramping in and out of my ward."

"What's that?" I said, but as I motioned with my head to this thing sticking up at the bottom of the bed the pain ran down the back of my neck, causing me to close my eyes, and the nurse said, "That's your leg, Mrs Leviston. And what caused that pain was jerking your head. Now what you've got to do is to lie still and be a good girl or else we'll have to say no to your visitors."

"But my leg?"

"It was broken. And your arm too."

Slowly I looked down at my arm. It was my good arm, and it was lying straight out and bandaged up to the shoulder. Slowly I realized that my head too was bandaged. Then I became aware of a tightness around my ribs. The only parts of my body that seemed to belong to me were my short arm and my left leg.

"Now no more talking. Just lie quiet and we'll make you pretty." A hand came out and gently patted my cheek; the voice was gentle too as it said, "You're a very, very lucky woman, Mrs Leviston, a very lucky woman."

A quirk in my mind that was still there said: Apparently a broken leg, a broken arm and an acute pain inside my stomach. Yes, I was a very lucky woman. . .

They washed me; they put my short arm into a clean bed jacket, the other arm of which was draped over my shoulder.

"There now, there now," one said.

Then they brought my breakfast. But they wouldn't let me feed myself, although I assured them I could use my short arm. But no, they fed me.

They were treating me like a baby.

"The doctor will be round shortly; he will be so pleased with you."

"Why?"

They looked from one to the other; then one laughed and said, "Because he thinks he's a clever so-and-so putting your skull to rights."

"My skull?" I put my hand up and touched my head. It seemed that I had a stiff cap on it.

"What was wrong with it?"

"You ask him, my dear, he'll tell you."

When, a short while later, a small dark-skinned man came into the room I had no need to ask, for he started straightaway: "Well, well! Merry and bright. That's more like it. How do you feel?"

When my answer wasn't immediately forthcoming he went on, "Perhaps not so merry and bright, eh? But how's the head? Aching a bit? Well, that's to be expected. Give it a few more days and you won't know you've got one, a head." More laughter, accompanied this time by murmurs from the sister and the nurse in attendance.

"Lucky little woman. Do you know that? That's what you are, a lucky little woman." His dark face was beaming. "Related to the cat family, nine lives. . . How's the rest going?" He had turned to the sister now, and she answered, "Very well, Doctor. Very well."

"Good, good. And the sooner we get the therapist on the left leg the better. But not yet, not yet." He was smiling at me again, and again I felt a child as he said, "We want no more trouble from you, you understand? You've got a whole arm and a leg" - he had called my deformed arm a whole arm - "and look after them, because I don't want to see you in that theatre any more."

"What day is it?"

He seemed surprised at my question. "Saturday," he said.

"What Saturday?"

He glanced at the sister, then laughed again, "This is Saturday, the twenty-second of September, nineteen eighty-four. God be praised."

The sudden effort to sit up straight brought a shudder through my strapped and stiffened limbs and the sister quickly to my bedside, "There now, there now," she said. "Don't jump out of bed all at once."

"Can't be September."

"Can't be September, she says, sister. Are we wrong?"

Sister smiled broadly as if the doctor had just uttered some great witticism, and she answered, "I don't think so, doctor."

"It was August when you were brought here from Hastings, the second week, wasn't it, sister?"

"Yes, doctor, the second week."

His face was near mine now. "You've overstayed your welcome, do you know that? And we'll have you on our hands for some time yet, so behave yourself."

I made no reply. My lids were blinking as I tried to reckon up how long it was since that Friday morning when I went to meet the Mohican . . . *Oh, the poor Mohican.* I'd forgotten about the Mohican.

"Has he been buried?"

"What?"

"Has the Mohican been buried?"

The three occupants of the room now exchanged glances, and the smile went from the doctor's face. He looked perturbed.

"That's . . . that's what I called him, the Mohican. He dressed like an Indian, and they stabbed him." My mind, I found, was rapidly sorting things out.

"Oh, *that* Indian." The doctor was nodding now, the smile back on his face. "No, he hasn't been buried, not yet."

"It's a long time since August."

"Oh, now, now, you mustn't cry. I can't stand women who cry because then I cry too. I must away. Be a good girl now. Be a good girl."

The doctor turned and, accompanied by the sister, went from the room. But the nurse stayed, and she wiped my eyes, saying, "You don't want red lamps when you've got a gentleman waiting to see you."

"Oh. Tommy?" I said.

"No, not Tommy, but doubtless he'll be here any minute. How is it you have so many men after you? And mostly big ones. There's that one from the north, Georgie, and. . ."

"Georgie? Gran's Georgie?"

"Well, I suppose he's somebody's Georgie. And there's the other one from the North with a complete shrubbery around his face."

"Mike."

"Is that what they call him? We know him as Doctor Kane."

"They've been here?"

"I'll say, and some more, and here's me can't even keep a boy friend. Now, behave yourself." She patted my cheek, laid my short arm on the coverlet, then went from the room. And the door had hardly closed on her when it opened again and a man entered.

He was a stranger; I had never seen him before. His neck was bandaged and he had one arm in a sling. He walked stiffly towards me; then pulling a chair up to the bedside he smiled at me. I looked at him: his hair was black, parted down the centre and flattened to each side of his head, yet it didn't reach his ears and cover the bald patches there. His face was pale-skinned. He had a straight nose and wide mouth and deep-set eyes of a dark brown colour.

He said, "Hello, Mrs Leviston."

That voice. I knew that voice. I looked downwards to his clothes. He was wearing a light grey suit and an open-necked shirt. His hand came out and lay on top of mine. I wouldn't believe what I was thinking, not even when he said, "John Drake, at your service, ma'am."

"The Mohican."

His smile widened and he nodded, "Yes, the Mohican."

"I . . . I thought."

"That they had done for me? I thought so too, and I wasn't the only one."

"You've . . . you've changed."

"No, this is me, or will be when my hair grows again."

When my face screwed up in disbelief the effect was painful for my skin seemed to crack and my voice was a mere whisper as I said, "You weren't really one of them?"

"No; only pretending. But it was a long pretence, over two years. In the end I . . . well, I really felt that I had become . . . the Mohican."

"You're a. . . ?"

"Policeman."

"Never!"

"Yes. Don't I look like one?"

"No, not at all."

"Well, I am. Detective Sergeant James Bainbridge, at your service."

"Not John Drake?"

"No, James Bainbridge."

"What happened to you, I mean after? It seemed to go in your neck, the knife."

"Well, it did somewhat, but just above the shoulder blade, and luckily missed the jugular. But it would have been Goodbye Mr Chips if it hadn't been for my connection. He had learned they were on to me, and he was about to get in contact when he saw me walk away from the shop. There was a signal he would have given me as he passed, but then he recognized you. I don't suppose you'll remember an American tourist with a slouched hat when you crossed the road? Anyway, he expected you to go into the shop and was about to pass you when you changed your mind and walked on. It was then he became aware of the car; he recognized the driver and immediately contacted a squad car. They arrived just too late to rescue you and pick the others up but soon enough to get me to the hospital. So there you have it, the story of my life."

"What was it all about . . . drugs?"

"Yes, drugs. And in a big way."

While he spoke I found myself sitting on the couch in that room and my head swam as I jerked and said excitedly, "I . . . I know where they are stored. In a dress shop, she's called Liz, a sort of boutique."

He squeezed my hand between both of his now, saying, "Yes, I know, my dear." He called me my dear so naturally. "I got the information out of you some time ago, and because of it the sister nearly finished me off; the effort had been too much for you and you sank back into yourself for two or three days. They wouldn't let me in after that."

"And you went there?"

"Yes, but in a bunch."

"Did you get those men?"

"Oh, they'd been picked up sometime before. Trucker and the psycho, and the ringleader of that little mob who went under the name of Bunty, they were clear for almost a week after they dumped you. And I don't suppose you'll remember a man and his dog walking along the cliff path that night?"

I started to grope in my mind, and then I saw a bounding labrador and I said, "Yes, yes, I do. Yes, I remember, especially the dog."

"Well, that man was a bit curious when later, and almost dark, he saw those two men that he had passed earlier on get into a car, but there was no sign of the girl they'd had in tow. There are some houses close by and he thought they might have been taking the girl home. That was until it came out in the papers that you were missing; and I was sufficiently round by then to give a description of the black car and the three that were in it. It all linked up, and the search for you began along the foot of the cliffs. Without much hope at first; they thought you would have been swept out to sea because the tides were high about that time and a bit rough. But you hadn't even reached the shore; there you were on a narrow jutting piece of rock and being held in place by some shrub. You hadn't fallen half-way down the cliffs. But when you landed you did yourself a great deal of damage, and they never expected you to pull through. You know, you're a miracle: there wasn't a part of your body that wasn't bruised or battered or broken, even your left leg, they tell me, is lacerated. Strange, that this" - he wagged my short arm - "should escape."

I had that frightened feeling on me again.

"What did you find in the shop?" I asked.

"What we expected, a good hoard. It would have brought in about two million pounds on the street. And not only that. She was petrified, Miss Liz, and to save her skin she blurted out quite a bit of very helpful information, something that we had been trying to piece together for the last four or five years. It was a connection with a yacht that was lying along the river and owned by a very respectable citizen and an old tub based in Hull that did trips across the channel and linked up with a foreign craft."

He drew in a long breath and slumped back in his chair before he said, "I'm glad it's over. I was sickened at times. And you know, it's the easiest thing in the world to take to that stuff, and I must admit it was difficult at times not to, especially being a . . . Mohican." He now pressed my hand and added softly, "I liked the sound of the Mohican and I liked you from the day we sat at Mum's table when I faced up to Stoddart. I felt we had a lot in common then; and we have shared quite a bit since, haven't we?"

I don't know if there was any colour in my face but it felt hot. To dampen down on my emotion I asked, "Didn't anyone know the truth about you?"

"No; that would have been fatal. I was sent from another area, and I was soon on the black list of the fellows in two of the stations. The only connection I had was the American tourist, Dave Radlett; we were in the same squad. Of course, he wasn't an American tourist all the time" - he laughed now - "he was a barrow boy one time until some of the real ones threatened to do him in. The same happened when he took up a paper stand. Oh, we were very versatile, we blokes. And by the way, it was Dave who collared our gentleman friend and his lady wife, Mrs Beckingtree-Holland. He's doing eighteen months now, and she's on probation. Oh yes; to say the least we are very versatile . . . and frightened out of our wits half the time."

"Oh, John."

"Do you think you could call me Jim?"

"No, I don't. I'll never be able to think of you as anyone other than John or the Mohican."

"That's a pity."

The look in his eyes brought the colour to my face again, and I asked, "How did Hilda not guess?"

"Oh, Hilda. Hilda never questions."

"Was she always like that? I mean, did she always dress like that?"

"No, no. Give her her due, she was almost a replica of May when I met her, but of course with only half of May's intelligence. But she's easily influenced is Hilda."

I said somewhat stiffly now, "She's a very nice girl really, I think."

"Yes, she is, she is, and she was much too good for a . . . Mohican or anyone of his breed. But as things are now . . . well."

I let my head fall back into the pillows. He had used Hilda. That wasn't like the Mohican. And he was being patronising towards her, and that wasn't like the Mohican, at least not like the Mohican I thought I knew.

"What does the family think of what has happened?"

"Oh, they are very chuffed. You can imagine it. Funny how people's opinions can be altered by the clothes you wear."

"Well, you can't blame them for that."

"No, I suppose not. But you know, the reason some of the kids dress up in this gear or dye their hair six different colours is mostly through boredom. You know, we're all imitators and gregarious: we live in mobs and we know that if we aspire to be different we're ostracized."

In the ensuing silence the door opened again and in came Tommy, and on the sight of me sitting up, my eyes open, he let out a long drawn, "Oh . . . h!" placed a great bunch of flowers on the side table, then came round the bed and, bending over me, he took my hand, which I'd taken from my visitor's, and holding it tightly pressed it against his chest, and he said, "Oh! my dear. How wonderful. You're looking grand."

"Don't be silly, Tommy." I closed my eyes. "I'm plaster from head to foot; how can I be looking grand?"

"Don't talk back to me, woman; when I say you're looking grand, you're looking grand." He bent and kissed me on the lips, and when he straightened up he looked across the bed to where the Mohican was standing now, and he said, "Isn't she marvellous?"

"Yes, she's marvellous, and I've just been telling her so."

"Good. Good. Oh." He bent over me again and, taking my face in his hands, he squeezed it, and again my skin seemed to crackle. "We'll soon have you out of that. And I've got news for you."

"I'll have to be going now."

We both looked to where the young man was standing very straight in spite of the fact that his neck and arm were bandaged, and Tommy said, "Be seeing you then."

"Yes, be seeing you. Goodbye, Mrs Leviston."

"Goodbye . . . John."

The Mohican smiled, then turned about and went out.

"Nice fellow that, brave as they come. My goodness me! To think what he's been doing all this time. I take it all back what I said about him. Anyway -" Tommy now pulled a chair up to the bedside, then went on, "I was right in a way, he wasn't what he appeared to be. And like you, he's lucky to be alive. Oh, darling." He now hitched the chair nearer to the head of the bed and, stroking my cheek, he said, "You've got no idea what I've been through all these weeks."

It was still in me to laugh. My head shook, my arm and my leg shook; I daren't let my stomach or my ribs shake, they were too painful.

And now he was laughing out loud, saying, "That was funny, wasn't it, saying that to you. But you know what I mean: I've been in agony every day, and they've had to throw me out; I've become a perfect nuisance."

My face was wet. Then after a moment, as I sat looking at him, I suddenly thought of Harold and asked myself why I hadn't thought of him before.

"How's Harold?" I said sharply. "Where is he? Who's had him?"

"Harold's fine. He's with Janet, and she's going to bring him this afternoon. But he's been here a dozen times already. And you know, I don't think you need worry any more about the fight for priority in our affection for you, we've come to a sort of truce. And strangely, he seems to think your living or dying depended solely on me, and he promised he would do anything in the future if only I would see that you would be all right. Strangely, too, he's gone off the Mohican since he knows he's a policeman; in fact, he blamed him very verbally for getting you into all this trouble. And you know, he was right. And I blamed him too. I wanted to murder him at first, that was when you disappeared; policeman or no policeman, it made no difference. By the way, did he tell you that the Captain and his lady had been picked up?"

"Yes. Yes, he did."

"But it didn't come about through what they had taken from you; the Captain, at his original game, had been getting things on approval including a nice little bit of jewellery, and, of course, giving a wrong address. And you'll be pleased to know that you've got your miniatures back, but not your rings."

"It doesn't matter."

"You tired, my dear?"

"No, no. I was just thinking what a lot of stock we put on possessions, and yet they are only ours for a very short time. All that collection in the china cabinet: they all belonged to somebody else, going back down the years; they're no use to them now as they'll be no use to me some day."

"Come on, come on, stop thinking in that way. As I said, I've got some news. How would you like to go to sea?"

"I wouldn't; I'm not struck on the sea, I'm seasick."

"Well, you'll have to get over being seasick, I'm buying a boat. Oh no, I mustn't just call it a boat, it's a yacht."

"You're not."

"I am, and with you in mind. You'll love it."

"You'll never get me on a thing that depends on sails. . ."

"This doesn't depend on sails, it's got twin screws and Volvo engines. And they're dependable enough. Oh my dear, wait till you see it. It's a peach; I've never seen anything like it. He's sorry to part with it himself . . . Mr Percy Liddle."

"Then why is he parting with it? It's likely got a leak somewhere."

Tommy laughed loudly now, saying, "*Spring Fever* wouldn't deign to have a leak. No; he's selling her because he's going back to Switzerland. He's got a business there. He had one here but like many another it's losing money, and it's an expensive business keeping a boat in harbour if you're only going to use it at holiday time."

"What about the expenses to you, or whoever buys it?"

"I can afford it."

"How much is it? I mean how much is it costing?"

"Well, I'm getting him down a bit. He wanted thirty-five thousand for it."

I nearly lifted from the bed, then pulled my hand from his and held it to my head.

"Oh, I'm sorry, dear. Does it hurt?"

"Yes, it hurts. And that sum hurts too. You must be mad."

"No, I'm not mad. That boat today would cost between sixty and seventy thousand and be cheap at that. If things weren't tight all round I wouldn't stand a chance of getting it for the price I am willing to pay."

"It'll take all your money."

"Don't be silly. During the last two years, dear Mama's little fortune has made more capital and I don't use it, I'm a working man earning a salary. And anyway, if I lost every penny I've still got that property in the West End. I could sell it for a fortune now and would do so only the damn tax man would grab so much of it. And I'm not really used to that yet. Don't worry."

"How big is it?"

"About thirty-five feet. And it has a beautiful saloon upholstered in green and gold, carpets right through. It sleeps six, and has a real double bedroom with bathroom and shower. And that room has everything, wardrobes, dressing-table, lounge couch, you wouldn't believe what they can get into thirty-five feet. There're two smaller cabins, single bunks, and then there's another two singles which I understand were used by the crew."

"It needs a crew?" My squeak hurt my throat.

"Well, he had an ex-merchant navy officer as captain and another fellow who cooked and did general cleaning duties . . . oh, the galley. You'd be amazed. It's a kitchen, and has a real washing machine."

"Never!" There was a deep sarcastic note in my voice, and I closed my eyes. Apart from being tired by Tommy's enthusiasm and the thought that his boat would be wasted on me for he'd never get me on it no matter if it turned out to be a luxury liner - the cruise I'd spent with Nardy had proved that neither of us were sailors - I wasn't feeling well.

"I've tired you. I'm sorry, dear. I'm thoughtless. But . . . well, I imagined it would cheer you up. Anyway, if we never put out to sea in it, it would be nice just to go and sit in it at weekends. People . . . do you know, they have boats that have never gone under London Bridge or moved up river. Look, I'll be quiet; you go to sleep."

I did not protest and say, No, I'm all right; I kept my eyes closed and my mouth shut. I was tired and I was in pain. Although very little of my body seemed to belong to me, it nevertheless registered aches and strange pains, especially the lower part of my stomach. I must ask about that. I wished Tommy would go. I wished everybody would go, especially the Mohican. Why had I said that? He had gone. I had a great desire to sink into that peaceful nothingness again. But not to die, except if I was going to do it properly, for I didn't want to go through the experience of being dragged back into life.

I knew the nurse had entered the room and I knew that she was standing at the other side of the bed looking down at me. Then her whispered words came to me: "She's very tired. I'd let her rest."

Tommy was asking her a question. I didn't know what it was until I heard the answer and the nurse saying, "Oh, some long time yet, weeks, weeks. It's very early days."

I don't know how long I slept this time but when I awoke I was conscious of a small hand holding mine, and I lay for a while savouring the feeling before I opened my eyes; and there, standing close to the bedside, was Harold.

"Harold."

He did not answer me. Then I heard Janet's voice come from the other side of the bed, saying, "Well, say hello to Mrs Nardy. You've been talkin' enough about what you're goin' to tell her."

Still he didn't speak; but his eyes became wide and damp like my own, and when he bent and laid his head on top of the hand that was holding mine the tears flowed gently down my face. And Janet's voice was stringent, yet with a break in it: "There you are now," she said, "see what you've done. The nurse'll turf you out. I told you."

"Oh, Janet." I turned my head towards her.

"How are you, dear?"

She had never before called me dear.

"Better, Janet. Fine."

"Oh, yes, you're fine." Janet's head was nodding vigorously now in denial.

"I've got three stars."

It was as if he knew what would please me most, and I said, "Never!"

He nodded, sniffed, and when his grandmother said, "Use your hanky. What have you got one for?" he dived into his pocket, took out a clean square and blew his nose; then looking at me with the look of the old Harold, he said, "She always keeps on . . . Gag. Me Uncle Max says that's what they're goin' to get her for Christmas, a big one, a gag." He hunched his shoulders as he looked across the bed at the frowning Janet, and I looked from one to the other and felt back home.

"What did you get the stars for?"

"Singin' and writin' and . . . an' behavin'." His lips were nipped in; his eyes were sparkling, laughing at himself.

"Wonderful."

Now bringing his face nearer to mine and his voice taking on that rapid, non-stop, chatter that I loved so much, he said, "And they're all suckin' up, wantin' to be me friend, all 'cos of you an' the Indian, an' the racket. And Millie Stott's mother asked me to go to tea, she did. She was waitin' outside the railin's and she asked me. But I'm not goin'. . ."

"You are." Again I looked from one to the other. They were exchanging glances, and now Harold said, "She's soppy, Gag."

"She's a nice little girl, what I've seen of her. You should thank your lucky stars someone like that takes an interest in you, clodhopper that you are."

Oh, I definitely was back home, and it was lovely.

"Ah, Gag."

Janet was looking at me now, her eyes twinkling. I said to her, "Has he been a good boy?" And she pursed her lips and wrinkled her nose, but then, her face straightening, she said softly, "Yes, ma'am, yes, he's been a very good boy. And so upset. Like all of us. Oh, ma'am" - she reached across and caught my hand - "what you've gone through. And all through the Indian an' meetin' him in my house. I felt sort of responsible, we all did, all the lads. They were so bothered. You know, our Rodney and Max, they took a day off an' went down to help them search after that man came forward an' said where he had seen you. And they had just found you when they got down to Hastings. Nobody thought you would live, you know." She paused, then said, "Oh! ma'am, you were in a dreadful state."

I forced myself to smile now to prevent myself from crying again, and, nodding towards my leg, I said, "I still am, Janet. They've got to feed me, wash me . . . the lot."

She sniffed now, then straightened up. "We haven't got to tire you else that nurse'll be on us again," she said.

Indicating Harold, I asked quietly, "Has his father been around again?"

"Oh." Janet raised her eyes to the ceiling, saying, "There's a tale there. You won't believe it. I can't believe it, I just can't. I'll tell you some other time."

"Me mum's comin' back."

"You shut your mouth, young 'Arold."

"His mother's comin' back?" There was apprehension in my voice, and Janet said, "It's a long story, but it's got nothin' to do with him." She jerked her head towards Harold. "You're all right; so's he; an' if I could laugh about the whole affair I would, especially at Stoddart, but I can't. Oh! our Maggie."

My hand was tugged, and I looked at Harold as he asked quietly, "When you comin' home, Mrs Nardy?"

"I'm not quite sure, Harold. Next week. . ."

"You'll be lucky." We both looked at Janet. Then again I turned my attention to Harold, saying, "Soon. As soon as possible because I miss you."

When his arms jerked upwards and around my neck I almost screamed as the pain shot down my spine, but I closed my eyes and with my short arm I held him to me. His nose was pressed into the only part of me that didn't seem to be bandaged up, a space above my short arm and below my chin. And when it became wet I said, "Now, now, you'll have me crying and then the nurses will go for me."

His words were smothered but I heard them, and when I answered, "I love you too, darling," Janet got to her feet and made her way to a table near the window on which was a huge flower arrangement in a basket. After a moment she turned and said, "I . . . I think you've had enough, ma'am. I think you've had enough. Come on you. Come on."

I pressed my son from me, because that's what he was, he was my son and the love I had for him was of a quality I'd never before experienced. I could have given him birth so close was the feeling I had for this child, and he for me. Oh yes, and he for me.

He was standing now with his head bowed, rubbing his nose on the side of his first finger, and I endeavoured to bring things back to everyday normality by saying, "Harold Leviston, what have I told you about that finger and your nose?"

"Oh, you!" He was groping for his handkerchief again and when he put it to his face he made great play of blowing into it while his eyes blinked at me.

When we kissed goodbye, he said, "See you tomorrow."

"You'll not."

I looked at Janet.

"Well, you're not fit yet, ma'am."

"Of course I am . . . please."

"All right then. Well, I'll let one of the others bring him because they're all mad to come. Oh, I must tell you." She came and bent over me and her mouth moved from one side to the other before she said, My 'Arry sent you a message, ma'am. 'Give her my best respects,' he said. Did you ever! Give her my best respects. I said to him, 'That sayin' went out with your granny.'"

"That was very nice of him, Janet."

She sighed. "Yes," she said, "I suppose it was, because he never gives a damn, I mean a thought to anybody but himself. Yes." She laughed now. "Huh! Yes, I suppose it was when you come to think of it. . . Come on, you!" She held out her hand; then looking at me tenderly, she said, "Take care. The house isn't the same. It won't be until you get inside again." And at this, she grabbed her grandson and without further ado made for the door; and when from there he shouted his last goodbye I lay back and closed my eyes, and smiled.

*

I had been asleep again. I was always wanting to sleep; I was so tired. I remember they woke me up for dinner, which I insisted on managing myself after they had cut up everything to size. Yet when the nurse came to take the tray away she said, "You've hardly touched a thing."

"I'm not hungry, nurse."

"You've got to eat."

Yes, I had to eat, but what I wanted more was just to sleep, peacefully sleep, because when I slept now I dreamt. I dreamt that all my limbs were moving: I was walking; I was running; I was sitting; I was standing; I was chasing Harold and Sandy across the heath. . . Sandy. I never asked where Sandy was. Oh no, he couldn't be left on his own from Janet leaving in the early afternoon until she returned the next morning. My worry must have shown on my face for the nurse asked, "Now what's the matter?"

"My dog. I don't know what's happened to my dog."

"Oh, your dog. The white poodle?"

"Yes, the white poodle."

"Oh, I understand your caretaker's looking after him. He and his wife brought him the other day. They kept him in the forecourt; the husband thought you might be able to see him out of the window; he didn't know you hadn't come round. I wouldn't worry about him. If you were as well as him you would do, my dear. What you've got to worry about is yourself, and eating. "

I wondered as she fussed over me how she and all her like managed to keep this caring attitude for one and another of those that passed through their hands. I was sure I couldn't do it. They were a special breed; but all different. Some were a bit stiff and proper, never thinking of calling you, my dear, but giving you your full title while doing everything that was required of them.

Later that night, as I dropped off to sleep, I knew there was someone else who was caring for me, and very deeply, for Tommy was still sitting there, just as, I understood, he had done most nights since I was first brought into hospital.

*

I had been transferred to a private ward and visitors were allowed in any time. However, they didn't usually put in an appearance until after the doctor's round which I had come to know was usually over by eleven o'clock. But on this Sunday morning the breakfast tray had hardly been taken away when a head appeared round the door. The bush around the face seemed to get greyer every time I saw it, and on this appearance I again caused a pain to shoot down my spine as I tried to turn on my side as I cried, "Mike! Oh, Mike! Where've you sprung from?" I was muttering the words into his beard as he kissed me.

"A quite comfortable hotel, madam. I came down last night late on, couldn't get away earlier. Jane had arranged to come with me when at the last moment her dear mother arrived. You've never met my mother-in-law, have you?"

"No. No, Mike." I was smiling widely.

"Well, she's the original stand-up comic's target."

"Oh, Mike."

As he pulled a chair up towards the bed, he said, "She's not really; but she comes on the hop, no phone message, nothing, just lands on the doorstep and expects her only daughter to wait on her as she did before we were married. . . How are you feeling, dear?" His voice had dropped.

"Which part are you enquiring about, Mike?"

He chuckled. "Oh, you're reviving," he said; "I think my journey's been unnecessary. Well, we'll start with the head. That got the most bashing."

"It aches."

"It's bound to. But he did a good job on you, he's a clever fellow. They don't come any better, so I understand. Your leg and your arm. Oh, that's ordinary, just compound fractures, they're nothing." He pulled a face. "How's the middle?"

"I don't know, Mike. What did they do to the middle?"

"Oh, I think they untangled your guts. Put a couple of rivets or so in your pelvis and sorted it out generally."

"Oh, is that all?"

"As far as I know." He caught my hand now, saying, "You're the luckiest girl alive. My God! You should have died with that sub-dural haematoma."

"What's that?"

"Well, to put it simply, it's a blood clot between the bone of the skull and the brain. That's why you were fluctuating in and out of consciousness."

"Really?"

"Yes, really. It was a tricky business. He had to drill a burr hole in your skull and aspirate the blood clot. It was touch and go with you for a time. I hope those three get their just deserts, the same as Stickle got his. Odd that you had to get rid of that pain only to have a worse one taking its place. Anyway, attempted murder will take care of them for some time, I'm sure of that. But by! you do pick 'em, don't you, the men in your life?"

"Yes, I seem to, don't I? But don't forget there was Nardy, and before him George, and now Tommy, and all the while, right from the beginning, you."

The whole bush of hair round his face moved as he muttered, "Stop your soft-soaping." Then he added, "But it's good to see you looking . . . well, different. I hadn't much hope the first time I glimpsed you."

"You've been before?"

"What do you think? I've been twice. You spoke to me the second time, and you know what you said?"

"No?"

"Hamilton."

"I didn't."

"You did. Had he come back?"

I tried to think, then said, "Yes, yes, I think he did."

"You are going to marry Tommy?"

"Oh." I thought a moment, then said, "Yes. Yes, I suppose so, sometime."

"Don't make it sometime, make it soon. He's a good fellow. He's another Nardy, only twice the size."

"There could never be another Nardy, Mike."

"They say there's never a good but there's a better, but in this case I'll say he's as good as."

"Have you met the Mohican?" Why should I talk about the Mohican when we were talking about Tommy? "I mean since he stopped being the Indian."

"Yes; I've met him once since he reverted to himself and I take back all I said about him. He's a brave man. They've got to be, doing that kind of job. Over two years he played that game, so I understand; it's a wonder he didn't become an addict himself. I said he was, didn't I?"

"Yes, you did. He's a nice person, Mike, very nice."

"I've no doubt of it, none whatever." He put his head to one side, then asked, "How old is he, do you think?"

"Twenty-seven, twenty-eight."

"Oh, I wouldn't have thought he was that; a bit younger I would have said, twenty-four."

"I thought they had to be a certain age before they got into the C.I.D."

"Oh yes, yes, perhaps. Well now" - his tone became brisk - "this is a short visit, my dear, because I promised Jane I'd be home shortly after two, so I'll have to catch that eleven o'clock, and before I leave I want to have a word with your man. Sister tells me he should be around about this time, being Sunday."

As he looked at his watch I said, "It was good of you to come, Mike. I'm . . . I'm so grateful. It's been almost as good as my Monday visit to the surgery."

He now rose and bent over me, saying, "Nothing will ever be as good or as amusing or aggravating as those Monday morning visits. Do you exclaim 'wh . . . at' to the doctor when he comes round?"

"Yes, every time."

He laughed. "That was a funny habit you had, wasn't it? I've never heard anybody exclaim what! like you did."

"There weren't many patients like me, Mike."

"No, you're right there. By, you're right there. Well, my dear. . ." Again he kissed me, and I put my hand onto his thick hair as I said, "Give my love to Jane, and thank her for sparing you. She's a very understanding woman. Goodbye, love."

He patted my cheek, walked two or three steps backwards, saluted, then turned and hurried out.

I loved that man. Yes, yes, I did, I loved him, and I wasn't going to differentiate between a father and a brother or a husband or a lover, I just loved him.

I knew that Tommy wouldn't be in until later in the afternoon because he had run down to Brighton to see Bella, who too was ill.

It being Sunday, however, I knew there would probably be visitors after lunch; but the only one I was looking forward to seeing was Harold.

I had just settled myself for yet another nap when the door opened and the nurse called, "You have some visitors, Mrs Leviston." And there, as large as life, were Gran and George.

"Hello, pet."

"Hello, love."

They were bending over me.

"How you feelin'? Eeh! what a mess-up." That was Gran. "My God! lass, where've you gone to? You were little afore, but look at you!"

I hadn't been able to say a word. They were now seated close together at the side of the bed and my voice was thick as I said, "How lovely to see you."

"Not half as lovely as seein' you, lass."

I smiled at George. He was looking older: his hair was quite grey, in fact it was as if I hadn't seen him for years. Gran looked the same. She was ageless. And the next moment she proved that her tongue too had not altered, for she said, "Eeh by! you're the one for notoriety, aren't you? Gettin' yourself into the papers. My God! for two days you hit the front pages, all mixed up with Indians and gangsters and drug runners. We couldn't believe it, could we, Georgie?"

At this point, leaning towards me, Georgie picked up my hand and said, "But she was a hero . . . female-like, heroine."

"Well, it's all how you look at it; she might have been a dead heroine. You don't look half alive yet." And she put out her fingers and patted my face.

"Oh, Gran."

"What d'you say it like that for, lass? You could have been dead, all through gettin' mixed up with those funny people. You should never have left home; they're a queer lot up this end. I've said it afore, and I'll say it again. And when Georgie here came back and told me how you looked, eeh! I couldn't believe it. I couldn't come 'cos Mary was down with a summer cold. It hung on, and I had to see to the bairns." Gran was nodding as if to emphasize her words.

Mary and the bairns were her first concern now. How things changed; how people changed. But then, in this case, that's how it should be.

Gran leant towards me as she said, "Kitty sends her love."

The fact that Gran was telling me that Kitty had sent her love was in the form of a reproach. Whether intended or not, that's how I saw it, and that it all stemmed from my interest in Harold. And this seemed to be verified by her very next words: "It's goin' to be a long time afore you're yourself again, lass, and able to see to that youngster."

"Oh, it won't be all that long." I tried to keep my tone level. "And anyway, he's staying with Janet. She's seeing to him."

"Best place for him, among his own kind."

"Mam!" George's voice was loud. "I told you, didn't I, keep off it."

"Yes, I know what you told me. But I know what I think, and all this trouble started with him."

"Gran."

"Aye, lass." Her voice had softened.

"It isn't fair; you're hitting me when I'm down, because I'm not up to a fight."

"Who wants to fight? Not me. But you know me, I have to say what I think."

Yes, yes, I knew Gran: she had to say what she thought. But years ago her thoughts had been softer, more tender. That was when I had needed her.

It was George who now asked, "You in much pain, lass?"

"Not too much," I answered, "nothing that I can't manage. A bit of a headache all the time."

"My! they were a lot of dirty buggers weren't they?"

"Yes, Gran; they were a lot of dirty buggers."

My head, as I'd said, ached all the time, but now it thumped with her next words.

"It said in the papers the other day that they can't bring them to trial yet until you're well enough to give evidence. That'll be another big splash in the papers."

I closed my eyes and drew in a long breath. A court case. I'd never thought about that. Of course, I'd never thought about much since I'd come round. Things had to be triggered off in my mind, and Gran's remarks certainly triggered off my fear of being in a court. Even thinking about my past experience filled me with a sick dread, let alone the thought of facing those men again.

I was aware that George was whispering something to Gran, and for answer she dug him with her elbow; then bending to the side, she picked up her carrier bag and from it brought out a fancy wrapped box which she laid on the bed saying, "That's from Mary. It's chocolates. And this" - she now handed me a large envelope - "is letters from the bairns." Then dipping into her bag again, she brought out another small parcel, saying, "That's from me, it's scent."

"Oh, thanks, Gran."

"It's not cheap stuff mind, it's a good make."

"Of course I know you wouldn't buy anything but a good make." I now said, "You must have had to leave early."

"Aye," George nodded, "just after seven. But we were up from half-past five or thereabouts." He jerked his head towards his mother. "If she'd had her own way we wouldn't have gone to bed in case we missed the train. And don't those trains move! And now that we're here I thought it would be a good idea to take her round London." He again jerked his head towards his mother. "She might get to like it." And as he laughed she put in, "Never on your life."

"There are some beautiful parts, Gran," I said quietly, "and so much to see."

"There might be, lass, but it isn't places I'm concerned with, it's people. To my mind you get no response from big houses and palaces, it's the people that matter."

"Well," I felt forced to say, "there are some nice people live in the big houses and palaces. There's the Queen for instance."

"Aye, there is," George said with a grin. "Now that's something,

Mam, we might look in on her 'safternoon, an' she might give us a cuppa, save us having to spend out."

Surprisingly Gran answered, "She might an' all. I wouldn't put it past her, for she seems to be the only canny body in this neck of the woods."

Although it caused me pain in my chest and in my rearranged guts, as Mike had called them, I joined my laugh to George's.

But the next minute there was almost an explosion when he said, "If you want a lesson in bigotry you come to the north-east, especially from types like this 'un." He now dug his elbow towards Gran. "I've travelled the country in me time, as you know, lass, and what I found was, if you look for the bad 'uns you'll find 'em. And she needn't look any further than her own street, silly old jenny."

"What did you call me?"

"A jenny."

"That isn't me name. What you up to?"

"I know it isn't your name, Mam, it's another name for an ass."

I didn't listen to Gran's explosion, but I looked at George. He didn't change; he held no animosity: he had lost three fingers in the fire, burnt off to the bone, but he held no bitterness towards me. He didn't say, as his wife had done, if it hadn't been for my letting them have the house to live in they wouldn't have suffered as they did in the fire, and her youngest daughter wouldn't have been scarred for life. . .

As I had done once before after they left, in order, as Gran said, to have a meal before they got on the train, 'cos they weren't paying train prices, I criticized myself for feeling relieved of their presence, at least of Gran's; no, not of George's, never George's.

I must have been very tired following their visit for I went to sleep and I remember little of what followed that day except Tommy saying "Sleep, dear." And that's what I did for the next three days: I ate and I slept and my mind stopped working. I think this must have been the outcome of the numerous pills they had given me to swallow. . .

Towards the end of the week, however, I was feeling different, brighter, more alert. I no longer had a headache and, too, on the Friday morning the bandage was taken from my head, and although this had revealed that I was bald above one ear, I quite readily agreed with the doctor that all I had to do was to alter my parting.

It was on the Friday afternoon that I had another visit from the Mohican. I could never think of him by any other name; not that there was any resemblance to him in the very smart young man who took his seat beside my bed, saying, "What a difference! You look marvellous."

Why did people always say I looked marvellous? I'd never looked marvellous in my life. And so the answer I gave was, "Not even the term exaggeration could fit that remark," to which he replied "And the remark proves that you are yourself again." Then a little hesitantly he went on, "I thought I'd call in to say goodbye, at least for the present. I'm being sent home to my old station, but as soon as the case comes up I'll be back. It's amazing what's been unearthed: one thing's led to another."

"Are they going to make you Chief Constable?"

There was a touch of sarcasm in my tone, and he answered it, "Not yet. No, not yet." He pulled a face at himself. "Undercover men are just undercover men. There are a number of us."

"Are you taking Hilda with you?" I asked.

I saw the expression on his face change and his lips purse before he answered, "I shouldn't think so."

"Why not?"

"Well" - he shrugged his shoulder now - "Hilda belongs to a chapter that is past, or is passing."

"Just like that."

"Oh, Mrs Leviston, you know Hilda, you've seen her, you've heard her. Anyway, she understands. Even as . . . the Mohican, she realized there was nothing permanent in our association, there never is with the Mohican types."

"Or other types, I should imagine."

"You're condemning me?"

"I . . . I think Hilda's very fond of you and you used her."

"No, I didn't. Well, not in the way you mean; she picked me out. And anyway, look at us as we are now, chalk and very much cheese. Now if she had a mind like yours. We, for instance, recognized each other, didn't we, even when I was the Mohican?" His head had come forward; he was looking at me in an odd penetrating way. "How old are you?" he asked. And I just prevented myself from saying, "What?" but answered, "Thirty-five, hitting thirty-six. How old are you?"

"Twenty-seven hitting twenty-eight. There's not much difference between us age-wise, or any other way that I can see, and I recognized it the first time we met."

I pressed myself back into the pillows. What was this? Yet I knew what it was, and I knew he was right. Yes, I had felt something in him the first time we met. It was in his voice. I had felt my heartbeat quicken as it didn't do when Tommy was near me. Oh my God! this was silly, stupid really, ridiculous. I forced myself to turn my face to him and say in a heavy tone, "I have one adopted son, I don't want another."

"Oh . . . oh, don't be silly, my dear . . . Mrs . . . Leviston . . . Maisie."

"*Please.*"

"Please what?"

"Don't you be silly."

"Are you going to marry Tommy Balfour?"

"That's . . . that's my business."

"Then you are not sure?"

"Yes, I am sure of what I mean to do, but again I say that's my business. And . . . and now I'm very tired."

He stood up and looked down at me, saying, "End of act two, that's a good line to finish on, but the play has some way to go yet. Goodbye, my dear." Then quickly and before I could prevent him, he kissed me. And now he was smiling as he said, "And we've got that in common, too: we've both got bald patches behind our ears."

I did not look at him leaving the room. My heart was beating against my still painful ribs. What, in the name of God, was the matter with me! What was it that people saw in me so much that they could hate me to death, or love me? Nardy, Tommy, and now this attractive young being. There was something weird about me, there must be. It had come out with the horse. But this latest business: no; no, never. Pull yourself together. Yes, yes, I must, and when Tommy comes tonight I'll tell him . . . I'll tell him that I'll marry him. Definitely I'll tell him.

Tommy came as I knew he would, but I didn't tell him I would marry him.

Chapter 3

In whatever way my emotions were affected by the Mohican they were definitely put in their place the following day when I had a surprise visit from Hilda. The first part of the surprise was that she was no longer wearing her extraordinary get-up that had matched the Mohican's but was dressed in a green skirt and a three-quarter length coat to match. The white blouse had a bow at the neck and the whole outfit looked so simple, and so unlike Hilda that at first glance I did not recognize her; even her hair style was different, soft, hanging down onto her shoulders.

"Hello, Mrs Leviston."

"Hello, Hilda. Oh, how nice to see you."

"I hope you don't mind me comin' in?"

"Of course not. Of course not. Sit down."

As she sat down to the side of the bed she said, "I haven't brought you anything. Well, you see, I didn't think I would come in, have the nerve like."

"Why not? Don't be silly; why shouldn't you come in and see me?"

"Because of me mum. Not that I said I was comin'. She stopped May and Max. He wanted to bring Harold. And you know Max, or at least you don't, Mrs Leviston, but he'd make a cat laugh at times and Mum said it pains you to laugh."

"Oh, not any more; and it's good to laugh."

I was smiling widely now but Hilda wasn't, she was looking down at her hands and the two fingers that were seemingly picking another hole in the white honeycombed bed cover.

I waited for a moment or so before I asked, "Is anything wrong, Hilda?"

She lifted her head. Her eyes were blinking, and she looked away to the far window as she said, "I shouldn't have come, an' he'd go for me right, left'n centre, if he knew, for . . . for he likes you. He . . . he thinks you're very clever and understandin', and I thought - " she swallowed deeply before she brought her eyes to mine and ended, "you might have a word with him and persuade him like. I know we are different and I'm not up to his standards, I'm dim, like, I know I am. I know I am."

"You're not, Hilda."

Her eyes were blinking more rapidly now and her voice was slow and definite as she said, "Oh, yes I am, Mrs Leviston. Not if I'd been like May, things would've been different. But he's . . . he's a gentleman. He is you know, you know he is, Mrs Leviston. You saw the difference straightaway. He always said you could see below the skin."

She was again looking down at her fingers which were plucking more quickly now at the bedspread and her voice was a mere whisper as she said, "I love him. I'd die for him. I'd do anything for him. I'd keep in the background. I told him I would as long as he would let me be there near him. I said I would try to learn to speak proper an' all that, and how to act and. . ."

My short arm came out and almost dragged her fingers from their plucking and my voice was harsh as I said, "Don't denigrate yourself like that, Hilda! you're as good as he is any day."

"Oh no, Mrs Leviston." Her head was shaking.

"I mean it, Hilda. There's more things in life than being able to talk properly, as you say, and act as if you were somebody you're not. You've got what many people would envy, capacity to love, and that's a great thing, Hilda."

"You think so, Mrs Leviston?"

"I don't just think so, I'm sure of it. Now you get it into your head that you are worth loving, and you tell him so. Don't crawl, Hilda. Don't crawl."

"Oh, Mrs Leviston, I'll always crawl where he's concerned; he's just got to open his mouth. And . . . and Max is always singin' 'Less than the dust 'neath thy chariot wheels'. He sings it funnily, but . . . but I've often thought that's how I feel with regards to John. I can never think of him by any other name but John. And things would have been different if he'd let me keep the baby . . ."

She finished this sentence with her mouth agape; then, her hands linking together, she shook them as she said, "Mum warned me, I've only to open me mouth and I'd get somebody hung."

"You have a baby?" I'd pulled myself now from the pillows without any effort and was bending towards her.

And she muttered, "I could have had, I wanted to, but . . . but I had an abortion." Her eyelids lifted and she stared at me for a moment. "He wanted it that way. An' . . . an' Mum an' all, 'cos as she said, he'd never be able to work to keep it, an' what a life it would have had. Of course we didn't know then that he could have worked and was already workin' sort of. Anyway, it had to go. And . . . and I was bad after. I couldn't stop cryin'. I was sent away for three weeks so I could pull meself together. He was nice about it."

Gran's retort was in my mind. "Bloody hell!" she would have said. "He would be nice about it."

"I . . . I think if I'd had the baby I wouldn't have minded so much, I mean about now, being left. May's been a brick. She's taken me in an' looked after me 'cos I started that cryin' bout again. But I'm over it now. Well, I mean, I've got to face up to it like, haven't I?"

She had forced a smile to her face, but at this moment it was I who wanted to cry.

"May was for me comin' to you about him, but Mum nearly went round the bend. She swore what she'd do to me if I did. But" - her smile widened a bit - "here I am, and I know I'll get it in the neck but I had to try. Do you understand, Mrs Leviston?"

"Yes, Hilda, I understand. And you know something? And I mean this: I think you are too good for him, far too good for him."

"Oh, no, no, Mrs Leviston; he's educated an'. . ."

"Damn education!" The jerk I gave made me take my hand from her arm and hold my neck, and she said, "Oh dear! there I am upsettin' you."

"Oh, no, of course you're not; it's just when I jerk my head I think it's coming off. But to get back to what I said, or to say something further. I could only wish that you'd get over your feeling for him and find a nice young man who'd make a home for you and you for him. How old are you?"

"I'm on twenty-five."

I was again surprised for I had thought she was nearer the Mohican's age. . . The Mohican. How could I ever have thought . . . ? What had I thought? Again the pain went down my back as the movement of my head denied my thoughts. He was a snob, an upstart. Who did he think he was, anyway? After all, he was just a policeman.

"Will you speak to him if you see him, Mrs Leviston?"

I had to force myself to say, "Yes, yes, I'll speak to him, Hilda." I had not said in which way I would speak to him.

"I'd better be goin' now."

"You aren't at work?" I asked.

"I've been off these last two or three days. I wasn't feelin' up to the mark. The doctor gave me a note. Nervous debility, he said. Well, goodbye, Mrs Leviston, you've been so nice. Mum says you're always nice. She thinks the world of you, does Mum. She says it was a lucky day for her when you married Mr Nardy. She's meanin' about you takin' Harold. None of us can get over how you handle him, because he's a holy terror."

"Is he not behaving himself?"

"Oh. Oh, he's all right now, because" - she laughed now - "he knows he's got to be, else Mum'll tell you. An' you know, he's terrified of not comin' back to you. An' you know somethin' else?" She bent over me now. "It had the lads in stitches at first until Mum said, the next one that laughed she would kick his ar . . . smack his face for him, 'cos you see Harold says his prayers at night."

"He says his prayers?" My smile was soft, my voice was soft.

"Yes. Yes, he does, Mrs Leviston."

Harold saying his prayers. I had never made him kneel down and say his prayers. . . That must be the school. Bless them. Of a sudden I longed to be home with Harold and Tommy. Oh yes, with Tommy. My mind had strayed from Tommy. . . Damn that Mohican.

"Goodbye, Hilda. And just a moment." She was turning away, but I caught her hand again and said, "You won't believe this, but you'll get over him. I know you will. And you'll meet a nice fellow one of these days. You're too warm and kind to be passed over. He's a fool. Oh yes, he's a fool and he'll find it out one day."

She was unable to speak, her lips were moving in and out as she attempted to swallow, and hastily she turned from me.

She'd had a baby. He had made her have an abortion. And she had wanted a baby, especially his baby. Some men were cruel and cruelty didn't only come through ignorance, it came through education and the feeling that because of it you were different, superior, and of a class that wouldn't deign to marry beneath it. Make use of it. Oh yes, make use of it, as he had done of Hilda to help him complete the picture of the drop-out. I hoped I never set eyes on him again.

And I didn't for a week; and then I was sitting up and had more strength with which to speak my mind.

In the meantime I had another visit from a member of Janet's family, and this one not only surprised me but amazed me after I'd got over the fright of seeing her walking into the ward with her son . . . my son.

The only name for Maggie Stoddart was blowzy: she was big-busted, big-hipped, and with a wide face and mouth to match; her hair was dyed inky black, and her eyes were deeply mascaraed. What age was she? She could have been thirty or fifty. She had a bouncy air about her, and in the following half-hour I came to know that it would always defy whatever age she reached.

When Harold had tugged his hand from hers and run to the bed I put my arms about him but said nothing. Nor did he speak, he just looked up at me as I now turned my gaze towards his natural mother,

who said, "S'prised to see me, Mrs Leviston? I'm . . . I'm his mum."
And she thumbed towards Harold.

"How do you do?"

"Well, take a look." She patted her stomach none too gently. "I do seven and a half months."

What could one say to that except, "Do sit down."

She sat down, then said, "Don't look so worried; I've not come to try an' get him back. Oh, no, not me. Anyway, he wouldn't come. Would you?" She leant across the bed as she demanded an answer to this question from her son . . . our son. And he replied simply, "No, Mum."

"There you are, isn't that a dutiful son for you? Well brought up, speakin' the truth." She opened her mouth wide, to show a surprisingly fine set of teeth; then turning her attention to me again, she said, "You're still lookin' surprised. Wonderin' why I'm here, aren't you?"

"Yes; yes, I am a bit."

"Well, it's not that I want to put a spoke in your wheel with regards him" - she again nodded towards Harold - "not that I could because it's all been signed and sealed, but I thought I'd put your mind at rest about somethin' else that I know you haven't taken to, and that's his nibs comin' to claim his rights every other week or so. Gawd! that sounds funny, doesn't it?" Her large stomach and big breasts seemed to wobble in unison. "Claim his rights. But you know what I mean?" She broke off here to open her handbag from which she took out a fifty pence piece which she handed across the bed to Harold, saying, "Go on to the 'ospital shop an' get yourself a bar."

Harold looked at the money, then looked at me, and when I said, "Yes, go on," he went, but with evident reluctance.

The door closed, I looked at my visitor. Yes, I knew what she'd meant the first time. And now she went on. "Mum says she hasn't told you the full story."

"No; Janet hasn't told me anything, I mean with regards to yourself."

"Better comin' from me, I suppose she thought. Well, it's like this, Mrs Leviston. You know I was in for a divorce 'cos I was goin' to marry this bloke . . . I'm a bad lass you know." She leaned towards me and grinned widely as she made this statement. "He was the third bloke I'd made a mistake about since walkin' out on Jimmy. But anyway, when I found I'd one in the pot" - she patted her stomach again - "I thought it was about time I stayed in one place, so Ralph, this fellow, said we'd get married. So all I wanted was a divorce. And of course I'd given enough grounds, you could say, to let a battalion off the hook." Again she laughed. "Then, I ask you, what did Ralph do? The bloody swine. . . . Well, he was, an' I'll say it again, he was, he takes a pattern from me an' he scarpers. But James Stoddart wasn't to know that, was he, when down he comes to see me. My! I nearly fell off me perch when I opened the door to him. Well, the long and short of it was, his piece had done the dirty on him an' he was left with Doris and Gloria. By the way, I don't suppose you know that the kids aren't mine, they were his by his first wife. Anyway, we got to talkin'. . . Am I borin' you, Mrs Leviston?"

"Boring me, Maggie? No, I've never felt so entertained for a long, long time."

We laughed together now, and her hand coming on the shoulder of my still-plastered arm in no light slap definitely quelled my laughter and almost made me cry out. But I said, "Go on. Go on."

"Well, there we were sittin' tête-à-tête, as they say, 'aving a cup of tea, an' what 'e says to me is, 'You intent on goin' through with this an' marryin' him?' And I, like the good liar I am, says, 'Well, of course; what else can I do, Jimmy? You can see me condition.' And you know what? *Do . . .you . . . know . . . what, Mrs Leviston?* He said to me, 'I don't mind your condition, I've had it once afore if you remember, all I want is you to come back.' Well, I 'ummed and 'aaed and 'ummed and 'aaed; then finally thankin' God on the side, I said, 'All right.'"

Again her head was back; again she was laughing. Then of a sudden her laughter stopped and her face lengthened as she said, "I slipped up there, didn't I?"

"What do you mean you slipped up?"

"Well, what I said about 'im takin' me before in the same condition."

"Oh."

"Anyway" - she shrugged her big shoulders - "I think you've got a right to know; you see, Harold isn't his."

"No? He's *not his father?*"

"That's what I'm sayin', Mrs Leviston, Harold isn't his. Mind, he tells himself that he is, but at bottom he knows what he knows. That's why he's never been able to stand the kid, and 'Arold sensed this from the beginnin'. That's why he became such a little terror, I think. No, his father was the only decent bloke I've ever known. But I wasn't up to his standard, you know like, so he scarpered."

I was singing inside. Of course the boy had nothing of Jimmy Stoddart about him; but he had his mother's humour and impishness. Oh, yes, yes, I could see that. But Maggie was going on.

"You know, when I walked into the kitchen the other day I thought me mum would pi . . . kill herself laughin'. An' the lads, all they could say was, 'Oh! Maggie.' Like our Max said, I could take on a brigade of guards an' they'd all be worn out by the mornin'. Well, you know what I mean, Mrs Leviston.'

She was flapping her hand at me now. And yes; yes, I certainly knew what she meant.

"Anyway," she went on, "when things had quietened down in the kitchen I had a talk with Mum and she told me about the rumpus there'd been between him and Mr Tommy. Well, I said, I'll put a stop to that. It isn't as if he cares anything for the lad, it's just that he wants to be bloody contrary. . . . Excuse me swearin', Mrs Leviston." I excused her swearing. "Anyway, I said I'd take the girls back, 'cos, you see, they weren't mine no more than young 'Arold was his. So that's what I said, 'I'll take the girls back if you let go altogether on 'Arold. He's got the chance of a lifetime, something that I could never give him nor you. No, never you.' That's what I said. Oh, yes, that's what I said. I don't pull me punches." Again her mouth was wide. "So that's why I thought I'd come an' tell you meself. You've got no need to worry about any more visits from him. If 'e starts shoutin' about his rights, 'e'll get his rights all right, but I'll see they're curtailed." Again her breasts and stomach were wobbling. "Mind, not that I'd like to cut off from him, the kid, altogether, you know what I mean; now and again I'd like to see 'im. That's if you don't mind."

I put my hand out and laid it across her fat fingers, saying, "Of course, Maggie, of course. And I can assure you he'll be a credit to you."

For the first time I saw her show some genuine emotion. She turned her head away for a moment, sniffed, then said, "No credit due to me. I've . . . I've always pleased me bloody self. Made like that you see, where the other thing is concerned: can't 'elp it, sort of. I don't know who I take after. Likely our old man. 'Cos Mum always said he was determined to have a baker's dozen but she put the cork in at eight."

She turned to me now. Her eyes were blinking, her mouth was tight. "People don't understand; we're all made different, aren't we? Aren't we?"

"Yes, of course we are, Maggie."

"There's you, so nice'n kind an' normal like, who would think you have spent years talkin' to a horse that wasn't there and gettin' it to kick people's arses? I read your book. I did, an' I laughed till I cried, because, oh! God, the people that I've wanted to kick in the back of the front."

"Maggie! Maggie!" It was a groan now. "Please!"

"What is it?"

I was choking: "Please, don't make me laugh like this, it hurts all over."

"Oh! Mrs Leviston, does it?" She was laughing more loudly herself now.

The door opened and in came Harold. He looked from one to the other, then said, "You're laughin'."

"Yes. What d'you think we're doin', big head?"

He looked at his mother but didn't answer her; then he looked at me and said, "For a minute I thought you was cryin'."

"Were!"

"Oh, you!" He glanced at his mother again, then grinned and said, "That's what she does," before turning to me and asking, "What d'you want, a Smartie or a piece of Mars bar?"

"Ask your mother first."

He stretched across the bed, and I watched her take a Smartie, say ta, then pop it in her mouth.

When he offered me the packet I also took a Smartie and, laying it on the bedside table, I said, "I'll keep it for after; they'll be bringing the tea round in a moment."

And when presently the nurse entered with a tea-tray on which there were three cups and saucers, a teapot and water jug, and a plate of small cakes, Maggie exclaimed, "My! My! Isn't this nice now. This is the life. What I wouldn't give to have a fortnight in 'ere." And when her son replied quickly, "Don't be daft, Mum, you'd have to be knocked about to be in 'ere," she looked at him and said, "You're right. You're right, boy; you would have to be knocked about to be in 'ere, and I 'aven't been knocked about enough yet."

She turned her gaze on me, and the look in her eyes made me want to reach out to her and say, Oh, Maggie, Maggie, but she was laughing again, saying, "Will I play mother?" And so I said quietly, "Yes. Yes, Maggie, you play mother."

Chapter 4

Later, when Tommy came in laden down as if it was Christmas with a great bouquet of flowers, three books, and a bottle of perfume, that's what I said to him, "Is it Christmas?" And his answer was, "Yes, every day I'm with you."

Tommy was nice.

While describing to him the reason for Maggie's visit I had him laughing so loudly he had to put his hand over his mouth to still the sound.

"That family," he said. "You know, you should write a book about them, starting with the day Harold was made legal."

"That's the idea," I said.

"But you'll have to be careful how you introduce the Mohican: you'll have to be truthful and say he put me off from the start, yet you recognized something in him that neither I nor anyone else did . . . clever clouts!" He had picked up Gran's phrase, clever clouts.

I wasn't clever or even perceptive in this case: as a silly woman I had responded to the emotional appeal of a young man with a very attractive voice who had presumably opted out of the system. I felt ashamed that, after living with a man like Nardy and knowing a man like Tommy here, I could allow my emotion to be so affected by such an unprincipled individual. And there was another thing; he had a nerve, hadn't he, to imagine that I . . . Oh, shut up!

"What did you say?"

I hadn't realized that I had lain back and closed my eyes while facing up to the fact that yet once again I was a very ordinary individual, and in more ways than one.

"I was thinking."

"I thought you had gone to sleep. I've got a confession to make," he said.

"What have you done now?"

"I bought *Spring Fever*."

"The . . . the boat?"

"The . . . the boat."

"Oh, Tommy." I shook my head; then asked, "How much did you finally pay for it?"

"Thirty-one thousand."

"Oh my!"

"She's a beauty. I can't wait to get you on to her, and I promise you that she'll move no further than the Thames if you feel at all afraid; and I wouldn't mind that because she's just lovely to be in. I can't explain it. Captain Lee feels the same way about her. He's been with her as he puts it, since she was born, seven years ago. He saw her being finished off in the yard a week after he was made redundant because his company was cutting down on their line. You'll like him . . . Ned. He's a fine fellow. He's dying to meet you."

"Oh, be quiet!"

"Yes, he is, because he knows as well as I do that it depends upon you whether he keeps his job or not. It's down to practicalities now. I can manage her on the river, but I should need some practice before I could cross the Channel and go up the French rivers. Just think of it, Maisie." He hitched himself further towards me and took my face between his big hands, saying quietly, "We could have our honeymoon in France. Come on, how say you?"

I looked into his dear kind face and knew that I must stop stalling. Nardy had wanted it this way, and I did too. Yes, I did now more than ever. And just as I had felt grateful to Nardy for taking on this commonplace woman, as I knew myself to be, so I again felt grateful to Nardy's friend. But such were my emotions at the moment that I couldn't answer like a sensible individual with a simple "Yes," but had to say facetiously, "That seems quite in order, Mr Balfour."

"Oh, Maisie, darling." His arms were about me, his long lean face was close to mine, and his words came thick and muffled as he said, "I love you so much, Maisie."

That was the odd thing about it, the weird thing, the intensity with which I created love and hate in people . . . in men. Look at Stickle. At this thought I metaphorically shook myself, my mind crying at me, I'm not looking back on Stickle or my mother; I'm going to look ahead and count my blessings and realize that the love I've inspired is much stronger than the hate.

"Don't cry, darling."

"I'm not crying."

"No, of course you're not." He wiped my eyes; then softly he asked, "Do you think you'll ever be able to say you love me, really love me?"

He did not add, "as you did Nardy," because he knew that would be impossible, and I knew I could never love again as I had loved Nardy. But there were so many different kinds of love and so many levels of love, and I knew in this moment that on one of the levels I loved this man, and so I replied simply, "I love you now, Tommy, and I thank you for loving me."

He didn't kiss me, he just laid his head on my shoulder and said softly, "We'll make it soon, straight after the court case is over."

The court case.

The following day they took the plaster off my leg and arm and what followed was almost as painful as when I returned to consciousness. Yet, I forced myself to laugh with the therapist, the nurses and the doctor as they made jokes about the "two sticks" they had to get moving.

Three days later I was wheeled from the room to the therapy ward; and my efforts there to move "the sticks" were even more excruciating. But at last I was out of bed, which was wonderful.

And it was towards the end of the week that while I was sitting by the window the Mohican came in. He was carrying a bunch of flowers. They were roses, red ones, and as in such cases I guessed there would be the conventional dozen.

"Back to life?" He looked down on me.

"Yes. Yes, back to life."

"How do you feel?"

"Very well, fine in fact."

He continued to look at me; then holding out the roses at arm's length as a child might and in the same manner, he said, "Brought these for you."

I looked at them, then said quietly, "They're very nice, but you're offering them to the wrong person."

His arm dropped: he turned and laid the roses on a side table; then going to the bedside he lifted up a chair and brought it towards the window and, sitting slowly down on it, he said, "I thought we'd discussed that at the last board meeting."

"Not quite."

I looked at him. He was staring me full in the face and again I felt sorry that I'd found him to be other than the nice Mohican, and also I knew that I couldn't flail him with words as I would have done had he appeared shortly after Hilda's visit. So my voice was quiet as I said, "Your roses might have been of some solace to Hilda in place of the baby that she wanted and could have had."

I watched the expression on his face change: his colour deepened, the muscles under his cheekbones moved in and out; and his voice came from between tight lips as he said, "She was no more fit to have a child than I as the Indian was fit to provide for it."

Now my voice was angry as I said, "If you didn't consider her fit to have a child why did you give her one?"

"Well, if you want to know the truth, *Mrs Leviston*, it was because she pestered me. I never took up with her in the first place; she became my shadow. She got rigged out as she did because she thought it would draw me to her. You could say that I didn't give her the child, she took it from me."

"Then why did you keep on with her?"

"Because in that particular job I recognized she could be good cover. A loner is always under suspicion, but squatting with someone like her you were accepted. It's a dangerous business, which has been proved to you, I hope."

I looked back at him and heard myself say, "I'm sorry."

"And I'm sorry too." His expression altered.

"She loves you so much."

He tossed his head impatiently to the side, saying, "Only because she saw I was a little different from her usual acquaintances. Maisie" - he was gripping both my hands now - "don't you see it's impossible? What kind of a life would we have?"

"Perhaps better in lots of ways than with a girl you consider of your own class. And she would learn. Why, she came in here the other day and she looked so. . ."

He screwed up his face. "She came?" He had pulled back from me. "I thought it might be her mother or May, but *she came?*"

"Yes, yes, she came."

"Good God!" He got to his feet, put his hand to his head and turned towards the window and stared down onto the forecourt.

I said softly, "You would make something of her, make her what you want, she would learn. As I said, she would learn."

He swung round on me. "She would learn nothing. She is of a type. All she wants is bed; she's as over-sexed as a bloody rabbit."

On other occasions I would have laughed, and when he said, "I'm sorry," I muttered, "Oh, you needn't apologize." He came now and stood close by my side. "You see me as a louse, don't you?"

"No, I don't, John." The fact that I'd spoken his name changed the light in his eyes, and I turned my gaze from his and looked out of the window as I continued, "But I'm sorry for Hilda, for I know that she sincerely loves you. Whichever way it is, she loves you, and it's a pity you can't see it that way. But I understand." I looked at him again and watched him slowly smile, and then he said, "You know, you have a funny face, an appealing funny face."

There it was again, my heart knocking against my ribs. I brought my defences up and heard myself lying, "Huh! It's odd you should think that, that's what Tommy says. By the way, we're going to be married shortly."

His smile slowly seeped away and after a moment he said, "Yes?" And I replied, "Yes."

"Well, well! So life moves on. I hope you'll be very happy."

"Thank you."

Getting away from this touchy topic, I said quickly, "Have you any idea when the case will come up?"

"Oh" - he pursed his lips - "about three weeks' time I should say."

"How . . . how long will it last?"

"Who knows? We've picked up eight of them altogether, including your three and the woman. There'll be the drug charges first; I should imagine abduction and attempted murder - that'll be your case - will be on the last day or so. You'll be the main witness in that, naturally, you and the man on the cliff top. And me of course. So we'll meet again." He buttoned the middle button of his light coat, then said, "Well, I'll say goodbye."

"Goodbye, John." Then I added, "In a way, I should say I'm sorry we ever met because of what has transpired."

"I can endorse that wholeheartedly, *Mrs Leviston*." He stressed my name. "Oh yes, wholeheartedly." Then, pointing to the roses, he said, "Give those to one of the nurses; they may recognize their significance."

When the door closed on him I seemed to slump in the chair and I asked myself a question: If Tommy hadn't been on the scene, would I?

Yes, yes, I would.

Chapter 5

On the day I left hospital I felt a little like royalty. I had said goodbye to the night staff earlier on and they had paid me the compliment of saying I was the only patient on that floor who had never rung the night bell; and the day staff had said they were sorry to see me go. The doctor who happened to be doing his rounds when I was leaving jokingly cried at me, "I'm going to see you off the premises and make sure you don't break anything more of that gigantic frame of yours." And so, supported at one side with a walking-stick and by Tommy's arm on the other and flanked by the sister and doctor, I departed from the hospital and made for home.

And there was Janet waiting outside the lift, and there were tears in her eyes as she exclaimed, "I never thought to see you walk out of there again. Welcome home, Mrs Leviston, ma'am."

Her voice was almost drowned by the sound of Sandy's barking coming from the kitchen and she said, "He sensed you were coming, he's gone mad since Mrs Brown brought him up, but I won't let him loose till you're settled, else he'll have you over."

The flat looked strange, very large and sort of empty. The yellow drawing-room was still beautiful but aloof somehow. There was something missing. I said, "Where's Harold, Janet? I thought. . ."

"Well, ma'am, that's another thing: I left him at home; I just thought he would run wild an' all, an' you would want to get settled in. He's been like a cat on hot bricks this last couple of days, in fact, for weeks now. You're goin' to have a job gettin' him back into form. Anyway, I told them I'd give him a ring as soon as you wanted him here, and Hilda would bring him. She's back, you know, ma'am. She's been stayin' home for a time, but she's goin' to room with May as soon as May gets rid of the girls. They're goin' back to Maggie's. Oh, what a mix up there. I've got things to tell you you wouldn't believe. Maggie's settled in with him again like, but she said she wanted space to move around before gettin' down to housekeepin' again. And so the lasses are still at May's. Oh!" She looked at Tommy now, saying, "I can never believe she's one of mine . . . Maggie. I've bred some queer 'uns, but she takes the cake." She turned away, saying, "Everything's ready in the dining-room when you are. Oh, it's lovely to have you back, ma'am . . . lovely."

Tommy sat himself down beside me on the couch and, putting his arm about me, said, "I endorse that. You've been a very missed woman, if you follow my meaning . . . ma'am . . . How do you feel, darling?"

"Do you know, Tommy, I couldn't tell you, I really couldn't. I suppose I feel tired, but I had expected to feel elated just to be back here." I looked around this beautiful room, then said, "But strangely I feel flat."

"That means you want a holiday. Tomorrow, if you feel up to it, or the next day, we're going down to the boat. If that doesn't cheer you up nothing will."

"Tommy."

"Yes, my dear?"

"I know what's worrying me, it's the case. I'm . . . I'm terrified of courts."

"It'll be all right. Everything's been arranged, and you won't have to appear until the last day."

"How do you know?"

"Oh, I haven't been idle. I've had a talk with the barrister, and he said the Indian's bodily harm business will come up first, then the attempted murder charge against those three fellows; all you've got to do is to identify them. I don't think the woman will be charged with them except as an accessory or some such. Don't worry, all you'll have to do is just walk in and then walk out again. It'll be over in no time."

I remained silent whilst thinking, I hope so. Oh, dear God, I hope so. . .

Two hours later I was sitting on the couch with Sandy curled up at my side when Harold came bouncing into the room. I say he bounced, but that was as far as half-way up the room, for there he suddenly stopped, stared towards me, then did a little run and came and stood by my knee and looked at me.

"Hello," I said. "Haven't you anything to say to me?"

He didn't answer immediately; then he asked, "You better?"

"Yes; yes, I'm quite better."

"You'll not go away again?"

"No."

"Ever?"

"Not ever."

At this he knelt up on the couch, put his arms around my neck, then whispered something, and I said, "What did you say?" And now I heard his voice very small say, "I was frightened."

"What were you frightened of?"

"You wouldn't come back, an' I'd be stuck at Gag's."

I pushed him from me. "Oh, that's all you were frightened about, because you would be stuck at Gag's?"

"No, no." He made an impatient movement with his head, and when I laughed and pulled him towards me he said, "Oh! you. You're funny." He then added, "An' he missed you an' all." He put his hand on Sandy's head. "He 'owled and 'owled, had fits of it."

"He never 'owled and 'owled, he *howled* and *howled*."

He slanted his gaze at me and his response was, "Nuts."

"What did you say?"

He grinned, then demanded, "Where's Mr Tommy?"

"He's gone out for a while."

"To the boat?"

"No; not to the boat, to his flat; he wanted something. What do you know about the boat?"

"Oh" - he preened himself- "I've been on it. It's smashin', lovely. Oh boy! Uncle Max and Uncle Billy were bloody dumbfound."

We looked at each other. His head was bowed for a second before it jerked up and he said, "Well, that's nothin'. They were."

"Harold!"

"Oh . . . well, they all say it. Oh, I'm sorry, I am, Mrs Nardy, I'm sorry."

"All right. All right. But tell me, how did your uncles and you see the boat? And where?"

"Mr Tommy, he . . . he took us one day in the car. Oh, that car! Uncle Billy nearly cried over it. He loves cars. His is four wheels an' a biscuit tin. He made Uncle Max and Mr Tommy laugh when he said he'd exchange any pair of boobs for Mr Tommy's headlights."

"Harold!"

"What?"

"You mustn't repeat things like that."

"Like what?" He was definitely puzzled and amazed. "I never swored."

"Swore."

"Well, I never did."

"No; but you repeated something rude."

He looked to the side as if his words were imprinted there and he was sorting them out. Then his head jerked towards me and he said, quietly, "Boobs?"

"Yes." I made a deep obeisance with my head.

"Well, huh!" There was now a grin on his face. "That's nothin'. They're in the papers an' magazines; women 'ave 'em. And - " I drew in a deep breath as I turned my gaze from him, and he went on, "Uncle Max says some of 'em haven't even got their bootlaces on."

My gaze returned to him sharply.

"Bootlaces! What do you mean bootlaces?"

"Well." He demonstrated now with a finger pointing across each side of his chest. "Those bits they wear. He calls them bootlaces. An' down on their bell. . ."

"All right, all right, we won't go into that any more. But tell me" - my speech was rapid now - "what was the boat like? I mean, what did you think of the boat, besides it being smashing, lovely? What are the rooms like, the cabins?"

"Oh." He turned from me now, linked his arms about his knees, brought his feet up onto the couch and rocked himself as he attempted to describe what he had seen: "Well, it's green . . . and well, it's big like a house inside, and it's got rooms. Oh" - he turned quickly towards me - "you'd have to see it. As Uncle Max says, even on the outside it made all the other boats round about look like a heap of old odds and sods."

We said nothing: our thoughts were exchanged by our eyes which stared into each other. When I spoke I said, "Your Aunt Hilda's in the kitchen. Go and ask her if she wouldn't mind coming and having a word with me?"

He slipped off the couch, stood looking at me for a moment, then said, "Well, it's. . ." but didn't finish; instead he slumped away out of the room.

Uncle Max, Uncle Bill, all those uncles, it looked as if I had to start from the beginning again. One thing I should be pleased about, he had taken to Tommy. But Tommy was no fool: the boat was an asset on his side in the cause of future relationships. . .

Hilda came quietly into the room, and I said, "Hello, Hilda."

"Hello, Mrs Leviston."

"Do sit down."

"How are you feelin'?"

"Still a bit shaky, I'm afraid, Hilda."

"You look much better than when I last saw you."

"Yes; yes, I am. But I'm afraid I'm worrying about the court case. "

I hadn't been very diplomatic there, had I? But it seemed that I need not have worried because she said, "Well, that's natural; it will be quite a big affair."

I narrowed my eyes at her. She seemed different; she was dressed very nicely. And after a short silence she said, "I'm sorry for upsettin' you that day I called at the hospital. I should never 'ave done it. I upset you and you were so concerned for me. But anyway, I've got over it."

"Oh. Oh, I'm so glad, Hilda."

"'Tisn't nice to be chucked aside . . . thrown off, you feel like dirt, but as our May said, the only thing to do is to show him that he's made a mistake, and that's what I'm gonna do."

"Good for you, Hilda. Good for you."

"I've . . . I've left the factory."

"You have?"

"Yes. I'm workin' in the same hotel as May, chambermaid. But that's only a start. May says I can rise an' I will. Yes I will. An' you meet different kinds of people. As she said, you pick up their lingo . . . how they talk. And anyway, as she says, I can pay for lessons an' be learned to speak properly."

"Oh, don't do that."

"No?"

"No; don't alter yourself, Hilda. You'll speak properly all right, mixing with other people. Don't lose your identity, I mean don't change your character, because you're such a warm person."

The head drooped now and I saw the old Hilda, and her voice was low as she said, "I went through a bad time. I think I would have done meself in if it hadn't been for May. May's good; she'll get on. She's got a fellow now. He's in a very good position, he's an assistant chef in one of the big 'otels. He's goin' to have a place of 'is own, a restaurant. Oh, May'll get on. An' she says I will an' all." She was looking at me again. "You know, Mrs Leviston, there's supposed to be no class distinction, everybody's the same, that's what they say, but as May says, it's a lot of codswallop. And the lads say it an' all. Max says you can't get into the Conservative Party unless you have a twang. John Drake had a twang, or James Bainbridge as he is. That's what got me in the first place, the way he spoke. Well, it's over. But I'll let 'em see in the end. That's all I want to do, let 'em see."

"You'll come out on top, Hilda," I said softly; and she looked at me and, her own voice now low and her eyes blinking, she said, "I still love him though, Mrs Leviston. I haven't seen him since, but I was goin' to go to the court on the day, but May says that would be a mad thing to do. What do you think, Mrs Leviston?"

"I think with May, Hilda. Give yourself a year, perhaps longer. By that time you will have . . . well sort of acquired a veneer and if you were then to meet him again it would be on his own ground. You know what I mean."

"Funny; that's what May said: aim to be somebody; that'll make him sorry he turned his nose up."

"She's right, Hilda. Yes, she's right."

She stood up now, saying, "You'll be glad to 'ave him back." She jerked her head kitchenwards.

"Harold? Oh yes, yes."

"You won't 'ave to expect too much of him at first. The lads 'ave had a field day with him, went out of their way they did, not meanin' it badly, you know. Max is a caution, but he's very fond of him, in fact, he thinks it's a shame he's goin' to be spoilt, I mean, altered."

"Well, you can tell Max he won't be spoilt. And also tell him the only thing I'll aim to alter is his language, most of it having been learned from him."

She laughed now. "I'll tell him, Mrs Leviston, I'll tell him. Well, goodbye, and thank you . . . well, for listenin' to me."

I held out my hand, and when she took it I pressed hers tightly, saying, "Now I mean this, Hilda, I'm not just being polite, but I want you to pop in and see me every now and again when you have time, and we can have a talk."

"*You do?*"

"Yes, I do. I'll want to know how you're progressing."

She turned from me now and went quickly from the room, and I lay back and willed that she would come out on top and one day in the future meet the Mohican again when by the sound and sight of her he would have to eat his words.

Then I asked myself, if Tommy hadn't been in the way, what would I have done about her and her feelings for the Mohican, and her being Janet's daughter and Harold's aunt? For answer, I thanked God I had Tommy.

It was almost a week later when I saw the boat. Tommy first took us to meet the captain, who shared a house with his sister and brother-in-law overlooking the canal.

Captain Edward Lee, who asked to be addressed as Ned, was a stubby man in his late fifties. He was of Welsh extraction and had apparently sailed the seas since he was a boy. His brother-in-law had served as first officer under him in the merchant navy.

Tommy was retaining Captain Lee's services on a full-time basis, for two reasons he said: the house overlooked the canal and in the winter months he could keep an eye on the boat; the second reason was it would be one less on the dole and would help a man such as Ned Lee to keep his self-respect which was something that many men were losing. He was thoughtful, was Tommy. I had found that out in more ways than one.

At my first glimpse of *Spring Fever* I exclaimed, "Oh, my goodness!"

she looked so long and high. And when the Captain jumped aboard and pushed a gangplank down onto the canal bank, Harold dived up it like a squirrel up a tree; but I looked at Tommy and said, "Oh, no." Whereupon and without any further words, he stooped and picked me up, and at the top of the gangplank he put me into the arms of the captain and for the first time I was hoisted aboard.

Well, I looked from one to the other of the three faces looking at me; then I looked about me. This, I saw, was the wheelhouse. It was shining. The wood was gleaming; there were leather-cushioned seats at one side, and a high seat fronting the wheel and a panel of instruments. I said nothing. Then Tommy, walking quickly from me, went down a short flight of steps, turned and held up his arms, and with their aid I slowly descended the stairway.

"The saloon." He spread his hand wide.

I couldn't believe it; it looked so beautiful. It had the same impression on me as had my drawing-room when I first saw it, the day when Nardy took me there to cry and to tell him the truth about my life.

"Isn't it smashin'?" Harold was jumping up and down.

Still I said nothing.

Now I was being led through a door and Tommy was saying, "This is the dining quarter."

And it was a dining quarter, it was a dining-room.

Through another door, "Here's the galley," he said. "What do you think of it?"

What did I think of it? I couldn't believe my eyes. It was much better and more modern than the kitchen back at the flat and I thought that was good. As he described it to me, it had everything, and what I noticed, too, was that there were no portholes so far but windows, as one would get on the first-class deck of a cruise ship.

When I stood in the main bedroom I spoke for the first time. Looking from Tommy to the captain, then down to Harold, I said, "I can't believe it. It seems impossible to get so much into . . . well, this space."

"There's a bath," Harold had pushed open a door; and indeed yes, there was a bath with a shower and toilet.

"Come and see my cabin." He darted out, and we followed him along what I termed a short passage and so into another cabin, smaller but also beautifully fitted. And Harold, pointing, said, "That's my bed. And there's a space underneath it for Sandy's basket."

"Bunk. "

Harold now grinned up at the captain and repeated, "Bunk." And we all laughed.

"Who said you were coming to sleep on this boat?" Tommy was

looking sternly down on Harold now. And Harold turned his gaze on me enquiringly; then looking back at Tommy he stammered, 'We . . . ll, I . . . I th . . . thought . . . well the captain said -" And the captain, shrugging his shoulders expressively and holding out his hands, said, "Oh, it's got nothing to do with me, has it, sir?"

"No, nothing whatever, Captain."

And now I put in my say: "It all depends on how you behave yourself." And we stood looking down on the crestfallen face, and Tommy ruffled his head, saying, "Of course, you're coming. We couldn't manage to get out of the canal without his help, could we, Captain?"

"No, no, sir. He guided us pretty well the other day."

"Of course with the help of his uncles."

Now Tommy and the captain exchanged laughter and a relieved Harold became himself and cried, "There's still some more."

And there was some more.

When later the captain served us tea in the saloon with thin bread and butter and home-made scones, I looked at him and said in amazement, "Don't tell me you cooked these?" I pointed to the scones. And for answer he said, "I've had to learn a lot of things during the last eight to ten years, madam; and I've never believed in living rough."

"They're lovely. I . . . I think this is the biggest surprise of all, this beautiful tea."

"Tut! tut!" The captain tossed his head from side to side but was definitely very pleased at the compliment; then he said, "You like her?"

"How could I help it? But I must tell you, I'm no sailor, I'm terrified of the water . . . I mean, being so close to it."

"You needn't be afraid of sailing in her, madam; I've guided her through some pretty stormy waters. At least, I say I did it, but no, she did it. She's got a mind of her own, like all women."

I smiled at Captain Lee. I liked him.

"Would you like a run into the river?"

"I thought we were on the river."

"This is the canal, madam. It's a fine day; she'll be as steady as a rock. What about it?"

"Well, I suppose" - I looked at Tommy - "it's got to happen sometime."

Tommy took my hand and squeezed it, and when Harold jumped up, crying, "Good-oh! I can take her again?" the Captain said, "Yes, yes, of course, she'll need your help. I wouldn't dream of attempting to take her out myself."

Harold looked at me slant-wise: he knew he was being kidded and he couldn't find words to answer the captain in this vein, but he did it in his own way, and what he said was, "Baloney!"

And so we went up the river. And I sat in the wheelhouse and looked at the bows cleaving through the water, and of a sudden I felt happy and knew that I would come to love this boat and that it would show me yet another way of life. And Tommy sat quietly looking at me while Harold stood within the arms of the captain and presumably took the wheel. And when at one point Tommy leant towards me and whispered into my ear, "I love you," I felt that life ahead was going to be good.

I'd forgotten about the trial.

Chapter 6

I had been sick in the night; in fact, I had been sick for the past two weeks, the dragged-out time of the court proceedings of The Indian Drug Case, so termed by the newspapers because the Mohican had, of course, been the main witness in the trial which covered a sea captain, a yacht owner, a well-known business man, besides two pushers and the three men accused of attempted murder, and a woman who ran a boutique. The sentences on the captain and the yacht owner had been similar, five years each, but the business man, to most people's surprise, had been given eight years, for this particular man had used his connections abroad to bring the stuff into the country using various young people who found themselves stranded abroad or down on their luck. The other men were given two and four years respectively. But when the judge had come to sentencing the three men who were to stand trial for attempted murder his remarks were that he would reserve judgement on these men and their woman associate after the charge had been heard. And then he had praised the detective sergeant who had for two years risked his life in his endeavour to bring the convicted men to justice. And it had been a dangerous task, as had been demonstrated in the end when he had been attacked and left for dead by a drug addict. The sergeant could quite easily have taken to drugs himself; in fact, in order to suggest that he was one of them, he had deliberately punctured his arm with a needle. The whole community and all decent people, the judge went on to say, owed this man a debt of gratitude.

*

I had been in such a state before I left the house this morning that Tommy had insisted I swallow a glass of milk in which he had put a stiff measure of brandy. But this hadn't prevented my shaking inside and I was shaking now as I stood in the witness-box, after being brought into court by the usher as the first witness in the case. I had taken in the fact of the judge being arrayed in a long red robe with a white stole, and wearing a grey wig. He was sitting high up as if on a throne. Below him was a large table with a clerk sitting at the head of it and beyond this rows of seats occupied by the solicitors and counsel; those, as I had previously been told, for the prosecution on the right and those for the defence on the left. And above these was the dock. My mind seemed to blur to my present surroundings for I was remembering when I was last in court, before the judge had passed sentence on Howard Stickle and he had screamed at me that he would get me in the end. And he nearly had with his power of thought.

I was staring towards the dock; I could see his face. Yet there were four faces there, all blurred, but as the mist cleared from my eyes I saw the woman called Liz, the man called Bunty and then the one called Trucker, and then that dreadful one, Danny, and I started to whine to myself: I shouldn't be asked to do this, I'm not well enough. I'll pass out again.

I was once more walking along the top of the cliff with two of these men, one on each side of me holding my arms; I seemed to be lifting my feet up high. . .

The prosecuting counsel was now asking me to tell the court, in my own words, what had happened.

Haltingly I brought out the words that gave the picture of my meeting the Mohican . . . I actually said the name before changing it quickly to Mr John Drake, as I knew him to be named then. The judge looked at me kindly. I think there was a smile on his lips as he said, "Is that the name you gave to Detective Sergeant Bainbridge?" And I said, "Yes, my Lord."

When he turned his eyes from mine I saw him looking slightly to the left, and there for the first time I saw the Mohican himself sitting. He was looking at me and he smiled.

"Why were you meeting the . . . Mohican or as you knew him then, Mr John Drake?" the prosecuting counsel now asked.

I then hesitantly told him that I'd had some articles stolen from the house and Mr Drake had discovered some of them in an antique shop, and he had told me he would show me where the shop was, but he didn't want me to meet up with him.

"What happened when you did meet up with him?"

Haltingly again I described the fight and the car drawing up and the men getting out.

"Mrs Leviston," said counsel for the prosecution, "can you identify the men who got out of the car?"

I looked towards the dock and met the three pairs of eyes riveted on me. Again they merged into Stickle's face. I nodded before I said, "Yes. They are the men in the dock."

At this point the counsel for the defence stood up saying that his clients had already admitted all that had been said; the main issue now was their presence on the cliff-top at Fairlight on the night in question.

The prosecuting counsel said calmly, "We are coming to that." Then turning to me he said, "Describe what followed, Mrs Leviston, after you had been thrown into the car."

I told him.

"Can you remember anything that was said before?"

My mind became blank for a moment; then I seemed to be back on that couch and I heard the woman speaking and I told them what little I remembered and added how she had said that she didn't want anything to be done to me in her house. I recalled she mentioned the name of Benson and said she didn't want that to happen again in her house.

At the mention of this name, the judge now said, "You are sure, Mrs Leviston, that you heard the woman mention that name with regard to something in the past?"

When I answered, "Yes, my Lord," the judge wrote something down. Then once again he returned his attention to me, saying, "Kindly proceed, Mrs Leviston."

I now said, "Well, they talked a lot about how" - I lowered my head as I muttered - "to get rid of me. And it was the man called Danny who suggested the cliffs."

"What happened then?"

"I . . . I cannot remember very much except that after they stuck a needle in my arm I . . . I sort of became resigned: I knew what was happening yet could do nothing about it. The last thing I remember is being pushed in the back and the air rushing into me. That is all." . . .

"And that is all that is required of you, Mrs Leviston." At this stage counsel for the defence indicated that he did not wish to cross-examine me.

As I was helped down from the box there swept over me a wave of relief, yet at the same time I thought I was going to faint. I sat on the front seat, and someone took my hand and patted it.

Someone else called a name out and a man stepped into the witness box. I didn't know him. He took the oath, then the prosecuting counsel said, "Are you Mr Peter Dyke?" and the man answered, "Yes."

"Where do you live?"

"In Fairlight, outside Hastings."

"Where were you on the night of August 10th, 1984?"

"I was taking my dog for a walk, as I do every night."

"Can you describe to us anyone in this court you saw whilst out walking on that particular night?"

All eyes were on the man now as he turned to the dock, and he pointed, saying, "Two of the men there, the big one and the thin one."

"What in particular did you notice about these men?"

"I noticed that one looked like a boxer and the other didn't seem to be half the size, in fact not much taller than the young woman that was walking between them."

"What were they doing?"

"They were each holding one of the young woman's arms."

"What else did you notice about the men?"

"They were laughing; but the young lady looked solemn. I thought she must have just told them a joke. I remember the small man took her hand and wagged it."

"How was it that you recall such a small action as that? They were, in fact, only passers-by."

"Because sometime later I saw the same two men return to a car. I had passed the car earlier and the third man" - he pointed now - "was standing outside leaning on the bonnet. But the other two men hadn't the young lady with them now, and I was a little puzzled at this until I thought they might have been seeing her home; there's a path leading to cottages and houses further along the cliff top."

"What time of the evening was this?"

"I cannot say exactly but it was almost dark."

There followed some more questions, but I found I wasn't listening. My sickness had increased, I longed for fresh air. Someone said, take a deep breath. I did just that.

There seemed to be a lapse of time; then my head cleared and I listened to a man's cultured tones. It was the defence counsel speaking and he was saying, "Neither William Smith, nor Thomas Robberton, nor yet Daniel Foxbrown, deny they bundled Mrs Maisie Leviston into their car, and they admit they took her to Fairlight, which they reached about one o'clock, and that there they pushed her out of the car and this is the last they saw of the lady in question. However, they admit that she might have been in a dazed condition as they had given her a sedative prior to bringing her from London.

"Therefore I suggest she wandered and later fell over the cliff. In the meantime, the accused men went to Hastings, a few miles away, parked the car, had several plates of cockles and wilks. . ."

"I think they are called whelks."

"Yes, my Lord, yes whelks."

There was a titter of laughter in the court; I looked towards the public seats and saw Tommy and he gave me a smile, which did nothing to help me.

The defence counsel was now repeating, "Whelks, they had several plates of these, and later they visited two or three public houses."

"How many public houses?"

"Two or three, my Lord."

"They either visited two or they visited three."

"Yes, my Lord, but I'm only repeating what they remembered, because to relate my clients' words, they became rather full."

There was another titter.

Now the judge's voice rang out clear across the court; "I can see nothing to cause amusement in this case. Proceed."

He proceeded, saying flatly now, "My clients can prove that they had returned to London and had had a meal in the flat above their friend's shop well before dusk."

"You are referring to the boutique?"

"Yes, my Lord."

"You have a witness?"

"Yes, my Lord, the accused, Elizabeth Myter."

"Call Elizabeth Myter."

It seemed from where I was sitting that the woman had to be lifted into the witness-box. I couldn't hear her swearing the oath nor could I hear her giving her name, but the judge said, "Ask your witness to speak up."

When I looked up again the woman was muttering now. Half her words were unintelligible. But the gist of them was she had lived with the man known as Bunty for the past three years and her premises had been used to store drugs which he distributed, and yes, they had taken the woman with the intention of doing her in.

This last statement caused a commotion in the dock: it was the big fellow yelling, "She's a liar, a bloody liar. Just wait."

Two policemen were restraining the man, a voice was shouting, "Order in court!"

The woman was now almost gibbering as she said that she knew about the drug racket all right, but that she would never have anything to do with polishing anyone off. And the man Bunty knew that. She was then asked if any one of them had threatened her. And after hesitation, she replied, no, not really, but that she was frightened of one of them. And to the surprise of the court she named the man called Danny.

Why was she frightened of him? she was asked.

Because he was weird, wrong in the head, twisted.

The man Danny made no response to this, he just stared at her. . .

There followed more procedure. The prosecuting counsel spoke to the jury. The defence counsel spoke to the jury. Then the judge was summing up and when he had finished the jury retired to consider their verdict and the judge also left the court.

There was a stir in the court, then a movement of people. I had moved too. I was now standing in an outer hall. Tommy was by my side, and in front of me stood the Mohican. His look was kindly as he said, "It'll soon be over."

"What do you think they'll get?" Tommy was addressing him now.

"Hard to say. The old boy's against them, which is good, but it's amazing, you never know with juries, there's always one or two who like to sit back and show they're different."

"It must have been pretty rough for you all this."

The Mohican now looked at Tommy and smiled saying, "No; quite a holiday compared to the other business."

"Yes, I suppose so, but it's certainly put a spoke in the drug racket."

The Mohican made a strange sound in his throat as he said, "You said the word, a spoke, and that's all it is. They'll still get in somehow."

"After all you've done?"

"Oh, yes. What I've done had been done before. It'll be quiet for a time, but then they'll find other ways or means. Once you're hooked, it's either drugs or death. They won't recognize that the death comes through the drugs, they just think they'll die if they don't get them; and they'll get them."

I looked at the Mohican. I was searching for a word to fit his mood, and the only one my mind presented me with was, disconsolate.

His voice was kindly now when, looking at me, he said, "You want to take a long holiday when this is over."

I nodded at him, saying, "Yes, I mean to."

"She's going on a honeymoon." Tommy had bent towards him.

"Oh. Congratulations."

"I've acquired a boat; we're going to do the rivers, if not the channel."

"Very nice. I hope you'll be very happy." He was looking at me now, and I said simply, "Thank you."

Why did I feel sorry for him? Why did I wish. . . ? What did I wish?

I looked to the side now and there, standing at the end of the room, were three of Janet's family, Max, Greg, and Rodney. They were looking towards us but they made no move to come forward, and the Mohican, turning his glance towards them before looking at me again, said, "They would like to have a word with you but I'm in the way." Then on a note of ironic humour he added, "We don't want a punch-up in court, do we?" And with this he nodded at me and turned away, and Tommy, bending down, asked quietly, "What did he mean by that?" And I replied as quietly, "Well, you know he's dropped Hilda and the boys are not very pleased. He . . . he was made very welcome in the house."

"Oh, yes. Yes, I see the point. Let's go and have a word with them."

They all said in their different ways, "Hello, Mrs Leviston. How are you?" And I said frankly, "Feeling dreadful."

It was Greg who stated bluntly, "I hope that old boy gives the buggers what they deserve, life, and not just for ten years or so. If I could get me hands on one of them there wouldn't be any need to sentence him."

The other two nodded in agreement; then Max, touching on a lighter subject, said, "Glad to have the nipper back, Mrs Leviston?" There was a grin on his face.

"Very glad, Max."

"Has he been behavin' himself?"

"Well -" I slanted my gaze at him now and pointedly said, "It all depends, Max, on what you mean by behaving himself."

He took my point and said, "Like that is it, Mrs Leviston?"

"Like that, Max," I said.

And at this the three men laughed and Tommy said, "For my part, I always think the English language is very dull; it needs a bit of colour."

"You're right there." Rodney was nodding at him now. "And I think the youngster'll always bring a little colour in his chatter. Trust him."

And now I put in quickly, "And if I may say so, Rodney, I trust you not to help him, or any of you."

"Oh, Mrs Leviston." The heads were wagging, the grins were wide, and Max's widened still further when I said, "As for you, Max, we'll have to have a talk."

"Yes, ma'am. Yes, ma'am." He took on the attitude of a child to a teacher, and the laughter from the three of them caused heads to turn. . .

Two hours later we were back in the court again; the jury filed in; the foreman was standing; you could have heard the proverbial pin drop. The judge's clerk asked the foreman of the jury, "Do you find the accused guilty or not guilty?"

"Guilty on all charges, my Lord."

"And is that the verdict of you all?"

"It is, my Lord."

The three men in the dock remained still for a moment; then the boxer and the thin man bent their heads deeply, only the one who acted as chauffeur remained straight, there was even a smile round the corners of his lips. I could understand that woman being afraid of him.

The judge was speaking again, first to the jury.

"Ladies and gentlemen of the jury I want to thank you for the care and attention which you have given to this case. Lest any of you may have any lingering doubts as to the correctness of your verdict let me say that it is overwhelmingly supported by the evidence. The accused have already been found guilty by another jury of serious offences involving drug running which has had dire repercussions on thousands of lives. They were distributors of heroin and L.S.D., and when they were finally apprehended they had in their possession drugs with a street value in the region of two million pounds. I have had some despicable creatures stand before me in the dock in my time but never have I faced any as low as the three before me now. On their own admission they drugged this young woman and although she was unable to resist them they knew that she was quite conscious and would be in a state of terror when they cold-bloodedly tossed her over a high cliff trusting that the turn of the tide would take her body out with it and so cover up their dreadful deed. Fortunately the tide did not do as they had planned but the injuries which she sustained in the fall almost succeeded in ending her life."

The judge now turned his attention to the three men in the dock addressing each of them by name: "William Smith, Thomas Robberton, and Daniel Foxbrown, on the charge of abduction and attempted murder I sentence each of you to life imprisonment to run not less than twenty years, and on the charge of drug trafficking, I sentence each of you to ten years imprisonment to run concurrently."

There was no word or movement now from the dock, and the warders led the men down to the cells.

The woman remained in the dock. There were two women warders, one on each side of her seemingly to support her, and the judge, looking at her, said, "Elizabeth Myter, on the charge of harbouring drugs and assisting in their distribution, I sentence you to five years imprisonment. And on the charge of being associated with the three male accused and having knowledge of their intention to commit murder and in no way endeavouring to stop them, which you could have done by an anonymous phone call to the police, I sentence you to five years, the sentences to run concurrently."

Did I feel pity as I watched the woman being helped from the dock? No, I didn't, for she hadn't really been concerned with what would happen to me, only that it didn't happen on her premises. . .

It was over. Or was it? In the hall I came under a barrage of cameras and reporters, and when I found the Mohican pushed to my side and a camera lined up to snap us, the Mohican swiftly turned his back and stood in front of me; and there we were, close, and our faces almost touching. The next minute he had gone, pushing his way through reporters, and Tommy was shielding me with the help of Janet's three boys as we made our way to the car.

Once inside, I lay back and thought for a moment that this was the time when I was actually going to pass out; and then I told myself not to be silly, it was all over.

"You'll soon be home," Tommy's voice was soothing, calm, reassuring. It wiped the Mohican's face from my vision.

Janet, Harold, and Sandy, were waiting for me. Harold grabbed my hand, Sandy jumped all over me, and Janet said, "Well?" and Tommy answered for me, saying, "Life for the three of them, the woman five years."

"Good. Good."

A few minutes later, seated in the drawing-room, a drink in my hand, I looked up at Janet and said, "The lads were there."

"Yes, I know; they said they were goin'. Max has got a job an' all at last. I said he was riskin' things to take a day off but he said he wasn't going to miss it. Did . . . did you see John?"

"Yes. Yes, he was there."

"Did the lads see him?"

"Yes, I think they did, but they didn't speak."

"No, I told them to keep clear of him 'cos I wouldn't put it past them to have a go at him 'cos of our Hilda. Well, I'll get you somethin' to eat; I bet you're starvin'."

I did not say food was the last thought in my mind; and when she left the room and Harold, standing before Tommy and me where we sat on the couch, said flatly, "I liked the Indian," I almost burst into tears.

And it was Tommy who said, "So did we; we were very fond of him;" and he took my hand and looked hard at me and said, "Isn't that so?"

"Yes, yes," I answered; "we were very fond of him."

Tommy was no fool.

Chapter 7

It was a Friday towards the end of March, the twenty-ninth to be exact. Tomorrow I was to be married to Tommy and, as on the day I married Nardy, Gran and George were with me. They had arrived late last night. George had definitely intended to be present, but, apparently, Gran had deliberated, her excuse being, there were so many things to see to, with Kitty once more in hospital having another grafting, and Mary needing company at this time. And then there was the club: she was running an outing due to take place next week, the first one of the season. Oh, there were so many things she had to see to. Nevertheless, here she was; but keeping clear of the kitchen, for, as she had plainly stated, she couldn't stand that Janet: uppish she was, and her only a servant.

It was the word uppish applied to Janet that gave me the idea. And when I thought of Janet's family, the word caused me to gurgle inside. And I had been gurgling a lot inside of late. I was feeling so much better: I could walk without the aid of a stick; I had no more pains, either in my stomach, leg, arm, or head. Oh, my head was very clear now; and I had turned to my writing again.

But now I was determined to do something about Gran and her animosity towards Janet and Londoners in general. She was now sitting in the drawing-room turning up the hem of her coat which she considered too long. Tommy, who had last week started a month's holiday, and had spent his time between dashing in to see me, getting rid of his flat, and visiting the boat on which we were to spend the first three days of our honeymoon, the idea being that Captain Lee would take it to a mooring somewhere down the Thames, leave us on our own for three days, then bring Harold to join us before we set off to cross the channel - fearful thought to me - and, as he said, meander around the French countryside just as the boat's previous owners had been wont to do every year.

So now I went into the kitchen and Janet greeted me with, "I've cleared the two shelves in the pantry and the top half of the fridge for them caterers to put the iced things in. Now I'll clear the dresser. . ."

"Janet."

"Yes, ma'am?"

"Will you do something for me?"

"Well now" - she turned fully towards me - "I don't think you've got to ask that, ever, unless it's somethin' that nobody else in my position could do, such as drive a bus, or pilot a plane." She was laughing heartily now.

"I think it's going to be harder than either of those things."

"Yes?" She poked her head forward in enquiry.

"Sit down."

She sat down, and I sat down, and after looking at her for a moment I said, "Will you take Gran along to your house tonight and introduce her to your family?"

"Wh. . .at!"

It was so like my wh. . .at that I laughed and said, "You heard."

"Gran? Me! She . . . she can't stand the sight of me, that woman, she's. . ."

"She thinks you're stuck-up."

"Wh . . . at! me?" She was digging her finger into her chest now while her face spread wide in laughter and amazement. "Me stuck-up, with our lot? How could anybody be stuck-up with our lot? Now I ask you, ma'am?"

"Well, I know that, but she doesn't; she's never met any of your family. She's got this thing about southerners, and I think she's only got to meet Max, and Billy, and Joe, and the rest, and she'll change her mind. Quite candidly I think she'll call them her cup of tea."

"And what about me? She'll still think the same about me."

"No she'll not. I'm sure she won't when she sees you among your family."

"Oh ma'am, I couldn't do it. How could I go up to her and ask her?"

"You could." I pulled a face at her. "You can be very diplomatic when you like."

"Huh! Diplomatic. I don't even know the meanin' of the word. As for being it, how could anybody be diplomatic with our crew? Everything comes straight out." She covered her eyes with her hand and her shoulders shook as she said, "Oh! but you know, ma'am, I'd like to see her in our kitchen, yes I would, and Georgie an' all. But Georgie's different." She was looking at me again. Her eyes were moist and mine were too as I replied, "Yes, Georgie's different. He's been about a bit, has Georgie. He's always the same, no matter who he's with, king or commoner. "

"Yes, I like him. Our lads and 'im would get on all right together, but. . ."

"Yes," I put in, "like a house on fire. Well, what about it?"

"Well, give me time; I'll have to think about it. Well, how will I say it? how will I approach 'er?"

"As you say, think about it."

I got up and left her still seated, her face cupped in her hands now but twisted up with laughter. . .

Gran finished her coat; we had lunch. I said I was going to rest for an hour and she should do the same. I went into my room, not only to give Janet a chance to speak to her alone, but I really did want to rest or rather to think of tomorrow and the step I was taking. I wasn't afraid of it; I knew I'd be happy with Tommy, safe, secure, and I didn't mean money-wise.

I'd always considered that I knew myself: I'd had plenty of time years ago to get to know the person inside my plain frame, to probe into her mind and understand the reason why she said this or did that. When I'd fallen in love with Nardy it had been the first time I had experienced love, and during the comparatively short time we spent together I had seen myself as a very sensible and matter-of-fact individual; my emotions ran on straight paths: I loved, I disliked, and I hated. Oh, yes, I hated. I hated Stickle, although he was in prison and could not possibly do me any more harm, for twelve years that is. That was my first mistake. The second was when I imagined that my emotions could not be drawn away from their central point: I was too sensible to be affected by an attractive voice, two deep brown eyes, and a personality that at first was a mystery and then became attached to somebody who was very brave; only to respond finally to this like any young girl without the experience of life, of good men or bad. The Mohican had become Sir Percy Blakeney, the modern Scarlet Pimpernel.

I had thought about him a great deal after the court case when, for a moment, our faces almost touched. But Tommy's love had gradually pushed him into the background. And now I rarely thought of him except when I saw Hilda. Hilda was doing what she said she would do, making something of herself. Janet often gave me a progress report on her and always ended up by saying, "Oh! I never thought to see the day when Hilda would become sensible." And with the last report she said, "She beats May now. She'll go some place yet, our Hilda. Funny how things turn out: if it hadn't been for that fellow she would have still been the dimwit I always thought her."

So much for a mother's opinion of her offspring.

I lay thinking about tomorrow, not about the wedding, or Tommy, but about how the company would mix, because the whole of Janet's family would be at the reception. And then nearly all of Tommy's friends from the office, some of them, no doubt, who had attended my marriage to Nardy. And, of course, Mike and Jane.

There were sixty people all told invited. The flat would take them, but would they take each other? Well, that was up to them; we wouldn't be here after the first hour or so.

I closed my eyes and softly I said, "I'm doing right, Nardy, aren't I?" And his reply seemed to come to me, "Of course you are, dear. As Tommy said, I wanted it this way."

I had lulled myself almost into sleep when Gran's voice came at the door, saying, "Can I come in, lass?"

"Yes. Yes; Gran."

As I pulled myself up on the bed she almost skipped towards me, her wrinkled face stretched wide. She sat down with a plop on the side of the bed and she flapped her hand at me as she said, "You'll never believe it, not in a month of Sundays."

"Believe what in a month of Sundays?"

"Her! Her in the kitchen, Janet."

"Oh, my goodness!" I pretended to be upset and I closed my eyes and put my hand to my brow; and this brought quickly from her, "Now, now, it's all right. Don't get yourself in a tizzy; I'm not goin' to blow me top about anything. But listen, just listen, will you?"

I took my hand away and said, "Yes, all right, I'm listening."

She laughed now and her body began to shake. And then she said, "She's asked me and Georgie along to her place the night."

"Wh . . . at?" It was my old wh . . . at.

"Aye, you might say what? her askin' me along. I tell you, I couldn't answer her until she said, 'Oh, I'm sorry. You mightn't like it, you see we're rather rough and ready.' Then I thought to meself: What! her lot rough and ready?"

I put in here, as I shook my head at her. "I've told you before, Gran, that. . ."

"Yes, I know you've told me afore, but there's rough and ready and rough and ready, and I imagine very rough an' ready comin' out of that one."

"Well" - I shrugged my shoulders - "you've seen Harold."

"Yes, but he's a bairn and he's been knocked from dog to devil and so that's understandable. And it isn't only workin' men that swear, the nobs can do their share, my God! don't I know it. There's the Tweddles that live two doors down from our Georgie. He's supposed to vote

Conservative but you should hear him. As our Georgie said, he's worse on a Sunday in the pub, 'cos then his talk comes out under blasphemy."

I again put my hand to my brow, and as I did so I said, "Well, are you going?"

She drew in her lips and wagged her head from side to side, saying, "Well, as I said to her, if you didn't need me an' our Georgie, we could slip in for an hour. Anyway" - she now poked her face close to mine - "I want to see what the set-up is. She's always so damn particular here: everything in its place an' a place for everything."

"Well, that's how I want it."

"Oh, she'd be like that if you didn't want it."

"Don't forget, as I've told you, Gran, she worked for Nardy's mother from she was a young girl. She nursed Nardy from a ba. . ."

"Aye, aye, aye, I've heard all that afore. Anyway, I'll know more the night, won't I?" Her eyebrows moved up to her dyed hair, then she asked quietly, "I won't have to get dressed up, will I?"

"Oh, no!" My voice was emphatic. "Good gracious! no."

"Well, what I meant was, put on me suit that I've got for the morrow."

"No, of course not. You're keeping that, surely. Just your ordinary frock and coat."

"Yes. Well" - she rose from the bed- "I wonder what our Georgie'll say."

What Georgie said was, "Never! Maisie. She's accepted a booking to go round to Janet's. Can you believe it?"

"Not quite, Georgie."

"I'm expected to go with her. Mind, I thought old Tommy would be havin' a bachelor do, but he tells me, no. He said he's had experience of them and he wants a clear head for the morrow, else you could walk out on him at the last minute." He now chucked me under the chin, saying, "You wouldn't do that, would you? He's a nice lad. You've been lucky, you know, in a way, lass: two good fellas like that; they don't often come in pairs, good fellas."

"No, they don't, Georgie. I've known three good fellows, four in fact. The first one was called Georgie."

"Aw! go away with you." He pushed me from him, then pulled me back to him with his arm around my shoulder.

"Then there was Mike."

"Oh aye, Mike."

Musingly now, he said, "She's like a cat with nine tails, would you believe it? 'cos she's hated the sight of that woman, you know, never stopped talkin' about her back home. Eeh! she's a marler. By! altogether, women are queer cattle. All except you, hinny." Then he changed the subject abruptly by exclaiming, "Eeh! that boat. God above! I've never seen owt like it. An' you're goin' on your honeymoon on her. You know, lass, when I look back on your life, it's like something you'd see on the pictures, so much has happened to you. As Mam says, you're hardly ever out of the papers. But here's one that doesn't mind. They say back at the depot: 'Your lass is in the papers again I see.' Do you know that? You're known as . . . my lass."

I put my arms up and pulled his big grey head down to mine, and as I kissed him I said, "I'll always remain your lass, Georgie, because you were the first good man in my life."

Patting my cheek gently, he said, "Well, if that's the case I know now why I was born, 'cos, you know, at times I've asked meself why I was put on this earth. I'm not all mouth you know, Maisie, I do use me napper sometimes. But anyway, now I know."

On this he smiled, then turned slowly about and left me, and as the door closed on him again it came to me how lucky I had been: weighed against the disasters there had been four wonderful men in my life and of these three were still with me. Not every woman could say that.

Tommy had driven Gran and Georgie to Janet's. They were to get a taxi back. He had then spent the evening with me; at least, he had spent it with Harold and me until, at nine o'clock, I had bundled that gentleman off to bed, after persuasion I might say, lined with threats that I could easily change our plans and not have the captain collect him in four days' time and bring him to the boat. He had laughed at me and said, "But you wouldn't do that, Mrs Nardy, would you?"

And I had replied sternly, "Oh, yes, but I would."

He had appealed to Tommy, and Tommy had shrugged his shoulders and said, "I can't help you here, laddie. If she makes up her mind . . . well, you know her better than I do." This piece of diplomacy worked and Harold went to bed, and after I'd tucked him in I left him with his books and comics and a promise to come back in fifteen minutes to see him.

When I was once again sitting beside Tommy he did not look at me but towards the fire as he said, "What are we going to do about this . . . Mrs Nardy?"

"Do you mind so much?"

"No, no; not really, but every time I hear him say 'Mrs Nardy' I've got a feeling somehow . . . well, that you still belong to Nardy, that you'll never really be mine."

"Tommy" - I had taken his hand - "we've been through this in different ways. Nardy was a part of my life, a wonderful part, but that is past now. I won't say it's forgotten, I could never forget Nardy, but now there is you, and I love you, in a different way from how I did Nardy. Now don't ask me to explain which way, I can't, only I beg of you, be content to know that I do love you. I want to be near you; I want you to be near me; the house is empty when you are not here. I want to do things for you. Aren't these all facets of love?"

He made no answer but kissed me long and hard, and then I said, "I shall try to get him out of it. How would Mrs Tommy sound?"

"Not bad.". . .

It was around half-past ten when I said, "I'm going to throw you out." And to this he answered, "Oh, I'll wait till Georgie and Gran come back."

"No, you'll not. I'm going to get ready for bed; I want a good night's rest. Anyway, Georgie's got a key."

Taking me in his arms, he said, "This is the last night we'll be separated. What do you say?"

I looked up at him and solemnly I said, "I wish you were a little shorter or I was a little taller. Don't you think we look ridiculous together?"

"Terribly ridiculous."

"And you don't mind?"

For answer he put his hands under my oxters and lifted me off my feet. Now I cried at him, "Don't do that! It always makes me feel so small."

"Well, you are small. "

"Well, you needn't rub it in."

And so it went on, our silly chatter, until I almost pushed him into the lift. And when I entered the hall again I stood for a moment and looked round it. The house was empty except for Harold, Sandy, and myself; it would be the last night we should be alone together.

I now went into Harold's room. He was lying on his back, his arms above his head, the bedclothes were around his waist. I lifted them gently up to his chin and resisted bending to kiss him in case I should wake him; then I went into my own room, got into a dressing-gown, and went back into the drawing-room to await the return of Gran and Georgie because, as I told myself, I couldn't put off until the morning to hear Gran's reaction to the Flood family.

It was when the clock in the hall again struck the half-hour that I rose to my feet, thinking to myself, They're leaving it late. And it was as I made my way down the room towards the hall that I heard the distant sound of high laughter. When I opened the hall door into the outer hall and the lift stopped there almost tumbled out three figures, Gran, George, and Max Flood, and to use Gran's own expression, they were all as drunk as noodles.

As I backed into the hall they joined arms and came staggering towards me, singing now a favourite of Gran's:

> "Keep your feet still, Geordie hinny,
> Let's be happy through the neet,
> For we may not be se happy through the day,
> Oh gie us that bit comfort,
> Keep your feet still, Geordie lad,
> And divvent drive me bonny dreams away."

Definitely Max had been tutored because he was singing as loudly as they; and now, flapping both my hands at them, I cried, "Soften it! The child's asleep, and there are people now downstairs."

"Sorry, Mrs Nardy." Max was supporting himself with one hand against the stanchion of the door and he spluttered, "Had to fetch 'em home. Gran' night, Mrs Nardy, gran' night. Taxi waitin'." He thumbed. "Good-night, pal." He reached out and slapped Georgie on the shoulder; then looking at Gran, he said, "Good-night, old girl," and to this she answered, "Good-night, lad. Good-night, lad. See ya the morrow."

"Aye, see ya the morrow. Good-night. Good-night. Good-night, Mrs Nardy." Max was stumbling now towards the lift, and I rushed forward and pulled the door back and foolishly said, "Will you be all right?"

"'Sright as rain. 'Sright as rain. Good-night, Mrs Nardy. Good-night."

I did not wish him good-night but, pointing, said, "Press that button," then slammed the door into place and watched his grinning face disappear from view.

When I returned to the hall, Gran was divesting herself of her hat and coat, and with one sleeve still in her coat she rounded on me, saying, "Why didn't you tell me, eh?"

"Tell you what?"

"They were a decent lot. Best night I've had in me life. Eh, Georgie?"

"Splendid fellas."

"Stuck up you said they were."

"*What?*" I poked my head towards her swaying figure.

"Janet's lot, stuck up, that's what you said. Fine lot of lads, Janet's lot. Speak as ya find. Speak as ya find."

"Go to bed."

"Oh! Oh! Gettin' on your high 'orse, are you? D'you hear her Georgie? Go to bed, she says. Go to bed. Where d'you think I'm goin', Buckingham Palace?"

She now fell against Georgie, and he, being able to hold his drink better than his mother and sensing my indignation, said, "Come on, Mam. Come on. Talk 'bout it in the mornin'." He led her now towards the passage, but looking over his shoulder, he said, "Grand night, lass. Grand night. As good a pub as any I've been in. Good-night, lass. Night, lass."

Why wasn't I laughing? Why was I full of indignation? How dare Gran turn the tables on me like that? Well, I'd wanted her to get to know Janet's family, hadn't I? And she had definitely done that. But to come back in that state.

All the years I'd known them I'd never seen them drunk. I knew Gran liked her drop, and definitely Georgie could put it away, but they were now both paralytic. That was a northern term and the only one that really described their condition. . .

When I heard the bedroom doors close I thought, I should go and help her to get into bed. But why should I? No, no; I wouldn't. I turned round and went towards the hall door and locked it, and I was making for the corridor again when Harold appeared rubbing his eyes. Going hastily towards him, I said, "Now what's the matter?"

"The noise, somebody yellin'."

"Oh, it was only Uncle George and Gran coming back from your Gag's; they'd been having a party. Come on, back to bed with you."

When I tucked him up again and said, "Go to sleep now," he answered, "I don't want to go to sleep. I'm not tired any more. What time is it?"

"Nearly midnight."

He gazed up at me, then said slowly, "We're nearly in tomorrow."

I pursed my lips, raised my eyebrows as I said slowly, "Yes, we're nearly in tomorrow."

"When you're goin' to be married?"

My face sank into its usual pattern as I replied, "Yes, you know I'm going to be married tomorrow."

"Why?"

"Well." Candidly I was stumped for an answer that I thought he could cope with: I couldn't say, because I love Mr Tommy, that would have likely caused him to think that I didn't love him. I fluffed as I said, "Well, so that Mr Tommy can stay here all the time."

"He stays here all the time now."

"Not at night-time."

"If you get married he'll stay here at night-times an' you can't push him out."

"Well, I won't want to put him out. Now go to sleep."

I attempted to tuck him in again and he pushed my hand away, saying, "I don't want to go to sleep." Then he added, "You'll want to put him out if you get divorced."

"I have no intention of getting divorced."

"Well, you can't until you're married an' then you might."

There was logic in that. But why was this conversation taking place? I thought he had accepted the situation.

I said now, "I thought you liked Mr Tommy?"

He turned his head away, then bit on his thumb nail which I hadn't seen him do before and I repeated, "I thought you liked Mr Tommy."

"Sometimes."

"When are the times you don't like him?"

"When you like him . . . a lot . . . over much."

I had to remind myself that this child wasn't yet eight. His reasoning could have stamped him as being fourteen, or more. There had been a lot going on in his head that I hadn't been aware of; I'd been concentrating so much on his language and his manners that I'd skipped the fact of more important issues that must have been troubling him.

I sat down on the side of the bed now and, pulling him round towards me, I said, "Listen to me, Harold. I love you. I love you very much. You came into my life when I was very sad. Yes, I know, you lived here before that when Mr Nardy was alive, but when Mr Nardy died I was very, very alone and if I hadn't had your company then I might have become very ill in my mind. You understand?"

He said nothing, but his eyes were wide. "The fact is your companionship kept me sane. You meant more to me then than anyone else in the world, and you still do. I . . . I love Mr Tommy, but . . . but in a different way, a quite different way. The love I have for you is very special, nobody can take it away."

"Not Mr Tommy?" His voice was small.

"No, no. And he wouldn't want to, he too loves you. And he knows how I feel about you; we have talked about it. You are my son now and you will be his too. He will be a father to you. I know you have a real father." As I spoke I wasn't thinking now of Jimmy Stoddart, but I went on, "Who would you rather stay with?"

For answer he did not say Mr Tommy, but, "Not my dad. I don't like my dad." He turned his head away and as he did so I thought, someday I will tell him why he doesn't like his dad.

He hitched himself round now and asked softly, "Can I come and lie in your bed?"

He had never made this request before, and I hesitated a while before I answered; and then it was by evasion: "No, you're not going to get up again. I'll tell you what. Look, I'll lie beside you until you go to sleep." And at this I pulled the eiderdown to one side and got under it, and when I put my head on the pillow beside his, he put his arms around my neck and, bringing his head under my chin, he lay perfectly still. And I didn't speak, not until I felt something wet on my skin, and then I murmured, "Oh, my dear, don't . . . don't cry. Anyway, what are you crying for? There's nothing to cry about."

When I tried to press him away from me to dry his face he held on all the tighter, and when I heard him mutter something, I said, "What did you say?" and then more plainly his words came to me: "I thought you'd be like my mum when she got another man an' you'd go off. Although she said she wouldn't, she did. She said she'd come back for me but she didn't. An' you had Mr Nardy an' now you've got Mr Tommy, an'. . ."

"Oh, Harold." I pushed him from me and, my voice full of indignation, I said, "You didn't really think that I would ever leave you or let you go or be like your mam?"

"Well" - he choked on his words - "People do go off. Johnny Rankin's mum's gone off. He told me she had. His dad's on night shift, so he comes an' fetches 'im. People do."

"I'm not people, Harold. I'll never go off and leave you. You'll be the one to go off and leave me someday."

"No, I won't." He sounded like his old self. "I'll never leave you." His arms were once more tight round my neck, and as I stroked his hair I thought, here was I thinking I had an insight into people, imagining I knew what they were thinking. Clever clouts, as Tommy had called me, yet I didn't know what this child, this beloved child who was under my nose every spare minute of the day, was thinking, nor had I detected beneath his brashness the feelings that must have been troubling him for sometime, the insecurity that lay deep within him and which he had explained by the fact that a woman could somehow disappear after taking a second man into her life.

We held each other tightly for a long time. When his head sank into the pillow mine did too, and we both slept.

Chapter 8

I was aroused by someone shaking me gently by the shoulder, saying, "Come on, wake up! I brought you a cuppa tea. It's eight o'clock. Come on."

I twisted round and groaned. There was a kink in my arm. I opened my eyes and looked at the bright face hovering over mine.

"Harold!"

He was laughing. "You went to sleep in my bed."

Last night's scene flashed back into my mind and, pulling myself up onto the pillow, I said, "Oh, I'm sorry."

"Oh, that's all right." He wagged his head widely. "You were under the eiderdown an' I couldn't pull the clothes round me this mornin', so I got up."

"And you made me a cup of tea. Oh, that is kind of you. Oh, dear me, fancy falling asleep in your bed."

"Come on," he said now, "an' drink your tea. You've got to get up, you know; you've got to get dressed an' all that."

"Oh, yes," I sighed; "I suppose so. But I could just sit here."

"Don't be silly; Mr Tommy'll be around any time."

"Yes, yes of course he will. By the way, is Gran up?"

"No, Mr Georgie is, but Gran's moanin', she's got a thick head. I took her some tea in an' all."

"That was nice. I'm sure she'll be glad of it."

He stood and watched me while I drank the tea; then I said, "Well, I'd better get away to my room, hadn't I?"

"Will I put some toast on?"

"Yes, that would be nice, dear."

"Are you gona have a fry?"

"Not for me."

"Mr Georgie will want one, an' so will I. An' Gag's comin' early, she said she would, so I'll set the table, will I?"

"Yes, dear. Yes, you could do that."

He was near the door when he turned and said, "Funny thing."

"What's a funny thing?"

"Sandy. He went into your room and sniffed round and he couldn't find you so he's lyin' on your bed."

"Poor Sandy. I must go and see him; he's felt neglected of late."

The door closed on him and I lay back for a moment. Either my boy was completely reassured or he was putting on a good act, and I didn't think he was that clever yet.

I felt very happy.

When I entered the bedroom, yes, there was Sandy lying on the bed. On the sight of me he jumped into my arms, and as he snuggled his head under my chin I had the warm feeling that I had a family, and this morning I was to have a man to be at the head of it.

I heard Janet arrive, and I heard Gran leave the room next door, but I didn't go out to speak to one or the other; I should hear all about it later.

I had a bath, made up my face, then put on my clothes, except the costume in which I was to be married, donned a housecoat, then went out and into the kitchen to find Janet clearing away the breakfast things. She was on her own and when she turned towards me I could see that it wasn't only Gran who was suffering from a thick head; but she grinned at me and I at her. Then I said, "No need to tell me how it went."

"Oh! ma'am. I've never known a night like it." She put her hand to her head. "An' you know, it's the first time in my life I've known what it is to have a thick head. A drop of sherry's my limit, as you know, ma'am, but I couldn't tell you, if I tried, what I had last night. And Gran" - she now gave a short laugh - "you talk about 'Knees Up Mother Brown' you should have seen her with the lads. Oh! she's a star turn. She had the whole pub roaring; they think she's the cat's pyjamas. They couldn't knock her down; she had them all singing Geordie songs. I couldn't believe it, at least what I remember of it. And when we got home it started again. If Georgie hadn't reminded her that there was a wedding today she would have stayed there all night. I'll say this much, ma'am, your ruse worked all right."

"Yes, it worked all right for you, Janet, but she blamed me in no small voice when she got in last night because she said I had given her the wrong impression of you and your whole family."

She shook her head. "You know something? I think she'll be payin' London a visit pretty often after this, if you ask me."

"After last night, I've no doubt about it. Well, I'd better go and see her."

As I was crossing the hall I met Georgie who said, "Mornin', lass."

"Morning, Georgie. Have a nice time last night?" My voice was prim.

"Never better. Bugger me eyes! You should have seen her. I can only remember bits. Eeh! she was at the height of her form. I can tell you that, lass. And aren't they a nice crowd, Janet's folk?"

"Where is she?" I asked.

He thumbed towards the dining-room: "Hidin' her head, I think. Go canny on her."

I slanted my eyes at him, then went into the dining-room. She was sitting looking out of the window. She had her back to me, but she knew it was me, as her words proved when she said, "Now don't you start."

"Who's going to start?"

She remained still until I was by her side, and then, turning towards me, she said, "Oh, you might as well say your piece; if you don't say it now you'll say it sometime."

"I'm not going to say any piece, only with a face like that you'd think you were going to a funeral and not a wedding this morning."

"Aw, lass." She put her hand to her head. "I must have gone really over the top. A drop an' me aren't strangers as you know, but I feel I must have got attached to a hogshead last night."

"You enjoyed yourself though?"

She focused her eyes now on the outside scene of first-floor roofs and patches of garden, and after a moment she said, "Well, we can all make mistakes, can't we? But you've got to admit, from the look of her" - now her gaze flashed at me - "you'd never think she bred that lot."

"But I've told you before, haven't I?"

"Aye, you have; but you have to see them to believe them. All I can think of is that some of Nardy's mother must have rubbed off on her, her manners like." Then a twisted smile coming onto her face, she said, "Plainly it didn't rub off onto her family."

I pushed her.

She narrowed her eyes now as she looked at me, saying, "I see you're all made up. You nearly ready?"

"Yes; just my suit to slip on."

"Well, here you go for a third time. Eeh! who would believe it? And you're the one who imagined that nobody would ever want you. Do you remember?"

"Yes, yes, I remember."

"An' went an' married that maniac. You know" - she leant towards me - "there's strange rumours goin' round about him: what he was up to afore he did himself in or somebody did him in, one or t'other, 'cos from all accounts he was hated in there as bad as bairn abusers. But they were sayin' in the club he was dealin' in black magic. Now that's so far-fetched I told them they wanted to get their heads looked. How could he deal with black magic in there? He'd have no chance of startin' a convent in there, now would he?"

I stopped a loud explosion coming from my lips and said quietly, "You're thinking of coven."

"What?"

"What you're thinking of is called a coven. It's usually applied to witches, a coven of witches."

She stretched her nose, pushed out her lips, then said, "Well, I suppose you should know. Whatever it was, they said he started it. But some people'll say anything. . . How you feelin'?"

"All right."

She nodded, then said, "In a way you've had a bellyful, but in another way you've been lucky, you've had two men that are the salt of the earth."

She now bent towards me and her head emphasized each word as she added, "One thing I'll ask of you, for the future that is, keep out of the papers. It got that way I couldn't open the *Journal* or the *Evening Chronicle* 'cos there you were, headlines, an' I had to stand the racket at the club. So I'm tellin' you."

"I'll do my best, Gran." My tone was polite. Then changing it, I barked at her, "And now, you old misery, go and get yourself ready, and quick! We're due out in a half-hour's time."

She got to her feet, a tight smile on her face now as she said, "You don't change, do you?" And I answered in the same vein, "And I'm not the only one, am I?"

"Aw, lass." She suddenly bent towards me and kissed me, saying now, "Things haven't been right atween us for some time. That's all over. It's me, I know. You see, I . . . I thought I had lost you altogether, but now I know I haven't, you're still my lass."

We held each other tightly; then, pushing me away, she walked smartly down the room. But at the door she turned and said, "That bit was only soft soap 'cos I want a trip on that boat of yours."

When the door closed on her I stood blinking and smiling to myself. That boat of mine. In her eyes it was already mine. And there was no doubt, too, as Janet had suggested, that she would be making the journey from Newcastle to London more often in the future.

I went to my room, and there I got into my suit and four inch heeled shoes to give me just a little added height. Next I placed an apology for a hat on the top of my head and, looking in the mirror, I saw a woman in her middle thirties who, although still plain, did not look her age. Next, I picked up my handbag and matching gloves and went out and into the corridor, and across it towards the far end I could glimpse Harold's door was open and I could hear his voice talking rapidly to someone. I looked into his room, and there he was with Sandy. The dog had its forepaws on his chest and was licking his face and my adopted son was admonishing it in his most natural form: "Stop it; you soapy sod," he was saying. "If you spoil me tie I'll pull up your guts an' strangle your tonsils with 'em."

I did not rush into the room and upbraid him, this wasn't the time, but I stepped back and leant against the wall for a moment, repeating, "I'll pull up your guts and strangle your tonsils with them." That was certainly a new one.

As I made to walk away, there he was coming out of the room, half bent over, keeping Sandy down with one hand. He stopped, straightened up, looked up at me for a long moment, then said, "I . . . I wasn't swearin', not really. Well. . ."

This was no time for a confrontation, so I said, "Who said you were?"

"Your face."

"My face?"

"You always look like that when I'm swearin'."

"Oh. Well, if that wasn't swearing, what was it?"

"You . . . you mean about pullin' up the guts and . . ."

"Yes, yes, that's what I mean." I noticed we had by-passed soapy sod.

"John Rankin learned me it."

"Taught me."

"What?"

"Taught me?"

"Oh, well, yes, well I only said it 'cos of him." He stabbed his finger towards Sandy. "You see, he was jumpin' up an' upsettin' me tie."

He was wearing a white frilled shirt, topped by a bow tie.

I bent forward and straightened it, and as I did so he looked to the side, gave a yell and said, "There's Mr Tommy!" and darted from me.

I stayed where I was looking down the corridor into the hall, and there was this tall attractive man. He was always well dressed, but this morning he looked different, not younger, older, if anything and very, very handsome.

As that unnerving, irritating, and questioning thing called my mind opened a door yet again to ask, What did he see in me? I kicked it closed and turned swiftly and went back into my bedroom, and a minute later he knocked on the door, and when I said, "Come in," he came in, saying, "What made you disappear like that?"

"Oh" - I made a small face - "I wanted to bang a door."

"Bang a door?"

"Yes. I'll tell you about it later."

"Have you had trouble with his nibs?"

"No. Why do you ask?"

He smiled before he said, "He's just said to me: 'She thinks I swored.' "

"Well, he did, and brought out a new one."

At this point it struck me to ask myself why we should be standing here talking about my charge and not about ourselves? But I went on to explain how I overheard Harold's reprimand to the dog: "Soapy sod, I've heard before," I said, "but never, I'll pull your guts up and strangle your tonsils with them."

"What?" He was shaking with laughter.

"Just that: pull your guts up and strangle your tonsils with them." I too was shaking now, saying, "Did you ever?"

I fell against him. His arms were about me and his voice came over my head: "Well, there's one thing, my dear," he said, "we'll never be dull where he is. But then" - he pressed me from him and looked down into my face - "I'll never be dull where you are. That's your charm, you know." He looked me up and down. "You look lovely."

"I don't look lovely. Smart, yes, but not lovely."

"Why do you. . .? Oh, shut up! and come along, I want a wife."

We clung together again; then we went out and there in the hall was Gran, and George, and Harold, and Janet. But Janet wasn't dressed for outside.

Tommy now said, "Hello there, Georgie. Hello Gran. How did it go last night? Enjoy yourselves?"

Her face perky, Gran said, "Oh, she hasn't told you then?" She now turned and smiled at Janet, saying, "It's a wonder she didn't get that in, isn't it?" And then she added, "You should be comin', you know."

What a changed Gran. And Janet, smiling at her, said on a laugh, "I could never stand weddings. They recall the mistake I made many years ago. And anyway, somebody's got to see to the caterers." She now cast her glance towards me. "Everything'll be in order when you get back. So get yourselves away."

We were going into the outer hall when I stopped, and turning to Janet and for the first time in our acquaintance, I kissed her and said softly, "Thank you, Janet for everything right down the years, and especially for Harold." Then we held each other tightly for a moment until she said, "Oh, go on with you." Her nose wrinkled and she chewed on her bottom lip, then pushed me through the door into the outer hall.

Gran and Georgie were now in the lift, Harold was standing at one side of it and Tommy at the other, their faces bright and smiling, and they both said almost in unison, "Come on, if you're coming. "

And I went towards them and into another world.